Epic Of Porch

Inside the garden, Tchako, with Cheeko close behind, reached the bolted gate. Tchako opened a code box next to the gate and pressed in the code to open it. Both squeezed through as soon as it had opened sufficiently. Porch was about one hundred yards ahead. Tchako waved his prod and yelled for him to stop. Cheeko produced a stream of yelps. Porch's months of captivity had weakened him, so Tchako and Cheeko began to close in on him.

Porch was coming upon the moat. With great effort, he increased his speed again and leaped as far as he could, just reaching the ground on the far side. He rolled again, regained his feet, and headed in the direction he knew the gate to be. Tchako and Cheeko reached the moat and chose to slide down. They lost some distance and had to climb the far side, but were soon in hot pursuit. Porch ran between the pampas grass and the dense brush. Tchako and Cheeko were almost on him. He was running as fast as his pounding heart and heaving lungs would allow, but he dared to glimpse back, and just as he did, he saw a flash of orange leap from the grass and then another from the brush.

Epic Of Porch

by

Jonathan Holman

Commonwealth
Publications

A Commonwealth Publications Paperback
EPIC OF PORCH

This edition published 1997
by Commonwealth Publications
9764 - 45th Avenue,
Edmonton, AB, CANADA T6E 5C5
All rights reserved
Copyright © 1996 by Jonathan Holman

ISBN: 1-55197-573-4

Printed in Canada

Look deeply into the crystal and count the
strokes on the metronome.
It ticks for you and it ticks for me.
It ticks for time universal.
It is the heartbeat of the stars.
It holds the rhythm of your heart and the
measure of your mind.

To Jason
Enjoy!
Jonathan Holmes

PART I

CHAPTER 1

JASON

It was late afternoon in the early spring in the foothills below the mountains. On a high meadow, a young girl skipping along and carrying a willow basket on her arm was gathering spring's first gift of herbs and greens. Her flaxen hair was braided and hung down her back almost to her waist. She wore a simple cotton print frock pulled in at the waist which gave evidence of her blossoming womanhood.

She tarried often in her task to luxuriate in the radiance of the late afternoon sun, stretching her arms up to gather in the benevolent, warming rays and turning her face up to better breathe in the sweet air. Her delicate nose was lightly freckled, her lips, an untouched pink. Her laughing eyes reflected green in the meadow, or blue beside a deep pool. She wore no shoes, yet bounded with effortless grace across the meadow. When her basket was brimming with poke, dock and dandelion, with wild onion and garlic and even some asparagus, she stopped to pick some wildflowers for Granny.

Her buoyant giddiness in this springtime rebirth of nature's world gradually subsided into tranquillity. All was right with her world. The burgeoning rebirth of the hills she loved filled her with wonder as each turn in her path revealed a crocus blooming, a nesting bird, or a butterfly taking wing. She slowly wound her way home.

As the sun set over the western ridge beyond the

meadow and twilight forecast the coming night, she looked up to see the evening star assuring peace and well-being.

Suddenly, she was startled. This evening star appeared to be moving. She blinked and looked about her to take reference from familiar things, then looked up again. Yes, it was moving. It must be a shooting star. But no, its path was not a curving arc that finally burnt out. It was descending in a spiral orbit, growing from a dot into a disk. Abruptly, it changed course and accelerated back up into the dark. But just as quickly as she lost its course, she found it in another quarter, descending first rapidly and then more slowly, as if braking. It was coming down, ever more slowly and right for the meadow she was centered in.

The golden disk fell within the shadow of the farther ridge, below the fading rays of the setting sun. Fascinated, the girl could not move. It dropped lower and lower, now just floating. It seemed to dim itself further by some internal force. The girl could hardly see it, but it was coming directly toward her.

When it was fifty yards distant and ten feet above the ground, still floating without a sound, her fascination turned to fear. She bolted like a frightened doe for the edge of the nearest wood and hid in a patch of rhododendron, standing rigid as a fawn.

The disk touched the earth noiselessly and settled down. It seemed to absorb every bit of light that might distinguish it, almost disappearing into the darkness. She shivered and slipped down farther into cover.

After several minutes that seemed like several hours, a triangular appurtenance rose from an opening at its top. Noiselessly, it rotated a full circle, scanning the meadow. The girl saw nothing, but thought she felt a radiation as the antenna passed her. It circled several times, and she knew she felt a beam. The antenna withdrew into the disk as noiselessly as it had risen.

After another eternity, a faint amber light appeared along a crack on the side of the disk. Quivering with fear, the girl watched the crack widen into a rectangular opening. It was a door. Then the amber light fell on the bushes within which the girl was hiding. She dared not move a muscle. Suddenly, a man emerged. Outlined in the amber glow, he stepped out and looked all around. The door closed quickly behind him, blotting out the glow.

The moon had now risen above the meadow. It was full and lit everything with a soft silver light. The man was coming her way, and she could see him clearly in the moonlight. He appeared as tall as the tallest mountain men she knew. He wore a silver body suit of unknown material, and from the waist up, he was further encased in what she surmised to be some type of cermet armor. In his right hand, he held a heavy sword, and in his left a strange staff. He looked young, quite young, but his hair was so light it appeared almost white. He was heavily muscled and had a commanding presence.

Although scared to death, she felt strongly attracted to him.

Long winter nights of reading wondrous tales by the firelight told her that he must have come from the stars. Her heart began pounding so heavily she thought it would give her away.

As he approached her cover, she became disconcerted and her foot slipped into a bog of which she was unaware. Her foot bottomed on a sharp rock.

"Ouch," she whimpered, and the bushes rustled.

"Come out," he commanded.

She rose and moved toward him, head down, like a naughty child.

"Why, it's a little girl," the starman said, sheathing his sword.

"I'm not a little girl," she pouted, and then said fiercely, eyes flickering, "I'm a full-growed woman."

"What is your name?"

"Amilee."

"I am called Jason. You have hurt your foot. I will fix it. Balance on my shoulder."

She placed her hand on his shoulder and lifted her foot to him as he knelt down. Withdrawing a cloth and a small jar from a pouch on his sword belt, he first wiped her foot clean, and then with the palm of his hand applied some cream to the cut. Instantly the blood stopped trickling and the pain disappeared. Amilee sighed in relief.

Gently cushioning her foot, Jason looked up—from her foot to her ankle, to the dimples in her knees, to her curvaceous hips, past her engaging breasts, and on to her face.

"Yes," he said, "you are a woman and a very pretty one at that."

Again he bent down, pulled her foot to his lips, and lightly brushed it. Amilee was enchanted, flushed with a heat she never felt before.

He looked up and smiled. "Take me to your leader."

Amilee looked at him in astonishment, then giggled, but squelched it when she saw the earnest look on his face. She stammered, "This way," and strolled into woods along a barely discernible path, marked only by moonlight filtered through the trees. She looked back to see if he was following. He was, for he too was enchanted. He had forgotten the pleasure of being with a pretty woman, forgotten, it seemed, from spending eons in space time dedicated to an all-consuming mission.

Now, his mission interrupted, his senses peaked. He caught her scent of freshness and wildflower sachet. Amilee felt his forceful stride right behind her, so she picked up the pace. She could traverse this well-hidden path in her sleep.

Presently a light shone up ahead and marked a cabin. It was now fully dark and getting late. They came to a clearing. Jason could see several more modest cabins ahead, all dimly lit by lanterns and outlined in the moonlight. Amilee led him to one of these and knocked lightly. Jason heard a thump, some rustling around, and then the door opened. A slight man clothed in a long nightshirt and flannel nightcap held a kerosene lantern high as he could reach and looked at them, squinting over a pair of spectacles balanced on his nose.

Amilee said, "Preacher Wyndotte, we have a visitor come from real far away."

Preacher looked at the sturdy man dressed in strange attire, and again at Amilee. When he was satisfied that she had not been harmed, he said, "Come in and set." When they were seated, he looked at Jason again and said, "I better summon the council."

With that, he went to an ancient wall phone and cranked it. "Granny, Jethro...come over... Yes, I know it's late, but this is important. We have a visitor... No, not from the Corporation... Then who? Never mind, come over, you'll see."

Preacher looked at Jason, then at Amilee, again at Jason, and once more at Amilee. Amilee sensed suspicion.

In a moment, the door creaked open and in came Granny Gronx. Hardly a granny, maybe forty-one or forty-two, but she'd gotten her name because she was midwifing her second and third generation of young 'uns. She was the local healer as well. She knew her herbs and teas, and any number of remedies. She set broken limbs, poulticed black eyes, suctioned out snakebite "pizen," and cured colds and croup. But more than that, Granny Gronx was wise; her counsel was widely sought and usually followed.

She had adopted Amilee after Amilee's father had been killed in a knife fight and Amilee's mother had run off with a schoolteacher from Arkansas. They dearly loved each other. Now, as she sat down, she looked fondly at Amilee, who smiled at her. She noticed Amilee glance shyly at the stranger and blush. Granny looked at Jason and smiled. Though he was strangely dressed, Granny instinctively liked his looks, so she began calculating. It was late April. Courting was quick in the hills. A wedding in late June would not be too soon. She wondered if she had enough white satin and lace in her old cedar chest to stitch a proper gown.

Just then, Jethro walked in. He had to stoop to get his huge frame in the door. He nodded to everybody and sat down without speaking. He'd been to council meetings before.

Preacher Wyndotte rose to open the meeting. He was a small owlish man, local leader by position but more so because the community subscribed to his hard fundamentalism and unwavering faith in the "code of the hills." Jethro, when needed, was the preacher's enforcer of whatever social judgments he made. On the other hand, Granny's wisdom ameliorated the harshness of some of these judgments. Thus, the three as a team provided respected leadership to the local folk.

Amilee introduced Jason by name as a visitor who had landed in the far meadow in "some kind of helicopter." The preacher accepted this, and introduced himself, Granny and Jethro. Granny smiled and stuck out her hand, which Jason shook gently. Jethro scowled but nodded.

The preacher cleared his throat, looked at Amilee and said, "Girl, you may go."

Amilee looked at Jason and replied sharply, "I'm not a girl. I'm a woman."

Preacher Wyndotte looked at Amilee in disbelief at such an outburst. Granny interrupted softly, saying, "Amilee, make some hot herb tea for all of us—why, we should welcome our visitor proper."

The girl went quickly over to the stove.

Jethro finally spoke. "That warn't no chopper. I saw it coming down from far away. This man's from the Corporation or the guv'ment."

After a pause, Jason said, "I've come from very far away—from the stars."

"You not human then," Jethro replied.

All were aware of Earth's space exploration and the emigrations of the Millenarians from the Earth over the past century and a half. The three looked at him suspiciously.

"I carry the blood of my ancestors, a humanity borne by my people for six thousand years." Jason paused. "There were giants on the earth in those days, and also...when the sons of God came in unto the daughters of men, and they bare children to them ..."

Jason trailed off, but Preacher, astounded, picked it up. "...the same became mighty men which were of old, men of renown. Genesis 6-4."

"How do you know our language?" asked Granny.

"The Ancients watched this planet for thousands of years, and had scholars that followed all 2796 languages and dialects and the civilizations that have risen and died here. For them, it was but a minuscule part of their quest for universal understanding."

"You know all those languages?" Preacher asked.

"No, but I have a Selector-Teacher on board my starship. I used it when my mission sent me here. The ST impressed it on my mind during periods of galactic sleep interval. If I hesitate on any of your phrases, it's only because it was interrupted when my navigator selected your coordinates for emergency landing."

"Emergency landing?" asked Preacher.

"My navigator was—how would you understand it— was dying."

"Dying?" quizzed Granny.

"She has—died. You must help me resurrect her."

Granny replied nervously, "Well, I know all the cures and then some, but not to bring the dead back to life."

As Amilee brought the tea over, she overheard this talk of "she."

He has a woman, she thought, bitterly disappointed. She poured out four cups of tea and looked longingly at Jason, her hopes of idyllic bliss fading. Granny sensed the girl's thoughts, and her own visions of satin and lace and a joyous June celebration vanished. To prevent further grieving on her ward's part, she said, "Amilee, you better go now. It is very late."

Obediently, Amilee went out and headed for the cabin she shared with Granny.

Jason continued, "Granny, it is nothing you can do. I must have Preacher's help and Jethro's, too, but that will come in time."

"Oh," said Preacher. Jethro grinned, flashing large white teeth.

"You quoted a passage from the Good Book. What did you mean?" the preacher asked.

"The Ancients visited the Earth long ago. They found this race of men, much like themselves but very primitive. The women bore them children—'Men of renown,' some of whom they took with them back to their home in the far stars. They wanted to enlighten them, then, in time, return their children's children to Earth so they could enlighten Earth's people. The Ancients could not stay on Earth because of the First Law."

"The First Law?" Jethro asked quizzically, scratching his head.

"Yes," said Jason. "The First Law of galactic travel is non- interference with the natural development of galactic life elsewhere, possibly warping the space time matrix with unforeseen consequences."

"Who are these so-called Ancients?" the preacher asked.

"The Ancients, as well as your people, were my ancestors. Their race was old before yours was born. They are no more," Jason said sadly.

"Enough," the preacher said. "This is heady stuff for us plain folk. Granny, you got an extra room and bed. You put the stranger up. We'll talk again after we think about what's been said. The starman looks like he could sleep a thousand hours."

"Come," Granny said. She took Jason to her cabin, put him up in homespun comfort, and he too thought that he could sleep a thousand hours. He slept the rest of that night, the next day and the following night. But he could not allow such earthbound luxury to continue.

Before dawn woke the hills, he crept quietly out and returned to the meadow in which he'd landed his spacecraft. He went into it, then came out with a package which, when unfolded, appeared to be a large shroud. It was a wondrous cover, having beneath it a web of memory metal.

He threw it over the ship with a mighty cast, covering it completely. Next, he took an infrared laser, focused it, and the heat provided made the spines come alive to form what appeared to be an outcropping of the ancient limestone that underlay those hills. Then he took what turned out to be a spray container, and like an artist with a brush, further transformed the cover with exact hue and hardness to simulate a rocky camouflage. This done, he returned to the cabin, where he found Amilee as fresh as the morning dew, up and about, making breakfast. As he said good morning, Granny came out of his room.

"Mornin'. You slept like a log for a day and a half. You must be famished. Now go wash up and put on Harry's clothes. He's as tall as you but skinnier, so I let them duds out so's they'll fit you good."

"Won't Harry mind?"

"No. Years ago some fancy Noo York city wimin messed his head up and he 'lost' hisself down in West Texas. Tole me he won't come back. I laid the clothes on your bed—gonna make a mountain man out'n you."

"Yes'm," Jason replied, feeling as though he'd found a family after the loneliness of his voyage. He made good use of the steaming washtub of water he found in the room, shaved, put on the homespun underwear, rough trousers and checkered shirt and reappeared.

"Sit down, son," Granny commanded, already counting him as one of hers. Amilee smiled, lending a sunny radiance to the table, and whispered a morning blessing.

Granny noted Jason's eyes followed Amilee's every move. In turn, Amilee was cool and only spoke to Jason when he questioned her directly. Granny mused, decided to let it be, and continued to formulate her own plans. They ate hotcakes with sorghum syrup, a mound of sausage and bacon, and stewed apples in cream, and drank huge quantities of coffee.

Now, such events as Jason's great voyage, even in the twenty-third century, was so remote to these mountain people that it would be some time before they pressed him to continue his strange tale. Anyway, storytelling was the stuff for winter before a fireplace, and spring had just burst out all over. The people were preoccupied with cabin repair, plowing, planting—and gathering the first fruits of the season.

Not so Granny; although Jason joined the others in the springtime labors, she insisted that Jason have afternoon tea with her. Gradually, Jason revealed his story to her. He held the rank of scout commander in the Knight Order of No. The Ancients had formed this sacred military order from the men they compelled to leave their star cluster before they themselves destroyed it.

The Ancients had created a glorious empire, extending it to the very limits of their star cluster. For thousands of years, peace prevailed and they devoted themselves to learning and enlightenment, ignoring police and military functions. Populations on all the planets within the star cluster grew without bound until the resources that sustained them were stretched beyond sufficiency. War and rebellion came upon the peoples as various factions sought to survive. Pestilence struck. So, disdaining military service for themselves, the Ancients imported a race of warriors to quell the rebellions and restore law and order. The imported warriors acted quickly and harshly, as they had no fear of battle while the peoples of the planets did.

Peace again prevailed, but not for long, because the warriors became the masters of the people they had subdued. Then, horror of horrors, like cancerous cells, they quit aging and did not die. Something had happened within their genes. Nature's order of evolution became one of devolution. The race of warriors degenerated into loathsome creatures, and their number increased without bound.

Again the resources that sustained the planets diminished. So the degenerate warriors began to use the people they had enslaved as cattle to feast upon, raising them as such. Leaping through space in stolen starships, they advanced inward through the star cluster, conquering planet after planet, cannibalizing each in turn. Soon they threatened the very seat of The Ancients' empire. Nothing stood before them, and they were on the verge of expanding into other sectors of the galaxy.

The Ancients determined that eventually they would consume all life within it. Desperate to exterminate this scourge, they concluded that they must destroy the greatest civilization ever to evolve within the universe— their own empire, and the star cluster itself.

Their science was so great they could move the stars themselves. This they did, moving them into a colossal vortex that first swallowed itself in its own massive gravitational pull and then exploded in the most gigantic supernova the universe had ever experienced, one that

Earth has yet to see because of space-time distance.

However, this superb act of self-sacrifice was for nought, because a portion of the degenerate vermin escaped the maelstrom in the most advanced ships the Ancients had developed. Even now, they multiplied their numbers exponentially and spread throughout the galaxy, riding the gravity waves produced by the heaven-rending explosion meant to destroy them.

To Granny, Jason's story was mind-shattering, but she accepted it because she had already accepted him. Anyway, as it was nothing she could do anything about, she decided to bring him back to more mundane matters. She asked him about his present status. "You said you were in a group of some type. Do you have to go back to them?"

"It's more than that, Granny. I am dedicated to them. My order, The Knight Order of No, are the remnants of the descendants of the Earth Children originally taken to the stars by the Ancients, those forced to leave prior to the cataclysm. We are the succeeding generations of the original five hundred who formed the order. We are sworn by blood oath to fight the scourge until they are eliminated from the galaxy. We have fought them generation after generation, in sector after sector, yet they continue to press forward, spreading horrible destruction."

"But what can you, a single man all alone, do to stop them?"

Jason smiled. "I am on a mission. We of the Order believe that the scourge originated here on Earth thousands of years ago, as we ourselves did. We are looking for their source. I am not the first. Many have come here throughout your history. Evidence of our visits has been available to you."

"Oh, how is that?" Granny asked.

"North of an old town in California called Blythe, your early people recorded a visit thousands of years ago with 'geoglyphs,' great figures carved in the mountains. Your Indians fashioned others on sites along your Colorado River, near towns such as Silver City in New Mexico; Casa Grande, Arizona; Chihuahua, Mexico—Nazca, Peru."

"I don't know about such things, but Preacher Wyndotte does. He read the 'Great Books,' but then he sold them to Harry. Tell me some more."

Jason was pleased with Granny's interest, so continued, " At the beginning of your twentieth century, one of our missions failed. We believe it was on the verge of finding the source when it went down. There was a gigantic explosion on the other side of your world from here, in a place you call Siberia. Trees were knocked down and burned in a fan-shaped arc nineteen miles across from the direction the ship came in. Your Russian people call it the Tungus meteorite. After the crash, there was much radiation in the area, but the crash was not investigated for twenty years, so nothing identifiable was found.

"After the second great war of that century, Earth people were vaguely aware of some of our probes, calling them UFO's. Your country's air force kept tabs on reported sightings. Interest died out when you began your own space probes."

Slyly, Granny then asked, "But now you can't go back. You said your navigator died. Poor girl, what was her name?"

Jason laughed, much to Granny's amazement, saying, "I'm sorry, but I have confused you. VANA, my navigator, is simply a computer. VANA stands for voice-activated-navigational-aid. Your scientists would consider it highly advanced. Developed by the Ancients, copies were put aboard our ships when we were compelled to leave. Our order has used them ever since, as they are simple to fix whenever we are stranded."

Granny sighed, smiled and pressed on. "If it's not a woman and simple to fix, why do you call it such?"

"In deep space, our warriors become very lonely. A woman's voice is most soothing and it alerts us better than any other signal device. We become very attached. The voice becomes very real."

"Can you fix it? How long will you stay here? I was hoping you would settle with us."

"Granny, I've already started to fix it. You may have noticed I go off at night... Soon I'll need Preacher and

Jethro's help. I'll need some minerals that you have under these mountains... I may be here a long time... I wait for a message from the Order locating the source."

"So you have no woman with you. There must be one waiting somewhere for one so young and comely as yourself."

"I've not known many, Granny... I've given my heart to no one."

"Hummm," said Granny. Then she decided to change the subject. "I suspect you'll be runnin' off soon's the message comes."

"I'll have to...I'm sworn by Blood Oath to my mission."

"This 'Source'–why is it so important?"

"If the Order can find the source, the origin of the warriors the Ancients took to their star cluster, our geneticists can unravel their genetic code, compare it to the *Book of Life*, and determine how their death cells disappeared. This is heavy, Granny, but you're a healer and midwife, so you'll understand. Life throughout the universe evolved from simple cells to more and more complexity, all the way up to humans. Embryos from the seed of species are much the same, even look the same in early stages, be they lizard, rabbit or human. They all have tails. But for humans, there are genes in the genetic code that tell the growing fetus to get rid of the tail. It's also why we don't have webs between our fingers. Life conceives, develops, matures, mates to conceive again, withers and eventually dies. It is universal...except for that degenerate, loathsome horde.

"The Scourge can be killed, and easily enough, because we've done so wherever they spread, and though their bodies scream for death, they do not die naturally and always press on, spreading farther and farther. We are few and can't contain them—only delay their deathly spread. So we must find their missing genes and reconstruct the 'death cells,' as we call the living mix we seek. The Order has ways to inject and infect them. I am sworn to this—to the final battle."

"Then what will you do? Where will you go?"

"I haven't thought past my task and the final battle.

Maybe I'll wander among the nebula—between the stars—through the breathtaking beauty of this galaxy, discover where it all began and find, perhaps, a place called home."

Just then, Amilee walked into the cabin, hot, tired and dirty from work. She smiled at Granny, looked shyly at Jason, but quickly averted her eyes. Jason reddened and looked at her wistfully.

"Maybe you are home," Granny observed.

CHAPTER 2
AMILEE

During the long spring days the mountain people got used to Jason. When they saw how hard he worked and how well he picked up their ways they adopted him just as Granny had. They admired his strength and virility. They liked his gentle good humor and honesty.

So they introduced him to their main source of income— moonshine. They distilled thousands of gallons of unstamped sour mash each year in small remote stills. This was highly illegal, since the Corporation, through inter-governmental agreements, had an almost global monopoly on the production and distribution of spirits. Continual skirmishes between Corporation or federal agents and the mountain people had raged for the past one hundred years. As "Mountain Moonlight" was a superior product, untaxed and cheaper than the legal stuff; city dwellers sought it out.

If the "revenoors" found and destroyed a still, another would spring up in its place. Ingenious distribution systems devised over the years ensured that ample supplies were always available in the megacity. This drove both the government and the Corporation into spasmodic fits of rage, always abetted, because every time the revenoors caught and confiscated a wagon or truck of moonshine, the mountain folk hijacked a Corporation load, and the small villages, towns and clans equitably divided the legal stuff, replacing the lost moonshine. It came out that the city dwellers enjoyed an ample supply of fine moonshine, and the mountain taverns stocked the best Corporation whiskey.

Jason went on a number of "distributions" with Preacher, Jethro and his brothers, and this further cemented the bonds that had grown between them. Upon return, they related whatever adventure befell them with much braggadocio and exaggeration. That is, all but Jason, whom the Order had trained to avoid self-aggrandizement. The brothers took to doing it for him, as his part in their escapades was indeed daring. The more he protested at being singled out, the more the blarney blossomed.

As a consequence, he became the darling of a bevy of comely mountain belles; that is, all but Amilee, still heart stricken in the supposition that he had a female traveling companion. She never failed to note when he disappeared into his ship for hours on end. She could do nothing but maintain a cool distance from him lest her heart flutter up to her throat and burst right there.

At first, the young girls' attention flattered Jason, but soon enough their outrageous flirtation and invitation grew wearisome and embarrassing. He also feared that it would draw the resentment of the other young men of the hollow. Consequently, he politely came to ignore the foolish fawning and wistful signals that he was drawing. But Amilee's cool aloofness was disconcerting.

He'd felt his heart stir when he'd landed and first saw her. Now he found himself growing increasingly fond of her. She was kind and gentle, caring and selfless to the mountain folk around her. He loved her smile, her laugh and her unabashed affection for her mountain home. He loved her unassuming nature. Well, no matter, he had a mission to fulfill and would overcome his chagrin by immersing himself in it.

At last he was ready to seek Preacher and Jethro's help. So when he found them one day at a respite from their labors, he said to them, "I need to secure a mineral that until one hundred years ago you had in abundance under these hills."

"What might that be?" Preacher replied.

"Anthracite."

Preacher went on, "I'm surprised that you know that, but it's true. These hills used to abound with coal mines. They are most all played out now except at the deepest levels, and then you have to know where to look. It's difficult to bring up. That's why they been abandoned."

Jethro broke in, "Now we know you're not a revenoor, we'll give you all the help you need. I'll get my brothers, too."

Locating the sparse amount of anthracite left in the mines entailed searching decades-old archives hidden away in trunks and poring over faded maps and charts. They found long-forgotten shafts and miles of tunnels, all at great depth, some not even known to have existed when the mining companies pulled out. The entrances, most often caved in and overgrown with trees and shrubs, were found only after they had learned where to look from the old maps and charts. They traversed almost all of these before they came upon the prize that Jason sought.

After many days of heavy labor, they had secured an amount of anthracite sufficient to satisfy his needs.

Wiping the sweat from his brow and smiling, Jethro said, "I hope this is for a worthy purpose."

"Oh, yes," Jason replied. "I'll use this coal to form diamonds. I have the equipment aboard my ship. I need the diamonds to repair my navigational computer, VANA. I told you her demise forced my landing. Only diamonds have the reflection and refraction indices to operate it accurately."

Preacher laughed. "When you first spoke of that device, we thought you spoke of a real-life woman."

"Diamonds?" Jethro questioned with interest.

"Yes," Jason repeated. "I'll save a portion for you. I know they are highly prized by Earth people who live in cities. Perhaps you do as well. If not, maybe you can trade them for goods you'd rather have."

In the days that followed, Jason spent much of his time alone, first forming the diamonds and then positioning them in the computer. But he had a problem. He could not get Amilee out of his mind. This was annoying, because it affected his precision in aligning the diamonds, which was crucial to his success. He strove mightily to attain the level of mental discipline instilled in him by the Order, with no success. He could not get her out of his mind.

It was maddening. He saw her in his dreams. He took long walks in the woodlands and meadows, and saw her face in the clouds and in the flowers below his feet. He heard her laugh come out of the bubbling brooks he passed. He heard the rustle of her skirts in the breezes that cooled his feverish brow. Yet when he came upon her, she scampered off like a frightened doe.

His spirit waned. His countenance grew haggard. At last he went to Granny for help. He said to her, "Granny, I think I've got the 'ague' you described."

"You don't look well," she replied, putting down the silks and lace she'd been sewing upon. "I'll put you to bed, give you a tonic and see that Amilee is here to nurse you."

After two weeks of tea and tonic, Jason's spirit revived. His countenance flushed with new vigor. Amilee's tender care had conquered him. But now his passion burst through all remaining self-imposed restraints, and he surrendered to it. He had to have Amilee's love.

Somehow he would make her his betrothed. When he'd reached this resolve, he made peace with his heart.

Granny saw this and knew the time had come. Coincidentally, she'd just finished sewing the last bit of lace onto a beautiful wedding gown. After tea time in the afternoon of the chosen day, Amilee walked in.

"Oh, how beautiful," she said, noticing the gown Granny was fluffing. "Who's it for?"

"You will know soon enough," said Granny. "Now I want you to go see Jason and have him introduce you to VANA, whom he's revived."

"Oh, Granny—no."

"Yes, child. It's time to put some nonsense behind us."

Dutifully Amilee left. She had been born in the hills and would die in the hills. Dreaming sweet dreams that were never to be was just downright impractical. She would put it all behind her. She trudged along the path through the woods and presently came upon the meadow.

Jason was sitting on a log by the outcropping of fake rock that hid his starship. He did not hear the soft tread of her measured steps.

"Jason," she said softly.

"Amilee, dear Amilee," he said, startled.

"Granny said you would introduce me to Vana, whom she said you've revived."

"Of course, and it's time to show you my ship, *The Wanderer*. Come in," Jason said nonchalantly. He led her inside after pulling the camouflage aside. In the interior, Jason proudly showed Amilee the command instrumentation console, his intergalactic communicators, his provisions' pantry, his hygiene cabinet, his wondrous work table, an arsenal of mysterious weapons, and a large, luxurious sleeping lounge.

"Your sleeping couch berths two," she murmured dejectedly.

"Listen," he said as he flicked a switch and turned a dial.

"Greetings, Amilee. I am VANA, Jason's companion through time and space."

Amilee looked all about trying to see the woman who had such a mellifluous voice.

This puzzled Jason. "For whom do you look?" he questioned.

"I thought there was a flesh and blood woman."

Astonished, Jason chuckled. "Why, you silly goose, whatever gave you that idea?"

Amilee could not answer. Her voice was all choked up.

"Look here, it is my navigator—a computer, my most important companion. I could not do without her. Her name is VANA. Isn't she beautiful?" Nonchalantly, Jason pointed to a compact console of flashing lights.

But Amilee could not see. Her eyes were full of tears.

"Oh, Jason," she wept. Jason reached for a cloth to wipe her eyes, but her arms were about his neck.

The melodious female voice interrupted, "Greetings,

Amilee. I am VANA, Jason's companion through time and space. He is the best of men and I love him. I have heard much about you. Jason loves you and I shall love you, too."

Amilee pushed away to look at Jason. It was his turn to stammer.

"Yes, it's true. I love you, Amilee. I love you dearly."

He pulled her to him, and he kissed her longingly.

At last, Amilee softly backed away, put her hands to his face, and looked at him, saying, "Jason, I loved you when first I saw you and have never ceased loving you."

Jason gazed at her, and it came to him that Granny had told her nothing of him. He took her hands, sat her next to him on the couch and looked at her gravely.

"Amilee, I want to ask you a question, but before I do, I must tell you who I am, why I'm here, and what I must do."

She looked at him intently and listened to him carefully while he told her all that he had told Granny. Then he went to his work table and picked up a package wrapped in soft cotton cloth. He thrust it out to her and said, "This expresses how I feel about you. Now I want to ask you a question."

Amilee took the cloth, but anticipating Jason's question, put her fingers to his lips and said, "No, not yet."

She rose, and taking Jason's hand, said, "Come with me."

She led him away from the ship, out of the meadow and through the woods on a little-used path, higher and higher, into thick forest. Suddenly the forest opened into a glade that lay beneath a rock ledge beside a small waterfall. The glade could not be seen from below, as it was concealed by the forest, but it had a view of the entire valley below all the way to the next ridge line.

Jason and Amilee stood as one viewing the beauty that lay beneath. They could see the cabins of the small settlement that Amilee called home, the place called Bountiful. Smoke crept up from chimneys as fires were lit to ward off the evening chill. Lanterns popped on, casting light into the encroaching darkness.

Amilee looked up at Jason lovingly. "You wished to ask me a question. This is my secret place. I found it when I was a little girl. I vowed never to come here until I found enchantment. You have brought that to me. I shall answer your question here and now."

"I love you, Amilee, so much, so much. Will you marry me?"

"Yes, Jason, I will be your wife."

They embraced, then Jason said, "Open the packet, my darling."

Amilee unwrapped the cloth to find a lustrous pendant hanging from a doubled platinum chain. Two joined hearts were superimposed upon a lyre of gold. White diamonds and blue sapphires of unsurpassed brilliance alternated around the hearts, upon the face of which was inscribed:

"Hearts entwined together,
Spirits bound forever."

Jason whispered, "Open the latches to the hearts."

Amilee opened them. "Why, it is a double locket."

The inside inscription read: "Together we shall seek out and find the Birthplace of Wonder."

The right side of each were cameos of white jade, one the likeness of Amilee, the other Jason. While opened, a strange melody chimed.

Jason said, "It is *The Song of the Starman.*"

"Jason, I have never seen anything so beautiful."

"I fashioned it at my work table to express my love for you."

When they returned to Granny's cabin, there was a briskly burning fire in the fireplace and supper had been prepared. Granny was sitting in her rocking chair. "Granny," Amilee said breathlessly, "Jason has asked me to marry him, and I shall."

"I know," said Granny. "Here is your wedding gown. We shall try it on tomorrow."

Amilee blurted out, "But how did you..."

Granny interrupted, "'T'ain't no never mind, child. There's only one week left in June, so the ceremony will be held on the last day—I've arranged with Preacher. We shall have a grand celebration."

The following few days were busy for Amilee and Granny. They ran Jason off so they could make the rounds of the women folk to assign tasks and share the joy. It would be a woodland ceremony, followed by a huge feast. For the men, this would occasion a night of toasting, and later gambling. Anticipation of the happy event increased.

Jason went off to his starship in the morning to check for messages and to continue his watch. In the afternoon, he was free to wander off with Amilee. Jason was naturally taciturn, but he also judged that he'd said enough about his situation. No matter, Amilee was bubbling over with joy, and when they were together, she led him through the woods, describing the herbs and berries and all the things upon which the mountain folk partially subsisted. Invariably, just at dusk, they came upon her "secret place" to gaze in awe at the beauty unfolding when the sun sank down below the farther ridge and the stars blinked on. On the fourth evening after the announcement of their forthcoming nuptials, strangely, where the great arm of the Milky Way was rising, they saw some flashes and then a void where stars should have been.

Jason looked apprehensive. He spent almost the entire next day in his starship. When he came out to meet Amilee, his concern was evident. In silence, they made their way to the high glade. Jason held Amilee so close he could feel her heart beat. She sensed that only with great will did he look up to the rising arm of the Milky Way. She felt a start and then saw his despair. Again they observed the flashes and saw the void where stars should have been. They hurried back to Granny's. All during the night, Amilee heard Jason's fitful sleep in the adjacent room.

The next morning, Jason hurried out to his ship and stayed the day. Amilee went out to fetch him in the early evening and saw when he emerged through the hidden door that he had discarded his mountain clothes and wore the regalia of a scout commander of the Knight Order of No. Stricken, she ran to him.

"Come," she said. In silence, she led him up to the

mountain. In silence, they watched the sunset over the peaceful valley. At last, she softly said, "In two days, to the world, I shall be yours forever. But I have a strange foreboding that that is not enough. So now, this very night, I shall bond to you and you to me."

So under the star-studded sky, beneath the rocky cliff by the waterfall, they consummated their love. As they were returning down the mountain, they heard the anguished call from the spacecraft. They hurried to it and stood dismayed as they listened.

"EMERGENCY-EMERGENCY. ALL SHIPS, SECTOR SOL, ABORT MISSION. ABORT NOW. VECTOR SECTOR ALPHA OMEGA. WARP SPEED. SCOURGE PROBE BREAKTHROUGH. KON DEFENSE. DESTROY OR PERISH. DESTROY OR PERISH. ABORT NOW. EMERGENCY-EMERGENCY."

Jason looked at Amilee.

"You must go," she said.

He started off, stopped, then returned. "The locket. Give it to me."

She took it from around her neck and handed it to him. He pressed an indent underneath and it separated into two. He took the half with the cameo of her and put it around his neck. He put the other about hers and kissed her, saying "I'll have you with me in this locket."

Tearfully she broke away, then said, "Go and come back to me."

He ran to the ship, turned and yelled, "Stand away," then entered. As she backed away, the ship threw off its rocky shroud of deception and slowly ascended. When it reached one hundred feet, it accelerated in a brilliant flash and went out of sight. The remnants of the shroud disintegrated in flame. Amilee watched until the last ember burnt out and only a char on the meadow remained.

Granny was rocking in her chair when Amilee entered the cottage.

"Oh, Granny, he's gone," she wept as she knelt and put her head on Granny's lap.

"Oh, my child, my poor child."

At last, the heart-rending sobbing abated and Amilee

looked up desperately at Granny and said, "He said he would return."

Granny stroked her hair. There was great despondence in the Hollow as the wedding day came and went. All had seen the flash or heard the whispered whistle as Jason hurtled up out of sight, and they guessed Amilee's tragic loss. They nodded in sympathetic agreement when she said over and over again, "He will return. He said it himself."

July passed into August. Amilee's pain persisted, and it became evident that others too had noted the strange departure. Ominously they began to appear, in one's and two's, in sleek black electro-cars.

"Corporation men," Jethro noted to Preacher Wyndotte.

"Yes," said Preacher. "There'll be trouble if they learn we harbored the alien. Silence must prevail."

In afterthought, he said, "That girl shouldn't have enticed him."

"He would have gone right after he came," Jethro conjectured.

The dark-suited men first approached the children, who, frightened, said nothing. Gloom prevailed over the valley. The mountain folk cooled to Amilee's anguish, and that coolness turned to disdain. The dark-suited men found the scorched splotch of earth in the meadow. Their frequency of visit increased, and they appeared to be carrying weapons.

The old women of the hollow began to whisper, "It's that girl's fault; there'll be trouble."

Preacher Wyndotte called a meeting of all the settlement folk, to be held at night in the tavern in the guise of a harvest celebration. Granny tried but was unable to prevent the council from barring Amilee. A chill had already come to the hills when the meeting was held in early September. Granny, Preacher and Jethro sat at a table along the far wall with the village elders. Jethro's huge brothers, Mungo and Caleb, sat by the batten door entrance playing cards. Others sat at scattered tables and at the bar. They had been directed to eat, drink and dance as the fiddlers played their mountain melodies.

Preacher opened the talk, saying they had to figure a way to get the strange men away from their mountains. He felt the girl was the key. She had to be hidden, but they couldn't send her off because the strangers would most likely find her and force her to talk.

"It was all her fault," said an elder.

"Nonsense," Granny retorted.

"She should be shunned," said another.

"I never heered sech rotten cowardice in this supposedly stick-together clan," Granny said in a fury.

Just then, four men in black overcoats entered the tavern. Three spread out along the wall by the entrance, holding odd-looking laser pistols in their hands. The fourth, a man they called Professor, looked around and then walked over to the table where the council and the elders sat. He was tall but very thin. A pair of pince-nez glasses sat on his nose. He had a slight foreign accent when he spoke.

"Ve want to know many things, and you vill tell us."

"We are simple mountain folk who keep to ourselves and harm no one. We wouldn't know anything of value to you," Preacher answered.

"So you are the leader—you vill come with me." At that, one of the swarthy men by the door grabbed a little girl and pointed his pistol at her head.

"Do not harm these poor people. I will go with you," Preacher said.

So the "Professor" led Preacher out. The other three men followed. One hour passed, and another. Then there was a thumping at the door and the Professor pushed Preacher into the hall. Preacher was hobbling. His glasses were broken and there was a bloody cut on his forehead. His nose was swollen red and appeared broken. The Professor pushed Preacher into the chair beside Granny. Jethro grabbed Preacher as he collapsed into the seat.

Preacher rasped to Jethro as he passed out, "I told them nothing—didn't break the code of the hills."

Granny looked at the Professor and said, "You son of a bitch."

The Professor looked down at her and grinned.

"You're next." He grabbed Granny's shoulder, and as he did, a bodkin from her hair went into his left temple and came out the other side. In the same instant, Jethro's hunting knife flashed across the hall and entered the throat of the swarthy man standing next to the door as the man raised his pistol. Mungo's ancient blade, once called a bowie knife, found the bowels of the third and then his heart. Caleb cracked the neck of the fourth, whose weapon then fell from a lifeless hand.

Quickly, the dead men were pulled from the tavern. The women wiped up the telltale blood. Other men brought up a cart and loaded the bodies. After the moon had set, Jethro and his brothers headed through the September chill for the deepest anthracite mine they had explored many weeks ago. The mountain folk slipped out of the tavern, and when they reached their cabins, snuffed out their lanterns. Next, "long barrels" appeared which were pushed out of windows into the darkness of the night. Granny retreated to her cabin, shaken. She found Amilee had prepared a cup of tea for her. This she took in her old rocking chair by the window, and started rocking.

"It is a time of trouble, girl," she said.

Amilee knelt down to hug her. Then she said, "Granny, I'm pregnant."

"It's a time of great trouble," Granny responded, looking far out into the blackness of the night.

CHAPTER 3
AMILEE

Amilee sat at the rear of the old bus as it chugged south on methane at forty miles an hour. It traveled the ancient interstate system, which was in a terrible state of disrepair. The fares its passengers were able to pay prohibited traveling the Corporation Super Thruways with its toll stations. But Amilee was content, because the route the bus took carried her close to her destination and miles from Corporation-controlled highways. She'd spent many days on the road, but the thought of starting a new life for herself and the child she bore in her arms sustained her. The heat of late October here in West Texas surprised her. She'd never experienced anything like it in the mountains she'd left. She fanned both herself and the infant, asleep at the moment, the best she could.

After a bit, the baby became restless, so she put the fan down and began humming to him very softly. Her thoughts went back to the home she'd been forced to leave. She understood the "shunning," for the mountain folk's harsh code permitted nothing less. Granny had shielded her as much as she could, and she was grateful for that. She had stayed to herself in the cabin, for there were always chores to do. They couldn't take the fields and hills away, so she'd roamed them often, always alone. She'd been happy when the thought came to her, as it often did, that her link to Jason was growing in her belly. She was certain that someday Jason would come back to her as he'd said.

The infant whimpered a little, which broke her reverie. Gosh, it was hot. She dipped a little water from her thermos and wiped his face, arms and legs, then her own. She had to conserve what little was left. The child opened his eyes for a second or two, smiled up at her, and then went back to sleep. Gosh, she loved him so much. She too closed her eyes, and her thoughts went back to the mountains.

To her delight, and with Granny's expert help, the baby boy had been born healthy and strong. Her only sorrow was that she had been unable to share her joy with the mountain people she loved so much. She didn't understand when the trouble with the Corporation came why their anger toward her turned into such fierce hatred. They blamed her for all that occurred, and she'd retreated into the depths of despair. Even thoughts of Jason's return faded from her mind. Then the final horror came.

The Council of Elders led by Preacher declared her unfit to raise her baby. Why? Because she was running around the hills again, alone. What shame would she bring on them next? They would take him from her and remove the stigma of her transgression on the community.

As the child was beautiful, strong and healthy, they'd have no problem getting him adopted in the city. This she couldn't bear. Nor could Granny, so they formulated a plan. Amilee didn't know it, because Granny hadn't told her, but the baby had a godfather called "Ole Mulemilk." His real name was Harry Noah, and he lived far away in west Texas. He'd once been a mountain man but had left long ago. Granny wrote a letter telling him they were coming, and posted it that day.

Covertly and quickly, they prepared for Amilee's departure, because the Council, having declared Amilee's unfitness, planned to take the baby that very week. Preacher so told Granny, who feigned resignation to the Council's will. They packed a few clothes for Amilee and the baby, and a wicker basket of provisions. Granny then wound a small money belt full of gold coin from the cache Harry had left around Amilee's waist. Next they hitched Mule to the cart and stole out of the Hollow in the dark of night.

So Amilee was on her way before anyone suspected, destination a town called Pecado fifty miles south of Harry's spread. According to Granny, Harry received mail from there. Amilee was to leave the bus there and wait for him to pick her up.

Pecado thrived solely because of its remoteness. It was wide open to drinking, gambling and funning with fancy ladies. Far enough from the El Paso-Albuquerque megapolis, it was immune from the scandals the big city press liked to publish. But politicians, Corporation men and other citizens of substance with a penchant for "swinging" could reach it by helicopter in an hour. Neither Granny nor Amilee knew of this. The bus driver nudged Amilee when they reached the station in Pecado. Earlier he had implored her to travel farther, but there was no way she could.

"Señora, Pecado peligro! Pecado peligro! If you stay in Pecado, you will be in great danger."

Amilee understood him not at all, so she got off the bus.

El Ratòn, deputy sheriff, sat nearby, half asleep in the late afternoon sun on a dirty station bench. As evening came, the heat of the day was rapidly dissipating and the wind that had come up brought a chill. It was, after all, late October, and the coming winter would not be forestalled forever. El Ratòn slunk farther down on the bench and pulled his poncho up around him. He had been posted there by the Sheriff, who always wanted to know who had come into town. His eyes half opened as the bus rolled up. He saw Amilee get off with the tiny bundle in her arms, carrying her old valise and wicker basket. He saw her flaxen hair glisten in the setting sun as she put her bag and basket down, adjusted the wrap on her bundle, and put a wool coat on.

As the bus departed, she looked around. She did not really notice him, but he pulled his sombrero down over his eyes. He squinted, then grinned as he took in her fresh wholesome look, pretty features, and lithesome figure. He rose slowly and walked nonchalantly down the street. When he deemed himself far enough away, he quickened his pace over the cracked and broken sidewalk, and then almost ran to the café. He pushed through its door, looked around hurriedly, and saw the Sheriff in a booth. He hurried over and in fractured border lingo, called out, "Jefe, Jefe, a dulce, a gringo dulce."

"Shh, idiota, sit down," Chief Lobo growled, looking around. "Now, digame, tell me quick."

"A pretty young girl, alone, at the bus stop, with an infante," El Ratòn said, panting.

"She is alone?" the Sheriff questioned.

"Si, Jefe, si. I can have her when you're done?" El Ratòn queried, licking his lips.

"Quien sabe?" evaded the Chief. "Wait here."

Lobo left the café, straightening his shirt and pistol belt as he went out, then rubbed his star with his shirtsleeve. He strutted to the bus stop, imparting authority to his stride. Amilee shivered as she stood with her baby at the station. Granny had told her to wait there at four o'clock every afternoon, if she had to, until Harry came to pick her up. It was now well past four. Amilee thought anxiously that she had to get a room somewhere. She did not see Lobo approach.

"Señora," Lobo commanded loudly to get her attention, noticing the child, "why are you standing there? Why did you come to Pecado?"

Amilee, first startled, was then very much afraid when she looked at this man with the pocked-marked face, scarred eye and fierce mustache, until she saw his badge and knew he was an authority.

"Sir, I am waiting for my son's godfather."

"Si, your godfather, your hoosband, your tio, your caballero, your patron, so you say. I think you are a vagrant, no?"

"Oh, no, sir," Amilee pleaded, shivering. "My son's godfather is a man called Ole Mulemilk. Perhaps you've heard of him. He lives to the north of here."

"Ridiculoso, un hombre called Mulemilk, ridiculoso—no such thing," Lobo lied, for he had very well heard of the man called Mulemilk and the legends growing around him. Lobo knew he lived far to the north and that his mail was posted out of Pecado. Mulemilk had come into Pecado only once to buy provisions. He'd bought flour, seed, salt and coffee, and had paid in gold coin. Then he'd gone to the café for some tequila and chili. News of the gold traveled like wildfire down the main street, so before the man was served at the café, some girls from the palacio showed up to shower him with affection and suggestions as to how to spend the rest of his time in town. Mulemilk had told them in no uncertain terms to beat it. When the bartender tried to interfere, Mulemilk felled him with one blow, spat a mixed mouthful of tequila and chili on the floor and left. He never returned.

Lobo also knew the story of Purple the pimp, and the girls Purple had carried out to Mulemilk's rancho to try to seduce him. Lobo was scared of Mulemilk. But he thought he must have this flaxen-haired niña for his palacio. The Corporation gringos would pay much for her favors—soft and young—blue eyes, si–ojos inocente, si—truly a dulce.

"Sir," Amilee interrupted what she thought was a stern silence. He glared down at her.

"Sir," she said, conquering her fear, "it is growing dark and I must find lodging for myself and my child. I am sure that my child's godfather will be here tomorrow."

"Where does the hombre come from?" Lobo questioned.

"No Sech Place."

"No Sech Place—niña, you make fun with me. I do not tolerate insolence."

"Oh, sir, I mean no disrespect, but please do help me find a room." Amilee held out a small gold coin.

Lobo's hand shot out by habit, but he withdrew it quickly.

"Niña, now you bribe a law officer. Mañana I take you to the magistrate! Si—it will go hard with you. Yes, I will take you to a room, and you will stay there—until I come get you."

Lobo thought to himself this was going to be easier

than expected. Amilee thought to herself that everything would be all right as soon as Harry came to fetch her, so she followed Lobo to the Hotel San Antonio. Lobo told the clerk she was not to leave or it would go bad for him. Amilee went to the room assigned and, dog tired, pulled a blanket up and went to sleep with the child in her arms.

Lobo left. He was grinning and whistling to himself as he walked back to the café. Then he thought of Mulemilk and became solemn. "It must be legal—muy legitimo."

El Ratòn was still sitting where he'd been told to wait. Lobo slid into the booth, facing him. He leaned over conspiratorially and whispered, "En mi mano, en mi mano, right in my hand."

Lobo told El Ratòn that the girl was waiting for Señor Mulemilk, so they would have to be very careful—legitimo, muy legitimo. He told of the attempted bribe, but not of the gold coin. They would get a man to her room late that night. The next day they would take her to the magistrate, charging bribery and solicitation. It would be well documented if Mulemilk showed up. He did not tell EL Ratòn of the girl's gold in case there was more, nor of his other calculations—a year in the Palacio, another in the tents down the arroya for the muchachos, a final year in the woods near the prison. Then, muerte—death! It was always that way. They never lasted. He would keep the boy five or six years, then if he was healthy and comely, sell him down on the gulf coast, otherwise, muerte too.

"I can have her when you're done, Jefe?" El Ratòn implored again.

"Maybe sometime," Sheriff Lobo lied.

They left the café. They had not noticed that Nogales, the postman, was sitting in the booth behind. Nogales had listened intently when he heard the name Mulemilk, because Harry was a good friend who had always treated him well. He was a small, humble man. He had a large, difficult wife and twelve children. Just keeping food on the table sapped all his energy, so whenever Lobo passed him, he took his hat off and stepped aside. He wanted no trouble, and although he'd watched Lobo and his rotten ventures for many years, he saw nothing, heard nothing and said nothing. He knew what happened to those who crossed the Sheriff. But this was too much. So Nogales resolved, *I will help Harry. They will not get this girl.*

At midnight, Amilee awoke to a tapping on her window. She was scared, but she went on over to it. Seeing a small man outside holding up a letter, she opened a crack. He stood on a ladder.

"Shh," he admonished, and then he motioned for her to open the window wider. "I am Nogales, the postman, a good friend of Señor Mulemilk, or as his friends know him, Harry Noah."

Amilee accepted what he said, because she knew that few in the region knew Harry's real name, and Nogales was holding up a letter addressed to Harry. Amilee saw Granny's handwriting, so now she knew that the letter had not been delivered and Harry would not come.

Nogales said, "I am not due to deliver this until next week, but señora, you are in great danger, so I'm going to make a run tomorrow. You must pack your things now and come. I am going to hide you in the mail truck until morning. I've prepared a bed for you and the niño. You will be warm and comfortable. You cannot stay in this room because they are sending a bad man up soon.

"We'll leave at first light. It's always when I leave, so they won't suspect. El Ratòn was watching from across the street, so I gave him a bottle of tequila. He's asleep now. Come, I will help you."

Quickly, Amilee gathered up her possessions and the baby, and with Nogales' help they made it out the window, down the ladder, and into the rear of the postal truck. There was a mattress and blankets there, and soon enough, Amilee and the child were again fast asleep. Amilee had placed herself in Nogales' care. She had no other option.

Nogales drove to a safe place for the rest of the night, and at dawn, he left Pecado without incident. He traveled north silently for many miles. His postal truck was his

livelihood, so he kept it in good condition. It ran on
methanol. The fuel was expensive, so he ran it slowly to
extract as many miles as he could from the engine. Three
hours out of Pecado, he stopped, climbed onto the roof,
and looked back across the desert. There were no telltale signs of dust rising, so he was sure they were not
being followed. Nor would they be now, six hours from
Harry's place, because of Harry's reputation.

When he got back down, he found the baby awake
and Amilee rocking him in her arms and feeding him
the last bottle she had. Afterward, she climbed into the
cab. She felt secure enough to tell him why she'd had to
seek refuge with Harry. Then Nogales began to talk. He
told the girl about Pecado, about Lobo and El Ratòn,
about the surrounding countryside, and about his family. Amilee asked him to tell her about Harry. Nogales
knew nothing about Harry before his arrival in west
Texas, but he knew all the legends that had developed
since. Harry had been a good friend to him. He was a
kind and gentle man who just wanted to be left alone,
and he enforced that one way or another, but the gold
coins that appeared infrequently caused the legends to
grow. Just then, they came upon a sign:

KEEP OUT*MULEMLK*PROP.

NO WIMEN

Nogales said, "He especially wanted to stay away
from womans." Amilee blanched and looked at him carefully.

"A while after Harry got down here, about twelve
years ago," Nogales continued, "some womans in Sheffield heard about Harry's supposed hoard of gold and
decided to hit him up big for a donation to their Ladies'
Auxiliary, so they wrote him a letter asking for one. I
delivered the letter, which Harry never answered so they
decided to pay him a visit. They saw themselves as
"grande doñas" and thought their presence would in-
timidate him. Eight of 'em got dressed up in their Sunday best and rented a bus to make the long trip south
to his rancho and ask him in person. They opened his
gate, letting the stock out, and pulled up in front of his
little ranch house. When he didn't come out they started

tootin' on the horn. Harry finally came out. He wore his pistolas on a belt around his waist, had on a ten-gallon hat, boots and nothing else. He went on down the path to the gate in front of his yard to greet them, but by the time he got there they'd turned the bus around and were high-tailing it back to Sheffield. They never bothered him again."

Amilee giggled.

"Ah, señora, you are happier now, si?"

"Si," Amilee replied.

"Not far now, Señora Missy."

They chugged along in the old truck until about three in the afternoon, when they came upon another sign:

LAST CHANCE*GO BACK*KEEP OUT
ESPECIALLY FEMALE-TYPE WIMEN
MULEMILK*PROP.

Once again, Amilee blanched. Nogales didn't notice and went on to tell her the story of Purple and the three prostitutes from Pecado.

He concluded, "So, Señora Missy, that is why Harry put up those signs."

When he glanced over at her, he saw how uncomfortable she was and added, "Of course, Señora Missy, you're kinfolk, so you don't worry."

But Amilee wasn't sure. At last the ranch house came into view. Nogales pulled up at the gate and called out, "Harry, Señor Harry."

There was no answer, so he hollered several times more. They saw a light through a crack in the door, so he turned to Amilee and said, "He can't be far, Señora Missy. I will go check the barn. You check the house. He never locks it. He has some very good guards."

Amilee headed for the house, and Nogales the barn. Unfortunately, Nogales was wrong. Harry had locked the house. Amilee checked all around it, but found no way to get in. When she returned to the front, she saw Nogales coming back from the barn. As he approached, he called out, "Señor Harry is not there. He is in the house, no?"

Amilee shook her head and said he was not, but

Nogales assured her that he could not be far off, because the chickens were out and the stock was in the barn.

Then he said, "I am thinking to go back now. Then they probably would not miss me and think that I have brought you here—but I hate to leave you, Señora Missy. Maybe I stay or you go back with me."

Amilee thought on this. She did not dare go back and let those horrid men get her in their grasp again. Yet if Nogales stayed, maybe Harry, the way he hated women, would make her go back with him. If she had time to stay a little while and show Harry what a good help she could be, maybe he would let her stay permanently.

So she said, "No, Señor Nogales, you go back before they miss you. Besides, your family needs you. We will be all right. We will stay in the house until Harry returns."

She did not tell him she could not get into the house. Nogales accepted this as best he could, and with a "Vaya con Dios" left. Several miles to the north, Harry and his great dog, Hercules, had come upon his lost sheep. Their half-eaten bodies told him what had happened—no doubt the coyotes had gotten them, but he did not understand immediately why the coyotes had scattered before finishing their meal—well before he'd arrived. Their tracks indicated hasty departure. He circled around in larger and larger arcs.

Then he came upon the pugs. The mark and drag of her right foot identified the lion. He had tangled with her before. She was such a beautiful animal that he'd not had the heart to shoot her. He'd fired low with the shotgun to drive her off the body of that man, Purple. But when he got to the body, the man was already dead, white as a sheet with not a mark on him. She must have scared him to death.

Over the years, the man and the cougar had developed a healthy respect for one another. He saw her many times. But she never bothered his stock, so he didn't bother the deer and javalina upon which she fed.

He could do nothing more there, so he decided to

head back. He half expected the wind when it hit. The day had been unseasonably warm for October. In fact, the whole month had been. When he looked north, he knew that they were now going to pay for nature's delay in bringing the cold. A monster storm was coming in. He had to hurry. They were in for it—really in for it. He picked up a trot. Hercules stayed close to his side.

Back at the ranch house, Amilee too felt the wind and the sudden cold. How could the weather change so fast? She went around the house again, checking doors and windows, but couldn't budge a one. She thought of the barn. Nogales had been able to get in.

She bundled the child up with wraps from the valise, picked him up and headed for the barn. Halfway to the gate, she saw it, a large coyote. The coyote saw her, raised its muzzle to the sky and let out a series of yips. She turned back to the house. The wind was now raging, and the snow had turned to ice. She could hardly see, but she gained the porch. In its shelter, she wiped her eyes and looked back toward the barn. She now counted five dark shapes.

Oh, Harry, she thought, *come home, come home now.* She looked around and saw the wood bin. She wrapped the baby carefully and placed him in it gently. Then she looked about for a weapon. A thick straw broom rested by the door. She picked it up and looked toward the barn again.

More coyotes had gathered, but she could not see how many. Several now headed for the yard. They entered the yard, then hesitated while their leader approached the porch. Amilee moved forward to meet it. It snarled. She jabbed the broom into its eyes. It yelped and backed away. The coyotes hesitated again, huddling against the raging wind and pelting snow. Amilee backed up to the wood bin to check the child and her hand felt some short, stout pieces of mesquite. Putting the broom down, she shifted the baby and pulled out every chunk she could feel, dropping them to the front of the porch. The coyotes moved up. Two gained the edge of the porch. She hit each with a piece of mesquite. They backed off yelping, but three others moved up to replace them. Again they were routed by Amilee's missiles. She jabbed another with the broom. They backed up. The storm raged on.

In the respite gained, she took stock of her arsenal. She had only two pieces left. Desperate, she determined what she had to do. She remembered how the woodcock back in her mountains drew the fox away from her chicks by leading him away from their nest.

Quickly, she took the locket she wore from about her neck and put it around the boy's. She kissed him and bundled him back up, wrapping the letter from Granny to Harry inside his blanket. She put his now cold bottle to his lips, and placed him back in the bin, emptied the basket, and placed it over him as a cover. She put the valise on top of that. She picked up the broom, the last of her wooden missiles, and moved to the edge of the porch.

Again, a coyote advanced. She hit him with a missile and moved forward off the porch. The coyotes backed away, snarling. Advancing, she picked up chunks previously thrown and hurled them once more. The coyotes backed away farther from the porch. She reached the gate, thrusting with the broom. Drawing them toward her, she headed out into the desert through the howling wind and driving snow, farther and farther from the child in the wood bin.

She led them farther yet. All followed, forming a half-circle around her. Behind a rock not ten yards away, the big cat crouched, watching the drama unfold. The cougar hated those coyotes, so she too followed as Amilee led them away.

Harry and Hercules had reached the back of the house. They saw and heard nothing in the ferocious storm as they came around to the front. All sign had been blown away. Harry struggled to reach the door and unlock it. He thought he heard a whimper and, looking around, saw some goods lying around the porch. He collected these, noticing they were an assortment one would use with an infant. He threw these inside. Hercules was pawing at the wood bin. The massive dog had his snout inside. Moving fast, Harry went over, nudged the dog aside, and removed the valise and wicker basket. He saw the shivering child, its face red with crying. He rushed it into the house and placed it in the bed in the back room beside the cat. He lit the wood stove and told Hercules to guard.

It was now dark outside, so he picked up a flashlight and struggled out against the storm. Twice he circled both the house and barn looking for some sign of whoever had brought the child, and found nothing. The third time around, he heard the baby wailing loudly. He ran to the barn, threw feed to the chickens, placed fodder and oats in the mangers for the mules and cattle, milked a goat into a pail, and hurried back to the house. He heated the milk and a tub of water as fast as he could, then he bathed, changed and stuck a bottle of goat's milk into the infant's mouth. Famished, it quit crying long enough to feed. Next he threw the child's soiled clothing into a washbasin he'd put over the stove. He did not see the letter that fell to the floor. The child started crying again as soon as it finished its bottle.

In consternation, he put a teaspoon of tequila into the bottle, filled it again with milk and gave it to the child. Initially, the alcohol repelled the baby, but it was so hungry that soon enough it took the bottle. At last, the little boy went to sleep. So Harry fed Hercules and himself. Then he took his wet clothes off, bathed, dressed in his night shirt, and crept into bed beside the child. Hercules leaped up on the other side. Mephistopheles, the cat, crept up and wrapped himself around Harry's head, and Mortimer, the big black snake, slithered over and wrapped his long body around all of them.

What a night, Harry thought as he drifted off to sleep.

Morning came too quickly, he thought as he pulled himself up out of the fog of sleep. Hercules loomed over him, tugging at his nightshirt. Then he heard the squalling next to him and remembered the baby. He looked over. Mephistopheles was licking the child's face. The great snake had slithered off. He jumped out of bed and immediately looked to caring for the child's needs, imitating what he'd seen Granny do so long ago.

The blizzard was still raging outside. Tending the

baby was all Harry could do for that day and the next. The baby would cry itself to exhaustion and begin again as soon as it had breath. Harry surmised it was calling for its mother or whoever had brought it. On the third morning, a feeble sun forecast the end of the blizzard. The baby now was uttering but a feeble whimper. He fed it and it seemed content, willing to accept its new surroundings. It pulled up the locket it had about its neck and put it in its mouth. Harry withdrew it and looked at it.

He said, looking at Hercules, "This is strange, strange indeed." He put the locket back into the child's tiny hand and smiled. He thought to himself, *Providence has given me the child I always wanted*. He looked again at the baby, who seemed to be smiling back at him, and said, "I'll name you Porch, 'cause that's where I found you."

The child grinned up at him.

Harry was eating his breakfast when he spied the letter resting at the base of the stove. Curiously, he went over to pick it up. "Why, it's from Granny."

> *Dear Harry,*
> *I am sending you Amilee and her child. You are her mother's kin. She had great misfortune here and cannot come back. Take care of her and the babe. We have run on bad times. But don't come back here.*
> *All my love,*
> *GRANNY*

"Oh, my God!" he said. He leaped up, looked at Hercules, and said, "Guard."

He put his overcoat, boots and hat on, grabbed his long barrel, ran out the door to the barn, threw open its doors, and yelled to the hounds, "Come." They circled the spread until they found some tracks frozen in the ice, then laid bare by the wind—a woman's footprint and many coyote tracks. The tracks gave direction but no scent, so the hounds followed Harry. They trudged on for about a mile, at last coming upon a woman's shoe, then another. Harry found more coyote tracks and the pug marks of the great cat. He found his broom. The handle was broken. They searched all that day and went out again that night. They searched the following day, and the next. They searched throughout the month. But Amilee was never seen again.

CHAPTER 4
PORCH

The Great Blizzard of 2238 went down in history as one of the worst experienced in west Texas. But Harry had lived alone for many years before that storm and was naturally prudent. He'd laid in enough supplies to ensure that he, his household companions, and his stock survived comfortably. Winter was his time of reflection and contemplation. He continued to read and reread the "Great Books" that he'd bought from Preacher Wyndotte. He worked at his personal computer on theoretical mathematics and tended the baby. The baby, Porch, prospered under his gruff, loving care. Hercules adored the baby. Mephistopheles tolerated this newcomer's affection and in return licked his face occasionally. Mortimer lay torpid, wrapped around an owl's perch, dreaming of the forthcoming spring banquet when Harry opened the hatch under the hay in the barn.

By the end of April the following year, winter had lost its grip and spring came to the high desert. But Harry's world remained incommunicado with the rest of existence until late May. It was then that Harry saw the dust plume approach from the south and draw closer and closer until he could identify it as the postal truck. It pulled up to the front gate and Nogales got out.

"Amigo," said Harry, "you're six months late."

"Si, amigo, I have had much trouble—grande calamidad."

"Come into the house."

Harry fixed eggs, beans, bacon and coffee, while Nogales inspected the baby. "He's fine baby boy—bueno muchacho," he muttered.

As they ate, Nogales became increasingly apprehensive. Harry noted this and sadly reconstructed the terrible events the night of the blizzard. Nogales dropped his head onto his arms on the table and, weeping, confirmed that yes, he had brought a young woman with the child to Harry's earlier that same afternoon. He'd left quickly in hopes of returning to Pecado undetected so that Lobo and El Ratòn would not come after her. He told of the terrible fate they'd planned for her. The storm delayed him, though, and they saw him return.

Harry wrung it out of him that the Sheriff and deputy beat the man half to death in front of his wife and children, then took his milk cow as a fine for "obstructing justice" in face of the charges they had placed on the girl. Harry thought of justice, proper justice, so while Nogales finished his coffee and played with the baby, he wrote a letter to Granny. He explained as gently as he could what had happened, and related Amilee's heroic act.

He went on to say that he was going to hide his gold far from the ranch because he thought that eventually it would be stolen if left where it was. He wrote that should anything happen to him, he wanted her to recover it and use it bring up the baby. Separately he would send her a map detailing its precise location. He would bury it under two white crosses to imitate graves and fool intruders. Next he drew a crude but detailed map and wrapped it in a special package. He addressed both in big bold letters.

Nogales had by this time finished his coffee, gone out to the postal truck, and returned with a mail- order package. He presented it to Harry. It contained new clothes for the baby which Nogales had ordered months before with forethought and kindness. Since Harry had become the lad's foster father, he ordained Nogales the boy's new godfather in return, and gave him a pouch of gold coin to seal the compact. He told him to buy a new milk cow for his twelve children. Then he handed the letter and the package to the postman for posting.

Nogales had gained new spine from the injustices levied on him, despite his terrible beatings. As he was leaving, he told Harry that he was going to run for mayor of Pecado in the forthcoming June election. He thought he'd win because the townspeople were "muy simpatico" to him, feeling that Lobo and El Ratòn had gone too far. He promised that as mayor, he would get rid of the pair.

Grimly, Harry muttered, "You will not have to..."

But Nogales did not hear him, and said as he left, "Adios, amigo. Vaya con Dios."

Harry replied, "Vaya con Dios." Then he began calculating. It would take Nogales the rest of the day to get back to Pecado, a day or two to buy the cow with the gold coin, another for the news of the reappearance of gold to spread, then interrogation by Lobo and El Ratòn—they would steal his letters that night or the next—at least before Thursday, the day of the weekly mail pickup for posting out of the town. He had a week before they would be at the site—plenty of time if he started right away.

The next day, he took out his "long barrel." None in those regions had ever seen it. He cleaned it, oiled it, and checked it carefully. Then he took out eight bullets, two more than he figured he needed. They were steel-encased lead. He carefully scored the noses, ensuring symmetry so that he did not alter the flight ballistics in ways that he could not compensate. He took some cloth bags like those he stored his gold in, filled them with stone, fashioned two crosses and painted them white. The next day, he hitched the mules to his wagon and loaded it with camping gear, a few picks and shovels, the bags of stone, the two white crosses and his weapon. He told Hercules to get in, lifted Porch into the seat beside him, got in himself and drove off to the south and west. He reached the site he had chosen after two days travel late at night and prepared camp behind a hillock.

The next morning, he rose with the sun and paced off four hundred yards south. He dug two small holes eight feet apart, set the crosses in these, and placed a white rock on the ground about a foot from each. Returning to camp, he took out the long barrel, loaded it, and adjusted its sight to four hundred yards. He mounted the hillock and found a good prone position, lay down and fired a round, noting its impact from the dust that spurted up near the white rock. He adjusted the sight. Not much was needed in the morning calm. He fired again and saw the rock move. He fired at the second rock, and made another small adjustment. The second shot blew that rock apart.

He returned to the location of the crosses and dug a pit at each, two feet wide by six long and six deep. He placed the bags of stone in these and refilled the pits. He was ready.

He waited two days, letting Porch half crawl, half walk around the campsite and learn about the desert under the watchful eyes of Hercules. As the sun rose on the third day, he picked up dust far to the south. Hidden from view on the hillock, with the baby and great dog beside him, he watched two riders approach. When they spied the crosses they stopped for a second or two, changed direction, and made a mad dash for them. Reining up in a great swirl of dust when they got there, they leapt off their mounts, pulled shovels out of their saddle bags and began madly churning earth up out of the graves they found by the two crosses. Harry identified the two through his scope when the badges they wore glinted in the sun.

Harry watched them rip out the earth until they were knee deep. It was getting hotter and hotter as the sun climbed the sky. One wiped his brow and climbed out of the grave, went to his horse and pulled his canteen off the saddle. In a frenzy, he pulled on it in long draughts. The other followed. Soon they were back in the holes, digging. But their speed did not last, and their water breaks became more frequent. By the time they were waist deep, it seemed to Harry that a minute passed between each shovel of dirt. Then, almost simultaneously, he saw a shovel fly from each hole. Still the dirt flew. They must have been digging with their hands. Soon he saw a bag placed at the edge of one hole, then another and one from the other grave. More were lifted out. Then the two men climbed out.

Quickly, they poured out the contents, and even from his distance, he could feel their curses. Suddenly they stopped dead still and began looking around. They became very quiet.

It was time for Harry's act. He rose from cover with his long barrel, waving his arms and shouting. When they saw him, he began dancing around, slapping his thighs and laughing as loud as he could. The men ran to their horses and returned with rifles. He watched them take aim and fire. Their bullets fell far to his front. Then calmly, as their fusillade kicked up dust to his front, he lay upon the ground and took aim.

Lobo was reloading when he looked over and saw El Ratòn's head splatter like a melon hurled against a wall shortly before his own chest caved in. When the two reports from the long barrel reached their position, the horses bolted and headed south for Pecado.

Harry picked up Porch, called Hercules, and headed back over the hillock to have lunch in the shade of the camp. The great she-lion had observed these proceedings from some scrub not far from the grave site. When she saw Harry disappear over the hillock, she got up from her cover and went over to investigate what had occurred. Her two cubs, recently weaned, fell in behind her. Soon they were near enough to smell the blood, and the young ones whined their anticipation of fresh flesh. When the mother cougar reached the corpses, she sniffed at each body. This was not food, she thought, and to teach this to her cubs, she urinated on each body, and then led her babies into the distant hills.

Late that afternoon, Harry dragged the corpses to the graves Lobo and El Ratòn had prepared for themselves and pushed them in. Then he filled each with the earth they'd so furiously shoveled out. As evening fell, he loaded his wagon and placed the baby boy beside him on the seat. The dog leapt onto the far side. With a "giddyup" from Harry, the mules headed back to their homestead. They arrived exactly ten days from the day Harry had said "Adios" to Nogales, who was elected mayor of Pecado as spring turned to summer along the border.

Harry observed that year, the thirteenth year of his self-imposed exile, that the land was coming back. The overirrigation and overgrazing that had turned the land into spans of sand had stopped. Each spring, Harry noted more trees, more grass and healthier, more abundant wildlife. New growth cushioned the short but torrential downpours of summer, so they no longer tore deep chasms in the ground. The erosion and land subsidence that had left deep fissures and wide rifts pleased Harry when he'd first bought the land. Such desolation assured his isolation. Now Harry welcomed these changes. The boy had changed his perspective. He wanted to raise him in a land of beauty, a land of nature in harmony with itself, then leave it to him when the time came. Porch had added a new dimension to his life.

When Harry looked at him, he imagined he saw the boy's mother's beauty in his features and character in his heart. He wondered if the lad had inherited his keen intelligence and love of learning from a father about whom he could not even speculate. The boy's only legacy from his parents was the locket he kept constantly about his neck. Harry believed that the white jade image of a man engraved on it, worn away by his mother's kisses and washed away by salty tears, was the boy's father.

However, Harry's affection for the lad did not soften his upbringing. He determined Porch should grow up tough, able to face and conquer whatever challenges life put in his path. As he himself had done, he had Porch begin reading at three and through the Bible and Great Books by the time he was twelve. Harry was a superb tutor. He balanced Porch's serious reading, which he called natural philosophy, with fantasy to stimulate his imagination. Porch steeped himself in Greek mythology, the Icelandic sagas, King Arthur and *The Arabian Nights*. He dreamed of great adventure reading twenty-first century science fiction such as *Tales from the Far Stars*. He conquered an extensive compilation of mathematics, physics, biology, chemistry and computer science, acquiring a foundation of knowledge in the silence of short winter days and long winter nights spent in the room Harry had set aside for his own thought and reflection.

When the snows melted, life changed. Harry's flock of sheep and goats and herd of cattle became restive. They wanted to taste the sweet new grasses of spring. They needed outside pasture. So Porch became shepherd and herder with Hercules and then Ulysses, Hercules' son, at his side.

The cougars respected the dogs and rarely attacked the combined herd, but coyotes were constantly harassing, taking every opportunity to go after stragglers and cut them away from the safety of the main body. The Mexican wolf had returned to the area, and also considered Porch's wards natural prey.

Harry viewed the dogs as bodyguards for the boy as well as the animals, and had such confidence in them that he allowed the boy and the dogs to range far away from the ranch for many days. He taught the boy to shoot the long barrel as soon as the lad was big enough to man the weapon, and he trained him to throw the knife and ax with the skill of a mountain man. However, enthralled with the Old Testament story of David and Goliath, Porch refrained from using these weapons and trained himself to use the sling with such proficiency that he could kill a coyote or wolf out to fifty yards. He found that with a very long staff, he could leap across most of the gullies and washes and vault up the steep embankments that slowed him up when he was chasing a predator. He learned to run very fast when he heard the yipping of a coyote or howl of a wolf.

When Porch was fourteen, Harry and he learned that the Corporation had bought the postal service from the federal government. Almost immediately, the new owner, for the sake of efficiency, cut out service to Harry's rancho. So Harry bought Porch a bicycle, and the boy and Ulysses acquired the obligation of riding south to Pecado once a month to pick up the mail. Thus Porch became fast friends with Nogales, the postman and mayor. He found out Nogales had known his mother and pressed the man to tell him about her. Nogales spoke of her beauty, sweetness and character, but was reticent about saying more. This led Porch to think of her often, and made him curious about his father. And always then, terrible feelings of insecurity hit him. There must be a way to find him, to find out why he left. If he found him, his insecurities would vanish. He was certain of that.

At times he would take off the strange and beautiful locket that he'd worn about his neck for as long as he could remember. He tried to distinguish the features on the cameo, but could not. Often he took it off to listen to the strange and beautiful tune it played when he opened its face. From its construction, he imagined part was missing, which served to deepen the mystery surrounding it. The inscription on the front was worn away, and all that was left of a second inscription on the inside were the words "seek out and find the Birthplace of Wonder."

One night, out on the desert with Ulysses and the mixed herd after the moon had set and only dim embers of the fire remained, Porch looked up to see that the great arm of the Milky Way had ascended. The stars twinkled like ten thousand diamonds and cut a blazing swath from north to south across the vault of heaven. He thought to himself, *Somewhere out there must be 'the birthplace of wonder.' I shall seek it out and find it.*

It was at that moment he determined to attend the Space Academy of the Western Alliance. He would become a starman. After he returned to the rancho, he told Harry what he wanted to do.

Harry smiled and sadly said, "I was hoping the day would never come when Providence would lead you off to your destiny, but I see that day has arrived. You are ready. Tomorrow we will go to Pecado. Nogales will know how to go about obtaining your entrance."

CHAPTER 5
THE ACADEMY

The forest broke on both sides of the road to reveal the massive arch that framed the entrance to the highly esteemed Space Academy of the Western Alliance. Porch stood before it in awe. A three- storey house would fit neatly beneath it. His journey north by electro-train and electro-bus had been long, but he'd refused air flight, as he'd never seen much of his country before. He knew he faced five long years of constant direction, close supervision and intensive study.

He'd even chosen to walk the last five miles to the entrance from the small town that had grown up nearby to serve the stream of tourists that flowed through The Academy during the summer respite. He had with him a small suitcase of clothes and a pouch of gold Harry had given him for his initial expenses. As he started to pass through the arch, he looked up and saw the inscription "To The Stars and Beyond."

He stopped for a moment and looked at the right foundation. A large bronze plate bearing the inscription THE SPACE ACADEMY OF THE WESTERN ALLIANCE was displayed upon it. He looked left and saw a small shield. On the shield's black field was a red griffin rampant. He recognized it immediately. It was the figure used to mark stamps after the Corporation took over the postal system, the logo of the Corporation. A bronze plate below the shield was inscribed with but one word, "Benefactor."

Porch walked through the arch and down the roadway about a hundred yards when he came upon another surprise. Before him loomed a high monument almost as large as the arch he'd just passed beneath. A giant disk slowly rotated in a gyroscopic housing, hung on an inner gimbal by two spokes, or rather rays, since many others jutted out from the central disk in all directions.

A tablet in front of the monument explained the symbolism. The disk represented a blazing sun, its rays the radiation stream that emanated from every such sun in the universe. The inscription on the tablet explained that the emblem was awarded to the Academy when it first opened its gates in hopes that graduates would go forth and find such suns nourishing habitable planets. When Porch looked back up at the monument, it had rotated so that the other side was now facing, depicting an ancient mariner's compass, its rays the cardinal and intercardinal points. Even lesser rays were included, completely boxing the compass.

Porch thought of Harry and how the old man had taught him, when he was a boy, to find direction so he'd never lose himself or his flock even in the worst desert sandstorm. He missed Harry already.

Then eagerly, his eyes went back to the inscription. It told him the Mariner's Compass was awarded to celebrate the first earthmen to reach another sun, explorers led by Rodriguez, or The Navigator, as he came to be called. He was an early Academy graduate. Porch looked at his watch. Still early, he continued on at a leisurely pace, coming upon the Mall of Heroes, those who had made Western space achievement possible. They were all there, engineer and astronaut, the early ones—Goddard, Von Braun, Yeager, Sheppard, Glenn, Armstrong, Aldrin, Collins and the Challenger Seven; and from the twenty-first century, Hammershmidt, Choi and Ironwood. The statuary was both elegant and awe inspiring.

As he continued, he passed side streets that led to academic buildings, laboratories, playing fields and the Grand Parade. Far distant to the right, he glimpsed the

Colossus of the North, as they called it, the huge domed stadium that made athletic events possible even on the coldest days up here on the Canadian Shield.

The Alliance had selected this hard environment to drill the harshness of space into the students. To his left, he saw the towering cathedral which paid homage to the Universal God. Straight ahead a structure dominated all that surrounded it. It was the Command Headquarters and Administration Building. Its central tower portrayed a starship lifting off. Extensive connecting side buildings housed barracks and dining facilities for the ten thousand strong Cadet-Midshipman Brigade, a mouthful seldom used, as the students were simply called Candidates until they graduated as officers into the Space Force.

Porch had been instructed to report to that building. He did this, and from the minute he gave his name until he got to his room later, he was swept into a swirl of sweat. Authorities took all his belongings and gave him a receipt; next, shower, shave, close-cropped haircut; down a line for initial uniform issue; put it on. Everything was done at a dog trot with an upper-class detail fanning him along. Then, lined up with other newcomers, he was sent to lunch.

After lunch, into another line of newcomers, all taught the fundamentals of close order drill by a candidate corporal named Tchako—left face, right face, turn about, forward march, this way, that way, squad halt. The numbers kept increasing as members of the new class reported in. Porch's squad became a platoon and then a company—with left turn, right turn, to the rear march, compa-a-n-y halt. The drill continued until these newcomers would embarrass neither themselves nor the Academy when they marched to the Swearing-In Ceremony later that afternoon.

The company now stood at attention while room assignments and a raft of directions were called out. They were dismissed to retrieve duffel bags full of initial issue clothing, report to their rooms, put their equipment away, prepare their new uniforms and wait until called to sign in at the company orderly room.

Porch ran up the five flights to his room. His superb physical condition checked any fatigue. Quickly, he put his clothes and other regalia away, and sat down to shine his shoes, intending to dress quickly when his call came to report to the orderly room. Each floor had six rooms separately assigned to men or women. The ratio had settled out over the years at about three to one.

He would live on the fifth floor the entire year that he was a Grub. The following year when he became a Fledgling, he would move down a flight. And so it progressed. He would become a Hawk the third year, then an Eagle, and in his final year, he would reach the exalted status of Condor and live on the first floor.

As Porch sat at the desk shining his shoes, a giant figure filled the door. Porch looked up to see a huge black man enter the room.

"Hello, roomy," the black man said, smiling and speaking in the clipped English of Eastern prep schools. "I am Bertram Beauregard Bokasi, but you can call me Bo."

Porch didn't quite hear him and replied, "Boy?"

Fire raged in Bokasi's eyes. "Whitey, you call me 'boy' again and I'll knock you six ways to Sunday."

Porch lurched back, astounded at such strange behavior. "I'm sorry, very sorry, I must have misunderstood you."

Bokasi read the white man's face, and when he saw the shock and heard the sincerity in Porch's voice, he grinned big and his large white teeth illuminated his face. "I grew up in the underculture of the New Chicago inner city where words, some words, are still never spoken—where you from, you don't know these things?"

"My name is Porch, and I'm from west Texas," Porch replied, still careful, "but I never heard of any inner city in Chicago."

Bokasi began to put his clothes and equipment away, and while he did, he told Porch his story. His grandparents, both sides, had fallen victim to drugs and, consequently, early death. His parents, each orphaned at an early age, grew up in a series of foster homes, but mostly on the streets of the inner city. They met and found strength in each other. They had nothing until they had the baby, Bertram, and they then declared to each other that they had something, everything. They doted on him, and steeped in the faith that their unity gave them, they protected him from the evils of the street and taught him its perils. They schooled him intensively, and his intelligence shone through, as did his strength and his agility. He grew to giant size. So regardless of his intelligence, the Eastern prep schools courted him for his athletic ability, particularly in football.

His parents saw this as a ticket to a better life and signed him off on scholarship to the best in the East. Then the Space Academy scouts found him and signed him, confident that with him as fullback rounding out the other talent they had secured, they could build a contender for the international collegiate championship.

Bokasi told his story matter-of-factly and ended saying he would do the best he could, hoping it would be enough. Then he asked, "What about you, Porch?"

Porch told him about Harry, Ole Mulemilk, as strangers called him. He told him about the western desert and the mixed herd he'd shepherded. He told him about the lion, the coyotes and the big dog. He told him about the Great Books, the fantasies he'd read, and the Bible. He told him about how he'd been fascinated by the story of David and Goliath and came to rely on the staff and the sling as his protection and weapons of choice. He told him of the land subsidence, the crevasses formed, why he'd learned to vault and run like the wind. He told him he'd made up his mind to win the pole vault championship for the Academy. He too would do the best he could and hoped that it would be enough.

Bokasi's folks had been such a strong factor in his life that he did not believe a man could make it without such, so he was curious about Porch's folks and asked, "What about your folks, Porch?"

"Harry's all the folks I've got."

"No mama or papa?"

Porch was silent for a moment. The story of Amilee that Harry had told him was personal and painful, but he liked his new, huge, friendly and forthright roommate, so he decided to tell him the story of Amilee. He began with a dry throat, and when he got to the part where Amilee had lured the coyotes out into the desert during the blizzard, he could only stammer the words out, ever so slowly, eyes down on the table.

When he looked up, he saw a tear roll down Bo's cheek.

In a muffled voice, Bokasi said, "I'm sorry, Porch."

Silence ensued for a minute. But then Bo pressed on. "How come you came here?"

Porch got up and retrieved the locket that he'd always worn, but decided to wrap in muslin and keep in his locker until he learned if he'd be authorized to wear it while in uniform. Unwrapping it, he handed it to Bo, who was astonished when he saw it.

Bo picked it up and examined the lyre, the two hearts, and the sapphires and diamonds. He turned it over and heard the strange tune when he opened it up. He looked at the worn cameo and said, "It's a man's face. Who is it?"

Porch said, "I don't know. It may be my papa."

Then Bokasi read the words "seek out and find the Birthplace of Wonder." He looked at Porch quizzically.

Porch told him of the starry night out on the desert when the great arm of the Milky Way was rising and he'd read those words again and again. It was then he'd vowed to become a starman and find "the Birthplace of Wonder."

"That is why I came here."

Bokasi extended his massive arm and grasped Porch's. Porch clasped his in turn and asked, "Then we're friends?"

"More than that," Bo replied. "Brothers."

He returned the locket to Porch but said, "I have a strange foreboding that you should hide the locket."

"Where?"

"There is a hill behind the barrack with some granite boulders. We could find a place. Only you and I would know. It would be safe."

"Tonight," said Porch. Just then an intercom blared,

"Room five-oh-six, candidates to the orderly room—move it, candidates—move it, on the double."

It was a female voice. Porch and Bokasi hurried to the orderly room and reported to the company clerk, a comely Haitian female corporal named Olivia O. Olive. Bokasi looked at her with interest and grinned.

She said, frozen faced, "You see something around here you wanna buy? Wipe that big ugly grin off your big ugly face and report over there to Captain Brightwood—at attention, maggot."

Bokasi froze and braced. "Yes, ma'am," he blurted out, hurrying over to where Captain Brightwood sat behind a desk with a raft of papers and a sign-in ledger. He came to rigid attention.

Now in front of Corporal Olivia O. Olive, Porch too braced after observing what had happened to Bo. In no way did he want to expose himself to the wrath of the diminutive but fiery corporal. He kept his eyes straight ahead but swore to himself that he could feel her eyes looking him over and searching for the tiniest infraction.

Captain Bonnie Brightwood was looking over Bokasi's paper. She was indeed a bonnie lass. Her father, Dr. Amos Brightwood, professor of Cold Temperature Engineering at Cal Tech, was the engineer who had gained international fame when he developed the superconducting cermet that retained frictionless electron flow at room temperature. The Doctor had been doubly lucky when such fame, most times unheard of for engineering drudges, had helped him win the heart of Bonnie's mother, a beautiful actress who graced the early twenty-third century tri-di screens. The professor and actress married, loved each other ardently, and Bonnie grew up privileged in a famous close-knit family. As she grew older, she became determined to make it on her own. When she announced to her parents that she would attend the Space Academy, they were somewhat taken aback, but knowing their daughter, they quickly came to support her decision. Leadership, academic achievement and superb accomplishment as a gymnast had won her captain's bars and a company command in this, her fifth and final year at the Academy.

Bonnie Brightwood was indeed a beautiful, healthy girl. Her rich chestnut hair, slightly wavy and of lustrous sheen, was her crowning glory. It set her apart when she was in full dress for parade, contrasting splendidly with her jaunty tri-corner cap set off by a pale blue plume. Her gymnast figure draped a uniform of midnight blue trimmed with azure in such a way as to make her a presence quite pronounced when she marched by, leading her company.

But she was not dressed for ceremony at the moment. Rather, she wore a utility uniform and was all business when she looked up at Bo and softly said, "Your name please, mister."

"Bertram Beauregard Bokasi, ma'am—but you can call me Bo." Bokasi knew he'd fumbled again even as his words issued forth, and he braced again to bear the onslaught to come.

Bonnie had dark brown eyes that could, as she desired, mesmerize, show deep compassion, twinkle with gaiety, or induce extreme discomfort. She chose the latter and a tone of voice that matched the mood of her eyes when she replied. "I shall address you as Mr. Bokasi, or if ever I choose less formality, as Bertram. Now sign in here, *Mr. Bokasi.*"

Instantly, she had reduced this six-foot-four-inch tall, three foot wide, all muscle and power, two hundred and eighty-five pound Grub to rubble. Bo picked up the pen, dropped it, picked it up again, dropped it, picked it up again, signed in, and came back to rigid attention.

"Dismissed!" said the Company Commander.

Bo did an awkward about-face and marched to the door, passing the frozen-faced Corporal.

"Doubletime," the Corporal called out, her eyes twinkling as he passed her position.

"Next," called the Company Commander.

Porch marched up smartly, saluted and came to rigid attention, for Harry had drilled him a bit before he'd left the rancho.

"Name," Bonnie asked without looking up.

"Porch."

"Full name!"

"Porch."

"That's all?"

"Yes, ma'am."

"What kind of name is that?" she said, looking up.

Startled, she noticeably blanched, although the first-year man standing before her, eyes straight to the front, did not notice. She thought to herself, *My gosh, what have we here—Adonis come to life—and the fates have assigned him to my company.*

She looked at his wavy flaxen hair, his steel-gray eyes, chiseled features that were set off in a muscular but slim six foot-two frame, and she felt a warmth deep inside slowly rise to surround her heart and make it pump a little faster.

Easy, girl, she whispered to herself. *Get a grip.*

Porch's answer interrupted her thoughts. "It's the only name I got, ma'am. Mulemilk—er—Harry gave it to me when he found me on the porch of the ranch during the blizzard."

I can't believe this, an innocent farm boy yet. Oh my, she thought.

Then, again in command, she said, "Sign in here, Mr. Porch." This done, she dismissed him.

In a stirring ceremony at sunset that evening, the new class took an oath of fidelity to the Western Alliance and to the Academy.

That night, the Company Commander's sleep was troubled. She tossed and turned—dreamt of strong arms around her, kisses on her lips and throat. She shivered in a strange new aloneness and pulled her pillow to her breasts. Now too warm, she wrapped her thighs around her quilt, sighed and woke with a start. She said to herself, *Get real, girl. He's just a baby, five years your junior.*

She went over and opened her window as wide as she could, but in her consternation, did not hear the slight commotion on the hill in back of the barracks where Porch and Bokasi were burying a locket.

CHAPTER 6
CHALLENGE

Major Wolfgang Werewick took his position to the left front of the company after it had formed up, as was his habit. This was his third year at the Academy, and the third company he had been assigned to as officer-advisor. Each had been in a different regiment. He liked being moved around. It broadened his awareness of what was going on in the Brigade, both on the surface of everyday life and amongst the undercurrents. It allowed him to sift out and find exactly the right mix of a man for his first love, the Sword and Saber Fraternity, which he sponsored.

The Major had supreme self-confidence when he was facing down a company waiting for inspection. He loved this part of his job. He sensed his power. He could see the apprehension in the eyes of every candidate lined up in front of him, from the company commander on down through the platoon leaders, the sergeants and corporals, and into the ranks themselves. He knew he looked good as he pulled on his pearl gray kidskin gloves, adjusted his midnight blue visored cap, and smoothed his white silk scarf. He had tied his withered left arm to his side so that it would not move, so that no wrinkle appeared on his sleeve or arm of his uniform blouse. He wanted all to note its immobility. This was part of the legend.

Some said he had his shoes constructed to add two inches to his height. Some said he used a cosmetic to enhance the dark red scar that ran from the lower edge of his left eye down across his cheek past the outer edge of his full lips to the center of his chin, ending just above its cleft. He also wore a thin, carefully trimmed mustache, also suspected to be darkened. But Werewick knew he was a legend, and if he primped, he felt so privileged. He was the bastard son of an early space hero, one Mineas Oberon. Oberon had seduced his mother the night of her coming out ball at the old Waldorf Astoria. All hell broke loose because Francesca was also the daughter of the Chairman of the Corporation, and in that organization's ethos, the dishonor she brought to her father was overwhelming. She was already in trouble because her birth marked the end of seven generations of male succession.

When her father found out about her pregnancy, he turned her out of his house with a meager stipend and told her to stay away from the family. She had to fend for herself during a difficult childbirth. Although she would not name her lover, the Chairman became convinced that the man was Mineas Oberon. Oberon disappeared before Francesca came to term, and several years of investigation uncovered nothing. Gradually the famous man's disappearance was forgotten. It stayed so until a survey ship returning from the Oort Cloud found a single spaceman fully clad for deep space traveling just beyond the planet Pluto on a trajectory that would carry him out of the solar system. The surveyors found the body cryogenically frozen, with the man in a kind of repose. He almost looked as if he was pleading a cause. It was Mineas Oberon.

Later events changed Francesca's life and that of her child, but Werewick never forgot the story of his origin. At fifteen, he stowed aboard a survey ship bound for the asteroid belt. When through miscalculation the helmsman threw the ship into an uncharted meteoroid shower, causing heavy damage, he replaced the dead bow gunner, and with fanatical courage fended off sufficient missives to allow the ship to escape. This earned him an ensign commission bestowed by the commander of the survey fleet, the Admiral himself.

Still underage, he signed on a mission to the Oort Cloud. Beyond Pluto, the tough crew, filled with fanciful fears engendered by weeks of travel through unimaginable blackness, became restive. After the distant sun, a last beacon back to earth's reality, disappeared into the void, they mutinied.

In those days, ballistic and laser sidearms were prohibited, since wild and indiscriminate shots would puncture the ship's outer walls and cause immediate decompression, destroying the ship, or at least damaging delicate electronic or photonic equipment. Hence, the Captain and a his small complement of officers were constrained to use sabers against a much larger force of mutineers armed with cutlasses stolen from the ship's armory. They were hard pressed until Ensign Werewick, fighting with maniacal fury, turned the tide in a chaotic melee. In the final battle in the engine room, Werewick forced the mutineer leader Grolub's face into a radiation port, where the fusion stream ate away his nose and part of his jaw. The huge Grolub's fight and that of his fellows was gone. In that fight Werewick lost the use of his arm.

He was promoted to full lieutenant, and he spent three more years with the fleet on ever more adventurous missions. Then he came to realize that there would be no more promotions unless he got an education. He was offered admission to the Academy, but felt too old to enter. He went elsewhere, graduated in three years, and returned to the fleet.

That was a decade ago. Werewick knew that this was his last year of duty at the Academy. He would again return to the fleet, in line for command and promotion. He would shed the land lubber rank of major, by custom awarded for shore duty, and revert to lieutenant commander and then commander. So he stood there proudly, waiting for the Company Commander to report her company ready for inspection. This would be his cue to push out his bemedaled chest, make a final tug on his blouse, march swiftly forward to take her salute, and begin his inspection. His decorations, lustrous and polished, gave credence to the legend of the little man. He wore the Medal of The Sun, the Iron Asteroid, the Galactic Talisman with two Star Clusters, and many other awards.

As he awaited the Company Commander's signal, he slowly moved his gaze down the ranks of new faces, hesitating at Bokasi, then stopping as he appraised his potential. Mentally he told himself that perhaps the giant would make a champion with a cudgel but certainly not foil, sword or saber, weapons which required a certain degree of finesse. His eyes moved on down the ranks. They passed Porch, returned and fixed on the tall blond youth. His eyes narrowed. Werewick was transfixed. He'd never seen such a perfect specimen—tall, long arms, thin. He had to have him. This one, properly trained, could carry the S&S Fraternity to the Olympics. Werewick was elated.

Just then, Captain Brightwood called her company to attention, turned and reported ready for inspection. Werewick strode over like a lead actor entering the scene from side stage. He took her salute and beckoned her to follow as he proceeded slowly down the ranks. He took great care to observe the condition of each candidate, calling out whatever delinquencies in dress, equipment or appearance met his practiced eye. He sped up a bit as he approached Porch. When he reached him, he stopped, turned and faced him squarely. Slowly, he moved his gaze over him, back and forth, up and down. Then he backed off a foot, stared hard up into the candidate's eyes and said softly, "I want you, mister...for the Sword and Saber Fraternity."

There was silence, and the Major put his face up to Porch, very close, and said quietly, "Didn't you hear me, mister? I want you. I want you for our fraternity. I will make you a champion, a world renowned champion. I want your commitment now, mister, now."

Porch stammered out, "No, sir, I am committed to track and field—the sprints, distance and pole vault. I promised Harry."

The Major stared at Porch and the scar on his face reddened and puffed out. "Mister, I am not used to hearing no. What I offer would be of great benefit to you. You have a tough year in front of you. Your trials could be eased. Do you understand?"

"Yes, sir, I understand. No, sir, I must stand for the vault and running. I promised Harry."

Major Werewick was livid. He made a left face and hurried up the rank without stopping. Captain Brightwood and the company clerk, Corporal Olive, who was noting demerits, followed as required.

When Bonnie passed Porch, she gave him an incredulous look and said, "I'll talk to you later, mister."

Werewick stopped well beyond the last file in the squad and wheeled about. "Captain Brightwood," he snarled, "I want that man, Porch, changed to Tchako's squad. Put Bokasi in Olive's in exchange. That is an order."

Brightwood flushed but said, "Yes, sir."

Normally, the company commander had assignment prerogatives, but since it really didn't matter to her, she complied without question. She was not about to cross a senior who could damage her career. Werewick continued his inspection rapidly. Bonnie wondered if this was a result of his obvious anger or some less apparent reason. Knowing Werewick's reputation for studied coolness, she tended to discount anger. Werewick did stop at Squad Leader Tchako's position and engage him in quiet conversation. Bonnie knew that Tchako was a long-time member of the S&S Fraternity—come to think of it, so was Cheeko, Tchako's assistant squad leader. Both were devoted to Werewick to the point of obsequiousness, and Cheeko was so servile and condescending to Tchako that Bonnie thought she might be observing an unhealthy relationship. She had meant to separate them, but in face of what had just occurred she felt she'd better wait and monitor the two over the forthcoming year for anything out of order. She would talk to Candidate Porch.

As soon as Werewick completed his inspection and departed, she called over Tchako and Corporal Olive. She gave them Werewick's transfer order and then dismissed the company, except Bokasi and Porch. She informed them of the transfer, turned Bokasi over to Olivia, and told Porch to wait. Privately, she told Porch to think long and hard about his refusal to enlist in the Sword and Saber Fraternity. She spoke positively, pointing out that Major Werewick was a renowned swordsman, and if he said he could train Porch to championship stature and the fame that went with it, he could. She told him that life would be easier for him during the tough year ahead if he had Major Werewick on his side. But Porch was adamant. He'd told Harry that he was going to be a track and field man, and that was what he intended to be.

Very well then, Bonnie turned Porch over to Sergeant Tchako and left the quadrangle. Tchako squared off in front of Porch and braced him up at rigid attention, tighter and tighter, until Porch was sweating profusely. After an hour, he marched him back to the barracks and dismissed him. Porch knew he faced a tough year. In the meantime, the diminutive Corporal Olive had circled her new acquisition several times to size him up. Then she came to the front of the giant who was standing at rigid attention before her, placed her hands on her hips, and starting at his feet, gradually looked all the way up to his face. She exaggerated, leaning back so as to see him properly. Bokasi dared not look down and stayed at rigid attention.

Suddenly she stepped back and yelled, "Do I see a smirk on your double ugly mug, you lug of a pea-brained thug? Pull your shoulders back until those blades crush your backbone! I want to see your chin inside your collarbone! I see nothing funny inside this quadrangle except a big overstuffed gorilla who has yet to learn how to soldier. So we'll start to instruct him with some close order drill! Atten-shut-right face-forward harch-hut to-hut to-hut to, to the rear- harch, hut to-hut to, squad haaalt, about face, by the left flank-harch, hut to-hut to, by the right flank-harch..."

And so Corporal Olive marched her new charge around the square for almost an hour. Then she marched him back to barracks. From the orderly room window, Bonnie had watched her subordinate. She said to herself as they approached, "Boy, Olivia really likes him."

In substance, Porch and Bokasi had become too visible. Had they had the good fortune of staying as inconspicuous as most of their classmates, their first year may have been at least tolerably miserable. They did not get much rest—Bokasi under the watchful eye of Olivia O. Olive, and Porch tormented by Tchako and Cheeko on the premise that he could be bullied into the S&S Fraternity.

During the summer, candidates received basic military training and orientation into their chosen careers, accomplished through a series of tri-di telelectures. After man's first step beyond the earth to the moon, the superpowers called off the Cold War and established a moratorium on nuclear war. They turned their attention to space after rebuilding devastated economies. Space became the new outlet for national ambitions and international alliances. By 2020, a permanent moon base had been constructed. The first Mars landings followed in 2026. A year later, scientists established a total spectrum telescope base line in sun orbit at one earth radius. They began probing the heavens for star systems whose emissions showed the chemistry of life. In 2030, the first space-based laboratory-factory was put into Earth orbit. It was a great wheel almost three miles in diameter. It rotated slowly, one revolution every five or so minutes to provide a false gravity for the vast array of living quarters, administrative facilities and tourist accommodations located along its rim. Its axis housed solar power plants, zero gravity labs and production lines. In the next twenty years, these laboratory-factories became bi-axial, then tri-axial. They evolved into tubes, then long hollow cylinders.

Advances in superconductivity increased the magnetic squeeze on ultra hot plasmas, harnessed them, and made their hydrogen-helium isotopes fuse. Ram jet fusion engines became a reality, transforming the great space cylinders into interplanetary travelers. The mammoth ships generated magnetic field lines that extended out millions of miles and sucked in the very ylem of space, compressed it, fused it and blasted it out again in fierce jet streams.

In 2060, the fiery visionary Thaddeus Moses Winter collected the downtrodden, disinherited and discontent, one hundred thousand strong. He named them Millenarians and called them forth for the First Emigration on the great starship *Leviathan*. With the charisma and religious fervor of Moses of old, he led them on the first star trek to a new promised land. In 2090, his son led the Second Emigration. The Third Emigration followed in 2130, and the Fourth in 2180... Such lectures continued all summer as the new class was molded into a spaceman fit. Fall came and brought with it the teeth of the academic year. In these northern climes, the sun set soon after it rose. The orders of the day were darkness and icy cold. Porch and Bo steeped themselves in the toughest curriculum of a Western Alliance university. Bokasi made honors math and science after the first trimester examinations. Porch, having read the Great Books and been tutored by Harry through the years, qualified to skip much of the liberal arts portion of the first year agenda. He knew Spanish well, while Bokasi had learned French from some years spent in Haiti, where his parents had been teaching. So both advanced to new courses in language theory and evolution. This would help them later as starmen should they be thrust into other worlds of new civilizations and required to learn their languages quickly.

In football, Bokasi, though ineligible for varsity as a first-year man, was making a name for himself as a fullback and linebacker. That year, the Space Academy varsity faced as fierce opposition during weekly scrimmages as they did on game days. Bokasi and a man called Eric the Red led the first-year men to several victories over the Academy veterans. Porch also was doing well. He set new Academy records in distance running that fall, and the varsity cross country team looked forward to his participation the following year.

Since both were of intercollegiate caliber, they had their meals at the training tables where hazing, by tradition, was never allowed. This gave them respite from the harassment their classmates faced during mealtime at the company tables.

Other times were another matter. Corporal Olive was constantly on Bokasi's back. But her hazing was minor compared to what Porch had to endure. He was always "on visit" before the supper formation to his squad leader Tchako's room for extra instruction. Sometimes it was spaceman lore. He learned to recite the dictum from the earliest days—Sputnik, Vanguard, Explorer. He knew the heroes. He had to learn the hardware—Gemini, MOL, Apollo, Skylab, the shuttles, the Martian Lander. He could give the engineering details of Moon Base. It was all contained in the "Blue Book" issued to each new candidate.

Sometimes Tchako's additional "space instruction" required him to do a hundred pushups, a hundred sit-ups, or hold his ceremonial rifle in one hand and one of Tchako's broadswords in the other in a free space position—which was on his belly with neither arms nor legs touching the floor for the full ten minutes of the visit. He was required to recite Blue Book material while doing this.

The assistant squad leader Cheeko, Tchako's roommate, was always there to help with the torment. Cheeko liked best to brace the Grub up, forcing him to put his chin into his neck as far as it would go, to pull his shoulders way back and suck his stomach "into his backbone." Cheeko gave his commands an inch from Porch's face and followed the orders with a steady stream of invective, most of the time going over the edge of good taste. But worse than all the physical or mental abuse was Cheeko's omnipresent foul breath and slobbering, some of which hit Porch square in the face. The hazing continued through the winter and into the approaching spring. It was designed to make the Porch give in and join the S&S Fraternity.

Major Werewick fomented the hazing and monitored it sub rosa. Since neither Tchako nor Cheeko by regulation could give demerits, Werewick took on that job, seeing to it that Porch was always close to, but never over, the limit that would cause automatic expulsion. Porch endured without complaint.

Only Bokasi was fully aware of this debilitating treatment of his close friend and roommate. It enraged him and almost broke his heart, though Porch never spoke of it. Finally Bokasi's own morale bottomed out and he could not conceal his anguish. His own mark in the company was constant good humor and jovial spirits no matter what the situation. When this disappeared, his own squad leader, tormentor and mentor, Corporal Olivia O. Olive, knew something was up. She wormed the full extent of Porch's treatment out of Bo and promptly went to Captain Brightwood to discuss the matter. Bonnie Brightwood was aware of Tchako and Cheeko's efforts to break Porch. But she was also aware they had Werewick's support. Porch's stubborn refusal to join the Sword and Saber Fraternity was still on her mind. She thought Porch foolish. Werewick invited few to join, and when he said he could make him a champion, she believed it. He had done so with Tchako.

Tchako was as big as Bokasi and looked as powerful. He had come to the Academy under circumstances almost identical to those that had brought Bokasi here. He'd been a highly solicited football prospect. Terrible anger arose among the football coaching staff when Werewick diverted him, but no one had dared face the Major off. They all were aware of his legendary status in the Space Fleet, and they also knew of his connections in the Corporation. Tchako's classmates had been taunting and derisive when he left the football program, but he'd garnered new respect from them two years later when he won the world broadsword title in the unlimited weight division. Most disliked him for his churlish ways, and they all kept their distance.

Cheeko was another matter. Bonnie was totally contemptuous of him for his braggadocio and bullying behavior. As he progressed through the Academy, he seemed to get nastier. Bonnie believed she detected a streak of sadism in him. Her dislike for him came well before he'd become Porch's tormenter, so even though she felt the Grub had brought it on himself, she felt she must act. She knew Olivia had good instincts. If Corporal Olive thought something should be done, no doubt it should. She thought about it for a while and then came to a decision.

She had it within her authority to make temporary or brevet appointments, as they became called. Normally, these were made in the next class under as a matter of training or to award examples of extraordinary leadership. So, much to the wonderment of the entire company, she appointed Tchako brevet commander for the evening formation, which required his presence at First Call, ostensibly to supervise the company officers, check the formation, and carry out whatever administrative functions were the order of the day. She was confident that Major Werewick would not contest such recognition of one of his favorites. This would obviate his ability to keep Porch on visit every night. Similarly, she made Cheeko a temporary squad leader, requiring that he too be present at First Call. He could still harass the Grub, but he would have to do it in front of his classmates and he himself would be under the direct supervision of his own platoon leader, who was a just man of good common sense.

Although most of the company thought that their commander had taken leave of her senses, Olivia understood right away what Bonnie had accomplished. She gave her a high five, although such conduct was totally inimical to good order and discipline.

Tchako's appointment puffed him up like a great toad. He strutted before the company with all the bravado he could muster. Likewise, Cheeko assumed grave authority and began dressing down his squad, including his own classmates, for the slightest infraction. And he would not give up on Porch.

Though contrary to Academy regulations, he decided that he would have the first-year man report to him in the basement of the barracks at 10 p.m., right after release from quarters and one half-hour before Taps. He figured that the Grub would not dare report him, and even if he did, his punishment would be light. Anyway, by tradition, his classmates were bound to rally around him, and they would bring the roof down on Porch if he made so much as a whimper. So Cheeko took it upon himself to have Porch report to the basement for "posture correction" sessions. He first braced him up and then asked as protocol demanded, "May I touch you, mister?" It was required that Porch assent. Cheeko started out with shoulder adjustments. After several weeks of these subterranean "calls," the areas of posture adjustment changed. Cheeko's hands often went to Porch's well- developed pectorals and then lingered on his buttocks. Porch knew something was wrong, but his isolated west Texas youth had left him somewhat naive. He asked Bokasi what he thought of such "training."

Bokasi exploded. He said, "Good God, he's feelin' you, man! I gotta clue you in. Next time he do that, you knock him six ways to Sunday."

"What?"

Bokasi clued him in. The next night, Porch knocked Cheeko six ways to Sunday and all hell broke loose in Captain Brightwood's company. When Bokasi heard the noises, he rushed down the five flights to the basement and got there in time to see several of Cheeko's classmates holding Porch away from his tormenter. Then he saw Cheeko get up from the floor in an astonishment which quickly turned to cold rage. He slapped Porch hard in the face before anyone could restrain him. Candidates were pouring into the basement from all over. Tchako arrived, followed by Captain Brightwood and Corporal Olive.

Cheeko started shouting, "I challenge the Grub. I challenge him, a fight to the finish."

Bonnie got order restored and began questioning the two men as to what had happened. Cheeko screamed again. "He hit me when I was correcting his posture. He dared hit me."

Bonnie turned to Porch and asked, "What do you say to that, Grub?"

His face flaming red with embarrassment, Porch did not answer.

Bokasi, sensing his roommate's plight, broke in. "Captain, ma'am, he was feelin' him. He's got no right to make such advances."

Bonnie glared at Bokasi, then slowly turned toward Cheeko.

Tchako broke in, "That's preposterous."

Cheeko shouted, "I challenged him. I demand satisfaction."

"That's absurd. There will be no fighting in my company. We will settle this in civilized fashion," Bonnie retorted.

"To hell with you, woman. I demand satisfaction and I'll get it." Cheeko screamed.

"You don't have any choice, Bonnie," Lieutenant Lippinscott, Bonnie's executive officer, said calmly. "By tradition, a challenge issued must be met, either by the Grub or his stand-in. It's been eighty years since Ironwood whipped six in a row in such a situation, serving tradition. But the Brigade will have it no other way."

"I want to fight him," Porch said grimly.

"Since he challenged you, Grub, the choice of weapon is yours," Lippinscott went on. "Shepherd's crooks."

Laughter broke out, but the exec said softly, "We don't have such weapons here."

"Very well then," Porch replied. "The yeoman's staff, three inches thick and eight feet long."

Some were still amused, but most thought maybe the Grub selected well. Although quite a fencing champion, Cheeko was unfamiliar with such a weapon. Tchako, though, was not amused, for he doubted Cheeko's abilities with any weapon other than sword, saber or foil. He said, "Grub, after he's through with you, you'll stand against me."

"Mister, you gotta go through me first," Bokasi interjected.

"You challenging me, Grub?"

"You heard it, man," Bokasi replied.

"My pleasure and my choice of weapons—unsheathed broadswords," Tchako said smugly. The crowd gasped.

"Aw, come on," Lippinscott argued, "that's taking unfair advantage. The Grub has never even held a broadsword, and you're an international champion."

"You heard his challenge. We'll fight like I said, or he can quit now, like the coward he probably is, and apologize. Any of you don't like it can have a turn when I'm through with him."

"I don't like it," Bonnie said.

"You want to fight me?" Tchako looked around, then said, "OK, I withdraw. The big man can hide behind a skirt."

"We'll fight," Bokasi demanded.

Captain Brightwood held her hands up. "I am not through with this," she said, "but it is two minutes before Taps, everyone except the two Grubs, Tchako, Cheeko, Lippinscott and Corporal Olive return to quarters. No use getting the command structure down on our backs. We'll settle this within the Company and the Brigade. Go!"

The onlookers filed out except those requested to stay. When all had left, Bonnie asked Cheeko, "Is what the Grub alleged true?"

Cheeko reddened and replied, "What do you know, you fancy whore?"

Porch leaped at Cheeko. Lippinscott restrained him. Tchako cursed Cheeko. "You damn fool," he whispered, "you know how popular she is."

Lippinscott looked at Cheeko and said with disgust, "If there is anything left of you after Mister Porch is through, you'll fight me and the rest of the seniors in the company."

Bonnie looked at Tchako and Cheeko and said quietly, "I've had enough of this for tonight. Tchako, you're relieved of your brevet rank of captain and reduced to private. Cheeko, you are relieved also and reduced to private. Now return to quarters or I'll charge you both with conduct unbecoming an officer and forward the charges to command, come what may."

Taps sounded. She continued, "Now, the rest of you, out of here now."

As they left, Corporal Olive looked up at Bokasi and said, "You fool, that man is going to kill you."

CHAPTER 7
THE DUEL

News of the forthcoming duels spread quickly through the Brigade. All knew the code of silence concerning such internal brigade affairs, so the information did not reach Space Command authorities. Morale was mixed; low in Captain Brightwood's company, because its members knew Tchako and Cheeko and felt that they had acted despicably, and high elsewhere because certain candidate entrepreneurs promised camcordisk delivery within an hour after the fights' conclusion. Captain Brightwood was pensive and curt the next several days.

She held several meetings with her classmates over what to do. Almost all believed the duels must be held. Porch would get the beating of his life, and Tchako would kill Bokasi. She could not allow a killing in her company. She had at least got the bouts delayed for thirty days. Bokasi would get some training, but the outlook was bleak.

She contacted Captain Ironwood, who commanded another company in the same regiment. He was the grandson of the renowned explorer and early Academy graduate. Ironwood had been a member of the Sword and Saber Fraternity several years before, but had dropped out shortly after Major Werewick took over as sponsor. He had never told anyone why. He was a good man, still highly rated as a broadswordsman. He agreed to give Bokasi intensive training over as many days as were left before the duels, but he held out very little hope for the man.

Bonnie held a number of brainstorming sessions with Olive. She kept saying, "We must do something, but right now I don't know what."

In return, Olive would pat her commander's shoulder and say, "We'll think of something," hardly believing it herself.

After reflecting on his situation for several days, Tchako found himself in a quandary. He thought he'd easily dispatch Bokasi. He knew he was disliked intensely, but he relished his reputation as a bully. It really didn't matter. Those who disliked him would soon fear him. Others could simply hold him in awe. But he didn't like standing in the ranks. He blamed Captain Brightwood. She had no reason for relieving him as brevet commander. It was Cheeko who had insulted her. She'd been completely unfair. He missed strutting in front of the company. He missed dressing down the candidates for infractions. He missed the resentment he could see in their eyes when he chewed them out. He missed the power.

But why had Werewick not intervened? The Major could see that both he and Cheeko were now standing in the ranks. Well, he'd fix the bitch. He would get headaches right before the next several supper formations and go on sick call. Cheeko could report his illness. This would surely draw Werewick's attention to check on him. He would tell Werewick most of what had transpired. He would cite Brightwood's command and leadership failure as leading to the duels. Of course he would not tell Werewick that his duel with Bokasi was to be with unsheathed swords. Werewick would not suspect because rubber coverings sheathed broadswords in all competitions. He smiled to himself when he thought that he had enough on Werewick so that the Major could do naught but take his side. Why? Hadn't the Major marked Porch for special treatment? It would all work out very nicely.

Of course Werewick noticed Tchako and Cheeko standing in the ranks. But he was too wily to take notice. Nothing official had been brought to his attention.

They'd probably done something dumb which was being handled within the brigade. Captain Brightwood was no fool. If he questioned her, there would be an inquiry. An inquiry would bring an investigation. The Sword and Saber Fraternity would no doubt be brought in.

Well, Tchako and Cheeko could take their humiliation. It probably had something to do with that man Porch. He'd come down hard on him and wasn't through yet. He was a patient man and eventually he would have him. So Werewick ignored Tchako and Cheeko.

For three days straight Tchako missed the evening formation, which Cheeko duly reported. He was ignored, so he began soliciting attention from anyone who'd listen. Finally he went to Lieutenant Lippinscott and told him about the severity of Tchako's headaches—how painful they were. That night at dinner, Lippinscott reported what Cheeko said to Captain Brightwood. Bonnie listened carefully, then turned to other matters. After dinner, walking back to barracks with Olive, she mentioned Tchako's reported headaches, saying she believed he was faking it.

Suddenly Olivia stopped dead in her tracks. "Ah-ha, that's it!" she exclaimed, and she began laughing and doing a little skip step.

Bonnie watched for a second or two and then, smiling, called out, "What's wrong, girl, has your head come loose?"

Olive continued, "Trust me, Captain, trust me." Then pointing a finger to the sky, she said, "Salvation is at hand. 'Bye now. I got things to do and people to see."

She ran off as fast as she could. As she ran, she thought to herself that she would start that very night, so she altered her course and headed for the Academy's central library. Once there, she went to the video files. Searching these, she found that what she wanted had never been transcribed to video disks. She headed for the stacks that housed the African Collection, and, searching these, picked out three ancient books on African tribal history. She checked these out and headed back to the barracks.

She read till Taps and lights out. Thereafter, she

continued to read by flashlight, concealed under a blanket from the duty officer should he come around checking. Tomorrow was Saturday. She could nap in the afternoon if she got tired, but she had to be ready by Monday. Saturday morning, using her authority as company clerk, she called together a detail of Grubs and gave each one a trophy from the company display case, saying all badly needed cleaning and shining. She told them not to return them until so ordered and then the trophies better be spotless. Next, she went to the materials lab and talked her old professor out of some memory metal extrusions. At the chemistry lab, she secured twenty pounds of hard wax. As a member of the art club, she was entitled to withdraw a set of acrylic paints, brushes and a pottery display stand. With these items in hand, she was ready to begin. She worked all weekend.

In the meantime, Bonnie received the first report from Captain Ironwood on Bokasi's broadsword training. He'd been working with the Grub for about a week. Ironwood told her that if he had six months he could train the man to defend himself successfully, but with the time he had, it looked pretty hopeless.

She checked on Porch. The classmate she'd asked to watch him work out reported that the Grub appeared pretty nonchalant, that he didn't seem to be working too hard. Infuriated, she called Porch in and chewed him out for an hour. The only response she got from him was "yes, ma'am" and "no, ma'am". She dismissed him and contacted Olivia. All Olivia would say was "not to worry." It looked hopeless.

Monday evening after supper, several fourth class Fledglings nosing around the orderly room discovered the redecorated display case. It stood in an alcove in the small anteroom. There was a jet black drape on the three inside walls and bottom which set off an almost godlike figure of a heavy set, well-muscled youth wearing a breech cloth. The figure was marvelously detailed, head held high, long hair flowing back, shining eyes, mouth open in what appeared to be an heroic cry of victory. The figure was about two feet tall, but extending forward and up another two feet was the figure's stout right arm grasping a broadsword. Likewise, its left arm extended high in a gesture of victory. The acrylic paint was blended with such artistic skill that it made the figure appear almost alive. Soft lighting from above illuminated the figure beautifully.

Word of the redecorated trophy case spread through the company like wildfire. Crowds of candidates packed the anteroom to examine the figure and debate its origin and symbolism. Then it came to them. It looked exactly like Tchako. Someone told Tchako and he rushed to the orderly room to view it. At first, he was very suspicious. But after thinking about it and discussing its significance with Cheeko, he concluded it portended his forthcoming match and victory. Already the company was paying homage to his prowess.

Bonnie saw the work and called Olivia aside. "What's going on?"

"Trust me," Olive smilingly replied.

Again, Tchako puffed up like a toad and began strutting about the company. Even though he'd been unfairly reduced to standing in the ranks, they so much as admitted he was a force to be reckoned with. Miraculously his headaches disappeared. For the next several days, he was his old self again, scowling down those who dared meet his eyes and bullying those who did not.

The matches were drawing near, now but ten days away. Bonnie queried Ironwood again. He was dejected. Bokasi was giving it his best but Ironwood doubted that he would last more than a round.

During this dark and dreary part of the Academy year, anticipation of the bouts gripped the brigade. The only conversations broached and conducted in whispers were of the matches. Heavy betting began. Odds settled at one hundred to one that Bokasi would win, twenty to one that he would survive, and twenty-five to one against Porch. Vast amounts of money were placed in escrow.

Four days before the matches, which were set for 2100 hours on a Saturday night when Taps was normally scheduled at midnight, Tchako's headache returned. He felt feverish. He went on sick call and Cheeko reported his plight to the company. This headache was real, and a doozy at that.

One of the underclassmen in the company happened by the statue and noted that it had gained a tight band about its head. As well, its countenance appeared to have changed from a heroic celebration to a grimace of agony. The lighting which had come down from the top now flooded up from the bottom in an orange glow, and the case was warm to the touch. The candidates looked at each other and speculated on these changes. The heroic figure now appeared more like an effigy.

Tchako ignored these postulations as superstitious nonsense. In any event, if the headaches persisted, he could overcome them with one of the amazing new sedatives available at the dispensary. But the trickery, if that is what it was, infuriated him. By morning, his headache was gone.

That afternoon, he doubled his workout time with the broadsword and exercised furiously, flailing at the heavy target bags with such intensity that he cut several in half with one stroke apiece. He also hurt his shoulder. The whirlpool bath was of little help. He went to look at the statue. The constricting headband was gone, but there was a rose thorn embedded deeply in the right shoulder. The orange glow had turned reddish and the case was warmer. Tchako found himself sweating profusely. Then he noticed that the figure's arms had dropped lower. There was a definite grimace of pain on the face.

Foolishness, he snarled to himself. *This is the age of reason. Belief in witchcraft died out in Salem six hundred years ago.*

That evening at supper formation, a whispered undercurrent of taunting began—voodoo—voodoo. Tchako bent his will to ignore it. In a little more than two days' time, he would show them who was paramount. The following morning, the pain and fever had once again disappeared. That afternoon, Tchako practiced with a fury that bordered on the berserk, his awesome blade cutting through every target in sight. Ironwood had quietly entered the site of his workout to assess the man's skill. Tchako faltered but once, losing his balance upon swinging a mighty blow. He fell on his hip and gasped in pain, but nevertheless rose immediately and continued in unabated fury.

Ironwood left in awe and went to see Bonnie. He paled as he told her, "Bokasi is a dead man."

Bonnie was terrified and called in Bokasi. She pleaded with him to surrender to Tchako and beg for mercy. All Bokasi would say was that he would not embarrass the company when Tchako killed him.

Tchako finished his workout, and after he'd cooled down he found the pain in his hip and thigh excruciating. Ignoring the whirlpool, he limped back to the orderly room to look at the statue. A hat pin was stuck in the right thigh of the figure. He'd had enough. He went to Bonnie's room and demanded that the figure be removed, that no matter who the company sided with, he deserved fair treatment.

"As fairly as you are treating your opponent, a man unschooled in the weapon, but yes, I will have the offending figure removed," she said in haughty retort.

Once Tchako had left, she called in Olive and told her to remove the statue. "No problem, Captain," Olivia replied.

The next morning, Saturday, the day of the fateful bouts, the figure was gone from the trophy case, and in its place, the company trophies stood, shined to a glitzy sparkle. Tchako awoke, feeling like a million dollars.

Lippinscott led a company detail which laid out a fighting square in the subterranean baggage stowage area designated for the matches. The detail put wooden barricades around its periphery and provided board seats on boxes for the judge, timer and official witnesses. Lighting was subdued for secrecy. Places were set aside for the referee, seconds and corner men. The duel master chose video-disk operators by lot. There was a small first aid station with bandages, tape, medicines and stretchers for use between rounds. Rounds would be three minutes with one between. Fights would continue until surrender, incapacitation or death.

By eight that evening, all who were to participate in managing and administering the bouts had gathered. Brigade Commander Stark was judge. Regimental Commander Yomohiga, a martial arts expert who could trace his roots back to the samurai of old Japan, was to referee. By eight forty-five, Porch and Cheeko's corner men and seconds were in place. Their match, stemming from Cheeko's challenge, the "casus belli" of the entire affair, had become small potatoes, a dull preliminary to the gut-wrenching drama that would unfold in the broadsword match. So what if Cheeko trounced the Grub? Who could care: hadn't the Grub really started it?

Nobody there, save Bokasi, knew of the years Porch had spent in the desert guarding Harry's herd and flock when their lives and his, too, had depended upon his skill with the sling and the staff.

At nine o'clock sharp, the judge called Porch and Cheeko to the center of the arena or "ring" and elucidated the rules. They were simple enough. The opponent's body could be hit anywhere. Should one's opponent slip on blood or sweat, the other must retire to a neutral corner until the referee called him back to the combat. The seconds and corner men could repair damage and revive their fighters with water between rounds. The bout would continue until one or the other begged for mercy, or was knocked senseless or killed.

Next, the senior first-aid man required first Cheeko, then Porch to hold his heavy staff high while he checked wrist bands and ankle wraps for evidence of fraud. He checked bare feet, breech clothes—their entire bodies. He used a laser medometer to check their eyes, and a breathalyzer to pick up evidence of drugs or stimulants. He did this slowly, with great care which added to the suspense. When he finished, the referee returned the two men to their corners.

The timekeeper hit the bell for round one. Cheeko came out quickly with a snarl, rushing at Porch. He feinted high, then struck low. Porch parried and dealt Cheeko a resounding blow behind his ear. Blood flowed. Cheeko reeled back, astonished. The audience sat up and gasped. They had not been prepared for this. Cheeko's rage returned and he rushed Porch again, feinting low and aiming high. Porch easily caught his staff, pushed it up and hit Cheeko in his gut. Cheeko staggered back. Now Porch advanced. He made a double feint, then delivered two quick blows to Cheeko's side and left thigh.

Cheeko cried out in pain and backed off, holding his staff far out, attempting to push Porch back. Porch saw fear in his eyes. Around they circled, Porch advancing, Cheeko retreating. The bell resounded, ending round one.

The audience was buzzing in astonishment. Bonnie left her seat in the stands, and coming down to ringside, went to Porch's corner. After his corner men ministered to him and wiped his face, she whispered in his ear, "Make it last, mister. Make it last."

The bell for round two sounded and the men advanced from their corners. The round was a repeat of the first, as was the third and the fourth. Round five came and went, and Cheeko's thrashing continued. Porch tempered the force of his blows to his opponent's condition. When Cheeko appeared on the verge of collapse, he checked his strength of delivery. When Cheeko appeared revived, he increased their force. For fifteen rounds, the fight continued.

When the bell for round sixteen sounded, Cheeko staggered out, motivated by hatred, preserved by painkillers. Porch moved to the center of the ring, lowered his staff and stood there unguarded. Cheeko raised his staff to strike but fell to the mat, out cold.

The judge declared the match ended, and the referee held Porch's arm up in victory. The onlookers sat in stony silence. They had yet to fathom what they'd seen. The stretcher men carried Cheeko out. Porch exited the ring.

At a quarter past ten the timekeeper signaled the next match to begin. The judge called for Tchako to enter the ring. Tchako stood up, looked around menacingly, pushed a barricade aside and entered. Unsheathing his broadsword in a great sweep, then holding it out, he swept his broadsword high, then held it across his chest, waiting for Bokasi to enter. High up behind him, just below the rafted ceiling, a drape fell down and behind it appeared the statue, flooded in blood-red light. Tchako looked up and cursed. One of his corner men from the S&S Fraternity grabbed Cheeko's fallen staff to dislodge it, make it fall to the floor and break into a thousand pieces.

"No!" Tchako screamed, remembering that what happened to the statue had happened to him. The corner man retreated. All eyes turned to the statue, gleaming in bloody red light. A deep bass chant, at first barely audible, then heavy and reverberating, filled the chamber. Voom—boom, boom boom. Voom—boom, boom boom.

Tchako sweated profusely, his eyes transfixed on the statue. The referee called him to the center of the ring. Tchako watched the statue. The light illuminating the figure changed to hot iron red. He noted that the arm holding the broadsword was lowering. The other arm, once held high in victory, was faltering, slowly falling to the statue's feet. He'd hardly heard the referee. Now the medic stood before him, indicating that he should hold his arms high for the medical check. Tchako strained to raise them. The beat of the chant, quicker now and louder, continued.

Voom—boom, boom boom. Voom—boom, boom boom. The referee turned Tchako around and nudged him back to his corner. He called Bokasi out and repeated the rules. The medic checked him and he returned to his corner. The chant grew louder, the beat faster. It seemed of ancient origin—out of the heart of the Dark Continent.

The judge nodded to the timekeeper. Ironwood told Bokasi to defend himself only. The bell rang. Tchako came out, straining to rush to the attack, but it took all his energy to hold his broadsword up and out. Bokasi slowly circled. VOOM—BOOM, BOOM BOOM. VOOM—BOOM, BOOM BOOM.

Tchako lunged, making a feeble sweep with his sword. Bokasi caught the blade and turned it aside. He twirled behind Tchako. Now he could see the statue. Its arms had sunk to its waist and now its torso was lurching over. He looked back at Tchako, who was reeling to stay upright. He circled, watching his adversary carefully. Tchako attempted to lift his blade and deliver a blow but could not lift it above his waist. Beads of water streamed down his body. Bokasi looked up at the statue. It seemed to be melting. The miniature broadsword was resting on its base. He looked quickly back to Tchako, now almost bent double, broadsword on the floor.

The audience gasped as the figure melted, hot wax pooling at its base. Hearing the gasp, Bokasi looked up, then quickly back to Tchako. Tchako folded onto the mat, his murderous weapon beside him. He began whimpering and drew himself up into the fetal position.

"Mark his flesh with your sword, Grub," the judge called down.

Bokasi moved quickly to do as told, then backed away as the slight chest cut bled. Once done, Brigade Commander Stark rose to give his judgment. He called out, "I declare this match finished, not to be repeated. Only superstition and fear have been victorious."

The light on the pool of wax that had been the effigy slowly faded out, as did the hypnotic chant. Onlookers began to leave. The aid men moved into the ring to tend Tchako's slight cut. Then they hoisted him onto a stretcher and carried him out. Bokasi grabbed Porch in a bear hug to celebrate Porch's victory and his survival. Then he moved to pick up his weapon.

Bonnie and Olivia came down to the ring. Porch saw Bonnie and came to attention. She picked up a cloth from his water bucket, rang it out and wiped his face. Putting the cloth down, she put her hands on his temples, drew him to her and kissed him, full on the lips—sweetly, ever so sweetly. Porch felt his heart pounding out of his chest. Seeing this flustered Bokasi, and as he turned away, he dropped the weapon he'd just retrieved. Olive was watching him, and when he bent over, she picked up Tchako's discarded broadsword and with its flat side, swung it with all the strength she could muster, hitting Bokasi full on his rear. Startled, he rose up quickly and turned to face his new assailant. Olive looked at him and said, "You owe me, mister. You owe me big. I saved your big black ass."

Bokasi grinned.

CHAPTER 8
THE OPERETTA

Porch and Bo went to church the following morning. Worship over, they returned to their room and hit the sack, slept all afternoon and, privileged to skip supper, slept till Monday reveille. Bonnie, after Sunday services, spent the day catching up on long-neglected correspondence. She wrote her parents a long letter. Among them, only Olive was really busy that day.

That afternoon, she gathered sufficient fifth-class volunteers to help her return four massive quadraphonic speakers to the Theater Guild. She had three times the number needed, as the video disks of the previous night's matches were already distributed. All wanted part in an historic occasion in Space Academy history. Making use of the extra help, she sent one with twenty pounds of wax to the chem lab, another to the materials lab with the memory metal, and yet another to the art club with paint, brushes and stand. She returned the other gear and the three ancient volumes to the library herself.

Next came the reckoning. As Theater Guild treasurer, she'd bet the entire treasury at one to twenty on Bokasi's survival. She collected the vouchers due and went over to the theater to re-establish the account. As she made the deposits, she began humming to herself, voom-boom, boom—voom-boom, boom boom. Then she giggled.

But Tchako and Cheeko were not so easily defeated. Early that morning, they'd left the barracks, Tchako leading and Cheeko hobbling behind. It didn't matter if they were caught off limits. After Major Werewick heard their story, they knew he would overlook the infraction, as they intended to blow the whistle on the entire proceedings of the past several months. They arrived at the North Tower about 8:00 a.m. and went directly to his rooms over the vehement protests of the old crone at the front desk. Major Werewick was highly irritated that they had the temerity to come up to his suite without being announced and disturb him on a Sunday morning. But caps in hand, they begged him to hear them out. He bade them enter, took a seat, and listened to an hour of piteous complaining. When they finished, he said he'd take care of it and told them to return to barracks and stay there until he had done so.

After they left, he made a few phone calls. By two that afternoon, several special investigators from the Corporation had secured a warrant from the Academy staff judge advocate to apprehend them. The Corporation men took them into custody at two-thirty. The Commandant's office had their resignations by three and Tchako and Cheeko were off the Academy grounds by four, destination unknown. Werewick hated losers.

April came. The dark winter days and terrible cold would soon release its relentless hold on the Academy. Porch's torment had ended, but however he tried, he could not get out from under the load of demerits he was getting from Werewick. He was always within two or three of expulsion.

He tried not to let it get him down and made his outlet athletics. Track season had begun. Bokasi also was on the team, competing in the shot-put. Another classmate who hurled the javelin joined the pair. He was called Eric the Red because of his flaming red hair. He was also a football teammate of Bo's. They became inseparable on the track field, and as occasion permitted, around the barracks. When together, they were almost happy.

In early April the news broke that Olivia was selected to produce the annual Midsummer's Night Candidate Operetta, quite an honor for a second classman.

She was elated. This performance was an extremely popular Academy tradition. It marked the end of academics and the beginning of Graduation Week with all its ceremonies.

That evening, as Olivia completed a round of inspections, she happened to pass Bokasi on his way to the showers. He slapped against the wall at attention to let her pass. To his amazement, rather than growl at him for some oversight, she smiled prettily and said musically, "Good evening, Mr. Bokasi."

After she passed, Bo continued down the hall, embarrassed should someone see him, because his heart was pounding so heavily. He made it safely. Olivia had hardly noticed Bokasi, as her mind was on the forthcoming production. She was in a quandary as to what operetta or musical to perform. The Theater Guild had many light operas and old Broadway shows on hand. It had the modern ones, such as the popular *Jumping over Jupiter* and *Neptune Blues* by Pennyweight and Pound. Sometimes the Academy had candidates in residence with sufficient talent to write and produce original shows, but this was risky. The archives contained several notorious bombs. She had confidence in her ingenuity, creativity and admin skills, but when she thought, *Could I pull it off?* she felt queasy and short of breath. Besides that, there was the time factor—two and a half months.

Suddenly, the most magnificent basso profundo she had ever heard rent her thoughts. She stopped to listen. Sounds reverberated down upon her in great waves. They were coming from the shower room of the floor she had just departed.

In the shower above, Bokasi was soaping himself under torrents of hot water, oblivious to the world around him. Happy over his encounter with Corporal Olive and unable to contain himself, he had broken into his all-time favorite spiritual, *Old Man River*. Olivia was, for a moment, transfixed. But then she turned to retrace her steps upward. When Bokasi finished showering, drying and putting his robe and sandals on, he slung his towel over his shoulder and stepped back in the hall to return to his room. Olivia was standing several steps below him. When he saw her, he stopped. Olivia began singing a duet from *Porgy and Bess*.

Bo came in at the male part. Together, they sang a beautiful rendition. Olivia slowly climbed the stairs as she sang. When they completed the song, she smiled and said with soulful sincerity, "I've found my male lead for the Midsummer's Night operetta."

Bo was a bit uncomfortable with her starry-eyed look, so he tried a little bit of levity, saying, "Who dat, ma'am?"

Olive ignored his smart-aleck answer, continuing, "You, Mr. Bokasi."

"Yes, ma'am, I know I owe you. I do. I certainly do," he said in mock servility.

"Quit it, Bertram, and come with me." She took him by the hand and led him back to his room. Porch was studying number theory. He jumped to his feet at attention. Olive extended her hand to Bo and then to Porch. "I recognize you both as full-fledged candidates, no longer conditional to me. Call me Olivia from now on."

"I prefer Bo."

"Oh, I really like Bertram," Olive said musically.

Bo decided he did, too, the way she said it.

"Now to business—Bo, I really do want you for the operetta. Would you do it for me?"

"Yes, I'd really like to."

"Very well then, now we're keeping Porch from his studies. Can you take a little extra time from your track practice tomorrow and come to my room? I want to tell you about The Theater Guild."

"I'll be there," Bo replied.

Bo met with her the following afternoon. She related the history of the Guild, told of the honor bestowed upon her in being selected to produce this year's musical, and of her desire, yet fear, of trying to do an original work. She felt the talent was there amongst the company of actors, but time was so short that they would have to have a story that would almost write and set itself to music. There were notorious past failures. So she surmised they should seek safety and produce something well loved and easy to put on.

It just had to be good. She wanted it for Bonnie's last year and for the Guild. But whatever was selected, she wanted him for the lead male singer. His voice was just too magnificent to keep under wraps. Next year they'd do something original—then somewhere, she'd find a theme upon which to build a whole new production.

After their talk, Bo returned to his room just in time to get ready for the supper formation. Olivia's enthusiasm caught him up. He wished that he could think of something. After supper came studies. He helped Porch, who asked a question on some of the math, which Bokasi the math whiz easily explained. Porch could tell, though, that Bo's mind was elsewhere.

After Taps, Bo lay on his bed, thinking about Olivia's desire to do an original musical. Finally he drifted off to sleep. At four in the morning, he woke with a start. He felt he was freezing to death. He looked over to the window. Porch had it wide open and was leaning far out, looking up at the stars. Bo whispered out as loudly as he could, "Man, are you daft? Its freezing in here."

Porch didn't seem to hear him. He seemed entranced. Bo got up and went to the window. Porch said, as if to no one, "It's beautiful up there, full of hidden mystery. See, there is Polaris, the North Star, at the end of the Little Bear, and in the opposite direction, the constellation Cassiopeia. Go around from there and you see the yellow star, Capella, then the brighter Regulus and Arcturus, blue Vega, then Deneb and you're back again. I've got to get out there."

"Well, you won't do it with pneumonia. Shut the window, man."

Porch pulled back in and shut the window. He turned around, looking sheepish, and said, "I think my father is still out there somewhere."

It hit Bokasi like a ton of bricks. He started to yell out, but caught himself and said in a whisper, "Porch, the operetta—Olivia could do your story—nobody would have to know it's about you or who. It would live forever as a legend, a tribute to your mother, a sweet, sad tribute to love. What do you think?"

Porch frowned and was silent for a long time. Then he relaxed his face and replied, "You'd keep it a secret, you know how personal it is to me—use different names and places."

"You know you can trust me."

Again Porch thought about it for a moment, then he said, "I think she'd like that, yes, maybe my father would, too—wherever he is, or went. But you could tell Olivia. I wouldn't mind that."

The next day, Bo asked Olivia if he could see her that afternoon. He said he knew a wonderful story—he was sure she'd want to use it for her production. He suggested for confidentiality she come to his room. She assented and at four that afternoon entered. Both Porch and Bokasi were waiting.

After greeting them, she said," Shoot."

She listened intently as Bo outlined the theme, "It's the saga of a star wanderer, a mighty knight warrior who comes down from the vault of heaven searching for the seed of a galactic scourge that is spreading through the cosmos and wasting all human life in its path.

"Though he and his comrades have fought this terror for decades, nothing can stand before it. It is a menace to the entire galaxy. The knight has made a Holy Vow to find its origin—the key to its destruction..."

Bo paused to gauge Olivia's reaction. His enthusiasm had caught her up. "Yes, yes, go on, go on," she pleaded.

"He meets this beautiful girl in a hidden community, a fairyland kind of place—like–like Brigadoon. They fall deeply in love. Many are suspicious of this great hero, his strange arrival and stranger story. The two are to marry, but an urgent call comes from deep space commanding that he return to fight in a great battle looming up far beyond the Pleiades. By blood oath, he must return.

"After he has departed, she bears the fruit of his love, though unwed. Denounced, she becomes an anathema to this community of ancient and fundamental values. She is cast out to wander on her own, looking for safe haven for herself and her infant.

"She finds that there is none and so, alone and exhausted, she hides her child where he'll be found, and goes out into a blizzard to lure a ferocious pack of carnivores away from her baby. She kneels down to succumb to the storm, singing of her tragedy and long-lost love."

"Wonderful," Olivia said, enraptured, and then she looked at Porch. She knew enough about him to guess the origin of the story, so she patted his arm and said, "We'll make it a glorious tribute."

The next day, Olivia, with Bokasi in tow, went to see the president of the Theater Guild and had Bo lay out the storyline he had proposed. The president accepted it immediately and called for a meeting of the entire Guild that Saturday.

In the interim, Olive assembled a writing team to flesh out the story with acts and scenes; contacted the set designers and got them started; and set up an audition schedule with the audition committee.

She took Bo everywhere she could, occupying all his spare time. He had to secure his track coach's permission to reduce his practice time to twice a week. That gave him more time to satisfy Olive's demands. She saw him as her successor and wanted him to learn everything. She was a human dynamo. She made him her scribe, her secretary and all around "gofer."

She had plenty of problems to solve. The major one was to keep her songwriter-composers in line. Dunsmore, Dunston and Dorfman were fine candidates who would someday become excellent starmen. But as songwriters they were temperamental, spending more time arguing than composing.

However, Olivia got them started, telling them she needed some songs by Saturday for the auditions. At the auditions, Bokasi was the unanimous choice for the male lead, and Olivia the female. The rest of the cast was selected quickly, and all members of the Guild were thrown into a frenzy of activity. They had two months and ten days before dress rehearsal.

Of course this was going on while the academic

schedule was racing toward its own crescendo, that year's final examinations. Bokasi also had to contend with the track schedule. He'd never been busier. Before he knew it, April had passed into May. Somehow, he was able to keep up with everything.

The first week in May, Olivia took him around, checking out all elements of her production. She saved her temperamental composers for last. When she entered their lair, she found them squabbling. But when they saw her come in with Bo, they abruptly changed their mood. They were always courteous to performers who they knew were key to their own success.

"Hey, chief," Dunsmore called out, "we've got some great stuff here for you and Bo. How 'bout tryin' it out?"

He handed the music to Olive and said, "Read it over while Dorfman picks up on the refrain."

While they were reading, Dorfman started with the melody. Then he picked up the harmony, and finally full orchestration. It was a duet for the male and female leads. Olivia and Bo nodded when they were ready. Dunston counted the beat, pointed to them and ordered, "Take it away."

Bo started.

"*Do you wonder—ever wonder, where is the birthplace of wonder.*"

Olivia came in. "*Yes, I wonder—always wonder, where is the birthplace of wonder.*"

So they continued through the song.

"*Oh, little one—my precious one, it is my heart that you have won.*"

"*If I dream—please wake me not, if I'm awake—I'll never sleep.*"

Inspired, Dorfman continued as if possessed, on and on. The duo kept right with him, giving their very best.

"*I come with lightning, wind and thunder—to take you to the womb of wonder.*"

They went through the work to the finale. "*He rode away on a blazing rocket—And's now but a mem'ry in a golden locket.*"

The three songsters rose as one, clapping loudly, and then for once shook each other's hands and patted one another on the back. So they practiced the after-noon away, enjoying themselves immensely.

At last, Bo and Olivia got up to leave, and as they left, an old man stepped out of the backstage shadows. He appeared to be blind.

Olivia said, "Why, it's Gideon."

She went up, grasped his hand and appeared to drum and scratch on it—GIDEON, I WOULD LIKE YOU TO MEET BERTRAM. Then she took Gideon's hand and held it out to Bo.

Bo took it, shook it, and said, "Pleased to meet you, Gideon. You can call me Bo."

Olivia drummed and scratched out—BERTRAM SAYS HE'S PLEASED TO MEET YOU. Gideon hand signed that he too was pleased to meet Mr. Bertram. Olivia translated. Gideon faded into the shadows.

Olivia told Bo about Gideon. According to medical authorities, he was a blind deaf-mute. But he seemed to have a strange extrasensory perception. He worked odd jobs around the Academy, for the Theater Guild during its season, and the rest of the year as janitor in the North Tower, where senior bachelor officers had their quarters. Gideon had appeared, literally, from out of the sky in a command space launch about twenty-four hours after the *Black Locust*, a solar wind cargo ship, had blown up. He was the sole survivor of that misfor-tune, able to spiral down using earth gravity to avoid falling into the sun. Then, by skipping off the earth's atmosphere, he avoided burning up during re-entry. He did crash land in a dense forest fifty miles north of the Academy. When the search and rescue people got to him, he was delirious. He kept repeating—slavers, slave ship, slavery—tie the tether, tie the tether. He passed out on the way to the hospital and had never spoken since.

About a week later, the songsters asked Bo to come over and review a song that they had written for his character, the star wanderer. He entered the stage door and continued to the stage through a dark corridor. He heard music ahead and his mind went to meter and melody. Then he heard a whisper. He stopped and peered into the darkness. It was Gideon, and reflected light gave his open eyes a strange glow.

"Gideon, I thought you couldn't see, hear or talk."

"I see what I need to see, hear what I ought to hear, and talk almost never. Tie the tether—tie the tether. Beware for your roommate, Porch. Beware of that wolf, Werewick. He is evil. He is an incubus. Beware of the Sword and Saber Society, an inner circle of the Fraternity. They perform strange rites with lotions and leather. Tie the tether—tie the tether."

Gideon disappeared back into the shadows, and Bo wondered if he'd heard the mad rantings of a demented old man. He continued on up to the stage. Once there, he sang the song the three D's had prepared. It was a sad cantata wherein the heroic star wanderer lamented his lost love, but he was not up to his usual brilliance. Gideon's warning stayed in his mind and the songwriters questioned his performance. Was he troubled? Could they in any way help? He said no, thanking them and admitting he had something on his mind. He excused himself and left.

When he found Porch, he told him of the odd warning, suggesting he be alert and very careful. Congenially, Porch said that he would, but his life had become so much better that he did not give Bokasi's worry much thought.

May had come and with it some warmth. Migrant birds had returned to the nearby woods and their songs filled the air, cheering all. The first small wildflowers were blooming. Final exams came; both Porch and Bokasi did credibly well in spite of the diversions that had afflicted them. But there was no respite after academics concluded.

The traditional spring clean up and spruce up, a prelude to the late June graduation, began. The winning company in each regiment received weekend furloughs for every candidate. Even the lowly Grubs were to have an afternoon in the local town. They had not been off the campus except for two football trips the previous autumn.

Bonnie had the entire company hopping. Her competitive nature made her relish the competition and covet the award. And she and her company won. The discriminator was that the trophies in the orderly room case were shined, something no other company thought to do.

The weekend before Midsummer's Night, Bonnie's company collected its gratis furlough, and that Sunday, Porch, Bo and Red Eric acquired the promised passes into town. Porch's companions were so high spirited that even Porch was in a buoyant mood, although Major Werewick had just the day before assessed two more demerits against him, putting him right at the limit.

Sunday was a gloomy day of intermittent drizzle, but that did not dampen their spirits, for their undirected ambulation was itself pure luxury. They found a small café and soda shop where they ate a pizza apiece and a half-dozen hot dogs and washed it all down with strawberry sodas. As they were leaving the shop, the sun came out and washed the town in brilliant light which dazzled off the wet roofs and turned the puddles in the streets into a glowing amber color.

Eric asked if they would wait while he checked some fishing tackle in the store next door. He said he intended to spend his time fishing off the coast when he got back on summer leave to Nova Scotia. Porch and Bo agreed they would, so the three pulled their rain capes over their shoulders and left the shop. Bo and Porch waited outside, savoring the clean fresh air and the late afternoon sunshine. How could they feel better, they asked each other.

Then they saw their company commander, Captain Brightwood, across the street. How wonderful she looked in her space blue rain cape and jaunty tri-cornered cap. Her auburn hair shimmered in flashes of ruby red light. They stood, frozen by her beauty and self-consciousness, too, for they did not know the protocol. Should they cross and greet her, or, uninvited to disturb her solitude, let her go her way?

There was no time to ponder, because three street toughs rose and blocked her way. The leader of these spoke a vulgar invitation and moved forward to grab her. Before he reached her shoulder, he was on the ground, groaning and holding his groin. The other two then moved forward. Before Porch could overcome his surprise, streetwise Bokasi had crossed over and, from behind, grabbed the two by their necks. He held them high, then slammed their heads together and dropped them unconscious at Bonnie's feet.

"My compliments, ma'am," Bo said with an audacious sweep of his hand, bowing deeply.

"Why, thank you, Mr. Bokasi. But as you see, I can take care of myself," Bonnie replied haughtily, but there was a twinkle in her eye as she stepped over the scum and continued down the street. Bokasi grinned.

In the meantime, Porch had walked to the corner, where he could not help but meet her. Bonnie reached the end of the sidewalk, meaning to cross, when Porch came up. She saw him, smiled and said, "Mr. Porch, it's nice to see you."

Porch tried replying, but the words stuck in his throat and out came mumbo jumbo. Flustered and red as a beet, all he could do was look at his feet. Could he save the day? He saw that Bonnie stood before a wide puddle just off the curb in front of her. As he looked at those shapely legs, he thought of the story of Sir Walter Raleigh, who, as a knight so long ago, had stood at a puddle before his own queen. Quickly, he pulled off his rain cape, and with a flourish, laid it across the puddle at her feet.

Bonnie, astonished, wavered for a second or two as to what to do. But then she smiled, stepped on the cape, and crossed the puddle. Safely across, she turned just as Bokasi drew up. Looking at both, she said, "You two Grubs, in the span of a minute, have brought back the age of chivalry, now dead seven hundred years—how endearing."

Porch retrieved his soaking wet cape as Captain Brightwood walked off. He watched her go and sighed. His love for her was unbounded. Then he looked back at Bo. Bo was as pleased with himself as he was, so they celebrated with a high five and said softly to each other, "Aw-right."

But perhaps they shouldn't have, because not far away, another figure stood in the entrance to a bookstore. He had observed the incident from start to finish. Major Werewick said to himself as he watched the pair walk off, *I have him now.*

CHAPTER 9

THE FENCING MASTER

Oftentimes, Midsummer's Night in the high latitudes cast a spell all about. This night, 21 June 2255, was no exception. It seemed the sun refused to sleep, and when it finally dipped below the horizon, it was for only an hour or two. So twilight ruled the evening hours. The languorous air had a quality of magic. Nothing seemed to move or disturb and so served to focus all attention within the Academy on the Theater Guild's production.

The matinee had gone on as scheduled at two that afternoon. The Candidates Fifth Class were required to attend. It was suggested that the Fourth and Third attend as well, because the evening performance, scheduled to begin at nine, was reserved for the two senior classes, the staff and faculty. These shows were so popular that few needed to be urged. This year's production was highly touted, so *The Star Wanderer* played to a full house. There wasn't a dry eye in the audience when Olivia, playing the heroine, sang the final number and succumbed to the blizzard.

When the final curtain came down, the cast received four curtain calls and again sang several songs on request. Bokasi got one curtain call and could not leave the stage until he repeated his final solo, *The Star Wanderer's Lament*. Next Olivia was called and amidst cheers and clapping, repeated several songs. Then together, she and Bo delivered a duet. Dunsmore, Dunston and Dorfman next appeared to receive their plaudits. Finally,

Olivia came forth again to receive the producer's praise.

After supper, Bo had an hour or two to relax before the main performance. He sat down on the stoop in front of his barracks. Many candidates came by to congratulate him on his performance. He grinned as he thanked them for their kind words. His good friend, Red Eric, came up and gave him a pat on the back. But Eric had also seen more in the early afternoon's performance than others who did not know Bokasi as well. He decided to needle Bo a bit.

"So, Bo," he began, "that little lady who plays opposite you is more than acting. She's really sweet on you."

"Aw, go on," Bo retorted, flushing. "She'll be gone in one more year and I'll still have three. She's too smart to fall for me."

"Oh, don't deny it now. I know what I saw. You've gone from pariah to paramour, thanks to *Ole Man River*, and you're just as sweet on her. Your days are numbered man. She's gonna get you."

"Aw, cut it out." Bo said, grinning.

Just then, Porch came up. He congratulated Bo on his performance. Then he said, "I'm going running. Eric, you want to come along?"

Eric was about to answer when the loudspeaker blared. "Candidate Porch to the orderly room—Candidate Porch to the orderly room. On the double—on the double."

"Well, I better get over there, maybe next time, Eric. Good luck tonight, Bo."

No trouble, he worried as he ran over, but the evening's magic was gone for him. He reported to the charge of quarters.

"Porch," said the CQ, "report to Major Werewick at his quarters in the North Tower immediately."

"But sir," Porch blurted out, astonished.

"But sir, what?" the CQ replied without looking up.

"It's not authorized to leave the Brigade compound, nor are Saturday night calls legal."

"What are you, Grub, some kind of barracks lawyer? If the Major says he wants you now, he wants you now, and I'll issue you a pass to go to the North Tower."

"Yes, sir. Sir, may I ask a question?"

"Grub, you are getting tiresome. What now?"

"I only got a tank top, jogging sweats and track shoes with cleats on. May I return to my room and dress?"

"No, damn it," the CQ shouted. "He said now, mister, now!"

"Yes, sir."

Then the CQ looked up and relented a bit.

"OK, go get one of those hand-me-down cloaks out of the locker in the corner while I make out your pass, and wear that."

He completed the pass, handed it to Porch and said, "Get going." Then he smirked as the Grub left the orderly room in the ridiculous outfit. Anguish filled Porch's heart as he ran north. He followed side roads and woodland paths as much as he could to avoid being seen. He covered the six miles in a bit over thirty minutes as the cloak slowed him down.

"The Towers", as the candidates called them, at last loomed up before him. He'd never seen them before. Designed and built sixty years before, they rose high above a granite cliff. Their solid foundation was perhaps an allegory of Earth's tenacious hold on man as he grasped for the stars. But to Porch, looking up in the twilight, they appeared more medieval than space age.

He did not delay for more than a glance so that laxness too would not be counted against him. Nor did he wish to show fatigue, a sign of lost control. But he had not anticipated the staircase, running up flight after flight from the roadway at the bottom of the hill to the pedestrian entrance. He did double time to the top, and when he reached the massive aluminum and glass doors leading into the foyer, he was breathing hard.

He entered, and heard a resonant chime announce his arrival. Looking about, he saw a lobby desk and went over to it. An old woman looked up and when she saw his garb, she sputtered, "What manner of creature have we here?"

Porch showed his pass and said, "I've been told to report to Major Werewick."

The old crone cackled, "Another little bird for the

Major's bird cage, huh? Well, he picked a good time—
yes, he did, indeed he did, with everybody gone to the
op'ry."

"Which apartment?" Porch asked, trying to conceal
his rapid breathing.

She squinted at him and said, "Way up. The little
hawk has his aerie on the thirteenth floor though there
be only ten, hee-hee."

"How do I get there?"

"On your legs, little pigeon. Candidates can't use
the elevator unless the stairs are blocked, and that's for
me to say, hee-hee."

She squinted at him again and said, "You look a
little pink and I can feel your steam, young stud. You
better get recharged before you face him. The elevator is
over in the corner. Take it."

Porch thanked her and went toward the elevator.
When he got to the glass doors, he saw the shield of the
Corporation engraved on them. He entered and pushed
ten. Soft music enveloped him. He was encased in glass
and could see all around. The gracious lobby was as
large as a ballroom. Its ceiling rose fifty feet above a
floor carpeted in thick blue pile. Great marble columns
were tastefully interspersed with potted silver birch and
illuminated in artificial light. A grand chandelier hung
from the ceiling.

The elevator rose so slowly that the ascent seemed
interminable as he passed floor after floor. But its slow
pace and the calming effect of the music allowed him to
regain his composure by the time he reached ten and
got off. There was a short hallway and some more stairs.
There was no carpeting, only highly polished black granite flooring. The cleats on his track shoes clacked loudly
and he tried to tread softly. After he had climbed the
stairs, he reached a door.

This must be the Major's apartment, he said to himself. He knocked and waited. No sound came from within.
It seemed eerie. At last the door opened.

"Come in," the Major commanded, "and stand there
in the center of the room where I can see you—at attention, mister, hard attention."

Werewick circled him silently, then stopped at his front. He had no shirt on, only black fencing tights and soft slippers. He was sweating profusely. He had a fencing foil tucked under his withered left arm. He walked around Porch again. While he was behind him, Porch took a hasty glance around the dim room. It was very large but sparsely decorated. An easy chair, side table and floor lamp that he could hardly see were on his far right. A door there evidently led to a bath. A full-length mirror hung more to his front beside that door and a long cork strip ran up to it. The wall in front of him was bare and extended left to the entrance of another room. This entrance was half covered with a drape, and the other room was so dimly lit that he could only see a foot or two into it. A wide oak cabinet with partially open glass doors was in front of the left wall. The case housed an array of swords, sabers, cutlasses and hand weapons of all types. Some covered dishes and a type of console sat on top of a plain bureau beside the oak cabinet.

As the Major came around him again, Porch quickly brought his eyes front, but Werewick caught him and said softly, "You're quite inquisitive, Grub." Then he was silent again.

Flustered by Werewick's strange conduct, Porch decided to report, and blurted out, "Candidate Porch reports as ordered, sir."

"Silence. You were not given permission to speak. Just look at you—dressed like a buffoon—hardly a military uniform."

"Sir, request permission to make a statement."

"Then speak," the Major said softly.

"I was told to report immediately, dressed as I was."

"Very well. Go on."

"Sir, I request redress."

"Redress! You should be seeking redemption for your foolishness. You were observed throwing your rain cape down in a mud puddle for another candidate to walk on. Wanton destruction of Academy property is twenty-five demerits and a month of detention in quarters. But already you have reached the limit. Had this infraction been recorded, you would be drummed out of the Academy. You know that."

"Yes, sir."

"Look at what recalcitrance to my overtures has brought you. Now get rigid, mister, rigid. I want to see you sweat.

"You interrupted me in the middle of my exercises, but perhaps it's just as well for you to watch a master at his work, for maybe, just maybe, there's yet a chance for you."

The Major walked to the mat. When he touched the cork strip, soft rose lights came on from above. He grasped his foil and raised it in salute–front, right, left–and he brought his head around as if to acknowledge an imaginary audience. Then he dropped the blade to the mat. When it touched the strip, soft music filled the room. As the beat got faster, he brought his weapon to "on guard," with his withered arm dangling limply at his side.

Suddenly he lunged forward, parried, thrust, feinted and lunged again to reach the mirror. His deft advance amazed Porch. He could not see where the foil's pommel ended and Werewick's arm began. As Werewick retreated to the end of the strip, the music beat faster and the lights turned amber. He advanced again, faster. His thrusts had more authority; lunge, parry, beat, thrust, parry, riposte, glide, lunge and he was to the mirror—now back again quickly and forward yet faster. Porch could not keep up until the finale, a full lunge stopping a micrometer in front of the mirror. It was a fascinating ballet.

Then, in a flash, Werewick dashed toward Porch and swept the blade across his throat, ripping through the Velcro fastener that held the cape around his neck. It fell in a heap at his feet. Porch felt the blade whisper by, but did not flinch. Nor was he touched.

Werewick said quietly, "It's grown hot in here and I must not lose your attention—for I am the master here, and you the pupil."

Porch thought to himself, *He trying to makes me crack. I must hold steady.*

Suddenly, the Major barked out, "Hard attention, mister. Get rigid. I want to see those shoulders touch your backbone."

Porch braced harder. Beads of perspiration wet his brow.

Werewick headed to the weapon cabinet. He wiped down the foil with an oily cloth, put it in its rack, and replaced it with a saber. Then he took another cloth from the bureau and wiped his own face and arms. Porch heard some chains rattle and several deep growls in the other room. But he could see nothing through the darkness.

Werewick said, "My pardon, Grub. I must recess to feed my pets."

Clamping the saber under his withered arm, he went to the bureau again, took a cover off a tureen that sat upon it, and withdrew from it a roast as big as a melon. "Come," he commanded.

Two huge dogs, black as night, dragging heavy iron chains, rattled forward into the room as far as their restraints would allow. One, long haired, was half as high as a horse; the other, much more massive. They growled upon seeing the meat, anticipating a feast.

The Major tossed the meat high, pulled the saber from beneath his arm, sliced the roast in half, skewered each piece as it fell, and tossed a piece to each of the dogs. They wolfed the meat down, then looked up, expecting more. Werewick went to the bureau and brought back a large chunk. He tossed it up, but this time simply skewered the meat and tossed it between the dogs. The long- haired one, a wolfhound or borsoi, was quicker and snatched it up. But before it could swallow, the mastiff had its throat and, snarling, threw it down. The borsoi relinquished its grasp on the meat, and the mastiff gobbled it up. Werewick continued to feed them, sometimes one piece, other times two, until they had eaten their fill. At that point, he went over to them. The borsoi leaped up, put its paws on Werewick's shoulders and licked the little man's face. Standing on its hind legs, it was a full head taller than its master.

"Good dog, Sodom, good dog," he said lovingly, petting it. Then he commanded it down and went over to the mastiff, which nearly knocked him over when it jumped up. He hugged the beast and said, "Good boy,

Gomorrah, good boy." He then commanded, "Back now, back," and the dogs retreated into the darkness.

Werewick said, as if to no one, "Splendid animals, the devil dogs—a gift of the Corporation, bred and genetically altered for size."

He wiped his hands and face again, picked up the saber, and returned to the cork strip. An hour had passed. The lights over the long mat burned red as Werewick began furious exercise—lunging forward, thrusting, cutting, parrying, feinting, slashing—always to the mirror and back, over and over, ignoring Porch.

At last he stopped. He was dripping with sweat. Holding the saber at rest, he walked over to Porch and looked him up and down, circling him again. Finished, he turned toward the mat, and Porch saw that long red gashes covered his back from his shoulders to his waist.

Suddenly Werewick whirled about and swept his saber across Porch's shoulders, cutting through both loops of the tank top. The top fell to Porch's feet, leaving him naked to the waist.

"So, Grub," he said, "you gaze upon my stripes and gashes, earned in fierce space fighting. Not so you, unblemished in the blush of youth, untarnished by time, unmarked by battle, not yet corrupted by lust. The ancient Greeks with all their statuary could not do justice to your physical beauty. Not so me, red and ugly—crippled, too."

Werewick returned to the cabinet, replaced the saber, and took up an epee. He returned to the strip and began another exercise set, going through its drills at dizzying speed. Suddenly he rushed Porch and lunged, flicking the young man's flesh so lightly that only a small red mark was evident right at his heart.

He said, "You're marked now, Grub—no longer unblemished."

Porch survived again without flinching or showing fear. He kept telling himself under his breath that he would not yield—could not yield. Werewick returned to the weapon's cabinet and next drew out a broadsword bedecked in gold and gems. It glittered under the red light and took on a fearsome appearance. At the console on the bureau he pushed several buttons and turned a few dials, as if tuning the device. He returned to the mat and this time stood stock still.

As he waited, Porch imagined that he heard an almost imperceptible sound of Scottish pipes in the far distance. He listened intently. His mind was not deceiving him. The sound of the pipes marched into the room and rose to such a crescendo that it hurt his ears. The pipes stopped and a highland warrior in full battle regalia emerged before him on the mat. It was a holographic image. Lighting changed to dim gray-blue matching an overcast sky above the Highlands. The Scot wore the tartan of the Black Watch and held his own huge two-handed sword at the ready.

The Major bowed as if meeting an old foe, then rendered a salute. The Scot returned both, then stroked his great orange beard. His eyes gleamed as he eagerly anticipated the combat. He leaped to the on guard position, as did the Major. Both approached warily. Each seemed to know the other's skill. A reckless attack by the Scot opened the action. He lunged. The Major parried, feinted and thrust, scoring a hit on the Scot's forearm which was dutifully recorded by the console's photonics. The Scot made a lumbering retreat on legs as large as small tree trunks. They battled on, each scoring many hits, but none sufficient to incapacitate. At last, the Scot brought the sword down from above in a mighty stroke, intending to cut his adversary in two, but the Major leapt aside and thrust his own blade home. The Scot crumbled to the mat as his image faded and disappeared.

Werewick walked back to the weapon cabinet, picked out a cutlass, and returned to the cork. The music changed to a Caribbean beat. Lighting turned sea green, and a new specter appeared. He looked to be a pirate from the Spanish main, and the color of his face indicated that he was Creole. There was no pre-match courtesy. The pirate simply charged, delivering great swipes with his cutlass. After a series of feints, the Major pierced his heart and the apparition quickly faded out.

Werewick wiped his blade as if to clean it, returning

to his cabinet for another weapon. This time, the lights burned tawny yellow, as off an African savanna, and the music had an African beat. A tall Zulu warrior carrying a leather shield and iron-headed assagai came into focus. He wore a white feathered headdress which almost touched the ceiling of the room. Werewick had chosen a saber. The Zulu advanced, dancing side to side, continually thrusting his spear. Werewick quickly dispatched him.

Next came a Roman Legionnaire with short sword and shield, accompanied by music meant to convey heavy leather sandals treading up the cobbles of the Appian Way. A French musketeer who almost skewered the Major followed. Then came a Confederate cavalry Officer, a Russian cossack, and a British fusilier.

On they came, a ghost army raised to taste defeat. The skilled ballet had turned into a danse macabre. Porch grew numb. At last the lights got bright, the music quit, and Werewick turned his attention to the weary Grub.

He said, "I see in your eyes that you grow tired. Very well, now that I've shown you my profession, I'll show you my hobby."

He went over and again circled the young man. Porch thought the man must be mad. Next Werewick left the room and went into the shower. Porch heard the water come on and gush for a long time. He was sweating profusely and even its sound was now refreshing to him.

Soon Werewick returned, wearing a purple robe, loosely closed, with a towel slung about his neck. He reeked of wintergreen. As he approached Porch his whole nature seemed changed from what it was but a minute ago. He smiled and said, "Mister, you may relax now. The lessons are over."

Then he took the towel from around his neck and softly wiped the perspiration from Porch's face and upper body. After he was through, he dropped the towel and withdrew a bottle of lotion from a pocket of his robe. He opened it, smiled solicitously, and said, "This will make that epee mark and sting disappear in seconds."

He poured some lotion onto his fingers, and lifted

them to apply the lotion to Porch's body. As he did, he
pursed his lips and his eyes seemed to glaze over. He
touched the young man's breast and then his hand went
down to the drawstring of his running pants. Porch's
reaction was instantaneous. His hand's went under the
little man's armpits and he lifted and hurled him across
the room. The Major landed heavily. His head struck
the oak bureau, which knocked him out. Porch bent
down to pull his undershirt up and then turned around
to retrieve his cape. As he did, he heard a rustle and
turned. The Major partially revived and moved toward a
lever to release the chains of the devil dogs.

Porch shot over, and as Werewick got his hand on
the lever, he stepped on it hard and twisted his cleats.
He heard Werewick's bones crush. He felt a jaw snap on
his own foot and saw the snout of the borsoi clamp down.
The dog had been able to stretch enough against the
chain to reach him. He yanked his foot away but could
feel warm blood seep out.

Werewick snarled, "You're dead meat, Grub, dead
meat." Then he passed out again. Porch pulled the limp
body back toward the bureau and lowered the heavy
oak piece over his body to restrain him. Then he ran
out of the apartment. He ignored the elevator. *Too slow*,
he thought as he found the staircase and bounded down.

CHAPTER 10

FLIGHT

As Porch ran through the lobby of the Towers and out the door, the old crone shouted, "Give up—give up, there is no escape."

He did not know if she would call the authorities. He would chance it. If she did, maybe he'd see them first and get past them. Only the most junior would be on duty with the big show going on—an advantage. They would probably be more hesitant to react to a call from such as her. But then, she had no idea of what had happened. Maybe she wouldn't sound the alarm.

No matter, time was of the essence. When he hit the roadway below the stairs, he fell into the long strided lope with which he was so comfortable. The sun had finally set and it was a very dark, moonless night. It would be dark for an hour or two before the sun returned. He kept to the shadows. He damned himself for what had happened. Bo would have known what to do. Tired and sore from standing rigid for so many hours, his almost effortless pace cleared his head and he was able to stifle panic.

It had cooled off considerably and the fresh air helped relax his muscles. Soon they no longer ached. His strength returned, a blessing of youth and superb conditioning. He began to formulate his plans. He knew that his days at the Academy were over. He was certain that he should not head back to Harry's. They'd look there first. Maybe he should head for the Eastern

Megapolis, find a job, and lose himself among the teeming millions until the search ended.

Presently, the quadrangle came into sight. When he reached the stoop to his company barracks, he pulled off his track shoes and silently went up to the orderly room. Good! The Charge of Quarters was asleep. He sneaked past him to the credits dispenser and pressed in his personal code, withdrawing the balance of his account. There was plenty of money. The finance people had placed the gold coin Harry had given him in escrow and he'd spent little of his candidate's monthly stipend. He pocketed the credits and again crept past the CQ.

So far, so good. When he was out of range of hearing, he raced up to his room, tore off his jogging pants, and raced to the shower. He gave himself two minutes, but he had to get the stench of his experience off his body and wash the dried blood from his foot. When he got back to his room, he treated his foot, bound it, and pulled the clothing he'd decided to wear out of his locker.

He selected his space blue warm-up suit. It was darker than any other issued garments. He put it and his black running shoes on and threw a few other articles into a duffel bag, including the jeans and plaid shirt he'd worn when he entered. He was lucky. Just a week ago, candidates had been allowed to retrieve non-uniform items from basement storage, anticipating the month's leave they would get after graduation. He grabbed some personal effects from his bureau. He thought of the locket. He would retrieve that next and be on his way. He scribbled "Good Luck, Bo" on a piece of paper and felt an almost overwhelming pang of sorrow. He doubted that he would ever see him or Eric or Captain Brightwood again—or even the Academy, which, in spite of everything, he'd come to love.

Suddenly he heard it, a distant howl, accompanied by a series of sharp throaty barks. Porch shuddered; the devil dogs. He realized he'd left enough of a blood trail for them to track him. Then he heard a multitude of theatergoers. The show had ended and they were returning. Their voices were boisterous and happy. There was some singing of the songs from the show. He listened and heard another howl, followed by booming staccato barks. The dogs were closing fast. He realized he could not go out the front door; the candidates would impede him or witness the direction of his flight. There he was, five flights up—trapped.

He thought of the firebox in the hall outside his door. He ran out and broke the case which sounded the alarm. Pandemonium broke out, because those returning, as well as hearing the alarm, also saw the dogs bearing down on them. They had no idea the dogs were only after Porch. They scattered in every direction, trying to escape. In just a few seconds the dogs and theatergoers mixed in a wild melee. There were screams and curses all about. Soon fire sirens on approaching trucks added to the bedlam.

Porch pulled the fire hose into his room and pushed it out the window, lowering it to the ground. He looped the duffel bag over his shoulder and half rappelled, half slid down the hose. He saw lights coming on in the rooms as he passed—no time to pick up the locket. He swore to himself that someday he would return and retrieve it.

An alley ran south behind the barracks to a sally port not far away. He began running along it. He went through the sally port and crossed the street in front of the Grand Parade. When his feet hit the soft grass, he looked back. Space police with lights flashing on their squad cars were coming up. Candidates were still scattering. Apparently the dogs, distracted by the crowding and by multitudinous new scents, were circling, trying to retrace the blood scent.

Porch did not hesitate, but began his loping stride. The soft grass was silent beneath his feet and the darkness of the moonless night cloaked his desperate course. Only feeble light from the stars gave evidence of his passing. Beyond the parade lay several miles of athletic fields and training grounds. Then there was a dense patch of woods, a moat and the perimeter fence. It was now about an hour before sunrise. He hoped, by first light, to be at the bus stop at South Space Side, the dinky little town where he'd laid his cloak at Bonnie's feet and the trouble started.

Two dim streetlights marked the road at the far end of the parade. He crossed it and ran onto the athletic fields. They were familiar. He'd spent much time there. He could pick out the vaulting pit as he ran past. Bitter grief welled up in his throat. There would be no more competitions.

He cut short this self-indulgent thought when he heard the distant howl. The devil dogs had again picked up his trail. Fierce throaty barks followed, closer, cannon-like in their reverberations through the still night. Great fear poured adrenaline into his being and he increased his pace. He knew the dense woods ahead would slow him down, particularly with the barrack bag, which, though only half full, seemed to be growing heavier. But he could not abandon it, because it contained his civilian clothes. He would be picked up immediately if spotted in his official Space Academy warm-up suit. The howl and the barks were closer now. He crossed the last open field and crashed into the woods loudly, then fell.

As he fell, he turned over, and upon getting up and looking back, he saw two forms two fields away racing toward him. They not only had his scent now, but also his bearing from the noise. Closing, they sensed the kill, so their howls and booming barks changed to raging snarls.

Porch tore through the brush. The young saplings and tough vines seemed to come alive to whip him and bind him tight. At last, he could see the dim lights marking the perimeter fence. He had thirty yards to go to get to the narrow open firebreak that lay before the six-yard-wide concrete moat. The dogs crashed into the woods behind him. His broken trail eased their way and they were but a few yards behind him when he broke free of the woods. He cast the bag across the moat and with a running leap powered by desperation, hurled himself across just as the borsoi broke into the clearing behind him.

He hit heavily, but his left foot gained purchase on the concrete lip of the opposite bank. His right shin crashed against the wall, but he fell forward and was able to pull himself up. The dogs braked violently, then ran right and left seeking easier passage.

Porch hopped to the fence dragging his bag and leg with the bloody shin. He grimaced in agony as he surveyed the twelve-foot height, horrified to see three strands of barbed wire jutting outward above. He shoveled the bag upward in a desperate heave to cover the wire. Leaping up, he grabbed at openings in the chain link fence. The toes of his sneakers found holes between the links as he clawed his way up. In a few seconds, he reached the topmost strand of wire, which he felt beneath the bag. Luckily, it had held fast. He was able to bend his legs up under him in the fraction of a second before the borsoi leaped up, and avoided its snapping jaws.

The animal had leaped far enough across to dig its front paws into the turf above the channel wall and then scratch its way up the concrete embankment. The mastiff was in the channel trying to pull itself up, with back feet flailing and toenails scraping, snarling in rage and frustration.

Porch tumbled down the other side but his bag remained caught in the wire at the top. He leaped up and tried to grab its strap, which hung down. The bag did not come loose. He dared not touch the wire in an attempt to climb back up and retrieve it, as he'd most certainly loose a couple of fingers to the fangs just a foot or so away. The wolfhound leaped high and tried to scratch its way over, but fell back again and again. With each leap, it tore open its paws and yelped hideously. The mastiff found a way around the moat, and in a frenzy, caromed repeatedly off the fence, hitting it with all its weight. The sturdy fence reverberated up and down its length, clanging loudly, but held fast.

Porch looked around, saw a sapling, wrenched it from the ground, and hooked it under the bag. The animals on the other side thought he was taunting them, and their fury increased. At last the bag tore loose and toppled to his feet. He snatched it up and was off down the hill heading for South Space Side. The town was not far through the woods. The first glimmer of dawn was evident in the east.

CHAPTER 11

APPREHENSION

He woke with a start. Bright lights were everywhere, yet somewhat distant. It was dark, night, but what night? Had the bus not moved? No, his surroundings were different. Gradually the fog befuddling his weary mind cleared. He remembered through a fitful sleep the seemingly never- ending, winding road, continuing through the forest, uphill, downhill, hour after hour, through a long day. Did he dare hope it? Yes, it must be true. He had gotten away. It came back to him. He'd been there a year ago, on his way north to the Academy. He was at the border terminal. He would have to find another bus here. He became alert. Providence was with him, but for how long, he wondered. Utmost care was in order.

He sat up and noticed the worn old coat he was wearing. Where had it come from? His hand went to his head. He felt the cap. Then he remembered trading his Academy running suit to the vagrant at South Space Side for the cap and the coat. At least the suit would not now be an immediate clue to his whereabouts. He quickly exited the bus, first for a men's room.

As he exited, he noticed that the driver was rewinding the destination scroll above the front windshield. The driver stopped at a new heading, New York. He hurried on to the washroom, thinking maybe he could just continue on that bus. He hoped the wait would not be long. He couldn't afford that.

Coming out of the washroom, he saw a vendor sell-ing sandwiches and sodas at a small stand. He bought several sandwiches and a soda. The vendor looked at him oddly when he handed him new credits, surely out of character for one dressed as he. He left the terminal building quickly. As he approached the bus, he noticed them.

There were two men, one very tall and slim, the other a bit shorter but heavily built. They were peering into the windows of the bus that he'd just left, as if looking for somebody. Was it coincidental? He had to be sure. Staying out of their line of sight, he hurried to the rear of the bus and climbed up to the little-used outside top luggage rack. Creeping forward along the top to just above them and slowly edging over, he peered down over the side. He could hear them talking. "Ess, come over here," said the massive man. The tall one moved over.

"I see no one of his description."

"It had to be this bus. There was no other from that far north."

"Well, come on, Ess. If he's not on the bus, he may be over at the terminal—maybe someone's seen him."

Both hurried away and headed for the terminal. Stricken with fear, Porch leaped off the other side of the bus. He saw another about fifty yards away. Throwing his duffel bag over his shoulder, he ran over. As he went around the rear, he saw that it was loading. A large baggage compartment forward of the rear wheels stood open. A porter was dickering with a couple not far away. While the porter's attention was diverted, he threw his duffel in and crept in after. Pushing bags aside, he slipped into the very back and pulled bags over himself for concealment. He lay still and prayed that liquid hydrogen fueled the bus so its exhaust would not asphyxiate him. The porter came over and, slamming down the lid, shut him into blackness.

Shortly thereafter he heard the turbo-engine roar and he felt the bus pull out. From the whine of the engine he knew it burnt hydrogen. Providence was still with him. He felt the bus turn into the highway and gain speed. As it did, he heard sirens blasting in the terminal behind. He began sweating profusely and felt like holding his breath. After a while he relaxed as the bus continued on.

Losing all track of time in the utter blackness, his tired body again overwhelmed him and he fell fast asleep. He did not wake until the bus stopped and the compartment cover opened. He rubbed his eyes as light flooded the compartment and looked at his watch. It read three o'clock. He wondered if he'd crossed a time zone. As he tried to get his bearings, several porters began unloading the baggage.

Halfway through this task, one saw him. The porter looked puzzled for a second, then yelled, "Hey!"

Porch clambered out with his stiff muscles complaining each inch of the way. He looked up to see the porter about to blow a whistle.

"Don't," he cried out, holding up a fistful of credits. Pressing these into the porter's hand, he slung his duffel over his shoulder and hurried off into the crowd. As he moved along, he looked up and saw a huge sign—CHICAGO TRANSPORT. He was in Greater Chicago, the Midwestern megapolis. Certainly he could lose himself here amongst the teeming millions.

It had become very warm this far south of the Academy, so he took off the overcoat and folded it over his arm. He kept the cap on, and pulled it down farther to cover his eyes. He thought that he would begin growing a beard. The sun was over his right shoulder, so he was walking southeast, he believed toward the inner city as the streets, buildings and people were becoming shabbier.

Presently he came upon a small restaurant—really a hole in the wall. It was very dirty, but he went on in and slouched down in a corner booth. He'd had the two sandwiches and soda about fourteen hours ago and his hunger was enormous. But he wouldn't order anything out of the ordinary and bring attention to himself.

His hunger abated somewhat when he saw the caked ketchup and dirt filling the cracks in the vinyl table top. But he ordered, and when the eggs came, he could taste the powder from which they'd been reconstituted. Soybean meal adulterated the sausage. The Federal

Surplus Food Program was at least reaching these rotting enclaves of the great city. The steaming coffee masked the meal. When finished, he ordered a quart of milk and several fruit pies to carry out and got ready to leave. Taking sufficient credits from his wallet to pay the tab, he slipped them first on the floor under his shoe and rubbed them around in the grease and dirt. Then, picking them up, he crushed them further and went over to the register to pay. They were accepted as a matter of course and he did not receive any inquisitive looks.

Porch set out again, moving toward the heart of the inner city. As he continued on, he stepped over boozed-out derelicts and averted his eyes from the solicitous smiles of a number of hookers. Then he thought he heard several sets of footsteps to his rear. He quickened his pace. Presently he came upon another hooker. As he needed a ruse to check on whoever was following, he stopped and pretended to dicker with the lady. She looked him all over and said, "Anything you want, baby— for free."

Porch saw three men loitering not far behind as he smiled at her and said, "No, I guess not."

He began to walk away, so she said, "Aw, come on, honey. I'll throw in a hot meal."

The men followed. He looked across the street and saw a junk man pushing a cart full of metal scraps. The man stopped every few feet to pick up the beer cans and glass bottles along the curb. He crossed over and approached the man. Within a moment, he had traded the old overcoat that he was carrying for a stout iron bar. He continued on. Those following did so as well. When he got to the end of the block, he turned and began to walk directly toward them, holding the bar in front of his chest. The men stopped and, backing away, found an alley to their right and quickly disappeared.

Porch continued, deeper and deeper into the inner city. Several blocks later, he came upon a sign in a bay window. It said—ROOM TO LET. Night was soon to fall, so he stopped and looked at the old brownstone. It was three storeys tall. Bay windows stuck out by the entrance, all heavily curtained and sorely in need of washing.

At the entrance, three stone steps led up to a door which appeared tightly shut. Still weary, he surveyed the building. Should he keep moving to deepen his cover, or hole up until he'd reconstituted mind and body? The day had gotten so hot, and the heat from the pavement penetrated his shoes and was burning his feet. He chose to stop.

He climbed the hard steps up to the stoop and knocked on the door. There was a stirring inside, followed by heavy footsteps. A rattle of chains followed and the door opened a crack.

"Whozzat?"

"You advertise a room?" Porch questioned.

The door opened wide and a large black woman confronted him.

"You got fo' bucks and no woman—we Christian people," she emphasized, using the old term for money.

"Yes, and no woman," Porch responded. She opened the door but still shielded the entry with her large frame. Placing her hands on her hips, she looked Porch up and down. He winced against any hint of recognition, but her eyes remained placid.

"OK, pay in advance. It's plain but clean," she said.

Porch handed her credits equivalent to four dollars. She handed him an old iron key.

"Upstairs in front, above this parlor. The lavatory's at the end of the hall. Keep your door locked and window down—we got air," she ended haughtily.

Porch went up, stowed his duffel bag, and looked the room over. After showering, he returned to the room, locked the door, pulled the shade down, sat on the bed, drank the quart of now tepid milk, and ate the pies. Then he lay down on the old mattress with creaking springs beneath and luxuriated in the coolness. He quickly dozed off.

Downstairs, the woman completed her work in the kitchen and sat down to rest. She too dozed off. About seven o'clock, there was a rustling at the door. She opened one eye and listened. She heard a key in the lock twist. The door opened and in came her man. She could see that he was tired as she nodded at him. He nodded back and came over, patted her shoulder, and handed her a rolled- up newspaper. She watched him out of the corner of her eye as he went to the kitchen. She heard him open the fridge, take out a beer, and pull the tab. He went to sit down in the small dining room, and she could see by the flickering light that he had turned on the small TV she kept there for the "soaps." This was a nightly ritual, and when he turned on the TV, she knew he was not ready for supper. The sound came on and she heard the announcer say something about the 326th All Star game.

Baseball, she thought. Now she knew that he would not be ready for several hours, so she leaned back in her rocker and opened the paper. She had all the time she wanted and would not have to hurry through the front section to get to the Abigail Flanders column, "Advice to the Lovelorn," before he interrupted her.

First she looked at the daily lottery numbers—no winner. Then her gaze went up to the headline—CRAZED CANDIDATE ATTACKS SUPERIOR. She mumbled to herself, "If we'd stayed on Earth liken we s'posed to, wouldn' be no trouble."

She read on—something about a man being hideously maimed, a famous hero, also attempted murder, then the felon escaped. There was column after column in the Corporation paper. She got to a description of the assailant. She read over it a second time, then saw the words "know the whereabouts of" and "reward."

She paused, stopped reading and her eyes drifted up to the ceiling. She sighed, rose slowly and, carrying the paper with her, went over to an old wall phone. Looking at the paper and then the phone, she punched in a number.

Night enveloped Greater Chicago. In the room above the parlor, Porch's sleep had turned fitful. In a dream, he imagined that huge bloodhounds surrounded him in a swamp where he was entangled in vines and sinking deeper and deeper into a wet black ooze. He cried out. Suddenly, bright floodlights flashed on all about

him and lit every inch of the swamp. He shielded his
eyes from the glare with a hand that he was able to
untangle. Then he perceived that he was free of the black
ooze and, laying supine on a bank, completely dry.

Gradually, consciousness seeped into his mind. He
was holding his right arm up and shielding his eyes
from the glare of flashlights directed at him from just a
foot or so away. As his eyes adjusted, he saw just as
many old-fashioned cocked revolvers aimed at his head.
Instinctively, he made a taut spring of his body, but so
many arms grabbed his limbs, he could not move a
muscle. Seeing resistance was useless, he relaxed.

A voice called out, soothingly, "Quiet, boy," then,
"Let him up."

He attached the voice to a well-dressed gray-haired
man standing at the foot of the bed. The gray-haired
man commanded, "Get dressed."

Porch rose and began to pull on his clothes. As he
did, he saw that the hands that had held him down
belonged to some six or seven Chicago policemen. They
kept the revolvers trained on him. He put on his shoes
and stood up. Rough hands pulled his arms behind him
and manacled him. The gray-haired man asked, "Is this
your duffel?"

Porch nodded and the gray haired man picked it up
and said to the police, "OK, boys, take him to the car."

Porch felt a blue sleeve go through each arm and
clamp it tight. Two policemen began to drag him along,
following two others. Two more followed these. The gray-
haired man brought up the rear.

Porch spoke out, "I can walk."

The gray-haired man said, "Gently, men, gently—
the boss doesn't want him mussed up."

The policemen relaxed their grip and Porch followed
the first two down the stairs with the two that held him
alongside. When they got to the first floor, Porch saw
another man who was wearing a somber black suit
standing beside the landlady. This man questioned the
gray-haired man, "Is he the one?"

"Without a doubt." The black-suited man handed
the landlady a wad of credits. She gave Porch a cursory

look and began counting, "One thousand, two thousand, three thousand, four..."

They motioned Porch to move and the entire contingent left the house. Porch saw an immense limousine at the front curb. A policeman opened the rear door and several others shoved him inside. Porch heard the gray-haired man say to them, "OK, boys, the Corporation will take it from here. Here's your receipt. I'm sure the boss will call the Commissioner—you can look forward to an early Christmas."

Porch found himself in the center of the rear seat. A swarthy-looking black-suited man sat to his left. The gray-haired man entered and sat to his right. Two others occupied side seats to his immediate front. The black-suited man who had handed the money to the landlady got into the front beside another man. The chauffeur turned on the ignition and the hydro-turbo revved up. The limousine pulled smoothly away from the curb and headed down the dark street. None of the men looked at him, nor did they utter a word.

CHAPTER 12
INCARCERATION

The limousine headed west, passing quickly through the inner city and the business district on the west side. Nobody spoke. Porch had fleeting glimpses of Lake Michigan behind him as they sped along. Soon they passed suburban residential sections, entered a freeway and then the Corporation Superthruway—ignoring toll stations. Finally they turned off onto a private road.

Porch saw the field lights of a small air terminal coming up. The limousine stopped at a heavily guarded gate and was waved through when the chauffeur showed a pass. The vehicle drove up to a terminal strip where a jet-copter was waiting with its rotors slowly turning. It was black as coal and had the red griffin logo on its side.

"Get out," the gray-haired man commanded. Porch felt the swarthy man's revolver at his ribs as he turned to follow the gray-haired man out. The gray-haired man headed for the chopper, and as he did, the jet whined to a higher pitch and the rotors increased rpm. The three got into the back compartment. Porch noted that his companions looked out intensely through the open doors, both right and left, with revolvers cocked. Then he saw cupolas amidships. Each had a gunner at the ready sitting before a large laser blaster. The pilot pushed the throttle forward. The jet engine whine rose to a scream as the overhead blades whipped the air, biting into it. The chopper lurched forward on its skids, hesitated, then rose quickly. The pilot pushed to maximum power and banked hard right. G-forces acting like giant unseen hands crushed the chopper occupants back into their seats. The pilot continued his circle, rising rapidly. When the lights of the field were far below, Porch's captors ceased their vigil and closed the rear doors. The amidships gunners also relaxed and sat back away from the laser blasters. As the chopper circled, Porch saw a thick cloud bank hovering over the great city behind. In a moment, they were in those clouds, and blackness enveloped everything but the dim instrument panel forward.

The pilot set his course and turned on the engine silencer. Quiet prevailed except for a barely audible thumping of the rotor blades. Porch felt despair and anger at himself for not controlling his destiny better. Save for occasional well-cushioned bumps caused by air turbulence, he lost all sense of motion.

The chopper sped on into the night. At last he sensed a slowing and a gradual banked turn to the right as the helicopter descended. Its skids hit and the pilot cut power. It was still dark. Porch felt a revolver in his ribs again as he followed the gray-haired man out.

When he gained his footing, he felt that he was standing on solid concrete. There were several dim blue landing lights around, shielded to be seen only from the air. By their light, he could see they had landed on top of a blockhouse. A glimmer of red now showed on the horizon, but how far they had traveled, or for how long, he did not know because the gray-haired man had confiscated his watch when he was first manacled. Two guards prodded him forward to a hatch that led down into the building. As he went down concrete stairs, he heard the helicopter roar off into the night. Again, the gray-haired man brought up the rear as the entourage descended. The staircase led to a narrow passageway lit with dim incandescent bulbs housed in wire cages. The main passage led off into equally narrow side passages every hundred feet or so. As they moved along Porch saw heavy steel doors fitted tightly into heavy steel frames, alternating side to side. He guessed that these

were entrances to individual cells. Each had a square
opening at eye level closed by an outside sliding cover.
Porch surmised these were used to pass food and drink,
or possibly for surveillance, inspection and communications. They descended to another level, and Porch saw
the same monotony of narrow passages, flanked by
massive steel doors, all painted a dull naval gray. They
continued down to another level. Here the air was cooler,
and then they came down to where it was absolutely
cold.

They met a huge man, evidently the jailer. He held a
heavy steel door wide open and a guard behind Porch
pushed him through and into a cell. The gray-haired
man entered behind Porch and said, "You will stay here
until called. Obey all regulations enumerated in the
manual that you will find on the desk.

Porch asked sullenly, "Is there to be no writ of
habeus corpus?"

"That has been decided. The Corporation owns you,
lock, stock and barrel—mind, body and soul. Cooperate for reasons that will be made apparent if you don't.
When I depart, disrobe and put your clothes in the chute
in the corner. Shower and put on the issue clothing that
is on your cot. I have a receipt to give you for items
taken from you which are to be returned if it becomes
appropriate." The gray-haired man departed and the
heavy door swung shut. Porch heard its lock clang into
place. He found himself in a windowless, fully venti-
lated concrete cell about fifteen feet wide by twenty long.
It contained a cot with mattress and blanket, a steel
table and chair, a combination shower, sink and toilet
in one corner with an exercise machine next to it. All
but the chair were attached to the wall. A single caged
amber light shone from the ceiling and another was
caged and half-shielded above the table. The cell was
spotless. He would do as told. He would be a model
prisoner. They might, at some time or another, let their
guard down. He disrobed, put his clothes in the chute,
showered and donned the issue clothing. For outer garments he had a black tunic with the emblem of the red
griffin rampant upon it, beltless black trousers, and a

pair of black athletic shoes. Everything fit as if he had been expected.

Before long, there was a sound at the cell door. It opened and a man dressed as he was entered with a covered steel tray. The huge jailer he'd seen stood at the cell door. He thought to himself that the man carrying the tray must be a trustee. That brightened his hopes. But the other man equally dampened them. He must have weighed three hundred pounds. He had a burr haircut on a bullet head that seemed squashed into a short bull neck. He wore a white tunic over black britches tucked into a pair of jack boots. He wore a gun belt and carried a stout oak truncheon. He had little piggish red eyes and wore a perpetual scowl.

The trustee placed the tray on the table and left. The steel door slammed shut. Porch took the cover off the tray and saw that, for whatever reason, they were concerned with his well-being. It was laden with fruit, eggs, bacon, pancakes, a ladle of syrup, a slab of butter, a quart pitcher of milk, and a large pot of coffee. He ate with relish. It was his first good meal since his troubles began, and he knew he had to rebuild his strength for whatever lay ahead.

After he'd finished, he read over the manual of regulations. He'd completed most of it when the cell door opened again. The jailer entered carrying a scrub brush and pail of water full of cleanser. Bullethead put these down, pointed to Porch's breakfast tray and utensils, and said, "Chute."

Porch quickly placed them into the chute in the corner. Then the jailer pointed all about the cell, then to the pail and brush and said, "Spotless." He left.

Porch went about this task fervidly, as it gave him something to do while he formed his thoughts. The manual said he must keep his mind and body in good condition while in captivity. Obviously they'd put the exerciser in the cell for this purpose. What about mental activity? He was authorized as many books as he wanted to read. He would spend as many hours daily as he could spare, reading books—books on geography, first on North America and then the rest of the world and its people, their languages, habits and customs. He would learn about every square foot of the earth, its terrain, and its climate. He fully intended to escape, and when he did, he had to know where to go, what to expect, and how to make his escape permanent.

As he finished scrubbing his cell, the steel door opened and Bullethead returned to inspect Porch's work. Satisfied, he picked up brush and bucket and started to leave.

"Books," Porch said in a loud voice.

"Books?" Bullethead responded with incomprehension in his voice.

"All you can obtain on geography." Bullethead left, scratching his head with his free hand. The steel door slammed shut and Porch went over to the cot to think out a schedule—personal hygiene, meals, police cell, exercise... After he'd arranged it mentally, he thought he must track the days. At the next meal, he broke half a tine off a fork. The metal bed frame should be a good place to keep a calendar. He could mark that. He rose from the cot and lifted the mattress.

To his surprise, he found a calendar. There were rows and rows of neatly inscribed marks. He began counting but stopped when he reached a thousand with many rows to go, at least as many as he'd counted, and half again more. He became miserable when he realized that a previous occupant had been isolated there for seven years. Later that day, another meal was brought—steak, potatoes, salad, ice cream, coffee. They fed him well. He wondered why. He made his toilet, lay down and went to sleep, waking again when the cell door opened. The trustee with the jailer behind brought breakfast.

Another day—he began the routine he'd outlined in his mind: personal hygiene, eat, police cell—scrub it down well, exercise. Several days passed. Then one morning, several trustees entered, carrying a four-foot cube. They set it down in a corner. Bullethead, following, said simply, "Books."

After they'd departed, Porch went over to the cube. It was a plastic box. When he opened it, he was amazed, then elated. There were books—hundreds on geography, containing detailed maps and charts, meticulous treatments and extended treatises on North America, South America, Europe, Africa, the Far East, both poles and the oceans of the world. There was a cornucopia of information—topography, people, flora and fauna, climate and ocean currents. Bullethead had followed the regulations to the letter, and the system he had become enmeshed in had responded, perhaps mindlessly. He added the books to his routine. He pored over them, then quizzed himself repeatedly.

The days passed. He was interrupted only for meals and cell cleaning, but at random times, the slot in the steel door would open and Porch could see little pig eyes dart around the cell. Bullethead could not bring himself to believe that his charge ordered the books simply to read them, but rather for some underhanded purpose.

Porch ended his day by inscribing a mark inside the marks of the cell's previous occupant. The fresh marks, lacking tarnish, enabled him to count the days that passed. He reckoned it was a late September morning when the gray-haired man returned. He was reading at the time. The gray- haired man looked at Porch's book and then the others, neatly stacked in the corner.

He appeared puzzled at first, then said, "Don't even think of it. There's no way. Didn't you notice the precautions taken bringing you here? Didn't you see the absolute security?"

Porch did not answer, so the gray-haired man continued," Anyway, your time has come. The Chairman has deemed sufficient time has elapsed so that few recall a crazed candidate who tried to murder his superior officer at the Space Academy, and failing that, maimed the man. Even fewer care."

Porch reddened but still said nothing.

The gray-haired man went on, "The Chairman, though, remembers well, and will never forget, because the man you crippled is his stepson and was his heir apparent. He will have justice, he has said to me, many times, yes, many times over. So you see, you are in his hands and will be brought to justice, and the world will not care nor even know, as you have been forgotten and the Corporation will not be embarrassed by whatever should come out. The Corporation will try you fairly. Official witnesses from the government and the Academy will be present. I am a lawyer, personal assistant to the Chairman, who has assigned me to defend you. I will do this with all the vigor I can muster. So henceforth, consider me your friend and counsel."

The gray-haired man stopped talking and appeared anxious for Porch to respond. Porch still said nothing. After a moment, the Lawyer said, "Very well, there will be plenty of time to hear you out. We go now to meet the Most Important Person who has summoned you. Shower, shave, look your best. I will wait outside your cell, and I'll assume I have your word to do nothing foolish such as trying to flee, for I don't wish to have you manacled. You'd only be caught and charges doubled. Quickly now, get ready."

The Lawyer left the cell. Porch got ready as quickly as he could. The uniform provided had the same cut and color that he'd become used to wearing but was much finer in all respects. He was provided black shoes that shone like glass, black trousers with razor-sharp creases, and a pullover shirt of fine angora wool. The pullover had the griffin emblem. He thought of the symbolism. He was truly a property of the Corporation, like it or not. When he'd dressed, he moved cautiously out of the cell, stopping just beyond the steel door. *Damnation*, he thought to himself, *I already have a prisoner mentality. I must act with dignity, as a free man.*

The Lawyer was waiting for him and he scrutinized Porch from head to toe. Porch was immaculate. He stood erect, with the countenance of a man unconquered. Nobody would have believed he'd been locked up for three months. "Excellent," said the Lawyer. "The Chairman demands perfection. Follow me."

The Lawyer led him up the narrow corridor and then into a much wider side passage. They came to a set of double doors, and when they had passed through, Porch found himself in a finely appointed entry, one hardly characteristic of a high security prison. He had been held on the ground floor rather than deep underground as he had imagined.

They continued through a set of glass doors to the outside. A limousine waited below them beyond a marble staircase. It was a heavily built armor-plated brougham which mounted a laser weapon in a recessed cupola in front of a thick anti-penetration front windshield.

When they reached the vehicle, its chauffeur opened the door for them. He invited Porch to enter rather than shoved him inside. The Lawyer followed. Inside, Porch found himself sitting on a deeply cushioned leather seat. He looked out the large side window. Some distance away, he saw several one-man aircarts hovering. As the limo moved off silently, its turbo-engine almost inaudible, he could see the aircarts follow. They hadn't relaxed security. The limo went around a large oval in front of the detention center and Porch could see the entire front. He could hardly believe its beauty. It had a facade of creamy Italian marble with feigned windows, high, narrow and arched. There was a beautiful fountain in the center of the oval. It was a huge structure. From the air or at any distance, it must have appeared to be a museum or gallery of fine arts. Porch wondered how many unfortunates were jailed there.

He turned his attention to the roadway. They were traveling east on a secondary road. His immediate past study paid off. From his surroundings, he knew he must be somewhere in the American Midwest. After several curves and a few small hillocks, the brougham crested a larger hill and a tall wrought iron fence appeared. Heavy vertical bars, capped with spearheads, were embedded in a three-foot-high brick base which also supported taller brick columns capped with concrete every fifty feet or so. Small rotating antennas on top of the columns gave themselves away as surveillance devices.

The fence paralleled the road for mile after mile. At last, they came to a set of colossal columns into which a side road turned. Massive wrought iron gates barred the entrance. The brougham stopped and the chauffeur punched a code into some buttons on his dash. The gates silently opened. Porch saw the red griffin on each pillar and that each gate had the emblem he'd not seen since he'd left the Academy—the blue shield with black griffin above a black rose.

The Lawyer sensed his puzzlement and said, "You may have guessed that the red griffin rampant is the logo of the Corporation, but the other is used only by the Chairman. It is his coat of arms, and it inspires love and respect, or fear and anguish, wherever it is seen. God help anyone who displays it without his personal approval."

They drove through the gates and the road widened into a broad avenue. Lombardy poplars one hundred feet apart graced each side like silent sentinels. These were special, genetically altered against disease and for long life. Porch was amazed. Each was over 150 feet tall. He saw green lawn beyond them, extending right and left as far as the eye could see.

The Lawyer smiled and said, "Meant to impress—it is through that gate and along this boulevard that the powerful of the world—those so privileged—pass, presidents and premiers, cardinals and kings, chairmen of parties and chairmen of boards."

He pointed right and left and continued, "What you see is rugged, water thrifty 'designer' grass that grows in a thick mat only two inches high. Soon we will come upon the biofarms."

Porch said nothing, awed by the spectacular grandeur of the drive. Now he saw in the distance groups of trees between which grazed diminutive deer. He suspected genetic alteration. Farther out he saw a barn and silo, some pens and a small farmhouse. The ethereal beauty of the place amazed him. It was storybook. He looked past the Lawyer to the right of the road and saw a mirror image of the left.

The Lawyer interrupted once again, "It might look quaint but important work goes on at those farms, not only in animal husbandry, but also with plant genetics. We grow blueberries the size of grapes, grapes the size of tomatoes, and tomatoes as big as cantaloupes. Have you ever seen pink cotton or green gardenias? You would be amazed. These biofarms circle the estate, and the Chairman maintains a personal interest in the work that goes on. He has an even greater interest in zoology and paleozoology.

"The Corporation maintains valuable gene pools of animals that now would be extinct because of the predations of man. It has brought fossil species back into existence through genetic manipulation or genetic engineering... Yes, backward engineering. Soon you will see examples of this work, if only a few. The Corporation maintains plantations and preserves vegetation from all over the world, from the polar regions to the equator, to carry it on. We will use the results of this work as Earth colonization into the galaxy continues."

Porch saw in the Lawyer's face the obvious pride the man felt in being a member of such an organization, and he wondered how well he would be defended. Presently they came upon a huge hedge, or rather barrier, of Osage Orange—ten feet tall and thirty feet thick. It looked impenetrable. The road passed between at a guard shack where the limousine stopped and the driver handed a paper to one of the guards. Porch could see a row of aircarts behind the guardhouse.

The Lawyer said, "Only aircarts and special helicopters are allowed beyond this point. The airspace above is a restricted zone; not even commercial air traffic may fly over. Should they, they are intercepted or shot down."

Now they came upon a swamp that looked primeval.

"It is teeming with life, dangerous life." They passed the swamp to fields of heavy grass and the Lawyer shouted, "Look!"

Porch looked over and saw three mammoths pulling large swaths of grasses into their mouths. Farther out, he saw an auroch, some ibex, and a herd of strange-looking horses.

"Primitive ancestors of Przhevalski's horse," the Lawyer said.

Suddenly the horses began to run and, just as quickly, their run turned into a stampede. Porch soon saw the reason. Three choppers, flying very low, were pursuing the animals. When they were just above the last three, they lowered padded grapplers and lifted the animals into their bellies. "They are culling the herd of the least fit. Hurry on, driver, our guest must see their disposition," the Lawyer directed.

As man increased his speed, Porch noticed that the poplars on the sides of the roads were getting smaller. There was a small rise ahead, and when they had topped it, he saw the Corporation Headquarters in the distance. It was a Renaissance palazzo of dolomite marble, glowing golden in the morning sunlight. An extensive piazza in front met a grand staircase set off by side balconies. Side wings extended beyond the main building with additional piazzas and balconies, and fountains adorned the place. A hundred or so windows on three floors appeared to the right and left.

The Lawyer smiled and said, "The marble glows pink at sunset, and at night, fully lit up, it's even more beautiful."

They approached a fence and final set of gates, beyond which there was a bridge. The Lawyer commanded the driver, "Stop on the bridge."

"Get out on the left and you will see a grand drama," he promised Porch.

When they were standing on the bridge, he pointed to the three choppers they'd seen but a minute ago. The aircraft slowed, then hovered about half a mile away. Porch watched each one lower the horse it had captured in a belly sling. The slings released as the horses' hooves touched the ground. Each began to run directly toward the bridge. A section of fence to the left of the gate behind them was rising. The lead horse, closing fast, was now but a quarter mile away, with the other two close behind.

Suddenly a streak of tawny orange raced out from a clump of Pampas grass on the right, and another rushed forth from dense brush on the left. They were great cats and they brought their prey down in a flash, dispatching the horses with a thrust from jaws that harbored saber-like incisors. They roared their conquest with fangs dripping red as the faster horse escaped through the passage in the fence.

The Lawyer said nonchalantly, "You may have noticed that those are saber-tooth tigers—very efficient killing machines—nature maintaining an ecological balance—survival of the fittest—the Chairman believes strongly in that."

Porch took another look at the fearsome beasts. They were tearing huge chunks of meat from the horses. He shuddered.

The Lawyer continued, "Our geneticists brought them back from prehistory—and they have grown lazy. Learning that their prey comes in threes, they never bother now to chase the first. We've tested. If we release only one herbivore, it can run right past the cats—almost leisurely.

"But you can imagine what superlative guards they make. Notice the area to which they are confined, past the final fence around the headquarters. But look to the end of this bridge and you see a concrete wall, flush with the higher ground around the headquarters. It rises like a great ocean wave, breaking this way. It has been engineered to just above the height those beasts can jump or scale. On the inside, looking back, you can't even see the moat. Nor is it apparent from anywhere inside the building. Ingenious, to say the least. But come now, we must hurry along."

They got back into the limousine and drove over the bridge, up a great circular drive with a magnificent central fountain and stopped at the marble stairs that led up to the grand entrance.

The Lawyer told Porch to follow him and led him up the steps through massive bronze and glass doors into a huge lobby. Side halls led off as far as Porch could see. A grand chandelier hung down from its mooring three floors above, and before them, left and right, rose a double staircase which ended at a high balcony above. Below the balcony at the far end of the lobby was a three times life-size portrait.

The Lawyer pointed to it and said, "That is a painting of the Founder. He is revered today by all employees of the Corporation. Look around you on the walls. The portraits that you see are those of his successors through seven generations. But come now—up the staircase."

Porch followed the Lawyer up and they came to a set of ornately carved double doors just off the balcony.

"Inside," said the Lawyer as he opened them.

Porch went in and found himself in a large ante-room. He could hear an opera by Verdi playing softly. Several large leather sofas faced each other in the center. Others were spaced along the walls with chairs and writing desks. Marble end tables with inlaid gold set off the sofas. Thick pile Persian rugs covered the floor and Renaissance masterpieces covered dark wood-paneled walls. He could pick out Giottini, Uccello, Bellini and Botticelli. But the most striking work was on the far opposite wall between two interior doors. It was a painting of one of the most beautiful women Porch had ever seen. She had a haughty look, with both fire and flirtation in her eyes.

The Lawyer whispered to him, "It is Francesca, seventh generation from the Founder. She married a man named Werewick to give her bastard son a name. Werewick died mysteriously—just as the boy's natural father did. The Chairman was her second husband, and he loved her very much. She was a brilliant, wild and witty woman who had a lust for life. Unfortunately, she was killed when the auto she was driving at high speed overturned some fifteen years ago. She was, of course, Major Werewick's mother."

Porch swallowed hard.

"I want you to sit over there until Don Belisarius is ready to see you. Don't move from there, or it will go very hard for you."

Porch went over and sat at the corner writing desk the Lawyer pointed out. The Lawyer went into the inner office. Porch could see a video camera trained on him. On the desk in front of him was a large but rather thin volume. It was bound in black leather and had the red griffin rampant embossed upon it.

He opened it up. The title read, *THE CORPORATION, A HISTORY*. He turned the page over and came upon a quotation from the Bible. He thought this strange but read on—"And the Lord said unto Satan, 'Whence comest thou?' Then Satan answered the Lord, and said, 'From going to and fro in the Earth, and from walking up and down in it.'"

CHAPTER 13
THE CORPORATION

The beginning of the twenty-first century was scary. The people who lived through it said, "Those were the days the devil roamed the earth, walking to and fro, back and forth, creating havoc."

Satanic cults emerged at the end of the twentieth century and grew without bound. Ritual slaying of animals was widespread. The story that Good Friday was the Black Sabbath persisted. Rumored sacrifice of babies and young virgins ran rampant. Drug lords took control. Corrupt nations wasted their wealth and became moribund. Terrorists with twisted dogmas ran amok and filled the streets with blood. The dread disease ravaged amoral millions.

In the early decades, nature exacted its due. Depleted ozone made melanoma epidemic. Acid rain decimated forests and poisoned waters. Intense "greenhouse" heat blanketed the earth, parching field and farm alike so that famine stalked the land—then spawned great tornadoes and fierce hurricanes. Polar ice caps melted and oceans rose. Millions succumbed to raging waters.

The world was out of balance and shook in agony as great earthquakes destroyed cities and towns. Falling stone and steel crushed millions. But then long dormant volcanoes erupted, spewing clouds of dust which cooled the lands and oceans—and provided particulate upon which water could condense and bring back rain and snow. Ice caps advanced and oceans receded. The

Great Earth Mother, Gaia, was healing herself.

Earth's people were chastened. There was half the population of fifty years before. But those who lived through those days looked back and said, "The earth is healing itself. There is hope."

Then along came a man, at first little noticed in the turmoil. Guiseppi was his name. Garbage was his game. He gave his place of business as "Down-in-the-Dumps" with a phone number that people remembered. They called. He hauled—first with one truck, then two, then ten. "Cash for Trash" emblazoned the sides of his growing fleet. But his real genius was disposal. By the year 2020, there were no more landfills. Air pollution prohibited burning below 2000 degrees, and incineration above that temperature had become prohibitively expensive.

Selective recycling made him a winner. When the other fellow recycled eighty percent, he did eighty-five. When his competition reached eighty-five percent, he was at ninety. He peaked out at ninety-nine percent. He located his disposal plants on wasteland and called them New Earth Resource Plants.

"It's all in the way you look at it," he said.

He used all the tricks of twenty-first century engineering to chemically and physically alter, separate, segregate, collect and collate waste. He exploited gravity, specific gravity, electrolysis, hydrolysis and ion exchange. He employed high speed centrifuges, supercooled magnets and microfilters. He enlisted bacteria and fungi. He transformed wastes into minerals, metals, fertilizers, fuels, feed and building materials; converted worn-out tires, pulverized concrete, and reclaimed hydrocarbons into highway surfacing. He recycled plastic into gasoline. He fed purified paper to his cattle and they relished it. He provided work for thousands.

With tight managerial control, his profits grew and grew. He was tough. He quickly defeated rivals and political foes. But harmony and growth were his long-term objectives, so he reduced his fees to just above cost whenever he could, as his major profits came from reclaimed materials, regenerated hydrocarbons, and cogenerated electric energy. He wanted to benefit all.

In 2060, when the Millenarians chucked it all to follow Thaddeus P. Winter to a new promised land amongst the stars, he bought up the lands they left at bargain prices and built greenhouses of recycled aluminum and steel, glass and plastics. He called them facto-farms and planted them beneath vast solar energy fields. Soon each facto-farm produced one hundred thousand pounds of foodstuffs per week. He wasted nothing and provided work for hundreds of thousands.

Guiseppi, the founder, died in the year 2080 and the people built a great statue in his honor with one word at its base, Benefactor. He left as a legacy to his son a mighty corporation that he'd started as a tiny company in 2010. Bruno was as smart as his father and twice as ambitious. He stamped the Corporation with the sign of the Griffin and vowed to make it renowned the world over.

As chief operating officer, he began to diversify and soon controlled most of the national electric grid. He started acquiring pipelines and moved into transportation, forming an engineering subsidiary to build a new superthruway system, bypassing the old interstate system. He adorned these highways with handsome bridges and awesome tunnels and made it a toll system. Few could afford not to use it. Next he bought up trucking companies and in a few years had a near monopoly. Railroads followed, then shipping, both inland barge and ocean transport. Soon he owned most port facilities and dry-docks. Computer nets, telephone, radio and tri-di television came next. By 2100, he moved into construction and heavy manufacturing; automobiles, trucks, farm equipment, locomotives and ship building.

Bruno passed on in 2129 and was laid to rest beside Guiseppi, leaving a commercial empire to his son, Silvano. Bruno hoped the boy would lead it to even greater grandeur, but Silvano had no interest. He would sneak away at every opportunity to roam the forests, hills and mountains. Bruno thought that someday his son would come around, but also knew not to leave anything to chance. So though he left the chairmanship to Silvano, he named an astute board of directors which kept everything operating efficiently. Growth was put on hold and the Corporation became a money-making behemoth, which was fine with Silvano, who spent his days wandering the woods as a happy camper.

Silvano met Diana D'Ambrosia at an Earth First rally at Stanford. When he first saw her, he thought he was looking at a wood nymph. She was tiny, had nut-brown hair, dark eyes, and the deepest tan he'd ever seen. When he found out that she too was nuts about trees, he married her, and the woods and forests became their single passion. They came to live for trees—trees, and nothing else. With the dividend flow that came from the Corporation, they bought up marginal farms and deserted ranches. Then with supertech biology, herbology and plant genetics, they planted super trees.

They confined their efforts to North America first, hiring thousands to reforest the Northwest, the Rockies and the California coast. They camped in the woods and moved from stream to stream as their projects progressed. Diana bore Silvano a son whom they named Urbano, backpacking him along on their sojourn. They created a great northern forest that began in the American Midwest and went north to the Arctic tundra. They repeated their efforts in the Northeast and South, then moved their work worldwide, tackling next the rain forests as money flowed into their coffers. The couple grew old together, died, and were buried under a stand of Douglas fir.

As Urbano poured a last handful of fragrant soil over their grave, he said to all about, "I hate the woods. I hate the forests and the jungles. I hate the mosquito swarms, the poisonous snakes—sand in my hair, mud under my fingernails, and thorns in my toes. I'll never go into the woods again."

So he moved to the megacity and began to run the Corporation from the most lavish penthouse he could find. He called himself the Great Indoorsman. But as Urbano was a little lazy and none too bright, the Board watched over him closely. Still, corporate affairs began to languish. So the Board found a second cousin for him to marry, hoping to recover the leadership genes of his forebears. They also built the great estate that is now the Corporate Headquarters and persuaded him to move there so they could watch him more closely yet. Urbano died at the turn of the twenty-third century at the age of sixty-one after a long and undistinguished career. His only notable accomplishment was siring Dominic.

Dominic inherited the helm at the tender age of twenty-eight. The Board of Trustees pointed out his youth and suggested a surrogate until he'd gained some experience. Dominic would have none of this, and said, "I'm going to turn this corpulent behemoth back into the juggernaut it once was."

Then he offered each trustee a golden parachute or the sack. The entire board chose to retire, leaving Dominic with all the marbles. He had the genes of his forebears and was both politic and ruthless. He believed in tradition and loyalty. Soon the Corporation became a "Family." He demanded total fidelity from all his subordinates, then treated them well.

He began with a three-pronged offensive. First, he greased key political palms. Next he bought up a high percentage of the public debt. Last he began a ruthless economic attack on his competitors, both national and international. Within a few years even his heavy contributions to political campaigns and cultivation of those who held the reins of power was not enough to quell outspoken dissent against such accumulation of economic power. The media began yelling about instituting harsh new antitrust laws. Congress started to react to the hew and cry.

Dominic simply showed the government what would happen if he unloaded the debt instruments the Corporation held. Congress cringed and antitrust legislation melted away.

What was good for the Corporation was good for the country.

The government and the Corporation made a pact. What was good for one had to be good for the other. Dominic had also learned a lesson. He bought up as much of the media as he could get his hands on. They ceased to be a threat. He bought up schools and colleges and heavily endowed those he could not buy directly. He would train generations to come that the Corporation was a benevolent father to all. Nor did he stop with institutions of higher learning. He bought up preschools and day care centers to teach the little ones the same.

He continued his heavy expansion, now mostly in the international arena and in the Western space effort. Only one thing marred his life plan. He had not produced a male heir, try as he would, with wife after wife. At last he resigned himself to the fact that the line of male succession was broken. His first wife had borne him a daughter, Francesca. As he watched her grow, he saw in her the same wit and aggressive spirit that he possessed. He thought to himself, *The name might be lost but not the genes.*

So he satisfied himself that he had an appropriate heir and came to dote upon his daughter. As she grew into a young woman, her beauty grew with her. Dominic indulged her beyond all reason. But on her sixteenth birthday at her coming out ball at the old Waldorf Astoria, catastrophe struck. A handsome adventurer and space hero seduced her. She became pregnant, and so dishonored the family. Enraged, Dominic sent her out of his house and forbade her ever to return. Then he exacted his revenge on her paramour.

But his spirit languished. He tried to recover by visiting the children at his centers. He would watch them for hours, marching before him, phalanx after phalanx of day care kids, wearing the red griffin, singing the Corporation songs and chanting the mottos. It helped not a wit. He was beside himself, living in a sea of sorrow.

As well, Dominic's ruthless ways had gathered for him an ocean of enemies. He reached his fiftieth birthday the very day the first attempt to assassinate him occurred. Now, very aware of his own mortality, he remembered he had no heir. His thoughts went back to Francesca and the son she had borne.

He sent out agents to find her and the boy and report their circumstance. They found her in Cannes. She'd married a man called Werewick to give her son a name. "Duke" Werewick claimed to be a nobleman of ancient English peerage. Dominic's agents brought back glowing reports of the boy. Again he had hope. The family genes would survive through the boy. He would rehabilitate Francesca. He sent his agents out to negotiate her return.

About the time of the reconciliation, another attempt on his life was made. Fortunately he had just hired a new chauffeur, a man recommended by his cousin, who ran the New Chicago subsidiary. The chauffeur, Belisarius, was small and wiry and had a reputation for meanness. His fierce eyes were constantly alert as they darted around looking for trouble. Dominic surmised the man's size disguised his toughness and would throw prospective hit men off guard. Three assassins struck at high noon as Belisarius opened a limo door for the Chairman in downtown Houston.

Belisarius put himself in the line of fire, took two hits, one in the shoulder, the other just above his heart, but killed all three with his own weapon before he went down. He grew very close to the Chairman and his status in the Corporation rose meteorically. Dominic came to trust him implicitly, made him chief of security, and used him for many ticklish assignments. In return, Belisarius' loyalty was absolute.

The reunion with Francesca came joyfully, but not so for her new husband, the Duke. When Werewick saw the opulence that surrounded Francesca, greed suffocated wit. He had been given a large-salaried sinecure, but this was not enough and he began to badger the Chairman for a bigger piece of the action. His complaints became incessant. When they continued to go unheeded, he began to treat Francesca badly. He absented himself for long periods and soon was seen in the company of other women. The Chairman told Belisarius of the humiliation Francesca had to bear.

Within a week, Werewick's lifeless body washed up on the shore of the large lake at the north end of the estate. Belisarius found the body. An autopsy reported suicide and the unfortunate Werewick was given an elaborate funeral to assuage his widow's grief. Dominic made Belisarius Francesca's personal bodyguard.

In 2228, Dominic died. He'd been loved within the Family and hated by his enemies, but countries around the world honored him at his funeral. Francesca became Chairman in face of unspoken queasiness within the executive suite, unspoken should such misgivings reached the ear of Belisarius. Francesca, however, held the corporate reins with a gentle hand and directed the affairs of the Corporation with considerable skill. Misgivings were soon forgotten.

Francesca looked upon her bodyguard as a funny little man until she perceived his fierce devotion. He became her confidant and then her closest consultant. When she saw his sincere interest in her son, young Werewick, she asked him to marry her. He agreed at once, as he'd always loved her but thought her unattainable, and Francesca found the happiness and security she'd searched for for so long.

For eleven years, Francesca directed the Corporation with Belisarius at her side and the Family prospered immeasurably. Both loved the power they wielded, but cared little for its trappings. Francesca had but two interests outside her family and the Family. She loved horses and adored fast cars. Normally, Francesca was content to be chauffeured everywhere in her limousine. She would sit back with her telephone-telecaster, computer, or fax machine, a glass of Amaretto in her hand, and do Corporation business around the world.

Her passion for fast cars reached a pinnacle when she acquired a hydrogen-fueled Scalia 101, which could do 0 to 60 in 3.2 seconds and had a top speed of 300 KMH. Occasionally, she would sneak over to the estate carriage house and take the Scalia out for an hour or so. She drove as if possessed along the superthruways, the old interstate and the local roads with her police scanner on until she was certain that she had the entire complement of state, county and township squad cars in mad pursuit. Then she would return exhilarated.

She never got caught.

On a late summer day in September of 2240, Francesca's luck ran out. Swerving to avoid an errant chestnut colt standing in the road, she ran headlong into a high stone wall. The Scalia exploded in an angry blue burst of burning hydrogen. There was no trace of Francesca. Belisarius was voted chairman of the Corporation.

****

Porch had reached the last few pages of the leather-bound volume when he felt a hand on his shoulder. He put the book down and looked up. The Lawyer, standing over him, said, "The Chairman is ready to see you now. Come with me."

CHAPTER 14
THE TRIAL

The Chairman sat musing at the turn of events. For the fifteen years since Francesca's death, he'd had absolute authority within the Corporation. It had been his totality for her memory, as well as for the power. He'd built it from the giant corporation Dominic had left into the megalith it was today. And now this insignificant boy had destroyed his hopes that Francesca's son could take his place when his time finally came.

He sat there and turned away from his huge desk, stroking the large black cat sleeping on his lap. At the high French window, he could just see the lake at the north end of the estate. The beauty and grandeur that surrounded him were now at risk of disintegration. He could not let that happen. He had to will himself to live long enough. He was in his seventieth year.

The reconstructed stomach and bladder of animal tissue as well as the kidney and liver transplants resulted from the beatings he'd taken as a kid in New Chicago because of his small stature. But those beatings had forged his fierceness and the fearlessness that had carried him to this pinnacle of power. The bullet he took above his heart would have left him dead without that first transplant. But that heart did not last, nor did the one from his retarded third cousin. But the one now pumping hard, taken from the big Irishman, Hammer—that was a heart. It gave him new vigor. Yes, Hammer killed two men before they subdued him. He'd had no qualms about the sacrifice of those men. The Corporation needed him much more than anyone needed them. He gritted his teeth over his second set of implants as he thought, *At least my mind is mine and performing as well as it ever did.*

He heard the knock on the door across his office and pressed the button on his chair. The Lawyer entered with the prisoner, Porch, and stood the man before the Chairman's desk. Slowly, the Chairman turned around.

Porch watched him turn, a wizened little man, very old, in a gray silk pinstriped suit. He wore a black rose in his lapel and was stroking a black cat. Porch thought to himself, *So this is the famous and feared Belisarius X. Belisarius.* He looked into the Chairman's eyes—piercing, black as night, and saw in them the onslaught of fury directed at himself. He did not blanch.

The Chairman looked at him for a long time before saying, "You have destroyed everything that I have worked for for the past thirty years. You attempted to murder my stepson, and failing that, tore up half his face and rendered useless his one good arm. He is now in a sanitarium, disheveled and incoherent, his life and career ruined."

Porch parted his lips, ready to reply.

"Shut up-a your face. You are not worth the slightest indignity this great house has been made to suffer. Because of your youth, I will show compassion. My stepson requires remedy. This great house requires reparations. My personal honor requires retribution. I give you two options. Choose correctly and I will forgo reparations and revenge."

Porch broke in, "I only acted in my own defense."

"Evidently you are more rash than has been reported. If you only acted in your own defense—why did you run? Why did you become a deserter? Answer!"

Porch spoke in the face of the Chairman's rage, "I knew there would not be a true judgment—the word of a first-year candidate against a hero."

Belisarius replied, "Listen carefully. You will be tried—so you'll have your chance to tell your side. Be aware that our computerized judge and jury eliminate the false emotions and muddle- headed thinking that clever lawyers have pulled from befuddled witnesses and jurors in the past. Logical analysis of testimony and statistical analysis of circumstantial evidence accurately confirm the truth of any matter brought before the court—especially the veracity of witnesses. We measure pulse rate, alpha pattern, breathing, body moisture, heart rhythms, stomach pulsation—change in the lymphatic and autonomic nervous systems electronically.

"I have assigned my right-hand man to defend you. He is the best there is, but the consequence should you be found guilty is more than you may wish to endure. Should you plead guilty and throw your self on the mercy of the court, the court shall only extract remedy. Since you have no property save yourself, you shall be indentured to your victim to serve him as his manservant at his pleasure. You would be well treated and allowed to retain your rationality.

"Should you plead not guilty and be found innocent, of course you go free. However, should you so plea and be found guilty, you would be sentenced to a "mind scrape," then still given to your victim for his pleasure and never go free. Think, boy, before you say. A mind scrape is not a pleasant thing. Our methods and machines erase synaptic pathways and redirect neuronic responses. We can make you manic depressive, paranoid or schizoid, or a combination of all three. Or would you like to be obsessive-compulsive, compelled to wash your ears with caustic soap over and over every twenty minutes for as long as you live? We can simply erase your mind and all your past—make you crave to supply whatever your master should require. So what shall it be?"

"Not guilty," Porch replied.

The Chairman looked at the Lawyer and said quietly, "You have thirty days to prepare your client's case. During that time, the youth shall be our guest in the suite that befits our hospitality. See to his every comfort. Take him away!"

The Chairman turned back to the window and

sighed, "What a shame—such a fine, handsome youth—courage etched in his eyes—honesty illuminating his face. But what must be, must be. Life is hard." He scratched the cat behind its ear, and it purred contentedly.

The Lawyer motioned Porch to follow him and they left Belisarius X. Belisarius' baronial suite. Once out of the office, a guard took up position on each side of Porch. The Lawyer led them down a long wide hall, its length paneled with the choicest of woods. They passed office after office, where evidently the Corporation conducted its world-wide businesses. Illuminated paintings that would have been at home in the Metropolitan, the Louvre, or Prado adorned the corridor's walls. At its end, another double set of stairs appeared, set off by a carved wooden triptych of medieval origin—another priceless artifact. The Lawyer turned left and began climbing the well-worn marble staircase. Winding around, the party soon reached the third and top floor. Almost immediately, the Lawyer turned right into a spacious suite. The silent guards posted themselves on each side of the double door entrance. Beckoning Porch inside, the Lawyer swung his arm around the plush suite. A sofa and chairs surrounded a low coffee table in the living room. There was a large screen tri-di TV, a writing desk with chair, and a dining table upon which rested a silver tea service. A bar occupied one corner, and French doors led out to a spacious balcony. The bedroom contained a large four poster, several chests for clothing, and another writing table and tri-di. In the bath, gold fixtures adorned the creamy marble counter of a double sink below a wide mirror. A smaller room contained a toilet and bidet, partitioned off from a sunken tub.

The Lawyer noticed Porch's quizzical look. "The Chairman is a worldly and most gracious host. He provides for the needs of all his guests in the best old world tradition. I will leave you now. We must begin to prepare your defense early in the morning."

When he'd left, Porch returned to the outer room and saw a covered dish dinner flanked by a flask of wine, a jug of milk, and a pot of coffee. It smelled divine.

Famished, he sat and ate. When finished, he continued his survey of the suite. He looked into the chests in the bedroom—fine prisoner garb consisting of black slacks and pullover with red griffin embroidery. In the outer room, he went through the French doors onto a wide balcony. He looked out at the estate's wide expanse. Even from this height, the moat with its clever parapet could not be seen. He could see the inner iron fence and wooded park farther out, and was high enough to make out distant hills beyond the estate. He thought of free-dom. Leaning far out over the balustrade, he saw that the balcony overhung sheer marble walls with no pro-trusions to climb down.

A giant apple tree grew in the center of a large gar-den below. Its spread was amazing. Hundreds of golden apples were ripening on its limbs. A path wound around the tree, skirted by roses flowering in every hue. The garden lay between two lower wings of the palazzo, closed in by a high wall on the far side. A small wooden door in one corner of the wall led out. It looked closed tight. If he could get down somehow but not out that door, he would have to scale the wall, but it too looked very smooth.

Looking down again, he saw two men looking up at him, so he knew that he was under close surveillance. He went back inside and happened to look up at the crystal chandelier. It was beautiful and very ornate, with hundreds of multifaceted crystals, but something seemed out of place. Cabochon cut crystals circled its base at the ceiling. Why should they be so cut when all others were faceted? He pulled the writing table over, placed the chair on top and climbed up for a closer look. The crystals were lenses that surveyed the entire room. There was a like chandelier in the bedroom, so he knew that everything he did would be observed.

Suspicious, he searched the whole suite. Cleverly concealed microphones and motion detectors were eve-rywhere. They left nothing to chance. He went out on the balcony again and he looked down. The two men came out into view. He looked a final time at the far horizon and dreamed of freedom, then told himself that at least this night he would be free. He put all thoughts of captivity out of his mind, went over, sat on the sofa and flicked the tri-di on.

Swishing through the channels, he came upon a football game. To his surprise, the Academy was playing the University of Tokyo at the New Coliseum in LA. He turned the holocast volume up as high as he could stand and smiled grimly at the thought that his monitors must enjoy the game too. It was exciting. The University of Tokyo had won the International Cup the previous year. The second half had begun. The tri-di speakers blasted, "IT'S BEEN A THRILLING GAME, FOLKS, WITH THE CONDORS HOLDING ON TO A FIVE-POINT LEAD. SHOULD THEY WIN, IT WILL BE THIS YEAR'S BIGGEST UPSET."

The holographic images were so clear and substantive that Porch felt he was at the stadium. The imaging crews panned the crowd. My gosh, he thought he saw Captain, now Fleet Ensign, Brightwood. The crews panned back. Yes, it was her. He loved her so hopelessly, and there she was sitting with a bemedaled, high ranking officer.

She had graduated, so Porch guessed there had been no investigation after his disappearance and at least no trouble for her, for which he was thankful. He watched the teams struggle up and down the field and was further cheered when he saw Bokasi at linebacker and Eric the Red at noseguard. The Condors fumbled.

"THE SAMURAI RECOVERED THE BALL ON THEIR THIRTY-FIVE. THIS MAY BE THEIR LAST CHANCE TO GO AHEAD—SUSHI IS QUARTERBACK, THERE'S THE SNAP—HE'S BACKPEDALING—RED ERIC'S AFTER HIM—HE'S THROWING LONG. THE WIDE OUT, KAWASAKI, IS CLEAR—HE'S GOT IT AT THE FIFTEEN—ONLY ONE MAN BETWEEN HIM AND THE GOAL—HE'S GOT HIM AT THE ONE-YARD LINE—THIS IS IT—TEN SECONDS ON THE CLOCK—TOKYO TIME OUT—THEY'RE BRINGING IN THEIR BEEF, THE SEVEN SUMO—ITS GOING TO BE A RUN—STRAIGHT AHEAD—THERE'S THE SNAP–SUSHI, QUARTERBACK SNEAK–HAS HE GOT IT—NO–BIG BO BOKASI BROKE

IN AND STOPPED HIM INCHES FROM THE GOAL—
THERE'S THE GUN—THE CONDORS HAVE WON—
TOKYO'S WINNING STREAK IS BROKEN—THERE'S
PANDEMONIUM—ACADEMY CANDIDATES ARE RUSH-
ING OUT TO CARRY THEIR TEAM OFF THE FIELD."

Porch clicked the tri-di off, and as he did, his own
reality hit him. He got up wearily, undressed, turned off
the lights and got into the bed. The injustice of it–he'd
been a good candidate. He would have been a good
starman. The terror of his capture and what was to come
burst upon him. His terrible insecurities returned.

He was afraid, terribly afraid—away from the friends
he'd made, away from Harry, alone, that was the hard-
est part, the terrible aloneness. A great sob welled up in
his throat and his frustrations and fears rushed out in
great uncontrollable spasms. He gave in to his feelings,
turned his head into the pillow and cried like an infant
for what seemed an eternity. Gradually, he regained
control, feeling ashamed. But the weakness of venting
his feelings had exorcised them and he found new
strength. He felt as tough and unyielding as a piece of
case-hardened steel. He thought of Bonnie, of Bokasi,
Olive, Captain Ironwood and Brigade Commander
Stark—they'd treated him justly, with kindness and
friendship. He could never implicate them and jeopard-
ize their futures, which he would if the full circumstances
of his plight came out, so he knew what he had to do,
turned over and fell into exhausted sleep.

He awoke, refreshed, as the sun reflected a rainbow into the room, through the prismatic cut-glass windows. He went through the setting up exercises that
Harry demanded of him from as far back as he could
remember, then hurried to shave and dress. A breakfast was waiting. He ate hurriedly, finishing a cup of
coffee when the Lawyer entered.

The Lawyer said, "Before beginning, I ask you one
last time to change your plea. In a plea bargain, I can
get very favorable terms."

"I am not guilty and cannot plead guilty."

"You are foolish. I don't think you understand what
you face."

Porch did not respond.

"Very well then. Begin when you first entered the Academy and tell me everything that happened that entire first year."

The Lawyer removed a small disc-recorder from his pocket and clicked it on. Porch had determined the night before that if he was to be railroaded, he would not join the charade, nor implicate those who had stood by him. So he said, "Porch, Candidate Fifth Class, serial number 137137."

The Lawyer reddened, but said smoothly, "I am here to help you. If you don't cooperate, I have only records to go on...and your record is abysmal. We know much more than you think. We know all about Harry. We know how and where you grew up. We know who shielded you at the Academy. We know that you refused to obey the lawful orders of your squad leader—a duly appointed authority. We know that you ambushed him with the help of that big black man and that you beat him black and blue. We know that you wantonly destroyed government property. Now let us begin again."

"Porch, Candidate Fifth Class, serial number 137137."

The Lawyer closed his disc-recorder compact and rose.

"Very well," he said, "I'll return tomorrow. I hope you have come to your senses by then."

He returned the following morning, and the following, and then for the next thirty days, but Porch's response was the same.

The day of the trial came. Porch was escorted under heavy guard down what seemed to be miles of corridors to the courtroom. The court was magnificent, appointed in the style of centuries past, high ceilings, chandeliers, marble columns and oak paneling. But something was different, very different. Besides the Lawyer and himself, only three others were present. They sat in the rear of the room at positions marked Government Observer, Academy Observer and Corporation Observer. The three men looked dour.

To the front, a large, black and ancient computer

was positioned behind the bench. Porch looked to the jury box. Large all-white computers sat in two rows, six to a row. These too appeared ancient. He turned to the Lawyer and asked, "What happened to the twelve good men and true?"

"Those computers are more than adequate and better than men, for they strip out all that is extraneous, judging only facts and weighing only evidence."

"But they are ancient and I believe use vacuum tube technology," Porch protested.

"They are but half as old as the law they judge."

"All rise." The metallic sound came from a gray computer on the left of the bench which Porch imagined to be the bailiff. The Lawyer nudged him to stand. He looked to the rear and saw that the observers too were standing.

"Be seated," came from the black computer behind the bench.

The gray computer continued, "The First Superior Court of...is now in session."

It intoned the words so fast that Porch could not pick them all up. Then a rapid succession of words emanated from the right. He looked over and a red computer was sounding with a myriad of lights flicking on and off. He imagined that one to be the prosecutor. The black computer then asked if the defendant was present. The Lawyer said yes and inserted a button disc from his disc-recorder into a slot in a blue computer to his right. The black computer ordered the trial begun. A continuum of gibberish clicks began. Lights on the red prosecutorial computer were blinking on and off in a blur. Clicks and lights from the bench interrupted these occasionally. The Lawyer whispered to Porch, "They are conducting the trial in binary."

The clicking and blinking between computers continued, faster and faster until only a buzz filled the courtroom. Now the blue computer began clicking and the red one became silent.

"Our defense," whispered the Lawyer. "Hope for the best."

Within a minute, all three computers were buzzing.

"Cross examination and consideration of the evidence."

Porch blurted out, "This is Alice in Wonderland!"

A mechanical arm holding a large gavel slammed down from the rear of the bench.

"Quiet in the courtroom," the black computer boomed. "Defense Attorney, silence your client or I'll have his mouth taped and hold him in contempt."

The Lawyer rose, apologized for the outburst and assured the black computer that such would not be repeated. He sat down and looking at Porch, pursed his lips with his finger over them and said, "Shush."

Buzzing among the three computers continued for a few seconds, then all went silent.

"Jury deliberation," whispered the Lawyer.

Clicking and blinking began among the white computers, proceeding at a furious pace. Then they too went silent. After a second or two, the black computer rasped, "Defendant rise."

The Lawyer nudged Porch to his feet again. The black computer asked in a metallic voice whether the jury had reached a verdict.

"We have, Your Honor," intoned the white computer on the front left. "We find the defendant guilty on all counts."

"Guilty, guilty, guilty, guilty..." each white computer of the jury repeated in sequence. The entire trial had consumed three minutes and thirty-six seconds.

CHAPTER 15
THE VAULT

The next day, the denial of the appeal took a minute thirty-six seconds. Four orderlies then whisked Porch down to a first-floor clinic. They stripped him, put him on a table, and a man, purportedly a doctor, examined him. The man reeked of garlic. Once he completed the exam, the four orderlies scrubbed him as if he was a piece of meat. They wrapped a loincloth about his hips, strapped him to a stretcher, and carried him down another flight to a very small steel cell. There they placed him on an incline and strapped his thighs, chest and forehead down. They clamped his wrists and ankles down.

The orderlies then pulled a two-foot disk into position in front of his face. It had a red and white swirl pattern. Next, they placed a tube in each of his ears. They left the cell and the disk started whirling. Soon enough, Porch felt its power. He could concentrate on nothing else. He felt as though he was swirling through an indefinite and undimensioned space. He closed his eyes, but as soon as he did, his ears filled with the screech of a thousand fingernails scraping a thousand blackboards. He had to open his eyes before his head blew off. The screeching stopped, and he felt his mind yielding to the disk. He reached back into his memory and thought he heard Harry calling, "Use your will, boy. Use your will."

Then he remembered the techniques of

autohypnosis Harry had taught him in conjunction with his studies of Eastern mysticism. He began to build a wall in front of his subconscious and told himself his will was stronger than the disk. He told himself the wall was there and nothing could enter his inner mind. He could feel the wall. He could feel success. Then, inadvertently, he closed his eyes and the screeching wail entered his ears once more. He felt his wall come tumbling down. Quickly, he opened his eyes and told himself to bend like the bamboo in the wind, to use the disk to reinforce his self-hypnosis. The wall began to build up again, block after block, higher and higher. He reached the deep sleep of a plenary trance and hour followed hour. At last, the cell door opened with a clatter and white frocks surrounded him, shaking him awake.

The smell of garlic was all pervasive as the "doctor" stood over him. "I am Dr. Cevello. How do you feel? We must soften you up for your therapy."

Cevello began probing him with a variety of instruments. Porch looked at him and said, "You monster."

Cevello replied, "I am a doctor, a scientist. I do not make moral judgments. You are a convicted felon. You have no right to moral judgments. I know what you're doing. Hypnosis will not help you. Others have tried. It only prolongs my procedure. Give it up. Submit. Sooner or later your wall will come crashing down and your brain will accept my eraser. Feed him now."

The accompanying orderlies unstrapped his wrists and one handed him a bowl of gruel and wooden scoop.

Cevello grinned. "Plain fare but nourishing, a mixture of proteins, starches, minerals, sugars, vitamins and fiber. We want your mind, not your body, which you must keep well-toned and fit. You will be allotted an hour at day's end for exercise, supervised, of course. Now eat."

Porch ate the tasteless stuff like an automaton, for he too wanted to keep his strength up. When he'd finished, they strapped him back down and left as abruptly as they had come. The disk began its relentless rotation. After some hours, the cell blacked out. This was his sleep period. Morning came and the disk began. Its swirling patterns varied rhythmically to lock onto his subconscious brain waves and establish an all-consuming dissonance that would disrupt and destroy them. He re-entered his autohypnotic trance as the disk's attack on his mental stability continued, interrupted only when his captors brought the bland gruel or came to let him relieve himself. It went on until late afternoon, when again he heard the steel cell door open. He remembered he'd been promised an exercise period.

"Unholy Satan. It's Tchako!"

Tchako stood before him, grinning hideously, with a heavy whip in one hand and a metal probe in the other. He snapped the whip in Porch's face and said, "I would live one hundred years in hell if I could use this on you now. But following the mind scrape, you must be awarded to your future custodian without blemish."

Tchako stuck the whip end against Porch's throat, and with his face an inch from Porch's ear, he whispered, "Your stupid obstinacy at the Academy forced the disbanding of the Dueling Club and my dismissal, but revenge is mine. Tomorrow I'll show you an example of the mind scrape. You'll love it."

Porch spat in his face. Tchako drew back and cursed. He pushed his electro-probe into Porch's gut. Porch was thudded with a heavy low frequency jolt. He felt his liver would blow apart and his kidneys burst, but no mark was left on his flesh. While he was groaning in pain, Tchako removed his straps and said, "Straighten up and precede me. You must exercise."

Tchako pushed Porch through a narrow passage, up some stairs, through a door to the exercise yard and handed him a pair of running shoes.

"Put these on and get moving or you'll freeze to death."

It was mid-autumn and the evenings had grown quite chilly. Porch, already beginning to shiver, put the shoes on quickly. He rose and began to run down the path that appeared to circle the yard. Tchako yelled after him to stick to the path or taste the prod again. Porch picked up his pace and began to warm up. Things were familiar. He was in the garden he'd seen from the suite where he'd first been lodged. The immense apple tree, gnarled with age and full of golden apples, was in the center of the yard. Beautiful roses, in hundreds of varieties, including the much ballyhooed blue and the black variety reserved for the sole use of Belisarius, grew along the path. He reached the far wall and saw the tightly bolted gate. Coming around again, he saw a wooden garden shack. He had not seen it from the balcony, as it was directly beneath. An old man, probably the gardener, was piling brush next to the shack. He did not look up as Porch passed. Around Porch went, again and again, faster and faster, as his body screamed for the exercise and his mind savored the respite from the terrible turning disk. An hour passed before he heard a whistle and saw Tchako signaling him to return.

Tchako made him take off his shoes, took him back to the cell, strapped him to the incline and started the disk swirling. He left without fanfare and Porch faced three more hours of mental torment. The following morning, the disk began to rotate as soon the lights came on and Porch began to feel a pyschophysical force hammering at the wall he had erected in front of his inner mind. He wondered how long he could hold out, and was almost glad when Tchako entered to begin the exercise period.

Tchako said, grinning evilly, "I promised you a treat today, and you shall have it now. Cheeko, come boy, come." Cheeko padded into the cell on all fours, stark naked, with a dog collar around his neck.

Tchako patted him on the head and said, "Good boy. Now roll over." Cheeko rolled over and panted like a dog.

"Dead dog, dead dog," commanded Tchako, and Cheeko rolled onto his back, held his limbs in the air, and closed his eyes.

Tchako laughed. "He thinks he is a dog. He was given to me as a toy after the mind scrape. The coward was about to tell all during the Academy investigation. The Corporation got to him first."

Tchako sneaked up behind Cheeko and jabbed him

viciously in the rear with his prod. Cheeko howled in agony as Tchako laughed and laughed. Cheeko began to whimper piteously.

Tchako commanded, "Lick the prisoner's feet." Cheeko obeyed as Porch, disgusted, tried to kick him away, but his feet were tightly strapped down. "Now pee on them." Cheeko lifted his leg and did as commanded. Porch felt the warm liquid trickle down his feet. Tchako could hardly control his laughter.

At last he said, "Cheeko, you're a worm. Now get out of here." Cheeko dropped to his belly, clamped his feet together, arms to his sides, and began to writhe out of the cell. Tchako released Porch's straps and they followed Cheeko out of the cell.

"OK, Cheeko, stand up and follow us out," Tchako ordered.

When they were outside, Porch put on the running shoes and began to round the path. Tchako commanded Cheeko to watch Porch while he sat down on a bench by the entrance to take a nap. Porch had completed two laps around the path when he heard a voice as he ran around the far end. He could not locate the sound and kept running. The next time around, he came upon the gardener who was hobbling down the path under a great load of brush. He could barely run past him. When he came around again the old man dropped his load in the path, then bent to pick it up. With the path blocked, Porch slowed to jog in place. The man said, half loud, "I am Gideon."

Porch reached back into his memory and whispered, "You were at the Academy. Everybody thought that you are blind, deaf and mute."

"They think so now, they do, they do. They tested me and I fooled them. Still they brought me here, suspicious that I knows too much. But I sees what I needs to see, hears what I ought to hear, and talks almost never. Tie the tether, tie the tether. Tomorrow I gather the golden apples at the top. I have a long pole, a sturdy pole, a pole made of sprong. On the day that follows, the pole will lie in the path. When you see the fire in the brush, do what you must."

Gideon secured his load and hurried along as Porch ran past. Porch thought about what the old man had said. When he passed the shack, he noticed that the pile of brush along its side had grown to a giant size. Continuing around the path, he again approached the wall. There was a concrete drainage ditch that ran along in front of the roses that bordered it, not far from the wall itself. That would give him purchase. Just then he heard the whistle and turned, still running, to where Tchako and Cheeko were waiting.

The following day, he waited for the exercise hour with both trepidation and anticipation. He felt the wall shielding his inner mind slowly crumpling before the onslaught of the disk. Yet hope of escape, if all went right, buoyed his spirit. Tchako entered the cell and said, "I have a real surprise for you today. Come in, Cheeko."

Cheeko entered, wearing a dress, high heels, a wig and make-up that made him look grotesque.

"Cheeko enjoys being a woman much more than a dog or a worm. A wonderful thing, the mind scrape."

Porch felt disgust as Tchako continued, "Cheeko, you're a tart, a trollop, a bimbo. Do your dance." Cheeko began mincing around the cell, swaying his hips and fluttering his eyelashes.

After the ludicrous performance, Tchako said, "Enough, Cheeko. We must take the prisoner out for his exercise."

As soon as Porch was halfway down the track, he saw Gideon pulling apples down with a long hooked pole and basket attachment. He kept running. Tchako once again napped on the bench.

In the next twenty-four hours, Porch felt further erosion of his will by the force of the disk. It had to be this exercise period. Tchako and Cheeko came to get him, and soon he was outside shivering as he picked up his pace. Dark was closing in, each day shorter. Sure enough, Porch saw the pole, now without hook and basket, beside the path. He ignored it, continuing around. As he passed the garden shack, he saw Gideon bending over the brush. Once more around, and as he approached, he saw a sizable blaze. Gideon had run off to get a hose. Tchako and Cheeko also saw the conflagration. There must have been flammables in the shack. The fire now lit up the entire garden.

"Fire, fire," Tchako yelled. Cheeko started baying like a hound. Alarms began to ring inside the mansion. Porch approached the pole, bent and picked it up in stride. He found the balance and increased his pace to a dead run as he approached the wall. He hit the far concrete curbing and lifted off with a mighty leap. He had retained the grace that had won him the championship. When he reached the top of his arc and released, he heard Tchako shouting. He went over the wall, dropped and rolled as he hit on the outside. He was on his feet and running immediately.

Inside the garden, Tchako, with Cheeko close behind, reached the bolted gate. Tchako opened a code box next to the gate and pressed in the code to open it. Both squeezed through as soon as it had opened sufficiently. Porch was about one hundred yards ahead. Tchako waved his prod and yelled for him to stop. Cheeko produced a stream of yelps. Porch's months of captivity had weakened him, so Tchako and Cheeko began to close in on him.

Porch was coming upon the moat. With great effort, he increased his speed again and leaped as far as he could, just reaching the ground on the far side. He rolled again, regained his feet, and headed in the direction he knew the gate to be. Tchako and Cheeko reached the moat and chose to slide down. They lost some distance and had to climb the far side, but were soon in hot pursuit. Porch ran between the pampas grass and the dense brush. Tchako and Cheeko were almost on him. He was running as fast as his pounding heart and heaving lungs would allow, but he dared to glimpse back, and just as he did, he saw a flash of orange leap from the grass and then another from the brush.

The male saber-tooth snared Tchako and tossed him into the air. The female grabbed Cheeko, threw him down and began devouring a leg. Cheeko shrieked. The male, less hungry, released Tchako to run, then began to play with him as a cat does a mouse. He tossed him into the air, and when he came down, ripped most of the flesh off his back. Tchako lingered another twenty minutes while the beast mauled him.

As Porch had hoped, the electronic eye opened the gate to the fence as he approached. He was through and into the woods. He slackened his pace to catch his breath and pick his way through brush which was whipping his nearly naked body. It was now totally dark. Sirens from the mansion broke the night stillness. Searchlights swept its immediate environs. Porch heard choppers revving up and air carts taking off. Packs of hounds were yelping at their trackers to get started.

They began a deep-throated baying which Porch took to mean they'd picked up his spoor. They sounded frightened. No doubt they heard the saber-tooths roaring their kill. Porch crossed the woods and found himself in the fields where he'd seen the mammoths. He came upon heaps of mammoth dung and stomped through it, hoping to confuse the hounds. He saw a herd of auroch and ran toward them. They became fidgety, began to trot, and then ran. They too must have heard the roaring of the big cats.

Desperately, he threw himself on the back of a huge bull. Pulling forward, he grabbed great masses of neck wool and hung on for dear life. The auroch bellowed, stampeding. Luckily the beast headed away from the tumult behind. On and on it ran, mile upon mile. They reached the perimeter swamp, and the crazed animal plunged into the mire, lost its footing and went down head first into dark waters. Momentum hurled Porch forward onto a soggy bank. The auroch moaned in agony, its neck and front legs broken. Porch found his footing and slogged forward, finding a moss- and fern- covered rise among some granite boulders.

Exhausted, he lay down, lungs heaving and muscles aching. Swamp creatures in a frothing and bloody feeding frenzy quickly enveloped the auroch. Porch saw genetically altered cold water piranhas, fierce flesh-eating turtles and alligators. He shuddered and pulled himself higher, finding a hiding place under clusters of

Paleozoic ferns. And just in time, as a swarm of helicopters closed in from above.

Bright searchlights rent the dark, weaving bands of light across the swamp. Each was accompanied by four or five air scooters, flitting much lower, back and forth, up and down, avoiding trees and brush. Light beams reflected the froth and flashes of the feeding frenzy, and the choppers dropped down to examine the boiling, bloody waters. The horns and skull of the auroch protruded above the muck, and the searchers concluded that a panicked beast, frightened by their noise and lights, had stampeded to its demise in the swamp.

Satisfied, they gradually moved off, continuing their patterned search. Porch dared rise from his cover, cold, wet and shivering uncontrollably. He knew he must move on or succumb to exposure and die right there. Stiff muscles caused him to lurch against a fern as he rose. A late-departing air scooter picked up the movement and shot down toward his hiding place. Too eager, its operator hit a dead standing tree trunk and the scooter flipped him out. It then righted itself and drifted down to the ground and automatically cut off.

As luck would have it, the other choppers and their swarm of air scooters drifted farther away. The downed rider stayed still, and after a time, Porch approached his body. By a fluke, the man had broken his neck against a boulder on impact. Certain the man was dead, Porch removed his clothes and put them on. He put his running shoes on the man. They almost fit. He pushed the corpse into the murky waters and within a minute the swamp creatures were there gorging themselves anew. He threw his loincloth in, hoping that it and whatever remained of the grisly feast would prove his demise.

He found some emergency rations in the pockets of the uniform and quickly consumed them. The rations plus the uniform and overcoat warmed him, and as his strength returned, he looked to the air scooter. Again, good fortune—it had settled onto a bed of moss and ferns without discernible damage. He set it upright. Trained on a similar vehicle for Academy sentry duty, he quickly figured out the controls.

He reckoned it was well past midnight, and a ground fog was rising from the swamp, so he mounted the machine and restarted the hydrogen turbines. He pushed the throttle to quiet and slow. Gradually, the machine rose. Without lights and hugging the fog, he headed for the main gate landmark. When he saw its lights a few hundred yards south, he crossed the main road just inches above the pavement.

There was no alert, so he continued about a mile east, rising to clear the trees. Then he cut south and cleared the ornate iron picket fence and brick wall. The early fog had thickened, so he set the vehicle to fly just above it.

As soon as he dared, he gave it full throttle and whizzed off, setting the autocompass due east. Looking at the fuel gage, he figured he could make seventy miles. He rejoiced at his luck and prayed that it would hold. At the hint of first light, he came upon a river. It was fairly wide and somewhat sluggish. From the direction of the dawn, he judged it to be running north to south and believed he had come upon the upper reaches of the Missouri.

He changed the scooter's direction north to follow it. The fog was holding and about thirty minutes later, he almost ran into an antiquated suspension bridge. He throttled up just to clear it and then throttled back to hover over it. Checking the fuel gage, he saw it was time to abandon the vehicle. He peered down at the river below and saw a number of mud flats.

If he abandoned the cart here, there was a good chance it would disappear into the ooze. Throttling down level to the roadway crossing the bridge, he swung over and bumped the structure hard. He reached across, grabbed a cable, secured it, and abruptly cut turbine power off. He swung across onto the bridge and watched the scooter plummet to the river below. He felt most fortunate when it sank out of sight. He chose to run north and found that the bridge ran into a dirt road overgrown with grasses and weeds. *Apparently not often used*, he said to himself.

The sun's first rays lit the roads, forcing him to run at an adjacent woods' edge. After about ten miles, the sun was well up. He had thrown the overcoat across his shoulder, but still began to sweat. Abruptly, he came to a dead end where an ancient gate, rusted and made of welded pipe and wire, hung on its support by one hinge. He pulled up, opened it slightly and squeezed through, pushing it back in place. Looking around, he saw a large sign. Much of its paint had peeled off, but he could still read:

WILLOW WIND COMMUNE ~
ESTABLISHED 2053 ~ MILLENARIANS

Gosh, over a century old, he said to himself.

Far down an almost hidden path and across several fields, he saw some stacked hay, a large house and a barn, the latter two severely weathered. The sun was becoming oppressive, so he headed guardedly for the hay. Apparently unobserved, he made for the largest stack and quietly crawled into it, pulling it back over his body until he was completely covered deep inside. He fell into a deep sleep.

When he woke, he did not know how long he'd slept—several hours, or even a day and night. He pushed enough hay aside to peek out. By the sun's position, he figured it was late afternoon. He saw an old man and a little girl about fifty yards away. The man was hoeing vegetables and gathering turnips and cabbage. The little girl was playing with a large rubber ball. She bounced it again and again, then, tiring of that, began kicking it and running along after.

Suddenly, she kicked it hugely. It caromed off a furrow directly toward his hiding place. She chased it, laughing and skipping along. It slithered into the hay, stopping close to the overcoat at his feet. She parted the hay cautiously, looking for the ball. She saw it and the coat. Slowly looking up the coat through the hay, she saw him and froze, wonder in her big blue eyes. Porch pursed his lips with a finger over them. "Shhh..." he pleaded.

Without making a sound, she slowly withdrew her ball. Her look of wonder changed to puzzlement. When she was clear of the stack, she rolled the ball back to where the old man was hoeing. She meandered back toward him slowly, pausing every few seconds to look back toward the stack. At last she was too far to see anything. The old man put his hoe into a nearby cart with the vegetables he had gathered and called out, "Becky, come now. It's supper time."

Becky turned abruptly and skipped away as if nothing had happened. Afternoon turned to evening, and Porch saw lights go on in the house. About an hour passed when the door opened and a small figure emerged. He watched, and again the little girl headed for his hiding place. He thought he should have fled while he'd had the chance, but wouldn't now as he didn't want to scare her.

As she trudged closer, he noticed that she was balancing a large tin pan in one small hand and carrying a pail in the other. She set these down at the edge of the hay, peered into the dimness, and then ran back to the house.

Porch came out of the hay after she'd re-entered the house and found that she had brought him several slabs of ham, large chunks of cheese, a loaf of bread, and a pail of milk. Hungry as he was, he wolfed the food down, wondering why she'd brought it. Then he remembered—she was a Millenarian, a movement founded on the principle "to share all we have." His heart welled up and he did a very foolish thing. On the tin pan, wiped clean, he took the knife provided and scratched—ANGELS ABOVE LOVE YOU, LITTLE BECKY.

Night had fallen, but the light from the house provided enough illumination for him to see quite well. He pulled on his boots and the overcoat and quietly headed toward the barn. Inside, he flicked on the pen light he'd found in the overcoat and flashed it all around. What luck! Trunks were piled on trunks, all full of clothes or other gear. The Millenarians must have left the stuff when they headed to the stars. He discarded the uniform and hid it in the bottom of a trunk. Then he outfitted himself in heavy clothes for traveling, made up a massive pack of knives, whetstones, a hatchet, some nails, several canvas bags, pieces of harness for bowstrings and slings, a sleeping bag and waterproof sheet, extra undergarments and socks, and another pair of boots. Looking farther, he found a store of apples, onions and potatoes. He filled a large sack with some of these, then added oats, coffee and sugar. He put the tin pan on a chopping block and placed in it the fat roll of credits he'd found in the guard's wallet.

Ready to depart, he hoisted the pack and sack and left the barn, heading north. He knew he'd soon reach Silvano's North Woods. It began to snow. Good, it would cover his tracks. If he reached the woods, he felt he could escape and survive. Was it his destiny to be a fugitive for the rest of his days? He wondered if he'd get to the stars to search for his father. He wondered if he'd ever see Bonnie again.

CHAPTER 16
BONNIE BRIGHTWOOD

One year later, Bonnie sat in her office at United Space Technologies. She had come in early by habit to read the newspaper and drink her morning tea. UST, a Corporation subsidiary, combined the remnants of McDonnell Douglas, Boeing, Hughes, TRW, JPL and some smaller companies that fell on hard times after their government contracts were canceled in the late twenty-first century. The government maintained a permanent project office at UST because of the cozy relationship Dominic had established with the government.

UST's successes were notable. They had constructed the moon bases, produced the first three series of interplanetary frigates, the first and subsequent classes of warships, and the great solar wind sailing ships. They had put the all-spectrum telescopic survey bases in sun orbit. These had already pinpointed a thousand distant intergalactic planetary systems and analyzed mass, temperature and composition sufficiently to predict which would support life. Now, collaborating with the governments of the Western Alliance, UST was engaged in the one-thousand-year Mars project.

Bonnie was assigned to this project. She was disappointed that her fleet assignment was cut short, but when Commodore, now Rear Admiral, Sven Petersen personally asked her to accompany him to the project, she said yes. She knew that when a flag officer made such a request, a junior officer did as requested. As well, ambitious Bonnie knew a promotion went with the assignment—a promotion most didn't get until they'd served at least two years. She was now Lieutenant Brightwood.

She had come to Petersen's attention by resolving supply problems that had plagued the flotilla for years. But more than that, when the flotilla was operating against the space pirates off Neptune, his flagship, to which she was assigned, took a laser hit which destroyed the opcenter and killed its complement. Very coolly, she'd gotten the destroyed section sealed off and an alternate operating.

The new assignment was a real plum. The Mars project was in its inception, although the idea was over one hundred years old. The government, Fleet and Corporation had cajoled the other members of the Western Alliance to support an effort to increase the mass of Mars enough to hold an earthlike atmosphere. Martian gravity had to be increased so that ionized hydrogen and oxygen would not bleed off, preventing water retention. Meteor accretion from the asteroid belt would do the trick. The concept was simple: suitable asteroids would be kicked out of orbit into trajectories intersecting Mars, and Mars would capture them. When enough had been captured, the planet would be bombarded by ice comets from the Oort Cloud. These would eventually provide sufficient water for oceans and an atmosphere to form. After that, life, starting with the simplest cells, then bacteria, amoebae, fungi and mosses would be introduced. Gradually higher forms would be brought in. It would take a long time; current projections calculated a thousand years, but enthusiasts predicted technical advances would decrease the time required exponentially.

Once again, population pressures on Earth were causing even the most vocal opponents of the plan to agree that something had to be done. Otherwise the Earth would go through another period similar to the horrors of the early twenty-first century. At last all agreed to try the plan because emigration to the stars was so costly it alone would not solve the problem. To demonstrate feasibility, the Government, the Fleet and the Corporation agreed to push the first asteroids out of orbit and onto a Mars trajectory within two years. Hence all assigned to the project were engaged in frenetic activity to meet deadlines.

Bonnie had been working in supply for several months as an expediter. Supply routes up and down the West Coast linked up east- west arterial networks. To meet engineering schedules, the identification of a high-speed data system, funding and directed materials were needed. Items moved continuously on the Corporation's electro-rail system or over Corporation superthruways in Corporation trucks. Stoppages caused by natural disasters, hijackings, sabotage or breakdowns had to be met head on and defeated. This was Bonnie's job. She responded well, which pleased the Admiral. Rumor suggested she would be selected soon as special assistant to the Admiral.

She was sparkling with happiness this particular morning because her friend, Ensign Olivia O. Olive, now graduated from the Academy, was due to report within the hour as her assistant. Bonnie had persuaded the Admiral to make a by-name request for her. Meanwhile Bonnie had time to order breakfast from the robo-caterer and catch the day's events on her newscaster. She switched it on.

The newspeaker was showing tri-di pictures and commenting about the ongoing summit between Western Alliance, Eastern Confederation and Asian Association leaders, and the Central Asian Autonomy dictator, Marshal Tukanon. For twenty-five years, Tukanon had kept the major power blocs on edge, playing the fears of each off on the others.

Bonnie thought out loud, "When will the world be rid of that monster?" She commanded, "NEWSTEXT SUMMARIES," and the voice interpreter switched to text which Bonnie read as she had breakfast. US Space interceptors had captured a pirate freighter with a cargo of methane from Triton. It was a solar sailer, believed to be a slave ship. An international fashion show had opened in Madras. Bonnie noted that and decided to pick it up that night. The Tasmanian Devils had defeated the Brazilian national team in the World Cup Soccer playoffs. Shrieker rioting was increasing in many sections of the San Diego-Los Angeles megapolis.

She said to herself, *If the metropolice doesn't get that nonsense under control, our supply routes will be in danger.* She scribbled a note to the Admiral. Then she sat bolt upright.

"SPACE ACADEMY DESERTER AND CONDEMNED FELON PORCH STILL AT LARGE. MAIMED SUPERIOR OFFICER. RESPONSIBLE FOR DEATH OF TWO GUARDS AND POSSIBLY MURDERED A THIRD. EXTREMELY DANGEROUS. APPROACH WITH CAUTION. ONE MILLION CREDIT AWARD FOR INFORMATION LEADING TO CAPTURE. CONTACT SPECIAL AGENTS ESS AND GEE THROUGH LOCAL POLICE."

Bonnie was flabbergasted. "Porch, a killer, no..." She knew he'd run away from the Academy just before she graduated, but never found out why. She thought that as much as he wanted to be a spaceman, he would have returned to face whatever had made him run off. After she'd reported to the Fleet, she'd heard about an investigation of the Dueling Club and its disbanding for certain demeaning rituals. She knew those two toads Tchako and Cheeko had been dismissed, but everything else remained a guarded secret. She felt both anger and pathos. She was angry because Porch had been so pigheaded. He was a natural for fencing with those long arms and slender torso. With his grace and agility, Werewick would have made him an international champion. Again, superb swordsmanship was highly regarded in the Fleet. It would have enhanced his career immeasurably. She wished she could have drummed some sense into him. Then she felt a certain warmth. No man should have been born so handsome. She remembered how he'd laid down his cape for her so she would not wet her boots, and sighed aloud, "My poor sweet Grub, I hope he escapes."

She turned off the newscaster, gathered up the breakfast china, and called for the robot to take the pieces away. Olive would be there soon. Maybe she'd know more. She would ask her after they'd discussed her assignment and duties. Turning to the computer files to see what needed attention, she soon was deeply engrossed in the overnight activity and hardly noticed the soft knock at the door.

"Hello. Anybody home?" In walked Olivia, looking smart in her gold striped ensign's uniform. Olivia saluted and started to report. Bonnie ignored her and rushed over with a big hug.

"Hello, boss," Olive said. "When I was offered the chance to work with you again, I jumped at it."

Bonnie took over. She asked about Olivia's health and trip out. She would stay with Bonnie. They didn't wear uniforms on the project, so she'd arranged several shopping trips so Olivia could acquire a new wardrobe. How much time did Olivia need to settled? Olivia wanted to go to work immediately.

"Very well," said Bonnie. "For starters we'll review this laser-op disc on the project. Sit over there." Bonnie started the machine. Twenty minutes later, the machine shut down. Olive looked at Bonnie and said, "Impressive."

Just then a robo-page signaled to enter. When Bonnie granted permission, it entered and intoned mechanically, "The Admiral would like to see you."

The Admiral would not allow intercoms because he felt they degraded decorum and electric emanations could be monitored.

"Follow me," crackled the robot. As they entered the anteroom of the Admiral's suite, he heard them and called them in. He sat erect behind a large oak desk. He introduced himself to Olive, welcomed her to the project, inquired as to her trip out and whether she needed anything, then bade them sit down on a sofa at the side of his desk.

Petersen had just turned forty and was graying at the temples, which gave him a rather distinguished look. He was not overtly handsome, but rugged and very polished. He loved the space service and the people in it, treating superiors, peers and subordinates alike with genuine respect and esteem. They returned his regard for them with great admiration and fondness. He was at the forefront of every mission he led and a quick rise to flag rank resulted. He was a Commodore at thirty-eight and now a Rear Admiral. But he was brusque. When Bonnie and Olive were seated, he said, "Lieutenant Brightwood, you are now my special assistant for supply operations. Ensign Olive's file impresses on me that she can step right into your shoes as expediter. Spend sufficient time with her to make sure they fit."

"Yes, sir," Bonnie said smartly. She had come to adore the Admiral, not only for his spectacular service in the Fleet, but also on this job for his kindness and sensitivity to his staff. He was brusque, and stern when necessary, but he had a knack for lightening things up when they became overly tense.

"Down to business then," he said. "I am particularly concerned with the riots in the metro areas. Foolish as they seem, they are occurring with increasing frequency astride our supply routes, and we have some critical structural materials coming in this month for the first space station monitoring Mars. The metropolice seem incapable of handling the situation. There have been beatings and some deaths. That's not the way the government or the Corporation deal with the public. Bonnie, formulate a plan to quell this unrest, to stamp it out once and for all with no killings, no beatings. The anti-corporation media will be everywhere. We must avoid bad publicity if called upon to assist or even take over if the locals continue to mess things up. Ensign Olive can assist you. She might as well get her feet wet. Have the preliminaries in hand by the end of the week and brief me." Bonnie gulped audibly.

The Admiral's eyes twinkled. "You can do it. I have full confidence that you'll find something the more experienced and hidebound staff would never think of. That's all."

Bonnie felt foolish about overreacting, but she was glowing inside because he'd said he had full confidence in her. Olivia sensed her pleasure and smiled at her as they left the office. Now it was the Admiral's turn to feel uneasy. He'd always felt awkward around the fair sex.

On the occasions that he was becoming seriously involved with a woman, he'd found himself transferred to
a new and difficult assignment which demanded his full
attention. He and the lady thereupon drifted apart. Since
he'd now turned forty, he believed he should remain a
bachelor, so he tried to put the ladies out of his mind.
But since Bonnie had come on board a year ago, he
found her on his mind more often than he wished. What
a magnificent woman. He found himself wishing he was
fifteen years younger, and wondering if he'd have a
chance. *What foolishness,* he thought. *You can't turn
the clock back.* He pushed these thoughts out of his mind
but could not resist one last glance as she exited his
office. He sighed, then went back to dictating the direc-
tive he'd been working on.

"We should get started," Bonnie said to Olive. "First
we'll review the intel-discs, then get you settled in my
apartment. This afternoon an extensive reconnaissance
of Los Angeles and the trouble areas is in order."

By early Friday morning, Bonnie had sketched out
a draft plan on compu-disc and Olivia had completed
the graphics showing prospective operations. Knowing
the Admiral's desires, Bonnie had also prepared a one-
page summary, a detailed exposition of the plan, and
personnel, logistic and funding appendices. He would
then be at liberty to read the plan in summary, or read
it all before he questioned her. She felt ready to brief
him, and sent the robo-page out to secure an appointment. It returned and stated that the Admiral would
see them both immediately. When she and Olive entered his office, he was watching the newscast on the
latest developments. He shook his head as he asked
them to sit down, and said that the riots were worsen-
ing and he suspected the media were fomenting the
demonstrations. He asked Bonnie for the papers that
she was holding and began to read the summary.

"Humm," he said halfway through. When he got to
the bottom of the summary, he looked at them both
incredulously. All they could muster in return were apprehensive smiles. Bonnie said to herself, *Oh boy, I think
we blew it with this brainstorm.*

But Petersen said nothing, flipped to the detailed plan and began reading it carefully. He started smiling when he was halfway through. When he was about finished, he began to chuckle, and by the time he put the paper down, he was laughing uproariously. Bonnie didn't know what to think and noticed Olive scrunching down beside her trying to make herself smaller. She looked over at Olive and thought she saw genuine terror in her eyes. Chuckling to himself, Petersen thumbed through the appendices. At last, he looked over at the two fearful girls and said as he wiped away tears of mirth, "I think it would work. Why, I know it would work, completely dispelling the riots."

He began chuckling again and said, "If we have to implement this plan, it's going to go down as a classic in riot control. You have my approval and authority to pull the resources together. Work with the operations people and begin training the teams. I'll talk to their chief and get him on board. I'll also brief the higher ups.

"If the city calls on us, I imagine we can be fully ready in two weeks. Well done, ladies, well done, and thank you. That's all for now."

Petersen began chuckling to himself all over again as Bonnie and Olive departed. They both felt limp, and in unison breathed a sigh of relief as they closed the handsome oak doors to the Admiral's suite behind them.

CHAPTER 17
THE SHRIEKERS

The Shriekers were an offshoot of the Millenarians, splitting away because they could not accept a philosophy of non-violence. They did not believe they could achieve the social change they wanted under such constraint. They relished confrontation and created pandemonium through chanting and shrieking. Early on, they adopted a pantheism of gods, devils and spirits from old Earth religions. As the years passed, this pantheon became very real to them and was now guiding many of their activities.

Currently, they were in the throes of a "back to nature," "harm no living creature" movement. They wore dung-colored robes of sisal and hemp, and headbands of jute to distinguish themselves and their movement. They ate only yogurt and yeast, truffles and other fungi, some of which were psychedelic. They grew their yeast and fungi in dung and pasteurized excrement.

They had gathered to protest the Western Wool Growers Convention in Los Angeles. To them, shearing sheep was an abomination. When nobody paid attention, they increased the size of demonstration and shrillness of complaint. Still no one paid attention, so they began to riot, and local looters and thieves gathered to make the most of the accompanying chaos.

The situation worsened through the summer and into the fall. By mid-October, the Mayor of the Los Angeles-San Diego megapolis saw that he had lost control.

The Shriekers realized that they had gained the upper hand and now were pressing to push their advantage home.

Their leaders called for a massive rally at the old Coliseum in downtown Los Angeles on Halloween day, when the spirits returned to Earth. Their followers would come from all over the country.

When he learned of this, the Mayor decided to call in the Army the very next day. That morning, when he came in, he saw the small black envelope resting on his desk. His hands trembled as he opened it and withdrew the note. He scanned the text, "...Unfortunate conditions and lack of control in LA-SD most grievous...Inimical to commerce... Mars Project deadlines at risk...Expect media field day in the event of an Army blood bath...Your re-election at risk...Pass control and responsibility for resolution to Corporation acting through UST Project Office...BELISARIOUS." The Mayor gulped as he picked up his secure phone and dialed the number he'd been given.

That morning, Olive was a few minutes ahead of Bonnie, and when Bonnie entered, she said, "Good morning. You just missed the Shrieker High Priestess on the ZVS a.m. show. That lady's something else."

Bonnie smiled. "Yes. I've caught her act before. I didn't know she'd come to town. Something big must be brewing."

"And read this column by Marylou McGrew in the *Times*. She really rakes the Mayor over the coals."

Bonnie perused the column, "Whew, vitriolic to say the least. She's one nasty old lady."

"She needs a good dose of salts," Olive replied, laughing.

They heard the robo-page enter. "The Admiral would like to see you as soon as possible." In a few minutes, Bonnie and Olive were seated in the Admiral's office. His eyes were twinkling when he looked at them and said, "Well, it's a go. The Mayor's rejected the Army and called us in. I've asked the Western Army Commander to send a team of observers. We'll show them what Fleet planning can do. The Shriekers are planning a massive rally at the old Coliseum, October thirty-first. We'll give them a Halloween party they'll never forget. I've passed implementing orders to Operations and our field commanders and notified the higher ups. We'll work with city and local police, state police and the FBI. Lieutenant Brightwood, I'll want you in the Operations Center when we begin. Wear your uniform, as I'll ask you to escort the Army folks. Ensign Olive, you're new to the area and relatively unknown. It would be fitting for you to circulate amongst the demonstrators and record proceedings at the Coliseum. We'll want a record of what happens to counter any media distortions down the road. Come back right away if it gets rough. It's not your job to get mixed up in anything. Any questions? If not, that's all for now."

For several days before the end of October, men infiltrated positions several miles out circumscribing the Coliseum. The metropolice augmented with robo-cops occupied the nearby university and other critical installations. FBI agents and state police began tailing known troublemakers. The night of the thirtieth, huge black vans bearing the red griffin emblem were pulled into selected streets several miles out from the ancient stadium. Hundreds of Corporation special agents and rangers from the Fleet debarked from them.

The thirty-first dawned drizzly and unusually cool for that time of the year in southern California. Followers of the High Priestess sneaked into the stadium before dawn and erected a platform for her, high enough so all could see her. Just at dawn, ZVS brought in its most powerful communications van, set up antennas, focused, and tuned them into its worldwide satellite system and began the mobile generators. They set klieg lights on poles around the platform because of the dull and overcast day. Shriekers in their dung-colored robes and headbands began to dribble in shortly after dawn and became a human tide before the wet, cold day was an hour old. With them came Olive, dressed in burlap that looked as though she'd slept in it. By nine o'clock, two hundred thousand strong filled the stadium.

Donaldson Rotter, ZVS heavy anchor, showed up

promptly at ten, angry because his chauffeur could not get through the teeming masses and drive right up to the communications van. When he entered the van, he found his producer already there with the show's director. He gave them a curt hello before he sat down in front of his make-up man. Donaldson hated them both.

The director started right in on him. "It's up to you, Donaldson. We've got to give the public a show."

Donaldson didn't answer, but took the director's comment to imply that he, the heavy anchor, last of a breed, need be told how to do his job. He was seething inside, so he took it out on the makeup man, "Dummy, when I say heavy tanning cream, I mean heavy. There are klieg lights out there."

The producer interrupted, "We need a happening, a real happening. The ratings are up for grab. If ZVS doesn't top, the Corporation net grabs the whole ball of wax, and sooner than later, we're belly up."

Rotter snarled at the make-up man, "I want ruddy cheeks, damn it. More rouge. Those lights wash out everything."

Just then, a roar swelled up from the crowd. The High Priestess had mounted the stand. "FU-FI, FU-FI, FU-FI...FUNGI, FUNGI, FUNGI."

"Donaldson, get out there. Get her riled up."

"I know my job." Rotter retorted angrily, then screamed at the make-up man. "Power eyebrows, you nincompoop, power eyebrows, more mascara. You act like you're paying for the stuff out of pocket."

The director ignored him. "Make that pussy...cat spit."

The producer picked up, pleased with the analogy, "Yeah, spit and snarl."

Rotter shouted at them, "I'll savage her, dammit, savage her. Now get out of my face." He got up and went out the door in his safari suit to face the wind and rain, and the soon-to-be savage crowd.

"FU-FI, FUNGI, FUNGI."

Fufi Fondle was an aging tri-di stage and screen star. From the causes she espoused, some thought her a little bit dipsy. But she knew how to work a crowd.

She'd discarded her weatherproof burlap cape and was up on the platform with her arms raised, swaying and swinging. Her passion for aerobics had kept her fit, and she flaunted it. She wore a designer burlap blouse cut for maximum cleavage, pulled tight at the waist and held in place with a wide belt of red coral-embossed silver. Below that draped a mini-mini skirt. A Navaho Squash Blossom neckpiece of silver and turquoise adorned her shoulders and open throat. Her woven jute headband, overlaid with silver and coral, matched her belt. She wore high heels and silk stockings, never mind that the worms had been boiled alive to separate them from the silk they had woven. Fufi was a fashion statement in sackcloth. Donaldson, shielding his face from the drizzle, did not look up until he'd reached the steps to the stand. When he did, an involuntary *wooh!* blew out of his lungs. Fufi was now pumping her arms and jogging in place. She was oblivious to the small raindrops pelting her face. Rotter said under his breath, "Wow, Sheena of the Jungle with legs all the way up to her...oh-oh. I wonder how she keeps high stepping in those heels?"

He regained control and muttered, "Got to get on track. If I work this one right, ZVS will be the Big Enchilada for a long time to come, and when my contract comes up, it'll be stock options and get rid of those two clowns. Fufi, you're mine, baby, mine."

Rotter mounted the steps, shouting over the din, "Media here. I have credentials."

Two huge men, Fufi's bodyguards, moved to block his progress.

"Stand aside...media...with worldwide coverage," Rotter demanded. The men folded their arms above him and looked down at him as if he was some sort of insect.

Behind them, though, Fufi had stopped. "Boys, boys," she panted, "did I hear media...worldwide coverage? Let the gentleman through."

Rotter mounted the stand and walked over to the High Priestess. Fufi smiled sweetly and began munching on a stalk of teosinte, her ample bosom heaving.

Rain and perspiration from her hair and face mixed and ran down her throat and into her cleavage in little rivulets.

"Yes," she murmured. Not far away, Olivia was watching. She held a micro-camcorder concealed in a tube of lip gloss focused on Rotter. Now she trained it on the pair. She turned the mini-mike on her hip full up to catch the interview. A technician not far away shouted up to the stand, "You're live, Mr. Rotter."

In his deep stentorian voice, Rotter began. "This is ZVS, worldwide, Donaldson Rotter, your reporter. I am at the old Los Angeles Coliseum where the Shriekers are protesting the Western Wool Growers Convention. Here, with me, is their high priestess, Miss Fufi Fondle. Tell me, your worship, just how many of your followers are here today? The stadium looks packed." He handed her the mike.

"There are two hundred thousand Devotees inside the stadium, ...and untold numbers outside." Fufi said coquettishly. Loudspeakers picked up her words from a mike she had concealed in her bosom and blared them forth.

"FU-FI, FU-FI, FU-FI,....FUNGI, FUNGI, FUNGI."

"Why are you demonstrating against the Wool Growers? They seem innocuous enough."

"Why, you know, they shear sheep and things."

"That seems hardly enough to get upset about," Rotter retorted.

Fufi stammered and looked at him vacuously. "Well, it hurts the poor babies and they get cold."

"FU-FI, FU-FI, FU-FI," the horde clamored. Fufi looked triumphant.

Donaldson smiled and continued, "I understand that you have undertaken many causes during your career, Miss Fondle."

Fufi was radiant. "Oh, yes. I always wanted to make a difference."

"FU-FI, FU-FI, FU-FI."

"I remember," Rotter agreed, "you were a famous peace activist some years ago when the dictator Tukanon was threatening the Far Eastern Association. I recall you visited him. What did you tell him?"

Fufi looked at him vacantly and after a few seconds said, "Why, I told him to be nice and quit sending soldiers out on everybody's borders."

Rotter smirked. "And tell me, Lamb Chop, is it true that you bedded him down to persuade him to come over to your view?"

Silence shrouded the stadium, and then like a great ocean swell, a roar of fury rolled forth. The Shriekers raised their battle cry, "TURDS AND CURDS, TURDS AND CURDS, TURDS AND CURDS."

A great human wave poured out of the bleachers, heading for Fufi's platform. Fufi was dumbstruck. She turned white as a sheet, and then began to redden. She stepped back, took aim, and threw a round house punch at Rotter. Rotter stepped inside to belay the blow and threw his arms around Fufi. She began clawing and scratching as he tried to hold her fast. They got twisted up in the microphones and then the klieg light cables. These bound them together tighter and tighter, and they twirled and twirled until they looked like a pair of whirling dervishes. Riot police appeared out of nowhere, dropped Shrieker disguises, surrounded the platform, took Fufi's guards into custody; and began fending off the surging crowd with night sticks. The crowd, thwarted in their effort to reach the High Priestess, surged around the communications van and turned it over. Communications were cut off, and the klieg lights went out. Pandemonium reigned.

Wailing like banshees, the Shriekers headed for the exits. Fufi was tearing and scratching while Donaldson tried to immobilize her. On and on they struggled, neither relinquishing their hold on the other. Tiring, their furious waltz changed into a slow dance. Suddenly, the microphone wires snapped loose. The couple lurched to the back of the platform and the cables gave way. They fell to the soft grass beneath the stand. Fufi landed on Rotter and they continued to roll. At last, Rotter pinned her arms. Looking down at her, he gasped, "You make me crazy."

Breasts heaving, breathing hotly, Fufi broke free,

threw her arms around his neck and begged, panting, "Take me...take me now." She put her open mouth to his and began tearing at his clothes. Groaning and moaning, they rolled into the darkness under the platform. Olive switched her micro-camcorder to infrared and followed them.

Shriekers poured out of the stadium, ready to riot. Bonnie's brigades were ready as the vanguard headed up the main thoroughfares. Looters, arsonists, and diverse thieves brought up the rear, setting fires, smashing windows, and breaking down doors. But as quickly as they set fires and made break-ins, fire fighters put out the fires and metropolice made arrests.

Soon surging crowds of Shriekers approached the planned perimeter on the main streets. Looking ahead, they saw huge black vans with red griffin markings. High rubber dams filled with water extended from the vans to the buildings facing the streets. Rangers and special agents stood in front of the vans, waiting for them. The Shriekers slowed, then stopped. But the mass of humanity behind pressed forward all along the perimeter and diverted the front ranks into narrow side streets. Horrible specters waited there.

A leader screamed, "Look, look ahead. It is Hecate and a host of diverse spirits."

Again the press of Shriekers stopped, awed at what approached. It appeared to be a witch with a band of wraiths, in reality rangers and special agents dressed for Halloween. A loudspeaker blared, fed from a microphone hidden in the witch's robe.

"Maybe Hecate, maybe not, perhaps the Witch of Endor, ready to call Saul, and even Samuel, up to prophesy your fates. Come close, closer yet. I'll tell of your deaths, then feed you a banquet fit for those about to die."

The witch and wraiths moved toward the Shriekers.

"Ohhh," the mob wailed, backing up. Then they turned and ran as best they could, seeking refuge in the vans.

On another street, a leader shrieked, "See ahead, the Furies, Daughters of Gaea, sprung from the blood of Uranus. All three are there. Pick them out, Tisiphone, blood avenger, and there's Alecto the implacable, and I see Megaera, the jealous one. Back away. Run, run for your very lives."

This horde too sought safety in the vans behind.

Not far away, another shrieked, "The Four Horsemen, up in front, coming toward us, agents of war, famine and pestilence. Count them. One riding a white horse, another red, and there's the third atop a black, and the pale horse leading is mounted by death himself. See his skull under a cloak, black as the blackest night, and he carries a scythe to reap our souls. Brothers and sisters, the Apocalypse is upon us. We have transgressed. Seek refuge, seek refuge now in the vans behind us."

In every direction, around the perimeter witches, warlocks, ghosts and goblins herded the Shriekers toward the vans. Rangers and special agents invited the Shriekers, completely cowed, into the vans in sets of ten. In a first compartment, they were sprayed with a tranquilizer mist that calmed them down. Willingly, they passed into a second partition. Here they were made to disrobe completely, and their clothes were sent down a chute. In a third compartment, they were hosed down with hot water laced with disinfectant, and blow-dried. Then they moved forward to the front of the vans. Here they were issued, one by one, a fig leaf, stamped with the word SHAME on their buttocks, and released outside into a cold drizzle to run back, naked, from whence they came.

In ten hours, one hundred vans processed two hundred thousand Shriekers. The following day, one hundred vans stopped at the Gentle Sisters of Mercy, other charities and a number of shelters to donate two hundred thousand sets of cleaned clothing, sandals and boots to the poor and homeless. Great piles of burlap were incinerated, which ended the famous Shrieker riots of 2256.

That day, as Bonnie and Olive were preparing their after-action report, the Admiral called for them.

"I am delighted," he said when they entered. "No

deaths, minor injuries, no bad press, and the Shriekers dispersed. Our supply lines are again free of threat. We can get on with our mission. The Mayor called. His metropolice caught many known criminals in felonious acts, and they can now be put away for a long time to come. He gave us his thanks and hearty congratulations. I want to pass his kudos on to you with my own—well done. Any questions?"

"No, sir," they said in unison as they rose to leave.

"Oh, one more thing–the Chairman is flying in," Petersen said, his eyes twinkling. "He personally wants to meet those persons responsible for such a grand plan. Prepare to brief him when he arrives this afternoon. Nothing fancy; off the cuff is enough. We'll record it, and the recording can serve as the after-action report. I'll call you when he arrives."

Bonnie and Olive worked furiously, skipping lunch, to prepare their briefing. Luckily, they had the video and schematics from their initial planning, which needed but little alteration to tell the story of what happened. They just had time to freshen up at four o'clock, when the Admiral called them to the conference room. He introduced them to the Chairman, the Chairman's lawyer, and the Chairman's burly bodyguards, who nodded a curt hello. Bonnie presented the overall action. When she'd finished, the Chairman asked how she'd ever thought of dispersing them by taking away their clothes and modesty.

"Sir," she said, "There is no intelligence in stomping feet, raised fists, and 'Dick and Jane' chants. If people wish to act like savages, they should dress as such, that is, with no clothes at all."

"Ah," the Lawyer agreed. "If they act like animals, treat them as such."

"No, sir," Bonnie replied. "Animals have dignity. These people had none."

The Chairman smiled. The Admiral said, "Please now, Ensign Olive, relate your activities for the Chairman."

Olive painted verbal pictures of what had occurred at the Coliseum, focusing on Rotter's interview with the

High Priestess and the antics that occurred after his final abusive question. She ended by saying, "I have a complete record on video, sir."

The Chairman retorted, "Hardly enough, if the past serves as any example, to shut them up. How have you managed that?"

"I sent copies of my recording to both, requesting that he confer with his wife, and she her husband to determine if it was sufficiently newsworthy for public release. Both replied they thought not, and the sooner the entire incident was put to rest, the better. Both promised never to refer to the episode again nor take part in such rebellious activity."

"Be specific, young lady," the Chairman demanded. "What happened that they volunteered such cooperation?"

Olive blushed, then hemmed and hawed. Bonnie spoke up, "The pair was copulating under the stand."

With that, the briefing ended.

****

Flying high above the weather on his return to corporate headquarters, the Chairman had been napping. He woke and mused to the Lawyer, "That young lady, Lieutenant Brightwood, is forthright, to say the least, just the type we need in the Corporation—young, energetic, full of new ideas which we could surely use—the other as well, once she has a little more experience. I must have them."

"I doubt they'd leave the Admiral–they showed such devotion–nor the fleet, as they've just begun their careers."

The Chairman smiled and said, "Get me the President."

In less than a minute, the Lawyer replied, "She's on the phone, sir...the gold one at your side."

CHAPTER 18
FENRIR

Far to the north that Halloween night, a man clad in a caribou coat with a wolverine hood was striding on snow shoes through a deep conifer forest. He had a sling at hand should he flush a rabbit. He carried a long bow and quiver full of arrows to use against larger game at longer range. He'd crisscrossed the great North Woods, never stopping more than a day or two in any one place. When he looked up at the airspace above, which he often did, a heavy blond beard glinted in the moonlight. His face was hard and weathered. It had lost the blossom of boyhood. He had put on some twenty pounds of heavy bone, massive muscle and steely sinew.

Porch had not heard or seen the choppers for six months. All trace of man was missing at these latitudes. He came upon many abandoned drilling rigs, pumping stations and rusting pipe lines, left in place when the oil ran out a hundred years before. And timber was not cut now to spoil the forest's pristine beauty. He had weathered many hardships, bitter cold and gnawing hunger, attacks by bear and wolf, and come out the better for it. That he endured filled him with new confidence and washed away the naiveté of youth.

He stopped dead still. Fling went his sling, and a rabbit, plump for the winter ahead, would make his supper that night, augmented by the roots, herbs and birch bark tea he carried. He decided to eat right there and selected a sheltered hollow under a tall spruce that would dissipate smoke from his cooking fire. He set his heavy pack down, took out a magnesium stick, shredded off a bit into some dry moss and wood shavings, and set the shavings burning with a flint and steel. He built the fire up with very dry brush so it would burn hot with little smoke. He cooked, ate quickly, then spread out the embers of the dying fire, covering them with snow.

Shouldering his pack, he headed toward the river a mile or so farther north. He thought he could break through the ice where it narrowed at the bend and ran fast, and hook or spear a fish. He should also be able to find shelter under its banks. He'd just about reached the northern tree line. There was an open area he'd have to cross before he reached the river. Beyond the river, open tundra began. He hurried along as the feeble sun would soon rise. The moon reflecting off the snow was dangerous enough, but he dared not cross an open space in daylight.

By the time he reached the clearing, the moon was setting. He looked up and saw the Great Bear Constellation in the north. In the south, Orion was rising. Almost directly overhead, the Pleiades, seven little sisters, were shimmering like so many jewels. He felt his heart throbbing with the sadness that had begun to torment him. He thought of the locket buried deep beneath the boulder that only he and Bokasi, working together, had been able to lift. Those twinkling little jewels seemed to be calling, "Retrieve the locket, Starman, retrieve the locket and go to the stars."

He was halfway across the open area when he heard the soft flutter behind him. At first, he could not see them. Then he picked up a glint of reflected moonlight, then another, and a third. They were about fifty feet off the ground, zooming back and forth. One seemed to be coming directly toward him. He froze. It turned and went back. They seemed patterned in thousand-meter blocks. They could not be much bigger than hummingbirds. From their small size and the surveillance net they were weaving, he deduced that they were passive infrared drones, probably limited to a fifty-meter pickup.

Then he heard the dull beat of the mother ship farther south. No doubt there were other choppers nursing other swarms of drones both east and west. He began to run. He had to make it to the river before they picked up his body heat. He hoped he could find a snow drift there to burrow into. He reached the ledge above the river and cast his pack down. He saw what he believed to be a drift and leaped down next to it. It was a drift, quite large. He dug his way into it, turned and pushed open an air passage. He was completely covered under many feet of snow. He believed the cover sufficient to block his body radiation and lay still.

An hour passed, then two more. He dared not move. Now another danger seized him. When at last he tried to move, he found his legs numb. His body heat had melted the surrounding snow into ice which held him in a vise. He tried his arms and found that they too failed him. He became sleepy and began to feel warm in spite of the cold. He shut his eyes and a dream formed. He was back as a babe snuggled in his mother's arms, but when he looked up at her, she had no face. He shuddered and willed himself to wake, but felt so warm he thought he'd sleep a bit more, and then a bit more. The cold had gone and he just didn't want to struggle anymore.

But something fearful was digging its way in and a primitive life force deep within him impelled him to wake. He felt a huge paw on his shoulder and thought a bear had found him. He opened his eyes, looked up and saw the leaden eyes of a great wolf peering down at him, a wolf as white as the snow that covered them. He could feel its hot breath on his face and was certain it would now crush his skull in its massive jaws. He closed his eyes, resigned to this fate. Better, he thought, than flushed by the drones outside, recaptured and returned to an awful captivity. Sleep overcame him again, and he dreamed of the monstrous wolf of Norse myth, Fenrir. He saw that great beast appear, straining against its binding for this world to end, its eyes gleaming like the coals of a white-hot fire.

CHAPTER 19

REASSIGNMENT

On the third of November, Bonnie was again called to the Admiral's office. When she entered, he was gazing out the window.

He turned and smiled. "In our business, lass, it appears that the only constant is change. Sometimes new vistas open, and so it is for us. The President has ordered me back to the Fleet."

Bonnie looked glum and replied, "We'll miss you, sir."

He continued, "There's more. You too are leaving. You are to report to Harvard for their intensive management course. It leads to a postgraduate degree. Unfortunately, you have only been allowed six months residency. You have to finish in a non-resident status."

"I'll do my best, sir."

"I'm sure you will. Captain, soon to be Rear Admiral, Oglesby is replacing me here at the project. He is a fine man with a genius for organization. Ensign Olive will enjoy working for him. She will replace you immediately, and effective today, she is Lieutenant Olive. The Service rewards outstanding work."

"Oh, I am so happy for her. May I go tell her?"

"Lieutenant, hear me out. Don't be so impetuous."

"I'm sorry, sir."

The Admiral grinned. "I'll not go back to the Fleet immediately. The Corporation has established a military position on its board of directors, ostensibly because sixty percent of its business is now with the Fleet or in space-related business. The Chairman made a by-name request directly to the President for me to occupy it, and she approved his request, so I must detour to the Corporation Headquarters for six months to get things set up. I'll form a liaison office there before I return to the Fleet, where I'll take command of the Neptune Squadron. Incidentally, I am being promoted to vice admiral."

Bonnie could not contain her glee. She threw her arms around the Admiral and gave him a big kiss.

"Oh, how wonderful for you," she exclaimed.

"My, my, you are impetuous." The Admiral reddened.

Bonnie backed off, aware of her breach of discipline and stammered, "Oh, I'm sorry, sir. How unprofessional of me... I was just so happy about your good fortune."

The Admiral ignored her apology and continued, "You will join the liaison office when you complete your term at Harvard. I asked for you specifically and told the Chairman that the office should be headed by a lieutenant commander. He passed my request to the President, who directed your assignment and immediate promotion."

Bonnie forgot herself again, threw her arms around the Admiral's neck and kissed him again, full on the lips. "Oh, thank you, sir," she exclaimed. This time the Admiral kissed her back. Then he said, "Bonnie, go now and tell your friend Olive the news."

Bonnie departed the Admiral's office walking on air. *Why*, she thought to herself, *it's the first time he has ever called me Bonnie rather than Lieutenant Brightwood.*

****

High above the stratosphere, winging east on the one-and-a-half-hour flight to the Boston suburb of the Eastern Megapolis, Bonnie was thinking of all the things that had happened in her life the past few years. *Destinies, destinies*, she thought. How was it and why was it that she should be so lucky?...born with a silver spoon in her mouth...always the best of everything...already a Lieutenant Commander in a profession she loved. Well, she had toed the mark, given her best, and taken whatever fortune offered.

Yet she felt a bit guilty. Then suddenly her mind went back to Porch. She wondered if her poor Grub was still alive...such a fine young man...why had fate treated him so badly?...a foundling who struggled so hard in life...who'd only asked to be a starman, and yet had that taken from him so strangely...well, when she got to the Corporation maybe she could find out what had happened."

"Destinies, destinies," she sighed. Would their paths ever touch or cross again?

CHAPTER 20
RETURN

Porch awoke in a very strange place and he felt a great weight on his body. Groggily, he looked up and found the great wolf lying on top of him. The wolf began licking his face. He struggled to move. The wolf crawled off and began to tug on his sleeve. Evidently, the wolf wanted something of him. He looked around. There was a dim light from the entrance to whatever he was in. He saw his pack close by and guessed the wolf had dragged that in, too.

What accounted for such strange behavior? Did the animal have abnormal intelligence? Had it been around men before? It was uncanny. He could but wonder and thank whatever grace had led the wolf to treat him as it had. He pulled his pack over and groped inside, retrieving the small flashlight he'd saved for emergencies.

Flicking it on, he looked about. As he'd seen in his dream, the huge wolf was white as snow. He was in a hut of sorts, maybe a long-abandoned prospector's or geologist's cabin. There was a table and chair in a corner, a cupboard against one wall, and a potbellied stove centered in the room. Snow buried a window on another wall so deeply that no light shone through. Another wolf was lying on its side not far away. It looked sick. The great white wolf was tugging him toward this one. He slid over to assess the problem.

The second wolf was female, appeared lethargic, and was feverish. She had a piece of antler stuck deep in her paw and the wound was festering. Porch pulled a piece of cloth from his pack, pulled the piece of antler from the wound, and cleaned it as best he could. The female snarled, tried feebly to snap at him, then lay back and whimpered. Porch found the biopowder he carried in his pack and shook it into the wound. He figured that when the infection had been destroyed he could go back in, wash the wound out and check for broken bones. He wrapped some deerskin he carried for slings around the wolf's paw, and bound it loosely.

Next, he crawled to the door, rose, looked around and slowly moved outside. It was snowing heavily. He walked around, straining to hear drones buzzing or chopper blades beating the air. Hearing nothing, he was satisfied that the searchers had left. He stumbled on the frozen carcass of a caribou. The wolves must have killed it and dragged it to the cabin. Perhaps it was the animal that had wounded the female.

He returned to the cabin to further explore. Lo and behold, a stack of wood chopped to length for the stove was not far from the door. Behind the stack, four very gaunt whelps looked out at him timidly. They must have been born late in the season and were still trying to nurse. He tested the stove with a bit of moss and it drew, although poorly. Then he carefully built a fire inside. He figured the snow falling outside would mask the smoke. As the smoke rose up the vent, it melted the snow blocking its passage and the stove drew better. It became quite warm in the cabin.

Looking further, Porch found a lantern and some fuel, and lit it. It shown dimly. He inspected the cupboard. There was coffee, cans of powdered milk, sugar, salt, a few spices, some bags of flour, and cornmeal. My gosh, the stuff must have been a hundred years old. He tested the condiments and the flour against his tongue. They were still good, preserved by the cold. He found some pots and pans, so went back outside with two of the pots and filled them with fresh snow. Back inside, he set them on the stove. When the snow melted and the water warmed, he opened several cans of powdered milk and stirred in the contents, adding a bit of sugar and a dash of salt. He went back to his pack and with-drew a bladder-like skin canteen. He had fashioned it long ago by wrapping and lashing a pouch of deerskin around a piece of rubber hose from the Millenarian barn. He wrapped a bit of deerskin around the nozzle and filled the canteen with warm milk, then went over and picked up a cub by the scruff of its neck. It protested vigorously until it tasted the warm liquid in its mouth, and then began to suckle greedily. Porch set the pup down when it could take no more, refilled the canteen and fed the others. When all four had their bellies full they waddled back over behind the woodpile and went soundly to sleep.

Porch next picked up his hatchet and the empty pots and returned outside. He butchered the frozen car-cass, got some more snow, and prepared a warm broth. When this was ready, he took a ladleful to the injured female. She snarled and snapped at him but became quiet when the great white wolf sounded a low growl. He lifted her head and forced some of the broth into her mouth. Soon she fed vigorously, ladle after ladle. After she'd had enough, he shared the remainder with the great white wolf.

Then he refueled the stove, closed the hut door, and went over to a corner to sleep. In an instant, he found himself under a pile of pups. They went back to sleep on top of him. The great white wolf snuggled beside his dam and that pair too went to sleep. The next morning, the pups licked at his face and pulled and tugged at him until he was fully awake.

Again, he prepared their "formula" and fed them. Then he prepared a stew and fed the female, male and himself. He also made some coffee and a few hoecakes.

The biopowder had cleared the female's infection, so he cleaned the wound. In the weeks that followed, the female recovered and the pups waxed fat, in fact, quite roly-poly. Porch took to calling the great white wolf Fenrir. The wolf responded to the name and they began to hunt together. Other wolves joined them. Fenrir es-tablished his dominance and indicated the man was one of them. Though he was leader, he subordinated himself to Porch. As the winter wrapped the land in cold and ice, game became scarce in the pack's range. Porch came to think they should move on.

One day he found a packet of maps of the entire north country. It had fallen behind the cupboard in the hut. "Wow," he said to Fenrir, who looked at him blankly but sensed his excitement, "contoured maps charting terrain all the way east to Hudson's Bay and south to the Great Lakes."

Porch knew he'd stayed in that place too long—much too long. He thought back to the call of the Seven Sisters. Yes, it was time to leave. Surely the pack would follow. The maps would save a lot of time. He would follow a course skirting the lakes, making best use of river valleys and avoiding the few settlements that remained in this part of the north.

With the wolves accompanying him, he could adopt an ingenious deception. He fashioned a hood from a caribou head with a set of antlers and attached this to a coat of caribou hide. In mid- December, he shouldered his pack, put on this artifice, and began his trek. He set a pace he could maintain indefinitely, eating and resting six hours at night. Fenrir scouted the way, the female and the pups stayed on his heels, and the other wolves followed. To any air observer, it would appear that the pack was closing on an exhausted quarry.

Four months later, he reached a wooded hill overlooking the Academy and the wolves became extremely skittish. They had never been so close to civilization. Porch knew they must return to the wilderness or soon be seen by day or heard at night, and killed forthwith. He called the great white wolf. When it came loping up, he threw his arms about its neck, then scratched its ears and chin. He pointed back to the northwest and signaled the wolf to go. At first, the animal didn't understand, but by repeatedly running back toward whence he'd come Porch imparted his meaning. So Fenrir called the pack, took a final look toward Porch and headed north.

Sadly, Porch turned to the scene below the hill. He was on the north side of the Academy. Winter was ending and green showed through the snow. The sun shone most of the day now. In the distance, he saw the high tower of the headquarters, the main parade, and the woods he'd crashed through to escape the devil dogs. He picked out the barracks behind which they'd buried his locket. Finally his eyes fell upon the North Tower Apartments. He shuddered. "Time to devise a plan and then get some sleep."

CHAPTER 21

INSPECTOR TUESDAY

Inspector Tuesday North Bear entered the Chairman's outer chamber, and even he was impressed by the opulence of the room. The room gave a sense of untold wealth and power. His escort, who had introduced himself as the Chairman's counsel, motioned him to a chair.

"Be comfortable," the Lawyer said, smiling. "I will inform the Chairman of your arrival."

Tuesday surmised, *These people don't request, they command.*

The Lawyer crossed the deep pile rug, quietly turned an ornate gold knob on one of the double doors and entered the Chairman's office. After enfolding himself into the soft leather chair, Tuesday looked around, examining everything, a habit from so many years on the force. Even in the subdued lighting, he immediately noticed the striking auburn-haired woman in a Space Fleet lieutenant commander's uniform sitting in another corner. He sensed that she'd watched him enter but now chose to ignore his presence. Her demeanor told him that she too had been summoned. She glanced at him briefly when she felt his eyes on her and immediately looked away. What studied poise and aloofness; it was if she belonged in this place. His black eyes passed on, as he, too, was comfortable with himself.

Inspector Tuesday was a cop with twenty years on the force. He retired when the mayor of New Chicago passed him over for chief, selecting a younger man. The younger man had degrees in psychology and socio-scientific criminology. He had been to the right academies and police schools, graduating with nigh-perfect marks. He had not, however, been through Tuesday's alma mater, the school of hard knocks. Tuesday never made a fuss. He just went private.

To Tuesday, there were good guys and bad guys. That was it. If he was hired to apprehend a man, that man was a bad guy. He did whatever it took to bring him in, walking, crawling, on a stretcher or in a body bag, without remorse. He was cold as ice about his work. That is what the school of hard knocks had taught him. He became visibly upset only a few times early in his career when his mates kidded him about an ancient video character, a certain Sergeant Joe Friday. They jested that Tuesday was always three days ahead of Friday. It was not funny to him. They had twenty-second century technology that Joe Friday could not have dreamed existed.

The door to the inner chamber opened and the Lawyer motioned for Tuesday to come in. Inside, sitting behind a massive oak desk in a large high-backed leather chair, was a small and very old man. Tuesday estimated him to be in his eighth decade. However, the old man's piercing eyes gleamed with shrewd intelligence. He looked Tuesday directly in the eyes and said, "Your reputation precedes you. I hope it proves correct." The Chairman waited for Tuesday to answer.

Tuesday replied, "I do my job."

Belisarius went directly to the point. "A convicted felon who escaped from here well over a year ago is still at large. He is extremely dangerous. He deserted the Space Academy after maiming his officer supervisor in an unwarranted attack. He is responsible for the deaths of his two keepers, and we believe he murdered a security guard while escaping. There is a one million credit reward for his capture. I will raise that to two if he is brought back alive. I would have him by now except for blunders by my own agents. We believed he went south. We no longer believe." The old man became silent.

"Why are you sure that he is not in the south?"

Tuesday asked. . "We know he was a foundling raised by a man called Harry on a ranch in west Texas. My operatives questioned this man as to his adopted son's whereabouts. They had lie detector beams trained on him. No lies were detected but my operatives decided to get rough with the old rancher. They took him outside to hang him up by his heels. Now their story becomes confused. Tell them, counselor..."

The Lawyer continued for the Chairman. "The two men are known as Ess and Gee... They said they were attacked by animals...a great dog named Ajax...with a mule, some goats, several huge black snakes and some black cats. The man, Harry, got the upper hand and had the animals herd our men into a barn and forced them down a hatch into a place swarming with rats. They escaped after two days and headed south to a town called Pecado. The old man had many friends down there, where he is known as Ole Mulemilk. Evidently he called or radioed the Mayor about what the men-had tried to do to him. The Mayor, by name of Nogales, who is also sheriff, and his deputies were waiting for Ess and Gee. They took them before the judge, also Nogales, and tried them for assault. Found guilty, Judge Nogales gave them a choice–tarred and feathered and run out of town never to return, or spend six months in their jail. Before choosing, he showed them their prospective cell. It was full of huge black snakes. They chose to leave town, were duly tarred and feathered and paraded down the main street past the new Mulemilk Elementary School, the Mulemilk Library, the Mulemilk Senior Citizens Home, and the Mulemilk High School to the outskirts of town, where they were released. This is what they reported to the Corporation."

Tuesday smiled. "Why doesn't this powerful Corporation send a couple of companies of men down there and raze the town?"

The Chairman replied, "We did that once...back East. It did not help us. It only created continuing problems...that have lasted to this day. So that is no longer the Corporation way. We work quietly, and must be effective the first time...whatever it takes.

"If we fail...which is not often, mind you, we find another way. That is why I called you in. You find the felon Porch and bring him back, whatever it takes. You will be on a most liberal retainer. Two million, if you bring him back alive. Do you accept?"

Tuesday replied, "The chase is important to me, the money is not. I'll bring him in...alive if I can, dead if I must."

The Chairman turned to the Lawyer. "See to it that Inspector Tuesday gets whatever he needs to start at once."

"Yes, sir," the Lawyer replied, and he motioned Tuesday to follow him out. When they reached the outer chamber, the Lawyer walked past Bonnie and said, "It will be but a moment longer, Commander."

Tuesday looked at her and said politely, "Good morning, miss." She nodded but looked miffed, and Tuesday remembered that she had arrived before him and had been kept waiting. Tuesday thought to himself that the Chairman must want this fellow Porch real bad.

CHAPTER 22
THE LIAISON OFFICER

Bonnie wondered who the wiry little man was. He looked hard as nails and cold as ice. His black eyes and the scar on his cheek, which looked like a claw mark, strengthened his scary appearance. But he'd smiled when he greeted her and was certainly polite. No matter, she had finally arrived at the Corporation Headquarters and would be working for the Admiral again. She hoped to see him soon. She knew that she had fallen in love with him. The Lawyer returned and stood in front of her. She quit her musing and looked up.

He said, "The Chairman will see you now, Commander."

She was a little apprehensive and tried not to show it.

It will be all right, she told herself. *The Admiral said just stay cool, but the Corporation is one of the most powerful entities on Earth. I hope I'm not in over my head.*

She rose and gave the Lawyer her brightest smile, straightened her skirt and blouse, touched her hair, and followed the Lawyer into the Chairman's office.

The Chairman stood up and said, "Welcome, Commander. It is so good to see you again. I am very sorry to have kept you waiting, but I had business that could not be delayed. Please sit. I hope your sojourn at Harvard was pleasant and profitable to you."

"Yes," Bonnie replied. "I enjoyed it very much." She had not really remembered how small and old the Chairman was, nor had she been close enough at the briefing to see the force in his eyes. They emanated power. But she concealed any impression of being startled.

Then the Chairman threw her a curve. He glowered as he sat back down. "I understand you know the felon Porch."

"Yes," she answered evenly. "He entered with the new class—my final year there. He was assigned to my company."

The Chairman continued to probe. "I understand that you stood up for him on several occasions."

Bonnie replied forcefully, "Yes, I did, because he was unjustly accused and unfairly treated. I did it in accordance with both Academy tradition and Academy regulations."

"He was asked to join the dueling club which my adopted son, Major Werewick, coached, an opportunity afforded very few, and he refused."

Bonnie went on the offensive. "I am surprised that a man in such a powerful position, with such awesome responsibility, would immerse himself in such trivial detail about something that could hardly concern him."

The Chairman flushed, looked at her fiercely, and spoke very slowly. "This position is built on and sustained by information ...information as timely and detailed as required. That murderous whelp maimed my son, a true space hero and contender for this chair when I pass on. He did untold damage to me and this corporation. My son is now in a western sanitarium to recuperate from his wounds. The felon Porch was convicted of the crime in a fair trial devoid of human emotion which weighed all evidence with total accuracy and fairness. The felon submitted nothing in his own behalf upon which to be found innocent. Then he as much as murdered several others when he fled from here."

Bonnie did not back down. "I have the highest regard for Major Werewick. However, the incident to which you refer occurred just as I graduated and left the Academy. I know nothing of the trial. But that young man was one of the finest I ever met, honest, kind, compassionate toward others, perhaps naive because of his youthful isolation. All he ever wanted to be was a starman. I do not believe him capable of murder. If he offered no evidence to protect himself, I can only believe he found his trial fraudulent and presented no defense to shield others. That is his nature."

The Chairman sought a final advantage and said, "The felon is comely to a fault and of magnificent physique. I've also been told your interest was based on desires far different than any desire to see justice done. Is that not true?"

"Sir," Bonnie said coldly, "that does not deserve an answer."

Belisarius kept his gaze on her and was quiet for several moments. At last he said, "Very well, I know where you stand on this issue, and I must say I admire your mettle. But that is not why you are here, and I will address that now."

He shifted in the big chair as if to emphasize a new subject, and continued. "As you no doubt know, Admiral Sven Petersen was nominated by the President to our board of directors and subsequently seated by us. You are to head the Fleet Liaison Office, which he established here. I expect you to act for him in his absence."

"In his absence, sir?" Bonnie questioned.

"Yes. The President sent him back to the Fleet several days ago. He will return as soon as his squadron cleans up pirates lurking around Jupiter base on Ganymede. He expects to complete his mission in six months, but I need somebody now and he has told me that you have his full confidence."

The Chairman didn't realize he had just thrown Bonnie the biggest curve of all. She had no idea the Admiral had left. She concealed her disappointment and said, "I'll do my best, sir."

"He established a small permanent staff to keep him apprised of our activities relating to the fleet... Are you listening to me, young lady?" He'd caught her.

"Oh, yes, sir, I just had no idea that the Admiral was not here."

"What I have to say now is most important. Intel

has picked up rumors of a strange device under development in Israel, a machine that circumvents the very fabric of space time to send objects and even humans across the galactic void in no time, or now time as it has come to be called. It uses some known and some new principles of quantum physics to do this.

"Should these reports prove true, a revolution in the affairs of men will occur and change the future history of mankind. Whichever political alliance on this planet succeeds in gaining control of the device will control the planet itself. Our intelligence also reports that huge amounts of capital, megacredits, are needed to develop it further. I intend to secure it for the Corporation...and...the Western Alliance. We must proceed cautiously. We are gathering information now. You will receive whatever we come by to transmit to Petersen. Security is vital. That is all I have for you now. Get settled in as soon as possible."

Belisarius turned to the Lawyer and said, "See that Commander Brightwood has the best we have to offer."

The Lawyer motioned Bonnie to follow him out.

CHAPTER 23

TRACKING

"Where is he? Has he reported in?"

"Yes, sir," the Lawyer said. "He sent a coded Ultra-FAX."

"Well?"

"It had but one word, TRACKING."

"Very well. We will be patient," Belisarius said, annoyed.

Inspector Tuesday was in the middle of a bridge over the silt-laden river. He watched the Corporation crew pull the battered air cart from the mud it had been buried in for almost two years. They'd grown impatient with him, but other Corporation operatives had found nothing. His meticulous work was paying off.

Inquiry about the habits of the saber-tooth and examination of what was left of Tchako and Cheeko revealed they'd been ambushed as they chased the felon. Their own stupidity caused their demise. A man running for his life could hardly have set it up, and he found the guard's skull in the swamp. Dental records proved it his. The skull showed the fracture that killed him. It had minute particles of granite embedded in it. The nearby boulder showed microscopic pieces of bone and traces of blood in one place only, and there was no other granite nearby. The man had been killed when somehow he fell from the aircart. The felon did not kill him. Nevertheless, he'd been tried and found guilty, so Tuesday would bring him in. After that, it was none of his affair.

The crew pulled the aircart onto the bridge deck and Tuesday spent the rest of the day examining it. He found paint and steel fragments that matched bridge materials. He did not find any more granite, but did find slivers of wood that matched swamp species. He surmised the aircart hit a branch, overturning when the guard located the escapee. Excited about apprehending him, the man got careless. He would keep these findings to himself. He knew his employer was in no mood to deal with them. He next had the aircart washed, slowly and carefully, sieving the silt through ever-finer filters. After meticulous examination, he found several strands of cloth and some advanced polymer that matched standard guard overcoats and boots.

When he finished, he sent the crew and aircart back to Corporation Headquarters and returned to his van for the night. That night in his van, he took out his map and circumscribed a circle of a twenty-mile radius centered on the bridge. *North, south, east, or west,* he mused. *West, back to the Corporation, hardly; east to New Chicago where he was first captured; south, the easier way but one of greater risk; north, the hard choice but least expected in face of the approaching winter. Considering the fugitive's courage, I will look that way first.*

As the sun broke the eastern horizon the following day, Tuesday stood before a sign with words barely legible: WILLOW WIND COMMUNE ~ ESTABLISHED 2053 ~ MILLENARIANS. The bottom part had broken off. He looked over and saw a gate half open and half off its hinges. He walked through it and up toward a distant house.

As he did, an old man carrying a pitchfork approached. A little girl followed closely behind. The old man raised his right hand and said, "Peace, stranger. Welcome."

Tuesday noted the other hand gripped the fork tightly as he spoke. He replied, "Peace. My name is Tuesday, and I'm looking for a man, a tall man, who came through here about a year and a half ago."

"Been no man to my recollection."

The little girl looked around the old man's leg, put a

finger to her lips, and made a sound, "Sshh..."

Strange, thought Tuesday.

"Come join us for some breakfast," the old man said, and started back to the house.

As they walked, the little girl looked up at Tuesday and asked, "Is he your fend? He was my fend."

"Pardon me?" said Tuesday.

"Quiet now, Becky. The stranger needs to sit a spell and have some breakfast, and so do you," the old man said gently—then, to Tuesday, "Nobody comes here anymore, 'cept the mailman and sheriff—once in a while. We are alone. There has been nobody. She is lonely and has a big imagination."

"But she said..." Tuesday protested.

The old man looked down at the child and asked, "Did you see a man, honey? Tell the truth, now."

Becky looked at her grandfather like she had said something wrong and was being admonished. She put her small hand to her mouth and thought and thought. Finally, she looked up, first at her grandfather to see if she should say more, and then at Tuesday. Finally, she said, "Wasn't no man."

"You see, sir, there was nobody. We are honest folk, Millenarians. We would tell you. Now let's break bread together."

Tuesday let the subject drop. But the next day, he returned with the sheriff. He was carrying a big, beautiful doll. The old man was doing his chores when he saw them approach and greeted them. "Good morning, Sheriff. I see my visitor from yesterday is with you. Good morning, Inspector Tuesday."

"Mornin', Josh. How's things?" the Sheriff asked.

"No complaints, Vern," the old man responded.

"Inspector Tuesday here is a private investigator. A very bad man is at large. Mr. Tuesday thinks Becky might tell him something that would help find the man. It's OK, you got to help us, Josh."

"Very well, come into the house. Becky's inside."

In the living room, the old man beckoned them to sit down and called out, "Becky, come here, please."

Becky came in, saw the two visitors, and ducked

her head shyly. As she did, her eyes caught the doll which Tuesday had placed on the sofa beside himself. Her eyes got big as saucers. She had never seen anything so beautiful.

Tuesday said, "Her name is Beth. I think she wants to come live with you, Becky, but she wants to know about your fend. She thinks he might be the man I'm looking for."

Becky's eyes remained riveted on the doll. At last, she looked at Tuesday and said emphatically, "Wasn't a man...was an angel."

"Why do you say that, Becky?" Tuesday questioned.

"'Cause he came out of the sky."

"Out of the sky?"

"Yes. He was in the haystack."

"If he was in the haystack, why do you say he came out of the sky? Did you see him come out of the sky?"

"Sometimes Grampy lets me jump from the loft into the haystack. Don't you get it—you jump into haystacks at the top, from the sky. So he came out of the sky 'cause he was in the haystack, so he was an angel. Grampy said angels were far away, high in the sky."

"Oh, I see," Tuesday said.

Finding belief at last, Becky brightened and continued, "Yes, he was a soljur angel."

"You mean he was wearing soldier clothes, like a uniform, perhaps an overcoat?" Tuesday pressed.

"Yes, and boots," Becky said as she went over and touched the doll's fingers.

"Besides, he knows angels," she said. "Show you." She ran from the room and then came back holding out a tin plate which she handed to Tuesday. "See, I gave him something to eat."

"But angels don't eat," Tuesday said.

"Soljur angels do, and they come from the sky 'cause I saw some at the fair with Grampy. They ate some food after they came down from the sky on big sails."

Tuesday looked at the scratchings on the tin plate. ANGELS ABOVE LOVE YOU, LITTLE BECKY. Then he looked at Becky and said, "I must go now. Beth here has decided to come live with you. She too loves you very much."

Becky ran over and hugged the doll, which was as big as she was. She touched the doll's blue silk dress and felt her blonde curls. The little girl had never seen anything so fine. She hugged the doll again and said to her, "Beth, you will have a nice home with me and Grampy. We will play together all the time."

Tuesday smiled, got up and, looking at her grand-father, asked, "Mind if I look around?" Josh said that it would be all right.

By noon, Inspector Tuesday had found the guard's uniform under the clothes in the barn. He then began to systematically search the farm, using a wide beam organo-spectrometer which he called his trash reader. Just before dark on the north side, he found remnants of an apple core, then another. Almost picked clean by ants, some stem, seeds and peel remained. He fed samples through his saliva and sweat readers. The barcode output matched what he had collected several months before in the fugitive's cell.

When he saw this, he grinned. The hunt was on. He had location and a line of direction. He arranged with the old man, Josh, to leave the van in storage on the farm until he called the Corporation to transport it else-where. Then he went back to it and removed the equip-ment and provisions he would need. His "finders" and his "readers" fit neatly into a small case. He would stay in touch with the Corporation via satellite through his omniband transceiver. This instrument would also give him his own location within a foot or so. He packed two month's supply of food and fuel capsules. Next, he un-loaded his "strider," as he called it, from the van. It was a force enhancer which looked like a cross between a fourteenth century suit of armor and a twenty-second century space suit. It was neither.

Rather, it was a semi-rigid, air-conditioned and heated cermet body suit. Multi-levered and internally powered arm and leg pieces were attached to the suit. The leg pieces extended four or five feet, so an operator could skim along five yards a step at speeds to sixty kilometers an hour. Its electro-pack provided sixty days' motive power, and Tuesday carried a spare. The spare and his other equipment fit on a back rack. A multi-purpose visored helmet topped the suit. It had omnispectra visual capability to include X-ray and ultraviolet down through infrared and microwave. Acoustic ear pickups could deaden a rocket engine to a whisper, or boost sound sufficiently to pick up a vole tunneling beneath a foot of snow. Tuesday mounted the strider and snapped two laser pistols on the left and right side of a belt, and behind those his stun guns. He was now ready to go. Josh had watched these preparations in amazement. Tuesday gripped his hand to say good-bye, pressing a roll of credits into it. The old Millenarian refused them as rent for van storage, but accepted them when Tuesday said they were for the child.

Tuesday North Bear adjusted his visor, extended the strider legs, and headed north at a fast clip. He loved the great North Woods. One of the "Morning Star" people born on a Tuesday, he wore the mark of the grizzly on his cheek. He was a child of the north, conditioned to the cold. As a youth, he learned the woods and their sign. He learned to track the bear and the wolf, the otter and wolverine.

His father died from alcoholism and his mother soon after from sorrow. The Mission took him in and taught him to read, write and do math. He learned the white man's ways and came to love the Fathers doing the holy work of Jesus. He worked hard to learn all they put before him.

And he met Laughing Water. They grew from childhood together. Her dark eyes reflected the innocence of the fawn and mirrored the peace of the doe. When she spoke, he thought he heard the bubbling brook. When she sang, and she sang often, it was like the thawing breeze of springtime rustling through the pines. When she laughed, it was like a thousand ice crystals breaking off the spruce and tinkling to the ground. When she came near, she carried the scent of wildflowers, and her breath the sweet grass of high meadows. He loved her deeply.

As he moved north, searching back and forth with his fire finder, the sorrow came back. He remembered when she left the Mission to enter a novitiate. He found and entered a nearby seminary to be near her. When they found her with child, the blue-eyed brothers accused him of fathering the blue-eyed child she bore and drove him away from the holy work of Jesus with words that impaled his heart. So he walked away from hunting lost souls to take up the work of hunting the men who harbored them.

When Tuesday found the char of an old fire, he decided to stop for the night. He was near an icy stream. He dismounted the strider, peeled off his clothes and plunged in. The water refreshed him. It drove the sadness away and brought back the harsh world he lived in. He built a fire and supped. Then he removed the thermo-cocoon from his pack, disabled the strider, and with a laser pistol nearby, crawled in and slept.

When he arose in the morning, he activated his stool finder and found evidence of the fugitive. He continued north and spent the next twenty days tracking. With the science he packed, it was easy to distinguish the fugitive's trail, with all its convolutions, from any other. Then he followed what was freshest. When he reached the shack on the bank of the river, he became confused. There was heavy sign of wolf. And evidently wolves had dragged his quarry's body into the shack.

Had they dispatched him there and made a meal? It was perplexing till he saw the potbellied stove which had been used less than a year before. Wolves did not use fire. He dug into the soft earth floor of the cabin. He found discarded tins of milk product, coffee grounds, several utensils, and other refuse. He tested the utensils for saliva and found a match. Somehow the fugitive had allied himself with the pack that used that shelter. Then he found the maps—a complete inventory of North America from the pole down to latitude forty-five. No, several sheets were missing—those that headed east from that position.

Tuesday thought about what he had found. He went out of the shack, held his transceiver up, and sent a message to the Corporation. "TRACKING—SEND VAN TO SPACE ACADEMY—SOUTH ENTRANCE."

CHAPTER 24
THE LOCKET

Porch was ready. He had circled the Academy the night before to ensure there were no surprises waiting for him when he left the grounds heading south. He'd hidden his pack near the south gate, where he could easily retrieve it, and left all his weapons except his sling with it. He intended to walk out the south gate this time. The sling would suffice for what he expected he had to do.

After night fell, he moved to the north gate, stopping at the fence where heavy woods bordered the entrance grass and hurled his deerskin over it. Then he headed toward the gate, staying out of the guard's line of sight. He distracted the sleepy guard by hurling a stone against a metal road sign just beyond the guard shack. The sign rang loudly. When the guard went to investigate, he slipped inside the gate and, crouching, ran to where the deerskin lay. He put it over him and continued south, creeping past the North Tower.

He reached his old barracks without incident and found the granite boulders on the hill behind. A rush of adrenaline hit him when he found the mark on the great stone he had traveled so far to reach. He shoved the boulder aside with a mighty heave, the same that took both him and Bokasi to move two years before. Panting heavily, he rested a moment, then dug into the soft earth beneath. Unerringly, his fingers found the plastic pouch containing the locket. Elated, he let out a great sigh but quickly covered his mouth so as not to be heard. It was so quiet. He knew that at this time of the year, all candidates were studying for final exams. He looked toward the barracks. Every room was lit, full of cramming students.

He wondered which was Bokasi's. Bo would now be an honorable third year Hawk. He thought he should try to find his friend, but quickly discarded the notion as most foolhardy. He felt himself then the loneliest man on earth, but took solace in the recovered locket. Withdrawing it from its pouch, he opened it and read the words, "...seek out and find the Birthplace of Wonder."

At this very moment in the North Tower, Ess was playing solitaire. Startled suddenly, he looked up. "I can smell him, I tell you."

Irritated, Gee snarled, "He's not such a fool as to come back here. Ever since Texas you've had no sense."

Ess growled, "He's here, I know it. Come on, he's ours. He's ours at last." He moved to release the dogs.

Gee cautioned, "You better be right, or we're done for sure."

Porch heard the howls just as he put the locket around his neck and said to himself, *Just as I thought, the devil dogs.*

He felt for the sling and pouch of stones on his belt, then put the deerskin back on and began running south on the same route he had taken two years before, making good time to the streetlight south of the parade. He discarded the skin there and continued south to the gravel road bordering the playing fields. He stopped there and took the sling from his belt. He started to pull two missiles from his pouch but stopped, bent down, and selected two well-rounded plum-sized pieces of gravel from the road.

Better, they'll trace these to right here, he thought grimly.

Just then the devil dogs reached the lamppost. Ferociously, they began tearing the deerskin to bits. Porch loaded his sling. The borsoi looked up. At that moment, the missile from the sling hit it in the right eye and it went down. The mastiff quit tearing at the skin. Porch let the second stone fly and hit the animal on the center of its forehead. He knew from experience that both were either dead or incapacitated. So he continued toward the south gate leisurely, exited, and retrieved his pack.

He felt good with the locket around his neck again. He reached up, touched it, and thought of his mother. He knew she came from a place called Bountiful in the eastern mountains. While imprisoned, he had located it in an atlas. Her kin might still be there. He would go there. Surely they could tell him her story and perhaps his father's.

As he continued through the night, his feeling of well-being ebbed and a strange foreboding came over him. He felt a fierce new element added to those arrayed against him, something that would pursue him to doomsday. Perhaps he could find refuge amongst his mother's people against such strange, unreasonable fear, but the insecurities that plagued him returned and flooded his psyche.

He continued south and reached the Appalachians and West Virginia. He got to the ridge above Bountiful expecting to see the town beneath, but saw nothing, no roads, no houses, no sign of life. He climbed down to the valley and began a search. He found a path, intentionally concealed. Farther on, he found the foundation of a dwelling long gone, and then another. There were remains of hearths and chimneys, all overgrown with vines and weeds. Suddenly his eye caught a wisp of smoke rising from the ground. He went over to look, and as he reached the place, the ground gave way beneath him and he fell amidst an avalanche of dirt and rubble, down, down and down.

CHAPTER 25

PURITY

Purity Wyndotte was Preacher Wyndotte's granddaughter. She had just reached sixteen and was in love with love and poetry. In the year just past, she had lost her childhood plumpness and had blossomed into a fresh and nubile beauty. She was like a ripe peach. The young men inhabiting the underground town of Bountiful had noticed. Preacher Wyndotte noticed that they had noticed, so he increased his vigil over Purity's activities tenfold. He was very concerned, because grief burned his soul over an incident that occurred many years ago with another young lady of their clan.

Purity was a bright child. She whiled away the hours reading poetry under the lanterns that dotted the underground town, especially during the winter when surface activity was limited. She read everything in the considerable library Granny Gronx and Preacher had saved from the fires. Recently, one of the older girls, whose parents did not watch her closely, introduced her to the racy pulps published by the underclass press.

Had Preacher caught her with these, he would have birched her good, but she salved her conscience thinking she was just learning the things any young girl should know. She dreamed of a world that did not include any of the "churlish louts" that lived in the band below. She tolerated them, as they were essential to the small society's well-being. She tolerated them like the coal dust that flowed through every tunnel, every shaft and every cavern of the underground town. It penetrated her clothing and permeated her skin.

On lady's day, when the sentinels proclaimed "all clear," she loved bathing in the pond below the stream that ran through the valley. She loved to wash her dark hair and loll there, bare, dreaming of love, letting the cool water flow over every part of her. She learned to swim a great distance underwater and pull herself out without a sound into the reeds that grew in the shallow waters around the pond. The people had been drilled on this, because one never knew when the sentinel's special bird call would alert all to take cover.

Purity had just finished *Odes of the Underculture*, one of Rene's pulps, the lyrical style of which set her to dreaming. Suddenly, a thump from far above and a series of loud crashes came from the air shaft not ten feet away. Finally, amidst an avalanche of rock and debris, what appeared to be a large and furry animal landed on some bales of Granny's herbs and mosses almost at her feet. She knew better than to scream out, because those who hunted them hurled debris down open holes in that area of abandoned mines hoping to find the sites occupied by her clan. But she was frightened almost to death.

She dared not move, though her instinct told her to run. When it was apparent the downpour had ceased and there was no movement from the heap at her feet, curiosity got the better of her. She edged over to the pile and touched it. She felt warmth. Then, running her hand toward the top, she felt a thumping and heard heavy breathing.

"Land o' goshen," she said to nobody in particular, "it's alive." She gently pulled the face up by the dirty blond hair and leaned over in astonishment. "It's a man, a young man with a dirty blond beard." She moistened the lilac-scented handkerchief she always carried and brushed the grime from his face. "Ooh," she giggled, "he's purty, real purty." Then she ran to get her grandfather. When she found Preacher, she blurted out what had happened and what she had found.

"Slow down, child. You say it's a man?" admonished Preacher.

She grabbed his hand and pulled. "Come on, Papa, come see for yourself." She pulled him toward the side tunnel from which she'd popped a minute before.

Preacher hollered back to Jethro, who was working nearby, "Get men with a stretcher, and some water and towels. A man's probably bad hurt. And fetch Granny."

He hurried down the tunnel with Purity, and when they reached Porch, she proudly displayed him. Preacher checked his pulse and breathing, and then for broken bones. He found none, but, frowning, he confiscated the knife and sling he found at Porch's waist. He made Purity repeat what had happened. She did so with carefully selected diction calculated to please him, and then asked coquettishly, "He's so purty, Papa. Can I keep him?"

Preacher would have raged at anyone else who made such a request, but his granddaughter was the image of his long-dead daughter and the apple of his eye, so he said quietly, "No, Purity, he is not one of us. We allowed another stranger to stay long ago, and suffered terrible pain and grief. We'll get Granny to fix him, and if he's not a Corporation or guv'ment man, we'll send him on his way."

Purity pursed her pretty lips and pouted, "But Papa, I found him, and I need a man."

"No," said the Preacher.

Jethro arrived, carrying towels and water, with Caleb and Mungo bearing the litter. Granny Gronx was close behind.

Setting the water down, Jethro nudged Porch with his foot and said, "Looks like a spy to me."

Caleb agreed. "Yeah, let's get rid of him now."

Mungo grinned gleefully. "The shaft—let's throw him down the shaft with the others."

Preacher said authoritatively, "None of that now. Put him on the litter. We'll find out soon enough."

Granny growled sharply at the four men, "You're forgetting the code o' the hills, now—back up, and let me look him over." Admonished, the men backed away.

Granny moved over the figure, then drew back, startled; passing years had not dimmed her memory, nor time her sight. Tears now blurred her eyes. She knew immediately who he was. She choked, sputtered and claimed coal dust had gotten in her eyes. She wiped the tears quickly so that the others, sizing her reaction, would not also guess who he was. For she knew his life might then be forfeit. She confirmed no bones were broken. Then she found a huge welt on his head.

"He's been knocked cold," she said, and put a compress on the lump. "Now put him on the litter and tote him to my infirm'ry."

The men lifted Porch onto the stretcher and followed Granny. Purity brought up the rear and every few steps tried to gaze around the men at the man she considered her prize. Shortly, they got to the underground room that was Granny's "infirm'ry."

"Set him by the tub," she commanded, "'cause I got to wash him up, and he's a big 'un. Then get out."

The men left, but Purity lingered. "Can I help, can I help?" she implored.

"You know better than that, chile," Granny answered.

"But I ain't never see'd a man," Purity protested.

"And you ain't about to see one now, and use the good English your Grampa taught you." Granny retorted. "Now go over to that chest marked 'J', where I been savin' homespuns these many years, and bring me the best and longest nightshirt you can find, also some underwear, a pullover and trousers for after I get him fixed— big boots, and socks, too."

Granny got some soap, scrub brushes, washrags and towels, then began heating water while Purity brought the clothes. Then Granny said, "Now skat."

"Aww," said Purity as she left.

Granny went over to the unconscious form and began stripping off his clothes. As she pulled his shirt off, she saw the locket, which confirmed what she already knew. Again the tears came, tears of joy. She looked at Porch and saw Jason's and Amilee's love combined in his features. It was the banished child now grown to manhood. She knew she must remain mute about her discovery. She took the locket that would give him away and put it in the bottom of the chest marked "J".

After a few more tears, she went determinedly about her task. It took all her strength to get him in the tub, where she scrubbed him clean, top to bottom, as she had the babe so many years before. Then she pulled him back down onto the litter and wiped him dry. As she began to apply her poultices, powders, then bandages on his cuts and bruises, Porch came out of his fog and began to get his bearing. He looked up at her and asked, "Where–where am I?"

Before she could answer, he saw his nakedness, and, turning red as a beet, began frantically to search for a cover.

"Be still now, boy," Granny commanded. "'T'was I that pulled you from your mother's womb and spanked the life into you, just as I did your ma, and I love you 'most as much as I loved her. I am your nearest kin."

"Granny, Granny Gronx," Porch said loudly, elated.

"Shh. Some here don't hold to my affections. Now, I got you fixed, so put that nightshirt on and get over on that cot. You'll rest there till I know for sure you're healing."

Porch sat up, still a little woozy, and pulled the nightshirt on. As he did, he did not feel the locket about his neck. Before he could ask Granny its whereabouts, she interjected, "I put it in a chest that only I know about. It will be safe. You dare not wear it here. You would be found out. Rest now. I'm going to get you some grub. I'll be back shortly."

Porch did as told and felt himself relax, more than he ever had since his escape. Sleep overcame him, and he did not awake until the following day. When he woke, he felt refreshed. The cuts and bruises he'd acquired in his fall were minor. He was ravenously hungry. Granny had him rise, clean up and shave because she wanted to see how he really looked. Then she brought in enough food to feed him and several others. While he ate, Purity peeked into the "infirmr'y" from behind the curtain Granny used to close it off from the outside.

She saw Porch alone, so she pinched her cheeks, bit her lips a bit and sauntered in, as though looking for something. Porch said hello.

"Oh, hello," she replied. "I'm Purity-the one who found you-I hope you weren't hurt bad-I'm sixteen and fully grown up and I don't like the boys here because they are rude and don't know how to treat a girl-We have to live down here in the dark and coal dust because bad men from the Corporation and revenoors from the guv'ment are always after us-It's so hard to stay clean-I love to bathe in the lake when its "all clear" time naked, and let the cool water run all over me and wash my hair-Do you like to swim?-I love to lie stark naked on the bank and let the sun warm me-Preacher won't let me do that anymore, since the rude boys sneak up and peek at me through the reeds-Do you think I'm pretty?"

"You are very pretty, Purity," Porch replied, smiling.

Encouraged, Purity continued, even faster, "How did you get here?- Where did you come from?-Are you a Corporation man?-Are you from the guv'ment?-Do you have folks?-Are you married?-Do you have a lover?-I know you're different from the boys here-You're the handsomest man I ever seen-Are you going to stay with us?"

Porch chuckled. "Purity, you go so fast, you make my head swim. Let's just say I'm a guest on a quest."

"Oh, how romantic-Just like in all the poems-I want to go to the perfume islands and sit on golden sand beside a turquoise sea-I want to see enchanted castles-Can I go with you?-Will you take me to New York City?-I never been anywhere, not even Webster Springs-Would you peek at me through the reeds?-I'd let you."

"Purity," Granny Gronx said sharply as she entered the clinic, "what are you doing here? Prob'ly talking the pore man's ear off. Now go off and do your chores, or I'll tell Preacher and you'll feel the birch."

After Purity had left, Granny continued, "Don't mind Purity. She's smitten with you."

Porch tried to rise.

"No," said Granny, pushing him back on the cot. "I gonna keep you here several days so I can talk to you alone. You must tell me about yourself, your whole life, and why you came. Then I'll tell you about this place, why we live like this, and why you must be careful. Can you start now? We haven't much time. They'll be asking."

"Yes," Porch answered. He told about Harry, and about his boyhood and the night under the stars when he swore to become a starman to search the heavens and try to find his father. He told about the Academy, his flight from there, and his unjust trial and captivity. He told about escaping to the far north. He told it all, and then he said, "That's all of it and why I came here. I must know of my parents, the ones in the locket."

"Well, listen well. You are a child of love, and I will tell you all." So Granny related the tale of the man from the stars and how he stole the heart of her beloved Amilee, the mother that Porch had never known. She told why she was banished and of her desperate flight to Harry. She told of Corporation men who burned Bountiful out and that even to this day hunted the townsfolk down. At last she said, "The men here will question you at length. Tell them only the truth, but not all; that you were a foundling, raised in the West, with ambition to be a spaceman. Tell them about Academy and what happened. Tell them how you beat the Corporation, and all that you've done till now. They hate the Corporation because of what happened here. Show them your skill with the silent weapons, and they will ask you to be a hunter. We cannot hunt when evil men are listening and would hear the long barrels. Game is plentiful here now. Certainly you were hunting when you fell down the shaft into this place. Now rest till you're mended."

Porch recovered fast and was up in a few days. As Granny forecast, Preacher and Jethro questioned him at length. His story impressed them, and they returned his sling and bow. They asked him to stay a fortnight and hoped he'd help fill the common larder with venison-, rabbit- and wild acorn-eatin' pork. Preacher showed him around the underground town they'd converted from the played-out mines, then proudly showed him the underground distillery and its product, their main source of credits. He explained its operation and how they vented the fumes and smoke to the surface, operating mostly at night when there was a wind, but sometimes during rainy and foggy weather, and always with a lookout. He also showed him the shaft where two thousand feet below the Corporation men who had burnt them out rested.

Porch was guardedly accepted. But there was a problem. Purity followed him around whenever she could, which did not go unnoticed. The Preacher admonished her, to no avail. Porch treated her as he would a little sister. Other young maidens tried their wiles on him, too, which infuriated Purity. One day, she got into a hair-pulling, wrestling squabble that Jethro had to stop. He went to his brothers.

"This is no good," he said. "We must do something. The man will be here a month, maybe longer. Remember what started the troubles."

Caleb said, "Put Mungo to watching her. He hates wimmen."

"Yeah," Mungo said, sighting down his long barrel. "Thar oughta be a bounty on 'em at three hundred yards."

Jethro thought again and said, "We'll all watch her— him, too." Some days later, Mungo caught Purity sidling up to Porch while Porch was eating lunch. He pulled her aside before she got to him.

"Purity," he growled, "you keep goin' on bout that man and I gonna pull your panties down and whup you good."

Eyes flashing, Purity retorted, "I'll bet you'd like to, Mungo. Prob'ly get your jollies that way." Then she ran off.

Thereafter, Mungo seethed with a rage, not only for Purity, but for the man who had brought this new trouble. Porch did not know this, nor did the others. They accepted him for his exceptional hunting skills. Many pleaded with him to stay past his intended departure time. They could not remember eating as well, as summer grew old and turned to autumn.

One day during a spell of Indian summer, Porch

was particularly fortunate. Well before the morning ended, he had bagged six rabbits and two young pigs. The band would feast that night. He began the ten-mile trek back to the town site fully loaded. Sweating under his burden in the heavy heat, he reached the stream above the pond. He did not see her, but Purity was wading in nearby shallows collecting rushes for Granny's baskets. Purity saw him and decided to conceal herself. Porch trudged past and took the fork leading to the pond rather than the hamlet.

Where is he going? Purity wondered, deciding to follow. He stopped at the pond, put his burden down and began to disrobe.

Land o' goshen, she thought, *he's going to bathe hisself.* She remembered then, watching him, that it was men's day at the pond.

Porch was now bare naked. He tested the water temperature with his toe and dove in, swimming rapidly to the rock in the center of the pond. He gasped at the water's cool embrace, gathered some rough moss from the rock, found some leftover soap, and scrubbed himself down vigorously. After finishing, he dove back into the water to rinse himself, and swam over to a half-submerged rock. Then he set himself to basking in the warm sun, eyes closed against the rays. He tensed when he heard a slight splash behind him, but before he could turn, small fingers closed firmly over each of his eyes.

"Guess who," he heard.

"Purity," he whispered hoarsely, "no!"

He raised his hands to pull back her fingers, but as he did, she pulled her hands away to grasp him firmly around his chest. He felt her cool wet breasts pressing hard against his back, and then all her warmth against him. She pulled him tighter, kissing his neck and shoulders.

"I love you, I love you," she exclaimed, wrapping hers leg around him. He felt her thighs against his buttocks.

"Love me," she begged, "love me."

Desire rose in him as he felt her supple form twist around to gain his front. Shocked at his own body's response to her advance, he broke free.

"No, Purity, I am not for you. Soon I must leave this place. I cannot betray your grandfather's trust and hospitality."

He dove into the water and swam rapidly away. When he reached his clothes, he pulled them on quickly and retreated into the brush. He looked back and saw Purity sitting on the rock, dejected and sobbing. He waited as she slowly regained her composure. At last, she dove into the water and swam slowly back to the rushes. Porch collected his weapons and game and headed toward the township entrance. When he got there, he placed his weapons in the hollow tree he found nearby. He did not want to emphasize his difference from the men in the band who all carried long barrels, particularly since he, with more primitive weapons, was the superior hunter. He carried the game below where his good fortune and skill was hailed.

Dinner that night was joyous except for Purity, who was sunk in misery. Porch tried to signal with a smile that he was still her friend and would not betray her passion. She would have none of it. Every time he met her glance, she would avert her eyes down to her plate. He felt her anguish.

Neither knew that Mungo was watching, highly suspicious of the silent interplay he observed. As Porch continued his day to day activities, the incident slowly passed from his mind.

Preacher asked him to join their marketing activities. The underground distillery was highly profitable. Their contraband spirits were renowned in the East, especially in the megacity a hundred miles away.

After one arduous back road trip to megapolis distribution points, the band returned late. A late- night dinner revived their spirits though most, very tired, turned in immediately. Porch delayed to bathe in a primitive tub and soothe his aching muscles in hot water provided by the fires that cooked the corn and barley mashes.

Refreshed, he retired to his assigned sleeping ledge, which was dug out of a wall in the cavernous hall reserved for bachelors. His large frame fit comfortably. He had a mattress filled with sweet grasses, a feather pillow, rough woven sheets, and a heavy quilt for cover. A curtain on the outside stopped drafts and provided privacy. Porch shed his robe, placing it on a peg beside his clothes, and slid between the sheets under the quilt. Warmth came quickly to his naked body.

Granny had told him all she knew of his origins, so he began to plan his departure. He would continue south. He had to get away from the Corporation and on to the stars. Freeport in the Caribbean was the most active spaceport of the unaligned nations. The interstellar ship captains never questioned those signing on as ordinary spacemen, and they had recruiting offices all along the Florida Keys. With these thoughts running through his mind, he gradually fell into a welcome sleep. Some time later, the dreams came. He imagined a soft warmth beside him. He sensed himself wrapped in tender arms with a pair of moist parted lips on his. He turned in his sleep to respond to this sensual pleasure. His arms entwined around a female figure, and the sweet fragrance of lilac water entered his nostrils. Slowly the dream turned real as he savored full warm breasts. His tongue sensed the flavor of coal dust and he woke up. "Purity," he whispered.

She was sobbing quietly as she placed wet kisses all over his neck and chest. Then she moved her pelvis, desperately seeking union. "I love you so much. I want you so much," she whispered. Suddenly, the curtain was yanked back.

"See," yelled Mungo, "I told you."

"Off him, girl, and out," a voice commanded, and hands grabbed her roughly, pulling her from under the quilt and off the shelf. Other hands covered her nakedness with a blanket.

"You'll get the switching of your life tonight, girl. Now off to Granny while we deal with this treachery," Preacher shouted.

Porch looked the blinding light of many torches. Squinting his eyes, he saw a number of long barrels, all pointed at him. He heard them cock.

"Shall I shoot him now, Preacher?" Jethro questioned.

"No. Out of there, boy. Put your clothes on." Preacher demanded.

Porch hurriedly put his clothes on.

"Perfidy," shouted one.

"Caught red-handed," yelled another.

"Throw him down the shaft."

"Hang him now."

"Get the noose. Be quick, before they hold the justice up," Caleb said to Mungo. Several men grabbed Porch and bound him with more ropes than he could count, with arms behind, legs together so he had to hop. Mungo returned with a noose, put it around his neck, and pulled it tight.

"Let's hang him now," Caleb shouted.

"To the shaft," Mungo screamed. The Preacher, thoroughly shamed by his granddaughter, stood glumly by, silent. He had lost control. Mungo pulled on the rope and Porch hopped along, held upright by rifle butts and barrels stuck in his ribs and back, and the eerie procession proceeded along the tunnels with torches reflecting red off dripping walls where anthracite still clung. The mob continued to scream, and soon the shaft loomed ahead.

"Get a plank," shouted one.

"Throw the rope over the beam above the shaft," another directed.

A small figure moved from a side tunnel to the front, blocking the shaft. It was Granny Gronx. "Stop," she hollered, palms up. The mob stopped instinctively and became silent.

"He is an innocent man. Purity tole me all." A muffled dissent rumbled through the mob.

"We caught him red-handed," Jethro contended angrily.

"Yes," screamed the mob. "In the act, the very act."

Again, Granny held up her hands. "Preacher, come here and I'll tell you all the girl tole, then you can be the judge. As fur the rest of you, 't'ain't none of your bus'ness, 'cause you ain't her kin."

Preacher moved to where Granny stood and Granny whispered in his ear. The preacher nodded and groaned in sadness when Granny told about the pond. The mob strained forward to hear, but heard nothing.

Finally Granny said, "Now, Preacher, tell 'em."

The preacher said sadly, "Release him. He is innocent."

The mob was furious. "No, no. Hang him now. Red-handed, in the act, we caught him in the act. The stranger broke the Code o' the Hills."

The end of the rope around Porch's neck sailed over the beam above the shaft. Caleb grabbed it and pulled it taut.

"Stop," Granny shouted once more. "You heer'd the preacher. The man is innocent." Then she lowered her voice to a whisper. "Now you remember so many years ago, you ran off a young girl with babe in arms. Shame, shame. That's when the sorrows started. It'll happen again, even worse."

Caleb strained on the rope and Porch was stretched to his toes, gagging. Caleb growled, "He broke the Code o' the Hills."

"He ain't broke nothin'," said Preacher, "'cause I'm goin' marry 'em up in the morning."

"No, no," screamed the mob. "We don't want him here. The girls don't look at us anymore. String him up."

Mungo grabbed the rope from Caleb and gave a mighty yank. Porch was pulled off his feet, choking, as his body swung perilously close to the shaft. Preacher grabbed his legs just in time and held on for dear life. Granny moved toward Mungo and shouted, "Leggo, Mungo, or you're a dead man."

Mungo lessened his grip and Porch's feet hit the ground. Granny faced the mob, eyes blazing. They moved back a step. Granny yanked a bodkin from her hair knot. Grasping it tightly, she held it high in her left hand and pointed it toward her right palm. The fierce needle flickered wickedly in the light of the torches. The mob stepped back and grew still. Throughout the cavern, every eye watched the needle.

Granny whispered, "Enough." She thrust the needle through her palm, withdrew it, and threw it at the
feet of Jethro, where it twanged ominously. She rubbed
her bleeding right hand onto to her left and held both
up to the crowd.

"I'm calling up the most unholy hex o' the hills,
who'er I touch with these bloody hands shall be dead
afore morn." She moved toward the mob, hands out-
stretched, palms up.

They faltered, shrank back; their retreat quickened
and became a rout till none were left. Granny pulled a
handkerchief from her petticoats, wiped her hands and
bound her right one. Then she said, "Preacher, you take
the man with you tonight, and keep him trussed up. I
wouldn't bet a hoot on him seein' the light o' morn if'n
we took him back to his bunk. We'll marry 'em up in the
morning."

Preacher made Porch, still tightly bound but out of
the noose, hop along in front of him to his own quarters. Granny spotted Purity, still wrapped in the blanket, trying to look small in a nook in the wall of the
cavern. She was moaning softly. "Don't hurt him. Don't
hurt him, please," she said.

"Come on, girl," Granny said. "We're gonna marry
you up to him in the morning, and we have little time to
fix you up a wedding dress."

Purity's countenance changed from one of dismal
sorrow to radiant happiness in the blink of an eye. "You
are?" she choked joyously.

"Come on." Granny prodded her. They marched off
to Granny's, passing Porch, slowly hopping along in front
of Preacher. Purity looked over and, smiling triumphantly, blew him a kiss with one small hand, still wet
from wiping tears away. When Granny got Purity to her
place, she had the girl put on a nighty and started holding measures of silks and satins against her chest.

Purity said timorously, "Granny, I see'd that beautiful ole weddin' dress in the bottom of your keepsake
trunk. Couldn't I wear that one?"

Granny replied angrily, "You speak good English,
girl, you been taught, and what are you doing, goin' in

my trunk?" Purity did not reply, but looked down, shamefaced, at her feet. Granny was quiet for a long time. Then she said, "That gown is very precious to me, but I suppose it would be fittin', seein's who you're marryin', but we'll have to let it out, 'cause my long ago darlin' was mighty slender for a mountain girl. Well, let's get started."

They worked the night through. The wedding was set for noon. Porch was allowed to shave and shower, under heavy guard. Granny brought some men's finery from the chest marked "J", and insisted he wear it. After he dressed, she put the locket around his neck and stuffed a pouch of gold coin in his pocket, which she said was a wedding present from Harry. He was again bound hand and foot.

At high noon, the entire population of Bountiful assembled in the underground chapel. Preacher followed by Jethro, Caleb and Mungo, all designated best men, led Porch, hopping along, to the altar. Each held his long barrel, cocked and ready. Granny sat in as mother of the bride. A mountain girl began to sing *Take Me Home to the Magic Mountains* in a beautiful soprano. She followed with several others, and the anticipation of the audience rose. At last a quartet of fiddlers began Mendelssohn's *Wedding March*. Purity came up the aisle on Preacher's arm, looking radiant.

As the party approached the altar, Preacher held up his free arm. He placed Purity beside Porch, and, turning to the audience, said, "'T'ain't fittin' a man should be all trussed up before our holy cross." So he took out a bowie knife and cut Porch's bindings free. Then he turned again to the audience and said, " But 't'ain't prudent to leave this man free till he prop'ly married to Purity."

With that, he held up a pair of ancient iron handcuffs and snapped one cuff on Purity's right arm and one on Porch's left. The assembly guffawed. Then he walked to the front of the couple and began, "Dearly beloved..." Porch heard but little...finally..."Do you, Purity, take–"

"I do, I surely do," she interrupted.

The rumbling began high overhead, faint at first, then increasing to a roar as great boulders came crashing down in a major cave in, landing between the wedding party and the audience. The rubble that followed reached a deafening crescendo as it filled in behind and buried Jethro, Caleb and Mungo. The boulders continued breaking through honeycombed levels of abandoned tunnels below the chapel and created a huge chasm in front of the assembled people. Dust filled the chamber and it was impossible to see a thing for several minutes.

Instinctively, Porch had grabbed Purity and shielded her beneath him as a shock wave threw them to the ground. The violence continued for what appeared to be an eternity, but in reality, subsided into eerie stillness in less than a minute. Aftershocks maintained the terror, but finally these too ceased. Porch was covered with dirt but was not hurt; nor was Purity. He got up and pulled her up, brushed her off gently, and brushed himself off. The convulsion silenced her, but he saw terror in her eyes. He looked toward Preacher, who had been knocked cold. He looked around and saw the chasm ripped across the chapel floor. He heard people moaning and scurrying away. Directly behind him a huge pile of rubble covered Jethro and his brothers.

"Come on," he yelled at Purity, "dig." Working frantically, they cleared away sufficient debris to uncover Jethro's head and one arm, which he had used to shield himself. Next, they uncovered Caleb's huge head. Both were out cold but breathing. Porch heard a cry to the left and dug out Mungo's head to his neck. Mungo was awake but groggy. Porch looked toward the altar and saw a strong beam of light illuminate the cross. Looking up, he saw a large tunnel-like hole all the way to the surface.

Without a second thought, he lifted Purity, still cuffed to him, across his shoulder in a fireman's carry and started to climb up the tunnel. The knowledge that he was several hundred feet to freedom spurred him on even though he slipped a foot back for every three up. When he reached the surface, he set Purity down and fell to the ground beside her, gasping for air. Purity stayed quiet. When he regained his breath, he sprang to his feet, lifted Purity to his shoulder and headed for the hollow tree to recover his weapons. Gathering these, he ran down to the pond. There, he again set Purity down and pulled off her veil, gown and slippers. He ripped off a strip of her petticoat, dipped it in the water and washed her face. This brought her fully back to her senses, and he saw in her eyes that the shock of the cave in had been replaced by fear of him. She began to scream.

Nevertheless, he threw her once more across his shoulder, leaving her wedding things by the pond. Hurriedly, he started off. He knew there wasn't much time. Rounding the pond, he plunged into the shallow stream and loped off to the east. It took all his will power to keep moving. After six miles, he slowed and stopped where an intermittent falls strewn with boulders and cobbles intersected the stream. Purity was exhausted, her screams reduced to involuntary heaves. He put her down and stretched her handcuffed wrist across a hard-edged outcrop of granite. With his free hand, he picked up a heavy rock and pounded on the iron links holding them together. Old and rusted, they quickly broke apart. Then he lifted Purity up.

She tried to shrink back, but he pulled her close and said softly, "Little sister, it was never meant to be. I am a fugitive. You'd have no happiness with me. I must say good-bye now."

She replied, "I'm going to die, surely die. I'll kill myself."

"No, Purity, go back. Your grandfather and Granny love and need you. Do as I say." He kissed her cheek and was off running south.

After half a mile, he heard the hounds, but judging their calls, knew they had not picked up his track. The stream had obliterated it, and it would take Purity a long time to get back without shoes. He thought, *They won't continue long for fear of giving themselves away. Then they'll say good riddance. But I'll sure miss Granny.*

Back where he left her, Purity sat by the stream, sobbing. She didn't move for an hour. Then, with a heart-rending sigh, she rose and slowly headed back upstream. Gradually her sobs subsided, and eventually the pond came into sight. She meant to recover her shoes and the gown and veil, remembering how much they meant to Granny. Suddenly, she stumbled and fell on what appeared to be a large pack. She sat up and saw a smaller pack, slightly open, next to it.

Curious, she thought. She opened the cover and saw some books, sheets of music, and what appeared to be handbills. She pulled a handbill from the pack. It was one of those one would see on a post, advertising a coming event. At the top, she read:

TOBIAS T. TUCKERMAN ~ IRONMONGER ~ TIN-SMITH ~ POET

TROUBADOUR EXTRAORDINAIRE and then in smaller letters—Songs of the Mountains, Songs of the Hills—Songs of the Rivers and Rills—Sweet songs, sing-a-longs Love ballads, too—Some are Ribald, Some are Rowdy.

"Well, I declare," Purity said under her breath. She dug further and pulled out a picture of a young man plucking a guitar.

"Why, he's cuter than a pup dog, and a poet, too."

Then she heard a faint whistling from the direction of the pond. She put the papers and the picture back in the pack, closed it carefully, and set it down. Stealthily, she crept forward. Through some reeds, she saw a young man sitting on the partially submerged rock scrubbing himself vigorously and whistling under the bright summer sun.

"Ooh," she murmured, stripping off her clothes. She pouffed her hair, pinched her cheeks, and nibbled at her lips. Slipping into the water, she dog paddled out so as not to muss her hair. She gained the back of the rock without him hearing her, then slipped her hands over his eyes.

"Guess who," she whispered, with a warm breath, into his ear. "I'm Purity, Purity Wyndotte. Hand me the soap so I can lather your back." He did and Purity began rubbing very gently. He shuddered and tried to look behind, but Purity moved so he could not see her.

"What's your name?" she asked, nibbling his ear-lobe.

"I'm Tobias—T. Tuckerman," he gasped as Purity pressed her warm breasts against his back and slipped her leg over his thigh. He groaned as she put her arms under his and began to soap his chest.

"What do you do?" she asked.

"I'm a troubadour and a–uh–mender of things," he stammered.

"You'll fit right in—if'n you can mend a pore girl's heart," Purity continued, twisting around to reach his mouth in a hot throaty kiss. "Are you married, Tobias T. Tuckerman?"

"No, no," he sputtered.

Out of the corner of her eye, Purity saw Preacher and Jethro coming over the rise toward the pond, carrying their long barrels.

"You will be soon," Purity said as she reached down to claim his manhood for her own.

CHAPTER 26

ESS AND GEE

She softened up when he handed her the hundred credit note and was downright deferential when he said he was from the Corporation. Although Hester had not been up to the Tower apartment in years, she volunteered to show Tuesday the way. When they got there, she croaked out, huffing and puffing, "Open up, open up."

There was no response, so she banged on the door, shouting, "Open up, Ess, open up Gee, you have an important visitor."

"Who is it? We see nobody, you old whore."

Hester cursed and spat. "You'll see this one, or it will go the worse for you. He's from the Corporation."

Tuesday heard heavy chains rattle, and the door cracked open. A hoarse voice asked, "What does he want?"

"Ask him yourself."

The door opened and Tuesday held up his Corporation ID. The man motioned him in and slammed the door on the old woman.

"I'm Ess, and he's Gee," he said, nodding to Gee. Both wore heavy bandages.

Tuesday asked, "How did you get so banged up?"

"In Texas, but it's none of your concern. Now state your business," "I have been commissioned by the Corporation to bring in the felon, Porch. I believe you know of his whereabouts. Was he through here?"

"Arrh," they growled, "that's our job. When we heal,

we'll go after him again. You stay out of it, you hear?"

"That was your job and you failed miserably, so co-operate with me. Should you not, the Corporation will be told. You know the price you would pay. Perhaps you'd like to meet the great cats close up."

Ess and Gee were immediately silenced. They looked at Tuesday with leaden eyes. "He was here," Ess said.

"Did you see him?" Tuesday asked.

Ess got up, went to the dimly lit back room and brought back a sodden bit of fur. "This was his. The hounds brought it."

Tuesday examined it and tore off a corner for later analysis.

Again he asked, "Did you see him?"

"We found a fresh-dug pit behind the barracks. It was his doing."

"Take me to it," Tuesday commanded.

"We can't leave. We're caretakers. We'll tell you where to go."

Ess described the location and how to find it. As Tuesday left, Gee moaned, "He's ours. You can't do this."

With his earth teller, Tuesday found the dug-up earth. He also found minuscule shreds of fur. His sweat teller revealed some of Porch's perspiration, confirming he'd been there. But what was of such value that the man traveled fifteen hundred miles, at great personal risk, to return to the Academy and dig it up? It was a mystery he could not fathom. He continued following the trail, which led south. He found the spot where the fugitive dropped the fur and ambushed the hounds. The trail then led to the south gate and broke. Tuesday searched along the perimeter fence. There was no sign at all. The trail was irredeemably lost, obliterated months later by scores of graduating candidates leaving the Academy. Their friends and families had trampled over all evidence of the man. Was the man that clever? Had he deliberately exposed himself and left by the south gate, knowing such evidence would be totally destroyed later?

But his own hunch had paid off. His van was there at the south gate, where he had instructed the Corporation to put it. It had been a long day, and he was glad night had fallen. At least he would have the van's comfort after so many months on the trail. He had begun dismantling his strider when he heard them coming. After he finished putting the machine away, he clicked on the van's headlights. There was a short delay before he picked up the black shapes in the beam. He waited until the nearest had begun its leap. He could see the blood lust in its eyes for a split second before he vaporized the beast with his laser pistol.

My God, they are huge, he said to himself. He thought of the felon standing up to them with a silent, crude weapon, most likely a sling. Then he blasted the second into nothingness.

By morning, Tuesday knew what to do. Though he'd lost the felon's trail, he now knew the man had come back to the Academy. He'd begin at the beginning, not with the felon's trail, but his foster father, Harry's. Harry had gone to west Texas from the East. Why? He must have had roots somewhere. Possibly his adopted son would seek refuge there. He also remembered the boy had been brought West from the East by his mother. Question? What was the connection? He would find out. When he did, he reckoned he would find the fugitive. What did he know about the old man? He was a legendary marksman with the antique long barrel—highly intelligent, evidently well educated—schooled the boy—maintained a celebrated library—fabled hoard of gold—hated women. Corporation records established when he bought the west Texas ranch. This gave him a starting point.

Tuesday drove the van down to the Corporation's Consolidated Computation Center in the Eastern Megapolis' Philadelphia suburb. Soon he had cyberspace saturated. Nothing turned up on Harry Noah. But Tuesday knew no information was in itself information. He called up inconsistencies. The great universities of Harvard and MIT each showed in past records one more student graduating in the year 2218 than their personnel departments had on class rolls. The same was true a year later at The Wharton School of Finance. In 2225, subtle blips in otherwise stable stock and commodity markets showed that someone who controlled an extensive portfolio sold out and bought gold. In the same time frame, a poor church in mid-Manhattan began an extensive expansion program, paid for with cash.

Tuesday paid a visit. Examination of parish marriage records showed a page missing for a certain day in June for three successive years. He put an advertisement in the *New York Times* offering a large sum to any woman married on one of those days to one Harry Noah. A woman named Dulcie identified Harry as a very wealthy but intolerant red-neck stockbroker whom she had married on the first date long ago. A woman named Druscilla identified Harry as a seedy ex-husband interested only in sex, and a woman named Dorcas came forward and identified Harry as a hillbilly former spouse who had needed extensive guidance in everything he did. All conceded he was a hick whom they should not have married but were induced to divorce for considerable sums of money.

It was coming together. An intelligent, well-educated man of backwoods origins had amassed a fortune on Wall Street, then tossed it all after three bad marriages and tried to isolate himself in west Texas. Next Tuesday surveyed social security numbers and found a number missing in a sequence assigned to births in a town called Bountiful in the Appalachian Mountains in 2196. But Bountiful did not appear in census records or on maps after 2239. Corporation records indicated extensive activity in that area preceding Bountiful's disappearance. There was something about a UFO, but Tuesday was denied access to Corporation files explicating whatever happened. Nevertheless, Tuesday packed up and headed for Webster Springs, West Virginia, in the heart of the Appalachians. He was dead certain he was tracking.

CHAPTER 27
CARACABANA

Porch was uneasy and could not account for it. Providence had been on his side so many times. He had escaped the unmentionable destiny the Corporation had scheduled for him. He'd recovered the locket and successfully found his roots. He'd been able to depart Bountiful a free man, able to continue his quest. He'd been hunted for so long that he'd developed a sixth sense that told him somebody very formidable was now on his trail. He traveled all the way to Harper's Ferry before he found a hacksaw at an ancient machine shop to cut the iron cuff from his wrist. Only laser cutting tools, unsuitable for his purpose, could be found elsewhere. He picked up the ancient Appalachian Trail below Harper's Ferry and was now almost to Georgia. The trail was little used these days. The masses of the Eastern Megapolis, immersed in creature comforts, shunned it as too primitive. They made their nature excursions to local Smell-It, Taste-It, Feel-It Hologram shows. Local folk never traveled far, fearing conscription into some distasteful government or Corporation program. They also feared the great bears, ferocious boars, man-eating cougars, and huge wolves rumored to prowl the Trail. Signs of these abounded, but Porch had not seen any.

The trail had returned to nature and to him was a very pleasant place. But the turn of events at Bountiful saddened him. He had grown as attached to Granny as he was to Harry. He knew she had supported the wedding plans because his only alternative would have been the noose. He intended to write her, apologize for the way things had turned out, and assure her that all was well with him. He did so that night.

The next morning, he went into the nearest town, exchanged one of his gold coins for credits, and went to the post office to dispatch his letter. He addressed it to Granny's general delivery box in Webster Springs, bought a larger envelope, put it in and sent it to Nogales' wife in Pecado. That way, it would get to Granny with the least chance of being traced. When he went to mail it, the post mistress looked at him intently. Then as he departed, he passed the usual rogue's gallery of most wanted.

Suddenly he felt fear, for in front of him was a picture of himself and below that a caption: ESCAPED FELON PORCH ~ EXTREMELY DANGEROUS ~ APPROACH WITH GREAT CARE ~ REWARD FOR APPREHENSION OR INFORMATION LEADING THERETO, ONE MILLION CREDITS. Smaller print below listed his crimes, both alleged and proven. The photo showed him in his Academy uniform, a fresh-shaven youth. He knew he no longer looked like that after the many tribulations he had endured. But below was a very accurate computer projection showing him bearded and dressed in furs. Again he was lucky, for he had discarded the furs long since in favor of Granny's homespuns, and was clean shaven. He looked like an itinerant laborer. The poster described him as carrying a bow, a sling and many knives. He was relieved that he had left the bow at town's edge under cover. His knives and sling were artfully concealed, the sling under his checkered shirt, the knives in cases at his boots. The last few lines described him as traveling alone, usually through the woods.

Well, forewarned was forearmed. He departed the post office nonchalantly, but once out of sight, made haste to depart the town. He left the Appalachian Trail and continued south by southeast, feeling a new urgency to reach his destination. By late afternoon, he'd reached low hilly country. The weather was gentle in these southern climes in late October. He reckoned he was about a week from the Georgia-Florida border.

Late that afternoon, as he approached a crossroads, he saw two men dressed much like himself. Now a master of stealth, he approached them along the wooded edge of the dirt road without being discovered. He halted and crouched low behind a rock wall about fifty feet away where he could observe and hear them. They had dropped heavy packs similar to his and were talking, laughing and joshing each other as though they had not a care in the world.

He thought back to the poster in the post office–travels alone, it said. He watched them aim and shoot pebbles at some bottles lining the rock wall across the road with rubber slingshots. Not very good, he thought, one hit for every five or so shots. He doubted they could hit anything moving. Three bottles remained on the wall. He took out his sling and in rapid succession, smashed each one. The two men looked around incredulously as he stepped into the open.

"Howdy," he said.

"Wow," said the red-haired, stocky man.

"Awright," shouted the scrawny, wiry one.

"Howdy yourself," the stocky man said, smiling. "I'm Hackstraw, and this here little feller's Bernouli."

"How'd you do that? You gotta teach us," Bernouli broke in.

"What's your name?" Hackstraw asked.

"Joe, Joe Smith," Porch answered.

"Aw, go on. Bet you runnin' from the law," Hackstraw laughed.

Porch looked at him really hard but said nothing. Bernouli broke in again. "No offense, mister. We're runnin', too. I'm a carny man from Atlanta, and the big 'un here was conscripted for the federal militia and ran away. He ain't nothin' but a redneck farm boy."

Hackstraw laughed again. "Yeah, carny man, you mean con man and loudmouth." Turning to Porch, he continued, "Fur a little feller he's got powerful lungs that match his mouth, which gets him in trouble all the time. But no how we gonna turn you in. Now teach us how to hit them bottles. We got a powerful urge to eat some rabbit. We got a shotgun but done run outta ammo."

"Where you headed?" Bernouli asked, but before Porch could answer, he pumped himself up and said, "We're gonna make our fortune, sign on a shuttle down at Spaceport Carib to moon base, jump ship and get on a space freighter, or even a liner, and get out to the colonies where them millionaire miners abide. Heard there's plenty of girls. Only takes a couple of years to get there. Heard they need populators. Me and Hackstraw are real studs. Joe Smith, you oughta hook up with us."

Hackstraw said, "Big mouth means Millenarians. He don't know the difference, but they're real peaceable people. Knew some down around Moultrie. Anyhow, you're invited. Be fun. Now teach us the whirligig."

"Maybe I will. I intend to sign on the right ship when I find her, but you got to be careful. I've heard some bad things about Spaceport Carib. I'll teach you the sling in due time, 'cause first we've got to get some good leather. Meanwhile, let's rustle up some grub. Let's see how good you fellows are at foraging. You want rabbit? I saw a couple of fat ones back at that meadow beyond the woods. I'll go get 'em. Let's see what you can do."

"You're on," Hackstraw said, motioning to Bernouli. "Come on, I see a coupla farms up ahead—Joe Smith, we'll meetcha back here."

Porch had six fat rabbits roasting on a spit by the time they got back. "Two a piece," he said, grinning.

Bernouli held up a pair of hens. "I liberated 'em," he boasted.

Hackstraw unloaded a sackful of fresh corn, potatoes, tomatoes and carrots, and then unshouldered a watermelon.

"We eat," he said gleefully. "Joe Smith, you're a good 'un."

After they had eaten, Porch and Hackstraw sat back, satisfied, thereupon Bernouli jumped up and yelled, "Surprise." He pulled a sack of coffee beans out of his shirt, carefully crushed some beans on a rock and added them to a can of water. He put the can on the coals.

Soon he filtered the brew through a cloth and poured them each a tin. They drank the coffee silently. Finally, Hackstraw said, "Time to turn in."

Bernouli whined, "Aw, let's go into town and get some girls."

Hackstraw said to Porch, "He's got a one-track mind in his pants. But he wouldn't know where to put it if he found one willin'." He laughed crudely at his own joke.

Porch replied, "We'd better get some sleep and be out of here early. We've been here long enough."

"Ha, I knew you was runnin'," Bernouli chimed in triumphantly.

Each found a place to sleep. Porch drew a knife from his boot, holding it close to his chest under his blanket. Neither of his companions noticed, and all were soon fast asleep.

At first light, they ate the remnants of the evening meal and used the remaining coffee beans for another hot brew, which fortified them against the morning damp. As they traveled, they acquired some harness leather. Porch fashioned slings and taught his companions the basic skill. Eventually they were passably adept at bringing down a squirrel, rabbit, or even a wild turkey. They continued south without incident to the outskirts of Orlando, where Bernouli's big mouth landed him in jail.

Porch bailed him out after securing enough credits at a pawnshop with several gold coins. Hurricanes and the great ocean rise of several centuries before had ravaged Florida. Even now the peninsula was much reduced in size. Salt water destroyed earlier citrus and truck farming and still persisted in many wells. Poverty was extensive in rural areas. But a city dweller working for the Corporation in Orlando or employed at the Corporation's Kennedy-Canaveral Spaceport wouldn't know this. Nor would he see any poverty at Miami, farther south. The Corporation had rebuilt the city completely, using piers, piles and dikes throughout. Gleaming ivory skyscrapers, massive apartment complexes and wide boulevards extended for miles along the old waterfront now protected by a mighty sea wall. The city was booming, not only from spaceport commerce, but also because thousands of Corporation pensioners chose to spend their declining years in its well-organized security.

Porch and his companions had to avoid all Corporation activity, and so threaded their way past Orlando, Kennedy-Canaveral and Miami. Commerce not controlled by the Corporation passed through a transit point out on the Keys. Life was easy there. Rules and regulations were circumscribed, and the police had a price. On Highway 1, south of Miami, they hitched a ride with a Jamaican driving an electrotruck carrying vegetables. The driver was happy-go-lucky and talkative. When he learned the trio's intent to sign on as space hands, he got nervous and looked worried. He told them never to sign on with a street solicitor, but to contract only through a legitimate third world consulate and always keep their wits about them.

"Heed my words," he kept repeating as he let them out of the truck at Transit Town, as locals called it.

Porch said, "Let's check the consulates out right now."

"Consulate Row" was nothing but a line of modest cottages that had seen better days. The Indonesians had an emigration liner about to depart on a ten-year voyage toward the Pleiades, which myth had as their ancient ancestral home. South Africa had a freighter called the *Long Trekker* headed for a planetary system discovered in 2102 which they were colonizing. The Confederation of Micronesia-Melanesia had a small exploratory ship destined to survey some fabled water worlds near the beautiful star Sirius. But as nothing was immediately scheduled for moon base, they decided to sign on the South African freighter, as the trip duration was less than five years. They had two days free before the shuttle went up.

As the Key was small, they did not have to travel far to find a secluded beach where they could rest up before departure. After a swim and a supper of fish and crab, they settled on some palm fronds for the night. Each felt excitement about the coming adventure but felt apprehensive about what lay ahead and melancholy about leaving their Earth home. A great tropical moon swelled the latter feeling as it slowly rose over the sea turning the waters from azure to violet and capping the gentle waves in shimmering glory.

Well into the night they saw some figures approaching across the sand. Alert now, they watched suspiciously. But suspicion turned to interest as three slender girls drew near. Their silky white flesh gleamed in the moonlight and their scanty bikinis might as well not have been there.

"Hi," said one, her voice a melody riding the breeze. "I'm Peaches. This is Pixie, and she's Pussycat."

Pixie said, "I'm sure."

Pussycat said, "You can call me Pussy for short."

Peaches continued, "We came for a stroll on the beach and we're looking for some fun."

"You look like three fine gentlemen to me," Pussycat purred.

Pixie pouted. "There's a cabaret up the beach with music, dancing and drinking, but it's no fun for three little girls all alone."

"You girls are sure pretty," Bernouli drooled. "I'm Bernouli. This here's Hacksaw, and the big fellow's Joe Smith."

"Uh, uh, uh," Hackstraw choked, his tongue caught in his throat.

Pussy knelt down close to him, pressing her body against his chest. "You're sure a mass of muscle, Hackstraw," she whispered in his ear as she ran her fingers through the hair on his chest. "I'll bet you could content a girl like me..." she paused, putting her lips to his ear "...again, and again, and again." Hackstraw was putty.

Bernouli grabbed Pixie's ankle, pulling her down to him. She did not resist, saying, "You're mighty strong for such a little feller."

Bernouli leered. "I'm big where I need to be, pretty girl."

"Oooh," emoted Pixie, falling on top of him.

Peaches, sensing resistance, approached Porch deferentially. "Joe Smith, you look more like Adonis to me," she said, sidling up to him. Porch backed away, but Peaches pretended not to notice. She said, "Take me to the cabaret, lover."

Porch said, "Go away." Peaches was not deterred.

"Come on, big boy. I'll bet you're ready for a tumble."

Porch replied, "The Mountain Bard said, "'Tis a real disgrace, without any grace/To engage in a rut, when love is not."

"What's that supposed to mean?"

Porch grinned and said, "It means that I'm a bust at lust."

"Well, EFF you," Peaches responded.

Porch winced. "What?"

"You heard me, and I'll not repeat myself, 'cause I'm a lady," she said, hands on hips, as she turned and waggled her fanny in his face. "Best you'd ever get." Then she tossed her tresses and said, "Come on, girls. Adonis here doesn't want to play."

Pussy and Pixie both rose, each tugging on her catch. Hackstraw and Bernouli followed the two girls up. Porch looked at them and said, "I've got a powerful uneasy feeling that you two had better stay here."

Hackstraw grinned helplessly. Bernouli gazed upward and said, "I got a fire under my belly that's gonna burn my britches. Gotta go."

With Peaches leading, the two couples followed, so tightly bound they stumbled down the sand. Porch shook his head as he watched them zigzag down the beach.

Not far away, hidden in stands of palmetto, the Mulatto watched intently, and then, silently, by another path, scurried toward the cabaret. The neon script, flashing harshly, left to right, red, then green, then blue, spelled out, "CARACABANA—OPEN ALL HOURS." It lit the circling sand, shrubs and oncoming revelers.

"Wow," said Hackstraw.

"Oh boy, oh boy, oh boy," said Bernouli.

The dilapidated building had withstood wind and water for many years sitting on heavy concrete piles. Its wide verandah protected salt-encrusted windows and the double half door entrance.

"Come on, come on," Peaches admonished.

"Hurry, hurry," Pussy giggled. Hackstraw bit her on the neck.

The inside was flooded with orange light. A pall of smoke hung in the air. Spacemen, sailors and whores were dancing to a Caribbean beat. In a far corner on a low stage, five musicians were tapping out a rhythm on large steel drums, and a singer was mouthing a song into a mike. "Nikra-man-cum, bete-da-big-stel-droom, ain't-notin'-but-di-boom." The crowd blashed out a refrain, "FOR-DI-TIN-TA-TAB-BOO-LA-TION-OF-DI-GREAT-STEL-DROOM."

Peaches led them down a long bar to a table suddenly cleared of riff-raff by a huge mulatto wearing a tank top and red tarboosh.

"Honki-man-cum, drink-da-bota-o-rum, ain't-notin'-but-di-boom."

"TO-DI-TIN-TA-TAB-BOO-LA-TION-OF-DI-GREAT-STEL-DROOM."

As the party sat down, he hurried over to the bar. He briefly spoke to the bartender, then disappeared through a rear door. Behind the door, a staircase led down to a musty candlelit cellar housing row upon row of ancient casks. Passing these, he pushed open another door and descended into a sub-basement of dripping walls and ceiling.

He whispered harshly, "Foog, Foog, where are you?"

"Here, master," came a hoarse reply.

"Prepare two syringes," the Mulatto commanded, proceeding past more casks to a dingy corner where a cadaverous figure sat amongst flasks, vials, pestles and mortars. A dim green light shone on him and large tanks of sea water full of puffer fish.

"I have them ready. I sensed you would be recruiting tonight," Foog, the chemist, replied.

"Imbecile, you do nothing without an order," the Mulatto whispered loudly. He picked up a wooden stave and beat Foog on his shoulders.

"Perhaps you'd like another voyage with Nonose."

"No, master, no," Foog wailed.

"Did you use the proper amount of tetrodotoxin? Too much and all I'll have is worthless corpses."

"Yes, yes, exactly right, depend on it." Foog shuddered.

"Is the datura ready?"

"Yes, master,"

Upstairs, Hackstraw and Bernouli sat down at the table with the three girls. The place was still jumping.

"Inja-man-cum, di-fida-to-strum, ain't-notin'-but-di-boom."

"TO-DA-TIN-TA-TAB-BOO-LA-TION-OF-DI-GREAT-STEL-DROOM."

Peaches shouted over the din, "What can I order for you boys?"

"Beer," they shouted back in unison.

Pussy looked at Hackstraw and sighed. "I thought a big he-man like you would have a big he-man drink."

"Beer's fine."

Peaches glanced at her sharply and said, "Maybe they just got to get warmed up." She signaled the bartender. "Two rounds of beer and three Swingin' Swizzies." The bartender brought the drinks.

Hackstraw and Bernouli each quaffed a beer in one long continuous swallow, thinking to impress the girls. Then Bernouli reached for the second, belched loudly and asked, "What are Swingin' Swizzies?"

Pixie lifted the shot glass of strong tea to her lips, tousled Bernouli's hair, and smiled. "They get a girl in the mood, lover."

Bernouli proceeded to chug-a-lug the second beer.

Peaches said, "I declare, girls, we're with some real drinkin' men. You boys ready for something to really warm your bellies?"

Bernouli slammed down his tankard, belched again and, wiping his mouth with his sleeve, allowed, "I need something stronger."

Peaches caught the Mulatto's eye and said, "Black Scorpion's the specialty of the house, a real spacefarer's drink."

"Beer's fine," Hackstraw said, draining his second beer.

"Ohhh," said Pussy, leaping on his lap, "you're hardly revved up yet, muscles." She pulled her bra off and thrust her breasts squarely into his face. "Don't you want these, big boy?"

Hackstraw gulped, "I'm as horny as a hoot owl, love."

Peaches signaled the bartender, holding up two fingers. When he looked over, she pulled them across her pretty white throat. He poured white powder into two tumblers and stirred in a concoction of rum and molasses. He took the drinks over to Peaches. "Down the hatch, boys," she said, handing each a drink. Pixie and Pussy started fondling their men, and each one downed his drink.

"These big he-men are ready for some fun, Pixie. Why don't you and Pussy take them in back and show them all your tricks?" Peaches suggested.

"Come on," the duo giggled as they pulled the men up and led them off. Unsteadily, Hackstraw and Bernouli followed the girls down a dark hall and through a green door into a room at the back. As Pixie closed the door, Hackstraw fell to the floor with a dull thud. Bernouli followed him down. Both men began twitching spasmodically.

Within a minute, Peaches entered with the Mulatto. Each had a hypodermic which they thrust into the stricken men's carotid artery.

Pixie sighed. "Seems you'd let us have some funning with 'em once in a while before you drag them off."

"Yes," Pussy lamented. "I would have liked it with that big one."

"Shut up, whore," the Mulatto said, "or I'll send you up to the Beehive to entertain Nonose and his crew."

The two girls cringed. An outer door opened, and four men hurried in with rolls of heavy cotton batting and two pine boxes. They quickly stripped the comatose bodies, wrapped them like mummies, dumped them into the boxes, and nailed the lids shut. Then they picked up the boxes and were out the door and into the night.

The Mulatto handed Peaches a roll of credits and said, "Well done, but Tukanon needs more, many, many more." Then he too left.

****

Porch awoke at the first glimmer of dawn. There was no sign of his companions. Squinting against the rising sun, he covered a full circle looking for them. Then he crept over to their paraphernalia. Their goods were all there. Thoughts of the past night's encounter flooded his brain. He suspected they had brought great trouble on themselves. He hurried into his clothes. Stupid, but he felt a loyalty and duty to find them. He concealed all their goods in a stand of palmetto and trotted off, following the footprints that meandered down the sand. Shortly, he came upon the path that led up to the Caracabana.

In the early light, the club appeared a weathered gray and seemed devoid of life, although the sign said it was open all hours. Perhaps there was a power outage. Then he saw a dim light far inside. He climbed the few steps up to the verandah, crossed quietly and peered through the double half doors into the darkened interior. He saw a figure sitting at a table at the end of the bar, illuminated by a hurricane lantern. He pushed through the doors and walked toward the figure.

Halfway down the bar, he recognized Peaches. As he approached her, she turned and said, "Well, Adonis, come to get some of what you thought you didn't think you'd want?"

"I've come for my friends. Where are they?"

"Fast asleep and far away," Peaches replied. Porch caught a glimpse of the three big men coming up fast from behind the bar. He dispatched the first with a mighty kick to the chin. The second, who'd encircled his neck with a huge arm, went over his shoulder, crashing heavily on the table in front of Peaches. His body knocked her over, broke the table in half and smashed the hurricane lamp, which threw kerosene all over. The fluid ignited, spreading flames quickly. Porch caught the last assailant with a vicious punch which broke the man's jaw.

Suddenly, fierce pain flashing behind his eyes brought total blackness. The Mulatto slowly fastened the blackjack back on his belt. Peaches picked herself up, and after wiping her face with a cloth, looked at the Mulatto and snarled, "Let me take care of this one myself. Help me pull him in back. I've got the hypo, there's plenty of roll, and I'll have him trussed before they arrive with the coffin."

"Hurry then," the Mulatto agreed. "These flames are spreading fast." They dragged Porch into the back room, and the Mulatto ran out the back door, shouting, "I'll jack the Haitians up. This whole place will be burning in a minute or so."

As Peaches stuck the hypo into Porch's neck and began to strip him, she saw the locket. Greedily, she broke the chain and wedged the locket into her bra, concealing it under a breast. She had Porch naked and wound with cloth up to his chest by the time the Mulatto returned with the men and the coffin. She finished wrapping the body, and they lifted it, dumped it into the coffin, and hurried out. The Mulatto and Peaches followed.

The Caracabana was a raging inferno.

CHAPTER 28

THE COVENANT

Tuesday sat quietly. He figured he had been there for at least two hours. He could see a light through the sack they'd placed over his head when they bound him up. He thought it was a lantern. He smelled coal dust, so he could be down in an abandoned mine. He was glad they had left him for a while. He figured they'd made him hop at least two miles before lowering him into this place. He'd not been as tired since he was a boy. These people were tough. No wonder the Corporation could not put them away all these years.

He'd come unarmed. Perhaps that's why they hadn't killed him outright. They'd taken his transponder, but that was all. He still had his ring with its three deadly laser bursts to five meters; and he still had his watch, worth five bursts of disabling gas to ten meters. Of course he couldn't use these weapons with his hands tightly bound behind his back.

His van and equipment were safe at Webster Springs, so he decided to just wait it out. He would answer questions honestly, seriously doubting he could fool them, since they'd survived so long against a foe as formidable as the Corporation and won most encounters. He smiled thinking about their bootlegging and hijacking successes that gave the Corporation fits.

He heard a rustling. They must be returning. They pulled the burlap sack from his head. Squinting against the brightness of the lantern, he could see three big, bearded men sitting opposite. The largest spoke. "I'm Jethro. Who are you and why did you come here?"

Tuesday replied, "I am Inspector Tuesday, Tuesday North Bear. I am looking for a man named Porch."

The slight movement of Jethro's eyes told Tuesday he had hit paydirt, but he did not react.

Jethro asked, "Why are you seeking this man? There is no one here who goes by that name."

"He is a wanted man, and I have a contract to bring him in."

The second man asked, "Contract with who?"

Tuesday replied, "A contract with the Corporation."

"With the Corporation—let's kill him now, throw him down the shaft," the third man hollered.

Just then another man came into the lantern light and took a seat. He was tall but slight and had snow-white hair. He said, "Hold on now, we may live like troglodytes but we're decent folk. We ain't gonna kill him lest it's justified. Now, mister, say your name again."

"Tuesday North Bear."

"That's an odd name for a Corporation man. How'd you come by it?"

Again the third man demanded, "Kill him now."

Tuesday said, "Hear me out. It will be worth your while."

"Shut up, Mungo. You been nothing but trouble since the cave in."

The white-haired man said to Tuesday, "I'm Preacher Wyndotte. Guess you met Jethro, Caleb and Mungo here. Now answer my question."

Tuesday told them that he was a Cheyenne, had been a police officer for many years, and only a year ago had contracted to bring the man Porch back to justice. He finished by saying, "I'm my own man. I don't belong to the Corporation."

Preacher told Caleb, "Go get the Algonquin woman."

As Caleb left, Jethro said, "We got no truck with the Corporation. They burnt us out long time ago, and been huntin' us ever since."

Shortly, Caleb returned with a woman dressed in buckskin. She was tall and willowy and rather handsome. She wore her hair straight down her back and had eyes as black as Tuesday's. He thought to himself that she was foreign to these people. She came up and stood before the table. Preacher rose and spoke some words to her softly in her ear. She looked at Tuesday and began speaking to him in an Algonquian language. It was close enough to Cheyenne so that he could answer. He also used the sign language of his people. She responded in sign. He answered all questions she asked. Finally she turned to Preacher and said, "The man speaks true." Then she left.

Preacher said, "That's good enough for me. Untie him."

Jethro slashed the ropes that bound him. Tuesday stood up and stretched, then shook his body out.

"Tell us again," Preacher said. "What you want?"

"I want to know about the man Porch. I know he came through here. Your manner has given you away. I want to know why he came here, how long he was here, why he left, and where he went. I'll pay well for all you can tell me,"

"What will you pay?" Jethro asked.

"One million credits,"

"We can't take the chance," Mungo interjected. "Kill him now."

Preacher gave Mungo a stern look, then said to Tuesday, "I have to think on what you've said. I'll take your word to be our guest tonight and be here when morning comes. Now it's dinner time. Come wash up and sup with us."

The mood at the communal table was somber, and Tuesday felt suspicion all around him. He caught a glimpse of the Algonquin woman and saw her eyes on him. He couldn't figure why. After dinner was over, Preacher took Tuesday to his own quarters and told him he was to stay there because hatred of the Corporation ran so deep that he could not trust his own authority to keep him safe.

At noon the following day, Preacher called Tuesday into conference with Jethro, Caleb and Mungo. He said, "We've thought on what you said to us. 'T'ain't gold nor credits we want. We want a covenant."

The four then were silent to let Tuesday absorb Preacher's words, words important to them, and to Tuesday as well, because they were set to kill him if he answered no. Tuesday responded, "A covenant? What kind of covenant?"

Jethro said, "A covenant with the Corporation that forever more the Corporation will leave us in peace, and that no Corporation men will ever again come upon our valley and harm our people, nothin' less. We want it signed by the Chairman, 'cause we've heard there's honor in his word."

"Done," said Tuesday, "but let me go above ground to transmit your terms to the headquarters. I'll charge them to draw up a compact signed by Belisarius and gain for you much more, because you've treated me justly. Now return my transponder to signal."

Preacher said, "OK, you can go now. I'll have a man take you. You better be escorted in these parts, partic'ly with night comin' on."

"I'll ask them to send the document to general delivery, Webster Springs. Send a man there. You'll have it tomorrow."

Tuesday knew his risk but figured the Chairman wanted Porch enough to meet the terms he would set forth. The following day in late afternoon, the man Preacher sent returned. He had the parchment in hand, signed by Belisarius. The Chairman had granted all Tuesday asked and more. The Corporation would restore Bountiful to what it had been before and leave the people alone from that day forward.

"There's two copies," Tuesday pointed out. "One goes back countersigned after you've told me all I need to know."

Preacher read the text and accepted. Then, true to his word, with Jethro, Caleb and Mungo chiming in, he told the story of the man Porch, whom they believed just happened upon them when he fell down the air vent. They told Tuesday the man was nothing to them, but that Granny had taken him in and patched him up.

Though it was difficult for Preacher, he told how

Purity had fallen under the man's spell, and how he'd jilted her, then headed south, so far as the child could tell. He told of Granny's strange affection for the man and suggested he not question her, as she might try to lead him astray—if she spoke to him at all. Tuesday had surmised most of this and carefully led Preacher to what he really wanted to know—what had happened twenty years before.

Preacher did not discern the Inspector's interest, but as he had the covenant, he was glad to detail the tragic story of Amilee and Jason, her child and the locket, for it underlay all their troubles. This he did, concluding it was then that the Corporation sent men to find out what had happened there, and failing that, had burned them out.

Tuesday interrupted, "A boy and, you said, a locket. Can you describe the locket?"

"It was magnificent. The man said he had made it himself, of gold and jade, diamonds and sapphires."

"What happened to the woman?" Tuesday inquired.

"We don't know," Preacher responded. But Tuesday knew. He meshed what Preacher related with that uncovered in Philadelphia and what was in Corporation files. He thought to himself, *I'm on the trail of an extraordinary man.*

Before the evening meal, Preacher called his people together and read the covenant as a proclamation. It astonished them. Jubilation took hold and the women went off to prepare a feast that would be remembered for years to come. Tables were piled high with mountain vittles, and Tuesday was surrounded by well-wishers. During the meal, he caught the Algonquin woman's eye. Then a spoon tapping a glass marked the meal's end and the start of the festivities. People moved to a makeshift stage, calling out, "Tobias, Tobias," and Tobias T. Tuckerman rose and carried a guitar up to the stage.

Tuesday saw the Algonquin woman move to the side of the stage and followed her there, seating himself beside her. She did not move away as he feared. Tobias bowed, and all cheered and clapped their hands. A young girl moved to the edge of the stage and took a chair there. She looked lovingly at Tobias and then proudly out over the audience. Tuesday took her for the girl, Purity, whose story he'd heard.

Tobias began strumming his guitar and sang a sweet, sad love song. Before its end, he had his audience in his hand. He was a master showman, and he went on with song after song.

In snatches of conversation with the Algonquin woman, he found out her father was Lakota, living in Western Canada, and her mother French Canadian. Her Indian name was Maria Many Coup. She met a mountain man running moonshine across the border. He carried her off, married her and brought her back to Bountiful. Subsequently, he was killed in a running battle with revenoors. She'd stayed on at the underground town, as she had no place else to go. They treated her as one of them, so she stayed. Tuesday liked her matter-of-fact recounting and stoic acceptance of what had happened in her life.

Tobias now had the people singing, stomping and clapping. Some began to dance. Moonshine was passed around. It was a happy time. Tuesday felt his own reserve melting. He really liked these people. He would be gone in the morning, back on the felon's trail, so tonight he would let his hair down. Maybe, after a while, he'd show them the dances of his people. He reached over and took the Algonquin woman's hand. She did not pull it away.

CHAPTER 29

SLAVERY

Far to the south, an ancient boat put out from a wharf in the Florida Keys. As it labored out of the small harbor, the harbor master shouted, "Where are you bound?"

"Tortuga," came the answer.

"And what do you carry?"

"Coffins, coffins full of the detritus of space and the flotsam of the seas. We carry corpses home to their final resting place."

Deep in the hold, Porch lay in a coffin, one of the living dead, his heart all but stopped, and his breath imperceptible. Such was the power of Fugu—tetrodotoxin. Datura, added to the potion, induced disorientation to keep him in a mental gloom, slipping between real and nether worlds. He felt the roll of the ship. He heard the lap of the waves, the creak of the mast, and the chug of the engine. Day after day, he lay in a mental swirl. A deep sleep came—the sleep of the living dead.

At last he woke, and perception came out of oblivion. He was inside the edge of a vast white amphitheater which he saw through a slit in the shroud that bound his body. The glare through the dust-laden air burnt his eyes and the dust seared his throat. His breath came in fiery gulps. All around him and miles away across the pit, he saw hundreds of men like himself, chained neck to neck, bodies touching, squatting, kneeling in tiers that spiraled down to the bottom of the pit. At the bottom, a shuttle sat on a launch ramp like a fat black beetle. Not far behind, another sat on a roller awaiting its turn, then another, and another after that.

Suddenly, the shuttle, magnetically propelled, rushed up the ramp at amazing speed. When it cleared the pit, rocket engines roared and propelled it out of sight. Then he heard a hundred screams. "Arriba, up, up."

His iron collar choked tight, pulling him up when the men in front rose and started forward. They marched in lockstep like a huge centipede to avoid the lashes of dark men in wide-brimmed hats who continued to shout, "Arriba, vamos, go, go."

Each, with a whip in his hand and cudgel on his belt, worked in a sweaty frenzy to bring his whip down on the back of a man who faltered or slipped. "Alto ahi. Stop, down, kneel. Aqui, aqui." Again and again the whips came down. Porch looked down seemingly endless lines circling to the bottom of the pit. A second shuttle loaded line after line of shrouded, collared men, all prodded into the ship. He heard a whispering voice behind him. "Joe Smith, we been shanghaied."

He recognized Hackstraw. Behind Hackstraw, another voice, in a screaming rage, yelled, "Those whores got us good with Mickey Finns."

It was Bernouli. Porch heard the whips come down, again and again, between Bernouli's defiant shrieks. Finally, there was quiet. Up, march, stop, kneel. All day they continued. Hosed down once an hour, the long millipede of men wound down the pit and into the rear of the shuttles. These blasted out of the pit and out of sight every thirty minutes. At last they reached the launch ramp and the rear of the hideous black beetle that was their shuttle.

"They are slavers," Hackstraw moaned.

"Slavers, slavers, save us, save us," Bernouli shrieked. Down came the whips and truncheons.

"No help from here to hell," an overseer yelled as he beat Bernouli. Finally, their turn came. The overseers released the neck collars. Several men were dead already. "Those are the lucky ones," the slavers observed as they kicked the bodies into a nearby trench.

Up and into the hull they crammed, packed on wire racks, layer onto layer. The shuttle cast off as engines blew a mighty blast. G forces crushed guts against spines. Eyeballs bled, nostrils spewed forth blood, and empty stomachs threw up a meager gall. When the rockets stopped and G forces died, blood and spittle floated free all around, adding a wretched burden to the hot fetid air. They floated in black nothingness until they felt a docking and a port above slid open. Tier upon tier, they were prodded up ladders. Overseers below again pulled out the dead or nearly dead and those too weak to make the flight. They opened a bottom air lock, cast the pitiful creatures in, sealed the airlock, opened an outside hatch and blew the bodies out. These exploded from internal pressure, disintegrating into clouds of frozen blood, flesh and bone.

The overseers herded survivors into an internal processor which quickly stripped their winding shrouds, then forced them into a chamber where steaming jets of ammonia-laden water hosed them down. In another chamber, blasts of air dried them off. Then they were issued and ordered to don ancient space suits, many times patched and repaired. Slowly the ship got underway, creating a false gravity, weak but sufficient for them to follow the command that came. "Up, march, up march."

Ordered to a long, wide table, each was issued a flagon of gruel, then commanded to unseal and eat, which they did, ravenously, as such was their hunger. All but one, as far across the table, Porch heard Bernouli yell, "Putrid slop," and the whips came down.

Overseers wearing black to distinguish them from the orange-clad slaves stood behind the table, one to each ten slaves. And what cruelties they did not know, they had been taught. "Cease eating, eyes down. The Great One comes," they screamed.

Porch looked up and got a heavy rubber hose across his shoulders. "Eyes down, eyes down. It is the Slave Master," the guard above him whispered in hushed tones.

But Porch had seen enough. A huge man of at least three hundred pounds had entered the compartment.

He wore lizardskin tights and steel boots. A wide yellow belt encircled his waist, and upon it hung a huge oak mace. Above his shirtless torso to his neck, he was covered with vile tattoos of horned beasts, pentagrams and other signs of evil. He had no hair on his head or body. He had no ears at the sides of his head, but holes instead. His nose and upper jaw were gone, replaced with two flaps of flesh that covered a purple orifice and moved like gates as he gasped from breath to breath.

When he got to the end of the table, he turned and harshly rasped, "I am Grubol, Lord Tukanon's Master of Slaves. Look once at me, then never again."

All looked and shuddered as Grubol continued, "Once I was the handsomest of men, darling of women. Now I'm hideous, as you see. The meanest wench would run and hide from me—would die of fright should I even approach. One time pushed into a rocket's radiation stream, no features have I left, nor even hair to hide my head. I live only to wreak revenge upon all those brought into my domain."

Grubol carried a strange implement in his right hand which he began to twirl like a baton. It looked like a sickle. As he twirled it, it made a sickening whistle and seemed to glisten. He continued, "So I live for terror, terror alone, and YOU LIVE to serve this ship, this ship alone. NOW, EYES DOWN. Look up again, and you will taste death. You live to serve the ship and YOU'LL DIE TO SERVE the ship." He strode forward and rasped loudly, "ALL CHANT."

The overseers, looking down, obediently began, "WE-LIVE-TO-SERVE-THE-SHIP. WE-LIVE-TO-SERVE-THE-SHIP." The slaves took it up, "WE- LIVE-TO-SERVE-THE-SHIP. WE-LIVE-TO-SERVE-THE-SHIP."

"Chant again," Grubol rasped, and the overseers shouted, "WE-DIE- TO-SERVE-THE-SHIP. WE-DIE-TO-SERVE-THE-SHIP." The slaves took it up till Grubol commanded quiet. He turned then and strode back up the table. Quietly he rasped, "I am an expert shaver, and you slaves have stubble on your necks such as I cannot grow. All close your eyes and hold your faces high as I come by so I can rectify such insult. Do not shiver nor quiver nor shake. DARE NOT FLINCH."

He came upon a man and stopped. Quickly and obediently, the man closed his eyes tightly and held his head up to bare his neck. Grubol scrapped it raw with an upward thrust of his blade. He continued down the table and stopped again. Another man felt the cutting edge. He turned and crossed to the other side and stopped in front of Bernouli. Bernouli continued to hold his head down and Grubol shouted, "Lift your neck to the blade, slave."

Bernouli yelled, "Go to hell."

With a quick slice, Grubol lopped off his head, then looked around and rasped, "An expert shaver and skillful slicer."

Two overseers moved fast to pick up Bernouli's severed head and body. They threw both in the nearest chute, shut it tight and pushed the ejection button. Grubol continued, "This is a sailing ship which rides the sun's own wind, the photon-proton stream. You'll learn to hoist our sails, shift them smartly when we come about, then take them down again. We're bound for Titan, off of Saturn, to pump the methane rivers and mine the precious hydrocarbon ice. Look smartly to your duties if you wish to last a trip or two."

Grubol turned again and began to stride up the table. Suddenly he stopped and swung his blade with such force that another man's head was severed, and crashed against a bulkhead behind them and split asunder. "I said, don't flinch."

He continued on and exited a far passage.

"All rise," a loudspeaker blared. "Move to assigned corridors." Whips came down on those who reacted too slowly or failed to understand the command. Porch's group moved into a narrow spaceway, halted and turned to face shelves full of numbered space helmets.

Loudspeakers blared again, "Don helmets, don helmets. Lock helmets, lock helmets." Latches clicked and hatches opened above them. Ladders dropped down as loudspeakers blared again, "Climb and enter your helmet-numbered station; feet first, quickly, quickly."

Porch climbed up to the vast array of hexagonal

compartments. He found the one that matched his numbered helmet and slid in. It was a tight fit, with only enough room to move arms and legs a foot in any direction. The entry port closed and locked behind him. He found it hard to breathe. *What now?* he thought. Again a loudspeaker. "Fit pack and tether. Fit pack and tether." He looked up and saw a pack on a fastening and a tether on a spindle. He clamped the pack to a fitting on his suit and fastened the tether to one on his belt. The loudspeaker commanded, "Pressure suits—pressure suits." He saw a toggle switch on the pack and pushed it. Immediately a rush of oxygen-enriched air rushed into the suit, inflating it. Lights brightened the cell and he saw a reflection pass the window above his head. An overseer checked him through the closed port. The lights dimmed and then went out. "Sleep, sleep," a concealed speaker commanded, and a gas was added to the oxygen.

All slaves slept as the ship tremulously accelerated out of orbit, then cut its rocket engine. At an indeterminable later time, the speaker screeched and blasted Porch awake. "Lesson, lesson."

An ancient video monitor above him came on and began to show pictures of the ship's exterior. The speaker described each in turn, and the lessons progressed to the mast assemblies of the great solar sails. It taught the slaves the tasking sequence for unfurling these. The lessons went on repeatedly until duties were drummed into the dullest of heads. Each time boredom stole a slave's attention, a fierce electric shock jolted him back to the screen.

The ship was a solar sailer which sailed the solar wind between the planets. When shiny new, computers controlled the electric motors, servos and hydraulics that raised, spread, shifted and lowered gossamer sails extending out from masts one hundred times her length. One hundred years ago, she was queen of the airless oceans, the pride of North America. She ruled the void for fifty years until old age crept upon her. Her computers died, her motors quit, her servos shorted, and her hydraulics fouled, and she was ordered back to Earth to be dismantled and sold as scrap. But those who bought her were deceitful men, and smuggling hydro-carbons from Titan and the moons of Jupiter to a nearly depleted Earth brought rich rewards. They patched her up so men could work her sails and she could ride the photon breeze once more.

But soon enough, manual manipulation of her sails grew to suicidal risk, and only the meanest of men would sign to undertake such tasks. Murderers, brutes and cutthroats made up the crew. Then cunning masters found ways to indenture crews to endless years of servitude. Indenture became slavery when death became so certain that each new voyage required new crews.

Once a day as the lessons continued, the slaves were unloaded from their cells and made to strip and exercise like mice in rotating cages for a full hour to keep them fit. Overseers sprayed those who faltered with ice water until they continued or died. The slaves then stood muster, were hosed down in ammonia-laced hot water, led to the table and fed the same gruel they'd been fed on arrival. Grubol strode the table and kicked away the flagons of those who failed to chant, "WE LIVE TO SERVE THE SHIP—WE DIE TO SERVE THE SHIP." He severed at least one head at each meal and a replacement slave was forced up from a hold beneath.

One day, screens went blank and speakers silent. Sirens sounded throughout the ship. Amber lights lit each cell. With a great swoosh, the slaves were blown from the ship through fast-opening ports at the exit end of their cells. They swarmed into the void until tethers pulled tight and they found themselves on the beam or mast their speaker had described and screen dia-grammed. Upon command, each did as taught in his lesson. They pulled levers, worked ratchets, wound winches and windlasses, and drew taut cables and ropes, working furiously until the great gossamer sails were raised and spread. These felt the photon stream and billowed out, unfurling mile after mile in ghostly splendor. Lines stretched tight and pulled on beams and masts, and the great ship yielded to their urging. Gradu-ally it accelerated and gathered speed along the course set.

Exhausted slaves were reeled in and exits closed. Those slaves who failed to measure up had their lines released, and they drifted off into the void. Frozen grimaces marked their death throes as oxygen ran out and deep space cold sucked out all warmth. Their work was passed to others who then did double duty.

But always after muster, hatches opened and additional slaves prodded up from holds below replaced those eradicated. Month after month, the deadly sameness continued: SLEEP, LESSON, OUT OF CELL, STRIP, EXERCISE, HOSE DOWN, MUSTER, EAT, SUIT ON, ENTER CELL, SLEEP. Respite came when the ship entered the Asteroid Belt beyond Mars, and soon the slaves were praying to return to the routine they'd come to loathe. It seemed that they were vented out a thousand times to furl or unfurl the sails, to tack and then tack back, and to avoid those deadly lumps of stony matter whizzing by that could tear the vast array of flimsy gauze into fuzz and blast the masts and beams into smithereens and dust.

At last the Belt was broached. Porch had lost his nearest neighbors to the void, each harshly torn from his tether. This haunted him until the words "Tie the tether, tie the tether" came back.

He thought of Gideon, supposedly a survivor of the slavery he now endured. Gideon had saved him once, now maybe twice. He looked to his belt and saw the quick release and its control. One side would go and the other then sustaining so much force would tear the space suit open. Quickly he snapped it open and looped the tether firmly about his belt so that it would catch if release was ever signaled.

CHAPTER 30
THE NEW CARACABANA

Tuesday surveyed the burnt-out and rotting ruins. His fire reader indicated the conflagration occurred about three months before. He sifted through the wreckage to establish layout and smelled the nitrogenous odor of decaying flesh. His flesh finder led him to the west side of the ruin, where he saw numerous flies and beetles flying in and out of a small opening. He returned to his van and put on coveralls, a headpiece and boots—all impervious to gaseous and liquid poisons.

Then he went back to the opening, cast aside pieces of charred wood, and pulled some concrete block out of the way. He found steps leading underground. He slipped down these, probing with his flashlight. About a foot of water covered the bottom along a hall. Sloshing forward, he came to door. It was half burnt and yielded to a mighty push, breaking in two. Some two feet of mud had held it shut. He passed through into a storage room full of leaking casks on racks. Proceeding forward, he came to another small room. His flesh finder buzzed and flashed. A number of jars and flasks, stoppers and tubing lay around, half buried in mud. Broken glass panels had fallen from rectangular frames. He determined that these had been fish tanks, as the smell of rotting fish was pervasive when he tested the air through his mask. Probing the mud, he found large quantities of dead fish. *Pufferfish*, he thought to himself.

His foot hit something semi-solid and he scraped

away the mud, uncovering a ghastly white bloated body. The eyes had been eaten away. He nudged the corpse with his foot and the rib cage collapsed, revealing thousands of wriggling maggots. Tuesday thought he'd seen it all, but revulsion caused him to back away as nausea gripped him. He fought for control, and when he'd regained it, he took out his poison teller and dipped up specimens from the debris. The analyzer focused on tetrodotoxin, the dreaded bane of zombies. Searching further, he found a cache of hypodermics. He put several of these in his pack and returned to the surface.

Back at his van, he removed his protective clothing and burned it. He put on the garb of a drifter, concealed a laser pistol and stun gun in his boots, closed the van, hoisted his pack and proceeded down the shell road to the outskirts of the island town.

Shortly, he came upon the glittering NEW CARACABANA, built on a high cement slab, with steel encased windows and hurricane doors. It had a tile roof and was painted a garish pink. Its marquee flashed against the early evening twilight. "ALL-NEW-OPEN-ALL-NITE-GIRLS-GIRLS-GIRLS." Tuesday entered. Early yet, the place was half empty. Several sodden men were at the bar, and there were musicians on the stage tuning large steel drums. A girl in a bikini sat alone at a table at the far end of the hall.

Tuesday approached and said, "Good evening, miss? May I sit."

"Certainly, stranger, as you look like a fine gentleman to me, ready for some companionship and fun. I'm Peaches, and I hate to drink alone. Maybe you'd buy me one."

"Surely, little miss. You order," Tuesday said, smiling.

Peaches lifted her hand and signaled the barkeep. "Two, Olie, a Swingin' Swizzie and a Black Scorpion." She turned to Tuesday and, smiling sweetly, asked, "Come far?"

"Ah, yes," Tuesday replied. "I'm looking for a man called Porch. Have you seen or heard of such a man?"

Peaches pondered a bit and then said, "No, I don't

recollect such a man, but such a number come through here."

Strange, Tuesday thought to himself, *she seems to be telling the truth*. He decided to press further.

"He's a big blond fellow, quite young and, I'm told, a very handsome man. He is a fugitive from the law," Tuesday said, looking at the locket that dazzled between Peach's breasts.

Peaches fidgeted. "Why, there was such a man, but he called himself Joe Smith. He left here about three months ago."

She's still telling the truth, Tuesday thought, *but not all of it*. Olie the bartender brought the drinks over. Tuesday kept looking at the locket, then said, "That's a mighty beautiful pendant you're wearing, little miss."

Peaches became visibly nervous and her eyes grew big. She pursed her lips to a circle and said, "Ohh, I just remembered, I know a man who had direct dealings with Joe Smith."

"Can you take me to him?...right now?"

"Yes, just follow me." Peaches got up and motioned Tuesday to follow her out of the bar and down a corridor to a back room closed by a green door. She said, "He has his office in there. Go ahead through the door. I'll follow."

Tuesday opened the door, ducked the blackjack, and pulled and fired his stun gun. Supersonic carborane particles hit the Mulatto in the chest and stung like a million nettles, knocking him down and out. Tuesday turned, grabbed Peaches by the wrist in an iron grip, slammed the door shut and, seeing the bolt, locked it. As Peaches began to scream, he grabbed her mouth, crushed it shut, and pulled her wrist behind her and up. Spying rolls of heavy gauze, he pulled her down and hog-tied her, then gagged her mouth. Turning his attention to the Mulatto, he did the same with a double amount of binding. Then he pulled both bodies over to the wall and propped them up facing him. He pulled over a stool, sat down, and waited for the Mulatto to come around. Coming out of his daze, the huge man began to struggle.

Tuesday grabbed the man by his throat and put a hole through his nose with his laser ring, saying, "Continue to move or call out and I'll put a hole between your eyes." He pulled the gag down and commanded, "Tell me of the man called Joe Smith."

The Mulatto snarled and tightened his jaw.

"Very well," Tuesday said, reaching into the kit at his waist. He withdrew a mini-recorder, set it on the stool, and turned it on. He reached into his kit again and pulled out two hypodermics. He held one up in front of the Mulatto and tested a little squirt with his thumb and two fingers. "Fugu," he said, pushing the needle into the man's biceps.

The Mulatto gasped, "Stop, stop, I'll tell."

Peaches was sobbing not far away. Tuesday turned to her and said kindly, "Quiet, little miss, or I'll burn your ears off with my laser. Your turn will come." For the next hour, Tuesday asked and they told. Peaches and her cohorts enticed the men, the Mulatto shanghaied them and sold them to a world wide net of slavers. Thousands of men had been ensnared, doomed to serve and then die in the void.

When Tuesday had it all recorded, he rose, took the locket from Peaches' neck and went outside. He signaled the Corporation, using coded ultraburst to transmit his data. Then he transmitted the whereabouts of his prisoners to the FBI, state and local police. Corporation Special Police and FBI helicopters came in almost simultaneously. They handed men caught running from the nightclub over to local authorities when these arrived by squad car.

Observing this, Tuesday headed for his van. He drove south to the port and arranged for a Corporation freighter to transport it to Port of Spain, Trinidad. Then he called in a Corporation chopper to take him and his strider to Amazonas.

****

At Corporation HQ, Tuesday's report was immediately passed to the Chairman. After considering it, Belisarius changed the subject, asking, "How is he? "

The Lawyer responded, "Since we brought him back, he seems to have deteriorated. He only stares blankly at the ceiling above his bed. We fear it may be the incubation period of another HIV mutation. He may have contracted it from one of the attendants at the sanitarium."

"Has he spoken?" the Chairman asked.

"It's mostly gibberish. He wants his dogs, but as you know, that man Tuesday destroyed them."

"Good riddance. Pull Cevello from his regular duties and put him full time on finding a cure. Tell him to assemble the best medical team available. Do not spare the expense. I owe that much to Francesca."

"Yes, sir," the Lawyer said as he left.

CHAPTER 31
BONNIE BRIGHTWOOD

Late in the previous September, Bonnie skipped down the majestic front steps of the Palazzo and entered a waiting limousine. She was as giddy as a schoolgirl on her first date. The Admiral was coming for his first visit since she had been on duty at the HQ. She had not seen him since leaving Los Angeles.

Though she missed fleet duty, she accepted her new position as fleet representative to the Corporation Board of Directors as good for her country, the Fleet and the Corporation. She had worked hard and set up the best staff possible. Things were running smoothly. After her initial run-in with the Chairman, she felt that she had gained his respect.

The Board of Directors was indeed formidable, with experts in many fields: finance, economics, engineering, industry, agriculture, genetics, medicine. Their accomplishments seemed endless. She took refuge in the Admiral's reputation. They looked upon him as a real captain of industry for his superb handling of the Mars Project. Before being reassigned, he had finished phase one both below cost and on schedule.

Thoughts raced through Bonnie's mind as the limousine drove to the heliport. She had deliberately chosen the hour's drive out rather than ten minutes by chopper, as she wanted time alone with him before he got caught up in Corporation activities. Ostensibly, she was to brief him on current business, but she was in love with him and wanted a chance to discern his feelings toward her.

Thoughts of a personal nature crowded all others from her mind as the limousine stopped at the helipad. She wondered how she looked. The driver came around to open the door for her. It was a bit breezy and she had to grab the suggestion of a cap she was wearing as she got out. She had chosen the cap carefully, as it lent a military air to her outfit but did not impede the flow of her beautiful auburn hair. The Chairman wanted to downplay the Corporation's close ties to the military, so it was customary to wear civilian clothes at the HQ. Therefore, Bonnie wore a somewhat severe yet shapely indigo suit. It was one of the "power suits" she wore to board meetings. Yet she carefully expressed her femininity with a lacy blouse.

As she stood there, she wondered again how she looked. She did not notice the forklift operator behind her, who, unable to take his eyes off her, ran into a wall, spilling a load of produce all over the tarmac. Nor did she notice the man's supervisor run over, cursing. A sudden gust of wind blew her skirt up, revealing an alluring thigh. The supervisor promptly ran into the same wall, knocking himself out. She demurely pushed her skirt down just as the chopper arrived.

Her heart began pounding fiercely as she stretched her neck to glimpse the Admiral. He bounded down the steps as soon as they were lowered. *What a striking figure*, she thought. Even in his dark gray civilian suit, he was of such commanding presence that one would not mistake him for other than a military man. As he drew closer, she noted his rugged features and graying temples. She thought she would melt. He looked very fit except for a the slight limp from the sword thrust he had taken long ago.

"Lovely lady, I've missed you in the lonely hours, yes, and even in the heaviest fighting, my thoughts turned back to you." He took her in his arms, very gently, and hugged her. But all she got was a peck on the cheek in this very public place. Then he pushed back to look at her, and she saw in his eyes the deep feeling and desire he had for her. He'd answered her question, so in great joy she relaxed and squelched the sigh that came to her throat.

She turned and motioned the limousine forward. Had they been in uniform, she would have opened the door for him; but in civilian attire, he quite naturally reached over and opened the door for her. The driver came around and closed it. When he was again behind the wheel, she directed him to take them to Corporation Headquarters.

As the turbomotor revved up, the limousine took off smoothly. Enveloped in the aura of each other, they hardly noticed they were moving. He took her hand in his and squeezed it gently. Then, looking at her, he asked, "What's up?"

Knowing this was his signal to get back to business, she replied, "I have an agenda. There is a Board meeting, pro forma, mostly with reports on world-wide Corporation activities, financial, industrial, scientific, new initiatives and the like.

"But I have good information that the Chairman will have a present for you, of which he is very proud. The Corporation just completed operational tests on a new class of space cruiser, the Space Griffin. The Western Alliance has contracted for six at six billion credits apiece. The United States government will buy two for your flotilla. It's a hot number, which purportedly can reach point-nine michelson in just under an hour, full thrusters, of course."

"Good," Petersen replied. "We need them badly. It's difficult to make timely intercepts at all the locations the space pirates attack. We intercepted and destroyed several privateers near Neptune, but our scout ships found others massing on the main emigrant spaceways. They boarded and took a Voyager class liner before we could get there, then rerouted it as a prize to the planet Czinn, a wild and lawless place far from the new colonies. The emigrants that lived through the attack face a life of slavery. No doubt the women have already been horribly debauched."

Bonnie was shocked, "Let me rejoin the Fleet," she pleaded.

"I need you more here. You know that," the Admiral said simply, patting her hand. Bonnie sighed but continued her briefing. In a minute, they wound up the wide avenue that led to the grand piazza with all its architectural marvel.

"Imposing," the Admiral said.

"I think the Chairman is making a statement," Bonnie replied.

"Certainly of power and splendor," the Admiral mused, smiling.

The chauffeur stopped in front of the wide staircase leading to the main entrance. He hopped out, ran around, and opened the door for them. They went up the grand staircase, into the building, and up to the meeting, which then started promptly.

The Chairman greeted the Admiral personally and seated him to his right. All eyes were on him as the Chairman introduced him. Bonnie discreetly took a chair immediately behind him, and most then stole a glance at her, unable to resist her beauty. The Chairman called the meeting to order, and it went as Bonnie had outlined.

Petersen was highly excited about the new space cruisers. Two were assigned immediately by the Admiralty, the ship's complement completely trained. One would be the new flotilla flagship, should that be the Admiral's desire. The US President was a history buff, and she had directed the Admiralty to select a list of names from US Naval History. She chose to christen one the *USS Constitution*, and the other the *USS Hornet*. The Chairman broke into the briefing and said, "We doubled the effort to get these new warships on line ASAP, hoping you can make short work of those space vermin. I want the President to be in a position to release you for work here."

"What is their armament?" the Admiral asked.

The Lawyer, seated on the Chairman's left, spoke up.

"The best and newest double proton-antiproton beamers front and aft, high density photon torpedoes from four tubes, electron-positron streamers all around, and electro-gatling minislug penetrators fore, aft and amidships. These latter fire the steel-clad depleted uranium slugs at ten thousand a minute—sustained. Each cruiser can launch ten boarder craft."

"Formidable indeed," the Admiral stated.

As the meeting adjourned, the Chairman turned to Petersen and said, "You will be my guest for dinner tonight with Commander Brightwood. It is being held in your honor. I am very much looking forward to it."

"Of course," Admiral Petersen replied, "I, too, am looking forward to it." The dinner that night was spectacular. Petersen had an opportunity to meet and talk to most of his colleagues on the Board. All had been invited with senior staff. He was quite impressed with their wisdom and knowledge of the world around them. Conversation was titillating, confined to the arts, science, literature, even history and philosophy–anything but business. A string quartet provided background music before the company was seated. The dinner was formal, and the Chairman had asked the Admiral to make an exception to policy and wear his mess uniform with decorations, as he wanted to show him off. Before dinner, Petersen presented a diamond and emerald necklace of the highest quality to Bonnie. It was elegant and very sophisticated. She accepted it graciously, but wondered how he could afford it on military pay. She asked him laughingly if he had ransomed his soul to buy it. He said he had not but would do so gladly for her.

She chose an off-the-shoulder emerald green gown to show it off and set her hair in a high French twist held in place with a diamond clip. She looked ravishingly beautiful. They sat together at the Chairman's table with Belisarius and the Lawyer.

Fine crystal and exquisite china accompanied heavy sterling flatware emblazoned with red-gold inlays of the griffin rampant. Red roses decorated each table but the Chairman's. His centerpiece displayed the fabled black rose. Liveried footmen brought in tray after tray of sumptuous hors d'oeuvres. Main course choices included seafood crepes, roast baron of beef, rack of lamb, or baked ham in brandy sauce. There were salads without bound. Corporation vineyards offered fine California, French and German wines. Though the Chairman set a lavish table for his guests, he ate and drank but little, confining himself to a glass of Chianti, an antipasto followed by pasta, and at meal's end a dollop of spumoni with his coffee. They kept their conversation very light.

As the banquet ended and the Chairman rose to leave, he asked the Admiral to come to his office in the morning for private conversation on several closely held matters. He looked at Bonnie and said, "Bring the young lady. She also must know."

It was still early, so Bonnie took the Admiral's hand and asked him to accompany her into the garden for some fresh night air. She led him to a beautiful rose garden with a magnificent old apple tree in the center. She told him the garden was sacred to the Chairman, as his beloved Francesca was buried there. They strolled along silently, enjoying dimly lit paths accented by the last roses of autumn, the fragrance of which was all around. They reached the far end of the path and the Admiral stopped. He looked at Bonnie and took her in his arms. She came to him willingly. Encouraged, he looked into her eyes and stammered, "Bonnie, my darling, I feel like an ancient mariner and old spaceman with better days behind me as I say this to one so young and lovely, but I cannot help myself. I love you."

Bonnie replied, taking his rugged face in her hands, "Oh, my darling, I love you as well, and want nothing more than to be yours, completely and forever. I want you desperately."

He kissed her tenderly, again and again, and she returned each kiss with all the passion pent up within her.

The following morning, the Lawyer was waiting in the Chairman's anteroom and quickly ushered them into his office. Belisarius was sitting behind his huge desk in the commodious chair that seemed to swallow him up. When he heard them enter, he rose and invited them to join him around a coffee table. Besides the three of them, only the Lawyer was present. The Lawyer poured coffee as they exchanged pleasantries.

After a minute or so, the Chairman said, "I'll get right to the point. Corporation intelligence has confirmed that the space pirates your flotilla is operating against are paid and supplied covertly by the Central Asian Autonomy. It has become clear that the tyrant Marshal Tukanon has ordered this to divert the Western Alliance Fleet away from his real objective. I shall get to that shortly.

I have apprised our President of this. Although the CIA agrees with our assessment, she is cool to the evidence we've picked up. She doesn't believe Tukanon would dare go up against the Western Alliance and tends to believe his assertions of peace and brotherly love. She points out that ninety percent of the US defense budget is devoted to the Fleet, and says that she has full confidence in your ability to liquidate the pirates with the assets you have. We do, too, but there are other factors to consider.

"Within the Alliance, only the Corporation has maintained a strong HUMINT capability. We have a mole inside Tukanon's headquarters, and reports from him indicate Tukanon is preparing a first strike against the Alliance, specifically against the Corporation. Why?

"For two reasons: one, Tukanon believes that if he can destroy Corporation power, he can cripple the rest of the Alliance easily and then sue for peace on his own terms. The second reason is even more harrowing and has agonizing implications. Our agents have picked up evidence that somewhere in Israel a machine has been developed that circumvents the space time barrier; that is, the speed of light. We are told the prototype has already transported items—instantly, from one place to another. My best physicists say with sufficient power, the device has unlimited range. Should this prove true, it is not difficult to imagine its impact on the entire future of mankind. We cannot wait. The Western Alliance must have it.

Tukanon has tripled his Near East agents. If he acquires the apparatus first, civilization itself is in grave jeopardy. We have so informed the President. But her scientific adviser scoffs at the whole notion. To him,

'Nothing can exceed the speed of light.' He has so advised the President. With this advice, and because she is politically committed to keeping the spaceways open, clearing out the pirates remains her first objective. She would not release you, Admiral Petersen, to head an effort to secure the machine. Thus we've redoubled efforts to get the new space cruisers to you so you can finish your campaign quickly and be released to assist us."

Petersen responded, "I appreciate your dilemma and will finish the campaign as soon as possible. In the meantime, give your full confidence to Commander Brightwood. She has mine. By our contract, my seat on your Board has purview over all operational military matters. Therefore, refer them to her. She will act in my stead and keep me fully informed."

The Chairman sat bolt upright, for he was not used to being told what to do. He gazed intently at the Admiral and finally said, "Very well. I am sure she will soon be tested."

He rose then, signifying the end of the meeting. As he returned to his desk, he looked back and said as an afterthought, "Eventually Tukanon must be destroyed, quietly, without fuss. We can't afford to arouse the Orientals or Eastern Bloc. The balance of power is tenuous enough. Good day."

The Lawyer escorted Bonnie and the Admiral out of the suite.

The following morning Bonnie accompanied the Admiral to the heliport. When he was about to board the chopper, she could no longer hold her sadness. A tear flowed down her cheek. Petersen saw it and chucked her under the chin. "There, there," he said, "I'll be back before you know it."

Bonnie replied, "I'm so sorry, Sven. I'd hoped to do better, but I love you so much, I want to be with you all the time."

"Dearest lady," Petersen stammered, "it won't be long, I promise you. I'll be back as soon as the campaign is over, and when I return, there is a question I want to ask you." He turned then and hurried up the ladder into the chopper.

Bonnie's heart pounded as she thought of what she wanted to hear. As the helicopter lifted, banked and flew off, she whispered her thoughts to him, though she knew he could not hear. "Oh, my darling, I love you and want you so much, I intend to be yours no matter what."

CHAPTER 32

TUKANON

One thousand feet below the wind-swept steppe, Tukanon sat in his private viewing room pumping up his hatred for anything Western. He was viewing the latest tri-di snuff film from the LA underworld.

"Appalling," he muttered to his aide. "Those young girls were not enemies of the state. Run it again."

His aide pushed the rewind, then started it over. Tukanon began gasping. His eyes narrowed and he leaned forward as the snuff scene came into view. "Murderers," he exclaimed as the knife came down. "Run it again, only the snuff scene—in slow motion." He licked his lips. "Filthy capitalists—make money any way they can. Once more," he snarled, "quickly, or we'll be late for the council. Are they assembled yet?"

"Yes, Supreme Marshal."

Tukanon savored those words, quietly rolling them around on his tongue. Then he had the thought that after the final victory, he would add the title of Great Khan. Of course, it would remind his people of ancient glories. His thoughts interfered with the tri-di.

Well, he'd had enough for the afternoon, and he'd kept his generals waiting long enough. By now, they would be ready for his grand entrance. He stood up, a signal for his aide to stop the projectors and turn the lights on. This done, he snapped his fingers and his aide rushed forth with the Marshal's cape, brown gray with a blood red lining. The aide adjusted it to turn at the shoulders and display the lining. When Tukanon was satisfied with its drape, he marched out with his aide on his heels. He went down the barren hall toward his conference room. He liked its severity. It showed his singleness of purpose. Its cold steel chairs and table complemented hard concrete walls. The entire headquarters complex was deep below ground. Its great depth protected him, and justifiably so, for he knew he was the only true national asset his people had.

Before he'd seized power, they had nothing and were without purpose. Now they had a national purpose and a mighty war machine to fulfill it. The underground complex created a sense that the nation was on a continual war footing. He himself had not been above ground for ten years. All his troops and war machines were also underground, secure from attack.

As they approached the conference room, the aide rushed forward, flung open the double steel doors, entered, and came to rigid attention. He called out loudly with the flourish he'd practiced so many times, "Gentlemen, Grand Marshal Tukanon, Defender of the Nation."

Chairs scraped back. The generals rose as one, clicked the heels of their boots, brought right fists to their chests and came to rigid attention, eyes frozen front. Tukanon stomped in, went to his black leather cushioned chair, the only one in the room, threw his cape over its back in a practiced sweep, folded his arms, and looked suspiciously down the line of conferees. When he'd finished gazing at each one, he said," Be seated," sitting down himself.

"Mark the time now," he continued. "This conference initiates Operation Griffinslayer. You have six months for final preparations. Thereafter we attack at my command, put an end to the abominable Corporation, and set forth on our own road to glory. Now, in turn, report your status, Operations first."

"Maximum leader, we have completed trajectory calculations. Three hundred rocket assault platoons have trained to ninety percent. One hundred heavy stormer companies are at ninety-five percent proficiency. Fifty mop-up battalions and thirty occupation and police brigades are ready."

"Targeting," Tukanon growled.

The Staff Targeteer rose, cleared his throat, looked around and said, "We have targeted his twenty-five mirved treaty missiles with 252 megaton clandestine warheads for ninety-eight percent destruction at ninety-nine percent confidence. Our second wave will destroy twenty major command, control and communication nodes; two hundred industrial plants; and one hundred railheads, trucking hubs and shipyards. A follow-up bio attack will broadcast plant and animal pathogens over his agro-research stations and farms, depleting food supplies until we have consolidated our conquest."

The Targeteer paused and then, with a disparaging look at the computer specialists, said, "We must use too many assets against his treaty missiles, as our inferior computers cannot give us smaller CPE's."

The computer specialists gasped.

"Science!"

Science nervously exclaimed, "Supreme Sir, we have a problem. Solving magnetic and gravitational anomalies along chosen trajectories requires total capacity. Our computers cannot also solve real-time weather. We need the enemy's new ultracomputer chip."

The Marshal turned to the Chief of Covert Operations. "Obtain one within three months. Should you fail, I will replace you and declare you an obstructionist. The lives of you and your family will then be short. Send Tang. He is our best agent. Tell him to secure the ultrachip, or he will return to us a paraplegic."

"Logistics," Tukanon barked out.

"Glorious Father of our Nation, our twenty-five mirved treaty missiles have been counted down to T-minus one minute and put back on hold at T-minus one hour. All clandestine rockets are assembled. UN inspection teams do not suspect they exist. Rocket resupply is in place and depots are at eighty percent fill. We are on schedule."

"Intelligence!"

"Glorious Commander of All the Legions, our White House operative has charmed the American President,

Inez Garcia Lopez, into faith in peaceful coexistence. She has committed ninety-five percent of US military assets to the Western Alliance Space Fleet, which we have successfully diverted to a campaign against the space pirates. She has only half-trained militia available for defense. We are confident of complete capitulation shortly after our initial assault."

The Marshal was pleased and continued rapidly through Personnel, Propaganda and Psywar. He then turned back to the Chief of Covert Operations and asked, "Have you the details yet on that device being developed by the old Jew in Israel?"

Trembling, the CCO answered, "Not yet, Mighty Leader, but we have two agents now working as security guards at his facility."

Science interrupted, "Gracious Patron, we have determined that material, in small amounts, is being transported instantaneously from his test facility to a station in the Kalahari Desert."

The CCO was noticeably angered by the rude interruption of Science and broke back in. "Maximum Leader, we know that several facility guards are Corporation agents. We will terminate them."

"No!" Science exclaimed. "We must lie low until testing is further along. Terminations would alert the Israelis and the Corporation. You would ruin everything with heavy handedness now."

"Agreed," Tukanon snorted, glaring at the CCO. "That would be the dumbest thing we could do. Wait and see. No heavy stuff yet."

Thoroughly cowed, the CCO meekly said, "Yes, Mighty Marshal."

Tukanon turned to Internal Security and nodded his head.

"Savior of the Nation," the General charged with Home Front Security said nervously, "we have a small problem. Mothers of the nine and ten-year-olds called up for military training complain their children are too young for the arduous schedules imposed."

"What!" the Grand Marshal said incredulously.

In a quaking voice, Home Front repeated his charge.

With a sinister smile, Tukanon directed, "Publicly arrest twenty percent of those complaining and declare them enemies of the people. Allocate the younger ones to the junior officers and senior NCO's. When they have been used up, terminate them. As for the older ones, those now barren or soon to be, deposit them on an arctic ice floe. That will stop such unpatriotic whining."

"Yes, Munificent Marshal, immediately."

The conference continued through the night. At last, rising, Tukanon said, "That is all."

Again, his generals rose in unison, snapped to attention, and saluted with their fists. The aide draped the Marshal's cloak about his shoulders and followed him out. Down the hall, Tukanon said to his aide, "Targeteer showed no deference and was too confident. He may be an enemy of the state. Have him watched night and day, and if the slightest impropriety is discovered, I want him publicly tried."

As they reached the Marshal's austere quarters, he complained, "My brain is burning. While I prepare for sleep, mix me a sedative."

"It shall be done, Great Leader."

The aide went into the bath and mixed a double bromide, which he brought out to the Marshal. Tukanon downed it, flopped onto his bed, and fell into a deep sleep. The aide left strict instructions with the quarters guards that no one was to disturb the Great Leader.

Not much later, far above, a feeble sun rose in the East. Its meager light shadowed the few clumps of brush that dotted the arid, frigid land, and a dust-laden wind howled the birth of a new day. A shadowy figure moved silently from shadow to shadow and stopped at a deep hollow sheltered from the wind.

It was the Marshal's aide. He slid into the hollow and opened a small umbrella-like antenna which he pointed north, ten degrees off the vertical. He attached a transponder and flipped a switch. Within two milliseconds, a soliton burst transmitted a coded record of the past night's proceedings to a satellite high above which reflected the signal to the American Midwest.

An hour later, operators in the Corporation's war

room sent a condensed version to the Chairman. Four hours later, the Corporation transferred twelve million credits to the aide's mother's account in Hong Kong. Six hours later, his mother transferred nine million credits to the aide's wife in the Bahamas. She sent six million to her sister in Zurich with strict instructions to deposit the money into a secret numbered account. Her sister, who was also the aide's mistress, converted the money to a draft and flew to Buenos Aires.

CHAPTER 33

WAR PLANS

The Chairman was livid. He had personally visited the President with evidence of Tukanon's first strike plans, and she dismissed them out of hand. Her science adviser scoffed at the possibility of the Israeli device transmitting matter. Inez Garcia Lopez was cordial enough. She promised full cooperation for whatever additional defense the Corporation wished to construct, but no funding. She still refused to release Admiral Petersen.

Belisarius determined to go it alone. After returning to the Palazzo, he observed to the Lawyer, "I have the feeling that many in government would like to see the Corporation take a hit."

The Lawyer responded, "I get the same sense. Someone very close to the President has turned things around, convincing her Tukanon's preparations are a ruse induced by the pirates to take pressure off them. The science adviser is simply being pigheaded about the Israeli device."

"The President is surrounded by ideologues—impossible to tear away from cherished beliefs even with hard contrary evidence. Their rationales border on the metaphysical if they are hard pressed. Well, we must get on with it. Has Commander Brightwood been apprised of these events?"

"Yes, sir. She says her military staff is working up some plans."

"I never thought it would come to this. Tell her she

has all the assets of the Corporation at her disposal. And...oh, that other young woman, the sparkling one we met in Los Angeles, Olive, yes, Olivia O. Olive, bring her on board. There was a certain synergism between the two. Call the President for a transfer. She owes us that much. Oh, yes, and see that Olive is promoted a grade. In a few days, I want to see both. We haven't much time, six months and fifteen days, if Tukanon sticks to his schedule."

"Yes, sir," The Lawyer said, leaving the Chairman's office. Early in the morning two days later, Bonnie was in her office having her wake-up tea and toast. She was reviewing the videodisk of Tukanon's meeting and writing notes to herself about enemy capabilities and vulnerabilities. There came a knock on the door. She clicked the video off, put her notes in her desk and said, "Come in."

"Hello, boss. I've been told we're in a real pickle."

"Olivia," Bonnie exclaimed, rushing over to greet her long-time friend, "what are you doing here?"

"I was hoping you'd tell me," Olivia said, smiling. "I was on a reconnaissance in orbit around Mars with a group from the project office, when I got a message that at the request of the President, and effective immediately, I was reassigned to Corporation HQ."

Bonnie held her back and said, "And just look at you, all trim and slim in a lieutenant commander's uniform."

Olivia laughed and somewhat shyly said, "Yes, they told me the promotion was effective with the transfer, but best of all, I knew I would be working with you again."

Bonnie said, "Well, you'll get a new wardrobe, courtesy of the Corporation. Policy here calls for civilian clothes—just like old times on the project, huh?" Bonnie read Olivia into the great danger the Corporation faced. Then they went to work.

The following day, the Chairman called them to his office. "Ah, Commander Brightwood, so good of you to come, and Commander Olive, so good to see you again. Please be seated."

When they were seated, he looked at each in turn

and said, "I'll be frank. I was so impressed with your work in quelling those riots in Los Angeles last year, I asked that you be reassigned here for liaison duty. The present danger is such that I also asked for Admiral Petersen's immediate reassignment, but the President denied my request. You are both relatively inexperienced, and therefore may feel overwhelmed with the responsibility I am going to place on you. If you feel unsure of yourselves, I will understand. I can bring in any number of outside military experts to handle our defense."

Belisarius stopped, waiting for a response.

Bonnie replied carefully, "I see no present need for that, sir."

"Very well," the Chairman continued. "I want Petersen to sign off on whatever you propose. Now I'll repeat, you have all the resources of the Corporation at your disposal, and President Garcia Lopez has committed all US ground forces to our operational control if we need them. I foresee a plan, call it Griffin Counterstrike for want of another term, that relies on stealth and cunning rather than brute force. Brute force would disrupt the world-wide balance of power, releasing ancient hatreds and possibly unleashing a conflagration that could not be controlled by all the powers on Earth. Find a plan that calls forth an assassin to come in the night with a feather pillow to smother his enemy rather than a cudgel to bludgeon him, one who prefers the stiletto to the meat ax. The fate of this world may rest on our success."

Quiet descended on the room. Then Belisarius continued, "Thanks to our mole's love of money, we have real time surveillance within Tukanon's Headquarters with a direct link into our war room. This must not be mentioned again until we have struck and destroyed the monster. Good day, ladies."

Bonnie and Olivia worked meticulously over the next two weeks putting a preliminary plan in order. Using ultraburst codex, they flashed it to the fleet for Petersen's review. He signed off on it, and the two commanders briefed the Chairman, who gave it his unqualified approval. Orders were sent out. Military personnel, engineers and scientists converged on the Headquarters. Task I teams hardened facilities wherever they could against an enemy first strike. Archives comprising the Corporate institutional memory were transferred to safe havens. Task II teams considered the US Treaty Missile Counterstrike force dug in on the northwestern plains big fat flat targets. They selected new positions in the Rocky Mountains and the Sierra Nevadas in defilade to incoming warhead trajectories. Mining engineers bored new silos into steep mountainsides at varying heights. The added verticality increased enemy CPE's so much that statisticians computed that the enemy required thousands more missiles to destroy them than he had available.

Task III proceeded smoothly. Corporation shipyards fabricated huge bladders, and submarines towed strings of these to Gibraltar. They were filled there with the high density, high salinity Mediterranean waters that flowed forth in a huge cataract from that strait. The bladders were then towed underwater north to the Denmark strait and the Iceland-Faroe passage. Oceanographers selected anchorages there for them that would incrementally change ocean currents and alter high Arctic weather patterns. The teams then concealed high altitude drones in Greenland ice caves for cloud seeding.

Task IV encompassed highly classified computer operations.

Civil defense measures made up Task V. Corporation employees practiced evacuation procedures for implementation on warning of impending attack. All other Corporation activities continued normally to give enemy agents an impression of business as usual. Bonnie and Olive attended the usual staff conferences and Board meetings at Corporation Headquarters. When the quarterly Board of Directors meeting convened on first of December, Olivia came in late and took her seat behind Bonnie.

The Chairman looked at her in surprise and became visibly angry when he saw that she was in uniform. Such breach in standing policy amazed other Board members. One could hear a pin drop. Controlling himself, Belisarius said quietly, "Commander Olive, you know my policy against wearing uniforms at the Headquarters."

Olivia interrupted him, saying, "Mister Chairman, I worked five hard years at the Academy to earn this uniform, and I intend to wear it. I did not ask for assignment here, but was jerked from a job I'd settled into and summarily told to report here in two days."

Belisarius yelled, "Get that woman out of here!"

Two burly men came forward and ushered Olivia from the meeting. Belisarius turned to the Lawyer beside him and said coldly, "See that she is reduced in rank as soon as possible." He turned to Bonnie and said, "Commander Brightwood, report to my office immediately after this meeting. I want a full explanation of such conduct."

Bonnie gulped, "Yes, sir. I'm sorry, sir. I promise you this will never happen again."

Order restored, the Board meeting proceeded as scheduled. Rumors of Olivia's defiance of the Chairman spread like wildfire. Things got worse. Olivia continued to appear in uniform on Corporation grounds. Coworkers saw she was highly disgruntled and apathetic toward her duties. She was seen several times in New Chicago in the company of a dance instructor and contract male escort, a high lifer named Tang. While on leave, she lost heavily at the gaming tables of Las Vegas and Tahoe.

Shortly thereafter, the government of Japan returned several tightly controlled, highly classified nanotechnology computer chips to the United States. They had been found on the Tokyo gray market and confiscated. Another turned up in Buenos Aires and another in New Delhi. Certain software programs used in the newly developed ultracomputer disappeared. Nevertheless, preparations for Griffin Counterstrike continued, and the days hurried by toward Tukanon's showdown, scheduled for May first.

CHAPTER 34
WOLF MAN

"How is he?" the Chairman asked.

"The doctors say the growths continue—in the muscles and bone structure, particularly the jaw, becoming heavy, forcing the teeth forward and out—and hair, always growing, black as night. They also report they hear, even under heavy sedation, heavy-chested gurgling and scarcely audible deep-throated growls. They say it's the virus, spreading, always spreading. Outside guards complain of late-night howling—followed by unearthly silence. A guard said it sounded like a soul in deep distress.

"This morning, the doctors reported a trail of blood from the window to his bed. The guards found two sheep, their throats ripped out and unspeakably mutilated when they checked the grounds. But he was sleeping peacefully. They gave him a sedative and the latest experimental antiviral shots. Even under heavy sedation, his eyes opened, and though he didn't move, he muttered as they were leaving, 'I want my dogs. I need them soon.' Then he was quiet again. We've muffled his suite and put heavy bars on the windows and steel plates on the doors."

"My God," Belisarius said as he slumped in his chair. "Call Cevello to come up immediately."

"Yes, sir," Cevello said as he entered the Chairman's suite.

"Have you nothing in your chemistry, your genetic

biology to cure or at least arrest this disease?"

"It takes time and testing, sir. We've pored through the literature. This virus or retrovirus, whatever it turns out to be, is particularly insidious. It doesn't kill or so weaken its host that he dies—that would be suicidal to itself. Rather, it transforms the host environment to best serve its own needs for replication. We are seeing some manifestations of hydrophobia, not so much that our patient will not drink, but he resists water to the point of dehydration and then drinks in huge quantities. As he does, he seems to be in terrible torment. There is a description of a phenomenon from an ancient text similar to what we are observing. It is a condition called lycanthropia. Someone afflicted thinks himself a wolf. In ancient folklore there are stories of men who have become wolf-like or werewolves, but there are no present day cases of patients suffering from such a condition. Therefore, we tend to disbelieve that such a malady is real."

The Chairman listened carefully and then observed, "What you have done is not enough, nor can we afford to have him break out of confinement again. Cevello, move him to the cell in your laboratory, the one you use for your mind experiments; recondition it and keep him there, locked up night and day until you find a cure."

"Yes, sir," Doctor Cevello said as he left.

The Chairman pushed open the window behind his desk, muttering, "My God, how that man reeks of garlic."

CHAPTER 35

THE STRIKE

Half a world away, the wind stopped howling above the desolate plain. It began to snow; not much at first, for only little was expected over that parched land. But the snow continued, gently falling in increasing amounts, wetter, thicker and faster.

Five thousand miles west, the gulf stream, now less impeded by arctic countercurrents, flowed north, bringing with it heavy moisture-laden air in clouds that blew east, ready to freeze and drop a load of crystals on what lay below. Hummingbird-sized drones, unseen at the altitudes they flew, crossed the high cold clouds. They induced the clouds to drop snow upon Tukanon's death-dealing silos with a dusting of microscopic crystals. It snowed and snowed and snowed, two feet deep, then ten, then twenty, and still more.

Deep beneath that desert, Tukanon was irritated. He had not yet been able to review the tri-di's just flown in from Paris. The previews promised slave girls and branding irons. He scowled as he thought of burning flesh and screams of pain, muttering, "Disgraceful. Those girls could not possibly be enemies of the state—dirty, decadent West." These angry thoughts further fueled his hatred of the West. He worked with maniacal energy to ready his attack, checking every detail and driving his subordinates to load his first wave of rocket troops and follow-on air assault armies. He brought his missiles to T-five minutes. He'd captured what he needed from the ultracomputer, the high capacity nano-chips and the software to work them on his obsolescent machines.

That man Tang would get a high award. He'd smoothly seduced the black woman to play turncoat and provide them. Of course they'd found the viruses lurking within the software. Did the Corporation take them for such dolts? They found them easily, sophisticated as they were. For once, Tukanon was rather proud of his Science staff.

As for the treaty missiles, so what if the US moved them to sites he could not hit? In a counterstrike, what would they hit? Empty silos? Towns and villages? His surgical strike would hit so fast, he'd certainly have time to persuade Garcia Lopez that his quarrel was with the Corporation alone—fait accompli. Surely she would believe him and stay her hand. He would remind her a counterstrike would most certainly unleash the other power blocs in indeterminate ways. His aide entered the office.

"Yes," Tukanon said without looking up.

"Home Front wants an audience, Great Marshal."

"Well, bring him in."

Home Front entered and said, "Savior of this Nation, we have a small problem." Though Tukanon glowered at him, he continued, "The noncombatants left above ground report snow so heavy they cannot get to food and fuel supplies, or feed their animals in the barns."

"Complaints again, on the eve of this great enterprise. We have thirty days to final victory. Western surveillance satellites operate overhead continuously. The complainers can survive that long or die. We must not give our plans away. We must appear to be a peaceful country simply trying to survive the winter. Cut off all contact with those above. They are only old men, women and children. Put out the order 'FINAL COUNTDOWN-OPERATION GRIFFIN STRIKE-THIRTY DAYS: RADIO AND RADAR SILENCE UNTIL T-FIVE MINUTES: NO SURFACE ACTIVITY OF ANY KIND: SIGNED, TUKANON, MARSHAL.'"

So Tukanon crossed his Rubicon. And it snowed and snowed and snowed; slowly, thickly, no wind, no sound, a solid falling fog. All sensors reported the impending attack at Corporation Headquarters. Doomsday came, sirens began wailing at 7 a.m., ELINT's launch time. The twenty- minute time of flight was counted down.

But nothing happened. The sun rose on a bright shiny Midwestern day. And as it rose, the world-wide seismographic net began picking up a thundering series of quakes lasting thirty seconds, reverberating around the earth's circumference and through its core; measuring eight-point-nine on the Richter scale at source; violent explosions, all deep underground, muffled by an overburden of sixty feet of snow. The Central Asian Autonomy was no more.

The snow stopped, not to fall again with such intensity. Armies of the Eastern Bloc moved east. Armies of the Asian Association moved north. By gentleman's agreement, the Armies stopped along ancient borders. Order was restored. In six years, when the frozen overburden finally melted, survey teams would find radiation levels precluding excavation for hundreds of years to come. The surface was breached in one place only. Evidence of Tukanon's elaborate fortress was never found, but in that place remnants of an ancient wall were thrown up and life-size stone figures of ancient soldiers were found.

Archaeologists were further elated to find seven copper tablets sealed in a stone sepulcher with the bones of an ancient nobleman or king. These were taken to scholars at the Beijing Museum in the Forbidden City for intensive study.

****

"Yes, sir," Bonnie said to the Chairman as they were concluding the after action debriefing. "You might find a parallel between the snow overburden that sealed Tukanon's silos to a huge feather pillow. And you could equate the poisoned microchips and software to a stiletto from cyberspace. Allow me to ask Olivia to detail that part of the operation, as it was part of her task."

"With your help in establishing the deception, sir," Olivia began, "Tang became a most unwary accomplice. The first batch of microchips I acquired for him were authentic. He was clever. He placed some of these on the gray market so others as well as his own people would test them. Unfortunately or fortunately, depending on one's point of view, our own agents were too good at recovering them, hence the reports that they had been found in Tokyo and those other cities. The second batch that I acquired for him were subtly altered by our people. We doctored the molecular substrate with molecules that crystallize and short out on signal. Let me explain.

"We were pretty sure that Tukanon's computer experts would find and eliminate the viruses we put in the software codes, so we put a carrier frequency on one of these, the easiest to find. That frequency was the same as the background radiation of the universe. We guessed that they would see this, believe it nothing unusual, and eliminate it with the viruses. But its elimination triggered the doped molecules to become unstable, crystallize and finally, short the warhead firing trains. The shorts were irreversible and would detonate the warheads soon after fuse activation began. You might say we went one step beyond computer viruses and employed a computer cancer."

****

The Chairman said, "I wanted to catch you both before you went off on your leave and well- deserved rest. I've told you of the great esteem I have for both of you, so what I say is not precipitous. I have been thinking about it ever since Tukanon's demise.

"Commander Brightwood, I want you to accept a position within the Corporation as vice president for Operations and with a separate seat on the Board of Directors. The challenge such a position offers would be much greater than you could expect to find in the Fleet for many years to come. Your compensation would be commensurate with the position, many times what the Fleet can offer. I do not need to mention the additional prestige that position would bring you. Don't feel pressed to answer now, but think about it and tell me when you have returned from your vacation. Of course you would have to leave the service.

"Commander Olive, I want you to continue with the Corporation, initially as Ms. Brightwood's deputy. Further advancement in the Corporation would be highly probable. I would have your answer, too, when you return."

Bonnie was dumbfounded for a minute and hesitated to reply. But Olivia said immediately, "I beg your pardon sir, I would like to continue in this assignment as long as the Fleet permits, but I cannot leave the Service."

She then hesitated, but with a twinkle in her eye, continued, "During my fourth year at the Academy I met a young man who needed constant supervision. He will graduate next June and join the Fleet. I must be in position to catch up with him then, for I intend to make his continued supervision my life's work."

The Chairman smiled and said, "Very well. I understand and agree that matters of the heart take precedence over all else."

Bonnie smiled and said, "I wish my decision was as easy, but I must have time to think. The offer right now overwhelms me, sir."

"Very well," Belisarius said, and Bonnie and Olive rose to leave.

****

Now, Bonnie was ambitious, so when she left the Service and took the position with the Corporation, many said her ambition drove her decision. But the calculation that finally swayed her came from her heart. She knew that in the conservative halls of the Admiralty, eyebrows would raise and necks stiffen should the Admiral reach so far beneath his station into the lower ranks of the Fleet to take a bride—or mistress, if he must—and she was prepared for that. She suspected such would damage his career irreparably.

CHAPTER 36

TUESDAY

He'd circled the great Amazon Basin on his strider, moving at top speed in ever-decreasing circles for the past five months. He'd crossed vast splotches of searing caliche plain remaining from the destruction of the magnificent rain forest three hundred years ago. He'd camped beneath acacia trees on the dried hardpan where new jungle was beginning to take hold.

But Tuesday had to be sure. His sweat finder emitted its baleful buzz everywhere. But at last his sweat reader called out the fugitive's perspiration signature. He'd traversed a thousand paths to find it. The paths converged on a hub like spokes on a wheel. Now the hub stood before him as a vast island escarpment rising out of the jungle three thousand feet before it hid its top in the clouds.

A picture of inexpressible horror formed in his mind. Close examination revealed the trail was marked with bones and skulls resting in the half-buried shrouds of thousands who'd died on the march. No corpses remained, as Caracawas and armies of ants consumed all tissue in the first hour after the men fell, dead or nearly so. When he found the trail circling up the cliffs to the clouds above, he set his strider on climb. He reached the top a day later and found himself above the clouds and back into the blinding equatorial sun. A few hours later he reached the lip of a vast open pit.

He dismounted the strider and placed the sweat

reader close to the ground. Again it read out the sweat signature of his quarry. As he knelt there, he surveyed the entire scene. The pit was empty, but he saw through the acrid haze how the tiers wound around down to the bottom. Far below, he saw the rails and the scorched, scoured furrows that told of the rocket blasts. His teller continued to buzz the sorrow of the thousands of men who had walked that trail. Lost in his thoughts, he barely heard them coming up from behind, but his laser pistols were fast and spit six times, a fitting punctuation to the stop he'd reached. Behind him six men lay dead clutching the machetes they'd meant to wield. He rose, took out his transceiver, and notified the Corporation of the overwhelming crime he'd found. Others could complete the destruction of Tukanon's slave net.

He put the transceiver away, took out the locket he'd taken from the girl at the Caracabana, opened it, and read the words "to seek out and find the Birthplace of Wonder." Looking skyward, away from the blazing sun, Tuesday pondered whether such a grand and noble quest had been snuffed out. A deep melancholia settled upon him.

****

"How is he?" The Chairman asked.

"Physically, there is no deterioration whatsoever," The Lawyer answered. "In fact, he's more robust than ever. It's one of the strangest phenomena ever observed in the annals of medicine. I hate to say it to you, sir, but he no longer appears human. All his wounds have disappeared. His arm is no longer withered. He has become extremely muscular. His body is covered with black matted hair. His jaw has extended and become snoutlike. His teeth have grown sharp and pointed. His guards must chain him down, night and day. I daresay he could tear three or four apart if he ever got loose."

"Chain him down! I gave no such authorization."

"There was no other way, sir. He's become extremely cunning. If he had the least chance, he'd free himself, and we'd find throats torn out all over the estate. It's as if the virus colonies that infect him have a collective mind and control him totally."

"Has Cevello made any progress at all?" "He has identified the virus genus and calls it HIV 215. It is of the family that ravished the earth several hundred years ago."

"I thought that virus had been wiped out."

"The early one had, sir, but this is another mutation, one that does not cause host death, as it would only destroy itself. Rather, it transforms the host to best facilitate its own survival and replication. Nature still outwits man given enough time."

"We must defeat this thing. Keep him chained down and lock Cevello up with him. This will insure the 'good doctor' does his utmost to find a cure."

"Yes, sir."

CHAPTER 37

DEAD MEN TELL NO TALES

Admiral Petersen was in staff conference with the flotilla commanders when the message came in. He was quickly summoned. "ADMIRAL PETERSEN TO THE BRIDGE. ADMIRAL PETERSEN TO THE BRIDGE."

He adjourned the meeting, and hurried to the bridge. The Signaler handed him the message as he entered. After he read it, the Captain said, "Sir, we are in search mode now."

"Very good, Jim," Petersen responded.

"The Admiralty believes the ship is astride the Asteroid Belt, Quadrant II, Sector three, Earth vector 343 degrees."

"Captain," the watch interrupted, "we had it clear. It appears to have traversed the belt heading on a Saturn vector. Not clear now. Too much interference, probably the asteroids."

The Captain peered at the screen, then commanded, "Narrow search sector, beam on last reading and magnify." He looked again, straining against the increased clutter. "There, there," he said with some excitement, "it comes and goes. Check each echo three-di, vector course plot, scrub out all ordinary gravity orbit."

The ship's computers hummed. "At last," the Captain exclaimed, "the damned rocks are screened out. Range about one hundred million miles. Take a look, sir."

Admiral Petersen peered into the display. "I see

something, and if it is what I think it is, we may have what we want. Check register file back to 2150."

The Duty Yeoman voice-input the computer. "Check register file. Year 2150 to present. All manned space inserts. Orbits, Earth to Neptune. Solar plane first, then galactic plane plus and minus one million miles."

Computers hummed. The printer quietly began spitting a readout. The Admiral and Captain pored over the emerging listing.

"There," cried the Captain, "it could be that one, but I can't imagine she's anything but space debris by now."

"Secure history and construction specs," the Admiral instructed. "Then let's try an omniband burst of radar, but keep it microshort in case they're monitoring."

"Aye, sir," the Captain replied. The Yeoman called in the instruction and almost immediately a readout printed: "SOLAR SAILER: COMMISSIONED 2158: *USS LINCOLN*: DECOMMISSIONED, 2206 AND SOLD TO AFRICAN CONSORTIUM: SOLD TO SCRAP 2235: NO SALVAGE RECORD: BELIEVED OPERATING ILLICIT: CODE NAME BEEHIVE."

"We've had many rumors," the Admiral muttered, "that she's still in orbit, though good only for salvage, a beautiful ship in her time. Ironic if what I fear is true, that the old *USS Lincoln* is now being run as a slaver."

"We've got a fit, ninety-three percent," the Captain cried, "but the sails extend out to incredible length and breadth in the readout, and our echoes show nothing of such nature."

The Admiral smiled. "Jim, you're forgetting that even one hundred years ago, sail filaments could be made almost completely absorptive at high angles of incidence. Solar stream particles didn't bounce. Momentum transfer was almost one hundred percent efficient. The echoes are hull return only, nothing else." He then directed, "Signal Flotilla to proceed on present course, except *USS Hornet*. Cut speed to point-zero-five michelson. Hornet, follow flagship at one hundred thousand miles, close on my command only. Petersen, commander."

"Are we going after them, sir?"

"You bet. Our best chance to surprise them is to go in alone. We may be able to save some of that wretched human cargo and capture the crew. I'd like to see the slavers hanged in the Admiralty Yard on Diego Garcia. Let's go in fast to twenty million miles, then cut power and glide, total radar and signal silence."

"Aye, sir." The Captain then commanded, "HELMSMAN, POLARIS REFERENCE; SET COURSE, DECLINATION MINUS SIX DEGREES, TWENTY MINUTES AND THREE-POINT-ZERO-SIX SECONDS, RIGHT ASCENSION 172 DEGREES SIX MINUTES AND THREE-POINT-SEVEN SECONDS. SOLAR PLANE. ENGINEER, FIT ACCELERATION/DECELERATION PROFILE TO TEN G SUSTAINED. POWER UP AT MY COMMAND. ALL HANDS, GENERAL QUARTERS, FASTEN IN, MED SUITS ON, HEART-LUNG ASSIST, OXYGEN ASSIST, INDUCED SLEEP MODE. MARK TIME TEN MINUTES FROM NOW. Admiral, twenty-six hours to arrival."

"Aye, Jim. I'll be in my quarters. Call me an hour before battle stations. Get some rest yourself. Be better fit for the attack."

"Aye, aye, sir, I intend to."

Twenty-five hours later the Duty Officer called the Captain and once he was on the bridge, he called the Admiral.

"What's it look like?" Petersen asked as he entered.

"All systems up, sir, and they haven't spotted us yet. We've not picked up any active electromagnetics at all."

"Extremely lucky. Let's power in when we hit two hundred thousand. Lift the blackout then. No weapons till launch, unless they attack. I want to take her as a prize. Have the Gunnery Officer report now."

"Aye, sir. ALL HANDS BATTLE STATIONS. BOARDER TEAMS ASSEMBLE. PREPARE GRAPPLER SHUTTLES TO BOARD. NUMBERS ONE, TWO AND SIX FORWARD, THREE, SEVEN AND NINE AFT. GUNNER TO THE BRIDGE. GUNNER TO THE BRIDGE."

"Excellent. Let's launch at ten miles." The Captain pressed his command intercom and said, "Captain Ironwood, I'll take her in to ten miles and launch. Your marines ready?"

"Yes, sir," Ironwood responded, and sent his command out. "BOARDERS, FULL CERMET BODY ARMOR, SABERS, SWORDS AND STUN GUNS. LASER DEATH RAYS LAST RESORT. SHUTTLE GUNS ARMED AND READY. FIRE ONLY ON MY COMMAND."

The Gunnery Officer came running in. He saluted the Captain and said, "Aye, sir."

The Captain pointed to Admiral Petersen. The Gunner turned and saluted again. Petersen said, "Sebastian, I want to take her as a prize, so we won't use the main batteries. How good are your men with the gatlings?"

"Hit a pinhead at three miles with the laser range finders, sir. It's a relative velocity problem only, no gravity, no coriolis, no air resistance out here. Computers correct in nanoseconds."

"Good. We'll launch the assault craft at ten miles. When we've closed to three, use the gatlings to take out the masts and rigging, starting two hundred yards out from the hull. Move toward the hull every twenty seconds in fifty-yard increments, stop at fifty. We want to obscure his viewports from our hull, grappling positions without interfering with our own craft or blinding them."

"Aye, sir," said Sebastian. "Is that all, sir?"

"Roger. Go for it when we get there. Thanks."

Sebastian departed.

"We have a good chance to get all the way in," Admiral Petersen observed. "The Corporation's new hull cladding on these cruisers should mask us at nose aspect to ten thousand miles and then we're on top of them. I will go in as soon as the assault teams have breached. I don't want to miss this one."

Excitement rose as the assault teams readied themselves. Most were veterans of campaigns against pirates lying off Neptune. They knew their jobs. Swords were sharpened to razor's edge as the men preferred them to stun guns for close-in fighting. The twenty man teams, each led by a lieutenant, boarded the grappler shuttles one half-hour before expected launch.

Twelve thousand miles away aboard the Beehive, the mate hobbled onto the bridge from the dilapidated radar pod. His iron leg clamored against the steel plating of the bridge as he moved. He waved a cutlass ominously, but that didn't hide the terror in his eyes as he exclaimed, "Cap'n, they're on us, like hounds on the hare, one forward and another behind, to rip us asunder. Quick, the viewport, they're close enough to see direct." He wiped a sweaty arm across his dirty neck and shook his head. Globs of grease splattered about.

The one-eyed Captain looked up fiercely and said, "Be that true, I'll skewer the watch."

Panic sped them to the viewport. One look confirmed their dread. The Captain screamed, "By Satan's horn and all the demons of hell, they're here. Purge the ship of slaves. Blast them overboard now. Signal quick to Grubol to throw the lever. Without live count, should they take us, they'll have no proof, and our lawyers will get us off at Geneva. Better yet, they may divert and try to save the scum, dead soon enough, if not ripped apart by decompression, then frozen stiff in thirty seconds. If that happens, we cast off the masts like a lizard throws its tail, come about and hide in the asteroids. Be quick now!"

The mate had already hit the lever. A great horn sounded and the ship shuddered in a mighty exhale. Ten thousand slaves were thrown into the Cosmos and quickly died as tether release tore space suits open. Aboard the USS Constitution, the Captain exclaimed, "My God, they've cast the poor devils into the void. LIFEBOATS OUT. BE QUICK!"

"Belay that command," the Admiral said softly. "You'd find none alive. I've seen it often. They tear their suits apart as they blow them out. Dead men tell no tales. They're already in their graves, and most happily so, their torment over. Let them rest in the eternity of space, but make an all-frequency video record of the crime. We'll avenge them now. Let's go."

The Captain commanded, "BOARDERS BLAST OFF. GRAPPLE AND ENTER."

CHAPTER 38

JOE SMITH

Only Porch's inordinately quick reaction saved him from being blown out of the cell with such force that nothing would have saved him. The tether would have simply ripped off. As it was, he thrust his arms and legs out, gaining some purchase against the terrible pressure. He slipped out slowly, and once outside drifted toward the spar he was programmed to man.

But something was terribly wrong. He felt the suit leaking at the tether connection and his warmth rapidly dissipating. He knew immediately what was happening. One side of the quick release had opened. Had he not tied it through his tool belt, the suit would have ripped apart. He quickly snapped the open side shut. He looked back and saw that the tether had been released at its juncture in his cell. He pulled the tether to him and in a desperate gamble threw it over the nearby spar so that it would wrap around.

He was lucky; it caught and he pulled on it slowly, hoping it would not come loose. It held. He drifted over and grabbed the spar. He felt panic rising within him. Forcing himself to calm down, he secured himself and took stock. Looking around, he saw thousands of fellow slaves flying away from the ship. He knew their tethers snapped back just before release and ripped their suits asunder. He hoped their final agony was brief. His will was again succumbing to panic. He closed his eyes and looked away from them.

Once more, he paused to assess his situation. He had about twelve minutes of oxygen in his tank and the suit should stay warm for that time. His only hope was to get back to the ship and somehow inside. He had to hurry, so he started back toward the ship by moving down the mast to which the spar was attached. He felt vibration behind him and looked back. About twenty feet away, something caused the thick mast to break apart. Cermet dust and fiber glass were slowly drifting away. He saw a second mast blow apart about one hundred feet away.

Oh, my God, he thought, *someone is firing at the masts. Gatlings!* Then he saw six shuttles moving in fast and beyond them the Fleet cruiser. He had to reach the ship as fast as he could. He took a knife from his tool kit and cut the tether loose. He had to risk it. He would push along from boom to gaff and whatever else provided handholds till he got to the hull. Should he miss, he would drift off into free space and that would be the end. He determined if that occurred, he would rip his suit open and die quickly.

He took aim and pushed off, traveling about one hundred feet. He measured distance and direction to the next boom and pushed off again. He made another hundred feet, and as he got there, he felt more vibrations behind. The gatlings seemed to be following him. Panic rose in his throat. Again he quelled it, but he was breathing too hard, using oxygen at twice the rate he'd counted on. He had to increase his risk. This time he made a leap of three hundred feet, barely reaching a protruding stanchion. Again the vibration, and the gatling fire bit off another section of mast. He pushed off, landing about one hundred feet from the hull. He had to rest a few seconds to reduce his oxygen consumption. He was quivering with fear.

He waited about thirty seconds; all the time his mind was telling him the next gatling burst would tear him apart. Nothing happened. The gatlings had ceased firing. He saw why. The assault craft were closing on the hull.

This brought new danger and perhaps salvation.

He stopped his climb and held on for dear life. He knew that when they began to dock, they would use retro-rockets to match their motion to the ship's. He had to avoid the blast. One shuttle came in about fifty feet away. It blasted to hover and then magnetically clamped onto the ship like a leech. He felt some vibration along the mast, which indicated interior ripping as the shuttle's augers bored into the slaver. From an Academy lesson, he remembered that the shuttles would then blast openings from their undersides for the assault teams to enter. In a moment, the mast was steady and he pushed off again, but now he detoured toward a hatch on the shuttle.

As he approached, he read: "RED ASSAULT TEAM 1, USS CONSTITUTION." Then he saw the great eyes and gaping shark jaws painted on the fore. He felt giddy. He knew his oxygen was about gone. Desperately, he climbed up to a hatch. He saw an emergency button and pushed it. The hatch flew open and he flung himself inside. Sucking nothing, he searched for the emergency closure and pushed the lever. The hatch clamped shut. In the dim red light, he looked around and saw the luminescent control. He groped for the airlock switch and felt the force of the air against his helmet, filling the airlock chamber. He tore his helmet off and found his lungs involuntarily heaving. As he passed out, a light came on, indicating pressurization was complete.

Gradually he regained consciousness. Now he could open the interior hatch. He did this, pushed off, closed the interior hatch behind him and floated down into the interior of the shuttle. Battle lights were on, so he had sufficient vision to see around the interior. The shuttle appeared empty.

Looking around, he saw the hole blown into the slave ship. It was still open and he could hear the din of battle inside. He pushed off, floated down a corridor and came to the wardroom. All lockers but one were open and empty. Opening the closed locker, he found a cermet assault suit with full armor hanging inside. It was bright red with the name WARD, LT. stenciled on the back. He took it out and pressed it to his lanky frame.

It would be a tight fit, but he discarded his slave suit and put it on. Then he tried the magnetic boots. They fit better. He placed the slave suit and helmet in the bottom of the locker and put on the full-visored helmet and body pack. He looked around for a weapon and spotted a single saber in the weapon rack. He pulled it from its scabbard, hurried forward and pushed himself down through the assault tube. He had to avenge ten thousand and would if he could. Once inside, he heard the clash of arms farther forward.

He saw wreckage all around him. Dead men floated around the compartment. He recognized them by their uniforms as overseers and members of the crew. He started forward to join the fray, but hesitated when he heard heavy thumping behind him in the compartment below. Looking back, he saw an open hatch leading down into the bowels of the dread ship where the reserve slaves had been chained. He strode over to the hatch and peered into the darkness below. He twisted the dial on his helmet for IR vision and saw a figure dragging a heavy shape toward a glowing open port.

Porch recognized the white-hot ion stream of the auxiliary rocket engines flowing past the port to the rocket nozzles. With sword in hand, he slipped quietly through the hatch and climbed down a few rungs on the ladder to the deck below. He stopped high enough to get a view of the entire compartment. He looked again toward the approaching figure pulling the heavy load. "My God," he whispered to himself, "Grubol." He froze in place, but the slave master was so intent on pulling his load forward he did not see Porch. The open ion port across the compartment was almost opposite his position on the ladder. He thought it must be some sort of inspection station. He looked again toward Grubol and his load. Grubol's purpose suddenly became clear. He was pulling a space mine to cast into the ion stream. Its explosion would destroy everything within a hundred miles. Grubol was almost to the port.

Porch expected but one chance. The privation of months as a slave had taken its toll on his strength and agility, and he knew that he would be no match for the giant Grubol in an extended fight. Grubol was opposite the port. As he bent over to lift the mine and drop it in, Porch cast himself from his perch above and using the flip he'd learned as a vaulter, came at Grubol feet first.

His heavy boots hit the giant squarely on the back of his skull and pushed his head into the ion stream. It sizzled and burnt off to his neck immediately, and Grubol's headless body slid to the floor so thoroughly cauterized that no blood flowed. Porch's impact slowed him enough to let him pull his feet away from the port, and he crashed against the sustaining bulkhead and slipped to the floor below. He rose slowly and, seeing Grubol's heart still pounding in his chest, plunged his sword into it with all the strength he could muster, shouting aloud, "That's for Bernouli, you son of Satan." Then his exhausted body gave out and he collapsed next to the space mine.

Red-suited men with drawn weapons had entered the compartment. Several saw Porch's great leap and its result. Their leader shouted, "Medic," and one quickly ran up. Others came up and an explosive ordinance disposal team disarmed the mine. The din of battle, the clamor of boots on the metal deck ceased when the men saw the mine and realized what they had avoided by the breadth of a few seconds. The medic looked up and said, "Sarge, this man's wearing Lieutenant Ward's uniform. Who could he be?"

"I don't know," Assault Master Sergeant Carruthers replied, "but he saved us all and the flagship, too. Keep it under your hat till we sort it out. I'll talk to Cap'n Ironwood."

Just then, the call came down the corridor, repeated and echoed from team to team. "CLEAR AND SE-CURED—CLEAR AND SECURED—CEASE FIRE—COL-LECT DEAD AND WOUNDED—PRISONERS FOR-WARD—REPAIR TO SHUTTLE—REPAIR TO SHUTTLE."

"Red Team One assemble," Carruthers commanded. The men formed quickly, as they wanted to get back to the mother ship where showers, clean clothes and hot meals waited.

"Squad Leaders report."

"One wounded but walking, two detailed to prisoner guard."

"Two wounded but walking," Carruthers continued. "At ease. Medic, you and Wasniak litter bearers. Bring that man forward and lead the way back. Red team follow me in two columns. Last pair keep the rear secured till we're back on the shuttle."

Porch came around after they were aboard the shuttle. Carruthers had them prop him up on the seat next to him. He said, "You look OK. Don't talk now, but drink this stimufluid and eat this assault ration; it'll get your blood runnin' again. We thought you a turncoat slaver at first, but as gaunt and weak as you appear, I figure you to be a slave. I don't know how you made it. Think all the others were blown out and killed. After we get aboard the Connie and you get a shower, clean clothes, some more to eat and some rest, you and me gonna talk about it. I'm putting you in Lieutenant Ward's cubicle. Don't talk to nobody else till I say."

Soon the USS Constitution loomed into view through the port. The team's shuttle slowed and matched the big cruiser's velocity, then awaited its turn to board. Porch woke many hours later to Wasniak's prodding. "Hey, man, wake up, Sergeant Carruthers wants to see you."

Porch looked up at the fair-cheeked boy and asked, "Where am I?"

"Man, you're on the USS Constitution, best ship in the whole Fed Fleet, flagship of the famous Admiral Petersen, who I know personally. What's your name? I know you ain't Lieutenant Ward, 'cause he was kilt off'n Neptune."

Porch answered, "Uh–why, Joe Smith."

"Well, shake a leg," Wasniak said importantly. "Sergeant Carruthers ain't nobody to keep waiting. I'll take you to his cubicle. Man, you must rate, him puttin' you in Ward's cubicle. Ain't no ordinary spaceleg or gyreen gets a cubicle by hisself."

"How long have I been here?" Porch asked.

"Man, we been through four watches since the battle." Presently, they came to Carruthers' cubicle. "It's a tight fit," Wasniak said, "so I won't come in with you. Just knock on the door."

Porch did so, and a voice from inside said, "Come on in." Porch entered and found himself standing before Assault Master Sergeant Carruthers, who looked him up and down. Porch looked at the kind and forlorn brown face and thought, *Too many battles for too long a time.*

Carruthers asked, "What's your name?"

"Joe Smith."

"Well, Joe Smith, I still don't know how you did it, or even survived, seeing how gaunt you are, but you saved all our asses. Sit down on that stool there and tell me about it."

Porch began, "I was shanghaied off of Key Largo with two others when I went looking for them. They didn't make it..."

When Porch finished, Carruthers said, "You got guts, lad, real guts, and you're lucky, too. I'd like to keep you in the platoon if I can, but I gotta talk to Cap'n Ironwood about that. He's a good man. I haven't told him yet that Lieutenant Ward got killed. I might get it for that, but I got my reasons, so don't talk to anyone till I tell him, 'cause it might get to the Admiral.

"The Admiral's mighty strict, but mainly I got so much respect for him, I don't want to seem like a rebel or raw recruit. After I talk to Ironwood, I think the Cap'n will make him understand. 'Specially don't talk to Wasniak. He's a good kid, but he's got a big mouth. Raw recruit, first voyage, detailed as Cap'n Ironwood's orderly. Makes him feel important to have all the hot skinny. He trades information. We're gonna take good care of you. Want to help you recover. Already got you on double rations. That's all for now. 'Spect Cap'n Ironwood want to see you soon's I talk to him."

Porch rose and moved to open the door of the cubicle. On the outside, Wasniak pulled his ear away from the door and hurried off.

Soon enough, rumors ran rampant throughout the flagship. "Only one who saved himself." "Shanghaied off of Florida." "Ten months a slave." "Killed the giant slave master." "Saved us from being blown to kingdom come." "Sez his name's Joe Smith."

From then till the end of the voyage, Porch was treated with deference and great friendliness. "Way to go, man." "Bully for you, lad." "You need anything, let us know."

Though he could speak to no one, he smiled and nodded at the adulation he received. On double rations and with priority in the exercise room, he gradually got his health back and put on the weight he had lost.

The same afternoon Carruthers interviewed Porch, Wasniak returned to his cubicle. "Cap'n would like to see you, Sergeant."

"Right," Sergeant Carruthers said, and he hurried out. When he reached Captain Ironwood's cabin, he knocked and asked, "Cap'n, you wanted to see me."

"Yes, come on in and have a seat," Ironwood replied. "Let me push aside this after-action report. That slave you found, scuttlebutt's all over the ship. What have you found out?"

Carruthers told him Porch's story, then said, "Cap'n, I haven't till right now reported Lieutenant Ward's death. The pirates off Neptune got him. The man was wearing Ward's outfit when we found him. He got it from Ward's locker on the launch."

"Why, Carruthers? You know the regs. The Admiral's tough on that."

"Sir, the men were very attached to Lieutenant Ward. They didn't want to break in a new man. Besides, if Command assigned us a new lieutenant in midcycle, he's jest gonna get hisself kilt. We figured we oughta wait till next time out."

"Well, you're probably right," Ironwood responded, "but next time follow the regs. I'll square it up the ladder, so we'll let it go this time. What did you say the recovered slave's name is?"

"Calls hisself Joe Smith. Cap'n, I sure want to keep him in the platoon. Man's got a lot o' moxie."

"Well, we'll see. Keep him with you the rest of the patrol and in partial quarantine till we get a full medical workup. Can't tell what he was exposed to on that slave ship. I expect the Admiral's gonna want to go over the action with us."

The Admiral and the Captain were on the bridge when the First Officer came rushing in. He exclaimed, "Excuse me, sir. Orders. We're to return to Earth. Something happened back there that scared the pee out of the Prez, and for that matter, the entire Western Alliance. Has to do with Tukanon and the Central Asian Autonomy. I'm sorry, Admiral, you're being reassigned. Seems they want to beef up near-Earth defenses."

Petersen read the order from the Admiralty. He turned to the Captain and said, "Tell them we're on our way and signal the *Hornet* to return to the squadron, Vice Admiral Yama to command. Also tell the prize crew on the Beehive that we'll tow them to moon base for dismantling. I want strict attention paid to the new environmental laws, no flotsam or jetsam left in the solar system, or for that matter catapulted into deep space."

"Aye, sir," the Captain replied.

"Orderly, third watch, four bells, I want to see Captain Ironwood in the officer's ward room. Please set up an appointment."

Down below, Fleet Recruit Wasniak knocked at Captain Ironwood's quarters. "Six bells," he cried out.

"Come in," Ironwood responded loudly. He was cleaning rust-red stains from his saber. He grinned at Wasniak when he saw the tray with a pot of steaming coffee, orange juice and sweet rolls.

"Why, Recruit Wasniak, I believe you're bucking for promotion."

Wasniak blushed and stammered uneasily, "No sir–uh–yes, sir–uhh–I don't know, sir."

The youth was only sixteen, an orphan who had stowed away at the beginning of the patrol. Carruthers let him follow him during the slave ship melee and he'd acquitted himself well. But he was in absolute awe of this captain, whose prowess with the saber and whose ferocity in action was already legendary in the Fleet.

"Sir," Wasniak continued, "the Admiral's compliments. He wants you to report to Flag at 3rd watch, four bells."

"Ohhh, did Flag say what about?"

"No, sir, but I have it on good authority that you and Sergeant Carruthers gonna be promoted."

"And what is your 'good authority'?"

Wasniak hemmed and hawed.

"Come clean now, I'm growing impatient." Ironwood feigned anger.

"Signal showed me the file message."

"And how much did you pay him?"

"Two Neptunian commemorative gold medallions. He wanted three—said he'd really get his butt in a sling if'n he got found out."

"But he did show you the message, didn't he?" Ironwood asserted.

"Yes, sir."

"Wasniak, your butt's gonna be in a sling right next to his if you keep trading for information."

"But it's real good news, sir, I mean you gettin' a battlefield promote to major, and Sergeant Carruthers goin' to sergeant major. Also that man who ain't Lieutenant Ward 'cause Lieutenant Ward got hisself kilt of'n Neptune, the Admiral wants to give him a medal."

There was a long pause. Finally Ironwood said, "Wasniak, you know he isn't Lieutenant Ward, and I know it, Carruthers knows it, and so do the rest of the men, but the Admiral doesn't. He will soon enough, because I'm going to tell him tomorrow, and I got to explain why it wasn't reported, not you. Now you keep your lip buttoned. I mean it. You say one word and you'll have your ass in a sling much sooner than you think. Now you go tell Carruthers that I want to see that man right now—on the double, man—on the double."

Wasniak turned quickly to head out, and then stopped and turned toward Captain Ironwood again. "Something else, sir. We're headed back to Earth. Admiral Petersen's going to be reassigned."

"Wasniak, you're incorrigible."

"I am, sir," Wasniak replied, beaming. Then he frowned, and with a worried look, asked, "what's that mean?"

"Wasniak, get out of here and go tell Sergeant

324 HOLMAN

Carruthers what I told you to. Now! Move it."

Wasniak scooted and in a few minutes Porch appeared at the open door. "You wanted to see me, sir?"

"Yes, come in. I'm Captain Ironwood, Assault Team Commander, and I understand you're Joe Smith, a former slave."

"Right, sir," Porch replied, standing at rigid attention. "Caught and imprisoned off the Florida Coast."

"Well, Joe Smith, I won't burden you with repeating your story now. Sergeant Carruthers told me most of it. Anyway, we're heading back to Earth. You can make a full report when we get there. I think the Admiralty will want you as a witness against the captured slavers."

Ironwood stopped talking and looked at Porch intently, then rose and walked around him. When he sat down again, he said, "You know, Joe Smith, few but Academy men stand so well at attention as you are standing now. Some years ago, in my last year there, I trained a man at saber, a big black fellow, first-year man, Grub, as we called them, hell of a football player who'd gotten himself in a duel with a dueling champion. Turned out alright. That man, name of Bokasi, was standing up for his roommate, forget the man's name, who was bullied for months by two upperclassmen, real rotters. It came to a head in several duels. You have an uncanny resemblance to that man, except you're thinner. Heard the man got in further trouble later. Ran away from the Academy. Don't know why, because my class graduated and we left. So far as I know they captured him and tried him for murder, but he got away again and is still a fugitive. Some say he was framed. Nice kid as I remember, hardly capable of murder.

"Well, as far as I'm concerned, couldn't be you. Even if it was, think you'd deserve some help for what you did for all of us. Well—why I called you in, Carruthers and I thought you might like to sign on...good pay and lots of action. What do you say?"

Porch put him off by saying, "I'd like to think about it, sir."

"That's OK, and...oh yes, Administration called

shortly before you came in. The Admiral is going to award you a medal for what you did, The Medal of the Sun. It's a high honor. He wants to wait till we get back to Admiralty Headquarters at Diego Garcia so there'll be full media coverage and you can tell your full story."

Porch blanched. Ironwood looked at him and said, "You alright?"

"Uh...yes, sir," Porch answered.

Ironwood hesitated, then said, "Perhaps we ought to wait awhile. I think I'll extend you're quarantine for a few weeks on Diego Garcia. I'm sure the Admiral would delay the ceremony for a couple of weeks till you're fully recovered. That sound better?"

"Yes, sir," Porch replied.

"Fine. I'll talk to him. That's all for now."

Porch left Captain Ironwood's cabin deeply worried. He was sure that Ironwood knew his true identity, yet was convinced by his words that he would not turn him in or give him away. But the Admiral's ceremony, even though a great honor, would lead the Corporation right to him. What could he do? Absolutely nothing until they returned to Earth, except avoid drawing attention to himself. He would keep to himself as much as possible, but even this, carried to extremes, could have the opposite effect. He just had to stay alert and plan a quick departure once they landed. Perhaps he could find a boat or gain passage away from the island.

Days passed and Porch's worries continued, but he stayed calm. One day, loudspeakers blared, "TRAVERSING MARS ORBIT. TRAVERSING MARS ORBIT." Elation passed through the Constitution's crew and its warriors, for they would soon be home. They formed a pool immediately for the day, hour and minute to the closest second that Earth and its moon could be identified with the naked eye as separate disks.

This tradition had grown up in the Fleet since its earliest days and become almost sacrosanct. It was a great morale booster. The watch had the duty to call this time out as "Earth Ahoy," and give direction. It was the Captain's honor to confirm the sighting. If it was a true sighting, the watch was feted throughout the ship.

If the Captain declared it false, the Watch was required to don a fools cap and gown, parade through the ship and be subjected to much abuse.

Wasniak sought Porch out. "Hey, Joe Smith, come join the pool."

Porch smiled and answered, "I have nothing to bet."

"Well, I'm going to put ten credits in for you, same time as mine, 'cause I'm gonna win."

"Thank you, Wasniak—very considerate. I hope you're lucky."

"Not a matter of luck, a matter of science, and I got it all figured. You'll see."

Wasniak did win, much to the chagrin of his shipmates. Because of his reputation of finding out everything that happened during the patrol, some suggested he had some trick up his sleeve. When he heard of this, he protested vigorously but unconvincingly. Porch's share of the purse was one hundred credits. Now at least he would not be penniless when he got back. Soon the cruiser reached moon base.

Again Wasniak sought Porch out. "Hey, Joe Smith, come to the viewport and watch."

Together they watched as the cruiser released the tow. Moon base catapulted four retrorockets up to the prize. Spacewalkers from the Beehive caught them and attached them to selected points on the slaver's hull. The prize crew fired them up and slowly lowered the hulk to moon base for salvage.

"Wow," Wasniak shouted.

Porch said softly, "That demonic, accursed ship. I'll only be happy when its cermet is dissolved to slurry and its metal structure melted to liquid."

Twenty-four hours later, the cruiser docked at Admiralty Space Station One, located at the Lagrangian gravity null point. There, the crew loaded onto lighters and the captured slavers were loaded onto the prisoner barge. They descended to Earth.

CHAPTER 39

A FISHING TRIP

The *USS Constitution's* video record of ten thousand slaves blasted into space convicted fifty-seven slavers of ten thousand murders. Assault Master Sergeant Carruthers and Major Ironwood attested to the authenticity of Porch's deposition, given from quarantine at the Admiralty Hospital on Diego Garcia. It became a powerful adjunct to the Fleet prosecutor's case and negated pleas for mercy presented by the defense. So one week after the Constitution had returned to Earth orbit, the trial was over.

Before dawn the day following trial's end, Ordinary Spaceman Wasniak, just promoted from recruit, sneaked past the Duty Orderly in the quarantine ward. Stealthily, he searched from alcove to alcove, until he found Porch. "Joe Smith," he whispered, "Joe Smith, come quick to the window."

Porch rubbed his sleepy eyes, and after he recognized the boy, replied, "Wasniak, you dummy, if they find you here, they'll bust you back to recruit and confine you to several months of quarantine."

Wasniak retorted, "It's more than worth the chance, Joe Smith, 'cause I'm going to show you a sight you shouldn't never forget. Now come to the window."

Porch got up, put his arm across Wasniak's shoulder, smiled and said, "OK, I'd just hate to see you lose your hard-earned stripe."

The first glint of dawn illuminated the vast ocean to

the east, and allowed them to view the Admiralty Yard
through the darkness. About one hundred yards away,
they saw that a long platform had been erected during
the night. It was topped with a symbolic yardarm extending the platform's length. Fifty-seven ropes, each
ending in a hangman's noose, hung from this long beam.
They watched silently as a corps of drummers marched
into the yard and took up station before the platform.
The drummers took up a muted tap which slowly rose
in volume. Other figures now entered to witness the
proceedings, and the drummers began the Deadman's
Roll.

As the first rays of the sun split the ocean, Wasniak
and Porch saw three columns of men enter the court-
yard from the eastern side. The outer columns were
warriors bearing sabers sheathed at their belts and carrying side arms at port. In the column between, fifty-
seven slavers shuffled along, arms bound behind, heads
bowed to the inevitable that lay ahead. When they
reached the scaffold, guards on either side prodded each
one to mount the steps. When all had mounted and
stood before a noose, fifty-seven hangmen put slaver
necks in nooses. The drummers' beat now rose to a crescendo, then stopped, and fifty-seven traps were sprung.
Down the slavers fell to the end of their ropes, necks
snapped, and fifty-seven bodies dangled lifelessly below.

"Wow," Wasniak exclaimed. Porch felt nothing. Both
watched as flatbeds were loaded to haul the bodies to a
waiting scow which would carry them to sea for disposal.

"Well, Wasniak, show's over. You'd better skedaddle
before you get caught and lose that stripe."

When Porch was alone again, he went back to the
charts from the Admiralty library. Wasniak did not know
that he too had broken quarantine each night for the
past week. But for him, it was a matter of life or death.
He imagined Corporation men would appear soon on
the island and force the Admiralty to give him up. He
had bought sixty days of outdated Fleet rations from
the black market at the fishing village on the east side

of the island and hidden these under a pier on the west side. Water was a problem, but the fishing village also had neoprene bladders fishermen used. He filled these from a faucet that engineers had installed and run from the desalination plant for picnickers who used the nearby beach. He filled and laboriously carried these to his hiding place. Lifeguards kept a motorized launch at the jetty which he intended to take when he left. He would row out beyond the surf before starting the engine. He was ready to depart.

From the charts, he calculated that ocean currents would carry him west to Madagascar or the Seychelles. From there, he'd continue to Africa, go overland south to Capetown, or continue by sea north to Arabia. Then somehow he would head back to the Florida Keys. He knew he must recover the locket. It had become his brace on reality.

Tomorrow his quarantine would end and he could legitimately make a final check on the launch and his food and water cache. His medal ceremony was scheduled for the following day. He had to depart before then. Early the next morning, he gathered his few possessions and signed out of quarantine. The desk orderly cleared him and told him to report to the Red Assault Platoon.

Sergeant Major Carruthers and his men greeted him warmly when he arrived. At breakfast, he asked Carruthers if he could have a pass that day to tour the island and again savor the land and sea. Carruthers gladly granted this. Wasniak, sitting nearby, overheard Porch's request. When Porch was ready to depart, he ran up and hollered, "Joe Smith, hey, Joe Smith, let me go with you. I'm the best guide on the whole island."

Porch smiled, replying, "Not today, Wasniak. I need to be alone."

Looking downcast, as Porch had become his new hero, he asked, "You sure, Joe Smith, you sure?"

Porch saw the hurt and said, "Another time, my young friend, another time, God willing."

Wasniak turned away as Porch went off, but he was puzzled. What did he mean by "God willing"? Was something else going on? Maybe he could get it out of Major Ironwood. He went to the kitchen, picked up a pot of coffee and some sweet rolls, then headed for Major Ironwood's billet.

Porch did enjoy his tour. The breeze brought salt air in from the ocean. He removed his boots to feel the warm sand between his toes. He enjoyed the solitude, becoming lost in his thoughts. He took the long away around the island to do exactly what he told Carruthers he was going to do. So it was awhile before the pier came into sight. He looked around to see if anyone had followed.

Nobody was in sight. He meandered down to the water and waded in as if for no particular purpose, but he knew he would be able to see his store from the water as he approached the pier. When he saw everything in order, he continued wading to the base of the pier and climbed onto the wooden walkway. He saw the lifeboat still moored at the far end.

Suddenly, he heard a familiar voice behind him. It was Major Ironwood, with Wasniak in tow. Ironwood asked, "Thinking about going fishing, Joe Smith?"

Hiding his feelings, Porch answered, "It's a fine day for it."

"Yes, it is, but the fishing is much better down the beach and there are some Special Services launches down there reserved for the Fleet. Perhaps Wasniak would go with you. He knows where the big ones are biting."

"That would be good, sir."

"Well, I better return to quarters now. I've got Fleet duty tonight, but it's good to see you up, Joe Smith, and recovered from your long trauma. Good day. Come along, Wasniak."

Porch watched them depart. He was certain now the Major was on to him. Would he turn him in? He had to leave as soon as possible. He started back to the barracks and was halfway there when he saw them. There was no mistake, because he could never forget them. They were Corporation men. He hurried on. He had to sweat it out till dark.

Not far away, someone else recognized the Corporation men and became highly irritated. *The felon is mine*, Tuesday thought. *How dare they send others to take him.* He would have to hurry. He took out his man finder and began a sweep.

As twilight approached, Major Ironwood reported for duty at Admiralty Headquarters. He had just settled into the large comfortable office when the duty NCO knocked at the door.

"Come in," he called out amiably.

"Sir," the Sergeant said, "some men have come to see you. They say they represent the Corporation. They are seeking a man called Porch, believed to be using the alias Joe Smith."

"Oh," Ironwood said nonchalantly. "Have you checked their papers and authority to be on the island?"

"Not yet, sir."

"Well, do that, and check all credentials carefully. Security must be very tight on the island. Come back in when you're finished."

As soon as the duty NCO left his office, Ironwood picked up his communicator. "Wasniak, get over here as fast as your legs will carry you and then make it faster. Come in the back entrance. I'll be waiting there for you."

Two minutes later, Wasniak came running up and, out of breath asked loudly, "What's up, sir?"

Ironwood was waiting at the back entrance. He put his finger to pursed lips. "Quiet now. I want you to do exactly what I tell you, no more, no less, and in the exact order that I tell you. If you deviate one bit you're back to recruit. If you do it exactly right, I'll put you in for thirty day's leave and buy your round trip back to the States or anywhere else you choose to go."

"Yes, sir," Wasniak whispered hoarsely, breathing hard. He listened intently because it sounded conspiratorial, and conspiracy was what he dearly loved.

"You go find Joe Smith as fast as you can and when you do you tell him, 'It's time to go fishing,' nothing more. Then get Sergeant Major Carruthers and bring him back to my office. Do you understand?"

"Oh, yes, sir," and the lad took off like a rabbit. Ironwood closed the back door behind him and went back to his desk.

Just then the Duty NCO re-entered. He looked at the Major and said, "Sir, I've checked them out very carefully. They're legit."

"Well, we won't keep them waiting. Ask them to come in."

When they had entered, Major Ironwood greeted them courteously. "Sorry to keep you waiting—tight security. How may I help?"

"Well, that's the third security check we've undergone. Really now, we are from the Corporation," the spokesman complained. "We are looking for a man called Porch and have evidence that he is on the island under the alias Joe Smith."

"I've not heard of any man called Porch, but we do have a Joe Smith. Quite a hero, you know, saved Admiral Petersen's flagship, and as a matter of fact—all of us. He's up to receive a high decoration at an Admiralty ceremony tomorrow."

The name Porch came back to Major Ironwood as he pronounced it.

"That has been reported to the Corporation and we too wish to suitably reward him," the spokesman sneered.

Ironwood ignored the sneer and said, "How fine. The man you seek is in Assault Sergeant Major Carruthers' platoon, and I have already called for the Sergeant Major to come and take you to him. He'll be here in a minute."

Moments before, Wasniak had run into Porch's alcove and hollered, "Joe Smith, hey, Joe Smith, Major Ironwood told me to tell you it's time to go fishing. Bye now, I gotta go get Sergeant Carruthers."

Porch put down the chart he was studying, went to his locker, put on a jacket, grabbed the barracks bag containing his few belongings and some foul weather gear and went out the back window. He regretted he didn't have time to check out a weapon from the arms room. It was dark now, and he began a long-strided lope to the beach. He felt good, no more waiting and worrying. He was fully recovered from his long ordeal. He got to the pier quickly. Nobody was around. He went out to the boat and threw his gear in, jumped down into the water, and strode back to his cache of food and water. He finished loading, making two trips for the food and six for water. He got into the boat, put the oars out and cast off. He was lucky. It was ebb tide. He began pulling at the oars, pacing himself carefully, as it was quite far out to the surf. Although it was dark, he was most vulnerable to detection at this time. Still he felt good. For whatever reason, something told him that he would not be detected. Soon he was rowing through the surf. Several hundred yards more and he was riding a smooth sea. He stopped rowing and rested for a while.

Then he started the engine and turned it to its lowest setting to get the least noise and most distance. By the stars he knew so well, he set a southwest course, knowing he would pick up western currents which would carry him far from Diego Garcia before they turned northwest toward Madagascar and the Seychelles. He hoped he had enough food and water, but he had all the lifeboat could safely carry. He set the engine on idle and stowed his stores away.

Later that night, under the stars on the calmest of seas, he had time for reflection, and he became melancholy. He wondered if fortune would always deny him the camaraderie of men like Carruthers and Wasniak. Would he ever be able to serve with men like Ironwood and Admiral Petersen?

By the time dark had fallen over the island, Tuesday's man finder had done its job. He was tracking. The track was cold, but he had to begin somewhere. The trail led to the Assault Team Barracks. There he stopped short. Twenty yards away, a big NCO backed up by several members of his outfit were arguing heatedly with the dark-suited men.

It looked as though the spacefarers were about to take the Corporation operatives apart. He guessed what had happened. The blundering fools had allowed his quarry time to escape. No doubt the spacemen were protecting the felon. Well, he had no time for what he saw. He tuned his man finder back to broad search and hurried to the rear of the building. He picked up the track right away and hurried on. It led to the western beach. There he noted the lifeboat he'd previously seen was missing. He looked seaward, but it was dark, so he surmised the boat he saw beyond the surf was but an illusion, and the engine he heard nothing but the roaring surf.

Chagrined, Tuesday turned away from the ocean. *Damn fools*, he thought to himself. Hadn't they yet learned the quality of the man they were up against? He thought about it as he walked back toward the fishing village where he'd found lodging.

He wouldn't even try to mount an air search through the Admiralty. All airspace within one hundred miles was restricted, and without a doubt the Admiralty was in the felon's corner. The man not only had escaped the slave ship, by itself unheard of, but he'd saved a Fleet flagship to boot. Even with the full weight of the Corporation behind him, Fleet bureaucracy could delay search approval for weeks.

Anyway, he didn't want the Corporation to know he'd been on the island when these other agents so badly butchered the operation, and then associate him with them. He started analyzing weather patterns, wind directions and currents surrounding the island. He knew his own skills, so he fully expected to meet the felon at his first landfall.

****

"Anything from our operatives at Diego Garcia?"

"Yes, sir, late last night, a report. The felon eluded them."

The Chairman was silent for several moments, then at last said, "I feared as much. How about Inspector Tuesday?"

"Nothing, sir, not one word since he returned from the Amazon."

The Chairman sighed, then said, "That's all for now."

"Yes, sir." The Lawyer left.

The Chairman turned to the window and became engrossed in his thoughts. He had come to admire the felon. He had never known a man who had overcome so much.

CHAPTER 40

THE ANGRY OCEAN

The sun rose, a great red fireball, already angry at the coming day. Within an hour, its presence dominated the sky, obscuring the horizon and turning the sea into dazzle. When it reached its zenith, it blazed forth like a thousand arc lights perched atop Porch's makeshift mast. Nothing could withstand its awesome heat, neither cloud, nor bird, nor fish in the sea, and none were seen.

So it was for forty days—days that Porch lay under a tarpaulin, not daring to show himself for more than a minute or two at a time. There was no breeze, nor had there been in all those days, and only a little at night. So it was only at night that Porch raised his sail to navigate the path the stars pointed out.

He'd left the Admiralty's island sixty-three days before. He had fuel enough to keep the boat going for ten, but then a countercurrent took back all the distance he'd gained. So he pulled the engine out of the water and jury-rigged a sail. Now he was beset by calm, so he cut his food to half a ration and his water even more. That night a moderate breeze arose and buoyed his hopes again.

At last he saw a sight that made him overjoyed. A seagull hovered overhead, then landed on his prow. Taking heart, he hoisted sail, set course and imagined he could smell the exotica of Africa.

The following day, the blazing sun was back. But

now it made him uneasy, for instead of a calm, the breezes, full of dust, increased into a searing wind that sought him out. It was so desiccated it sucked the moisture from his lungs and he felt very soon it would as well dry out his blood. Soon he was too weak to even protest the scorching dust that burnt his skin and filled his nose and ears and eyes.

At last the wind shifted, bringing dampness and the promise of water. He rose to see what brought the change and over the prow he saw a black wall that was closing fast. Quickly, he pulled down his sail and mast, tied up all that was loose, pulled on his foul weather gear, roped himself in and cast out a sea anchor.

The rain, in scattered drops at first, was announced by peals of lightning and relentless rolls of thunder. Then it hit. The rain came down in torrents, pressed on by the screaming wind, beating horizontal to infiltrate every crack and opening, as the dust had minutes before.

The ocean changed its color now from bright blue dazzle to a sickening peridot green. Porch rode on in ferocious seas, prepared to suffer all the storm would deliver. The sturdy lifeboat swamped to the gunnels floated on by the grace of watertight bulkheads fore and aft. He had but one consolation. No one would find him there.

After many days, the storm abated. Worn-out winds blew their final blasts and the sun burnt through the sodden clouds. But soon enough above that equatorial sea, it re-established its original tyranny and blasted down on all exposed. Porch had lost his oars, his mast and sail, and now ran out of food and water. Salt encrusted, he tried to stretch a thin cover over his being, again seeking shelter from those hellish rays. The brilliant light confused his sight and confounded his mind. He began to think he saw boats everywhere. Were they mirages or delirium? He did not know. At last sleep came as he lay beneath his meager cover.

In a daze, he did not see the dhow approach, and it took a gaff in his ribs to bring him back to his senses. He heard laughter and shouting and found himself looking up into the eyes of half a dozen well-tanned men in a sea-worn boat. The smell of fish was everywhere. He hailed them in English and they replied in a tongue unknown to him. He thought it was an African or Arabic dialect.

They motioned him to come aboard, which he painfully did. Every inch of his skin burned from the past few days' treatment by the sun and salty sea. His muscles ached from disuse. Once aboard, his saviors gave him as much water as he would drink and then, as he revived, strong coffee and rough round cakes. One of those men knew a smattering of English and another of Portuguese. With his English and Spanish, he could communicate fairly well. As time went on, he would learn their Arabic. They were humble fishermen, so they said, bound for Aden to sell their catch, then up the Red Sea to trade in spices along the Arabian coast.

They considered his boat their prize and winched it aboard. They asked if he had money, but he had none. Then he could pay for his passage by working as a deck hand, and if he caught some fish and was worthy, share their profit.

They gave him a turban and some clothes as ragged as theirs and got underway. Porch proved himself apt with the lines and nets and worked himself in with the crew. He learned the cadence of their chants, the measured clap of hands and stamp of feet that eased the heavy work as they rolled along with the sea.

They were a jolly band but all showed nervous agitation whenever they spied a vessel that bore a naval silhouette. They would tack away under extra sail as fast as the winds allowed. Porch noted the dhow rode lower in the water than could be attributed solely to the fish they caught. He wondered why and found out one day. Some timbers below deck near the keel had come loose from their coir, revealing a false bottom. Elephant tusk and rhino horn, quite likely poached from an African game preserve, were packed beneath. They were living on the edge of danger, trusting the will of Allah to see them through. Surely they would meet the headsman's block the instant caught, and he along with them. "Inshallah—as Allah wills," they shouted, shrugging off the danger. But the upside was that they would skirt authority, and he had his own reasons to be happy with that. They came to shore at night, unloaded the fish, horn and ivory, and took on a cargo of spice. They continued up the Red Sea, trading at several ports.

Porch disembarked at Magnah, close by the entrance to the Gulf of Aqaba, as they would go no farther for fear of Israeli patrol boats. They had traded for western credits and gold and silver, and gave him an ample share of each along with a blessing. They had been boon companions during the hazardous journey. He owed them a lot.

But he could not tell them he would strike north for Israel's Haifa, which had commerce through the Mediterranean back to America. It would have cost his freedom and maybe his life. So he headed north in Arab garb, stopping at scattered villages for food and water. He traveled slowly as a Muslim pilgrim returning to the East.

In a month and a day, he reached the Israeli border, which he could tell by the strip of desolation. Stumps of trees, shell holes and signs warning of minefields marked it well. He skirted along the strip to find a suitable place to pass on through.

Presently, he found fresh tire tracks leading to a barbed wire barrier one hundred yards away. Hiding among some rocks, he awaited nightfall. He started when the moon came out and crept along one tread, cautiously probing the soft sand ahead for metal or plastic indications of mines. Midnight came and the moon was setting when he reached the barrier wire. There was a gate with a sign, marked in Arabic and English, PRISONER EXCHANGE POINT. There was room to crawl under and he was halfway through when the bombardment began—mortars and ancient weapons, still in use. He could smell the cordite. He thrust his legs and pushed under the gate as quickly as he could, wondering what he'd done to provoke the barrage.

He dared to stand in a gully on the Israeli side, and, creeping low, ran along it away from the demarcation barrier. He reached another road, perpendicular to the first and parallel to the border. This one was in defilade to the Arab side, so he found a spot to sit and rest. He could hear them, now firing, whump, whump, whump. Then he picked up their whistle and splash—blam, blam, blam. He thought for sure he was the target, but they weren't even coming close.

Machine guns began to chatter. Flares lit the sky. They floated down—nowhere close. It was an eerie sight. What was going on?

****

"The device has finished preliminary testing and is performing well," the Lawyer said.

"Excellent," the Chairman responded.

"The government has named Admiral Petersen its envoy to complete negotiations with the Israelis."

"Very well. We will send our Vice President for Operations. Now that we have Petersen back, I'll keep the tough old space bear close to the honey tree. Maybe that will decrease his constant effort to get back to the Fleet. I'm told he proposed and she said yes."

"They may elope, sir."

"I would be disappointed. I want to give them a wedding in the grand old style. It would be magnificent. Make such a proposal as an invitation, not a demand."

"Yes, sir."

"What have we now from Cevello?"

"Only bad news, sir. He is beginning to act irrationally. His assistants fear that he has picked up the virus."

"Indeed," said the Chairman.

CHAPTER 41

ABSALOM

Suddenly the firing stopped, and Porch heard a loud voice from the other side of the border. "Show yourself, you repulsive son of a camel."

Then, again—whump, whump, whump—tat-tat-tat-tat. Porch ducked behind the rise, but the mortar rounds landed a hundred yards down the road. Flares lit the sky again, and Porch made out a figure cavorting up the road, paying no attention to the mortar rounds landing all around him or the machine gun fire. The figure seemed to be doing a jig, skipping up the rock-strewn road, flares alternately outlining him brightly and putting him in silhouette. Porch watched a little old man in a jogging suit approach. It was incredible. In a bit, he could hear him sing.

"Dipsy doodle, oh, dipsy doodle, a little white poodle and an h'apple strudel—and so I courted the Colonel."

Again, mortars, machine guns and shouts from beyond the wire, "Bastard son of Jezebel, show yourself and feel Allah's wrath."

Now the old man, still fifty yards away, mounted a berm, stood up, stuck his thumbs in his ears, wiggled his fingers, and gave his tormentors the raspberry. This brought a furious fusillade, but to no avail. The man hopped down and continued his jig and song, "Dipsy doodle, oh, dipsy doodle, they're off their noodle. Piddledidoodle, pidoodle, pidoodle—whole kit and caboodle—and then I married the Colonel." Presently, he came upon Porch.

Porch ran out, grabbed him, and pulled him under the bank. The mortars, machine guns and now light artillery continued for a few minutes, then ceased. Porch looked at the old man incredulously. The man looked at him, laughed, held his arms out expansively, and said, "I've spied the lad who thought I was mad."

Porch couldn't help himself and laughed expansively, then said, "You know, you could get killed out here."

The man ignored his comment and replied, "I'm Absalom, out for my evening stroll," then he broke into song again, "I'm not some bum, from a Tel Aviv slum— since I married the Colone-e-e-e-l."

So exaggerated were Absalom's gestures that Porch laughed again and said, "They call me Porch."

"Ah-ha! I knew you weren't Arabian, even in that garb. You are an American, no?"

"Yes," Porch said, smiling. He had really taken to this little white-bearded fellow. Absalom sidled up to him and whispered conspiratorially, "I don't get this far normally. It's quite exhilarating. You want some Dentine chewing gum? It's old but good, hard to get in these parts."

Again, voices came from beyond the wire. "Stand up, you son of a dog, so we can keel you."

"Ai-ai-ai, nogoodniks all," he stood up and yelled toward the wire, "May maggots grow in your bellies, God forgive."

Porch pulled him down again as bullets whizzed overhead.

"Shah! Shah! They come." Four air scooters and a chopper came in low, made mid-air stops at the wire, and turned on search lights, probing boulders, hillocks and ravines across the barrier. Firing from the other side had stopped, but the scooters began firing lasers, scorching the earth beyond. They were bobbing up and down, in and out of cover, like popcorn in a popper, firing on the up bounce.

In the meantime, the chopper landed nearby and four burly men in Israeli uniforms jumped out and ran over to Porch and Absalom. One provided cover with a laser, two grabbed Absalom under the shoulders and ran with him to the helicopter, and the Captain in charge yelled at Porch, "Come on."

They loaded up, buckled in and the assault force was off in a flash. They completed the operation in less than a minute. The officer said, "Absalom, what are we going to do with you? You're going to worry the Colonel to death."

Absalom ignored his question and said, "Meet my friend, Porch. I found him sitting in the road. He's dressed like an Arab, but he's an Americanisher. A real mensch. I'll vouch for him."

"We'll run a check, but Intel's real busy now rounding up the late Tukanon's creeps."

"I'm going to take him home with me. He looks like my boy, Uriah, who was killed in your damn war six years ago."

"No skin from my nose if the Colonel says OK." The chopper hummed on.

The Captain announced, "Outskirts of Tel Aviv. We'll land at the pad by your apartment, but I'm personally taking you up to the Colonel this time."

Absalom patted Porch's arm, "She'll like you, a wonderful woman," he said proudly. "She's my wife and my life."

The chopper landed quietly. They dismounted and the Captain squired them up to a tiny second floor apartment where he knocked on the door. An ample woman with gray hair pulled into a bun on top of her head opened the door. "Yes," she said.

The officer replied, curtly but politely, "We found him again, Colonel—way up on the barrier road by the prisoner exchange point." He pulled a sheepish-looking Absalom forward.

"Bubelah," she exclaimed, grabbing him in her arms, squeezing the breath out of him, and kissing him affectionately.

The Israeli officer saluted casually and said, grinning, "I'll be off, ma'am. Keep him on a tight leash if you can. Good evening."

"Gottenyu! Absalom, you'll be the death of me yet."

Absalom freed himself, but was obviously delighted at her affection. He said, "I just needed to clear my head for some deep thinking. I found a young friend, an Americanisher."

Miriam, the Colonel, looked at Porch, put her fists to her cheeks, and cried out, "Ha Shen, you are our Uriah, come back to life."

"No, mama," Absalom said, "he is American. His name is Porch."

Miriam pressed her hands to Porch's cheeks and looked at him carefully. Tears came to her eyes, "You look so much like our dear, lost Uriah. Come, welcome. Your name is Portch, nothing else?"

"No, ma'am, Porch, with a soft c. Yes, that is all." Porch knew the time for deception was over. They had accepted him so openly.

Miriam replied, shrugging her shoulders, "Portch, that's all, Americans, never did I understand. Your are hungry, I can tell. You must eat. Absalom, take him and wash, then come, sit down."

She hurried to her tiny kitchen and when they were seated, began bringing out food, wondrous dishes, chicken and rice, lamb, palm hearts, artichokes, a tureen of vegetables, wine, bread and cakes. Porch demurred out of politeness from accepting seconds.

Miriam said "Eat" with such authority that he obeyed. He was famished. They spoke at length of Uriah, killed repelling a cross-border raid. They asked but little about him, as if learning his reality would lessen the illusion that Uriah had returned. Miriam stated she was a reserve colonel of military intelligence, but her life was politics. She was a member of the Knesset. She also said that since they killed Uriah, Absalom no longer accepted closed borders and border skirmishes. To him, they just did not exist.

After dinner, Miriam led Porch to Uriah's room, which was as he had left it that fateful night, and said," This is yours, Portch, as long as you stay."

Absalom came in a little later, after Porch had retired, and said, "I show you, tomorrow, my baby. You'll see I'm not completely the foolish old man I play. Good night, son."

The morning rose, cool but bright. Porch awoke to a tugging at his shoulder. It was Absalom. He whispered, "Come, come. Shower and shave. Miriam has breakfast." At breakfast, the old man wolfed his food and drank coffee with milk in great gulps.

Miriam admonished him, "Absalom, you'll choke—slow down." She looked at Porch and said, "His whole life, it's been."

In a few minutes, Absalom led Porch out. After walking through several olive groves and orange orchards, Porch noticed several men following them. Porch tarried a moment, as if to pick an orange. The men following stopped. Porch pulled Absalom aside, pointed out that they were being followed. Absalom assured him that they were Israeli security men.

Soon they reached a large hanger-like structure surrounded by a high chain link fence. Guards were all around. Absalom pressed a coder and escorted Porch through a gate to a small side door. He pressed a few more digits on the coder and the door opened. They went up a flight of iron mesh steps, then down a walkway of the same material. Halfway down, the old man leaned over a rail and pointing down, said, "That's Baby's brain."

Porch looked down at what he thought was a rectangular swimming pool with glass sides. Looking through the top was like looking into nothingness. Thousands of fiber optic filaments connected along the sides made the glass appear to have long translucent hair. Absalom said, "Those are input and output connectors. Each connects to a microcomputer. It is a whole network of parallel processors. Come over here and watch."

There was a small glassed-in control room behind them which contained hundreds of dials and rows of buttons along three of its walls. On the opposite side was a heavy window. Absalom stepped inside, twisted several dials and pushed a button. Power came on. Porch saw a dim pink glow coming from the computer. Absalom adjusted the controls and thousands of multicolored needle-like beams flashed back and forth, intersecting, flashing on and off and changing hue to every tint in a rainbow. It was beautiful. Porch was fascinated as the beams danced in picosecond flashes, suggesting pattern after pattern. He looked back at Absalom.

The old man was completely enraptured with his "baby." He began singing, "Bits and bytes, bits and bytes. Wondrous sights, these bits and bytes. Colored lights from bits and bytes." Then he looked at Porch seriously and said, "Baby solves Einstein field equations, tensor fields and vector fields, scalars, too—centered on the center of the black hole at the center of this galaxy, metrics down to femto-femto-millimeters, time to femto-femto-femtoseconds. She looks at all geometry, Reimann, Lorentz-Minkowski, Euclid as well, and checks out Maxwell's electric charges. She marries general relativity to quantum mechanics and solves a manifold of ninety-three dimensions. Am I being lucid?"

Porch grinned.

Absalom looked pensive and then replied, "Ah, the physical universe, though nothing matters in the ultimate then and there, everything counts to form the here and now. Don't you know that except for ancient supernovas you couldn't get a drink of water?"

Porch grinned again and asked, "Aren't you duplicating a lot?"

"Cross checks, my boy, cross checks. With the slightest error, Baby would ship an entity into another universe or create a pile of dust. I'll show you Baby's muscle. Come with me." Absalom led Porch past heavy lead-lined walls into another room. Superconducting coils of tremendous size surrounded a transparent sphere. They entered the first sphere and another slightly smaller inside the first.

"This is the Impulser, Baby's transporter. Magnetic fields and countervailing electric fields squeeze the space time web to make a singularity."

Porch looked puzzled. Absalom looked around secretively, pulled him close and said, "I've found the way to harness singularities and use the wormholes they connect. I can send an entity from here to there instantaneously."

"But no physical effect exceeds the speed of light, according to relativity. It would make time run backwards."

"Relativity does not account for singularities and wormholes, and anyway, Baby sends virtual particles, my boy, virtual particles—Baby's magic transformations are not real in the physical sense, but wherever they emerge, they transform back to what they were."

"Unbelievable," said Porch.

"Not so," Absalom replied, then grinned and said, "There is no hocus pocus. Particles are nothing but the focus of the locus of the energy contained within—down to that certain uncertainty with which we must contend. Am I being lucid?"

"For certain, Absalom," Porch said, scratching his head.

"Well, anyway, it works," said Absalom. Porch was intrigued, so the old man continued, "Now, my boy, I'll demonstrate Baby's magic, which you must learn, as I deem you now my apprentice, soon to be my assistant. Today I'm going to run a collimation to reduce parallax to quantum levels. Otherwise I'd get the dust I spoke of."

Absalom pointed to a small table and asked Porch to bring it into the inner sphere. He went over to a corner and picked up a vase of roses, a pitcher of water, and one dead rose. Returning to the impulser, he placed the roses on the table and adjusted the table to some marks inscribed on the floor. He pushed the dead rose into the vase and poured in water. Looking at Porch, he said, "My test for truth. Come now and watch."

Once inside the control compartment, he turned on a tri-di that sat above the instruments and adjusted it until a desert came into view. The picture zoomed in on a mud-daubed hut. "It is my station in the Kalahari." He took up a microphone and called, "This is QZB CONTROL. Come in."

A loudspeaker sounded, "This is QZB TEST, Dr. Tsetse." Grinning Bushmen around the hut began to wave.

"Come meet my apprentice. He is American. His

name is Porch." Absalom trained a remote projector on Porch. The tri-di receiver showed a Bushman dressed in a safari suit, wearing a red scarf and great wide-brimmed hat. He spoke and waved. The receiver above blared. "Glad to meet you, Mr. Porch."

"He's very formal," Absalom observed. Absalom again spoke into the mike. "Dr. Tsetse, I'm going to send a present for your wife. I will transmit in one minute."

Porch watched the screen zoom back into the hut. The picture settled onto a small table.

"We are ready," came Dr. Tsetse's voice. Absalom twisted several dials, pushed a button and Baby's brain began to hum. Porch watched the dazzling display of color, but shortly the light display settled into a static white pattern. Absalom observed, "Baby is satisfied we're on target." He pushed another button.

Porch watched the screen above and saw a vase of roses emerge.

Dr. Tsetse transmitted, "How pretty. My wife will be filled with joy. Thank you, Dr. Absalom."

"He insists on calling me doctor. Now wait a minute."

There was a pause and then Dr. Tsetse's voice came back. "A thousand pardons, Dr. Absalom, but one rose is dead."

Absalom smiled. "They never would tell before if something was wrong. They didn't want to hurt my feelings. I finally made them understand it was essential I know. Now once in a while I test." Absalom transmitted, "Yes, I sent you a dead one. It's OK."

"I am so pleased to learn its OK," Tsetse came back. "Now I have a gift for your apprentice. Please reverse field."

Absalom pulled a short lever that read "FIELD RE-VERSE" on a plate below it. Then he pushed the engage button. "We have reversed and sign off now, closing station. Good-bye and thank you, Dr. Tsetse."

"Come now," he said to Porch. Again Porch accompanied Absalom to the Impulser. Inside, a very old Krugerrand sat upon the table where the roses had been.

"It's very nice," Absalom observed as he handed it to Porch. For the rest of the day, Absalom worked with

his apprentice, gradually showing him the inner workings of his miraculous transporter, as Porch chose to
think of it.

As dusk fell, they returned to the little Tel Aviv apartment. Miriam greeted Absalom with only a bit less fervor
than she had the night before. Then she held her arms
out to Porch. "Come, Portch, give a poor old woman a
hug." Porch gave her a hug and kiss on the cheek. Satisfied, she moved away toward the kitchen, but Porch
could hear her mutter under her breath as she did, "He
is my Uriah, come back to me."

They sat down to another of Miriam's delicious sup-
pers, and after prayers, Absalom related to her the events
of the day and extolled his apprentice's ability to absorb
the theory and inner workings of his machine. Then
she in turn spoke of her day. She glanced at Porch often, then averted her eyes if she thought he noticed.

Both solicited his feelings about Absalom's work,
their home, and Israel in general. But when he tried to
speak of his past and his eventual departure, they looked
pained and quickly changed the subject. If he persisted,
or Miriam thought he would, she would say, "Eat, skin
and bones you are, Bubee." She would allow nothing to
break her reverie that he was her Uriah, returned! His
heart went out to her, so he decided to delay his departure as long as he could.

In the weeks that passed, he mastered the theory of
Absalom's Transporter, as he called it. He became adept
in working its programs and controls. They worked together, ten hours every day except the Sabbath. Absalom
gave him a coder for use in entering the secure area
surrounding the machine and promoted him to assistant. The more he learned, the more the wondrous device amazed him.

Except for Harry and Granny Gronx, he had never
felt such warmth and love as Absalom and Miriam gave
him. Thoughts of his inevitable departure saddened him.
One day, Absalom was more excited then usual, and as
they walked through the Olive grove and orchards to work,
Absalom confided that this day they would return an
emissary to his home planet in the star system, Vundercy.

"Who to what?" Porch inquired.

"A very important man who came by rocket. Even under the effects of time dilation at relativistic speeds, it took him four years to get here. His mission is so important he must return immediately. The Vundercy system is one of the first colonized by the Millenarians. They were warmly accepted by native peoples extremely similar to Earthlings and are being integrated into existing populations. The Ambassador has confirmed this and also told me their planet faces terrible danger. He came to Earth to search for clues to help them defeat the threat they face. He thinks he has found the clue he seeks and needs to return to analyze it properly."

After they reached the control room, Absalom, in a flurry of activity, pulled star charts from under counter shelves and began to set dials to convert the chart's right ascensions and declinations to spherical coordinates based on the galactic black hole. He had Porch check and recheck his numbers, then activated Baby's brain. Baby sought solution, iterating and reiterating the input until everything meshed perfectly, then she hummed pleasantly while the thread-like laser patterns in the great glass case slowly undulated.

Shortly after eight o'clock, a van drove up under heavy Israeli security, and a man wearing strange iridescent robes got out. The security men brought a large trunk into the hangar, then left as the Ambassador entered.

"I hope you were successful in Beijing, sir," Absalom said.

"Time will tell, Absalom," the Ambassador replied. "The fate of us all hangs in the balance. There is much translation and analysis yet to do. I hope sufficient time remains. Is all in readiness?"

"Yes," Absalom replied, and he introduced Porch. The Ambassador looked at Porch strangely. Then his countenance turned to incredulity as he nodded. This expression faded quickly as Porch heard him mutter, "No, hardly possible." Then he told Porch it would behoove him to learn the system well and paid him no further heed. Absalom noticed the Ambassador's strange manner and thought to break the awkwardness of the moment by saying, "I'm glad you brought the trunk, sir. We'll send that on ahead. I'd hate to send you on without a preliminary test."

The Ambassador asked sharply, "Are you uncertain of success?"

"No, only cautious. We've never gone so far, that's all. The equations are right on, and the computer is humming solution."

"No matter," the Ambassador continued, "it took me four years to get here. Time is running out. Send the trunk first. They can send payment back. I'll write an instruction. I've run out of credits. The Chinese set a dear price. Well, let's get on with it. Porch, will you help bring the trunk?"

Absalom led them to the impulser. "Place the trunk squarely on the grid in the inner sphere. OK, to control now."

Once the three were inside, Absalom signaled Porch to transmit. They watched the glow through the prisms leading to the spheres. The spheres were emptied with a blinding flash and a loud KA-SLAM.

"We better wait an hour before reversing. Is that time enough?"

"Yes," said the Ambassador, "but no more. I must get back."

Absalom said, "After you get there, leave a note or something at the other end so I'll know that you got back. I'll reverse field a second time."

"Very well." The Ambassador grew fidgety as the hour passed. Finally, with five minutes to go, he said, "Let's do it now." Absalom reversed field and pushed transmit. A large gold bar materialized.

The Ambassador cried out, "Good! Good! I'll place the payment outside the sphere, then stand at the center of the grid. Transmit when ready."

He shook Absalom's hand, nodded to Porch, then said, "Good-bye. I am forever in your debt." He entered the inner sphere, stood on the grid, waved and gave the thumbs up sign. Absalom pushed transmit and with a glow, a blinding flash and a loud KA-SLAM, the Ambassador was gone. After an hour, Absalom reversed field. An immense ruby appeared at the center of the grid.

"Wow," said Absalom, "now I can pay my electric bill." He said to Porch, "Let's go home. I am ready now to deal with the Americans."

Porch looked at him sharply. "You have business with Americans?"

"Yes. They bought the rights to Baby. I have negotiated for months in partnership with the government. This poor state doesn't have the money to scale it up to transmit on a very large scale to extreme distances. As well, tee hee, the government is angry at me. Every time I test at extreme power, I black out all of Israel. The people don't notice, as it's only for a nanosecond, but all the computer nets blank out. The bureaucrats go into a rage, tee hee. The Corporation is acting for the Americans."

"What! The Corporation is very evil."

Absalom looked both surprised and hurt as he said, "Oh no, it is the Benevolent Benefactor. Why, the Corporation destroyed the terrible dictator Tukanon without help from anyone. And during the great evil two centuries ago, the Corporation put America, yes, and even the whole world back on its feet. Come, you have believed the rumors of the underclassers and the undercultures."

Porch said nothing, but Absalom saw he had not convinced him.

"Come," he said, "you'll see. They are sending real luminaries to sign the final contracts as soon as they have made their first transport on the machine built from my plans. We will have a great celebration. You'll see."

Porch was in a quandary. He did not want to hurt these people. Maybe boldness was the answer. Could they suspect he was in Israel? There had been no sign of their operatives. Perhaps they feared jeopardizing the contract if someone tried to seize him. Perhaps they had lost interest. Then he remembered how quickly they had come to Diego Garcia. *Wishful thinking*, he thought. He would be wary.

A week later, Absalom was summoned by the government and told the Americans would be there in a week. He could not contain himself. He did his jig, whistling and humming, all the way home. The great celebration would be held in a large hall of the kibbutz. Time passed at a furious pace, with Miriam directing preparations to the smallest detail. Her affection for Porch had grown so much she now insisted that she and Absalom would adopt him as their son and announce his adoption at the celebration.

To make it special, he was not to come into the hall until they completed the "business," as she called it. Then he would enter and take the place of honor next to Absalom and herself. "That was how it would be," she said, as she laid a new suit out for Porch to wear.

The night of the banquet came. Absalom, in Miriam's tow, left early to greet the Americans and their Israeli and government guests. Miriam left Porch with a full set of instructions as to when and where he was to report. Porch protested weakly, but Miriam was adamant. Good-naturedly, Porch saluted and promised he would comply.

An hour passed, and Porch entered by a side door to take his position behind heavy drapes. He could hear toasting, laughter, cheers and clapping. Notables were being introduced by an Israeli aide. Then he heard Miriam's voice. She was to introduce the American delegation. "...and I have the great honor and distinct pleasure to introduce the renowned Admiral Sven Petersen and Lady Brightwood-Petersen, distinguished in her own right, heroine in the destruction of the infamous Dictator Tukanon. Admiral Petersen represents the United States of America, and Ms. Petersen, a member of the Corporation Board of Directors, represents the Corporation."

All the guests rose, clapping loudly. Porch was astounded. There was his beloved commander from the Academy. He had loved her hopelessly from the moment she'd pressed her lips to his after he'd trounced Cheeko so long ago. He found a parting in the drapes and peered out. Her beauty took his breath away. Her rich auburn

hair draped her shoulders and led his eyes to the magnificent diamond necklace gracing her lovely throat. She
wore a sky-blue gown, and over her shoulder draping
diagonally to her waist flowed the white and yellow ribbon of the Medal of the Sun, with its diamond-encrusted
medal pinned just above her breast. He surmised it had
been awarded her for the defeat of Tukanon.

A sorrowful happiness that she now belonged to his
personal hero, Admiral Petersen, whom he'd served but
never met, competed with a raging jealousy that she
was now forever lost to him. He watched intently as
Petersen rose to honor Absalom. Then he thought he
saw him. Yes, the wiry little man with a bear claw mark
on his cheek whom he'd first seen from cover at Diego
Garcia. He was standing toward the rear of the hall.
Porch noticed the bulge at his waist and remembered
the many strange implements he carried there. The man
cast his eyes about as though looking for someone. Instinctively, he knew him as his dreaded pursuer. He
suspected the man worked alone, but could not take
that chance. Were he apprehended here as a convicted
felon, he'd embarrass Bonnie and her new husband.
The shame of his arrest would crush Absalom, his mentor, and perhaps destroy Miriam, his adoptive mother.

It was more than he could bear. All of his insecurities returned, but providence intervened again and
flashed his mind back to the Ambassador and the
strange look he had received from him. He thought of
the picture in the lost locket and then he muttered to
himself, "Could it be? Could it be?"

He was sure he had nothing to lose as he ran from
the banquet hall and returned to the apartment. He
changed to working clothes and left the suit carefully
laid out. He wrote a note to Absalom and Miriam ex-
pressing deep regret for his unexplained departure and
thanked them for their loving kindness. He retrieved
the dagger the Arabs had given him and took a laser
pistol from Miriam's store, leaving the Krugerrand and
the few credits he had left in payment.

He ran through the olive groves and orange orchards
to the hangar. The guards recognized him when he used

his coder to enter but thought it not unusual because he had worked late into the night many times with Absalom. He went directly to the control room. Good, the settings for the Vundercy system had not been moved. He turned Baby on, and as soon as she began humming solution, he set the remote on ninety seconds and pushed TRANSMIT. He ran to the double bubble. The soft glow was increasing in intensity as he entered. Good, charges and magnetic fields were building. He centered himself on the grid. Then he heard the alarm. Lights flooded the hangar.

He could see Israeli guards running toward the control room. Others were running toward him. One reached the outer glass door of the sphere and began to open it, but KA-SLAM, he was gone.

****

The Lawyer reported, "Resounding success, sir. Last night's test results have just come in. Everything worked perfectly. Our engineers will do the stretch test today, two parsecs out, using the old man's coordinates since we're sure of them."

"Tell them well done. If everything goes well today, double their bonuses."

"Very well, sir. Anything else?"

"I heard the wailing again last night. Is there any chance?"

"Frankly, sir, no. Transmogrification is complete, for Cevello as well as his patient."

The Chairman put his head in his hands. The black cat in his lap whined and readjusted her position. At last, he looked up and said, "Terminate them both—immediately."

The Lawyer left quickly, glad to carry out the assignment. The Chairman turned back to the window. He could do nothing else until his order was carried out. Twenty minutes later, the alarm system's scream permeated everything. The cat leaped from his lap, jumped under the massive desk and began snarling. From his window, he saw guards run and mount air scooters, then head for the test site. He sat there, stoically, ready to accept whatever occurred. Ten minutes passed before the Lawyer returned with the Chief of Estate Security.

The security chief trembled, saying, "They were administering the injections. Somehow he broke loose, killed three guards and a doctor, ripping their throats out...released the other...ran south to the test site...countdown progressing...killed two engineers...somehow entered the impulser, and poof—they were gone."

PART II

CHAPTER 1
MIDLWURLD

Inaeternum! Incredible and unfathomable. He sensed eternity, a piece of forever outside time, beyond dimension. He had been where angels dwell, a flowing stream, incorporeal, and now again incarnate. Later he thought about it often.

He materialized at the edge of the great spaceport of Nork. As he emerged, a child screamed and ran to get his father. Soon a company of men surrounded him. They were armed with what he later learned were blasters. Scared, but not lacking courage, they approached. He held his arm up, hand out with palm facing, in what he hoped was a universal sign of goodwill.

He said, "I come in peace."

One cried, "To the magistrate." But another said, "No, wait, we'll greet him as a friend, as we have all others in years past. I'll vouch for him and be his sponsor. Parole him to me."

"Very well," said a third, and the men drifted away, leaving the one who spoke for friendship. This man was as tall as Porch, of sturdy frame and ruddy complexion. He strode up and extended his hand. "I'm known as Big Gwyn. You've brought another wonder from the far stars. I would learn your mode of travel, as I work on rockets, the starships that journey here. We've heard rumors of such travel but had no evidence till now."

Porch replied, "You were good to stand up for me. I am in your debt. My name is Porch and I come from a

star system about two parsecs distant. Its sun is called
Sol. My planet is Earth. I am curious as to why you
accepted me so readily."

Big Gwyn continued, "I knew you came from Earth
as soon as you spoke. We know of Earth, as all the new
ones came from there, the ones who call themselves
Millenarians. They have been welcomed here because
of their peaceful ways and their expressions of love and
kindness, as well as the heroic accomplishment of crossing the Cosmos. My grandfather was a Millenarian of
the Second Emigration. He spoke often of the great space
voyage. I accept the Millenarian philosophy of treating
a stranger as a brother.

"But I confess I had another reason. You look like a
man who knows of rockets. We are rebuilding a ship
that floundered here and was abandoned by its crew. In
years to come we hope to build our own star voyagers,
ships that can leave the Vundercy system. We need all
the starmen we can find to do this. Come with me. I
promise a job at a decent wage, plenty to eat and a place
to stay."

"You are too kind, but I gladly accept," Porch said.

"We have an hour's walk. Tell me of yourself."

Porch sketched out his life and admitted that he
was on the run. Big Gwyn's rejoinder was simple. He
would accept him for what he said he was. Many men
had come for many reasons, some to escape unfortunate circumstance as he had, some for adventure, some
to seek fortune. Soon enough their character was discovered and they were treated as their character demanded.

Porch said, "I know nothing of your planet or star
system."

Big Gwyn said, "Over your stay, you'll find it out, as
all is open to know and ponder. You have entered the
Vundercy system. Our sun, Vundercy, is actually a double star of which you shall learn more. It is one-point-
four solar masses. There are eleven planets. Three are
in the zone of life which begins with the third one out. It
is Megadamn, a hellishly hot, wet planet where few go
and few can live, full of grotesque beasts but valued for

strange fruits and useful drugs. The next one out is where we are, Midlwurld by name. The farther out that yet bears life is Ice World, inhabited by a sturdy race called Vikuns. Our science advanced after you Earthlings came about two hundred years ago, so now there is interplanetary commerce. Though, as I have said, we go no farther into space."

"I'm amazed," Porch said, "that Earthmen could meld into a species so foreign that one would think them incapable of hybridization."

"The learned ones say the Universe has humans throughout, but legend has it that our ancestors were Earthlings, deposited here by an ancient race which had learned their own civilization, a mighty empire of many worlds and star systems in a distant part of the galaxy, would be destroyed. They say those ancients sought to salvage intelligence and understanding and thereby save the Universe for order over chaos. I subscribe to the legend. Anyway, as it is, we are all human. Our blood has been mixed over seven generations. It was quickly blended because Earth men found Midlwurld women most exotic, and Midlwurld men found Earth women quite erotic."

"Interesting," Porch observed. They walked on in silence, each absorbing what the other had said. Then Porch came to wonder about the space time he had entered. Had he been transported many years into the future? Were his friends on Earth all dead, Absalom and Miriam, Bonnie? Emotionally, he could not accept that. Absalom had said that transport was instantaneous. He decided he existed in a universal "now time," that the hour passed since he left Earth was the same hour passed at Miriam's grand fete. This seemed consistent with Big Gwyn's description of the Millenarian's voyages through the void. No doubt they experienced a time dilation, but he remembered from Academy histories that they had left Earth in the same two hundred years of which Big Gwyn had spoken. Then he thought how little it mattered, as he would never see Earth again.

As Big Gwyn said, he found employment at the rocket port, as the natives called it. He became fast friends with Big Gwyn and his sidekick, Little Weejie. Both his Academy background and ignominious servitude aboard the slave ship had given him technical and practical skills in the work that went on there. Although immigration into Vundercy had slowed to a trickle, the spaceport was busier than ever.

Newer ships that ranged farther into the galaxy stopped there to be refit and for replenishment. Sometimes they had cargo to deliver or goods from other star systems to sell. Explorer craft stopped over before proceeding to virgin worlds. The citizens of Nork had plenty of work, and on top of that Big Gwyn and his compatriots were rebuilding the old starship abandoned there a century before to give Midlwurld its first capability to explore beyond the Vundercy system.

Six months passed. Porch found contentment, or at least respite from running. He continued to make friends among the Rocket Guild workers. They liked him for his sunny demeanor, humility and quick intelligence. And he was a good worker. They asked nothing of his background and accepted what he related. They knew he was an Earthman because of his dialect, and figured he had jumped ship from one of the transient vessels that plied the nearby star systems. He said nothing to dissuade them from this assumption, so except for Big Gwyn, who knew better, this became fact.

They taught him to speak the Midlwurld language; easy enough, as the English the Millenarians brought and the Midlwurld tongue, like the people themselves, had become so wholly intertwined. They taught him much about their planet, one quite similar to Earth except that its continents were smaller and more numerous and its jumbled landmasses made for abrupt climatic zones. Grasslands and forests changed suddenly to deserts and mountains, to lake country and marsh, then back again. No settlement or city was far from a sea, and Midlwurld was sparsely populated compared to Earth.

Porch asked about their second sun, which none had ever seen since its far elliptic orbit took seventy-six of their years to complete, and one of their years was two of Earth's. It was the stuff of fearful legends, a dark dwarf that hardly could be seen until it crossed the face of their primary star. Then their golden sun dimmed, turned iron red and had a dire aspect. Their seas churned, their mountains shook, and the winds raged. The Northern seas turned to haunting green and reflected icebergs which chattered, shattered, splintered apart and fell into the icy sea.

One night at the end of their ten-day work week, Porch and the others were paid and given a bonus. Little Weejie suggested they go to Mama Mia's for pizhu. Porch smiled at the odd delivery of the Earth word, though such was common. So off they went, he, Big Gwyn, Little Weejie and several others. They were a happy band, as their work was going well, especially on the starship. After they had eaten their fill of pizhu washed down with beer, Little Weejie suggested they round out the night at a public house with a little merriment. Rosy-hued girls with hair to match from a traveling troupe were doing dances, both exotic and erotic. It was said that some would grant favors, and on occasion a worker would find his heart's match amongst them.

Amidst the shows and drinks and song, a man named Rumermong told of a man who knew a man who talked to a boy who said some time ago he saw a man come out of a rock. Then another, one called Taleberry, said he'd heard it was a pregnant woman who saw the apparition and she said he came out of a tree. It scared her so much, she lost her child. And soon thereafter, another man appeared. Porch looked at Taleberry and asked, "You say another man appeared?"

"Oh, yes, I heard it from my wife." Rumermong, not to be outdone, chimed in again, "It's an evil omen that foretells the dark star's coming. Strange and cataclysmic things will happen." His eyes grew big as he looked around to see the effect of his words.

Porch caught Big Gwyn's eye. Big Gwyn said, "The hour is late. I, for one, have had enough, I'm going back to the boarding house and hit the pad. Tomorrow, with clearer heads, we can discuss this further, as we have the next three days off. Perhaps we should talk to our union man. Come, Porch, you've not been one for carousing."

The others too agreed to call it a night, and so they headed back to the boarding house. On the way, they met the district constable, who stopped them short. The Constable knew Big Gwyn.

"Big Gwyn," he said, "we're looking for a man not seen around these parts in the past, who, some children say, came out of a rock behind a tree. Crazy it sounds, but they've worried their mothers into a fright. The Super says we must canvass the district and question everybody. We'll begin tomorrow at noon. Please tell your men to stay nearby."

Porch made up his mind, then and there, that he would be gone well before noon. He'd leave a note for Big Gwyn. He set out early, musing to himself that running had become his way of life. He headed east, having heard that the farthest inhabited area from Nork was a small city called Edgetown at a place called Land's End. With his pack on his back, he quickly distanced himself from the spaceport and the surrounding service district. He continued past the new steel mills, and at the edge of the city, he saw a used car lot. If his bonus money would cover the cost, he decided to buy transportation.

He tested several trucks before the owner convinced him to buy a used "jup" of twentieth century Terran specifications which could be had for the exact amount of his bonus. Soon he was on the road again, well past the city. Noon, too, soon passed. It seemed the old jup had a top speed of about thirty miles per hour. The speedometer needle passed that mark only going downhill, and then laboriously. The Norkers, as citizens of that city state were called, had copied the specs exactly. They hadn't even changed to the metric system, which Porch had thought was universal. Pressing his foot on the accelerator, he looked again at the speedometer. It hovered right at thirty miles per hour.

Outside the city, the road turned from Macadam to crushed rock and now to just plain dirt. Porch thought the Midlwurld civilization quite skewed and wondered if the Earth people's arrival two centuries ago was the cause. In the space age, their transportation was hardly up to twentieth century Earth's. They had not developed aircraft, nor had any interest in doing so, as such would give each the ability to overfly the other's domain, which would be considered snooping and most impolite. They had used wood and coal for a thousand years but had only begun using petroleum and gas twenty years before. They knew about cermets and advanced computers, but their communications were archaic. He decided it was a matter of priorities set by their quest for starships, because the cost of bringing new technology across the void was measured in billions of credits.

Porch continued along the dusty dirt road when the jup, climbing a short but steep hill, began to sputter and choke. He coaxed it to the top of the rise, and before him lay an artist's pastoral as far as he could see, golden fields of waist-high grain interrupted by green pastures full of cattle grazing contentedly. Woodland-covered hills bordered vales where slow streams flowed. A citadel lay, high up, in the far distance. It looked like a cap on an extinct volcano, with high outer walls and a palace or castle in the center. He thought it must be the capital of one of the kingdoms of this world of kingdoms, commonwealths, and city states.

The jup caught on again and gathered momentum as it ran down the hill, dust blooming behind. Porch looked to his left and was amazed. The road seemed to bound two climatic zones. Desert lay out to a distant dusty horizon. As he scanned the expanse, he picked up a whirlwind of riders pressing down on the road. They rode toward him at breakneck pace. The jup halted just beyond a stone bridge at the bottom of the rise, its momentum used up where it chugged, choked and died. A thicket of bushes grew under several tall oak trees on his right. He got out to gaze at the riders and particularly their steeds, the renowned camel-horses which had the desert endurance of Earth camels and the speed of racing thoroughbreds. He was fascinated and wondered why they were racing. The long cloaked riders flashed scimitars in the late afternoon sun. Closer and closer they came. Suddenly he heard a voice from high up in the tree.

"Hide the jup in the undergrowth on the right. Hide it well."

Porch looked up to find the source of the instruction. The voice continued, "Do not tarry. You'd make a fine specimen for her stable, should they snare you."

Porch pushed the vehicle into the undergrowth and looked up again.

"Climb up here. Your life depends on it. They are almost on us. Hurry, before they see you."

Porch jumped up to a lower branch, looped up, and climbed rapidly into the dense foliage.

"Be quiet. Don't move. Make not a sound."

Porch again searched for the source of the voice, but did not find it. The riders were fifty yards away. Cloaks and black turbans fluttered in the wind they made. With reins in one hand, they whipped their mounts wildly, side to side. With the other hand, they smote the air madly with their blades. Porch saw they wore cuirasses of woven gold beneath their robes. They swept past swiftly, not seeing the pair in the tree, and were gone as quickly as they came, leaving swirls of dust to mark their passage.

"'Tis the Ruby Queen's company on a raid. Pity those swept up."

Porch dropped to the ground, followed by a wiry little man dressed in a cassock. He began talking as he looked around for his wide-brimmed hat, which had fallen behind him. "This road bounds the two kingdoms by the treaty the Wizard made them sign. But the riders flaunt the Treaty by their raids, which good King Szidrous overlooks. He'd be devastated if the wars started up again."

Porch recognized the habit of a cleric as he watched the man pick up his hat and brush the dust off. He smiled and said, "Why, you're a cleric, a monk, or perhaps a priest."

"Aye," said the man.

"Well, what?" Porch demanded, somewhat suspiciously.

"Brother, father, friar, monk, reverend, whatever pleases you."

"You're pretty far from Rome, Father," Porch chided him, laughing.

"Aye, or Worms, or Zurich, or Canterbury... But farthest of all from Jerusalem," he sadly replied, "and I've been waiting for you."

"For me?" Porch was puzzled.

"Yes, today is the day. Now is the hour, and here is the place, so said the ancient astrologer. I am his messenger, his servant and assistant, humble and willing to accept the wrath of my order to serve the Seer and his order, the Wizard who reads meaning into the hidden and secret scrolls of Nostradamus."

"What?" Porch said.

"Come, we cannot tarry."

"Why me?" Porch asked.

"You came to the place at the time appointed."

"But Nostradamus was debunked, discredited, centuries ago. The things he predicted could be said to mean any number of things."

"Shh, you don't know what you don't know. The world line changed, the Wizard said—long ago, when men broke the atom and put it back together again, fission and fusion, fuss and muss."

"Preposterous!"

"Not so," the Priest continued. "Not long ago, on Earth, in an obscure monastery near Salon in France, he found some scrolls, written in an ancient French hand, from the year 1557 anno Domini. There were three quatrains of Michel Nostradamus, unknown pieces, lost fragments of the eleventh and twelfth centuries: 'The Monk shall go...far from the source, to serve the Knight whose love was lost...A Priest to see the horde from Hell, unspeakable vermin, all consuming...A Universe lost to all that's natural...Unbearable, unbeaten, unbegotten abomination...Black the nebulae, dark the galaxy ...Frost before and fire after...The source shall send a golden one To quell the loathsome horde from Hell... By epic flight, late at night...Rotting the flesh, the consumer consumed.'" The Priest paused and looked at Porch, then said, "Come—on to Edgetown and the Tower of Astral. The Wizard waits."

Porch and the Priest pulled the jup from its cover onto the roadway. Porch thought for a moment, then threw open the hood and cleaned the carburetor. He refilled the jup's tank with gasoline from one of the jerry cans he'd purchased, got in and attempted a start. The jup sprung to life, and they were off. Later, as the last rays of sunshine played on the clouds above, turning them to red, orange and pink, they drew abreast of the fortress that Porch had first seen six hours ago.

"And what is that?" he asked the priest.

"That, my young friend, is King Szidrous' castle and palace. He is the Wizard's close ally, one of the few who understands the holocaust to come. His castle is in fact a citadel, the strongest in this land. It was begun by his great-grandfather when the Earthlings first came as a caution should they prove hostile, and a good thing, too, because it plays a part in the Wizard's strategy against the cataclysm to come. As you see, it has thick bastions and lofty barbacons ingeniously placed to be defensible all around. Its outer walls are thirty feet thick and twice as high. Its highest tower reaches up six hundred feet. Though the immigrants, Millenarians, as they call themselves, presented no threat, the desert kings turned evil. When the Ruby Queen's father, Abul, came to power, the tribes banded together. Under Turg, the Black Prince, who was the Ruby Queen's husband, they mounted many raids against the Szidrian people for slaves and booty. They were fierce and still are, believing that death in battle leads straight to grace for all eternity. Turg was killed in battle, and although the Wizard led the warring parties to a treaty, sporadic raids continue to this day. Shalimar, the Ruby Queen, grieved for a year and a day, then vowed she would secure a champion of Turg's mettle as an heir to follow her rule of the Desert Kingdom of Soome.

"She since has followed a very strange course. She seeks a man to sire her child and has decreed that he must be the strongest, most courageous man in all the land. Thus she maintains a stable of gladiators whom she pits one against the other to determine the most fit to take as consort and give her an heir. Many compete willingly to possess her, but the losers suffer a fate that men should not be made to bear. Many call her the Black Widow as well as the Ruby Queen. She must be approached with great caution. I saw her once when I went with the Wizard to Toome, the great tent city in the desert. She is most beautiful in a wicked, lascivious way. She has long hair, black as ebony, and flashing black eyes enfolded by long and delicate lashes, soft feathers that brush a man's psyche indelibly. Her skin is almond and her lips blood red. She costumes herself in a scanty halter with bare midriff and thigh-slit skirt or loose translucent pantalets, all meant to tantalize. She wears a large and brilliant ruby in her navel. She is said to be a sublime lover of infinite capacity and insatiable desire."

"I am surprised a priest would take such notice," Porch observed.

"I am first a priest but forever a man."

The Priest's long discourse was interrupted as they came upon some beautiful orchards. He said, "Stop here. This is a good place to camp for the night. There is a spring nearby. The gracious owner shares his bounty with weary travelers."

In his kit bag, Porch had some coffee and cakes. The Priest pulled out a pouch of sausage, cheese and biscuits. So they built a fire and supped quite well, topping their meal with apples from a nearby tree. The fire dimmed and the moon came up as they were having their coffee. Porch asked, "But what of King Szid? Is he living still?"

"Aye," said the Priest. "The good man, now an octogenarian, is very frail and I'm afraid, growing senile. He loves his subjects and they love him, but he absolutely dotes upon his daughter, a child of his old age and his only child.

"Her mother, Szid's queen, was a Vikun princess sent to seal a compact between Ice World and this. She came to love the King very much for his kindness and wisdom, but to everyone's sorrow, she died in childbirth of a disease unknown in that cold world. She had not the immunity built up in people here. It was a choice between her and the child—pity."

"Didn't you indicate the child survived?" Porch asked anxiously.

"Aurora is now grown, and the Ruby Queen's beauty pales beside her own. She is tall and slender, with silver-blonde hair and ice blue eyes that flash an opalescence when she laughs and are signature to her Vikun forebears. She is as pure as the morning dew and gentle as the dawn. It is fabled that should she wear a rose upon her shoulder or moonflower in her hair, it will not wilt.

"But her father has promised her in a blood pact to the Thurl of Ice World for a defense treaty and ties between the two worlds. That man, Prince Spauk, is a cobra, a cockroach, to say the least. Little does Szid know. But Aurora, poor Aurora, a dutiful daughter, has resigned herself to fulfilling that abominable contract to uphold her father's honor and for the sake of their people—pity.

"Even under the sadness of that marriage contract, she remains full of hope, joyful, kind and compassionate. Her laughter is as the tinkling of wine glasses. She wears below her ivory throat and above her sweet and sculpted breasts a single pearl of teardrop shape to commemorate her mother who died to give her life."

The Priest went on to talk the night away. At last he was silent. Sleep came only with the dawn, and then fitfully for both. High noon came before the Priest awoke. He splattered water on his face, then went over and shook Porch. "Hurry! Hurry!" he said. "The Wizard waits. We dare not be late."

Porch, now fully awake, said grumpily, "Well, I have but one can of gasoline left. After that we walk, and the Wizard will wait."

"No, no. If we start now, we'll be at the Millenarian border and Hodel's hostel late tonight. Hodel has a pump," the Priest replied.

They ate supper's remnants and went on their way, riding through pine forests and small towns, passing well-kept farms and humble villages. The road remained

rough, but was sometimes improved or even macadam-
ized at the entrances to the larger towns. Both men
stayed silent, still tired from the night before. At sun-
down, they reached a clearing where thousands of ravens
were beginning to roost for the night. As the jup passed,
the birds began a raucous clamor, cackling their indignity at the intrusion below.

The Priest spoke up. "They are ubiquitous in these
parts."

Porch looked up. They covered the sky as they flew
in to roost.

The Priest spoke again. "When the ravens gather
and grow silent, the great battle is nigh...Life hangs on
a song...A stealthy flight...in the dead of night."

Porch looked at the Priest but said nothing.

Close to midnight, they saw lights ahead on the side
of the road.

"That should be the border and Hodel's hostel," said
the Priest.

Porch pulled the jup up and parked it at the side of
the building. The Priest jumped out, went to the door,
and knocked gently. The man, Hodel, opened, and upon
seeing the Priest, bowed and said, "Peace, Brother, welcome. It is good to see you again. Come in."

The Priest introduced Porch to Hodel and his wife,
and arranged for a night's lodging and a purchase of
gasoline. Soon they were seated at a hearty meal and
quickly thereafter retired for the night.

At first light, the Priest woke Porch, saying, "We must
start."

Hodel's wife, jolly, plump and red faced, had a sub-
stantial breakfast prepared. Hodel sat with them and
listened while the Priest talked of his comings and go-
ings. When they finished, Porch filled the jup with gas
while the Priest took leave of their host. When Porch
pulled the jeep over to pick up the Priest, he heard Hodel
say, "The Great One will tell us what to do."

The Priest responded, "Your people must act on the
Wizard's word."

Hodel bowed, pressed his palms together just below his nose, and replied, "The Universe is one, and we

are one with the Universe. No harm will come if we heed the Great One's words. Peace be with you." He waved good-bye as Porch pulled away. Porch said, "I'm confused. He spoke of the Great One. Was he too referring to the Wizard?"

"Alas, that it was so. He refers to Thaddeus P. Winter IV, direct descendent of the leader who brought the Millenarians to Midlwurld. He has not accepted the Wizard's warning. So his followers never say yes or no. I fear a terrible consequence when the dread day comes."

They drove on, mostly in silence, for another day and night. The Priest notably brightened the afternoon of the next day when they came to what he called the Perfume River and passed the Crystal Lake.

"We are almost to Edgetown," he said brightly. "It nestles beneath Twin Chime peaks at the edge of the Eastern Sea. It is a university town founded cooperatively by nearby principalities and city states."

"Exotic names for rivers, lakes and hills," Porch observed.

"But descriptive," the Priest replied, somewhat huffily. "The founders wanted more attractive names than Land's End to enthuse the students they envisioned would come."

The rich odor of cloves rose from water lilies floating on the water. The lake was so clear they could see hundreds of crystals sparkling on the bottom. The Priest continued, "The waterfall chips off and spreads the crystals lying on the bottom as it tumbles down between Twin Chime Peaks. The crystals tinkle as they fall. The peaks look somewhat like bells if one has sufficient imagination."

Porch laughed. " OK, OK."

"It may interest you that the Wizard is also the chancellor of the University. He takes great interest in the curricula, as well as the students and faculty, insisting upon the best and most advanced."

As they passed through the campus, people of all ages scurried by, carrying loads of books and some video disk packs.

The Priest observed, "The Wizard insists on reading. He says only the written word sufficiently stimulates creativity and nourishes the imagination. He makes the faculty justify each video disk used."

Porch looked around enviously and thought maybe someday he could complete his education. The Priest caught his wistful look and asked, "What troubles you?"

"Really nothing."

"Let's stop at the student's union for supper. Everyone's welcome. A little rest won't hurt. We have a steep mountain road ahead of us."

An hour later, they reached the road leading up the mountain. After climbing the foothills, the Priest exclaimed, "There! You can see it now, the Tower of Astral where the Wizard resides."

Porch looked up and saw a fat, jet black, squat cylinder about four times as tall as it was broad. Porch could see the tower better as they took each switchback and wound on up the road. It looked made of obsidian, dark, glassy and hard, without windows or doors. They reached the base of the tower at the top of the mountain, passed through an iron gate and entered a small parking lot which had a solid wall about five feet high on its outside. Porch saw why. The fall was thousands of feet down. From this height, he could see Edgetown, where lights blinked on as dusk settled. The town must have been at least fifty miles away.

The Priest had gone directly to a portal that fit seamlessly into the smooth black stone. He touched a square of unnumbered tiles at the side in a preset sequence, and a ponderous stone door groaned open to a dark interior. The Priest beckoned Porch follow him in, and after they entered, the stone slowly ground back into place.

They were in a high-ceilinged entry hall shaped like the interior of a truncated pyramid. Ancient astronomical instruments and orreries were displayed on pyramidal stands around the room. Cold light shone up from below, illuminating each. The polished stone floor also appeared made of obsidian. It was inscribed with a great circle with lines radiating out from a huge diamond of at least three hundred carats set at its center. The center represented the Vundercy sun. Thousands of tiny diamonds were inlaid into the polished stone in pattern at ever-greater distances.

As Porch gazed in wonder, the Priest touched his shoulder. "'Tis a star chart of the heavens hereabout. Note the circles concentric to the Vundercy sun. They measure time in light years and distance in parsecs. Your solar system lies way out. Now, observe."

He pointed a ring he wore toward a wall and pressed the inside with his thumb. As the chamber lights grew dimmer, the tiny stars took on a brilliance. The Priest pointed his ring toward the wall and pressed it again. The tiny diamonds at the far edge of one thirty degree sector dimmed and slowly went out. Darkness came ever closer, like a giant hand, until its fingers almost reached the great central diamond of the Vundercy system. Porch gasped.

"The Wizard uses this display as a vivid illustration of the galactic cancer's spread. Enough! Come. We go to see the Wizard."

The Priest led Porch to a seemingly solid wall of obsidian. Again he pressed an obscure set of squares. A heavy stone block opened to a dimly lit elevator. They stepped in, and after the block moved back, the elevator rose swiftly, passing level after level. At last it stopped and doors opened. The Wizard stood before them.

He was imposing. A shock of steel-gray hair matched by a close-cropped beard framed his chiseled features and piercing blue eyes. He was solid and as tall as Porch. He wore a strange indigo silk gown embroidered with mysterious symbols in silver thread which made a wild dance when he moved—sinusoids, cycloids, spirals, serpentines, cubics and rhomboids.

He said to the Priest, "I see you brought him—well done." Then turned to Porch and asked, "How was your journey?"

"Interesting," Porch replied noncommittally.

The Wizard grasped his shoulders and held him steady as he looked at him and said, "Yes, he could be the one. Come—sit here."

He motioned both to a round table of polished ebony surrounded by three low chairs. A crystal obelisk of amazing clarity was centered on its top and crystal rhombohedrons on headbands had been placed at each chair. The Wizard indicated each should put the device on with the rhombohedron at his brow. This done, he reached into a chest at his feet and withdrew a small brass box which he put on the table.

He twisted a single dial on its top and the image of a metronome appeared deep inside the obelisk. Its pendulum began to move back and forth. The room slowly darkened and as it did, the crystal obelisk's luminescence increased to such brilliance that neither Porch nor the Priest could avert his eyes from the image. The pendulum gathered speed and its ticking became audible. The Wizard looked at Porch and said, "Look into the crystal and count the strokes of the metronome. It ticks for you and it ticks for me. It ticks for time universal. It is the heartbeat of the stars. It holds the rhythm of your heart and the measure of your mind."

Porch's thoughts were swept into the obelisk in a maelstrom. He entered a trance.

"Your mind is joined to mine. Your thoughts are in the crystal—all that you have lived, all that you have dreamed. Go back now, back to the beginning. All must be revealed. All must be made known.

"Empty your mind, your psyche, your very soul."

"Quod avertat Deus!" the Priest exclaimed.

CHAPTER 2
THE WIZARD

"Let him wake slowly. There is great danger. We have drained his mind, stressed his psyche, and pushed his emotions to the limit. We may have ravished his soul. Remember he has relived the agony of his life as it was projected above us."

Porch's eyes opened, seemingly without focus. The Priest bent over him. "Deo gratias!" Then he looked up at the Wizard with a hundred questions pressing him.

The Wizard said simply, "He is the one."

The Priest looked back at Porch, who had begun to move his eyes. He touched his shoulder gently and asked, "How do you feel? You have slept for four days."

Porch did not reply, but sat up instead. He did not recognize the Wizard immediately, since he had discarded his indigo robe with its strange silver symbols and dressed in a simple black tunic with black trousers tucked into high black boots. As it came back to him, Porch focused on the stern face and felt awe but no fear. He said, "I did not recognize you at first, as you changed your attire. Your strange robe is gone."

The Wizard replied, "In life's theater, men costume themselves for the occasion and the duty it carries."

Porch began to ask why his mind had been so violated, but before he could, the Wizard said, "It had to be done. We had to find out. You are the one. Get up. You'll be fine. I have much to show you. We have much to do. Night has returned. We will sup now." He looked at the

Priest and said, "Lead the way, Brother. Time is precious."

They dined in a golden room on pillowed chairs, on soup and bread, steaming tureens of vegetables, pheasant and hearty meats, and fine vintage wine, and finished up with coffee, cheese and fruits. The Wizard spoke of many things, Edgetown, the University, the Millenarians, the Desert Kingdom and Kingdom of Szid, of Midlwurld itself. When he saw his guests had finished, he said, "Come. It is time to show our young friend the Dark Star, and worse than that, the reality of what you, good Brother, showed below. Come, we'll take the stairs."

"Oh no," the Priest groaned.

The Wizard led them to a small door entering on a stairway. Up they went. The Wizard fairly flew, and Porch, for all his youth, could hardly keep up. The Priest fell far behind. Higher and higher they went, forty-four steps and a turn, then forty-four more, up, up and up, fourteen flights to another small door. The Wizard unlocked the door and bade Porch enter a pyramidal chamber. A large mirrored surface was centered there. The Wizard seated himself at a console and motioned Porch to one adjacent.

He said, "This is a camera obscura modernized many times with elaborate sets of mirrors and advanced optics. We sit at its focus." He pulled a lever, and high above four leaves on the pyramidal roof opened like a tulip revealing its bloom. Porch looked up through the opening and saw a black sky punctuated by brilliant stars.

The Wizard continued, "First, we'll look at the Dark Star." He pulled another lever, twisted a dial, and Porch heard the deep rumble of heavy optics and mirrors rolling into place. There was slight vibration as the great camera hunted its target and then settled into place. "Look at the focus in front of us and tell me what you see," the Wizard commanded.

"I see a dim blotch in a background of stars."

"Yes, that is Nemesis, the Dark Star. It formed soon after the birth of the Universe, farther away than the farthest galaxy we see today. It was blasted from its birthplace in a horrendous supernova that consumed its substance, all except its core. That core lived on as a dense white dwarf with its radiant energy almost gone. Passing close to the Vundercy sun, it bound itself as a mate, married by celestial mechanics into the binary orbit both follow today. It has become a cannibal, a vampire bride. On each orbit, as it passes our sun, it sucks of its gaseous substance in a swirling gravitational embrace and grows fat while its mate grows lean."

Just then the Priest appeared, huffing and puffing. He seated himself on the other side of the Wizard. The Wizard looked at him ruefully and said, "Brother, you must do better. The time of trial is soon to come. You're not much faster than a tortoise."

The Priest retorted, "Sometimes the tortoise wins the race." Then he looked at the Wizard and said ominously, "The Dark Star, all consuming, grows fat...only to die."

The Wizard ignored him, turned to Porch and said, "Mathematics forecasts that in two more orbits, Nemesis will have grown robust enough to again vent her fury, go supernova and degenerate into a neutron star. A century and a half from now, that awesome event will destroy the Vundercy system. That is why the University must advance this civilization. The people here must have sufficient science and wherewithal to journey forth to a new star system.

"Well, enough of Nemesis. The Night of the Conjunction is coming soon enough. When that errant star crosses our sun, this world will tremble. Seas will rage and terrible storms will roar, but such will only presage the greater danger to come."

He slowed the optics and said, "Now look up."

Porch looked up to the heavens and saw the bright star field half occluded by utter blackness. Black fingers extended forth. The Wizard dialed the console to increase the magnification and focus again, and Porch could see the utter darkness expanding, coming closer, like a gaseous cloud of unknown poison.

The Wizard pulled a third lever and the optics

groaned back as its housing port closed. He said, "That is the Scourge. We call them Throgs. They have devolved into a race of demons. I have fought them, along with a handful of others, the better part of my life. Yet we have not stopped them. They cross the galaxy riding gravity waves like surfers, gaining an impulse from each passing wave, in star ships of a technology known only to the ancient race. They lie deep in cryogenic sleep, roused each time they reach a new planet to conquer and devour its people. They have destroyed untold worlds in unnumbered star systems. We have but a few months before they reach us and much to do because we've found new hope. Come."

The Wizard led them back down the stairs into a study. Books, old and new, lined the walls. He went to a corner and pulled a chest forward. Porch glanced at it, and as the Wizard pulled it into better light, looked again more carefully.

My gosh! he thought, *I've seen that trunk before*, and the experience came back to him. Absalom, the Ambassador—was there a connection? It seemed a hundred years ago, but he was certain that was the trunk. He looked at the Wizard. Could it be possible? He couldn't be sure. He was left to wonder as the Wizard opened the trunk and carefully lifted out some ancient plates.

"Come over to the light on the table to inspect these better. They are invaluable, secured at great cost."

Porch and the Priest looked at them closely. They were bronze, covered with a thick gray-green patina. A black oxide surrounded and obliterated portions of the columns of characters.

After pausing for their examination, the Wizard continued, "They come from pre-dynastic China, from a land populated by a race called Tungs. It has taken considerable time, but I have deciphered the characters on the plates and translated them. Listen!

"'I, Wu, chief astrologer of the Northern Kingdom, in the Year of the Horse...the date is not readable...ordered these plates inscribed and buried, so someday they may be found, made known, and remembered.

'These are the last days. Barbarians are at our gates. The great king, Lu, is dead. His son, Shu, reigns. Shu is a wastrel. His days are numbered. He has given himself to drink and gambling. He has more concubines than he can count. He used the kingdom's gold to pay his debts. Still he drinks and gambles. He sold the royal store of grain to pay his debts.

'I cannot feed the concubines,' he said. 'What shall I do?'

'Release them to their families,' I said to Shu.

That I cannot do, said Shu.

From the heavens star gods came, searching for soldiers.

'It is an omen,' Shu said, 'we have the greatest warriors in all the Earth. I shall sell the star gods half the Army and feed the concubines.'

Barbarians came from the north.

'What shall I do?' said Shu, 'I have but half an army.'

'Build a wall to keep them out,' I said to Shu.

Shu built the wall and went back to drinking and gambling. Soon his creditors were again upon him.

'What shall I do?' said Shu.

'Sell your store of wine, your silks and porcelain, and send the concubines back to their villages,' I said to Shu.

'That I cannot do,' said Shu.

So once more he sold his soldiers.

Best in the world, he said.

Soon barbarians broached the wall.

'I have sold my army. What shall I do?' Said Shu.

'Build a terra cotta army and place it in the valley where the barbarians have broached the wall,' I said to Shu.

But a sandstorm came and buried the red clay army.

'What shall I do?' said Shu.

'There's nothing you can do,' I said to Shu."

The Wizard looked at his two guests.

"Fascinating," the Priest said. Porch nodded in agreement.

The Wizard spoke again. "Years later, buried with Qin Shi Wang, China's first emperor, a vast army of terra cotta soldiers was found, and as you know, the Great Wall stands there to this very day.

"But that's not the reason I've had you listen. The story contains the clue I've searched for for more than two decades. You see, the star gods of whom Wu speaks were the Ancients who destroyed their own empire in a mighty cataclysm to save the galaxy from that same scourge so close upon us now. Those warriors from the northern kingdom are the very ones whose devolution into degenerate beings, true demons, became the scourge whom we call Throgs. Their descent was marked when they lost the natural clock that causes all to age and die, a genetic program lost from their DNA. Now they grow like a cancer, never dying, but spreading throughout the galaxy."

The Wizard paused so his guests could think of what he'd said, then he continued, "But now we have a chance."

"I don't understand," Porch said.

"The descendants of those warriors still live on Earth, and they die like ordinary humans. Now we can trace them. I must secure a sample of their blood and tissue–their death cells–and have sent for such. One member of my Order is there, subordinate to me, but he is more my assistant. He is most trustworthy, an heroic man, an admiral in the Western Alliance Fleet. I cannot divulge his name, but if anyone can secure what I seek, he will. I'm sure of that."

Porch's head was in a swirl. He wondered if the Wizard spoke of Petersen. Had he been swept up in coincidence, collusion, fate or predestination? He wondered what his role in the terrible events that were gathering would be.

"Once the samples have been collected, we shall reconstitute the death cells. The Angel of Death has waited for those demons twenty-two centuries too long."

"You spoke of an Order," Porch said, searching.

"Yes, a little-known order, The Order of No, descendants of Earthmen like myself, who were first ordained by the ancients before they perished to destroy the Scourge or fight them forever.

"Nostradamus was one of us. We are now few in number, for such is the deadly toll of our combat, and it has fallen on me to command those left. I am Lord No."

A raven descended upon Lord No's shoulder as if to punctuate all he had said. He lifted it gently, took it over to a perch that Porch had not seen, and deposited it there. Returning, he said, "They are ubiquitous in these parts, for they have a role to play. Now, my son, will you join the Order?"

From all that Porch had seen and heard, a sense of destiny came over him, and he said, "As you desire, my lord."

"Very well, but before I add you to our roster, I must test your fidelity with a mission. You will carry a message to the Ruby Queen who rules the Desert Kingdom of Soome. She resides in the great tent city of Toome at the Oasis of Oome. I will send you with a guide and a safe conduct. She will listen, as I have her chit for service performed and her oath of support. You leave in the morning."

Lord No then turned to the Priest and said, "The time has come for the ingathering. Brother, it is yours to go to the land of the Millenarians and persuade them that no force in this world can stand before the horror to come. They must evacuate to the Szidrian citadel. I will gather the folk from the lands around here and then the great city of Nork. We too leave in the morning."

"Alea iacta est—the die is cast," said the Priest.

CHAPTER 3

THE RUBY QUEEN

Porch and his companion fairly flew across the dunes on camel-horses. The speed and endurance of these animals amazed him. They traveled for days, riding only at night to avoid Vundercy's blazing sun. They wore loose-fitting cotton pants and shirts covered by silk burnooses embroidered with silver and gems befitting a Wizard's ambassadors. Each carried a highly decorated scimitar at his side. The Wizard forbade them other weapons, saying his safe conduct would suffice. They refreshed themselves at small and rare oases. Mirages of such fooled them several times, but otherwise the trip was uneventful.

When they stopped to rest on the morning of the tenth day, Porch saw birds to the west, circling very high. He cried out and pointed, "Ravens, no doubt."

"No, my friend," Rashid, Porch's guide and traveling companion corrected, "probably vultures. The tournaments of Toome produce many corpses, which feed them well. The birds are a sign that we approach the Great Oasis of Oome and the fabled tent city. We should see it soon. I think we should continue, since we are quite close."

"Agreed," Porch said.

By noon, with the sun directly overhead, they saw the tent city in the distance, shimmering in the heat. As they approached, a troop of desert warriors rode toward them at full gallop, brandishing great curved swords.

Rashid motioned both to stop. He held his hands out to show he had not pulled forth his weapon. Porch did the same.

The riders swarmed around them, black cloaks blowing in the wind, golden cuirasses shining beneath. Their leader drew up before them, his scimitar held menacingly, and shouted, "Who dares violate the dominions of the illustrious Desert Queen?"

Porch held out the sealed paper Lord No had given him, which their inquisitor snatched from his hand, tore open, and scrutinized with fierce intensity. His voice softened and he said, "So you come from the Wizard, our great benefactor and close ally."

"That we do," Porch replied.

"I'm Harim Skarim Shareem, captain of the Queen's Own Camel-horse. State your name. I know this other, Rashid."

"They call me Porch."

"And what is your business?"

"We are envoys to the Queen on matters of great import."

"Very well, I will take you to the city, where you may beg audience. Show this safe conduct to all who seek to see it," Harim said, handing the paper back to Porch.

He took position at the head of the troop surrounding Porch and Rashid, raised his scimitar, slashed the air, and all raced off like the wind. As they approached the outskirts of the city, Shareem's warriors dropped off, leaving only the Captain with them. The fertility of the land skirting the city astounded Porch. He thought, *Water, it does indeed make the desert bloom.*

Fields of grain, pastures full of sheep and goats, lemon, lime and orange orchards were all around them. Fig and olive trees, gardens and melon patches surrounded small ponds. He glimpsed fishermen netting what he perceived to be great carp and catfish.

Then they reached the city itself, which was indeed splendid. Every color of the rainbow feasted the eye. Tents rose, some to sixty feet, all draped in harmony, festooned in stripes and diamonds or diverse arabesques. They rode up sandy alleys filled with stalls where vendors hawked wares in a noisy bazaar. Carpets, silks, robes and gowns, sandals and boots, and heavily jeweled swords and daggers were all on display. Fragrant spices, perfumes and flowers tantalized their noses, as did the sweet aroma of roasting meat and baking bread. Mounds of fruit and melons invited purchase by those strolling along the crowded passages. Children of every size and year, barking dogs and sleeping cats were everywhere underfoot.

They tread carefully along the crowded lanes, riding along for at least an hour. They passed a carnival and saw sword swallowers, fire eaters, snake charmers, belly dancers and stalls for fortunetellers. Pitch men stood in front of other tents hawking the secrets that lay within. They came upon a pastel tent guarded by fierce-looking men. Rashid leaned from his camel-horse to catch Porch's ear, whispering loudly, "It is said that slave girls may be bought inside."

Porch winced, and Harim Skarim Shareem, who overheard him, looked at him darkly. Now just ahead lay a narrow lake, or perhaps it was a moat, for an arched bridge with a sentinel on each side guarded its approaches. Small islands with feathery willow trees dotted the water. On the other side tall stately palm trees flanked the entrance to a golden tent, the highest and most extensive tent the travelers had seen. Harim Skarim Shareem looked back and said, "We come to the royal palace. Show the Wizard's seal and safe conduct to the guards as you cross. I leave you here."

Once across, the Captain of the Palace Guard invited them to dismount and asked them to follow him into the palace. Inside, attendants led them to the baths, rubbed them down with fragrant oils and spices, and brought them bread and meat, a heaping tray of melons, and fruity ices. Soon they were refreshed. Shortly thereafter, a heavy gong rang and reverberated through the tent. A huge man, at least seven and a half feet tall by Porch's estimate, and black as ebony, entered the chamber. He wore a massive turban fastened in front with a gigantic topaz, which further increased his fearful height. A gold-embroidered vest covered his broad, muscled chest and a wide silver belt held his bright red silken breeches in place. He wore a pair of silver slippers and had a huge jeweled scimitar sheathed at his side.

He bowed and pressed his right hand to his forehead, then brought it down in front of him. With great dignity, he said, "Salaam, Effendi, I am Brobdingnagia, grand vizier to the Queen and prime minister of the Desert Kingdom. I have been told that you are envoys from the Great Wizard. He is our close friend and ally. We owe him our good fortune and great wealth, for he found the outcropping and the seeps. He showed us how to dig deep wells and said, 'Drill here.' We did, and soon the wells brought forth the black liquid gold."

Brobdingnagia then reached into his vest and with great display pulled out a jeweled timepiece which he looked at carefully. He looked back at Porch and Rashid and said, "The Queen grants you audience now. Come."

They followed him, one on each side, treading silently on carpet after carpet as unseen persons pulled curtains aside to let them pass through chamber after chamber. At last, they entered a grand chamber held up by exquisite pink marble columns. Fountains, flowers and massive pillows adorned the chamber. At the end of a long red carpet, the Queen sat in a throne of gold and red velvet raised up on a pink marble dais. She was beautiful beyond description. She wore a golden band of diamonds on her forehead which channeled her jet black hair to flow down in waves about her almond shoulders. When she moved her head, her hair shimmered with a blue and silver radiance. Her deep-set black eyes were framed in long soft lashes that gave her curving eyebrows perfect symmetry. A sculpted nose and full red lips completed her perfection.

She wore a burgundy gown draped and pinned at her right shoulder with a large diamond brooch. Her gown was pulled tight against voluptuous breasts and gathered at her slim waist, held in place by a silver belt through which she had thrust a jeweled silver dagger. It flowed down past ample hips to fall open just above her knees, revealing long almond legs; sensuous stems fit to bear a sybaritic body. Silver slippers fondled her beautiful feet. Yet Porch could see a hardness about her. Beguiled, he thought of Delilah, Salome, Helen and Eve.

Brobdingnagia approached the throne and, bowing low, said, "Your Radiance, I have brought the two who rode in from the south. They bear the seal of the Grand Wizard, who was declared by yourself and Council a prince of the Realm. They carry a message and protocol from him." The Grand Vizier turned and motioned Porch and Rashid to his front, then pushed their heads down into a low bow.

The Queen replied, "I know the one, Rashid, by name, retainer to the Wizard. As to the other, the tall and comely golden one, I know him not." She gazed at Porch intently. "What is your business?"

Porch raised his head and stated, "We carry an urgent message from the Wizard."

"Hand it to me."

Porch stepped forward and handed the seal and documents to the Queen. She examined the seal, opened and read the documents quickly, then spoke to all, though she kept her eyes fixed on Porch. "The Wizard reminds us of our alliance and requests we join our forces to those of the senile old King Szid in a great war that will soon be upon us. What do you know of this, Brobdingnagia?"

"Your Exaltation, there is a portent, the day of the Great Conjunction, fearful enough with the winds that will blow and bring fierce storms upon us, then turn day to night, but worse than that, it presages an unholy terror to follow. Even now, each night in the canopy of heaven, stars blink out and an evil blackness comes closer.

"It is an intergalactic army of hideous creatures, more in number than all the sands of the desert."

"Ha!" said the Queen. "More yet, the Seer would have us come with all our legions, all our goods and all our people to reside within the imprudent fool's castle, crowded with thousands to wait the fate to come. We could not breathe the fetid air—we who ride a thousand leagues, a thousand times, in a thousand days. Such we could never do." She looked sternly at the two messengers.

Porch said, "It is your only chance."

The Queen laughed contemptuously. "You dare say that to the queen of the fiercest warriors who have ever trod this planet. We who sweep all before us. You would have us cohabit with the sweating, stinking masses who inhabit stone and wooden cities and wallow in barnyards with pigs and chickens. We should have you in irons for such suggestion, and would, save you represent the mighty Wizard, selected from amongst all others to be one of us."

Rashid trembled visibly, but Porch continued, "Though your cohorts are mighty in battle, though your legions sweep all before them, the fury to come is like no other in all the annals of recorded time. It is a horror that plagues all that is known–"

"Enough!" the furious Queen commanded. "Another word and I shall have your tongue on a plate, even though you are the Wizard's man."

Porch was silent and looked at her in awe. Her agitation radiated out like fire, enhancing her beauty. Her almond skin flushed pink and her dark eyes flashed brilliantly. Her bosom heaved and as she rose from her throne in her ire, her hips undulated voluptuously.

Hot blood coursed through his veins and he felt a lust that he could not quell. He felt the heat of her anger, and his nostrils picked up her exotic scent. He steeled himself to control any visible manifestation of his enormous salacity. She stood silent a moment to diminish her anger and then spoke in a rich contralto, "We know the debt we owe the Wizard, who showed us how to gain the precious black gold, that fluid that flows in seas so deep beneath our dunes. That material has made us rich beyond measure.

"We know the pact we made with him to join forces at his call when the time for battle comes. We shall reconfirm that now."

She drew a silver vial from her skirt, removed the top and held it up for all to see. She next withdrew her dagger from its sheath and pricked her finger with its point, letting seven drops of blood drip into the vial. She replaced the dagger, wiped her finger with a bit of silk, and corked the vial, saying, "We make a blood oath to which you bear witness, here and now, that when the Wizard calls the desert legions to battle, we will respond—with a fury that will shake this planet, its moon and sun."

Again, she looked at Porch, though she spoke to the Grand Vizier. "Brobdingnagia, draw up this oath on our finest vellum. I shall sign it with a flourish and stain it with my blood."

Brobdingnagia bowed deeply and replied, "As you command, oh Song of Songs."

The Ruby Queen then said, "When this is done, Rashid will mount our swiftest camel-horse and take the parchment to the Wizard."

The Grand Vizier started to lead Rashid and Porch away, but the Queen commanded, "Wait, the Golden One is not to leave. He shall dine with me in my chambers at ten tonight. My handmaidens will prepare him. Make sure he is well rested."

"It shall be done, oh Brighter than the Morning Star."

"That is all." She clapped her hands, strolled across the dais, and disappeared behind a drape.

"Come," said Brobdingnagia, and he led them out, passing Porch to a young maiden dressed in blue. She led him to a new chamber which was luxurious and cool. "Sleep now and gather strength," she said as she left him. For that, he needed no urging, and soon, to the soft melody of woodwinds, strings and chimes, he fell fast asleep on a pile of cushions. Some hours later, a dozen voices united in a tinkling of laughter awakened him. As he opened his eyes, he saw himself surrounded by as many handmaidens, veiled but scantily clad. One tickled his face and neck with a long feather.

"Are you awake now, Master Golden One?" she half-questioned.

Porch, startled, started to retrieve the clothing he'd pulled off. Several stayed his hands and others pulled him up. Before he knew it, they hustled him into another chamber, wherein he saw a large bath. The mar-

ble tub was filled to the brim with bubbly water. Over
his protests, the handmaidens pulled off his drawers
and half shoving and pushing, cast him into the tub.
They began to wash him, caressing his limbs with the
scented sudsy water. When he could not but help respond physically to their soft touch, they tittered and
giggled and pointed to his embarrassment.

"Oooh," gasped one. "Ahhh," sighed another, and
they all began to jabber in a strange foreign tongue.
When they had washed him to a pleasant tingle, they
pulled him out of the water, dried him off and massaged
his limbs with a perfumed oil, vaguely familiar. Then he
remembered the virile scent of desert santolina. He found
himself powerless to protest, so they dressed him in a
gauzy vest and loose white trousers. They combed his
hair, manicured the nails on his hands and feet, then
thrust his feet into a pair of sandals.

Just as they finished, a gong reverberated around
the chamber. All but two ran off, giggling and laughing.
The maidens left behind took his arms and pulled him
up. They led him through another series of chambers
and down some halls until they came to a gate. It was
solid jasper, framed by columns and an arch. Carved
on the arch were the words—TEMPLE OF ASTARTE.
The maidens spoke in unison. "Enter in," they said, and
then silently withdrew.

The gate swung open into a dimly lit anteroom. Great
vases of apricot blossoms filled the room, and tapes-
tries of fabled lovers festooned the walls. He crossed the
room and came upon a portal. Above it, PORTAL OF
ISHTAR was inscribed on an arch of crystal. It slid open
and led into another chamber full of statues of unclad
lovers in tight embrace, fountains, pink flowering orchids, and amaryllis wrapped tight, anticipating bloom.
He was puzzled, yet could waste no time in contemplation, for ahead two translucent peach-colored curtains
slowly parted. A wide white ribbon, inscribed THE CLEFT
OF VENUS with silver thread held them up. Crossing
these, he found himself in the subdued light of a high-
ceilinged chamber filled with a light fragrant incense,
perhaps sandalwood.

The Ruby Queen rested at one end on a high, wide divan, as luxurious as anything he'd ever seen, covered in dark pink satin. Several paces away, slightly lower pedestals framed the divan. And on each pedestal, a very large, sleek and beautiful black panther sat regally. Jeweled collars ringed their necks. The Ruby Queen had removed her headpiece and her jet black hair flowed down to cloak her creamy shoulders. A diaphanous drape constrained her large, full breasts. Her midriff was bare, and she used her navel as a bezel to hold a giant red ruby. Her luscious red lips parted in a smile that hinted of rows of lustrous teeth. When he caught her dark eyes, he felt he looked into the depths of female mystery that ranged from the beginning to the end of time. She half reclined, resting on an elbow. With her other arm she made a regal sweep, beckoning him forward, and said softly, "Welcome, Golden One. Now turn around slowly so my eyes may feast upon your beauty."

Her voice was so compelling that he followed her direction. Then, at a loss for what to do next, he bowed low and stammered, "My greeting, Your Radiance."

"Enough of that. Come here."

Porch approached till she could touch him, and she slid her legs sensuously down the divan, slipped up next to him and put her hand on his forearm. She ran it up to his shoulder, across his back and down, bringing it back to rest in his palm. Gazing into his eyes, she said, "Golden One, in my chamber you belong to me, and we are man and woman and my name is Shalimar. Whisper it into my ear."

She tilted her head and threw back her hair to expose her ear, then pushed it up to lightly touch his lips.

"Shalimar," he choked tentatively.

"Again," she commanded.

Better composed, he repeated softly, "Shalimar."

"Much better," she said.

Then she touched her lips to his. "Now we shall dine," she smiled. As if on signal, both panthers lay down.

"It would be a pleasure," he said, and as she turned away to call out, he ran his tongue around his lips where her print had been to savor again its spicy memory. Shalimar clapped her hands and called out softly, "Victoria, we dine."

She rose from the divan, pulled Porch up and led him around the panther, which ignored her, to a candlelit crystal table set for two. He helped her to her seat and took his opposite. The table was small enough for their knees to touch. She looked back at the big cats and said, "My guardians, lying there in such regal repose, are really pets, raised by my late husband, Turg the Magnificent."

A curtain parted at one side and a beautiful handmaiden entered. She wore a sky-blue gown with a scanty bra and wraparound skirt pinned at one side and opened there to reveal a well-turned leg. Her hair was a nutty brown of such sheen that it glimmered in the candlelight. She did not look at them or speak but served two silver bowls of cool vichyssoise, turned and left. Porch recognized her as the prim guide to whom Brobdingnagia had passed him earlier.

"She has the glow of youthful beauty, does she not?" questioned the Queen, her eyes flashing.

"She has indeed, but pales before Shalimar, the Morning Star," Porch replied carefully.

Very pleased, the Queen said, "Victoria, my handmaiden, is my confidant, and even more, a true sister. Now eat your soup. It's getting tepid."

The moment they finished, Victoria brought another tray bearing purposely small portions of oysters clad in a pastry, lobster in cream, and truffles in sauce. Fruit and wine completed the meal.

Shalimar said, "We'll take a demitasse of coffee and some chocolate on the divan. Come."

She pulled Porch tightly to her, an arm about his waist. As they passed the panther, it made a throaty growl, answered by the other with a loud roar.

"Be still, Bathsheba. You too, Luther."

She turned to Porch and said softly, "My pets grow anxious."

"Have they reason?" Porch inquired.

Shalimar smiled, "We'll see. Sit close beside me now."

Victoria brought in the after-dinner coffee, a golden goblet of liqueur, and a tray of chocolates. She set them on a table at the edge of the divan.

"You may go now, Victoria, till I call again."

Shalimar next lifted a demitasse to his lips and one to hers.

"Sip," she said. "This drought will refresh your palate and lead you to another hunger. It is an elixir of love."

Porch sipped the coffee. It had a fresh minty taste.

"Now," she said, reaching for the goblet, "the lore of love and chocolate, intertwined, lie in this cup with added spice and honey. It is a special mix—passion's potion. Put caution far behind you, Golden One, sip with me, and learn the art of love." She held the goblet to Porch's lips, and he sipped tentatively.

"Again," she demanded, and he drank heavily.

She took the cup and turned to where his lips had been and drank deeply. She turned it back to him to drain. Its delicate sweetness lingered in his mouth and had a strange effect. All around him save Shalimar faded out while his brain poured forth wanton desire and his loins a torrid lust. Her exotic, heady scent further enraged his passion.

She selected a chocolate from the dish and fed it to him with her fingers, which he kissed. He felt, then smelt her spicy breath as she drew closer. She kissed his lips, then took a chocolate in her mouth and mashed it against her palate. She placed her mouth to his, and with her tongue pushed the sweet syrup in, then rolled her tongue around, seeking his.

Bathsheba whimpered as Shalimar ran her lips about her new love's face and nibbled on his ears. She ripped open his vest and stripped it back, then pushed him down, kissed his neck and shoulders, ran her mouth about his chest and lingered to titillate his flesh with teeth and tongue.

The male panther moaned. Slowly, Shalimar continued down the sinewy musculature below his chest, searching out every ripple. Breathing heavily, he did not protest. As she circled his navel with her tongue, she pulled the drawstring to his trousers and deftly slipped them off his buttocks, then down his thighs and legs onto the floor. She then continued around his thighs and stopped at the treasure she sought out and now was hers. He gasped in erotic delight as she lingered there.

The male panther groaned, then roared as Porch moaned his ecstasy. Shalimar looked up and ordered, "Luther go, Sheba down."

In a flash, the great black leopards leaped from their perches, clashing just beyond the couch. The female snarled and swiped the male. They bit and clawed, tumbled, then rolled around, but shortly then, Luther took Bathsheba, with great jaws clamped on her neck, and pulled her to a dark divide far across the chamber.

Porch sat up, his chest heaving. But he was now delirious with desire. Shalimar pulled away to lean back on her cushion and let her scanty cover fall away. Breathing rapidly, she thrust a leg behind his back and with her other foot pulled him closer. With her other, she moved jeweled toes to the chocolates, grasped one and pushed it to his lips. He took it quickly, then licked her silky toes. He pressed his lips around her foot, its sole and heel, soft as velvet. He kissed her ankle, her calf, and as she wrapped her leg about his shoulder, he licked the moistness behind her knee.

She grasped his tousled golden locks, pulled his head into her hands and drew him slowly up her thigh. She held him there to moan the pleasure of his searching tongue, then slowly, very slowly, pulled him farther. Eager to sense all of her, he nuzzled the softness of her belly and reached the dazzling ruby in her navel, which was spitting bright red fire. She said softly to him then, "Come visit the sugar mountains and taste of their honey."

So she pulled him up to her heaving breasts and tumescent nipples. She closed her eyes and stroked his shoulders as he took his pleasure there. His lips crept then to the chasm in between, went round about and on to the moistness of her fragrant arms. Drunk with the essence of her body, he tasted of her neck and chin, her nose and eyes, and nibbled on her ears. She found his mouth with lips now taut, and pressing hard, her tongue thrust in. He thrust in turn, probing here, probing there in lingering abandon. She freed her arms from his neck, scratched down his back with nails dug in, seized his haunches to aid his thrust and pulled him deep inside. She wrapped herself around him with a tenacious grip and in a growing frenzy spurred him on so they could synchronize together, every quiver, every shiver, tightly bound, until they were released into great spasms of delight.

She gasped her ecstasy, and he felt crescendo after crescendo of wondrous release. She demanded of him, again and again, until she felt his vigor fading, then flipped him over as if possessed, clamped him deep inside and worked him to exhaustion. At last she slowed, bent down upon his spent and groggy body, and wrapped her limbs around him tightly, with all her flesh pressed to his. She held him to her for an indeterminate time. She kissed his lips one last time very sweetly, then bit him deeply on his neck very neatly. Shalimar, the Black Widow, had made her mark.

Porch lay still, the fire inside now but embers. He grew cold, very cold. Recoiling then, she pushed him off the couch onto the floor, rose, retrieved a robe, straightened her hair, stretched and rang a chime. Within the minute, a curtain parted and into the room strode six squat, hairy eunuchs, eyes down, carrying a net. They stretched it out and laid it down. It looked much like a web. They picked the supine body up and laid it, naked, limp, within, then carried it quickly out as quietly as they had come in. A curtain parted and Shalimar noted another dawn had come.

She hit her chime, this time twice. Victoria entered, pushing a cart on which rested a large golden tub full of scented sudsy water. Her mistress dropped her robe and stepped inside. Victoria bathed her, dried her off, oiled her skin, then dressed her in a fresh pink gown. Another maiden wheeled in a dressing table, put a stool before it and then removed the clothes strewn around, the towels and tub of water. She returned to remake the

Queen's divan. Shalimar went to the dressing table and picked up a hand mirror to gaze closely at her face. Victoria brought in a tray of creams and began to brush her lady's black tresses. The Queen, surveying her image in the mirror, said, "The years begin to take their toll. I must choose soon."

"Oh, beloved mistress, I thought that he might be the one."

The Queen, humming softly, asked, "Where is the Retin Triple A?"

"'Tis here in the marble jar, sweet mistress."

"Ah, yes," Shalimar said, dubbing it on. Victoria kept brushing her hair until the Queen remade her face. Then Shalimar rose, returned to her lounge and said, "Bring the box of favors, please."

Victoria went to a chest and withdrew a crystal box, saying, "Here, my heart's own."

The Queen took it and said, "He was good, very, very good, though somewhat inexperienced. In fact, he was quite delicious; the pheromones and aphrodisiac acted quickly and completely. He was close to equaling that huge and raging bull, the one who claimed he came from another world, a place called Earth, I think. Ah, what was his name? Oh, I remember–Eric, Eric the Red."

"Yes," Victoria said. "You awarded him two golden balls for his performance. It was just after he conquered the dark one, the highest award so far."

The Queen reflected back. "Yes, he was worthy of those." She opened the box of favors which contained lead spheres: bronze, steel, wood, gold and silver spheres. She picked up two silver spheres and toyed with them. "At least these," she mused.

"As you deem appropriate, Wise Queen," Victoria replied.

The Queen grew serious and said, "We must follow the royal proclamation. I'll choose my consort from between the two. We'll let the lists decide which is worthy to sire my heir. I'll pit them in mortal combat, one against the other. The winner shall be mine."

Shalimar then clasped the maiden's hand and lay back, gazing out with a faraway look in her beautiful dark eyes. The maiden stood motionless, and for several long minutes it was very quiet. At last the Queen broke the silence and said, "Oh, Victoria, why can't I ever be satisfied?" She became still again, then pulled up and said, "Victoria, come closer." The Queen slipped her arm around Victoria's waist and pulled the drawstring on the maiden's bra, setting her tender breasts free. Victoria sighed.

CHAPTER 4

THE TOURNAMENT

Porch awoke in a cell under a drenching of bucket after bucket of water. The water stopped and the previous day and night's events flooded his mind. He looked up into blinding sun, unable to see the figure standing over him, a dark shadow extending higher and higher.

"Wake up, Effendi. It is I, Brobdingnagia. The Queen likes you. You get to compete for her hand in marriage. Stand up. Your food is here. You must restore yourself."

Porch rose groggily. He was naked except for a loin-cloth. He wiped his eyes to better see the giant. Brobdingnagia grinned broadly. He said, "Tomorrow I come again to explain the rules. Today you rest. We have much to clean up after yesterday's tournament."

The giant bowed deeply, his right hand touching his brow, turned and left. A jailer brought in a great tureen of stew, a mound of bread with cheeses and fruit, and an ample supply of water. He set it on a table in front of Porch, then left, putting a chain around the cell's entrance and clasping it fast with a heavy lock. Porch pulled a stool from under the table, sat down and ate heartily.

After he'd finished, the jailer came back, removed the food, and left him a basin of water and some towels. Porch refreshed himself and then made a survey of his situation. The bars to his cell were stout. They bent to meet at the top. Sawdust covered the floor and there was a pile of straw in one corner. A heap of blankets lay beside the straw. Nights got cold in the desert.

The cell seemed center to a line of cells. Each held a single prisoner and most were sleeping, but Porch could see several pacing back and forth. The cells bordered an arena, a vast circular area to the north surrounded by wooden walls and barricades. He went to rest on the pile of straw but what he saw outside his cell interrupted him. Men were pulling a cart full of bodies toward a gate at the west end of the arena. High above, he saw buzzards circling. *Well*, he thought, *Rashid knew what he was talking about.*

Next he saw a group who, he guessed by their demeanor, were eunuchs. They were replacing sawdust that had a distinct red tinge with fresh. He thought of the Ruby Queen, surprised that one so beautiful and such a lover would have such a barbaric dimension. He was surprised as well at his response to her charms, unbridled lust, primal and carnal. Yet he could lose his heart, his soul and his very rationality to her. Why had the Wizard not warned him?

"Psst, psst." The noise startled him out of his reverie. A red-bearded giant was standing at the bars of the adjacent cell. Great shocks of red hair also covered his head. The man whispered again, "Psst, I am Eric, Eric the Red. At least people have always called me that. I don't mind, because as you see, it's true. I came from a faraway world, but don't remember how or why. I was with another, but he is gone. Everything is fuzzy.

"When I arrived, I found myself on a great desert, the one over the wall to the west. People here call it the Western Waste. I wandered for days without water or food, seeking shelter. I found some deep holes. I began to crawl down one. An unearthly scream came up from beneath. Something gripped, ripped at my feet. I withdrew quickly. Strange, unearthly howls followed. I ran far away, became deranged. Black riders came. They brought me here."

It was long ago, but came to Porch in a flash. This man had been a friend. He said, "I know you. We were candidates at the Academy. Do you remember Bokasi? You were teammates on the football squad."

"No. It is like a fog, a distant haze."

"What do you know of this place? Why have we been brought here?"

"Simple enough—we are gladiators. I have fought and won twice. Shh! A guard is coming. We cannot talk together. It is not allowed. They will think we are planning an escape."

Eric moved away, going to his pile of straw, where he lay down. Porch did the same. He had to think about his situation. Night came, then morning. As promised, Brobdingnagia came early.

"Ho ho ho," he shouted, "wake up, Young Warrior, I've come to tell you the rules and bring you a steaming breakfast. Wash up and eat. I will return when you are finished. I must inspect the others and see if they've survived the night."

When he returned, he announced, "Behold her Omnipotence's seal." He gave Porch a minute to observe the seal, a black twelve-pointed star encircling a blood red ruby. As Porch looked it over, the giant said, "First, Effendi, you are ordered into individual combat by her Celestial Majesty as stipulated in the laws of Soome."

"Why?" Porch asked.

Brobdingnagia's eyes grew big with surprise. "Why? Because the Queen said so, that is why. Is that not enough? Do you rebel? Do you wish me to take your head to her on a platter?"

He put his hand on the hilt of his scimitar ominously before he continued, "The Queen would be very sad if you did not participate. She might even weep. I could not bear to see her in such despair."

Brobdingnagia paused for Porch's answer, but Porch said nothing, so he began again, "The rules then... One: it is mortal combat, to continue until one contender is killed or yields. Two: contenders choose their own weapons, as many as they wish to carry. Three: weapons are limited to those that show individual prowess...no lasers, stun guns, poisons, etc., etc. Four: combatants are allowed shields of one meter diameter, no more, no less. Have you questions?"

"Yes," Porch replied. "Are helmets allowed?"

"No. The Queen likes to watch contestants' countenances to search out courage, determination, fear...or cowardice. You may wear a head band to keep your eyes clear. That is all."

"Is body armor allowed?"

"No. The Queen thrills to watch muscles bulge, sinews ripple in swift attack, and sweat glisten off a mighty back. You will wear only a loincloth. That is all."

"Are contenders allowed to train?"

"But of course. You may train in your cage. Beneath the stadium is a two-mile track where you may run for endurance. There are skill rooms to develop tactics, strategies and individual techniques. Each contender may use the arena for two hours a day, working with his trainers, who are provided by lottery. We have a skilled staff of warriors who have won in the arena. There are no losers, as those not killed are not suitable for such duty."

"And who am I to be pitted against?"

Brobdingnagia's eyes twinkled, "Why, I thought you guessed–the Raging Red Bull. I know you talked to him. The Queen likes him, too."

Porch felt sick. How could he go up against his friend? "Well," he said, "we may as well get on with it. I will begin my toning today. Be good enough to come tomorrow and I shall give you my specifications for weapons and ammunition."

"Very well, Young Lord." Brobdingnagia departed with a salaam, and Porch began his training. He returned to his cell for supper, quite tired. He lay down to sleep just as the sun set when he heard strange chanting in the adjacent cell.

"Yo-ho, yo-ho...she rode me like a whore and I grunted like a boar...yo-ho, yo-ho." He raised up on an elbow and peered over to see Red Eric pressing heavy weights up and down from his waist to high overhead. He judged the weights to be one hundred pounds apiece. Eric was chanting an up and down rhythm. "Yo-ho, yo-ho." He quit when he saw Porch watching and came over to the bars separating them.

"Psst," he whispered, "have you heard? We fight each other."

Porch rose and went over to where Eric was standing. "I know."

"You'll pardon me, but I must kill you—nothing personal, but I must have her. I've tasted of her once and want no other, ever. She has bewitched me. My passion cannot be quenched. She is my bread and butter. So when I pierce you with my lance, remember—it had to be, so die with a friendly thought for me."

Red Eric backed off and went over to his straw to sleep. Porch was sad, very sad, but he had no intention of giving up his life.

Brobdingnagia came at dawn the following day. "Greetings, Young Lord. Do you wish to choose your weapons now?"

Porch noted a deference in his voice. Perhaps Brobdingnagia would give him a chance. Should he win and marry the Queen, he would be the Grand Vizier's master too. The giant was taking no chances.

"Yes," Porch said, "I will choose my weapon now. I choose the sling. Here are the specifications." He handed him a drawing elaborated with notes. "And I want one thousand aluminum pellets, one inch in diameter, clad in steel, and one hundred lead pellets, also clad in steel. Most are for training, but one hundred aluminum and ten lead are for the contest. And I must have a device to hang from my waist that lets me retrieve either kind quickly without looking. It should be lightweight and spring-loaded. Give this drawing to your armorers. They can construct it."

"Strange weapon indeed," Brobdingnagia replied, puzzled. "I doubt you'll have a chance. Consider again, Young Lord, an ax, a mace perhaps; your foe is formidable. We have scimitars, swords, tridents and nets; even a bow and quiver of arrows would be better."

"You said the choice was mine."

"As you command, Young Master." The giant left with a deep salaam.

Porch began intensive training. Within a week, he was running twenty miles. He spent his time in the weight cage toning his upper body and arms. He devoted his two hours in the arena to practicing with the sling the artisans had fashioned for him. He became lightning fast drawing the pellets from the device on his belt. His trainer and seconds worked earnestly to help him prepare, as they would benefit greatly should he win. They set up targets on wires to dance up and down and move to and fro so that Porch could fire his missiles at them. Porch used only the steel-clad aluminum pellets when he was in sight of Red Eric's cell.

Both Porch and his trainer put on heavy padding, and Porch would fire his sling to hit him. His trainer would hurl javelins back. Porch honed his skills of jigging, weaving and ducking those hurled at him and learned to parry with his shield.

Red Eric watched all this, and Porch would watch him when he was in the arena. The powerful man could hurl his javelins in high arcs of over a hundred yards, in near straight-line trajectories and all the curves between. He could cast a fusillade in just as many seconds as he had spears. And Eric used his trainer as an opponent and dodged the missiles that came from his sling.

As the days grew nigh to the bloody judgment, Porch watched Eric split heavy beams bobbing on a cable. Then strangely, Eric ran up against a rapidly twirling carousel of thick bobbing logs. But he did not use his javelins, rather a thick lance. Porch thought to himself that it was an ungainly weapon which should be easy to dodge. But a voice of caution whispered in his ear— *easy to dodge if it's as it appears*. His suspicions rose when Eric's assistants built up a barricade which blocked all view from the cells. Unseen, Eric continued with the stubby lances, and Porch heard sounds of crashing and splintering.

When Porch's turn in the arena came, he found and examined several splintered posts which showed piercing at high speed with great force. Burn marks indicated fibers had been compressed violently and mashed aside. No man could produce such a piercing velocity with even the most violent thrust. There must be an auxiliary mechanism. He wondered if he would find an answer to this mystery in time.

Two days before the combat, Porch noted another of Eric's characteristics. Left-handed, he consistently circled clockwise. Casting his javelins, either singly or in flurries, he could retrieve those spent before he cast his total inventory. Porch must turn this to his advantage.

As the sun began its arc across the sky, promising blazing heat on the day of the combat, Brobdingnagia began his rounds. He stopped first at Red Eric's cell.

"Greetings, Mighty Champion. May this be the day of your greatest victory. I favor you to win because none can stand before you. There will be two preliminary bouts. Then you face the Golden One. I shall call for you. The prize is worth this world and another. Make the combat excite the blood."

He went to Porch's cell and said, "Greetings, Young Warrior. May you carry the day. I favor you to win because in the ancient tract the Wizard gave the Queen, there is a story of David and Goliath. This you re-enact, which favors your success. After two preliminary bouts, you face the Raging Bull. I shall call for you. The prize is worth the moon and stars. Make the combat excite the blood."

So both prepared, calmly and carefully. Their trainers rubbed them down and plied their flesh with oil to counteract the sun. Their seconds inventoried and checked their weapons. All was made ready.

Trumpets blared, signaling the matches to begin. The first contest pitted a tall blond Vikun, a spacefarer captured in a raid on Nork, against a swarthy fisherman who had wandered too far up the coast of the Eastern Sea. The Vikun carried a battle-ax, the fisherman a trident and net. The combat ended quickly after the Vikun, pricked in the side, rushed the fisherman, who was swinging his ax but slipped and fell. The man of the sea netted him, entangled him and plunged the trident into his heart. The crowd roared approval as six eunuchs came out with a rope and dragged his body to the gate in the western wall.

When the roar of the crowd subsided, trumpets blared again and two more combatants entered; it was broadsword versus scimitar. The match was long and hard. Weapons seemed to clang and clash forever, until the blade of the scimitar broke and the broadsword was at the enemy's throat. A plea for mercy rent the air, and since the fight had excited the blood, the Queen gave thumbs up.

This time, however, the eunuchs bore a stretcher to which a strange harness was attached. They placed the vanquished warrior on the stretcher and attached the harness. He was too tired to protest. Porch wondered what drama was about to unfold, but just then he heard the chains drop off his cell door and he was called forth.

The trumpets sounded with considerably more flourish than before. It was the main event. On cue, the contestants entered from opposite sides of the arena and met Brobdingnagia in the center. Brobdingnagia read them the simple rule of the contest. "Fight without quarter until one or the other is vanquished."

Porch and Red Eric looked at each other. Brobdingnagia continued, "Go, side by side, up to the Queen, bow low, and await whatever word she has to give you."

He preceded them as they marched up to the royal box.

Shalimar sat there in regal splendor, the diamond tiara adorning her head. She wore a low-cut white gown of fine silk. A broad red sash ran from her shoulder to waist, upon which she had pinned the twelve-sided ruby-centered star. Her jeweled dagger was attached at her waist. Her handmaiden Victoria sat beside her holding a parasol above their heads. The men stopped and bowed low.

"Approach, Red Eric," the Ruby Queen commanded. He did, bowing low again. Shalimar tied a silken scarf around his neck. The crowd roared, thinking she had chosen her champion. As Eric backed away, she turned to Porch and said, "Approach."

He did, bowing low. She handed him a pouch containing two silver balls, saying, "An award for a night of delight."

Porch strung it to the cord that held up his loincloth. As he did, Shalimar commanded, "Now turn about that I may gaze upon your beauty one last time." Porch did as commanded, then returned to his place. The Queen cried out, "Let the contest begin."

Brobdingnagia marched them to the center of the arena, faced them back to back and instructed them to step off one hundred paces, then turn. At the trumpet's sound, the combat would begin. He left for the Queen's side, where he counted one hundred paces and signaled the trumpeter, who sounded a stirring flourish of three measures.

As the last note faded, a javelin swished by Porch's ear. Porch looked toward the Redman. Eric carried a quiver of at least three dozen steel-tipped spears which he could reach over his shoulder and hurl in an instant. Beside them, in a separate quiver, he carried two of the strange stubby lances. He began to circle clockwise, as did Porch, who loaded his sling with a steel-clad aluminum ball.

In quick succession, Eric hurled three javelins, one high, one on a medium arc, and the last at twice the velocity, almost in a line of sight. They had a triangular pattern to catch their target right or left should he misjudge their arcs. During Eric's effort, Porch cast one pellet, then another to spoil the Redman's aim. Eric circled left, closing. He hurled another barrage of six javelins. Porch dodged and flung a volley of his own. They circled, feeling each other out.

Oddly, the arena seemed to be shrinking, and Porch saw desert warriors pushing the barricades forward into an ever-tighter circle. Porch thought, *The time for feinting is over.* In rapid succession he slung four balls, two at his opponent's head and two at his shoulder. He scored a shoulder hit, as Eric, shielding his face, did not pick up those aimed at his shoulder. Porch was now close enough to see the Redman wince.

Around they danced, ever closer. Eric was now retrieving spent lances from those he had hurled. Porch unleashed a barrage each time Eric bent over. An hour passed. He scored a number of hits on his opponent's shoulder, and he was creased on his side.

Blood flowed and he felt weaker, but he saw that Eric's ability to move his shield quickly was also deteriorating. The size of the arena had been halved. Eric lost six javelins which whistled by Porch and plunged irretrievably into the wooden barricades. They circled closer, panting, sweating profusely, their flesh glistening.

The Queen watched intently, enthralled with the combat. She did not see Victoria hide her eyes as another javelin creased Porch's side above the first slash. Porch had fifteen steel-clad aluminum balls left. Now he changed his tactic. Eric's reaction to the sling's fusillade had visibly slowed. He flung a ball at the big man's head. As Eric raised his shield to counter, Porch flung several at his groin. One hit its mark, and Eric cried out, gasping in pain. He recovered quickly, threw several spears in return, but his aim was way off. Porch repeated, this time toward the shoulder, another to the head. The missile hit the Redman's shoulder as he went to protect his head. Porch flung a flurry of three balls at his groin. Eric's shield went down to protect him, but not in time, and he groaned in agony. The first wound on Porch's side had caked, but the second was still seeping blood. Both men's bodies streamed with sweat. Again Porch's missile hit its mark. Eric staggered.

The Queen, watching, wondered whether her champion would be able to service her. Was he permanently damaged, unable to sire an heir? The Golden One was dashing her hopes. She grew irritated and called out to Eric to vanquish him immediately. They were ten paces apart when the red giant hurled his last javelin, reached over his back and pulled forth the first stubby lance. He positioned it toward Porch and slowly closed. Porch, seeing the lance close up, discerned its terrible secret. Eric charged and thumbed a lever. The lance telescoped out with lightning speed to triple its length. Porch pranced aside as its sharp steel head missed him by but an inch.

He was ready. He flung two balls at the big man's groin, and as Eric reacted to protect his vitals, a steel-clad lead ball hit his forehead with twice the force of the balls he'd suffered before. He staggered, but with great determination steadied himself and reached back for his last lance, pulling it forth. Porch was quicker, and another lead ball hit the giant in the middle of his forehead. Eric groaned, his knees buckled, and the last terrible lance fell with him as he crashed to the ground. He did not move. The combat was over.

Porch approached cautiously. Eric was breathing. His friend would survive. Porch folded his sling and attached it to his loincloth next to the pouch containing the two silver balls. As he examined the unsprung lance, his trainer and seconds came up. His trainer handed him a huge canteen full of water laced with minerals, vitamins and other potions designed to restore him. While he drank heavily, his seconds sponged his body, then toweled him off.

The eunuchs arrived with their stretcher and its odd harness. They placed Eric in it and strapped him down so that he could not move. He was gradually regaining his senses.

Brobdingnagia came up. "Turn to the Queen," he said. Porch turned to the royal box. The Queen was standing. She held out her hand and signaled thumbs up. Both men had fought bravely, victor and vanquished. Eric's life would be spared.

Shalimar motioned Porch forward, and he approached to stand motionless before her. She removed her broad sash, which she handed to Victoria. The crowd cheered as Victoria came down and bound his wounds with the sash, then returned to the Queen's side. Shalimar gazed steadily at Porch and said, "Long ago, by royal proclamation, those defeated and allowed to live were deemed unfit. We have an excision to make this so. This edict is written into the laws of Soome and must be obeyed."

She quit speaking and looked around at her subjects filling the stands. Silent now, they strained to hear the royal command. Shalimar withdrew her jeweled silver dagger and held it high for all to see. Its steel blade undulated from hilt to tip, each curve razor sharp. She put the dagger on a dish, handed it to Porch, then softly said, "Bring me the glands that rest in the pouch that lies between his thighs."

Porch was stunned and fell back, feeling sick.

Shalimar continued, "Dare not be squeamish. Use a surgeon's touch, not the hack and whack of a butcher. Now go and do as commanded!"

Porch turned and sadly went back to where Red Eric lay strapped, unable to move, bound in the harness fixed tight to the stretcher. The eunuchs had removed his loincloth. As Porch approached, Eric looked up. The terror in his eyes turned to sorrowful pleading. Porch heard his giant friend whimper.

He placed the dagger through the cord on his loincloth, picked the canteen up and placed its strap around his neck. Looking around at the crowd, he lifted its spout to his lips as if to sip and savor this final act of victory. The crowd hushed, awed by his cool demeanor, and awaited his awful surgery. But Porch could never do such a deed.

Quickly, he picked up the unsprung lance and raced west. He hurdled the inner barricades easily and when he came to the wall, he pushed the lance point down into the ground, sprung its lever and leaped. Its recoil threw him high over the wall. He rolled when he hit and instantly began running out into the Western Waste.

In the arena, the crowd had risen as one, aghast in disbelief. Such had never happened before in all the annals of Soome. The Queen was thunderstruck, for a moment shocked beyond speech. At last she turned to Victoria and said, "Have Captain Shareem call out the camel-horse. Brobdingnagia will perform the surgery."

Victoria replied fearfully, "Oh, gracious Queen, wisest of monarchs, consider..."

Shalimar looked at her sharply, but allowed her to continue. "...The Golden One has spurned the most lustrous rose of the desert. He won by trickery, not strength and prowess—shooting missiles whose path and force did change and could not be known. And now by fleeing shows cowardice, not courage. Is it not so?

"It has always been the champion who remains on the field. Who is there now? The Raging Red Bull you crave. Is not the Golden One but a fleeting fancy, soon to be a ghost? Will he not be a victim of the sun and its blazing heat...or if not, those unknown things that lay beyond the western wall that creep and crawl at night and howl when the moon is full so fearsomely as to curdle the blood? Think of the size and strength of the heirs you'll bear should you the declare the victor vanquished, and the vanquished victor. Certainly, all things considered, the Royal Proclamation will be served."

The Queen looked at Victoria and took her hand. Then she turned to Brobdingnagia, who had approached for her instruction, and said, "Repair the Raging Red Bull. He is mine."

CHAPTER 5
THE WESTERN WASTE

Porch ran. He ran until the Oasis of Oome was but a shimmering image on the horizon. He halted, fatigue about to overcome him. He checked his wounds in the shadow of a dune. They were not as bad as he had initially thought. Perhaps when his seconds sponged him off, they had had a curative in the liquid applied, or maybe there was a medicinal additive in the canteen his trainer had handed him. Nothing about the Desert Kingdom would ever surprise him again.

He felt lucky to have the canteen. Without it, surely he would perish. He knew he had to conserve what little of the laced water remained. He had to get back to the Wizard.

Wiping his brow and still breathing hard, he rose and trudged up to the top of the dune. He looked back, expecting to see a dust cloud of pursuing desert warriors. There was none. He guessed the Queen and her warriors were certain he would expire in the desert to be consumed by vultures before they found him, so why mount a chase?

He looked west and thought he saw distant mountains, but he had learned the desert trickery of strange mirages, so he could not be sure. If they were mountains, they were many days away. He wondered if he could make them. But he had no other option, so he had to try.

He decided to rest till nightfall, found another dune

that offered better shade, and lay down. Exhausted, he fell fast asleep. Contrary to his desire to wake and travel at night, he slept till dawn. He found he'd burrowed into the sand as protection against the night's cold. Wearily he rose and shook off the sand. He drank the last of the water. His muscles ached, but he knew he must continue and he headed west.

Gradually the sun took its toll, but he trudged on. The red silk ribbon, unfolded, provided considerable cover for his head and back. Gradually the terrain changed, the dunes replaced by hardpan covered with pebbles. He was glad the gladiatorial sandals provided for the combat were so well made.

He came upon a dry streambed and found a kind of creosote bush. Cacti took shelter underneath several of these. Careful to avoid the needles, he plucked several with the Queen's dagger, cut them open, peeled them, and chewed on the pulp. They tasted bitter, but contained moisture which refreshed him. He satisfied his thirst enough to continue on.

He found some burrows dug into the banks and went to investigate. Maybe he'd find refuge from the noonday sun. He threw a rock deep inside, heard nothing, so began to lower himself down. Halfway down, a hideous shriek erupted from below and something tore at his sandal. He quickly retreated and ran off a dozen yards. He pulled his sling from his belt, grabbed a handful of heavy pebbles from the streambed, loaded his sling and held it ready.

Nothing emerged. He waited. Then growls came from several burrows close by, which grew quickly into an unearthly chorus of howls. He ran from the place, shuddering.

Farther along, he reached the end of the wadi. He could again see the far horizon. Although the fierce sun bleached all color from land and sky, he was sure he saw a distant escarpment, giving him hope. He felt better. His wounds no longer bled. Dirty scabs covered both.

He trudged along, so intent on picking a feature along the escarpment to give him a heading, he didn't notice that the dazzling sun was dimming. Features bleached colorless by glare were taking on sunset colors though the sun was still high. Finally, startled, he looked up at the sun. It had turned blood red and a black streak had formed across its diameter. Then he remembered. Nemesis, the little cannibal star, the vampire bride, was crossing the atmosphere of the primary sun and sucking great swirls of matter from its face.

The Day of the Conjunction, the first epochal event forecast by the Wizard, had arrived. Gravitational tidal forces now reached the planets. Tectonic plates under Midlwurld's lands and seas groaned and shifted, unleashing momentous earthquakes and monumental tsunamis. Geysers burst forth from the bowels of the planet. Long dormant volcanoes spewed fire and lava. Even the atmosphere shifted.

Porch looked again toward the escarpment. A heavy fog was flowing down its cliffs. A hot breeze rose, and the light from the sun continued to dim. Now everything around him, the sand, the hardpan, the rocks and the boulders took on a reddish glow.

Suddenly, the hot breeze became a cool, then cold wind. It started to rain where it hadn't rained for fifty years. Huge drops of water like those of the summer squalls he remembered from his boyhood in Texas splattered down. It was most welcome. Closing his eyes, he lifted his face and opened his mouth to receive the beneficence. He glanced again at the sun. The black streak had spread. The star had turned dark red. Nemesis was creating a nuclear and chemical chaos.

The fog he'd seen approaching arrived. Soon he couldn't see the sun. The air grew heavy, now saturated with water. The rain turned to pelting hail, stinging his already burning flesh. The hailstones grew to marble size. He feared they'd grow larger. He had to find shelter, but it was hard to see, as he could hardly raise his head against the pummeling. But by sheltering his eyes and looking ahead, he saw a huge boulder. He ran to it and found shelter beneath its underside where the wind had shoveled out a depression in the hardpan, which was turning to ooze as water collected. He looked around. Rivulets of water trickled into channels. Residual heat in the rocks, boulders and hardpan melted the hail as it hit. The rivulets grew, further eroding channels. Water now roared into the wadi.

Suddenly the hail stopped. A strange calm settled. Then he heard the twister, like the whistle of a far-off freight train, then two, then three. Soon it would sound like a hundred, all racing toward him. He remembered it from his youth as the most awesome sound he knew. Fear struck him. He must dig down. Furiously, he scooped the ooze out from around him, forming a trench. Otherwise, should his sheltering boulder roll with the twister, he would be crushed. The whistling was now a thundering roar. He took one look around his boulder and saw it. The tornado came on with brutal power, its black funnel spiraling, swirling, spewing destruction, rolling boulders as though they were grains of sand. It spawned other funnels from its dark belly; whirligigs danced and skittered about like delinquent children as evil as their mother. On it came, pushing across the desert, sucking up all that it could plunder into its black underbelly.

Closer and closer, then it was there, as loud as the loudest rocket of the mightiest starship. It seemed to seek him out, crashing against his boulder to crush him if it couldn't suck him up. He lay beneath on his belly, his arms protecting his head. The boulder groaned and rolled. He felt its hard surface on his back. It pushed him deep into the ooze, then rolled away with the mighty wind. He was safe. He had survived. The fierce tornado left as quickly as it had come.

Not far away, in the burrows he'd passed, creatures not known on the planet before were stirring, stirring in the agony of advanced disease. The dry burrows had provided them with shelter against the wind, the rain, the hail and even the tornado that passed. But now they were aroused because they could not escape the water pouring into their holes in torrents. They were hydrophobic, and even the heavy mist-laden air maddened them. When they drank to serve their bodies' need, it was an agony. Their huge misshapen jaws ached, and their grotesque snouts burned as if the water was an acid. So two black, misshapen creatures exited their burrows, howling in the agony of the wetness all around.

The virus had entered its last stage of conquest and metamorphosed its host into a body of convenience for itself. Nodules, lesions and fissures erupted on the skin; hair grew, coarse and black, thick and matted; lupus, lupine, lycanthropic; men transmogrified; hands to claws, feet to paws.

The mist parted for a minute, and the creatures saw the demon eye that was the sun. That part of them still men saw their master Satan's eye, and howled their homage. That part now the demon wolf saw their age-old enemy, the cat's eye, and howled implacable hatred.

The mist closed again. One caught a spore and its fury rose to madness. It was the scent for which it had searched so long. In a throaty drawn-out howl, it alerted its mate. Both sniffed the soaking air, each breath a torture. But mind-numbing rage drove pain away and both began tracking, snouts close to the ground, growling softly, anticipating the bloody showdown to come.

The first moved slowly, not daring to lose the spoor, its mind inflamed to taste the flesh of the one who had brought it down. All pain now blotted out, it relished the thought of its canines closing on the throat, its claws ripping open the ribcage, of feasting on a heart still throbbing—soon, soon. The werewolf salivated.

Somewhat ahead, Porch had left his refuge. He'd been covered head to foot with mud and was washing in a ravine. Suddenly a sixth sense alerted him, a sixth sense now keenly developed in one long pursued by danger and death. It told him to beware.

He heard a rustling. Night was falling, but out of the corner of his eye he saw a black shadow approaching through the mist. In a second or so, his sling was in his hand and he'd grabbed up a handful of sharp stones. He positioned himself, ready to hurl, and peered through the gloom. One dark shadow now was two.

The first advanced as the second paused. He heard a sniffing and saw it down low to the ground. It looked like a bear or very large dog, but a wild thing. It stopped again, sniffing, while the second advanced. The first looked up and howled as it rose onto its two back legs, raising its forelegs. No, he saw they were arms. It had the appearance of a very hairy man. It saw him and stood stock still, snarling.

"My God, it can't be," he muttered to himself. He remembered the legends he'd read at night as a child, the legends that brought terror to his heart, made his hair bristle and brought cold sweat to his neck. He remembered how he'd snuggled close to his dog, mighty Ajax, who, sensing his fear, would growl, then lift his shaggy neck and howl. Porch knew he faced a werewolf.

Suddenly the mist lifted. The moon was full. The day of the Conjunction and its natural terrors were over. Was he pitted now against the supernatural? He did not know. He saw the creature clearly in the moonlight. Fierce yellow eyes glared at him. Teeth shone brightly and froth glistened at its snout.

He slung a sharp rock with all the force he could muster. The stone that would have killed a man hit the creature square between its eyes. It didn't seem to faze it. Maddened now, the beast advanced, arms or forepaws lifted to crush or tear.

Porch backed up and threw two more murderous missiles. Again he hit the beast square on, this time dazing it a little, but still it advanced. Then he saw the second, close by the first. It too rose to its hind legs. Desperate, Porch thought again of the legend—"silver bullets required to kill." Quickly, his hand went to the pouch the Queen had given him and withdrew a silver ball. The creature was now a mere six paces away. Porch hurled the silver missile with all his might and hit the monster between its hideous, hate-filled eyes. The missile embedded itself in the creature's forehead. It lunged as black blood erupted from the wound, and the creature went down at his feet gasping for life, but death came quickly.

The second beast charged. Porch hadn't time to reload. He dodged and tripped, falling to the ground. The beast turned and sprung down at his throat. Porch rolled and slashed out with the Queen's dagger. The dagger cut into the back of a hind leg. Black blood flowed and the creature howled. Porch got up quickly and began running, for he knew that if the beast was able to bite or scratch him, whether it killed him or not, the dread virus would infect him. The beast hobbled up, clutching its wound, and staggered forward.

Porch looked back, but in doing so, slipped again in the mud and dropped the dagger. He got up to retrieve it but didn't see it, so he reached for the pouch with the remaining silver ball. It too was gone, It had pulled off when he last had fallen. It was somewhere in the sea of ooze. He was defenseless. He got down on all fours, terror stricken, groping, desperate to find either. He paused for breath and to control his pounding heart. He looked around and saw nothing in the mud. He looked up and there was the werewolf, ready again to pounce. All the hatred of hell filled its bloodshot eyes. Porch couldn't move. He was paralyzed with fear.

The brute lunged, hurling itself through the air. At the final second, desperate for survival, Porch rolled aside, then over and over in the mud. As he pushed up to rise and run again, his hand hit a lump. It was the pouch. He grasped it and rose quickly. The beast had already recovered and was coming again, snarling its fury, howling its hate. It began to circle, now clearly outlined in the moonlight. Porch circled too, now extra careful of his footing. He loaded his last silver ball, his last chance to avoid certain death. As he moved back, the creature closed, intent to leap and tear out his throat. In a flash, the beast leaped and Porch slammed the silver missile between wide open slavering jaws. The missile penetrated to the back of the beast's throat, crushing its neck bones. It went down, gurgling and spewing forth black blood, twitching in paroxysms of agony, its final death throes.

Its contorted features relaxed as its chest made one final heave and the virus released its grip on muscle, meat and bone. An unknown force drew Porch up to look at the carcass. Through the matted hair, he recognized the features and the withered arm, and there was a faint smell of wintergreen about the corpse.

The other corpse was not far away. He headed toward it, but as he approached, the odor of garlic reeked in the air. He stumbled back, and back some more, facing the bodies, moving farther and farther away. He felt no relief, no comfort, though reason told him he should. Rather, he turned around and retched, then lost control of both bladder and bowels. Then he crawled off, still farther away. At last he rose to his knees, still shaking. He clasped his hands before him in prayer, praying prayers abandoned since childhood, rejoicing in his deliverance.

Naked now and holding only his sling, he rose to his feet and began to run. He ran like a man possessed. He ran through the rest of the night and into the dawn. His wounds opened again and began to bleed. Still he ran. He ran as the sun rose high in the sky. He ran until he could run no more. Then he fell and began to crawl.

He crawled to the top of a dune and found he could move no more. He lay there on his stomach and felt close to death. He turned over and looked up into the sun. He shielded his eyes with a palm when he first saw them, hovering, then descending. There must have been ten or more. The first one landed about twenty feet away. Then another flapped in. *My God*, he thought, *they're as big as camel-horses*.

He wondered to himself as he lost consciousness whether they would let him die before they began pecking and ripping at his flesh.

****

Hunter-Man dismounted and approached the still figure. Flight-Leader followed him, as did Scout. They stood over him. Scout prodded him cautiously but gently with a toe. Then Hunter-Man put his head to the fallen man's chest. He looked up and said to the other two, "He's still breathing, but weakly."

"Let's carry him back in the net," Flight-Leader suggested. "Ouregard will know what to do."

CHAPTER 6
THE ESCARPMENT

The Earthman looked up at the black dots passing over the escarpment, flying west. He was full of envy. They seemed to be flying in formation, but so high, he couldn't determine their size or type. And there he was, surface bound, after traveling across the cosmos, the equivalent of over seven light years, instantaneously.

He wondered what had become of his partner. A minute maladjustment of coordinates between the two in the transporter may have separated them. Well, he hoped his companion had had better luck than he had come by—first the infernal desert, then the strange comet running across the face of the sun, a phenomenon which he suspected of causing the ground tremors and storm that followed.

Well, no time to search. His mission was too important. He had to get out of the desert depression to make radio contact. There were no satellites to reflect signals on this world. That meant he had to climb the escarpment, so he continued to look for a way to the top.

Dust and caked mud covered his dark blue uniform. The storm made things worse. He pulled his scarf out and turned it around to protect his neck from the sun. He pulled the brim out from his cap for the same reason. His blouse was open, missing buttons, his trousers torn and tattered, his boots scuffed and battered. One had lost its sole, giving him a limp. As shabby as he looked, he wondered if an intelligent being would accept him as an envoy from a planet called Earth on an urgent mission.

He found water trickling down the face of the cliff, forming a small pool on the desert floor just before going underground. He was very glad for the water, but more than that, the water meant erosion, and that meant he might find a passage up the four thousand foot basalt cliffs that stood before him. He soon found a passage up. He'd eat, sleep and begin his climb in the morning.

Before leaving Earth, he had tucked a standard survival packet into his belt next to the stun gun and laser pistol. The fire glass and microgyrocompass had been useful. The desert was a good provider close to the escarpment. It yielded plenty of water, lizards and large rats that ran on their hind legs, as well as tubers and cactus pads. He'd kept his strength up quite well, he thought smugly as he watched the locusts roast on the small fire. He ate, removed his boots, placed his laser pistol next to his hand, pulled his cape over his head and went to sleep.

Up with the dawn, he ate quickly, drank plenty of water, filled his water pouch, and began his ascent. The ascent proved easier than he had reckoned. By noon, he was halfway up. He found a shaded crevice there that went all the way to the top, reaching it just before nightfall. He had entered a totally different world. To begin with, it was much cooler and the desert dryness was gone. A forested plateau five hundred feet below the top rim of the escarpment went west as far as he could see. Lakes dotted it. The trees of the forest, even from his distant vantage point, appeared huge.

He tried his radio, but got no response. He tried again–nothing. He kept trying into the night–no luck. During the night, he saw a distant light. He decided the next day he would continue to try to make radio contact with somebody, somewhere. If he was not successful, he would proceed on a bearing that took him to the light.

CHAPTER 7
THE ERTS

Porch spent thirty days in the wood cave resting in a straw nest before Ouregard let him out to mingle with the people, and even then, the Good Medicine had to give his approval. Root-Woman cured the two slashes on his side. She simply put on a poultice of leaves and resin when he arrived. A few days later the wounds were gone.

When Porch woke that first morning, the small man with the headdress was squatting beside him. He remembered that he must have appeared startled, because the man had patted his shoulder to assure him that he was all right. He'd said, "We are ERTS, Tree People...in your language. That is as close as I can make the sound, because normally we speak in a sound range too high for you big ones to hear. We know your kind but most of you don't know us because we are careful to avoid you.

"I am Ouregard, chieftain. I preside over ERTS Council with the Good Medicine, Hunter-Man and Root-Woman. Three days ago, Hunter-Man, Flight-Leader and Scout were hunting the grav-deer. A great wind came and blew them over the desert. They saw you and brought you here in a net, carried by the Condor-Steeds.

They brought you because they saw the Eye of BOKS where the sun should be. BOKS told the Good Medicine that we must revive you and send you on your way. I will come again tomorrow and we will talk some more. BOKS must tell me what I can say to you."

The little Chieftain came the next day and each day thereafter for thirty days, but until thirty days had passed and the Good Medicine said OK, only he, Ouregard, Root-Woman and the Good Medicine were allowed to approach him. Ouregard was quite blunt about it—they hadn't had a big clumsy one in their town for decades, and they didn't dare take a chance on contamination.

They threw the Queen's dagger and Porch's sling on the midden far below. They washed him, shaved his head, and dressed him in a feather "shirt and pants," as he would call his fuzzy coverings later. He simply pulled the shirt down and the pants up and he was dressed. They chose lemon yellow garments for him, since his hair was yellow. They said his hair would grow out, and until it did, they gave him a "sun hat" to wear, more yellow feathers woven in a bowl shape. Dressed that way, he looked much like them from a distance.

The second day, Ouregard said to him, "The mighty BOKS, great panther god of the ERTS, says your arrival foretells a terrible calamity to come. He is worried about his people, namely us. Soon he will come among us to protect us. He wants to know who you are, where you're from, and where you're going. Tomorrow you can tell me."

He came the following morning and asked, "What is your name? Where do you come from and where do you go?"

"I am Porch. I come from a place amongst the stars and am on a mission for the Great Wizard. It is about the coming calamity. I have no instructions to pass to you. I must return to him, and you should go with me so he may tell you what to do."

"We know of him, though he knows not us. When you are well, we will return you to him. We do not need his guidance. BOKS will tell us what to do. You will see."

Ouregard came every morning to check his guest's health. On the twenty-ninth day, he said, "Tomorrow I'll bring the Good Medicine. I am certain that he will lift your quarantine."

Ouregard told him that they were just as human as

he was, but genetically adapted to live in the trees ever since the mighty BOKS had brought their ancestors there. ERTSONG described that as having taken place long ago, and as far as he was concerned, that was sufficient for anyone who wanted to know how long.

Porch was eager to meet and mingle with the ERTS. They were fascinating, all diminutive. Porch estimated the men weighed less than one hundred pounds and the women about sixty. Ouregard told him that War-Leader, five feet tall and a solid ninety-eight pounds, was the largest. A delicate down which ranged in color from pinkish-white to a deep rose covered them. Their hair was almost transparent and flowed down past their shoulders. Their long, sinewy arms reached their knees. This greatly enhanced their climbing ability and added to their agility in gliding through the trees.

In every other aspect, they were human, and with their exquisite features, very beautiful people. Both men and women wore only light skirt-like coverings around their loins. He asked Ouregard, "How is it you know our language?"

Ouregard replied, "When I was young, we saw starships come like meteors out of the void. We were sore afraid. Great BOKS told the Good Medicine to send a youth to spy on the new ones. The council chose me, for I was fleet of foot and cunning. I went to the town of Nork, now the great city. But I was captured, and was so odd to them, they put me in a cage like a bird and made me sing.

"I learned their language then. But I was cunning. I found a way to flee. I stole the talk buttons and the device that swallows them and speaks their tongue. Others also listened, not many, but some, and they can speak their language, too. They don't know ours, nor can they hear it when we speak. Thus we are secure.

"Additionally, the trees speak to us in sounds you cannot hear. They tell who comes in the forest and when. We know each time a panther-cat sharpens its claws on a trunk.

"Tomorrow the Good Medicine will release you. Since BOKS has said you are a friend, I will show you our domain, from Edge to Center. Then we'll have a feast and take you back to where you say you go."

The next morning, Ouregard and the Good Medicine came early.

"Come," they said, "you are released from quarantine. The mist has risen and it will not rain until four o'clock. We have far to go."

Ouregard handed Porch a long sword with belt and scabbard.

"Put it on. You may need it should a wind-eagle come."

He led Porch out of the wooden cavern and onto the massive branch of a gigantic tree. The branch was as wide as a roadway, and the little people used it as such, pulling carts and carrying burdens along it. Ouregard beckoned him and he went to the side of the branch.

"Look down," the Chieftain cried proudly. Porch did, and was amazed. They must have been seven hundred feet above the forest floor. Some light filtered down and he could see great vines, patches of ground, and new trees rising where a giant tree had fallen.

"Now look up," Ouregard sang out cheerfully. Porch did and saw another three hundred feet of trunk with branches rising up.

"Our domain extends from fifty feet above the forest floor to fifty feet below the canopy top," Ouregard said matter-of-factly. "BOKS gave us the ERTS-deed when our time in the trees began. We have it enshrined in the Jubilee Tree. The forest floor belongs to the great black leopard, the panther-cat, who is BOKS' guardian of the forest. We have circled the trunk of each great tree with an iron guard. The panther-cat does not come above, and we do not go below. The fierce wind-eagle rules the sky above the canopy. We must be alert to where he flies. Come."

Ouregard led Porch along the aerial roadway. Porch noticed that Hunter-Man and War-Leader had fallen in behind with four small archers. As they traveled, they came to rope causeways hung on cords of rubber and jute. These led from tree to tree, as if they were side streets along the major road nets of the tree city. Bell-like structures hanging from hundreds of oaken trees were ERT roosts.

The oak trees were the predominant species of tree, but there were many other species, some with leaves as broad as blankets, others with leaves as fine as human hair. Porch had never seen so many shades of green. ERT women were gathering figs the size of melons from a broad leaf tree. Another tree bore nuts similar to walnuts, except they were as big as footballs. Other fruits and nuts ripened everywhere. Thick vines carried green melons. Fruit blossoms as large as dinner plates were well attended by honey bees as large as hummingbirds. Ouregard said his people were never without honey.

Most amazing were the beautiful epiphytes, mostly orchids, which matched the color range of the tree people. Some were as big as beach umbrellas. Ouregard said that spices were extracted from these. Edible lichens and mosses completed their abundant menu.

Porch followed Ouregard past wonder after wonder in a self-contained community of little people who never touched the ground. Golden-hued monkeys half the size of the ERTS were gathering huge oak corns, which the ERTS processed into flour, from the oak trees.

Stout hanging cages housed nests that wind-eagles could not break into to steal condor-steed eggs. They passed rookeries where the ERTS were training condor-steed young. Likewise, cage schools protected ERT siblings so their parents could work without worries that their offspring would be wind-eagle prey.

Ouregard signaled a stop for lunch, and Hunter-Man's soldiers gathered tiers of oyster mushrooms from the sides of oak trees, poked ladles into nearby beehives for honey, pulled ripe melons off nearby vines, and shared the food with all. After lunch, they continued their journey and reached the boundary of the tree city.

Ouregard said, "We hunt the grav-deer and grav-goats here. They provide our meat. It is the panther-cat's food, too, when the panther-cat can't find rodents and wild pigs feeding on fallen oak corns.

"Come and see how the animals got their names."

Porch looked down and saw a misty black figure stalking. Unaware, several large deer were grazing in a meadow just beyond the forest. The panther grew near and suddenly charged a buck. Halfway through its charge, the buck bounded high into the air, landing thirty yards away. All then cavorted off, leaping as if to defy gravity itself.

Ouregard said, "The panther-cats are not always successful."

Both he and Porch were so intent on watching the drama below, they failed to see the wind-eagle circling above. But one of the archers saw it and gave a signal inaudible to Porch. Ouregard hollered to Porch, "Watch out above!"

The wind-eagle came screaming in, talons extended. The ERTS all froze in place. Quickly Porch drew his sword and held it up. The eagle veered off. The large yellow object with the extended silver talon was more than it cared to tangle with. The unusual coloring of the ERTS suddenly became obvious to Porch. It was a camouflage nature developed over time, protecting them from the wind-eagles that could not distinguish them from orchids they had no interest in. Ouregard laughed, as did the other little people, at how effortlessly they had fooled the deadly bird.

"Come," said Ouregard, "we will stay at Fringe tonight with Forward-Observer and his Out-Guards. They have soft nests, good things to eat, and are a jolly group. Tomorrow, we will start early to reach Center by mid afternoon."

Dawn cast a rosy spell over the forest as they left Fringe. Everything was so beautiful in these colossal trees, Porch felt he was in the original "Forest Primeval." By noon they had reached the deepest part of the forest and stopped for lunch. Soon enough, Ouregard said, "We must reach the Jubilee Tree before the rain."

Off they went again by the most direct route. Several hours later, Ouregard said they were approaching Center, and then they came to the largest tree Porch had ever seen or could imagine existed. Of starship girth, it rose fifteen hundred feet above the forest floor.

Ouregard said it had been there since time began, and he led the party to a hollow in the tree. Inside the hollow, itself a large chamber, a fire burned in a wide iron dish, and in the center of that fire a higher flame rose. Ouregard asked the ERTS in the party to wait at the entrance and then led Porch forward. Porch saw a number of ERT maidens surrounding the fire.

Ouregard whispered in a voice of great reverence, "That is the ERTS Fire and the Eternal BOKS Flame. Neither must ever go out. That is why the sacred wood nymphs attend it day and night."

Beyond the ERTS Fire, an exquisitely carved oak throne sat on a highly polished slab of wood. A massive robe of panther-cat skin spread out on it. The panther-cat arms extended along the arms of the throne and ended in fearsome claws. High on the back of the throne, a fixture held a panther's headdress, with black ears extending above a crown. The panther's skull and upper jaw were attached inside to support it. Phosphorescent crystal eyes protruded from the eye sockets, and long sharp teeth stuck out below the upper jaw.

"This is the panther god, BOKS', imperial robe. He will wear it when he comes to rule," Ouregard said matter-of-factly, then, "The hour strikes four. The rain will come now. We will wait till five, when it will stop. Now I will show you the ERTS-deed. Come."

Porch heard the rain begin, a slow drumbeat of large drops which turned into deafening torrents of water accompanied by lightning flashes and deafening thunder. Ouregard led Porch to the case where the "deed" to the forest was kept. He pulled up the cover and stood proudly before an ancient piece of blue slate about four foot square. Porch looked at the slate. A fossilized oak leaf about three feet across was embedded in it. He imagined it could be anywhere from one hundred thousand to several million years old. It was a perfectly preserved relic from another age. The veins were etched in fine detail, and a leaf gall from an ancient irritation covered the fossil's center. Ouregard saw Porch's fascination with the deed and said earnestly, pointing to the gall, "You see there the exact location of the Jubilee Tree, and all those lines running out show the roadways, the trestles and the paths among the trees. The edges on the deed are the limits of ERT domain."

Porch saw several other imperfections. But Ouregard pointed to each in turn, saying, "This is the township of Cloud, this Pine Top, and over here on the edge Fringe, where we spent last night. Come."

He led Porch into an inner chamber closed off from the sound of wind and rain, where an old ERT of pale blue hue sat before a harp. His hair was gone, but he wore a long translucent beard to balance that loss. Ouregard said, "This is ERTSINGER. He keeps our history and tells our stories in ERTSONG. Let's sit and listen."

ERTSINGER began to strum the harp and sing ERTSONG in a singsong voice low enough for Porch to understand. He told of how the people lived on the southern plain before tree-time began and were content. He told of how the big clumsy ones stole ERT children to keep in cages and raise as pets, of how they gave the ERTS no respect because the ERTS were smaller, then drove them north with whips and canes. He told of how the ERTS crossed the Blue Shale Mountains and reached the edge of the great forest. He told of how the great black panther sat astride the blue shale boulder and blocked their way. He told of how they stood in the rain, shaking, sore afraid as the great black panther crept up to eat the ERT children. He told of how a lightning bolt came down from heaven in a clap of thunder to cleave in two the blue shale boulder. He sang out joyously that the rain then stopped, the sun came out, the panther was gone, and there in the rock was the deed to ERTFOREST.

ERTSINGER sang ERTSONG for an hour and more, sometimes loudly, sometimes softly, quickly and slowly, happily and sadly. When he finished, he rose, bowed and left through a door leading even farther into the Jubilee Tree. The deluge outside stopped as quickly as it had started. Ouregard said, "It is time to return. You have seen what BOKS thought important you see and you have heard what BOKS thought important you hear."

The trees outside were dripping, but a freshness in the air invigorated their stride and they were back at their starting point by nightfall. Ouregard told Porch to rest until ten o'clock. The feast would start then, and after it was over the condor-steeds would be ready to take him to the Castle of Szid.

Sharply at ten, Ouregard returned to fetch Porch. The little man wore the full-feathered headdress and full-feathered cape of ERTCHIEF. He also carried the ceremonial bowstaff, quiver and arrows. Midlwurld's silver moon was high in the sky. Festive lanterns had been placed along the roadway and branches leading to the festival. ERTS were gathering from all about. Ouregard looked at Porch and said happily, "The feast is to be held at Cloud on the great wind-pavilion. It is not far. Come."

As Ouregard and Porch moved along with the crowd, Porch noticed the Chief strutted a bit, apparently proud to have a big clumsy one in tow. Like any good politician, he greeted all who walked close by and waved to the rest. Presently, they came upon a platform as large as a football field held up by massive ropes suspended from six huge trees. Satellite platforms a little higher surrounded this central pavilion, and colorful canopies and nets were strung high above all. The fierce wind-eagle was not a problem after dark, but the cyclopean night-owl was.

A raised platform at one end of the Wind Pavilion was reserved for the ERT Council, its honored guest and other ERT notables such as Forward-Observer, who had come all the way from Fringe with several of his Out-Guards. The sweet scent of flowers placed around lanterns lent enchantment to an already enchanting place.

Hundreds of ERT families had gathered for the festival. Acrobats performed on vines and trapezes set amongst the trees above the platforms. Maidens danced the Feather Dances, and the Nightingale Chorus sang the Bird and Breeze Songs. It was well past midnight when ERT families began drifting away, many carrying sleeping young ones. Ouregard then told Porch of the plan to return him to the Wizard. He was to ride in a net carried by four great condor-steeds, accompanied by Flight-Leader, Scout and six out-riders, two far ahead and one at each point of the compass. They would travel at night resting well hidden in selected woods by day so as not to be seen. The condor-steeds fly very high to catch the southbound wind, because the lower winds were always northerly.

Ouregard reckoned five nights of travel, as their destination was at least one thousand leagues away. He said, "The condor-steeds are ready. Flight-Leader is bringing them. You may leave right away."

Ouregard rose along with the Good Medicine, Root-Woman and Hunter-Man to bid farewell. Root-Woman's apprentice brought a large package to Porch and presented it to him with a curtsy.

Root-Woman said, "Open it. It is our going away present to you."

Porch opened the package to find inside a large cape of lemon yellow feathers knitted together. The cape exactly matched the feathered suit he was wearing.

The Good Medicine said, "You must put it on before you leave. It is very cold at the altitudes the condor-steeds must fly. You will freeze without it."

Porch wrapped it around his body. He thanked the council profusely for saving him from the desert and healing him, and for all their kindness to him. Just then Flight-Leader descended with the condor-steeds and the net which he, Scout and the out-riders laid out. They bade Porch sit in the middle, and as soon as he was settled in, he felt himself rising. He waved good-bye to Ouregard and the council. The huge birds climbed higher and higher, and when they reached the south wind, they took a south heading to Szidrous. Porch looked down and watched the lights below snuff out till all was darkness. He felt a sorrow in his heart and wondered if he'd ever come upon the ERTS again.

On they flew through what was left of the night, then descended with the dawn to hide and rest. They rose again as the sun was setting, and did this each day that followed until the castle at Szidrous was in sight.

CHAPTER 8
THE SPACE WHISTLER

Some distance to the west, the Earthman watched the lights go out the night the condor-steeds began their flight to Szidrous. Those lights spurred him on, as they foretold of sentient beings ahead. He'd not seen any since he had materialized on the planet. He traveled on a vital mission and would find the man he sought or die trying. He had no luck trying to make radio contact.

He thought he'd reach the settlement soon, but for now he needed some supper and rest. He found a small lake with an island in the middle and decided to camp on the island. He'd run across three black leopards since entering the forest and used his stun gun on two. The third had followed him the last two nights and was tracking him now, but the cat would not come into the water. Each night he camped on an island in whatever lake he came upon. There were many, so he had no problem finding one.

This night was no exception, and as the Midlwurld moon rose, he felt secure. He had made a meal of some fish he snared, some cattail catkins and lily pad roots he found on the bank of the island. He wrapped himself in his cloak and lay down on the bed of reeds he'd piled up. With his stun gun in hand and a stout club nearby, he drifted off to sleep.

He did not hear the panther on the near shore growl its frustration at the water's edge, nor did he hear the eerie whistle in the atmosphere as a slight perturbation jostled the planet. A gravity wave had passed. It was a precursor to the dread sequence of waves on their way.

The panther noticed and growled again, annoyed. Its night-piercing eyes saw a strange black object rocking to and fro float down in the moonlit sky like an autumn leaf on a very still night. The panther watched the craft land softly at lakeside, thought perhaps there was a meal in the offing, and began to stalk. It crouched and crept toward the strange-looking pod. It was but a whisper away when the top opened and six strange creatures furtively emerged. Caution stayed the cat for an instant. It lifted its nostrils to catch the scent and was blasted with a stench so putrid that it winced in overwhelming nausea, flopped to the ground, rubbed itself in the dirt and weeds, and rolled in agony. Then it ran, whimpering, off into the night.

The dark creatures gathered, hissing and speaking in staccato grunts with a loathsome spittle splattering about. Their black saucer-like eyes flecked orange while they squinted around suspiciously. Their rows of saw teeth shone in the moonlight. As they huddled together, their backs showed leathery carapaces over furry skins. They had wide skulls, broad, flat noses, and even broader jaws. Each held a tri-forked weapon that looked like a small pitchfork with barbed tines.

One pointed to the water's edge and to the island where the sleeping figure lay. One behind the other, they entered the water and began to cross.

CHAPTER 9
AURORA

The great birds circled high as Hunter-Man waited for the moon to set. He intended to follow Ouregard's instruction not to be seen when they delivered their cargo. Porch, looking down through the net, saw the gripping panorama below. The Castle of Szid, truly a fortress, had its outer works sitting high up on an extinct volcano. The gardens and pools within, reflecting moonlight up, seemed tranquil enough, but just beyond was bedlam. Streams of people carrying lanterns flowed toward the castle from every direction; all pulled carts or drove teams of horses, mules and oxen harnessed to wagons full of possessions. They had heeded the Wizard's call to seek refuge in the castle before the terror arrived.

Hunter-Man signaled and the birds began their descent. The moon, not yet set, had retreated behind a cloud bank and the darkness was sufficient so that they would not be seen. As they drifted lower, Porch noted that the castle was huge, at least as large as the largest buildings he remembered from New Chicago.

The condor-steeds circled silently, lower and lower. They were but fifty feet above the gardens when suddenly a searchlight beam flashed on and spotlighted them. They abruptly dropped the net and pumped their huge wings to gain altitude and escape. Porch, totally entangled, fell with the net, which caught on an abutment and dropped him farther, until he landed on a balcony with a loud thump. The net pulled tight around him and he was so entangled he could not move.

Lights came on behind a set of French doors which opened to the balcony, and a slight figure in sleeping gown and silver robe burst out. Long tresses of golden hair identified her immediately. She was wielding a crystal dagger. Before he could utter a sound, she rushed over, pulled the net even tighter and then back to bare his throat.

Holding her dagger to his neck, she challenged, "Who dares invade the sleeping quarters of Aurora, daughter of His Majesty, King Szid of Szidrous and Princess of this Realm."

Porch, totally embarrassed, looked up at this beautiful woman who was about to pierce his throat, searching for the proper words to render a fitting apology, but his brain went numb and his tongue grew thick in his mouth. From what the Priest had said, this princess, this fairy princess, was all that he had told him. He was smitten, totally smitten with love for her. He muffled several more sounds as his affliction deepened.

Aurora questioned, "Are you some evil cutthroat who's come to assassinate a helpless girl?"

She pulled his head to the side and pressed the small dagger's point harder against his neck, which, though lethal there, was more an ornament than a weapon. Porch rolled his eyes to get a better view of his fierce assailant. Her eyes were flashing fire. "Speak!" she demanded. "Are you some awful creature come to force himself upon an innocent, some rude oaf come to besmirch a princess's reputation?"

Porch heard alarms ringing inside her quarters. Finally, he stammered, "Wait, wait. It's all a mistake. I was dropped here—in this net—from the sky—by the birds. I look for the Wizard."

She was more furious than ever. "Dropped from the sky by birds? Truly, sir, now I understand. You are a big buffoon who has taken leave of his senses. Yes, to the Wizard you shall go, and quickly."

Armed men were pouring through the glass doors.

"Guards, untangle him. Then bind him and remove him."

"Believe me, please," Porch pleaded, "I am the Wizard—Lord No's assistant, returned from a mission."

Aurora softened when she saw Porch's pitiful look, but questioned, "In such an outfit, covered head to toe in yellow feathers?"

The guards untangled him and bound him roughly. His hat fell forward over his eyes. Aurora watched and it came to her, flooding her memory. Her childhood, the videos—borrowed from the Millenarians to teach Szidrian children Earth language. *Sesame Street*, that was it. She became amused, totally tickled. She covered her mouth with a hand, but her eyes twinkled and tears of mirth began to flow. She pointed to the captive, and as they prodded him to hop out, his feet bound together, she giggled, "Big Bird."

Porch hung his head dejectedly. Her derisive laughter stung him like a nettle. The capricious Fates had dealt him cruel humiliation and everlasting mortification. Through no fault of his, he appeared a dolt, a babbling buffoon, a complete fool before one whose very shadow he now adored. It would have been better, he thought, for Red Eric's lance to have pierced his heart.

The guards pushed Porch, bound so he could only hop, through the double French doors and quickly out of Aurora's apartment. They hurried him along a corridor, then up some steps, more steps, stone steps, up and up, then through some doors, down another corridor, through another door and into a large chamber. They pushed him to the front, and before him, bending over and adjusting a telescope, stood the Wizard, Lord No. Another man was with him. He continued to adjust the large instrument, moving it up toward the vertical, then down and around. He stopped and muttered to the other man, "Good field of view now. When they come, we'll be ready. We'll get range and direction data, plus the meteorology to the General tomorrow."

At last, he looked over and said, "Ah, Porch, Rashid has preceded you by more than a month. Welcome to Szidrous."

The Captain of the Guard broke in and told how this intruder had invaded the Princess' private sleeping quarters, and when accosted, had the gall to tell some wild tale of dropping from the sky.

The Wizard listened patiently, then said, "He speaks true. He is one of my men, so you may cut him loose. Thank you for bringing him."

As the guards were releasing Porch from his bonds, the Wizard introduced the man with him as Orwell, Lord Chamberlain of Szidrous, next after the king in authority and affairs of state.

Porch was outraged, first because the Wizard had sent him off without giving him even a hint of what he might encounter at the Desert Kingdom, and again that he took his humiliating return so lightly. He asked, "Why was I not warned of the Ruby Queen and the customs of Oome? Did she not break the safe conduct?"

Lord No picked up the sense of betrayal in his young protégé's voice, but responded matter-of-factly, "You tarried there without protest when Rashid left, and overcome adversity with audacity and tenacity as I expected."

Porch was yet unsatisfied. "Why have I received such a reception upon return?"

The Lord Chamberlain said, "You have our sincerest apologies, but know that Princess Aurora is a precious jewel to us. I will explain your strange arrival to her after you have detailed it to us."

Now Lord No interrupted with some irritation, "It shall be made up to you. Now enough of this banter. We have much to do. Porch, go get out of that ridiculous costume and then return. Your room is down the hall. The door is marked, and I have left some uniforms there."

Porch left quickly, as he also wanted to get rid of the feathers. When he returned, Lord No asked for an account of his journey, which he gave, leaving out only the most personal aspects of his trip.

When he had finished, Lord No said, "Rashid gave us Shalimar's blood oath of assistance when called. I hope it does not come to that, and I know of the ERTS, though they know not that I know. I hope to spare them the coming terror. They are best off remaining in their forest. I will draw the enemy to us. It is part of the plan."

They continued to talk late into the night. Porch

asked about the Priest. "Has he returned?"

"Nay," said the Wizard. "We've heard nothing from him. The Millenarians are stubborn. They believe in what they call 'friendly persuasion,' and that no harm will come to them if they show signs of peace and love. They don't know the enemy we face. Unless the Priest can bring them in, they will perish. I hope he can persuade even a few to come. If not, I hope he does not linger until it is too late.

"Now we must get some rest. We have much to do in the days that remain. Tomorrow, after seeing the General, we will begin the inspection of all defenses. Good night."

Early the next morning, Porch set out with Lord No. The General was a photonic computer Lord No had salvaged from an errant warship that had come to Midlwurld. He had refurbished it to war game the coming battle and after that provide fire direction.

Porch questioned, "It appears quite old. Is it adequate?"

Lord No replied, "It has simultaneously defeated a hundred grand masters in a hundred moves in a hundred minutes at tri-di chess. I know the characteristics of our enemy, having fought them all my life. They are not sophisticated."

"But I am much surprised," Porch said, "that we isolate ourselves in this castle rather than fight them on the open ground."

"They are too numerous to so engage. No matter how fiercely we fight or destroy with our best weapons, there will always be more. The General shows we can survive a siege of many months. Our only real hope is to get the death cells before we are overcome. As I have said, samples of their ancestral blood are on their way, sent by courier. We must have them in time or we are as good as dead."

Lord No inspected the General and its operators, insuring that the firing data had been input correctly. Then he motioned they continue. The Lord Chamberlain joined them. They inspected the castle, all turrets and barbicans armed with laser and ballistic weapons.

On the way, Porch heard his name called out. He turned to see Little Weejie waving vigorously. Big Gywn was with him. Porch walked over to greet his friends, and Lord No followed. When Little Weejie and Big Gywn saw Lord No, they snapped to attention, saluting smartly. "Ready for inspection," Big Gywn called out.

"Take your ease, men," Lord No replied. Both men ran up to greet Porch, shook his hand vigorously and patted him on the back.

"We thought that we had lost you to those men doing the looking back at Nork, or maybe something worse when the Dark Star came by," Big Gywn said.

"The Wizard made us cap'ns when he called the people in," Little Weejie interrupted proudly.

Big Gywn continued, "We just about finished the big rocket ship. She's ready to go except for fuel loading and final checks." He became silent for a moment, then continued glumly, "If we got to fight these critters, we gotta win, or we'll never get to the stars."

"Come see our guns. We ready to go—mine first," Little Weejie urged. He led them out to an abutment supporting a turret which contained a huge ballistic gun. He opened the breech and motioned Porch to take a look. Porch saw the spotless chamber and shiny rifling down the tube. He said it was well-cared-for and Little Weejie beamed with pride, then, pointing to his crew, proudly said, "They my men."

Porch recognized some as his fellow workers from the Spaceport and nodded. One held a rammer. Two others stood by a loading tray. Another held a box of primers. Rows of large shells and canisters of powder stood behind them. Little Weejie then led them into another bay after unlocking a heavy steel door. Two rows of black canisters with the words "Projectile, Nuclear" stenciled on the side stood there. He said secretively, "These our last resort weapons."

Porch looked at Lord No and the Lord Chamberlain. Both men looked pleased at the high state of training and readiness.

Lord No said as an afterthought, "Also salvaged from the errant Star Ship which yielded the computer."

Next they visited Big Gywn's massive laser gun. Huge capacitor banks in vacuum encasements emitted an almost inaudible hum. Heavy copper cables connected them to induction coils surrounding a glass laser tube filled with strange green laser gas. Radiation and leak detectors with needles vibrating around the zero mark showed constant monitoring. Behind the gun and protected from enemy hits by thick steel plates were the rows of cold fusion banks that powered the laser. Big Gywn too was ready.

Lord No said, "We'll take our leave now. We have much left to check. Thank you. You have done an outstanding job."

Continuing along, they questioned the captains and put the gun crews through their drills. They did the same at the fire control centers, the observation posts and the communications centers.

In following weeks, they visited commissaries and magazines, checked cisterns and deep wells. They went out from the castle to the ramparts and outer works. They checked the security at the sally ports. Lord No had posted there the fittest soldiers, all ready for foray, raid, repulse or rescue. They went down below the castle into the bowels of the extinct volcano. It had been transformed into an underground city of long tunnels and vast chambers, level after level, carved from the heavy basalt. Refugees were settling in everywhere. Children were playing in all the nooks and crannies. The disruption in their lives was to them a great adventure.

At last, they had completed their rounds and returned to the upper levels of the castle. As Lord No led them along, he said to Porch, "For twenty years I've known that the Vundercy star system was astride the expanding path of the Throgs, and have cajoled the citizens of Midlwurld to understand the need for gun factories, steel mills and all the other plants we established deep in the caverns below this dead volcano. We studied the plans of ancient and modern weapons and developed, I think, a proper mix. My agents on the spaceways bartered for weapons we could not build ourselves. I am satisfied that we are ready for the on-slaught. The hour grows late. Report to me in the morn-ing. I have a surprise for you."

The next morning, Porch reported as ordered. Lord No smiled as he entered his quarters and said, "We have a happy duty to perform. King Szidrous' Birthday Ball is but a fortnight away. It is an annual celebration and may be the last time for merriment for many months to come. As well, it is time for you to make amends to the Princess."

Porch gulped audibly. He hadn't forgotten his lam-entable introduction to Aurora, but Lord No had kept him so busy that the pain of the first meeting had dimmed in his mind. Now there it was again, confront-ing him directly.

Lord No looked at him quizzically and asked, "Are you all right?"

"Yes, sir," Porch tried to believe.

"I told you that your sense of being slighted upon your arrival would be rectified at the proper time. That time has come. You will be required to dance with the Princess at the King's Birthday Ball. You do know how to dance, do you not?"

Porch felt feverish as his brain raced back to his childhood. He thought of the winter nights on Harry's ranch when Harry got out his fiddle and taught him the mountain jigs while Ajax danced around his feet, bark-ing and carrying on, and later, when Nogales and his multitudinous family had taught him the Latin rhythms. They'd said he had natural grace, but dancing with a princess was something else.

"I have not danced since I was a child, Lord No. You can hardly expect me to dance with a princess," Porch said lamely.

Lord No ignored his comment and said, "She loves the waltz. You must learn it right away. I have some tri-di video disks and a projector. Take them, listen, prac-tice and learn. You'll do fine."

"But what of a partner?" Porch asked, trying to es-cape his fate.

"None are available who would not gossip throughout the castle. Would you want that? The Princess would think you a double bumpkin."

"Oh, no."

"Then take this broom. After you have learned the steps, use it as a partner. This happy people take their dancing most seriously. Don't let the Order down. They hold in low esteem he who doesn't dance."

Porch left armed with the video disks, projector and broom. For the next eight days, when he had no other duties, he practiced in his room. He practiced as if his life depended upon it, for he knew he could not survive another incident in which he was deemed a fool. He practiced harder than he ever had to learn the vault, the sling, the staff or the long barrel. He skipped meals and cut his sleep short.

Before he knew it, the fortnight had passed. On the morning of the King's Birthday Ball, Lord No sent him a message. That afternoon he would demonstrate his skill for Orwell, and the Lord Chamberlain would decide where to put him on the Princess' dance card. Dance he did, with a palpitating heart on shaking knees and quivering ankles.

"You'll do fine," the Lord Chamberlain said. "I shall award you the fourth and seventh dances." No sooner had Orwell left when another visitor knocked on the door and called out, "It is Mendel, the tailor. I have your uniform for the ball."

Porch opened the door with a quizzical expression on his face. Mendel saw it and said, "The Wizard ordered it. He holds you in high esteem, almost like a son. It is an appropriate uniform for the Ball. I've put my considerable skill into tailoring it just right for you."

Porch was dumfounded. Certainly Lord No had never treated him with any such affection, but only as a subordinate.

"Put it on. We have time for minor adjustments if necessary. I know your measurements to a T, as I made your other uniforms."

After removing his work uniform, Porch picked up the trousers and put them on. They fit perfectly and were made of soft creamy white poplin reinforced to hold a perfect crease. A stripe of burnished gold ran the length of each side.

"It's real gold woven into the fabric," Mendel said proudly.

Porch picked up the jacket. The galactic spirals of the Order of No went around the high military collar. It had the epaulets of a Knight Commander of the Order. Surely Mendel had made a mistake. He wasn't even in the Order. He looked questioningly at the tailor.

Mendel ignored him, saying, "This symbol is attached to the right shoulder and loops around the right arm. It designates you as Lord No's aide. It too is made of gold, spun gold from the Wizard's own store. He thinks highly of you."

Again, the fit was perfect. Porch had never seen a finer uniform. Mendel held out a wide gold sash, saying, "This is a sash to hold a ceremonial saber, but since you go to dance and not parade, you will not wear a weapon. Nevertheless, it completes your uniform. It is my very best work. Take it off so I may press it again. Lord No said that you must be perfect. I'll have it back within the hour."

Mendel took the garments and left, whistling happily to himself. And as soon as he departed, a messenger came. "Lord No requests you be dressed and ready at seven. Report to his quarters then."

Porch wondered what came next. The day had been full of surprises. But he knew he could not dress perfectly. All he had was a pair of boots. He took them out and spit-shined them, as if he was still at the Academy. Maybe Lord No wouldn't notice. Mendel brought the uniform back, and as the hour drew near to his appointment, he put it on. He slipped into the boots standing up and carefully pulled the bottoms of the trousers over them. They almost looked like shoes. But how could he dance in them? The capricious fates had him again. Lord No invited him in when he knocked on his door. Orwell was with him. Lord No looked at him and said, "You look splendid. I hoped the Priest would be back for the Ceremony, but we can wait no longer. It is time to induct you into the Order of No. Orwell, Lord Chamberlain of Szid, is also knight adjutant general of the Order. He will bear witness to your investiture."

Lord No explained that the Order had but one purpose, which was destruction of the Throgs, the dehumanized demons spreading through the galaxy destroying all before them. He led Porch into a small chapel. Before them stood a sword struck deeply into a pot of clay.

Lord No said, "Before you stands the sword of the last emperor of the Ancients. He thrust it into the sacred clay from which, according to their holy book, their race was sprung. Then he made the fateful decision that his people would sacrifice themselves and the empire of Gaelos, which spanned a vast star cluster in a cataclysmic supernova, to destroy that black horde that even now is upon us.

"Just before the cataclysmic supernova that marked their noble act of immolation, he ordered the first man commissioned, the Lord of No, to carry that Sword of Empire in its bed of sacred clay with him for all the time they fought the Throgs. Then should the Ancients fail to destroy that terrible galactic cancer in the fire, that sword would be the standard of the Order and the knights should rally to it and remember the empire that was no more."

Porch swallowed hard, visibly moved, as Lord No commanded, "Go forward, kneel before the sword, and grasp it with both hands. As you repeat the Oath of Fealty in the secret words, you declare your life has the destruction of the Throgs as its single purpose."

He said the secret words which Porch repeated. Then he went before the altar and drew the sword from the clay. He touched it to the new knight's shoulders and declared, "I, Lord No, commander of the Knights of No, by the authority vested in me now appoint you knight commander in the Order of No."

He replaced the sword, motioned Porch to rise, and turned to Orwell, knight adjutant general of No, and said, "Record his name in the list of knights." He turned back to Porch. "Remember the thousand who have gone before, now all dead. Ten of us remain, including you."

Lord No then led them from the Chapel, saying, "There is a little left to do."

The Lord Chamberlain handed Lord No a decoration and a sash that Porch was sure he'd seen before. It was the Space Fleet's Order of the Sun.

Lord No said, "You have an advocate on Earth, a member of our Order. At his insistence you were awarded this decoration in absentia by the Admiralty."

He placed the sash over Porch's shoulder and pinned the diamond-encrusted medal on Porch's right breast. Then he said, looking at Porch's feet, "You think you can dance in boots such as those? You'll bruise the Princess' feet and crush her toes."

He went to a bureau, pulled open its bottom drawer and lifted out a pair of shoes. "Sit down and put these on."

Porch sat down, carefully removed his boots, and put on the shoes. They were brilliantly shined and of the most pliable leather he'd ever felt on his feet. He felt a great surge of gratitude and looked up at Lord No to express his appreciation, but Lord No interrupted, smiling, "Those are a pair of dancing shoes. They have a magic quality. With them on, you will glide around the ballroom floor most gracefully. Now come, the festivities have begun."

Soon they entered the Great Hall of the People in the center of the castle. It blazed with light from massive triple golden sconces on the walls and immense crystal chandeliers suspended from the ceiling. The hall was filled with people. The men displayed badges of rank and office with epaulets and sashes. The splendidly coiffured ladies were dressed in magnificent gowns of many fabrics and colors. Even the children were there, shined and polished. Porch felt a glow. What began as an evening of trepidation had been transformed into magic. He had a new confidence.

Lord No and the Lord Chamberlain were greeting people all around. He, too, moved through the crowd, hailing those he knew, introducing himself to others, and smiling at all. Lord No motioned to him and when he'd come to his side, said, "'Tis fitting we have such a

gala in the face of the coming slaughter. All is ready.
The Desert Warriors are poised to aid us at my call. The
Lord of Ice World, Prince Spauk, has received my signal
and replies that even now his hardy Vikuns are loading
their interplanetary longboats to come when we beckon.
But for now we'll celebrate the good King Szid."

Just then trumpets blared six regal notes and a hush
crept over the revelers. The King, escorted by his chamberlain, entered. The people stood rigid for a moment
and then burst into cheers for his good health. He proceeded across the hall as the crowd made way with great
difficulty because so many were pushing forward and
craning their necks to see him. He was old, bent over
and very frail, but the affection he felt from his people
gave spring to his step. He reached his throne set on a
dais at the far end of the hall, folded his purple robe
about him and sat down.

Again the trumpets blew a flourish, and Princess
Aurora entered, escorted by her aunt. The crowd hushed,
awed by her dazzling beauty. Then a murmur rippled
like a wave through the bedazzled audience and broke
in a crashing thunder of happy approval. She wore a
gown of white satin embroidered with tiny pearls around
a deep but soft V neck with a wide midriff band drawn
tight to show her tiny waist. She had a side sash screen-
ing her narrow skirt, slit to mid-thigh. Her silver slippers flashed with each step. She wore a diamond tiara.
Her light golden hair flowed around her shoulders and
framed the single teardrop pearl commemorating her
mother which she wore at her throat. A splash of miniature white roses graced her right shoulder.

Lord No whispered in his ear, "Such pure beauty
comes from a heart of perfect grace. Sadly, she is promised to Spauk of Ice world."

The Birthday Present Ceremony began. A person
had been selected, usually a child, from each town, hamlet, city or province to present a birthday present to the
king. He lavished his appreciation on each as they
passed, no matter how large or small the gift. After that
ceremony, the trumpets blared again. The King rose,
took Aurora's hand and led them to the banquet hall
across the curtains.

Retainers brought a sumptuous feast, during which Porch fought to keep his eyes off the Princess. But once, twice and then again he stole a glimpse to quell the hopeless thumping of his heart. The second time he looked, she caught his eye. Again the third time, she saw him look. He blushed and felt the fool, a ruffian of coarse, indelicate manners, and wondered if she thought him rudely staring. Little did he realize that many watched her every move, so she was quite used to eyes always on her. Had he been a different man, he would have been elated that his glances had been returned.

His thoughts were interrupted by another bugle's blare. All looked to the entry way as four men drew in a miniature coach which bore the royal emblem of Szidrous. An immense cake blazing with eighty-one candles sat on the coach. The King was visibly pleased as it was brought before him. The Lord Chamberlain handed him a bellows and with a vigorous pump, he blew the candles out, then said, "See that all are served." This his retainers quickly did.

When the cake ceremony was over, he rose, clapped his hands and said, "Let the dancing begin."

He took his daughter's hand and led her to the ballroom floor. The violins began a soft triple measure which Porch likened to an ancient minuet. As the full orchestra came in, the King guided his daughter toward the throne. At a break in the music, he stopped, bowed proudly, and handed her off to the Lord Chamberlain, then turned and took the steps up to his throne. After he was seated, the orchestra blared forth in a waltz which Orwell and the Princess led. Dancers filled the floor, and Porch found his partner, the Lord Chamberlain's wife, an outgoing and lovely lady. Both enjoyed the dance. The second waltz began, and Porch bowed and took a young lady from Nork to the floor. She pulled him very close and her body spoke her availability. He cast a worried glance toward the Princess, but her partner had her full attention. The dance ended, and as Porch bowed to express his thanks to the dark-haired beauty from Nork, a young man came up, gave him a sullen look and retrieved her quickly.

He next took in his arms a college girl from Land's End. She was bright and intellectual. Conversation was pleasant, but then in the middle of the waltz, another college girl cut in on her. The first said to the second as she relinquished Porch, "You have just broken our long and enduring friendship, Adelaide."

At intermission, the dancers refreshed themselves with champagne punch. Porch knew the name Aurora was next on his card. He screwed up his courage and moved to where she was centered in a group of admirers. He slowly wedged his way into the group.

She glanced up at him, and he said, "I am Porch, one of Lord No's company." He saw recognition come to her face. He went on hurriedly, "I am sincerely sorry about..." She reached up and put her finger to his lips and said, "Ah, yes, the Wizard spoke to me of you."

Again he tried to apologize, and Aurora broke in with a twinkle in her eyes. "The Lord Chamberlain explained your odd arrival. Do you like the waltz, Sir Porch? It is about to start. Place your arm about my waist and give me your hand."

The music began and off they glided. Porch felt confident. She had made it so easy for him. Now she was like a feather in his arms. Besides, he had the magic shoes on. Around they whirled. Around they glided. As they danced, she spoke of her fondness for the Wizard, a second father to her, she said. She asked how he liked Midlwurld, and about Earth. She asked about his boyhood. She asked him about his decoration. She made it so easy for him, he was totally enchanted.

The dance ended and she said, "Sir Knight, you either have a natural grace, or your dancing master was a genius. I suspect the former true. You made the waltz lovely for me. Thank you."

Before Porch could return her compliment, the Lord Chamberlain stood before them. "Dear Princess," he said, "the next dance is mine, but the King has called me to counsel. Perhaps this good knight would take my place?."

Aurora nodded a smiling assent. The music started and she came a little closer to him. Porch had never felt happier. He was in a world of dreams, and only she was with him. This time both were silent. As the dance ended, Aurora smiled at him. "Porch, I am certain you've broken many a lady's heart."

Just then, Lord No stood before the pair. "Dear Princess," he said, "My dance is next, but your father would speak to me. Perhaps this young man could substitute?"

Joyfully Porch took her in his arms again. The world had turned imaginary. When Lord No reached the King's side, Orwell said, "They dance beautifully together. Surely the shoes you provided are magic."

Lord No chuckled. "I only made a suggestion. He made them magic."

By the contract of his card, Porch knew the next dance, not a waltz but rather a medley of old Earth tunes, was his. There was a singer, Paglio, who sang in a soft and rich baritone. Now she snuggled into his arms, golden hair against his cheek, her breath on his neck. His heart was pounding, and he sensed that hers was, too.

Paglio sang, "...you and the night and the music." The two danced as one. The song changed, "...I could have danced all night..." Suddenly she stopped and looked up at him, flushed and breathing hard. She said, "Oh, Porch, you must know that I am promised..." she faltered slightly, "...in marriage contract to Lord Spauk... Prince of Ice World..." Porch detected sorrow as she went on, "...by my father, to unite our kingdoms and our worlds, to bring prosperity and strength to all...which I must honor for my subjects."

Then it happened. A moan and a shudder, almost imperceptible, accompanied an eerie space whistler. Everyone felt it. The music stopped. The first gravity wave had passed. Again, a great wave, mightier than the first, shook the castle and all inside. The whole planet jumped. She looked at him with fear in her eyes and said, "The hour has come."

King Szid rose and spoke with great effort, hoping all could hear. "Good citizens, our time of trial has come. Move with dignity to your places, prepared to carry out the tasks assigned by Lord No. I wish you Godspeed and Heaven's blessing."

A guard came to lead Aurora away. She had pain in her eyes as she said good night. Wistfully he bowed. Only a few remained when the third tremor lurched in, mightier than the first two combined. A chandelier crashed down. Luckily the floor was empty. Several fires started which men rushed to put out. Porch left. He was to meet Lord No in the high tower at the powerful scope and assess the situation.

The Wizard was there before him, moving the scope back and forth. Beyond the opening, Porch saw searchlights combing the skies. The Wizard looked at Porch and said, "The last gravity wave has passed. I discerned but three as I tracked them. The castle has held. They are landing now, far off. They know better than to land nearby where they would be destroyed before they could disembark. Come look."

Porch took the eyepiece and traversed the land. Fires were burning here and there, diminishing as they consumed their fuel. He pushed the scope up to the sky and saw them descending, slowly drifting back and forth, supported on some unknown force. They looked like dirty black pods.

Lord No spoke again. "Communications are up, and I've contacted the Ruby Queen to disperse her forces into the desert and hide in the dunes until I call. I've signaled Lord Spauk to embark. It will take the Vikuns a month to get here.

"I fear the Priest is lost along with the Millenarians. An awful fate awaits them and us as well unless the courier comes."

Porch looked beyond the walls. The pods were landing. They began to open.

CHAPTER 10
SPAUK

Spauk was furious. The Chieftains had told him Vikun
honor was at stake. They must embark. Who were they
to say? He was their Thurl, soon to be their king. He
would call the shots, not they. Yes, the message from
King Szid was unmistakable. He requested they embark
immediately. Szid was calling in his chit, invoking the
treaty. He knew that the necromancer called Wizard was
behind it. Should he lead his Vikuns into a fray not
weighted? Preposterous. If the Szidrians lost, what was
to be gained? Yet should he catch them on the verge of
winning but weakened, he could have it all. His eyes
narrowed. Of course, orbit and wait. So he would give
the order.

Spauk waddled back and forth, feeling better. He
had his dressing gown on and a heavy robe. He was
always cold. He wore his slippers, the ones with the
curling toes and a stocking cap with tassel. It covered
his long pointy ears, keeping them warm and pink. He
felt secure. These were the clothes his nanny dressed
him in long ago. He wondered what had happened to
her after he ordered her exile. Could it be helped? No.
She knew too much.

The clothes comforted him in times of stress, and
there had been much lately. He wore them only in his
sleeping chambers; outside they'd call them shameful,
and him, behind his back, shameless. But who were
they to set the dress code, they with their great horned

helmets, their shimmering furs, and all that iron and
bronze? He was getting worked up again. He paced faster
and faster.

The dwarf hunched farther into the corner. He'd seen
his master's black moods before and knew the fury they
could bring. He bore the marks of that fury. Spauk would
start spitting out scurrilous comments about those he
feared and hated, the Chieftains. Then he'd hatch aloud
the devious plan he'd follow. But Spauk continued pacing to calm himself down. Too much was at stake to
lose through unrestrained emotion. He had to keep
thinking straight. He knew his long pointy ears had reddened, venting the hatred and heat within, so he pulled
his cap up to cool them. His long pointy nose reddened
also, but the tip hung down so far beneath his nostrils
he could lick it with his tongue to cool it, which he did.
He waddled side to side as each long, wide foot flapped
down. He clasped his hands behind his back, clutching
the short whip. Now he spoke of what the dwarf had
heard so many times before.

"They laugh at me when I don't see, and then go on
and bow so deferentially when I do. 'Lord Spauk,' they
say, 'you're looking well.' 'Prince Spauk,' they sputter,
'so good to see you.' They think me ugly. Who sets the
beauty standard? 'Tis but the average of an average of a
race. What is ugly? The woolly warthog proliferates in
greater number than the sleek snow leopard.

"They think me of slow wit and ill temper. Yet I have
the cunning to rule, not they. I had the signet ring when
Nanny brought me from the marshes. Hidden there from
those who would have another, from those who would
have me slain. I am their prince, soon to be their king.
They accepted me when they saw that ring, worn by
each and every ruler back to the perilous voyage across
the void to find Valhalla. It is a sacred thing, a holy relic
from our origin."

He was quiet for a minute. He reached up and pulled
at a long lock of his coarse black hair. Then he wheeled
and pointed a long misshapen finger at the dwarf, who
cowed and wrapped his arms about his head.

"Aye, who sets the standard? They—with their

chiseled faces and hard gray eyes, not the prince? They—
with their massive muscles and square straight bodies,
not the king? Who, who? Those with the platinum locks
and soft gray beards? Who?"

Spauk raised the whip to strike the dwarf, shouting, "Answer me, answer now!"

"It should be you, sire. None other," the dwarf replied meekly.

Spauk nodded gravely and moved away. Then he
grinned sardonically, pulling on his scraggly goatee.
Again he whirled toward the dwarf, waddled over like a
duck and bent down. As he hovered over him, his eyes
narrowed. The dwarf whimpered, coiling up even tighter.
Spauk hissed, "Yes, I shall set the standard when I have
her, her kingdom, too. All will envy. I'll sire many with
pointed ears and noble noses. Rough black hair shall
be the rule, and long, wide feet the measure of the Court.

"Old Szid was wise to bargain for our added strength.
He said it was for his people and for mine, a benefit to
both. I know better. He wants our ores and gems. He
covets the shimmering, scintillating furs of the ice animals, more beautiful than those of any other world. He
knows we need his wheat, his oats, his barley, to make
the Vikun loaf—his honey, spice and malt to make the
Vikun mead, but the trade is not enough.

Since I own the sailing ships that float between his
world and mine, I'll set the price, not he. If the price be
too dear for him, it's not enough for me. But I'll shove it
down his throat once I get his daughter. The meat of
these cold valleys, the fish from our frozen seas grow
tired to the tongue. We must have more and other, and
I shall have it all once I get his daughter."

Once more he strode away from the dwarf. "She is a
prize young virgin. Already our minstrels sing her fabled beauty. The bards recite her purity and charms.
Already she commands the respect and awe, why, even
worship, of those who have sworn allegiance to me. They
say that since the contract was struck, sorrow dims her
eyes. But she has no right to fret. Her mother was a
Vikun, a baroness, no less. But I will tame that beauty
to obedience, with the whip if I must..." He hurried back

to the dwarf, bent over him and whispered hoarsely, "And should the whip not work...the iron and the tongs..." What do you think of that, faithful Scrofulous?"

"Hee, hee, hee," giggled the dwarf.

CHAPTER 11
THE THROGS

All night the spaceboats descended. Inside the fortress all were awaiting the unknown. There was enough food, water and ammunition to withstand constant attack for many months. But their ultimate survival awaited the Earth courier. Lord No had gathered his general staff in the war room at the great scope. They had voice and visi-screen to each gun position and all the redoubts. They monitored the landings throughout the night. The spaceboats opened like the seed pods they resembled. Black hairy creatures disembarked, disoriented, aroused from a cryogenic sleep of many years, propelled through the cosmos by gravity waves.

Each was about five feet tall and almost as broad as he was high. They wore vests and skirts made of pieced-together human bone. Tortoise shell helmets were strapped tightly to their squat heads. They had huge carapaces on their backs, so from the rear they looked like large roaches. They wobbled about on powerful squat legs till the oxygen they sucked in warmed their blood.

Then they began buzzing in their strange staccato language and gathering in groups of twenty to thirty. In each group, one was twice the size of the others. These were their leaders, in their tongue, the Bu'ji. All carried a small iron shield and trident that looked much like a pitchfork. They hardly resembled the men from whom they'd devolved fifty centuries before.

By morning, the plains from a mile beyond Szid's

fortress to the far horizons and distant mountains were covered with the creatures and their spacecraft. Now, in the morning light, the group in the war room watched larger craft come floating down. These carried heavy weapons, ancient and modern: ballistas, catapults, bronze and iron cannon, and huge siege mortars.

Lord No spoke. "Those weapons came from worlds they conquered. They discarded many more, such as lasers and anti-matter devices, because they did not understand their operation. I know their language and their ways. Come, we'll ask for a parley."

They left the castle and went to the far outer works, then climbed the rampart closest to the Throgs. At the top, Lord No took a hand scope and surveyed the field. He turned to Orwell and said, "They are still milling about. Their siege weapons are not ready. Their commander, the Big Boojie, has not arrived, and the Lesser Boojies have no control. I will work them into a frenzied, uncoordinated attack. Command our batteries commence fire at one thousand yards. We'll kill as many as we can. That will force them to reconstitute, which will give us what we need most—time."

Orwell gave the glass to Porch and transmitted the order to the gunners. Lord No took up a great electric horn and thundered out, "LEAVE THIS PLANET. WE ARE A PEOPLE OF PEACE."

After a silence, a buzzing began among the Throgs, rising into a thundering din. "T'THROG, T'THROG, T'THROG. BL'J, BL'J, BL'J." interpreted as, "Throgs, Throgs, Throgs. Blood, blood, blood."

When the din subsided, Lord No lifted the horn again. "I AM NO, THE DESTROYER. I HAVE FOUGHT YOU FROM THE BEGINNING, ALONG THE ARMS OF THE GALAXY, AMONGST THE NEBULA AND STAR CLUSTERS, BETWEEN THE SUNS AND THE PLANETS. I HAVE NEVER BEEN DEFEATED AND HAVE CUT YOU DOWN IN UNTOLD NUMBERS, GASPING IN YOUR FILTHY SPITTLE. NOW I RISE TO SAVAGE YOU AGAIN. I CURSE YOU AND YOUR DEMON PIG GOD, TORTOS."

This created great agitation amongst the creatures, for they remembered and knew what he said was true.

A great rumble rolled forth, "URKU! URKU! URKU!"

The Lord Chamberlain quizzed Lord No, "What—what?"

The Wizard said simply, "Kill, kill, kill."

A deafening swell of rage rolled in. In a mad, undisciplined horde, the Throgs charged, shields up, tridents forward, screaming and spitting. At one thousand yards, defender lasers opened up and burned, rushing Throgs to blackened crisps. They continued attacking throughout the day, thousands upon thousands, in an undisciplined stampede which was exactly what Lord No, the Wizard, wanted.

Beyond the horizon, in the land of the Millenarians, a different scene unfolded. It too began at daylight. The Priest, filled with fear, watched the landings take place around him and, inadvertently or not, took the one action that would save his life. When the gravity waves passed the night before, the ground around him quaked and he was knocked off his feet. He found himself lying next to a very large tortoise shell that had been overturned. The farmer who worked that field had inverted it and used it as a trough to slop his hogs. Though it had a terrible piggy smell, the Priest crept underneath. It fit him tightly, but he could move around a bit and stay concealed. He could see out well enough in front where the shell arched up.

He humped his back up and, like a tortoise, crawled up a small hill with the shell on his back. He saw Millenarians standing around below him, looking up, awestruck at the descending pods.

The Throgs began rounding up Millenarians at the end of their tridents or pitchforks like so many cattle and herding them into a large open area where they separated the children from the adults. They prodded the children into large barred cages on wheels and pulled them out of the Priest's field of vision. The circle of adults increased until it was several miles around.

Presently, a giant pod descended, and as the clamshell doors opened, the Throgs got down on their knees and bowed in obeisance.

The Priest heard, "Aka qzsital B'bg Bu'ji." As he had

learned a smattering of Throg language from the Wizard, he interpreted the words, "All hail the Big Boojie."

A tortoise the size of a battle tank emerged from the spacecraft, and on its back it carried a hulking figure, a replica of the smaller Throgs but ten times their size. The Big Boojie was their general. He wore the tortoise helmet and all the other gear stretched to fit over a ponderous belly so distended that it rested on his thighs as he sat cross-legged on a saddle strapped to the beast. His arms were thick and muscular. They rippled with strength when he moved. He carried a huge trident.

The Big Boojie's steed lumbered forth, swaying, claws ripping into the ground with each slow step. Its head extended forward on a long sinuous neck and undulated side to side as the beast moved. Its head was hog-like, with small peaked ears, tiny red eyes, and a great tusked snout.

Subordinate leaders pressed forward. These were the Lesser Boojies. They began waving up and down from their waists, arms extended in exaltation, shouting, "Bu'ji, Bu'ji, Bu'ji."

The Big Boojie moved to the front of the corralled Millenarians and stopped. The Lesser Boojies prodded them forward, segregating twenty men and women. The Priest recognized these as Millenarian leaders. Rank and file Throgs were setting up vats ten feet across. They built fires under these and stoked them with wood and coal, foraged and pillaged. Others formed a bucket brigade and filled the vats with water from the nearest sources. When they completed these tasks, a Lesser Boojie prodded a Millenarian forward to stand in front of the Big Boojie.

The Priest recognized him as Thaddeus P. Winter IV. Thaddeus ignored the prodding fork and raised his hands before the Big Boojie. He said, "We are the Millenarians. We have seen the darkness and the light. We are one with the Universe."

The Big Boojie delicately plucked him up with his thumb and forefinger and held him close to his flat leathery nose to smell. His big saucer eyes bulged out to get a better look. Again Thaddeus raised his arms and said,

"Peace, brother, and love."

The Big Boojie blinked and thrust Preacher Winter into his cavernous maw, biting through him at the hips. Thaddeus P. Winter's eyes rolled heavenward as life ebbed from his body. The Big Boojie poked the rest of him in, chomped down, chewed rapidly, spit out the head, and swallowed big. He grunted, wiping blood from his leathery lips with a big hairy arm.

The Priest was aghast. A baleful moan rose from the crowd and became a chant, "MOLOCH—MOLOCH, COME TO LIFE; IN A HOPELESS, HORRIBLE TIME OF STRIFE."

Lesser Boojies began nudging selected groups of people, mostly fat ones with lots of flesh, toward the cauldrons which were now bubbling. The chant began again, "BELIAL—BELIAL, UP FROM HELL, LIVING FLESH, HUNGER TO QUELL."

The Lesser Boojies jabbed several people, screaming, up ramps into each cauldron, then more and more. The din of scalding death was hideous. Beneath his shell, the Priest alternately prayed and wept. The rank and file Throgs began fishing bodies from the human stew, tore them apart, and devoured them voraciously. Ptui— they spit out the heads as the Big Boojie had done. The vermin that infested the pods streamed down. Each was about eight inches long and looked like a scorpion on a long centipede body. They quickly picked the heads clean, for they too had insatiable appetites after years in space.

As evening fell, the Throgs collected the skulls and stacked them into glistening pyramids. At dark, the Priest began to crawl toward water and in the general direction of the castle. He believed he had a chance. The Throgs avoided the tortoise shell covering him, though they had closely approached it that whole day. From what the Wizard had told him, he believed the shell was taboo.

Back at the fortress, the Throgs retreated, leaving a wall of burnt corpses behind them. Lord No's forces had no casualties. Though three of his lasers overheated and quit operating, it was a great victory. Lord No beckoned the Lord Chamberlain and Porch to accompany him. They circled the ramparts along the outer walls, congratulating the defenders. Morale was high.

On return to the war room, he collected the staff and said, "It will take them several days to reconstitute. Then they will attack again, using their standard tactics. First they will try to inspire fear in us. Then they will make some feints and begin an investment of our works. They are readying their siege mortars, heavy cannon, ballistas and catapults."

That night, beyond laser range, the defenders watched a macabre event. The Throgs brought up huge cauldrons from which they ate a human stew of captives, spearing ghastly pieces of flesh and grunting as they satisfied their hunger. A horned Throg danced before each of the fires raging below the cauldrons. The Wizard explained, "Those are the Lords of the Furnace, Throg shamans who rank after the Boojies. They are invoking the spirits of their dead to aid them in the coming days of battle."

As the Thyestean banquet continued, rank and file Throgs got up, disappearing behind a sulfurous pall of smoke, but Porch caught a quick glimpse of several re-entering the space pods. He looked wonderingly at Lord No.

The Wizard said, "They unveil their dark secret. They continue coming in untold number no matter how many we kill, because they are cloning." Porch and the others were horrified.

The Wizard continued, "We have a few days before the next onslaught. We'd better look to our weapons, sharpen our defenses, get some rest and...pray the courier comes."

When dawn broke several days later, the Throgs were ready, lined up in ranks of thousands. Behind them, they had constructed a huge pyramid built of the skulls of their victims. They had brought up massive iron mortars and other siege weapons to breach the outer walls. Their chant began, "T'Throg, T'throg, T'throg... Urku, urku, urku... Bl'j, bl'j, bl'j... Bu'ji, bu'ji, bu'ji."

On signal, Lesser Boojies raised white banners high

and Throg infantry raised their tridents, to which they had attached white guidons. Again, on signal they flipped them and dipped them into quivers they wore at their sides. Then they withdrew them in unison, now bright red, soaked in human blood. They began their advance as massive mortars boomed, catapults cracked and ballistas twanged. Szidrian ramparts were breached in several places as iron cannon balls and boulders rained down. Ballista shafts took their toll.

On and on they came. Among the defenders, casualties screamed, cursed or prayed, and died. Throgs streamed toward one great cut in the wall. Porch led one hundred men in a sally to turn them back, which they did with hand lasers, pistols, submachine guns, swords and knives in fierce hand-to-hand combat. Porch was badly wounded and they brought him back on a stretcher. Medics took him quickly to the emergency medical facility.

Defender lasers, cannon and machine guns spit forth streams of death, and the wall of Throg corpses grew ever higher. More rushed up to push the corpses forward and take refuge behind. By noon, Szidrian counter battery fire silenced the catapults and mortars. By dusk, the wall of death quit moving forward. The day's battle was over. During the battle, the Throgs dug a net of deep zigzag trenches into which they retreated as they withdrew. Lasers could not reach them there.

Throughout the day, Lord No had been indefatigable. He visited the most hotly contested salients, encouraging the men. He exposed himself as he felt necessary to the fiercest Throg bombardments and taunted the enemy. He directed a withering fire where it would take the heaviest toll. He visited the wounded and shored up those he felt faltering. Now he stood resolute as the Throgs withdrew. He was the rock around which the defense rallied.

He called his staff together and said, "Men, we did not hurt them enough today, so they will continue their attack tomorrow. It will be more difficult for us, as they will use the trenches and attempt to dig them ever closer. We must use high angle fire to reach them with our mortars and our cannon. Register these weapons on the trenches tonight.

"They will also dig deep holes as adjuncts to the trenches for their siege mortars and catapults, probably under the cover of darkness. We must root these out. They are our first priority. Now post the guard, tend to the wounded, and see that all are fed well. Then get some rest."

In the hospital deep within the castle, surgeons treated Porch's wounds. Except for Lord No's advanced medicines, he would have been dead. Many thought the Wizard's drugs were magic in their healing power, which was part of the mythology surrounding him. Porch was sleeping and ran a fever from filth-born poisons on Throg tridents. When Lord No visited him, he ascertained the young man would recover, and left to check the other wounded. By morning, Porch's fever broke.

When he opened his eyes, Aurora stood over him. She was haggard and worn from tending wounded around the clock. Perspiration beaded on her forehead as she bathed him and changed his dressings. But he thought he saw an angel. He tried to speak, but his mouth was too dry from the fever. She put her palm to his mouth, and when she had finished the last dressing, she lifted his head so he could sip some water. He saw great concern and compassion in her eyes as he looked up at her. Then she gently lowered his head back to the pillow, took out a fine handkerchief with the royal emblem embroidered on it, dipped it in a pan of bedside ice water and carefully wiped his face. When she finished, he feebly reached for it, took it gently from her hand and tried to tie it about his wrist. She reached over and tied it for him. He looked up at her again and saw tears in her eyes. She rose, turning to leave, but hesitated, turned back and placed her lips to his. Then she ran off hurriedly.

Porch returned to the outer wall three days later. For the next six days, he led a number of sorties with his chosen one hundred, slashing, cutting and pushing the demonic besiegers back wherever they threatened to break through. On the tenth day, the Throgs withdrew once more. He had not suffered a scratch. He wondered if Aurora's cloth at his wrist was a talisman of loving protection. His heart told him yes, though his mind told him no.

That evening Lord No drew them together and said, "Again they've suffered sufficient attrition to quit the field to replicate in their abominable way. We'll have several days to rest and rebuild defenses. We must look to it smartly. Note their trenches come ever closer, and as we destroy one section, two more appear. We must remain vigilant. They will begin mining operations shortly. When tailings appear, we can be sure they have, and we'll begin our countermine program. Watch closely. Make sure our underground listening posts are alert and our own miners and flame throwers ready."

On duty shift that night, Porch picked up a strange object seven hundred yards out. He called for Lord No, pointed it out and handed him the scope. Lord No peered through it and said, "Strange, it looks like a land turtle or tortoise. The Throgs revere them and keep them well away from the field of battle. I doubt it has any military significance, but keep an eye on it throughout the night."

As Porch continued his surveillance, he stopped and focused on the strange object. He felt certain it moved sporadically closer. At the end of his watch, he asked his relief to keep watching it. The following morning, he hurried to the tower. The Lord Chamberlain was already peering through the big scope. He asked Porch to look.

As Porch did, he said, "I am sure it moved during the night. It's now over by the large boulders. Wait! I see something—black letters on the boulders, possibly marked with char from the battlefield. Take a look."

The Lord Chamberlain took the eyepiece again. He said, "Yes, I see them, too. Oh...some Throgs are nearby. They also seem suspicious, but won't touch it. Lord No said it was a taboo. Look again, see if you can read the letters. They are in Earth language."

Lord No arrived as Porch scanned the letters. Slowly words formed on his lips, "LISTEN—TO—MY—CRY—FOR—HELP, BE—NOT—DEAF—TO—MY—WEEPING. PSALM—39:12."

He passed the scope to the Wizard. Lord No looked through and said, "It must be the Priest. Ah-oh, the Throgs have approached. They are kneeling in obeisance. They seem to be in awe of it. No, now they are sneaking toward it. They are picking at it with their tridents. Now they back off. Several Lesser Boojies are coming up."

Porch exclaimed, "I'll go get him. There are not many Throgs. We can make a lightning strike."

Lord No turned to Orwell and said, "Assemble twenty of the best, volunteers only, at the east gate. Porch will lead them. Hurry."

Porch met the men, armed to their teeth, at the sallyport. The Throgs had discovered the writing and had gathered to determine what to do. Porch and his men rushed out toward the shell five hundred yards away, covered by withering fire from the outer wall parapets. The Throgs ignored the fire when they saw the Szidrians approach and rushed to engage them. A huge immigrant from Earth's Russia called Rasputin kicked the shell over, grabbed up the Priest, and hightailed back to the fortress. Porch and his men covered, slowly retreating.

The Throgs finally broke off, unable to withstand their slashing steel and the withering fire from the parapets. At the last moment, Porch was pierced in the thigh by a trident. He turned and galloped off, hobbling like a wounded animal.

Rasputin reached the gate, dropped the Priest inside and continued running. Then he fell to the ground retching, so terrible was the smell from the Priest. Porch reached the gate and also fell, just inside. Medics grabbed him and rushed him to the hospital. The gate slammed shut. The Lord Chamberlain, who had been awaiting their return, directed that a fire truck be brought up and the Priest thoroughly doused. After his dousing, the Priest got up. He was somewhat wobbly but all right. Several men came up, wrapped him in a sheet of plastic and spirited him off to the showers for additional cleansing. A supply of disinfectant and a copious amount of soap awaited him there. He wept uncontrollably for several days before he could tell his story, and then wept again from the horror he had seen.

In the meantime, surgeons attended Porch, pulling iron shards from his thigh and applying the Wizard's bactericides to his festering flesh. Once again it was the Princess who bathed him and dressed his new wounds. He watched her, amazed at her tenderness, and was able to smile up at her as she went about her task. She pulled a chair up beside his bed, took his hand in hers, and sat there several hours.

The respite lasted several days before the onslaught resumed. Porch recovered and again led sally after sally where defenses proved weakest. Other warrior teams were pressed into service, but the main Throg trenches pressed ever closer and auxiliary trenches seemed to increase without number. Listening teams and seismograph operators ferreted out Throg mines, and the countermining operation destroyed all found by mining below them and setting explosives. Several times Szidrian miners and warriors broke directly through to the Throgs and destroyed them with flame throwers.

A month of continuous battle passed before the next respite and resumed again in just one day. The defense held but sustained ever greater casualties. The Throgs succeeded in bringing their heavy weapons still closer and breached the outer wall in many places.

They began to lob the heads of the ill-fated Millenarians over the walls and encapsulated the highly poisonous scorpion-millipede vermin in them. Lord No, recognizing the extreme danger, formed terminator squads armed with pistol lasers. He ordered them to circulate continuously and blast the vermin immediately upon hitting the ground inside because they quickly sped away from their awful carriers.

Another month of continuous battle passed before the Throgs again withdrew to reconstitute. The outer walls were crumbling and the defenders labored continuously on repairs. Lord No asked Porch and the Lord Chamberlain to accompany him on an inspection tour to encourage the defenders. They met some women bearing belts of machine gun ammunition up an emplacement under repair.

"What happened here?" Lord No asked.

"Ask Hedda. She is at the machine gun," came the reply. They reached the top of the parapet and came upon a woman boresighting the weapon.

"Hello, where are the men?" Lord No asked.

Hedda replied, "Dead—all dead, killed in the bombardment. We are their wives. My good man Henry fell here, so it is here that I shall meet my fate. The others feel the same."

She bent over to continue servicing her gun. Lord No fell silent as they continued on. They reached another high point and found a cadre of young boys, all orphaned. Their leader was twelve years old.

Lord No said, "It is time to call the Desert Warriors and Spauk's Vikuns. The Ruby Queen's warriors should attack from the north and Spauk should land in the far west and attack from the rear. We will coordinate their efforts by signal from the high tower. Orwell, notify me when they say they are ready. We will wait until the Throgs renew their assault and hold our fire until they are within two hundred yards of the fortress. Release our reserves of ammunition. I want the heaviest bombardment possible after we open fire and our allies attack. Porch, be prepared to counterattack with two thousand of our ablest men."

Seemingly endless Throg columns moved up that night. Lord No watched them with Porch and the Lord Chamberlain through the scope in the high tower. When the Throgs saw their advance unopposed, they came up out of the trenches and spread across the battlefield. They began digging more trenches toward the fortress. Lord No stated, "The Ruby Queen will attack as soon as the Desert Warriors hear our artillery open up. Spauk will attack the Throg rear simultaneously. Has he begun his landings? We have gathered no evidence of that through the star scope."

Orwell replied, "Strange. He signals the Vikuns are landing now."

"Very well. Transmit the attack order."

Beyond the walls, at 0557, the Lesser Boojies raised their bloody banners and the Throg infantry rose from their trenches with bloodcurdling screams. At 0557:15, Szidrian machine guns on the outer walls opened up. At 0557:20, lasers from the main fort began to sizzle. At 0557:30, the first rounds of Szidrian artillery landed and began to blast great holes in the attack forces. At 0600, there was sufficient light to see columns of dust on the northern horizon, and at 0610, the Desert Warriors poured over the dunes from the north with the fury of a Jahid, as they called it. They surprised the Throgs and cut a great swath through the enemy.

But by evening, Throg numbers stymied the Desert Warriors and began to push them back. There was no sign of Spauk's warriors landing. The Szidrians sent an emergency signal but received no reply. Lord No looked through the great scope and saw the long boats still in orbit. They continued to plead for landings throughout the night. Spauk did not respond. Word spread among the defenders that the Prince of Ice World had failed them, and they became terribly afraid because they were running out of ammunition.

Lord No called Porch in. He was imperturbable. He said calmly, "We must extricate Shalimar's forces. They have fought bravely and taken a great toll of the enemy. One hour before dawn, we will once again increase our barrage. Attack then with your two thousand. The Throgs will not expect another sally from here and will break off and retreat. As soon as they begin to withdraw, return."

As Porch signaled a preparatory order, there was a disturbance in back of them. It was Aurora. She said, "Here is one Vikun who will fight. I will accompany Sir Porch."

They turned and looked. She was wearing Vikun chain mail battledress and armor with a great horned helmet. She had two laser pistols at her waist and she carried a great Vikun sword. Yet she could not conceal her radiant beauty.

The Lord Chamberlain came in as though he had followed her. "Princess, why did you come here?"

"I must fight as the other women are," she said.

"Impossible," Orwell replied, cringing. "Dear Aurora, this kingdom cannot afford such. You represent all that's good from the past. When this is over, our people will look to you to lead them to all that will be good in the future. It can be no other way."

Her eyes found Porch. He was visibly distressed. Resignedly, she sighed, took off her helmet, lay down her sword, and returned to her quarters. Porch left to mount the attack and the intense cannonade began. His force caught the hell horde by surprise, and before noon relief of the Desert Warriors was complete and, as Lord No predicted, the Throgs were in full retreat. The Szidrians then broke off and returned. They suffered terrible casualties, and the hospital bays filled with the wounded and near dead. Porch reported back with his after-action statement and casualty count. He asked, "What of Spauk?"

"Treachery," Lord No replied. "We have about twenty days as the Throgs prepare their final attack. They will go through a period of double cloning, two to four, four to eight. Except for volunteers manning machine guns on the outer walls with our last ammunition, we must evacuate and confine ourselves to the castle. Inside, we will stand or die. Heads of household will be responsible to see that no one is captured alive. The Lord Chamberlain will carry out the withdrawal. Get some rest. You will be needed again."

Exhausted, Porch slept for several days. When he rose, he went to the outer walls to help with the evacuation. It was eerie. The Throgs had feasted on the corpses of the dead, and now in the far distance, Porch saw them marching off from all around the castle in chanting columns of thousands.

The following day, there was no evidence of them as far as the eye could see. The battlefield was quiet except for the buzzing of insects feasting on the offal that remained. Porch worked to aid Orwell until late afternoon. Then, bone weary, he left. He was as tired as he'd ever been in his life. Every wound he'd taken ached. He had to escape that loud and incessant buzz. But he knew most of his weariness came from his foreknowledge of what lay ahead. He looked at the cloth around his wrist and thought of her.

He doubted he could face her close up and reveal his sadness, but he thought he might catch a glimpse of her from the inner garden below her balcony. He longed for the quiet coolness he knew he'd find there. When he got there he saw thousands of ravens roosting in the trees. They began to cackle their annoyance at his disturbance below. Their crowing grew louder as he wondered what had brought them. Was it some inner instinct and anticipation of the carrion to come? Suddenly they ceased their cawing. He heard a beautiful song, one that he had not heard since his childhood in the little Christian church in Pecado. He listened as it gathered timbre and intensity. It was to him the most beautiful gospel song ever written, "AMAZ-I-NG GRA-A-CE, HOW SWEET THOU ART, TO SAVE A WRETCH LI-I-I-KE ME-E-I ONCE WA-A-S LO-O-ST, AND NOW AM FOUND."

A great lump rose in his throat and a tear came into his eye. He could not resist looking up toward her balcony. It was Aurora. His wounds quit aching and a great veil of peace enveloped him. He sat rigid to catch every note, rendered in a voice of such purity and love that he wept openly. She continued on, and when she finished, there was a great silence all around. He wondered where she had heard it. Then she began another song.

"DO YOU WONDER...EVER WONDER, WHERE IS THE BIRTHPLACE OF WONDER..."

Porch sat bolt upright. His mind raced. There was only one who could bring that song to Midlwurld. He ran toward the balcony and began climbing, grabbing vines, stones, whatever handholds he found.

"YES I WONDER...ALWAYS WONDER, WHERE IS THE BIRTHPLACE..."

He reached the wrought iron fence that circled her balcony, pulled himself over and landed in front of the Princess. Quite startled, she quit singing. "Why, Sir Porch–" she began.

He interrupted her. "Aurora, where did you hear that song?"

She replied, "Why, it was on this button disk I found on my balcony this morning, along with that other sweet song. I played it. Both were so heartwarming in this desperate time, I had to sing them. I thought it might be the only chance I would have. Look here! The disk was attached to this great black feather with this piece of bark wrapped in leather. There is a scratching on the bark." She handed the bark to Porch. It had one word scratched on it, "ERTS."

Porch picked her up and began dancing around and kissing her wildly.

"Sir," she screamed, giggling, "what is it about my balcony that makes the madness come upon you?"

Extremely embarrassed and bright red, Porch set her down gently. "Sweet princess," he said, "you may just have saved the kingdom, perhaps saved us all."

She looked confused as he went on sheepishly, "I am so sorry for my exuberance, but I'm certain you have found the courier. I must take the feather and the bark and find the Wizard. Please forgive me."

She reached up, placed her arms around his neck and kissed him as only a princess could. "You have brought hope to a desperate heart. Now go," she said, smiling.

He hurried out and as he raced to the tower, he began planning. Soon enough he reached Lord No and told him what had happened.

"We must have a glider, really, an ultralight powered hang glider. We need no more than that. I can build one with Big Gwyn and little Weejie. They know light-weight materials from their work on rockets. Yes, and that big man, Rasputin, the one who brought the Priest in–he builds racing bicycles. We can power the glider with pedals and cycling gears to extend its range."

Lord No was caught up in Porch's enthusiasm and called for the staff, along with Big Gwyn, Little Weejie and Rasputin. Porch and Lord No related the story and laid out their plan. Looking solemn, the Priest quoted, "WHEN THE RAVENS GATHER AND GROW SILENT, THE GREAT BATTLE IS NIGH. LIFE HANGS ON A SONG. A STEALTHY FLIGHT, IN THE DEAD OF NIGHT. We cannot lose!"

The Wizard smiled. "It is our only chance. We will

need a launch ramp here in the high tower. The Lord Chamberlain can see to that."

"Yes," Porch agreed. "I can get to the northwest mountains with the small amount of propulsion from the propeller-driven cycle train. The south wind will lift me high as it presses over those mountains. From there it is but two days to ERTFOREST. I can glide most of the way. I'll need at most two days there to find the courier, a day to describe our situation and enlist ERT aid, then three days back on the condor-steeds. I can carry water and high energy food, and strap on a two-way radio and beacon so that you can monitor my progress."

"Let's begin," Lord No said.

Porch was acquainted with airfoils. The Wizard knew them well. They worked through the night, and by morning, after six iterations on the computer, all agreed they had an optimum design. Two days later, Big Gwyn and company had a craft. They had just enough space to test it from halfway up the castle to the outer wall. Porch would leave that night.

"Godspeed," they hollered as he cycled down the ramp, gained speed, and became airborne. Soon he was lost in the darkness of the moonless night.

CHAPTER 12

SPAUK

Earlier, four hundred miles above Midlwurld, Spauk was sitting at the Commander's console on the bridge of the royal longboat. As he watched the battle on his visi-screen, he laughed gleefully and said, "A plum to pluck, a planet to plunder. Call the Chieftains in." The dwarf obeyed, and within a few minutes they came in, fear-some in battledress, wearing huge horned helmets, their broad chests covered with heavy breastplates over chain mail, shoulders draped in the scintillating furs of Ice World, shirts of thick wool and leggings of leather fitted to leather shoes. Each carried a round shield, long spear and sword of beaten steel.

A huge man stepped forward and said, "Sire, we must attack and save this world as the treaty binds us to do."

Spauk retorted contemptuously, "So, Baldor the Brave does command the Thurl, his prince, soon to be his king. Listen to me, all of you. My spies have just reported. The Desert Warriors have broken off their at-tack, leaving havoc in their wake. The Szidrian coun-terattack has been successful, and their fierce cannon-ade has blown great holes in the witless horde they face. The Throgs are running from the field. King Szid and that Soothsayer have yet ten thousand men, a regiment of women, and a band of boys in their fort. Let them fight and be weakened more, perhaps succumb.

"Then we strike and win a world. They will welcome

us once we destroy the aliens they cannot. And those below, battle weary, would be no match for fifty thousand Vikuns. They will be a vassal state."

The Vikuns leaders were aghast. "Why, that's unbridled treachery that spits on Vikun honor," Ragnor roared.

"Hear me out," Spauk demanded. "I follow exactly the Treaty words, 'come to the aid of each other.' We are here, are we not? Our attack must just be timely—for us. It's just judicious, is it not?

"There is a world to win down there, a world of soft climes, fair women for the taking, fields of heavy-headed grain, pastures full of tasty beeves. I shall reward you richly. You've sworn your fealty to me in blood. Will your 'Vikun honor' let you break the vow?

"We shall wait, but prepare now. I shall command descent when I deem the time is right."

CHAPTER 13

BOKS

Porch caught the south wind above the castle, and by pedaling constantly, maintained sufficient altitude to clear the Throg lines undetected. As morning came, he saw the northwest mountains looming ahead. When he reached their base, he began to circle, and the strong updraft carried him to ten thousand feet. The enclosed cabin retained sufficient heat to keep him warm during the day. He glided throughout the day. As dusk came, he ate the high energy bars and drank as much fortified liquid as he could, then began pedaling. He pedaled through the night to stay awake and to keep warm.

As the sun rose the next day, he saw ERTFOREST ahead. He was very tired but the sight of his destination revitalized him. By noon, he saw the Jubilee Tree looming majestically above the sea of trees. Suddenly an unseasonable wind came up from the west. It blew him off course and cost him several hours to track back. It was two o'clock by the time he got back to the landmark tree. He began to circle slowly down so the ERTS would not think him a wind-eagle.

But the torrential rain came, with downdrafts and updrafts. The glider bucked and tossed. A nearby thunderclap turned him over and down he fell, tangled up in the broken craft. He plummeted thousands of feet, faster and faster. *Well, this is it*, he thought, sorry to have failed the desperate people back at the fortress.

But just before he hit the trees, a net scooped him

up. He could see the great wings and hear the high-pitched buzzing, but was so disoriented from tumbling he had little sense of what was happening. He felt himself floating down. Then he hit and was released. When he disentangled himself from the broken craft, he determined he was on the same platform from which he had left so many months before.

Ouregard, the Good Medicine, Hunter-Man and Root-Woman surrounded him. Ouregard said, "Porch, you have returned in a very strange craft. Did you have a good trip?"

They laughed uproariously. Porch looked sheepish, then joined in their laughter, saying, "All but the last part."

Ouregard continued, "We have been tracking you since Forward Observer picked you up at Fringe. The Out-Guards signaled us."

After exchanging amenities, Porch related what was happening in the Kingdom of Szidrous, of the terrible war that was going on, the desperate plight of the people, and the grave danger the ERTS themselves faced.

After Porch had finished speaking, Ouregard said proudly, "Not to worry, the mighty BOKS has come. He will protect us."

Strange, Porch thought, but he had a sense of what might have happened, so he said, "Yes, it is mighty BOKS I've come to see. Perhaps his power is so great that he will save this world you share with others. Please take me to him."

"I don't know that BOKS will see you," Ouregard answered with some suspicion.

"But I've come to petition him."

Ouregard, the Good Medicine, Hunter-Man and Root-Woman huddled together, chirping in the ultrasonic language Porch could not hear. Shortly thereafter, Ouregard turned and stated gravely, "The Good Medicine says Mighty BOKS receives all petitions. It is written."

As a delegation, they led Porch to the Jubilee Tree, moving slowly against the pelting rain. When they arrived, the rain stopped and the sun shone gloriously through the trees.

"It is a good sign," Root-Woman allowed.

"Yes," Ouregard replied. "Let us enter."

They entered the dim chamber, and Porch strained to see ahead with eyes not adjusted to the dark because of the brilliance outside. Then he saw a man who looked as black as ebony sitting on the Imperial BOKS Throne. He was wrapped loosely in the panther god's imperial robe with his own arms and hands concealed under the robe's forelimbs and menacing claws. The half-panther head sat on the man's head, ears pointed up, iridescent crystal eyes glaring, and incisors gleaming just below his brow. Six ERT maidens, three on each side of the throne, were slowly fanning him with great condor-steed feathers. They were softly trilling an ERTSONG. Two more maidens lounged just below the throne, ready to bring food and drink and answer any whim.

As they approached the throne, Ouregard whispered to Porch, "Bow low obediently, or he cannot grant your boon."

They all bowed low, and as Porch then raised his eyes, he was astounded. "Bo—Bo Bokasi, is that you?"

"The one called Porch, come forward," BOKS commanded in a deep stentorian voice, grinning like a Cheshire cat.

Porch, not quite certain, moved forward and said, "I've come to petition the great BOKS."

Bokasi rose from the throne. Porch saw that his left leg was gone at the knee and in its place was a beautifully carved peg. Bokasi came down and lifted Porch high in a great bear hug.

Ouregard whispered to the other ERTS, "I knew he was an extraordinary man, but he knows BOKS, and BOKS knows him."

"The Golden One must be a god, like BOKS," Root-Woman whispered back fearfully, "and we have not shown the proper deference."

"Wow," said Hunter-Man.

"What if they leave us?" the Good Medicine worried.

BOKS spoke, "This is my brother. Treat him with honor."

"Yes, Mighty BOKS," the ERTS replied.

"Leave us now," Bokasi thundered.

"Yes, Great BOKS," they replied again. They left hurriedly and the maidens fluttered out behind them.

"Old friend," Bo said, "rumors persisted for years that you eluded your pursuers. I thought, was there a chance, I would find you."

"Your leg," Porch inquired.

"It is gone—but no matter, it's fitting for a spacefarer, just as it was for those who plied the unknown oceans so many centuries ago. I'll have the image of a fierce space warrior and many stories to tell."

"We've not much time, but tell me how you came here and why."

"Let me go back then—graduated from the Academy two years ago, always suspect because of my support for you. I learned what a raw deal you got, but still graduated high enough to make the Fleet as a first tour of duty along with Red Eric. Asked to serve under Admiral Petersen. That's where the action was. Bonnie Brightwood put in a good word. Petersen accepted us, and we served directly under Colonel Ironwood. Remember him? He said he was sure you were the man who escaped the slave ship but then disappeared.

We fought the pirates at War World, a huge iron satellite they put in sun orbit in the asteroid belt after Petersen beat them at Neptune, thinking they could conceal it. We totally destroyed them.

"Things got slow. Rumors of an urgent mission circulated in the fleet. Red Eric and I volunteered. Ironwood liked us, recommended us to the Admiral. We got transferred to the Corporation. Saw Captain Brightwood, who married the Admiral. I asked her about you. She spoke of a meeting in Israel—there were indications you were there, but she knew no more. The Corporation bought a machine from an old man, an eccentric genius. He called it Baby. They renamed it Transporter, and sent men to this planet.

"The Admiral said we were couriers and gave us some vials in canvas pouches. He said we must deliver them to a Lord No, also called Wizard, no matter the cost. We entered the transporter, a large double bubble and ka-boom, I was here. There was no sign of Red Eric."

Porch interrupted, "I know of Red Eric and will tell you when you have finished."

"Anyway, I landed in a desert—saw an escarpment which I felt I must climb, as my radio transmissions brought no response in the desert depression—after many days found a way up into a totally different land—lakes, meadows, a great forest in the distance. I saw a light and headed for it—at night it was like a beacon calling to me. There were large carnivores, panthers all around. They tracked me—I hit a few with my stun gun. For security at night found islands in lakes where I could sleep, as the beasts would not enter the water. There were 'gators, but they didn't bother me, seemed content with fish. Then it happened."

Bokasi paused.

"Go on," Porch urged.

"One night I sensed a nearby panther and waded out to an island—ate some fish I caught with some greens I found there and settled for the night. Several hours later I woke—don't know what woke me, the awful stench or terrible pain in my left leg. I thought a panther had crossed over but looked down and some gruesome creatures with big saucer eyes and huge toothy jaws were gnawing on my leg, biting out large chunks of flesh. Others prodded me with pitchforks. I killed three with my laser pistol and the others with a club I kept nearby. They smelt like death. I pushed them off the island into the swamp. Several 'gators came out but flipped off after smelling them.

"My foot was gone and most of my leg up to my knee. The pain was almost overwhelming, but I managed to cut the injured part away below the knee socket. I cauterized the stump in the fire, stopped the bleeding with a bandage from my survival kit, doused the wound with antiseptic and put on a mud pack. I went into shock with high fever. Sleep overcame me. I don't know how long I slept, but when I woke the sun showed late afternoon. I thought I was dying. The stump began to fester, but I was too weak to re-dress the wound. I managed to take some water and copolien tablets. I lay back sweating, bleary-eyed. I knew I was dying. High above I saw huge buzzards circling—come to pick a dead man's bones. I passed out.

I woke up here high in the trees. Ouregard and his council were standing over me. The pain was gone from my leg. I felt well. The stump was clean. Ouregard said that I had been there many days; their moon had come and gone. Hunter-Man had brought me. The Good Medicine and Root- Woman fixed me with roots and herbs and poultices, like they fixed the Golden One before.

"Ouregard asked my name—I said Bokasi. He looked awed and said, 'BOKS, you've come.' The others shouted for joy and sang out—'BOKS, BOKS has come.' Little people came from everywhere, bowing, pushing and shoving to get a look, shouting joyously. They talked to one another, but I could not hear them. They brought a kind of sedan chair decked with flowers and carried me here to the Jubilee Tree, singing and dancing along the way, shouting 'Mighty BOKS has come! Love him! Revere him! Serve him!' They had a ceremony and put me on the Imperial Panther Throne and covered me with this robe and headdress. Gorgeous maidens sang sweet, shrill songs and attended to my every need.

"I tried to dissuade them. They would have none of it. I told them of my mission—that I was a courier to a man called Wizard. They pretended they knew no such man, but by their faces, I could tell they very well did. At last they admitted they knew of the Wizard.

"I commanded that they take me to him. They said they could not, too dangerous. A great war was raging. I said Mighty BOKS would go away if they didn't. They said I was too big for the condor-steeds. I pointed out that the birds had carried me here, and they also had told me they'd carried a man called Golden One. They hemmed and hawed and finally said Flight-Leader would carry the pouch to Wizard. I said that I had sworn to my own leader that I would personally hand the pouch to Wizard. They did not understand that I had a leader, that there was authority over me, because I was BOKS, the Great Panther God. As they had mentioned a Golden One, I thought from all the clues I had the Golden One was you. So I sent a message that only you would understand—the great feather, a song and a piece of bark wrapped in leather, all entrusted to Flight-Leader. He said he would deliver it precisely where he left you, and apparently did, because here you are, my friend.

"Now tell me how you got here and how I can complete my mission."

Porch replied, "First I'll tell you of Red Eric, then all that has happened since I arrived, which I must do quickly, as I must go back a day from now with the pouch."

Bokasi felt the urgency involved and said, "We'll eat, then sleep. I stay here in the Jubilee Tree. I have a room with an extra couch. Tomorrow we'll lay our plans. I shall command the ERTS to help. I'm sure they will. They are sweet people."

Porch smiled and said, "I know."

Mighty BOKS clapped his hands and in the ERT maidens came with torches and lanterns. They had not gone far. He asked for food, and they brought a feast. While they were eating, Porch continued his story and concluded with, "...And so I must get the potion you have brought back to the Wizard, Lord No."

"And what is this potion?" Bokasi asked. "They never told me."

"It is ancient human genes that produce enzymes that trigger cell death, that makes what lives grow old and die. The genes were lost in the Throgs when they devolved from man into demons. Once the Wizard has them, he will increase them a thousand-thousand fold and more, then put them in a viral vector."

"Come, let's retire," Bokasi concluded.

The following morning, ERT maidens brought breakfast, and after they'd eaten, Bokasi clapped his hands and called for the Council.

"Sit," the Great BOKS commanded when the ERTS arrived, "and listen to the tragedy my brother Porch will now unfold."

The ERTS sat silently while Porch detailed the terror. They began to moan as he spoke of the Millenarians' fate and the prospects for the brave Szidrians if they did not get the potion in time. Soon the little people were weeping openly.

"We can help," Ouregard shouted.

"We must," the Good Medicine confirmed.

"Yes," repeated Flight-Leader, who BOKS had commanded to sit in on Council meetings. "My brave condor-steed riders can spread the potion amongst the demons from the night sky, flying high, then dropping low, unseen and unheard."

The ERTS' enthusiasm grew as they developed a plan. They began to trill in ERTSPEAK—octaves too high for Porch and Bokasi to hear.

"We will gain status."

"Become heroes."

"They will never again put us in cages and make us sing."

"And we are invulnerable since BOKS has come amongst us."

By noon, the plan was fully developed. Porch and Ouregard would return immediately with the potion, leaving the transmitter receiver, charts of the castle, and a map of the battle area with BOKS. They would stay in constant contact, and when the Wizard was ready, Porch would pinpoint Throg positions. Then Flight-Leader and Hunter-Man would come with a thousand ERT flyers in single column. There would be roosts at the castle if any were injured in flight. Two hundred would stay back in ERTFOREST as a reserve. The great birds would arrive at night after two days of flight. The Mighty BOKS would be carried by twelve condor-steeds in a net as they had lofted Porch. Ouregard would be at the castle on a perch, giving directions in ERTSPEAK and handing up bomblets of viral vector to each bird rider as they flew by. The condor-steed riders would deliver the potion as a fine mist on the Throg platoons. Porch transmitted the plan to Lord No in soliton bursts, and reported he was returning immediately.

The ERTCOUNCIL looked quizzically at Bokasi, who rose and, pulling the panther robe majestically around him, said, "ERTLIFE and people life are interwoven like the vines of a condor-steed nest. By saving people life, we save ERTLIFE. My brother Porch and Chief Ouregard leave immediately. We must train to go when called. BOKS has spoken." The council scurried out to do as BOKS bid.

A day and a half later, at night, Porch and Ouregard swooped down on the castle. Lord No and the Lord Chamberlain were waiting. Porch saw the withdrawal into the castle had been completed. The defenders, except for the volunteers who remained outside, were more secure. The lasers had been refocused to shorter ranges which would take less power and extend the heavy water supply for the fusion banks. Beyond the outer walls, the Throgs were moving up for the final assault.

Porch handed Lord No the pouch containing the potion. He introduced Ouregard, and the Wizard surprised the little man by greeting him in ERTSPEAK through an ultrasonic transducer. Ouregard was highly flattered and from then on would do anything the Wizard asked. The Wizard inspected the contents of the pouch, holding up each vial of toxin. He showed them the orange crystals and said, "We must take these directly to my laboratory and begin their increase."

It took two days to increase their measure to all that was needed, and then inject them into the viral vector by DNA snipping.

The Wizard said at last, "We must test the virus potency. Come."

They proceeded to the depths of the castle, and the Wizard led them into a small room. There were lockers on three sides and on the other, a heavy metal door with a thick glass window on its upper half. On the lower half, a sign read, "STOP—DO NOT PROCEED WITHOUT FULL PROTECTIVE COVER."

Lord No pointed each to a locker and told them to don the suits inside which were similar to space suits. Each suit had its own air supply. They put them on, and an inside attendant, after checking through the glass, opened the heavy door, ushering them in quickly. Porch looked through his glass helmet and saw four steel tables. Dirty, hairy creatures were strapped on each. They were Throgs, ambushed in the tunnels they had bored beneath the castle. Steel bands pinned their necks, bodies, legs and arms. They appeared tranquilized. Lord No saw one stir and said, "Watch and you'll see why they're sedated."

As the creature gained consciousness, it began thrashing about, attempting to break its bonds. Soon it began shaking violently all over. Its face turned bright orange, and its great saucer eyes bugged out. There were no irises, only a blackness that scintillated dull orange specks. As it became more agitated, the specks took on a fire. It began working its mouth, and its razor-sharp teeth sank into its own gums and tongue till orange blood was spewing everywhere. A technician took a syringe and sedated the Throg.

"We are ready to test," Lord No said to the technician, and he handed him a vial of the reconstituted toxin. Porch felt an instant of compassion for the horrible creatures. He said, "Why test? It will work or not. It is a zero-sum game. We either live or die."

Lord No motioned him aside and said, "What you say is true, but if we are doomed, then all must die. Only the Brotherhood may know this. When I first learned this planet was in the path of the Scourge, I placed a trillion megaton fusion bomb with a lithium hydride cobalt core deep within the bowels of the planet. It is yet unarmed, and I must have time to arm it."

Lord No paused for Porch to reflect upon what he had said. Then a fierce determination lit his face, and he continued, "If we are doomed to die, so must the Throgs. I am sworn to it."

He turned and signaled the technician, who pushed a pin through a rubber stopper on the vial, immersing the tip in fluid. He withdrew it and scratched its surface on the nearest Throg's arm. He moved to the next, and then the next, till all had been inoculated.

The virus' virulence was quickly proven. Within an hour, the Throgs were dead and shriveled as ageless cells grew old and died.

"Call the ERTS," Lord No said. "We'll begin loading the bomblets."

As the Szidrians loaded the grenades with their

deadly contents, the Throgs began their brazen movement forward. Since they received no opposing fire, they
ignored the trenches they had so laboriously dug. Lord
No called in the suicide squads from the outer walls.
The Throgs began a series of probing attacks to scale
the walls and gain the inner gardens. The Szidrians had
only the lasers to fend them off, but they did successfully for the next two days. From the high tower, Porch
and Ouregard traced Throg dispositions, locating each
position. Ouregard translated these into ERT
alphanumerics so he could call them out on the grid
system Bokasi had been given.

As dusk fell, Bokasi signaled he was ten minutes
out, and nine minutes later, twelve great condor-steeds
came gliding in, braked abruptly, and the Mighty BOKS
stepped from the net in which he had been carried. He
grinned at Porch, who introduced him to Lord No and
the Lord Chamberlain. Ouregard mounted the perch
from which he would hand the bomblets to the bird-
riders. The Szidrians formed a line to hand them up
from their containers.

A minute later the first bird-rider came in, and the
value of ERTSPEAK was profoundly demonstrated.
Ouregard chirped coordinates in ultrasonics four times
faster than anyone could in Szidrian or Earth language.
Every twenty seconds a great condor-steed swept in and
the bird rider reached down and grabbed his missile of
death. By dawn the last was on his way back to
ERTFOREST. None were detected, nor were there casualties, so effective was the Mighty BOKS' training.

When dawn arrived, the battlefield was still. Lord
No took the great scope in the tower and surveyed beyond the walls. Nothing moved. He saw score upon score
of shriveled Throg carcasses, their hair turned white
with age. The enzymes had done their job. Szidrian
scouting parties were sent out. When the first of these
returned and reported all dead, the call went out, "Let
the church bells ring. Sing the song of salvation. The
people have been saved."

In joyous celebration, the people thronged out of
the fortress to dance their jubilation. And their joy was

doubled when the farther scouts returned with a column of wheeled cages. They had found the captured children, shaken and full of dread at the horrors they had beheld, but alive and unharmed. The Throgs had fed them well to fatten them up so that their tender young meat could be used in a victory feast.

Aurora led King Szidrous out to the high balcony with Ouregard beside them. The ERT was the hero of the hour, as all night he had manned his post, directing the destruction. The King hailed the little man for his intrepid service. Then he hailed the people and their salvation. The throngs below responded with hearty cheers, with song and dance, and blew kisses of affection and great joy to their King and Princess and to the guest who stood beside them.

Porch stood among the crowd with Big Gwyn and Little Weejie, who had manned their guns for many months and now were free to wander. When he looked up at the lady on the balcony, a radiance fell on him that made his heart pound so hard he was sure it would burst right out of his chest. He did not feel the hand on his shoulder, nor hear the gentle salutation, so Lord No shouted into his ear, "Come, we must make our own survey and assess the Throg destruction, noting all and documenting everything so generations to come may take heed."

They formed a party to go out, himself, Lord No, the Lord Chamberlain, Big Gwyn and Little Weejie. As they reached the gate, Rasputin and Bokasi came up and asked to go along. They left on a ragtag assembly of horses and circled the fortress in ever-widening sweeps. They reached the battlefield's northern edge when a galloping rider summoned Orwell on an urgent call from the King.

Mute evidence of the Desert Legion's heroic stand diverted their attention from his abrupt departure. Something there caught Lord No's eye. He rode toward it and dismounted. After brief examination, he rose to full height and crossed himself, then waved the others up.

As Porch dismounted, he saw a tear in the Wizard's

eye. Looking down, Porch saw what grieved him. A slender skeleton rested at his feet, finger bones still clutching a jeweled scimitar. Beneath the whitened ribcage, resting in the dust, lay an immense red ruby. There the Ruby Queen had met her fate heroically, as all around her lay cut-down Throgs. Porch looked again and saw the enormous bones of another arm clutching an ax. It lay upon her bones, as if defending her, shielding her fragility. Tufts of bright red hair lay around the massive frame from which the arm extended. Porch turned to Bokasi, who had also ridden up, and, pointing, said, "Red Eric won his Queen, then fought beside her as he vowed he would, to the very end."

Porch looked at the others. They looked away, for they had no words to say. But then riders were coming from the desert to the north, so they waited silently. As the figures took shape, Porch could see Harim Skarim Shareem, captain of the Queen's Own Camel-horse, leading. Beside him rode Victoria, her pale blue gown trailing in the wind. They drew up, reined in their camel-horses, and hailed the group.

Shareem raised his scimitar in high salute and shouted, "We've come to build a marker, nay, a monument, over the body of our queen. She was a valiant lady, as desert tribes for years to come shall sing."

"We shall help you enshrine the memory of her noble deed," Lord No replied, "but we first must cleanse this place. Who rules you now, that I may secure the help we need?"

Harim replied, "The people have elected me king, and Victoria, who rides at my side and is my bride, their queen."

"Then, Majesty, before all else, have your people carry off the bones of those they loved. Then lay a pipeline from your wells and saturate the soil with oil, which we will set ablaze. When all has been consumed, we'll scrape the ground and bury this sullied soil."

"It shall be done, noble Wizard." King Shareem flashed his scimitar, and with his lady and their escort, wheeled about and rode furiously off into the desert.

As Lord No's party watched them, the Lord Chamberlain came dashing up. His face was ashen. He shouted, "Lord No, the King bids you come quickly. Spotters see horror near Nemesis in the great star scope."

The party mounted, rode back to the castle, went directly to the high tower, and were met by the sickly faces of astronomers on duty.

"What is it?" the Wizard demanded.

"Our fate is sealed," came the reply as Lord No took the scope. After a minute, he turned and looked at those who had gathered. Then he, who had been so stalwart through the terror, said with faltering voice, "They come again. Those we defeated were but a vanguard, a token of the horde that comes upon us now."

Silently each took the glass. When Porch's turn came, he took a look, then turned to Big Gwyn behind him. "They are approaching Nemesis, the cannibal star, as she orbits out from us. They could be landing in four months."

Lord No turned to the Lord Chamberlain and in a shaking, sorrowful voice said, "Come, we must go down into the belly of the planet, arm and set the doomsday bomb. We have done all we can."

Big Gwyn whispered something to Porch, who, for a minute, reflected on what he said, then hollered out, "No, wait!"

CHAPTER 14
RAGNOR, BALDOR AND OLAF

Far above Midlwurld, Spauk's Vikun fleet still orbited, so focused on the planet below, they were unaware of what now obscured the stars and blackened half the sky beyond Nemesis. Spauk was in a rage, waving his fists and yelling at the dwarf, "They didn't fight. There was no fight. Now we have no subterfuge. But still I'll strike."

"Strike now, Mighty Lord, strike now. Though they won, their army lies prostrate. They are exhausted. You will have it all," the dwarf Scrofulous screamed, jumping up and down.

Spauk grabbed the command communicator and shouted into it, "Vikuns embark. Strike now according to plan. Kill all who resist." Nothing happened. Furious, he spit venomously into the speaker, "This is your Thurl, your prince and commander. Strike now! Strike now! Embark immediately."

Still nothing happened. Spauk rushed from viewport to viewport with the dwarf following, looking for evidence of Vikun departure. Still there was no response. He was shaking with rage, but then he calmed down and regained his composure. He thought to himself, *Do I face an insurrection?* He sat down and began biting his nails. The dwarf came up and sat on the floor beside Spauk's throne. Spauk reached over and slapped the dwarf on top of his head. There came a knock on the steel door.

"Yes," Spauk called out regally. Three chieftains,

Ragnor, Baldor and Olaf, entered. The dwarf scurried to a corner and curled up in a fetal position.

"Sire," Baldor said, "we wish to introduce you to a political instrument of great merit. Its name is Assassin."

Ragnor drew forth a dagger. Its blade glinted in the light as he held it up.

"It's made of the finest Vikun steel, woven, then beaten into the sharpest of blades," Olaf allowed.

"It has grown hot and should be quenched; yea, cooled in the chilly streams of Ice World," Baldor explained.

"Otherwise a throat is needed. One slice would do, or a heart instead, the blade plunged in, the heart cut out, still beating," Ragnor exclaimed.

"Withdraw the Fleet," said Spauk with a feckless giggle. "We return to Ice World."

The Chieftains left and Spauk got up, picked up his whip, went over and beat Scrofulous until the dwarf was bloody, head to foot.

CHAPTER 15

THE FINAL FIGHT

They sat together in what began as a council of despair.

The Lord Chamberlain was glum when he said, "It just might work."

Lord No was grim when he said, "It's our only chance."

Porch and Bokasi were enthusiastic. But Big Gwyn and Little Weejie were ecstatic. They would finally get to fly the rocket and see outer space for themselves.

"The rocket is ready," Big Gwyn urged, "except for chem-fueling to boost us into orbit before we can safely shift to fusion drive."

"What about armament?" Lord No questioned.

Little Weejie could not contain himself. "We'll refit and use the lasers for close-in work. The fusion drive has plenty of auxiliary power. It is a deep space ship which has an electro-magnetic gun that generates twenty times the muzzle velocity of chemical propellants. We'll use the nucs of last resort you put at my gun—modify them to fit into a ferromagnetic sabot. They would go hundreds of miles."

"What about the fusing?"

"A piece of cake for me," Rasputin said. "I build clocks as well as cycles and can give you milliseconds from one to thirty minutes."

"What about fire control?"

"With your permission, we'll take the General, re-programmed for free space," Porch replied.

Again Little Weejie could not contain himself. "We'll modify the cargo loaders to handle the atomic shells."

"And how will you attack?"

Bokasi said, "We'll run along the wave front as close as we can, and use the lasers to blast a path avoiding collision and the atomics to fire deep into their midst."

Now Porch spoke. "The idea is to do as you did when the Throgs first assembled. Invoke them to fury. Divert them to attack us and follow like a swarm of hornets. You said they have no motive power, can only sideslip left or right, riding gravity waves like surfers ride ocean breakers. We'll head for Nemesis' fierce gravity field. Once captured, they will not escape the demon star's tight embrace. But we, with the great starship's engines, can pull away in time."

"It just might work," the Lord Chamberlain said.

"It appears the only chance," Lord No agreed. "Who will go?"

"We've agreed on four. They've elected me, Commander. Bokasi is pilot, as he's had experience with Earth Fleet. Big Gwyn is engineer as he rebuilt the ship and knows her inside out. He'll also work the lasers. They'll be on automatic mostly, and Little Weejie is gunner."

"What about me? Don't leave me out," said Rasputin.

"You have seven mouths to feed. The rest of us have none. As well, our lifeboat, the space launch, seats only four," Porch replied.

"It is suicide," said the Priest.

"A world will be lost if we do not go. Which is worse, four or forty million?" Porch replied.

"How much time do we have?" Orwell asked.

Bokasi answered, "The calculations show three months. Nemesis is six hundred million miles out, the Scourge a trillion. If we fly a great arc around the Vundercy sun, we will reach our initial firing position a month after liftoff at point-three michelson. We'll arrive as the enemy's forward edge approaches Nemesis. I'll pilot the ship parallel to and two thousand miles in front of their wave front. We'll have twenty-four hours to divert them. Then we must pull ourselves out or be captured by the demon star."

"Then we have about four weeks before liftoff," Orwell said.

"We better be loaded and ready in three weeks," Porch admonished.

Dividing into teams, they enlisted all able-bodied men to locate spare parts, cannibalize, rebuild and load the lasers, computer, ancillary fire control, automation servos and atomic shells into trucks and carts. Then they formed a well-guarded convoy for the trip to Nork, which they reached in a week.

Big Gwyn and Little Weejie assembled all the skilled shipfitters from their union, and soon they were swarming all over the rocket ship to install the fighting equipment. Large crowds of people gathered to watch the work. They were perplexed and asked why the great starship was being armed. The Lord Chamberlain put out a proclamation that they must be ready to defend themselves should Spauk come back. This was true, and as the people had heard of Spauk's perfidy, they accepted the proclamation as a logical explanation.

Two days before the mandatory launch, Bokasi made his checks and found all systems go. On the appointed day, the four warriors boarded and Commander Porch ordered liftoff. The powerful engines belched and fired, and as their blast increased in intensity, the great ship slowly rose under Bokasi's unerring control. They reached orbit in minutes that seemed hours, and Porch looked through the viewport one last time at the planet below. It was beautiful, except for the vast battle scar all around Szidrous. He could see the petrol fires still burning, and he thought of her.

Oh, how sad that our victory could not have been the end of it.

He swore determination to succeed. Bokasi signaled ready for fusion firing, which Porch so ordered. The ship trembled as the magnetic squeeze took hold and long electric tongues crackled out to ionize and suck in the thin hydrogen of space. The ship accelerated, and they felt the compressing G's. Bokasi pulled the ship on course, arced around the Vundercy sun, and soon the viewport showed Nemesis and the far black cloud. As the weeks passed, the extent of the cloud grew more ominous, blotting out more and more of the star field beyond.

At last, all stars were gone. Porch initiated an all-frequency probe, and Bo began his final turn to bring the starship tangent to the curved gravity wave upon which the demon horde rode. As they grew closer, their sensors showed that what appeared to be a black void had structure. The gravity waves were much more complex than first imagined. There was a series of them, some weak and dissipated, others many times reinforced, like ocean currents passing islands in their path. The demon horde had passed through many star fields that split the initial gravity wave and gave them great depth as well as breadth, and their number was many times past conjecture. They were amazed, but if they could solve that structure their strategy of diversion would be greatly aided.

Working with the sensors, Porch determined that each ten thousand pods clustered about one pod ten times as big, and as that one slipped along the gravity wave, moving left or right, ten thousand followed like a school of fish.

"That's it," said Porch. "It's got to be a Big Boojie command ship."

At a one thousand mile range, Porch ordered Little Weejie to train on the command ship on the flank. Weejie reported ready, and Porch commanded fire. Four minutes and forty-two seconds later a brilliant flash burst through the viewports. When Porch and Bo could look out again, the command ship was gone and sensors showed one thousand pods went with it. But the Throgs did not turn to follow them.

An hour passed. Porch located another Throg command ship, deeper in a much denser formation of surrounding pods. He ordered Weejie to train on it and fire. Twelve minutes later, another blinding flash confirmed by sensors indicated twenty-six hundred pods destroyed. Still the Throgs did not follow. Bokasi said, "Let's get closer."

"Bring her to one hundred miles, parallel," Porch commanded.

Thirty minutes later, the ship was on the new course. Suddenly it shook violently, passing through a gravity wave precursor. The view screen showed Throg scout ships to their front. Should they collide with any one of those, all would be lost. Porch alerted Big Gwyn. He already had the lasers on automatic, tracking ahead, and he began blazing a path through the forward pods. Little Weejie found another Command Group, fired, and atomic radiation consumed it. Still the Throgs stayed on course.

"We must go closer yet. Bo, bring her to fifty miles parallel," Porch ordered.

"We are passing through the advance guard. That should get a reaction," Bo replied. "I hope Gwyn's lasers hold out."

The lasers spit fire continuously, cutting a path through the forward wall of pods. Gwyn reported laser overheating. Weejie fired two more atomic shells, incinerating thousands. Still the Throgs did not divert. The ship began bucking furiously. They heard internal structure grind. Plates started popping. Little Weejie reported he had only four atomic shells remaining. Gwyn reported two lasers out from overheating. Weejie fired two more shells. Again, blinding flashes bit great holes in Throg formations. Yet they did not turn to follow.

Bokasi hollered out, "We are approaching the edge of our escape envelope. I can feel Nemesis tugging, velocity approaching point-six michelson and increasing."

"Look at infrared, port side—seventy degrees, a massive black object—deep in the formation."

"My God," Bokasi replied, "it looks as big as New Chicago."

"Might be the flagship. Pick it up, Weejie."

"Got it. It's at max range."

"Might be the imperial Boojie's flagship. Fire the last two nucs. We've got to get it."

Twenty-eight minutes later, Little Weejie screamed, "Yahoo, obliterated. Huge explosion."

"They're sideslipping, turning to follow," Bokasi

shouted in glee. "They are, they are."

"At last," Porch shouted. "Pull away. Big Gwyn, maximum flux. Chemical assist."

As the Throgs turned, they increased speed, and in their fury lost all sense of formation, coming in like a swarm of hornets. The starship began to lurch away, and they felt increasing G's as it battled Nemesis's gravitational clutch. It began again to vibrate violently.

"Not enough," Bokasi growled. "Nemesis gravity too great. I can see the star ahead."

Porch looked out the viewport. He saw the star ten degrees off the bow. It had already begun to ingest Throg pods, growing larger, pulsating like a living thing, thermochromatic, orange, brown and hideous.

"We've had it," Bokasi said, "but the horde's locked in, too, and they have no motive power. The demon star will consume us all. But we've saved a world, compensation enough."

Porch looked at Bokasi and yelled, "We still have a chance on the space launch lifeboat. Put her on automatic."

Then he yelled through the intercom, "Prepare to abandon ship. Seal space suits. Meet at launch bay— two minutes. We'll cast out all non-essentials and lighten our lifeboat up—twelve minutes to ship destruction."

He and Bokasi unstrapped from their seats and ran to the corridor. Threading past piles of dislodged equipment and broken structure, they made their way to the launch bay. Big Gwyn and Little Weejie were already there, pulling equipment from the launch. They had removed two of the four seats.

"What have you done?" Bokasi, first up, yelled.

"Max chem-thrust only lasts ten minutes. Must save two minutes for re-entry at Midlwurld. Even then, velocity vector sum shows only two can make it," Big Gwyn replied.

Weejie came out of the launch with the sensors, communications gear and oxygen tanks and cast them aside.

"Now for sure only you two can go. Weejie and I decided to stay. We want to see Nemesis up close," Big Gwyn said, laughing.

"No, we all go—take our chances. That's an order," Porch raged.

"First dumb one you've given, Captain," Little Weejie replied. "No way for four to make it. The vectors don't lie."

"I'll stay then. It's my mission," Porch yelled.

"And I shall stay with my friend," Bokasi said.

"No time to argue, only six minutes 'fore nobody goes," Big Gwyn said. He pulled his stun gun, set on low, fired twice, hitting both Porch and Bokasi square in the chest. Both men went down. Big Gwyn and Little Weejie hauled them into the launch, strapped them to the seats and set the controls on automatic count down and autopilot. They exited, secured themselves from being blown out of the mother ship, and opened the launch doors.

Porch and Bokasi, strapped down inside, couldn't move anything but their eyes. They watched the doors open. Big Gywn and Little Weejie came around to the side of the ship. The launch engine caught and the craft slipped forward, slowly at first. As it did, Big Gwyn and Little Weejie came to attention and saluted. Then voom, the launch plummeted forward at max power and began a programmed turn, trying to break Nemesis' grip.

Gradually feeling came back to Porch's limbs. He moved his arms, his legs, and finally his feet. Bokasi stirred. Porch looked over through tear-blurred eyes; his friend looked grim. Tears streamed down his face. G forces crushed them into their seats. Nemesis loomed larger through the port viewscope. The pressure of the frail launch's acceleration was awesome. Both hoped it would not disintegrate. Nemesis seemed to hang in space, pulsating faster as it ingested Throg pods at a prodigious rate. Then it began receding, slowly diminishing in size. The launch had broken its hold.

Porch and Bokasi could now move freely, so they unstrapped from the seats. Porch looked at internal pressure—two psi. He moved the air intake lever. The cabin began filling with oxygenated air, six psi, ten, twelve. He closed the intake and both removed their suits. They took inventory. Communications had been removed to reduce weight, except for a small MAYDAY transmitter which they turned on, hoping to alert Midlwurld of their survival. They had oxygen for two months, water for less, but the waste recycler was still intact. They could make it by keeping activity to a mini-mum. Their sensors showed they were three months from Midlwurld, with fuel so limited it must be saved for re-entry. The Vundercy sun was a far-off dot in their viewscope and Midlwurld was behind it, so they turned off their MAYDAY signal until they were outside the sun's shadow. They cut power when they came on course. Now they had nothing to do but wait.

Nemesis was now far to their rear, still engorging the black swarm. Within the month, the demon star belched and spewed out a mighty plume of plasma that blew it out of orbit and set it on a course to unknown regions. There it would implode from gluttonous accre-tion into a neutron star and some thousand years later collapse into a small black hole with a history that none would ever want to hear.

Far away on Midlwurld, the Wizard, Lord No, was waiting. The King's astronomers brought him the word. "We picked up the ship when it engaged the horde, re-cording many great explosions. But the star ship moved too close and was sucked into Nemesis. The black horde followed, to be engulfed by the demon star, so we are saved by the valiant effort of the four who went."

The Wizard replied in great despair, "We bear a bit-ter burden."

That night King Szid died, full of years and bur-dened by the trauma of the battles fought. Yet he found peace when they told him that the four who had gone had saved his kingdom.

But Aurora's anguish was grievously increased. She retired to her quarters and would see only Victoria, who came to Szidrous and stayed with her as long as she could. The King's funeral was held, and all who died were remembered then and there. Life slowly returned to what it once had been, as the people, sobered by their trials, bent to the tasks of reconstruction. At last, Victoria, too, returned to the desert and left Aurora alone in her grief.

****

They waited, seemingly floating in a silent void. They had no communications except the small transmitter, obscured from the planet they sought. They had spare food and water, and oxygen sufficient to sustain them as long as they stayed quiet. They passed the time talking, relating all that had happened to each since they'd been separated at the Academy. At last the day arrived when they rounded the Vundercy sun and, looking beyond, could see the far planets.

"Oh-oh," said Porch, "we're far off course, headed for Megadamn, not Midlwurld, and that planet now shadows Midlwurld, and again we are obscured from signaling our distress."

"Not to worry." Bokasi grinned. "I'll use the inner planet as a sling. With ten seconds of retro thrust, I'll slow us down as we approach, and her gravity will bend us around and head us right for Midlwurld. You'll see.

"Of course our subsequent re-entry into Midlwurld's atmosphere will then be fast and hot, and the landing very bumpy; that is, if our launch holds together one more time."

Soon they reached Megadamn, and Porch looked down through the viewport. He could not believe that that steamy, hot world was inhabited. Bokasi fired the retro rockets, and Megadamn gravity pulled the launch around. He stopped firing when he was precisely on course. In a month, Midlwurld came into definition. Porch was cheered to see the oceans and the continents. The planet was blue and brown, green and white and beautiful.

Bokasi said, "Prepare for re-entry. We'd better suit up and strap down. It will be hot and bumpy. And we'll land on the night side."

He fired the retros, and the launch descended into the atmosphere. The craft, though well insulated, began to heat. For a minute, they could not see out for the incandescence all around. Porch switched on the temperature gauge, but could barely read it for the terrible vibration...one hundred...one ten...one thirty...one sixty...two hundred degrees. At last the temperature stabilized. The craft slowed, and as the retro thrust ran out, Bokasi extended the wings and skids. The craft began its glide.

"I can see the lights of Nork, now the spaceport to the left, but the landing zone is not lit. Bring her around," Porch said.

Bokasi did so smoothly, then grinned. "We're on the glide path. Hang on." He turned on the front searchlight.

Porch hollered, "We're coming in too fast."

"Acknowledge, and if we don't flip, watch the fireworks when the skids hit... Touch down."

The craft hit hard, bounced, hit again and continued forward at great speed. Plumes of sparks trailed the skids.

"We're going to overshoot. Prepare for crash," Porch yelled.

The craft skidded off the concrete into the sand beyond. Finally it stopped, half buried in a high sandbank.

"Phew," they said in unison, "let's get out of here."

They unbuckled their belts. Porch tore open the launch door, and both men, sweating profusely and breathing hard, tumbled out, ran a few steps, tore off their helmets and suits, plopped to the ground and kissed the soil. Then they turned over and promptly fell asleep. A light rain was falling.

CHAPTER 16
AURORA

"She has been in seclusion these many months. She would see only Victoria, who stayed with her as long as she could. But now she is alone in her grief. She will see no one and eats but little. She goes to the inner garden at dusk to sit there alone for an hour or two. She knew you loved that place. Victoria said to me she feels your spirit there. She does not know you have returned."

"I am sorry," said Porch. "I can feel her anguish in my heart. I'll go to her now. It's well past dusk."

"One moment. There's more," the Wizard said. "I have a ring I crafted long ago for another. I give it to you to give to her. It is significant that you do. I know she loves you and you love her. Now take it and go to her."

"But she is promised to Spauk, lord of Ice World."

"Spauk be damned. He broke a solemn treaty, and his treachery is much more. This people owe him nothing, and she much less. She knows that, too."

Far below the high tower where Lord No spoke to Porch, Aurora sat on a bench in the inner garden. It was a perfect night. Spring had come and the moon had risen, casting a silver glow on the soft white flowers blooming along the winding path to the bench.

In her melancholy, Aurora thought how gracious Providence had been to spare this place from the desolation that lay beyond the walls. Her thought was interrupted as the great night moth came flitting up to taste the moon flowers on the vines behind her bench. It was as white as snow and as silent as the night. She imagined it a ghost as it flitted away, noiselessly, down the path from whence it came. But down that path beyond the moth an apparition did appear. It was a man dressed in white. She thought to herself that it was Porch. But eyes could lie in a garden such as this, because she knew that Porch was lost. Yet the ghost came on and stood before her. She was stricken with the thought that a grief she held so close and deep would play such a trick. Now he took her soft hands in his and knelt before her.

Porch pressed her hands to his lips and kissed them tenderly, then looked up but saw only silence in her eyes. Nevertheless, he began the speech he thought he'd never say, the speech he'd practiced so long as only a fantasy of his mind.

"Aurora, sweetest of princesses, beloved Aurora, I come to you in humble supplication. I have neither estate nor title. I bring only eyes to adore you, ears to listen for your sighs and song, lips to whisper my love. I have nothing to give you except my soul, my being, my body, my heart, and a love that will endure forever. Yet I do ask to be your husband and that you would be my wife. Would you take one so poor as I?"

She thought the words this ghost had said were the words she'd longed to hear so many times in the fantasy of her mind, so how could they be real? Then suddenly a breeze came up. She felt it on her face, and it was real. She looked at the hands that held hers tight and they were real. She looked into the eyes that looked into hers and they were real. So she said, "Oh, Porch, my darling Porch, yes, I'd take you...I'd take you if you couldn't see," and she reached down and kissed his eyes, "I'd take you if you couldn't hear," and she kissed his ear, "I'd take you if you couldn't talk," and she kissed his lips. Porch rose and lifted her to him so she could fold her arms about him. And as he did, she said, "And I'd take you if you couldn't walk, I love you so.

"Yes, I'll be your wife, your love, your mistress, the mother of your children. I'll be your friend and your companion to suffer your sorrow and share your joy.

Yes, I'll be your wife."

Tears of gladness flowed down their cheeks and intermingled on their chins as they embraced. Porch took the ring and put it on her finger. The silver moon smiled upon the peach trees in full bloom. A breeze came up, and as it kissed their blossoms, petals floated down to tickle the ground beneath. The great night moth hovered silently above to flicker its approval. All was right in Midlwurld.

CHAPTER 17
AURELIA

Early the morning of the wedding day, they had a memorial service for Big Gwyn and Little Weejie. Simultaneously, at the great spaceport at Nork, the Union raised a monolith with a great bronze plaque citing the pair's heroic deed. Thereafter, a grand parade was held at Szidrous in which all defenders marched. The Wizard said that such would mark the end of the terror. That afternoon, Aurora was crowned queen in the Great Hall of the People. Porch insisted her coronation precede their marriage, saying that only she could symbolize her people. But best of all, she said when asked about it later, she married Porch at twilight in the inner garden.

The Priest presided, Lord No and the Lord Chamberlain gave the bride away, and Bo Bokasi stood as best man to the pride of the ERTS, who sent one thousand as their delegation.

On that day, there was no time to tire, as a wonderful wedding feast was to begin sharply at nine that night. And the Queen in her first proclamation said it would be followed by a costume ball to make that day enchanting for the children. Aurora grieved to leave her husband's side after they'd said their vows, but when the last guest had passed to offer his or her affection and best wishes, she kissed him lightly and said with a radiant smile, "I shall go and dress for the fete tonight. I see the people are already gathering in the gardens."

He should do the same, she said, then meet her at

the entrance. Later, of course, he got there first so he wouldn't keep his lady waiting. As he looked around to admire the lanterns twinkling in all the trees in red and blue and green and yellow, a delegation of notables came up to him. They represented Land's End, Nork, Szidrous and other outlying towns and cities.

"Sir," said the spokesman, "we think it fitting since you are a legendary hero now married to a queen, that you should bear a title. We've researched the customs of old Earth and have voted to bestow on you the title of count, or earl, or baron, marquis or duke, or even better, we'll make you a prince, whatever you select."

Porch smiled and said, "No, it is enough for me to be consort to Queen Aurora. Anything else would be a conceit, but I thank you kindly for such consideration."

The delegation left, but a man he had not seen before lingered there and said he hoped that Porch would not come to regret his refusal. Porch wondered why he had said that, but the thought left his mind when Aurora arrived. She took his arm and they went to enter the gardens. As they approached the gate, trumpets blared, and soon enough they were caught up in the festivities. The people were in the mood for merriment. Most had worn costumes. Some were beautiful. Some were funny. And some were just outrageous.

A great bear of a man wearing a mask and dressed as a Russian Cossack came up and gave Porch a hearty slap on the back. Then he bowed and kissed Aurora's hand. It was Rasputin. Behind him trailed six little Cossacks and his wife, smiling proudly. Lord No was there, as was the Priest and the Lord Chamberlain. The people paraded their costumes and clapped roundly for all who passed.

The Wizard whispered to Porch, "I can feel the pain of the past melt away."

Then Aurora looked up at Porch and teased, "Where is Bo Bokasi? It would not be fitting for your best man to miss our fete."

Just then, there was commotion at the entrance. A shrill sound rose over the noise of the crowd and all turned to see what was happening. ERTSONG filled the air and twenty-four ERTS paraded in carrying a huge and wonderfully decorated sedan chair upon which sat BOKS. He was wearing the panther god mantle and headdress. Six ERT maidens on each side of the chair were fanning him with black feathered fans as they sang. The ERTS began chanting "BOKS, BOKS."

When the crowd recognized Bokasi, they too began cheering, most chanting "BOKS, BOKS." The faces of the small ERTS filled with pride as they gained such recognition for their panther god and such status for themselves. As they approached the wedding couple, Bokasi hopped off, grinning from ear to ear. He shook Porch's hand, lifted Aurora off the ground, and gave her a big kiss. The ERTS cheered wildly.

Porch said softly, "You look like a cannibal king."

BOKS replied, "Be quiet, human, or I'll have you for breakfast."

And so the festival continued. The ball began when the feast finished and all had eaten their fill of wedding cake. Porch and Aurora quietly left, but the revelers continued dancing till dawn, when the last of them went off, exhausted.

At last the time came when Bokasi determined he must return to Earth, for as he said, he had someone waiting for him there. Now was a very good time to leave, because a transporter station had been bootstrapped to Midlwurld from Earth, and the Wizard had just finished supervising its assembly. Ouregard, chief of the ERTS, was beside himself when he learned that BOKS intended to leave. But Bokasi told him not to fear, that he would return to ERTFOREST to say good-bye to the ERTFOLK and leave an appropriate message.

When they arrived, Ouregard assembled the ERTS from miles around at the Jubilee Tree and told Bokasi that he would translate his words into ERTSPEAK. So Bo began, "I, Lieutenant Bokasi of the faraway Earth Fleet, in truth am but an Earthling and must return to that faraway world, as I have work to do for those people. I will always remember the ERTS and the care they showed for me. Keep me always in your hearts, as I will you."

He paused and Ouregard dutifully interpreted, "I, Mighty BOKS of the pantheon of Heaven, in truth am also god of the Earthlings and must return to the heavens and minister to those people. My spirit will remain with the ERTS. Worship me always."

So Bo took his leave of the little people, returned to Szidrous, bid farewell to Porch and Aurora, and the Wizard transported him back to Earth. Then Lord No also left Szidrous for Land's End and the great university. He had a formidable task before him. He had to reconstitute the million- volume library. As the Priest told Porch, after the Throgs' initial foolish attack, the Big Boojie assembled the Lesser Boojies and told them to learn to fight smarter. So the Lesser Boojies went to the library and ate all the books.

Thus tranquillity came to Midlwurld. The fields filled again with cattle and corn. Industry rebuilt. Commerce grew. Science flourished. The people prospered. Aurora was a gracious queen and loving wife to Porch. A year and a day after their marriage, a sparkling daughter was born to them. They named her Aurelia, and all was bright in Midlwurld.

PART III

CHAPTER 1
SO IT SEEMED

Spauk had reformed, or so it seemed. For a year and more, he kept a calm demeanor. He wore a mask of reason, courtesy and affability. Even Scrofulous didn't duck when he raised his scepter.

When he first returned from Midlwurld, he gathered the chiefs and other leaders together and said, "Though our world is a crude and dangerous place compared to Midlwurld, we can improve our lot. We need to modernize. We will build a great spaceport, like Nork. We will construct new roads to make commerce easy. We need new egress to the seas to harvest the bounty there, and fishing boats as well. We need factories and dams for electrical power.

"Our traders return from Midlwurld and speak of the wonders there. We must catch up in science and technology. We too must have a great university, and new hospitals to care for our sick and injured. We must fashion new arts, great music, and refresh the old Vikun Sagas to rival the best of all the worlds we know.

"So I declare the royal treasury open to purchase what we need and pay the folk who will do the work. Whatever skills and expertise we don't have here, we'll hire from Midlwurld and other worlds as well."

The Chieftains were amazed, but they went out to the clans and told them what they had heard. When Spauk did as he said, they were no longer reluctant to accept him. Since he wore the signet ring brought from the world they left so long ago, they crowned him king.

"Let bygones be bygones," he said to Ragnor, Baldor and Olaf the morning after his coronation. He then decreed they be honored for superb counsel during the Vikun foray to Midlwurld. He awarded the hunting clan of Ragnor with a royal game preserve. Next, he deeded alluvial valleys in the Geyser Lake district, which grew bountiful crops even in the harshest years of Ice World winter, to Baldor's farmers. Olaf and his miners received rich veins of gold and silver. No other tribes, though they'd been there too, were so well treated.

To further show his change of heart and magnify his benevolence, Spauk sent the three to Midlwurld as Ice World emissaries. Everything fell into place, and Spauk was ready to do what he had to do.

"Come sit with your king at the table, faithful Scrofulous, and I will call for refreshments."

Scrofulous was flabbergasted, for never before had he been invited to sit at Spauk's royal table. His place was underneath, at the King's feet. Warily, he did as bid, climbing onto the seat. As soon as refreshments were served and the servant girl had gone, Spauk looked at him and said, "I have a long tutorial which, if you learn it well, will raise you and your brothers above all others in my favor and esteem. It concerns a secret mission for your hearty band, which, should you perform without flaw, will bring you rich reward."

The dwarf began panting with pleasure. "Yes, sire. Please go on."

"Should you fail or say too much, the lot of you will provide good sport for the King's Berserkers."

Thereupon Spauk spent many days coaching Scrofulous as to what the dwarf must do. Thereafter Scrofulous spent just as many days deep in the caverns beneath the castle in conclave with his cohorts. Then they too were ready.

In Vikun lore, to see a dwarf was lucky, and to touch one brought double luck. So dwarfs were always welcome wherever they might go. Short, Snort and Stuff went into the forests where snow deer sheltered themselves for the winter and Vikun hunters would be found.

The dwarfs soon found a band of five.

"Good day, noble Vikuns," they said. "What's been your luck?"

"Not very good," said a tall blond warrior. "I wish we'd seen you sooner so you could have touched our bows and spat upon our arrows. We're returning now to bring our families the scant meat we've found."

"A shame," said Short. "We wish we'd been here, too."

"Unfortunate," said Stuff. "I see your kill is lean and the skins are scarred. It looks like the wolven almost took them first."

"Too bad," said Snort. "We've been to Ragnor's fief, where game abounds. His people hardly leave their halls. The game they snare is plump, with pelts and coats and skins so fine, all are reserved for the export trade. The tribe grows rich, as good King Spauk promised when he awarded that royal preserve for Ragnor's valiant service."

"We also went to fight and did no less then Ragnor or his men," the tall Vikun replied, obviously rankled.

Stonehead, Stomper and Stubble wandered out to the farms.

"Come, let us touch you," the farmers called out. "Our luck must change. Our harvest is so meager we can barely feed our families."

"'Tis a pity," Stonehead bewailed, "how hard you work for a bushel or two while Baldor's clan hardly works to harvest much more. But then, Baldor's great service to the king brought him rich reward."

"We went, too, and did as much."

Scab, Scruff and Scar journeyed to the mountains and went down into the mines, where they heard some miners working below. Scar called out, "Come here, come here, I see a streak or two of ore."

When the miners came up, he said, "Look here, if you pick and dig, you might make a penny or two. Of course, if you were as lucky as Olaf's men, you'd pass such poor stuff by. We saw them lying exhausted from digging out a vein thick as a barrel of ale."

Then Scab whispered, "Perhaps villainy has been

rewarded. We've heard rumors that Olaf was one of three who threatened the King. Perhaps there was extortion."

The miners looked at him darkly.

Stump and Stoop went into the alehouses and bewailed Vikun dishonor. The Szidrians said the Vikuns broke the Treaty. But weren't the longboats there, ready to pounce? There was no fight. The King saw no foe worthy of Vikun steel. The Szidrians broke the Treaty, and Ice World was not to have the queen who had been promised.

Scrofulous covered himself with ash and went to the kirks and assembly halls, crying his grief. "Good King Spauk sits alone on his throne in the Great Hall of Thrymheim, immersed in sadness. He has no queen. She was lost to a commoner. He says there is no highborn lady to set a style or social standard for the Court. There is no queen to honor Vikun womanhood, no queen for the lovely Vikun ladies."

"Oh," the Vikun ladies lamented, "poor King Spauk, that lonely man, and woe to us, the Vikun ladies."

"Such could destabilize a whole society," Hulda allowed.

Scrofulous went on, "She was one of you, daughter of a Vikun baroness, daughter of the Ice World realm."

So the dwarfs traveled across the land sowing seeds of discontent, and on the trail they left, a proud people grew sullen. The master of deceit had set the stage. Spauk was ready, and he called the chiefs, the elders and all the Vikun leaders together at the Althing.

"Vikuns!" he said, "the people are morose and moody. Who knows the reason? Certainly not I. But as your king, I feel responsible for their happiness. Now you know, in Ice World years, we've been here soon five hundred. When the day arrives that marks it so, we'll have a month-long celebration, as grand as anyone has seen. We'll honor our heroes, kings and queens. We'll dedicate our spaceport, our hospitals, factories, roads and grand new university. We'll have feasts and balls and merriment, and our people will feel good again."

CHAPTER 2
THE INVITATION

The invitation arrived by special courier the day after Aurelia's first birthday. Aurora called Ragnor, Baldor and Olaf in for consultation. The three ambassadors had gained much favor at Queen Aurora's court with their honest charm and rugged stature.

"King Spauk," she said, "invites us to Ice World to celebrate the five hundredth anniversary of the Vikun arrival. He says, 'Let bygones be bygones, if Szidrians harbor such.' He proposes a new treaty with terms most carefully set so misunderstanding never occurs between our people again. Should we go, noble Vikuns?"

"Only if we go as your guard, and you should leave your consort here. Spauk would never harm you, gracious Queen, and though we've seen some change, we think treachery still lurks in his heart."

"But I could not leave my beloved husband behind."

"Nor could I let you go alone," Porch said.

"But there is more," Aurora said, "the Vikuns will honor my mother, who died for me. She lies in a crystal sepulcher beside her mother, a Vikun queen, in the Royal House of Eternity on Ice Moon."

The Special Courier broke in, "Yes, how could you not go and so dishonor your family name?"

Ragnor looked like he would kill the man on the spot, but Aurora said soothingly, "I shall go with Porch. It is my mother's land, and we are loved and honored there. As it is but for a fortnight, Princess Aurelia shall stay here in the Priest's good and careful care. The Lord Chamberlain shall direct affairs of state and administer the realm. We depart six days from now."

CHAPTER 3
ICE WORLD

They left on the newest Szidrian interplanetary cruiser, the *Gwynweejie*. It was one of the Wizard's advanced designs, built by the union at the Nork works. The trip would take three weeks. Ragnor, Baldor and Olaf accompanied them.

Once embarked, Aurora declared that Porch should learn her Vikun heritage and the Vikun history. Porch learned that it was by custom and part of Aurora's mother's marriage contract that on her death Aurora be returned to Ice World and buried on Ice Moon in the Royal House of Eternity. There she would lie in state forever beside her own mother.

Aurora said that the Vikuns had come to Ice World more than twelve hundred Earth years before. She said the Wizard had told her that in his search for origins he had found ancient runestones, originally from Scandinavia on Old Earth. When deciphered, these declared a Norse people, called Vikings, had accepted a promise from strange men they thought were messengers from the gods to carry them to Valhalla. The men came from the sky in fire-spitting dragon ships such as Norsemen had never seen. The strange men who called themselves Ancients needed the fierce Norsemen because a race of demons, whom they called Throgs, was destroying their empire, a glorious place in the heavens. The Wizard said that even then the Scourge was growing.

The Norsemen interpreted what these messengers

said to mean trolls were taking over Valhalla. They determined they would go to fight.

Trouble began on the journey when the Norsemen looked through forbidden viewports and saw endless darkness and unknown star fields. They began to suspect the strange men were messengers of deceit, because all Vikings knew that Valhalla was reached over a rainbow bridge across a misty river. They mutinied, so the Ancients stranded them on Ice World, which was much like the regions of Earth they knew.

Aurora told him much more during their journey, finishing as the *Gwynweejie* put down at Iceport. When they disembarked they saw that Vikun clans had gathered from all over Ice World. Throngs of people surrounded the ship and began pressing forward after the ship's engines cooled. All dressed in fabled Ice World furs which, though white, shimmered and glittered, as the fur reflected the faraway Vundercy sun. Except for wolven, which hunted in packs and needed to be seen to panic their prey, the white fur naturally evolved for both predator and prey, providing camouflage and breaking up outlines against the sparkling ice and snow.

A mighty cheer went up as Aurora descended from the ship and the people saw her dazzling beauty. But as Porch followed, the crowd became silent and pressed forward, murmuring, to see the man who had stolen the heart of the beautiful queen they considered their own. As soon as Aurora touched the ground, the Vikuns began a welcome ceremony. The Chieftains came forward to kiss her hand and pledge their honored allegiance. They wrapped a thick full-length ermine coat about her and handed another of black wolven fur to Porch.

They led the Queen and her consort to a huge sleigh fitted with silver and garlanded with greenery. King Spauk's personal ambassador mounted behind them. Six massive frost elk with antlers spanning twelve feet stood reined and hitched to the sleigh. They pranced and billowed clouds of hot breath into the icy air. When Aurora and Porch were seated, the sleigh master pulled out through the cheering, waving crowds. The women blew kisses, the men waved their broadswords, and the children threw flowers.

A retainer on a side seat offered them a Vikun draught which warmed their insides and brought a rosy glow to their cheeks. The sleigh master drove them around the new spaceport, which the proud Vikuns wanted them to see. But soon he stopped the sled at the new train station, and the Ambassador told them they would continue in a new high-speed train to the Vikun capital of Bifrost.

The train of two cars left Iceport, traveling at half its normal speed of 120 miles per hour, for the Vikuns wished to show and impress Aurora with the Ice World countryside. They coursed over the snowy tracks, up grade and down, and each passing hill and bend brought a new scene into view. Distant mountains sparkled white. Far-off glaciers cast a blue glow. All the ice scintillated and twinkled a rainbow of color: green, blue and red.

They passed frozen lakes full of skaters and ice boats. Skiers flew down long slopes and cast themselves into the air like graceful swans. They crossed high mountains above deep valleys where green forests covered the floors and split rapidly flowing rivers, and rose up to where the snow began. They passed farms and small factories. Game abounded. They saw gentle snow deer and regal frost elk. They glimpsed a fox tracking a hare, and high above, a great snow leopard, leaping crag to crag, stalking curved horn mountain sheep.

They followed a long valley where a hundred glass greenhouses stood column and file like a Roman field encampment. Around these, hundreds of geysers steamed, venting their heat into concrete slabs beneath the glass enclosures. The Ambassador proudly pointed out that a special fruit or vegetable for the King's table grew in each.

As they approached Bifrost, they passed a park where children cavorted on long slides with large ice otters, both sliding down to tumble together on the ice below, squealing and snorting in their fun-filled bonding. Aurora wondered why she had feared a trip among such fun-loving people. She looked up as dusk approached and far off in the indigo sky saw a brilliant evening star.

"That is Midlwurld," Porch said. Aurora felt a longing and snuggled closer to him. He felt her quiver through the furs.

As they entered Bifrost, the train slowed and finally stopped. The Ambassador again led them to a sleigh, a smaller one pulled by reindeer. He told them it would take them to their chalet, where Aurora's handmaidens would meet them. The sleigh coursed through the capital, where, once more, crowds of Vikuns cheered them. The streets were lit for the Festival of the Five Hundredth Anniversary. Colored lights shown everywhere, lighting up huge ice and snow statues of Vikun heroes, the Einherjar and their brides, the Valkyries. Odin, the Allfather, and Thor, his son, were there. They passed Freyja, most beautiful of goddesses, and a huge statue of the fierce wolf, Fenrir, in a mighty death struggle with Jormundgand, the snake that circles the world. Last of all, Yggdrasil, the World Tree, towered above them with every leaf, twig and piece of bark finely sculpted in ice.

They left the capital, passing through a well-guarded iron gate where the Ambassador took his leave. They wound up a mountain on a narrow darkened road, and light from the city reflected down from a mist-shrouded castle above. Anticipating a question, the sleigh master looked back and shouted, "We are on the royal road to Thrymheim, Lord Spauk's great hall. Soon we will arrive at your chalet."

They began passing chalets, brightly lit, nestling in nooks and crannies along the mountain. They slowed, and the driver stopped the sleigh in front of the path to the finest door they had seen. He jumped down, opened the sleigh's half door, and, bowing, indicated they should get out. The chalet door opened and six retainers ran out, followed by two tall and stocky Vikun women. The retainers unloaded Aurora's massive trunk and Porch's suitcase and carried the luggage into the cabin. The women approached, curtsied, and one said, "Welcome, lovely Queen. We are baronesses of King Spauk's court, handmaidens to your Grace, commanded to serve your every whim. I am Brunhilde, and she is Daggmar."

Aurora replied, "Thank you. Please meet my husband, Porch."

Neither looked his way, but Porch said kindly, "It is my pleasure to meet you."

Again, speaking only to Aurora, they said, "Please, gracious Queen, let us show you your quarters."

The women, one on each side, escorted Aurora up the path to the door. Porch followed. Brunhilde and Daggmar towered over Aurora. Both had arms as thick as young oaks. Their straw-colored hair was braided from the sides, wound around the back of their heads in circles and secured tightly with ribbons and pins.

The chalet was warm and inviting. A great fire crackled in the stone fireplace, and a huge white bearskin lay on the polished oak floor facing the hearth. Soft furs covered a quantity of leather sofas and easy chairs. Isinglass windows cast back amber reflections from the fire, from gas lamps on the tables and lanterns on the walls. An archway led to another room, centered with a large oak table laden with fruit, cheese and loaves of bread. One door led from there to a kitchen from which inviting odors drifted. Another door led to the Queen's private suite of bedroom, bath, powder room and several closets. A giant canopied four poster was centered in the bedroom, and on it lay a silk spread of royal blue covering eiderdown quilts, satin sheets and oversized pillows of pale rose. A deep pile rug of lamb's wool covered the floor.

Brunhilde said, stonefaced, "I hope these accommodations suit your Majesty and her escort."

Aurora returned a queenly smile.

"We shall leave you now to rest and bathe, should you desire, and to prepare your supper. It will be ready at your call,"

The Baronesses curtsied and withdrew. Soon Aurora and Porch returned from the suite, refreshed, and sat down to a heavy meal served by Brunhilde and Daggmar. There was a thick soup, followed by fish, fowl, bread and turnips. Sweet fruit, cheeses and wine followed. When they had satisfied their palates, Brunhilde brought Aurora a silver tray upon which rested a royal orb. It was a jeweled crown sitting on a silver eagle talon clutching a star sapphire as big as a grapefruit. A vellum note with a royal seal lay beneath. It was from Spauk.

In the note, Spauk flattered her on her beauty, declared his humble servitude, and wished that she and her escort, as he put it, would grace his table at the Great Hall of Thrymheim the following evening. The Vikuns would celebrate his birthday and renew their oaths of fealty. He suggested that the occasion would be a good time to discuss a renewal of the treaty between their kingdoms and increased commerce for the betterment of their two peoples.

Aurora handed the note to Porch, and as she did, Brunhilde moved as if to intercept it, but a scowl from Porch made her think the better of it. Porch read it, closed it and put it back on the tray. Then Aurora pushed the tray to the center of the table, rejecting the orb.

Porch said, "Tell the King it is our honor to accept."

Brunhilde ignored Porch and said to Aurora, "My lady, the King would feel a slight should you disdain the jewel."

"And I would feel an effrontery should you persist," Aurora replied.

"Very well, Highness. Then Daggmar and I shall withdraw until the morrow."

Brunhilde and Daggmar put on their hooded furs and went out into the night. A sleigh was waiting to carry them off.

Aurora smiled at Porch, took his hand, brought it to her cheek, kissed it lovingly and said with a twinkle, "We have this glorious night in this faraway place just for ourselves."

Porch smiled, pulled her to him, and nuzzled her neck. She pulled away and said coquettishly, "But first, I would walk with my handsome husband in the chilling air and upon the crackling snow. I want to feel frost on my nose and the icy wind on my cheeks, then afterwards your sweet body's warmth on my breasts will soothe away the cold."

They donned their furs and heavy boots and ran out into the night. New snow had fallen, and all about was pristine beauty. No track or print or wagon rut corrupted the scene. The moon hung huge in the sky and bathed everything in silver. Ice crystals sparkled everywhere. Aurora looked up at Ice Moon and thought of the bond that pulled her there. But she recovered quickly—there was so much wonder all about. She took her lover's arm and together they strolled along the road on the mountainside. Soft amber lights from several other chalets added to the beauty and mystery they found there.

As they approached their own guest house on their return, Porch slipped on some ice hidden beneath the snow. Both went down. Aurora landed hard on her bottom and cried out. Porch tumbled on beyond.

Laughing, she exclaimed, "That's no way to treat a queen!"

Porch laughed at her discomfort, so she grabbed a handful of snow, crawled over to where he lay sprawled, and pushed it in his face. Then, leaping up, she ran off laughing and calling out, "Big Bird, Big Bird, clumsy Big Bird."

Porch pushed himself up, slipped again, but finally got to his feet. He picked up a large handful of snow, packed it into a ball, and threw it while running after her. She had almost reached the door to the chalet when the snowball hit her in the back of the head. She slipped, startled, but Porch caught her in his arms, picked her up, pushed the door open and carried her over the threshold.

"I'll show you who's a big bird," he said, menacingly.

He knew he blushed whenever she so teased him about his oafish landing on her balcony, but it had become a signal of ardent, wanton desire on her part, when she made love with all-consuming passion. As he held her, she began kissing his face, nuzzling his ears with tongue and teeth, and nibbling at his neck. Once inside, he quickly pulled her clothes off, and she his. Then they fell, with bare skin, onto the enormous bearskin in front of the hearth. Soon the sweat of their passion mixed with the icy wet of the snow, and they reached the heights, gasping, hearts pounding, wrapped in one another. In the afterglow, he felt completed as a man, and she as a woman. Truly, they had become one flesh.

When his heart quit pounding and his breath came deep and even, he reached over and pulled a fur from a sofa to cover them as they lay on the thick white fur. She snuggled up to him, her soft breasts on the scars of his combat soothing the memory of those wounds. He lay still, so she pulled up onto to his chest, and as he caressed her back and bottom, she began to sing Szidrian love songs softly into his ear. As they lay in the glow of silent embrace, he asked her, "How did you come to love me, a wanderer, a man of humble origin?"

She replied softly, "Fury thrust me at you when you burst upon my balcony, but then I saw you helpless, entangled and embarrassed, lying prostrate at my feet. Whimsy overcame me, but I saw your vulnerability. Your need for love was so transparent, my heart just melted and I was yours. I came to see that you love me so completely—I see it in your glance—I hear it in your words—I feel it in your touch, that I love your love as well as you, my dearest."

He became silent, and after a while, she pulled him up and they went off to bathe together. Then, naked, they crept onto the great four poster and made love again. Then she clasped his face in her hands and brushed her lips against his eyes, his ears, his nose, and folded herself in his arms. She put her head against his chest, for she liked to hear the thump of his heart, and asked him to tell stories of old Earth. She had before, and usually he recited the ballads of the mountain people or told her about the Old American West. Such became part of their intimacies when time itself seemed to disappear.

This night, however, he felt a need to tell her of his life, that he too had never known his mother nor even his father. He told her of Harry and his life as a shepherd boy. He told her of Hercules and Ajax, and of the night under the stars when the Great Arm of the Galaxy beckoned him to his destiny. He told her of the lost locket.

At last, silence came upon them and they drifted off into deep and heavy sleep. The chalet grew cool as the fire reduced itself to embers. Blissful hours passed as they lay warm together, until Porch heard a shriek.

He sat up, startled. Aurora lay beside him moaning, cold sweat on her forehead. She was as white as the snow outside. She shivered, then cried out. Gently, he woke her. She looked up at him through wide, frightened eyes. "A banshee wailed—right outside the door. It is an omen. It cried out—'Leave this place. Leave this world, or onto death you shall be hurled. Go now, tarry not, stay no longer. Separate from this domain, or into a crypt you shall be lain.' You heard it, didn't you?"

"No, you had a dream, my darling. Surely it was nothing. It is all right now. I'll go have a look."

Porch leaped up, put on his robe and boots, wrapped his sword and pistol belt around him, and went out the door. He looked around. The moon had set, and a dense fog had settled in. He could see very little. Then he heard a rustling in some trees around the side of the cottage. Since he could not see well through the fog, he drew his sword rather than pistol. Warily, he crept over toward the source of the sound. There was nothing. Looking down, he saw some prints in the new snow—cloven hooves—a goat, or snow deer perhaps. But strangely, there were not four, only two. Maybe the animal was prancing up to feed on the branches. He looked around again and saw nothing, but then he saw a tree that looked oddly out of place. On what should have been bare branches, there were instead thousands of what— cotton balls? He approached, and as he did a piercing shriek accompanied thousands of ghost bats as they rose and fluttered off into the fog. He stood a moment in wonder, then returned to the chalet. Disrobing, he returned to his wife's side.

"It was nothing," he said. "A swarm of ghost bats."

Aurora looked up at him and smiled. "I guess it was only a dream."

He stroked her forehead and could feel her relax. She pressed up against him and they drifted off to sleep, but sleep was fitful for both the rest of the night.

CHAPTER 4
THE BANQUET

A sunbeam streaming in through a melted spot on the frost-covered pane hit Aurora's eyelid and the lash beneath flickered. She began to wake and in the fog of half sleep did not immediately remember where she was. The strange surroundings woke her with a start. She looked over and saw Porch still fully asleep. She leaned over and kissed his cheek. She looked toward the window where the beam streamed in.

Why, it's late in the morning, she said to herself. *We're normally up and about.*

The past night's fright came back and she shuddered. Then she heard the singing. *How beautiful*, she thought. It sounded like children. She listened and smiled. It was, it was—hundreds of little children. She jumped up with pleasure, threw on her robe, pushed open the window, and saw them all around the chalet, dressed in white furs, singing their hearts out. Her fear was gone. Quickly she bathed, threw on her clothes, and shook Porch awake.

"The children—the children, they've come to sing. Wake up, sleepyhead, and come see!" As Porch rose, she ran out past the kitchen where Brunhilde and Daggmar were bringing breakfast to the table. She opened the door to the chalet and the singing flooded in. The children saw her and redoubled their effort. She looked back to Brunhilde for an explanation.

"King Spauk sent them," Brunhilde said.

Aurora's fears and doubts evaporated. How could a king who knew how to bring such joy harbor evil in his heart?. She stepped out the door onto the small stoop and blew kisses to the little ones. The children sang song after song until the choirmaster lowered his baton to give them a rest. Now some older boys and girls, bell ringers, who had been silent, lifted their bells and began a lovely melody. After six bars, they muted them and Aurora could hear the chimes reverberate back, time and again, from different hills and mountains. Aurora was transfixed by the beauty of it.

Porch came up quietly and put his arms around her. He saw that she was so moved she had tears in her eyes. The bell ringers stopped and the children started again. When they finished, the choirmaster turned and bowed. Aurora blew kisses to the children as they bowed and curtsied. Then a little boy hardly higher than the snow he stood in valiantly trudged forward, and when he'd reached Aurora's feet, his head went down bashfully and he thrust out a bouquet of wildflowers. Aurora took them, handed them to Porch to hold and picked the child up, kissing him resoundingly though he squirmed his protest. After she released him, he ran back through his tracks to his place. The choirmaster bowed again, turned and blew a whistle, and the children began to run back to the sleighs that had carried them there, slipping and sliding, tumbling along, laughing and shouting. But they didn't stop there. They continued down to a slope where sleds and toboggans had been placed and began playing there.

Aurora looked up to Porch, a radiant smile on her face, and said, "I want to go sledding, skating and skiing with the children, as my mother did on this world long ago when she was a girl."

Porch smiled and said, "Come to breakfast first."

He led her back into the chalet. Daggmar handed each a steaming cup of chocolate. They sat down, hurried through the sausage, eggs and toast, then ran back outside.

They were soon in the midst of red-faced, tow-headed tots, sliding down the slope shouting joyfully. Before long, the children, in their innocence, hugged, pulled and tumbled all over the queen. About half an hour later, the choirmaster rang a large bell and induced the children back to their sleighs with hot chocolate and cakes carried there on a large sledge bearing the royal seal. As the children ran off, Aurora looked sadly at Porch and said, "Oh, how I miss my baby."

Porch smiled and said to comfort her, "We will return so soon I doubt Aurelia will know we have been gone. I am sure the little princess is thriving under our Brother's good and careful care. She also has Victoria and Harim who love her as their own, And don't forget Orwell, who would give his life for her, and all your loyal subjects, who would certainly do the same."

Aurora seemed comforted. She put her arm through her husband's and they trudged slowly back to the chalet. Brunhilde and Daggmar greeted them at the entrance. The place had been transformed. Yesterday's flowers had been removed and red roses abounded everywhere. Aurora gradually reddened.

"My lord Spauk has sent them, my lady," Brunhilde observed.

"Though they are beautiful and their fragrance heavenly, it is most improper to send red roses to a married woman. Perhaps Lord Spauk is unaware of that."

Brunhilde, out of earshot, muttered, "Lord Spauk is not stupid."

"What?" Aurora asked.

"Nothing, my lady. As I grow older, I find myself talking to no other, no doubt a very bad habit ."

"Please do speak up," Aurora replied, "and remove these roses."

While Brunhilde and Daggmar were removing the roses, a messenger knocked at the door. He handed a note to Porch from Ragnor, who said King Spauk had designated him, Baldor and Olaf to escort them to the banquet. They would pick them up at six that evening. At a quarter to six, Porch and Aurora were ready, and soon the ambassadors, now their trusted friends, arrived.

"It is not far," Ragnor said as they got under way.

"We take the sled to the base of the castle or hall, as we Vikuns call it. Spauk has installed several large elevators through the mountain up to the Hall. We shall take one of those."

Before long, they arrived at the elevator which conveyed them up to the Hall. They exited into the cavernous chamber in which the ceremony would take place. It had a medieval atmosphere. Huge round shields, high up, signifying the clans, adorned the walls. Great battle-axes, broadswords and maces framed the shields. Torches blazed below them. There was an open pavilion at the far end with a throne at its center and benches at its sides.

Spauk waited at the steps leading to the throne. Tall guards stood beside him. Spauk wore a thick ermine-trimmed red robe and horned crown designed to hide his pointed ears. A thick belt drooped around his waist, and a massive Vikun sword in a scabbard was attached to it. He strode forward to greet them, consciously attempting to diminish his waddling gait. As he approached, he hailed his ambassadors. "Ah, Ragnor, Baldor and Olaf, surely Odin has been good to deliver you back safely with Szidrous' lovely queen."

Ignoring Porch, he approached Aurora. Bowing, he awkwardly kissed her hand, trying not to touch it with his long protruding nose. He said, "My lady, your dazzling beauty belittles the notice preceding your arrival. You have struck my heart. My kingdom is yours."

Aurora replied, "Sir, your words are as generous as your hospitality and that of your people. Your kingdom belongs to them as well, so surely you need to keep it."

Such a gentle rejoinder surprised Spauk. The woman before him was more formidable than he'd imagined. He began, "Ah, my lady..."

But Aurora had not finished. She continued, "Now, King Spauk, turn and greet my husband, Sir Porch, knight captain general of the Order of No, hero of Szidrous, and my defender."

Spauk turned, puzzled. Porch was resplendent in his black uniform, its new gold sash, his accumulation of decorations, and the stunning epaulets and galactic collar insignia of a captain general of the Order of No. Spauk had not expected one so overwhelming. Porch saw awe and a touch of fear in his eyes. Spauk did not offer his hand, but bowed almost imperceptibly. Porch returned a slight bow but kept his gaze on Spauk's eyes. Spauk regained his composure and the fear disappeared, replaced by what Porch saw as hatred.

Spauk turned to Aurora and said, "My lady, it is time to begin the ceremony. My guards shall lead you to the throne on the pavilion, a place of honor, and it would be my pleasure if your escorts would sit on the benches to its side."

Ragnor broke in and said, "Certainly, sire, Baldor, Olaf and I should make the oath with our fellow Chieftains."

Spauk turned to him and said, "Ah, noble Ragnor, I wish to honor you as my ambassadors, and the Oath of Fealty is for the clan, not the man. Your surrogates will do as well. Besides, would you now desert the Queen? Please do as I have bid."

He turned back to Aurora and said, "My lady, Ragnor can explain the ceremony. I must leave you now."

He bowed and gestured that they should go on. The guards started forward, led them to the pavilion and seated Aurora on the throne with Porch and Ragnor to her right, Baldor and Olaf on the left.

Baldor whispered to Olaf, "He has isolated us from our fellows."

Olaf replied, "Yes, and perhaps put ambition in the heads of those who displaced us while we were away. Keep your hand on your sword."

"My blade is sharp and my arm is strong."

Just then a great ram's horn sounded and resounded up and down the chamber. The Vikun court and notables from the twenty-four clans filed in and took their places, standing about two hundred on each side of a broad central aisle. The aisle led to a shallow circular trench about thirty feet wide that lay in front of the pavilion. As the lords and ladies quieted, the ram's horn sounded again. Spauk entered, strode forward and took a place in the center of the ring. He drew his sword and held it up to his chest. Next, two retainers with large skins of whale oil entered and filled the trench.

Ragnor whispered to Porch and Aurora, "That is the Vikun Ring." Now a very old Vikun with a long white beard dressed in white robes entered. He carried a blazing torch and had a large leather-bound book under his opposite arm. A quill and ink pot suspended on a long thong hung from his neck.

"He is Odin's Scribe. He carries the Book of Clans," Ragnor whispered.

Again the ram's horn blasted. The old man bent down and lit the oil surrounding Spauk. It quickly blazed around the ring so high the King could hardly be seen in the center. Next, a retainer brought in an iron stand with a ring and tray. Odin's Scribe placed the torch in the ring and the book on the tray, and lifted the quill from around his neck. He then looked up and in a voice that belied his age called out, "The Procession of Fealty shall now began."

He opened the book and called out, "Arnvid of Arnuval."

Arnvid marched forth while a deep drumbeat marked his step. He passed through the ring of fire as though it wasn't there and placed his hands above Spauk's on the hilt of the sword, whereupon he renewed his oath of allegiance to king and kingdom. Then he turned and exited the ring through the flames as though he didn't see them.

Ragnor whispered, "The allegiance of he who falters before the flames is doubted, and he must face the Court of High Treason."

Arnvid shouted, "Five hundred kegs of mead for the royal cellars."

Odin's Scribe picked up his quill, dipped it in the ink pot and recorded Arnvid's tribute. There was a clatter, and four teams of oxen pulling carts laden with kegs came through a curtained entrance. They rumbled down the aisle and went out a side exit.

Odin's Scribe called out Askard of Skaggerak. Again a sturdy Vikun strode up the aisle to the measured drumbeat, passed through the flames, and made his

Oath of Loyalty. He turned back, went through the flames and proclaimed, "Four hundred barrels of kippers and pickled herring for the King's kitchen."

And so they came, one by one, until twenty-four had passed, and Spauk was richer by five thousand bushels of wheat, two thousand quarters of meat, one thousand flagons of wine, five hundred tubs of cheese, one hundred bars of gold, and several chests of gems, not to mention bales of furs, bolts of cloth and skeins of wool.

Trumpets blared the end of the Procession of Fealty. Odin's Scribe departed, and as the ring of fire subsided, Spauk stepped out, turned, and mounted the platform where Aurora and her escorts sat. He approached Aurora and boasted, "My lady, as you see by their homage, my people love me dearly. I want for nothing the people can provide, and can get more. Now please take my arm and I shall lead us to the feast, for the lords and ladies are hungry. Your escorts can follow."

What crass braggadocio, Aurora thought. She was coming to detest him, but by court custom had to allow him to escort her.

Spauk led her through a curtained archway, and before them stood the legendary Vikun long table. It was heaped with food, and waiters were bringing in more. Spauk seated her at one end to his right, and as there were only two places, Porch was relegated to the nearest corner. Ragnor took the seat beside him. Baldor and Olaf sat opposite. The feast went through twelve courses. The Vikuns ate like trenchermen but still had time for toasts, talk and much laughter. Spauk was strangely silent. Aurora tried to speak about a new treaty, but he put her off, saying there would be time to talk of such later. After the final course was served and consumed, Spauk rose and rang a bell. The lords and ladies fell silent. He rose and said, "It is time to honor the clans."

The great horn sounded. From the rear of the hall, a color guard marched forward, filing left and right around the long table to the measured beat of the deep drum. First they carried the white, gold and light blue Szidrian standard and then the black, gray and white flag of Ice World. Banners of all the clans followed, escorted by heavily armed men. The bearers, on command, placed the banners in stands and with the guards took position just behind, surrounding the table. The lords and ladies watched most attentively, then rose in a great Vikun cheer. Porch looked toward Spauk and saw that he was very pleased. As they sat back down, Ragnor touched his arm.

He said, "There is something rotten here. These men are not Vikuns from the Clans, but Spauk's Berserkers, outcasts and cutthroats. I'm going to get my warriors. Sit still." He rose to leave the hall.

Spauk saw him and called out, "Noble Ragnor, you must not leave now, for we have yet to conclude."

"Sire," Ragnor replied, "I must, I have an urgent call. I must relieve myself."

"Then go behind the curtain here," Spauk said angrily.

"Surely, sire, you would not condone such low vulgarity among your subject Vikuns before this lovely queen."

Chastened, Spauk hesitated, then said, "Very well, go then, but be quick. You will find great interest in my concluding speech."

Ragnor left and Spauk covered his indiscretion by calling for the Vikun anthem. All rose, singing vigorously. During the song, Daggmar and Brunhilde entered quietly, taking seats behind Aurora, who did not notice them. After all sat down, Spauk began his closing speech.

"Noble Vikuns, beloved subjects, this night you have done me great honor. My cup is almost full. On this day, our world is graced with Aurora, queen of Szidrous on faraway Midlwurld—lovely Aurora, more beautiful than the goddess Freyja—Aurora, daughter of Astra, a Vikun princess. Surely beautiful Aurora is one of us."

Spauk paused and the Vikun nobles rose, cheering and clapping. When the applause subsided, he continued, "Her father, king of that warm land a world away, promised by treaty to put her hand in mine."

He paused, rolled his eyes up and wailed in mock despair, "Oh Szid, you were a faithful man, but with your passing, your promise faded, for she married another. Alas, we have no queen to grace our throne. We have no queen to guide our ladies to gentle ways. Woe to the Vikun ladies."

He paused, looking around for effect, then looked down, as if too sad to continue. His long nose began to drip, but he wiped it with a sleeve, making it look like he was wiping tears away. The lords moaned and many ladies began to weep openly. Aurora was ashen faced.

"Szidrians say we made the treaty null and void because we did not fight when called. Not so; perhaps it was a quirk of fate or poor communication, but we were there. When I ordered strike, valiant Ragnor, bold Baldor and faithful Olaf said, 'Don't go,' for when we looked down on the battlefield from high above, the Host from Hell was dead. Midlwurld had won. None worthy of Vikun steel remained.

"Save for Ragnor, who has left, ask those who gave such counsel if what I say is so. Baldor and Olaf sit right here."

The lords and ladies were becoming agitated and began to drum on the table. Aurora was horrified.

"Silence," Spauk commanded, then paused, lowered his voice and, looking at Porch, said, "There is a man amongst us who claims to be her consort. We know not from whence he came. He claims it is that same star system that brought our forebears here. He is a commoner, eschewing royal titles. He would not be a prince or lord. That we know. My man was there. Would he destroy age- old, proven social order? We do not know."

Spauk lowered his voice still further, and the lords and ladies strained to hear. "There is no record on any starship of his passage, so how then did he get here? Some say he just appeared; if so, by what black science, I would ask?

"There is an answer clear. On Midlwurld resides a man called Wizard, who prophesies the future and knows about the past."

The people moaned and shuddered.

Spauk leaned forward conspiratorially. "Whoever heard of such, save from a necromancer? And the man who sits amongst us admits he is a disciple of that warlock. So I say to you that he has stolen this fair lady by spells, charms and unholy incantations. He is an interloper! This we must set right. So seize him, seize him now!"

Aurora screamed. Bedlam broke out. No match for the guards despite a desperate fight, Porch and Olaf were quickly overcome and dragged away in chains. Baldor was killed. Ragnor arrived with his men to storm the Hall, but Spauk's Berserkers, armed with laser pistols, heretofore not seen on Ice World, repulsed Ragnor and his men with heavy losses. Brunhilde and Daggmar rushed forth, covered Aurora with a heavy black coat, and carried her off.

CHAPTER 5

THE BARGAIN

Aurora stood at the thick glass window. It was twilight, and her eyes were fixed on a bright evening star in the western sky. But it was not a star, and she knew it. It was Midlwurld, her home, forty million miles away. Her eyes were dry, for no more tears would form, and only occasionally would a deep dry sob reach her throat. For thirty days now, she had been captive in Thrymheim's highest tower. She thought of Aurelia on that faraway planet. She thought of her husband. Did he still live? She was well attended by Brunhilde and Daggmar, but they did not speak to her except to issue instructions.

They told her not to touch the window's heavy glass because her hand could freeze to it, as it was one hundred degrees below freezing outside. Just opening the thick thermo-curtain violated their orders. A fierce and constant wind blew outside and sucked all the heat from her apartment when the curtain was open. Her rooms were ten thousand feet above the valley. She could barely see the river at the bottom.

Still, she had to look out at twilight to ensure she had some link to that faraway world that once was hers. As she looked out, the outside door rattled. She closed the drape quickly. The chambermaid, Gurtrude, came in to clean the room again, although she had cleaned it thoroughly that morning. Gurtrude dared not speak or even look at her. An hour later, she finished, and as she left, Brunhilde entered carrying Aurora's supper. After

setting it on the table, Brunhilde seated herself opposite the Queen's chair to watch her eat.

For the first six days of her captivity, Aurora refused to eat. She did this until Brunhilde and Daggmar
wheeled in a steel table with straps and an intravenous
feeding apparatus. It was then that Aurora determined
to keep her strength up for whatever lay ahead. So she
ate whatever they brought without relish.

As she ate, Brunhilde said, "My lord Spauk is coming tomorrow, so you must sparkle, and this apartment
must be at its best."

When Aurora finished, Brunhilde continued, "Sleep
now, my lady. Daggmar and I will be here at nine o'clock
sharp to set your hair, bathe and dress you. Lord Spauk
will be here at eleven."

The next morning, everything went according to
schedule. Gurtrude came again to clean the room, but
she had not finished when Brunhilde ushered Spauk in
at eleven, so she dived under the bed and lay there silently. Neither Aurora nor Brunhilde noticed her.
Brunhilde left. Spauk sat down at the table and motioned Aurora to sit opposite. He said, "You look beautiful this morning, dearest Aurora."

Aurora did not reply, so the King continued, "I have
the writ of the annulment of your marriage to the Interloper here."

Aurora asked, "Where is my husband? Is he still
alive?"

Spauk said generously, "Why, of course he is alive.
Were he not, you would be a widow, free to marry another, and there would be no need for a writ."

"I want to see him."

"Then sign the paper. You must sign it before we
can post the marriage banns."

"I will never marry you."

"I grow weary. If you'd rather be a widow, the Interloper will be tried before the High Court for witchcraft
and surely found guilty. Perhaps you'd like to light the
fire under his feet when he's bound to the stake. Sign
the paper. Here's the quill and your seal."

With no recourse, Aurora took the pen in hand and

put it to the paper. She hesitated, as her hand was trembling. Spauk reddened and his nose began to drip. His eyes narrowed to slits and he hissed, "Sign the paper. If your fingers are not able, I'll bring you his to use, one by one."

In great anguish, Aurora signed the paper and affixed her seal.

"I knew you would be reasonable. I'll post the marriage banns."

Sadly, Aurora said, "I want to see my husband."

"I shall take you to see him tomorrow."

Spauk left Aurora with her head in her hands, sobbing, which gave Gurtrude a chance to sneak out unseen. The following day, Gurtrude was again cleaning when Spauk arrived. This time, Aurora noticed her crawl under the bed but said nothing as Spauk greeted her.

"Ah, you are the fairest of the fair, dearest Aurora."

"And you, sir, are the unfairest of the unfair," Aurora replied.

"Don't rile me. Now come. Precede me."

Spauk rose, beckoned to Aurora, and pointed to the door. Two warriors fell in to the front. Spauk said, "Follow them."

The warriors passed along some back halls, then down a series of stone stairs, then down some more, through dimly lit passageways. The lower they went, the more humid and warm it became. Soon the stone walls around them were covered with wide trickles of water and moss. Finally they came to a balcony above a vast arched chamber. A five-foot wall fronted the balcony. Spauk led Aurora up to the wall. Looking down, she saw a stone floor fifty feet below with a deep stone pit in its center. She could not see to the bottom of the pit.

"Observe carefully, and dare not cry out."

He clapped his hands resoundingly. There was tumult below. A heavy door beyond a dark passage opened and fiery light flooded in. A dozen dwarfs with pikes prodded Olaf, bound in heavy chains, into the chamber. He was bleeding heavily from their savage prods. The dwarfs pushed him to the edge of the pit. Throaty snarls rose from the bottom of the pit as blood dripped down, and reached a crescendo that rumbled like thunder. Gradually the noise subsided.

Spauk hollered down, "Olaf, you are guilty of high treason to the Vikun state and king. Therefore, I sentence you to death in the jaws of the thunder wolven who await your throat below. What say you?"

"I've not been tried by The Council of Ten, nor any other court. I'm not guilty of treason or any other crime. If you must have my life, then so be it, but at least let me die like a Vikun with sword in hand so that I may reach Valhalla and fight again at Ragnarok."

Aurora rushed at Spauk, but the guards stopped her up short.

"You beast," she screamed, trying to wrench loose from the guards. Spauk turned. His eyes were slits, and he licked his nose with his tongue. But then he turned back and looked down.

He screamed, "You'll die as a craven traitor and find a place in the nether world. You'll never see Valhalla, nor fight again when this world ends at Ragnarok. Push him in."

The dwarfs with heavy lunges pushed Olaf into the pit. A growling, ripping frenzy ensued. Within a minute, it was quiet again. Spauk began giggling, and his giggles gradually changed into uproarious laughter. The dwarfs below heard him and began to chortle. Raucous laughter soon filled the chamber. Aurora put her hands to her face, sobbing, and backed away from the wall. Spauk grabbed her by her hair and pulled her back. "You asked to see your husband, and he's about to make his entrance. I would hate for you to miss him."

He hollered down to the dwarfs, "Bring out the Interloper."

Another dozen dwarfs, jabbing with pikes, forced Porch in and to the edge of the pit. He too was bound in chains, and in addition, naked. He had been severely beaten. Blood seeped from his wounds. Spauk pulled Aurora's hair up so that she was forced to look into the chamber. He whispered into her ear, "Look now at your champion and defender."

Aurora sobbed. Spauk pulled her back into the shadows and again whispered into her ear, "I can kill him now should you desire, and put him beyond his misery."

"No, no, I beg you," Aurora wept. Spauk let her go and went to the wall. "Enough," he shouted down. "Clean his wounds and cover him well. There is a chance for him to live. Remove him."

Dwarf hands dragged Porch back from the pit and marched him out.

"Go now, my lady, back to your tower. I'll come on the morrow and present your choices. Guards, take her back."

The next morning, he entered Aurora's chamber promptly at eleven.

"Sit down," he commanded. She did, and he sat opposite.

"Ah, my lady, you do look haggard and worn. But choose what's right and everything will be just fine. You have two choices. The first is best. Fulfill your father's legacy, marry me, and I will set the Interloper free. Reject my hand, refuse the nuptials, and you may watch him die in the pit as Olaf did."

Aurora's eyes widened in fear, but then disgust filled her face. Spauk felt she would still reject him as all who ever knew him well did, so he continued unabashedly. "More than that. You have an infant daughter, now well guarded. But even now, I have agents everywhere on Midlwurld. There will come a day, a time, a moment, when there's a lapse by those who now protect her. My men will grab her then, yes, kidnap her, carry her off, sell her as a slave on the brothel world of Cynn. Perhaps you've heard of that dark planet on the spaceways in another star system not far away. It is a world where pirates lurk and the meanest of men, debauched and brutish, congregate."

Aurora covered her face as Spauk went on. "But that's not all. For you see, I'll have you anyway, under the whip or by the brand."

Completely defeated, with nowhere to turn, Aurora said, "Very well, my lord, I'll marry you, but you must free my beloved in good health with means enough to leave this dreadful kingdom, and I must be assured your agents will never touch my daughter."

Spauk, elated, jumped up and did an awkward jig, saying, "I knew you'd see the light, my lady. I knew you'd set things right, my lady. I am an honorable man, you know, tee hee, so I will free the Interloper right after we marry, and you may watch him go. Tee hee."

Spauk clapped his hands and the ugly little dwarf Aurora saw at the Ceremony of Fealty entered. Spauk pulled a parchment from his robes and, handing it to Scrofulous, said, "This is the Proclamation of the Marriage of Ice World's king to Szidrous' queen. Distribute it to the Council and Clans. Send it to Midlwurld as well."

Turning back to Aurora, he said, "Our business is done, dear lady. We shall marry in the Great Kirk of the People ten days hence before all this world. Brunhilde and Daggmar will prepare you. Rest well."

Spauk rose and, half skipping, half waddling, went to the door. He was beside himself with glee and started hopping. He began to sing, "Oh, I shall be king of two realms—two realms, indeed two worlds, the greatest king in the Vundercy System. Indeed, indeed." His nose started dripping, so he licked it with his tongue and left.

Later, the dwarf Scrofulous creaked open the heavy iron door that led to Porch's cell in the dungeon and entered. He said, "Good news, Interloper, you will be healed, then freed. The woman you stole has annulled her marriage to you and will marry our king. Tee hee."

He held up the proclamation for Porch to read. Porch thought to himself she must have agreed to save his life, but he'd rather have died.

"Has the cat got your tongue, huh? Well, that's better than wolven got your throat." Scrofulous laughed, then ran out.

Several hours later, he brought a great tray of food and drink. Then a dozen little men brought a heavy tub of hot water, towels and soap. They brought heavy clothing, too.

Scrofulous instructed, "Eat hearty and clean your-self, then put on the handsome clothing, for it's cold outside and you have far to go."

The wedding day came for Aurora. The very moment Brunhilde and Daggmar entered her apartment to dress her, her mind no longer accepted what was happening. Shock made everything surreal. But they took her limp acquiescence for acceptance of her marriage.

Brunhilde beamed. "Why, I do believe, my lady, you've overcome your past intransigence. King Spauk will be most pleased. We must hurry. The Vikun wind boat is ready to take you to the great kirk."

"Oh, what a happy day," Daggmar allowed. "I do hope you have as many children as your lord and master, Spauk, desires."

They dressed her and wrapped her head to foot in a black silk cover. She perceived dimly that they led her out of the apartment and into the air boat. Now they guided her into a great church. Once inside, they stopped her on a center aisle. Ahead, she saw dimly a tall, skinny creature wearing purple robes and a horned crown.

Someone pushed her forward. In her trance, she saw thousands of eyes staring at her and she faltered. Then a vision of her beloved on the edge of a pit loomed above her. Dwarfs were prodding him with wicked pikes and he bled from many wounds. With great will, she pushed one foot ahead of the other and continued. Now she heard strange music from lutes and horns and wooden drums. The music stopped as she approached the man in purple robes. He looked at her with huge lust in his eyes. She thought he must be Satan. Another man in front of him stood before a dozen stands of burning oil. The other man was very old. He held a book. She remembered dimly Odin's Scribe. He said strange words. Then he stopped and looked at her, as did the man in the great horned crown who stood be-side her.

Terrified and trembling, she saw a vision of her in-fant daughter screaming, carried off by brutish men in black furs. The word "yes" formed on her lips. The man who stood beside her took her hand and placed a heavy ring upon her finger. Her hallucinations deepened further and took her over till she was again in the air boat that took her to that strange ceremony.

Her consciousness returned abruptly when she felt strange fingers groping at her female parts. She saw Spauk sitting beside her on the air boat and the reality of what had happened hit her instantly.

He had his arm around her and he was reaching over to kiss her.

Calculating to delay him, she squirmed free and gently removed his hand, then said, "Dearest husband, lord and master, you must save your searing passion for our wedding bed. Tonight I shall be ready and determined to please you in every way I may. Besides, you have a promise to fulfill, which is to release my former husband, whom you call the Interloper. This must be done before we find our bliss upon the marriage couch."

Spauk's eyes tightened into slits and anger rose up in him, but then he thought, *She's right. I should not be crass but gentle now, and find more sensual profit later. I'll satisfy my hunger with a simple kiss.*

He reached over to kiss her, but his nose started dripping, so he pulled back, and hoping she would not see, licked it with his tongue. He thought to cover his action by saying, "Ah, my love, all my life I've saved myself for you."

Unfortunately, his words came out as slobber, so he said nothing more the rest of the way back to Thrymheim. Rather, his thoughts ranged from how many children she could bear to how the combined kingdoms of Ice World and Szid could seize all of Midlwurld and then move to conquer Megadamn. His greed now extended not only to that hot world of endless jungle, but to rich spices, medicines, exotic fruits and nuts, and that glorious chocolate aphrodisiac. Why, he could even afford to be magnanimous and release the Interloper. The man was nothing to him now.

After the air boat set down at Thrymheim, Spauk bundled his sweet possession in his greatcoat, and in a show of masculinity, carried her to the gate and over the threshold of the castle. Once inside, he set her down and called for the dwarf Scrofulous, to whom he said, "Release the Interloper. Assure that he has warm clothing and provisions. We'll watch from the balcony above."

Scrofulous hurried on to do as bid.

In the dungeon deep below, Porch had heard the pealing of the chimes in the valley far below. Sadly, he surmised that that day his beloved had married the beastly king of Ice World. When the dwarf appeared, he confirmed that fear, saying, "Interloper, the queen you stole is now in the arms of mighty King Spauk. He said to release you with warm furs and food. When the cell door opens, take them up and go. A passage to the lower level leads outside. Make haste to the spaceport and leave this world. Hee, hee."

The dwarf left, and shortly thereafter the cell door swung open. Porch was free. Dressed in the warm furs, he took up the provisions, made his way down the passages, and reached the outer door. He pushed it open to an ice-cold wind and thought, *I must keep my strength and wit, for one day I will destroy that beast and recover my beloved.*

At a window far above, Aurora watched Porch exit, though he could not see her. She saw the anguish on his face. Then he picked up a trot, pushing through the snow toward the valley far below. Spauk, who stood beside her, said, "Now you see I am a man of my word. Go prepare for the wedding bed. Brunhilde and Daggmar will assist you."

After Aurora was led out by the Baronesses, Scrofulous came up to Spauk to report. Spauk said, "Release the thunder wolven on his scent at twilight."

CHAPTER 6
THE THUNDER WOLVEN

Porch had never been so cold, not even in the Great Northern Forest of Old Earth. But he had to build up his strength, keep his wits and formulate a plan to rescue Aurora; do it or die trying. Life without her was nothing. He struggled against the snow. The way down the mountain was steep, but this helped him. Where he could, he pulled the outer fur around him and slid. Twilight came. He was glad for the diminishing light but knew he must find shelter for the night. Maybe he could start a small fire for warmth, but he had to be wary. The dwarf had implied that his release was unconditional, but he did not believe Spauk would let him escape to return another day.

Then he heard them far above, the wolven. He listened. They were closing. He had no weapons and without them, he had no chance. They would overcome him and devour him quickly. He increased his pace, taking greater chances, leaping down higher crags to lower. If he broke a leg, it would be all over, but it also would if they caught him before he gained the wherewithal to make a stand. He was coming to the tree line. Should he climb a tree? No, if they treed him, he'd freeze to death and they'd have their meal anyway. He continued for another hour. Then he saw the fire geysers far below.

If he could reach them, possibly the wolven would lose his scent, or he might find some pine boughs and make some firebrands. He continued down, faster and faster. Blow the rock outcrops, he could take greater chances. Their howls and calls to one another were louder. They had spread out, possibly to surround him before he could reach the geysers. He increased his pace again and came to a ledge where he rested while surveying a way down. A sixty-foot drop-off ended in a snow bank. Four hundred yards remained from there to a lava pool at the edge of the geysers. The snow bank was narrow, with rocks on each side. He began to descend. A black furry creature leaped at him. The wolven had caught up. He dodged, caught its midsection and hurled the wolf to the rocks below. He saw another following, so he made a quick judgment and leaped off the ledge.

Hitting the snow bank, he began tumbling ever faster. Toward the bottom, the incline lessened, as did his velocity. He stuck his arms out and slowed further. As he slid, he felt heat radiate his face. He came to a stop at the bottom of the slope about fifty feet from the lava pool.

He struggled to his feet and again felt the intense heat. Even so, it was so cold that the snow almost reached the edge of the pool, as it reflected most of the radiation away. He looked around.

The cliff from which he leaped loomed up fifty feet behind him. Tall conifers stood to his left and right. He was in a cul-de-sac. He would have to make his stand there, as there was no time to pick his way around the pool and fiery geysers beyond. He felt he stood at the edge of hell. He pushed through the snow to the conifers and found some heavy branches in the debris littering the forest floor. He began picking up the stoutest and smelled the heavy pitch inside.

Good, he thought, *firebrands*. He carried what he could to the edge of the lava. The intense heat had melted the snow there into mud, so he had to be careful not to slip. He put the brands down and rested, breathing hard. He hoped the wolves would attack one by one when they reached him. Then he could wound them badly and send them scurrying off. But he knew that was not their nature, so he prepared for multiple attacks. He picked up a brand, reached over and touched it to the hot lava. It flamed instantly and he quenched it in the snow just as fast, for he had none to waste. Then he turned to face the attackers who were sure to come.

The first one burst out of the brush, pulled up short and looked around slyly. Seeing him, it snarled. Then, left and right, the others came. They, too, saw him and snarled, showing gleaming fangs. They were cunning and not about to attack one by one as he had hoped, but rather waited till their mates, fifteen in all, arrived. They formed a semicircle, waiting. Then their leader appeared from the shadows to the right, huge and black as night. It moved to the front of the others and looked at Porch, and its eyes reflected the hot red fury of the lava pit beyond. It looked around, as if to count its fellows. Snarling its dominance, it then looked back at Porch. Growling, it began to twist its massive head up and around and snap its frothing jaws to show its dreadful fangs. Porch thought of Cerberus, guardian of the gates to Hell.

He crouched down, picked up a brand and, reaching behind, touched it to the lava. It flamed instantly, and as he brought it to his front, the black leader rushed forward with a hideous growl, then stopped short in a feint. It was a signal, for two of the wolven on its flank attacked. Porch thrust the torch into the muzzle and eyes of the first, blinding it. It dropped to the snow, wailing in agony, but the second was on him. Twisting, Porch avoided its leap and got an arm under its hindquarters. With a mighty heave, he cast it into the lava pool. Its body exploded when it hit and was rendered into steam and char. Then a third clamped onto the heavy fur sleeve of his arm and began shaking its head to tear it off. Porch ran the brand up and down its furry back, but it did not release until its fur was consumed in flame. Then it succumbed, dying at his feet.

Now three others moved forward more cautiously, and Porch was able to burn them with the brand. The rest of the pack saw the demise of their fellows and did not move. The black leader barked a command and snapped its jaws furiously. The other wolven moved forward slowly, then stopped. They would advance no farther. Sensing their revolt, the leader advanced, zigzagging, seeking an opening. Porch's fire brand was going out. Observing this, the huge wolf lunged, eyes gleaming red. Then, from behind Porch's right shoulder, a white streak propelled itself forward and went for the black wolf's throat.

Instantly, there was a tangle of black and white fury, snarling, rolling, flipping, turning. The black leader fell, bleeding from a throat torn apart. Porch saw his savior, a large white wolf. He watched, bewildered, as the great white wolf, front paws astride the vanquished, lift its head and howled its victory.

Then it turned and stared at the remaining thunder wolven. All cowered as the victor's gaze fell on them. It approached each in turn. growling, and as it did, each rolled on its back, feet up, and whined its submission.

Porch was beside himself in wonder. He thought of the icy Northern Forest and an incident now long ago. His lips and tongue formed the word "Fenrir," independent of his mind, which would not accept the notion. *Could it be*, he thought, *that somehow, within space time, a force of such power that it can bring together a bond made once and meant to last forever? No, it cannot be, yet it seems to be.*

The white wolf yipped, then howled, and the thunder wolven ran from there, disappearing into the dark gray forest. The white wolf looked at Porch, then approached. Porch dropped to a knee to greet it. The wolf licked his face, and Porch gave it a long hug. Then it grabbed his sleeve and tugged, so Porch rose to follow. It led Porch around the lava pit and picked its way along a path between the geysers, gingerly leaping rock to rock. The path led up a slope. At the top, there was an opening into a rock face surrounded by steaming fissures. The wolf disappeared into it. Porch followed and found himself within a shallow cave. It was quite warm inside. Looking around, he saw a freshly killed snow deer. The wolf stood beside the kill and looked up at the man as if in invitation.

Porch found a sharp stone on the cave floor and cut

off an ample hunk of meat. He still had the burnt-out firebrand, so he sharpened it to a point by rubbing it against the wall. Skewering the meat, he roasted it at a hot spot just beyond the cave entrance. He ate his fill, as did the wolf, right from the carcass. Melted snow provided drink. His spirits rose; with shelter and food he could rebuild his stamina for the tasks ahead. The wolf was already lying down, so he lay his head on the animal's flank. They were soon fast asleep.

A dream came from deep within his mind. He was with his beloved, strolling through the garden of Szidrous castle, where he had proposed and she had accepted. She was smiling up at him in bright sunshine. She put her soft hand to his face, then reached up and kissed him. Twilight came. They could see the lights of the castle come on and the stars come out. There was merriment all around.

Now he was in a high vaulted room, but Aurora was not there. Hundreds of candles burned along the walls. Then at once they all blinked out. Now he was again outside. Aurora was not there. The lights from all the windows of the castle, at once, blinked out. Porch looked up at the stars, and they too blinked out. He was thrust above the planet far beyond the galaxy. He saw all the galaxies that had ever been in space and time. They too blinked out. Blackness consumed eternity. Existence was extinguished. He woke to a hollow drumbeat in his mind. Something had happened to his beloved.

CHAPTER 7

TRAGEDY

Brunhilde and Daggmar took Aurora to the bridal suite and began extolling its magnificent appointments. Looking at the marriage bed, Aurora noticed a battery of lights and devices just below its canopy.

She asked, "And what are those?"

Brunhilde answered matter-of-factly, "Those, dear bride, are video cameras. Lord Spauk wishes to record the beauty of his copulation." Aurora gasped in horror. Brunhilde ignored her anguish, but Daggmar tried to gloss over the shock, saying, "Look at your marriage bed, dear lady. See how soft it is." She went and pulled down the cover, then continued, "It sags in the middle, so you can cuddle together."

Aurora whimpered. Brunhilde said, "Come to the bath. You will adore it. Only the purest glacial water is pumped in and heated."

Aurora followed her into the spacious bath. There was an immense dressing table, several large closets, mirrors on three walls, and in the center, a huge transparent tub of crystal-clear leaded glass. It had a thick sealskin pad on its bottom.

Brunhilde said, "My lady, your generous master provided the cushion so you'll not bruise while bathing. He will want to watch you bathe and join you on occasion."

Aurora cried out in anguish. Again Brunhilde ignored her, but Daggmar, to cover the shock, said, "We brought your trunk and your personal things from Midlwurld. Come, I'll show you."

She showed Aurora the toiletries. Next to them sat the star sapphire orb she had rejected. Brunhilde said, "Tomorrow, after you have consummated your marriage, my lord Spauk will crown you queen. Then you may place your scepter beside the orb. We must bathe and dress you now."

"No, I'll bathe and dress myself. You may wait outside."

"I beg to differ, dear lady, but as your handmaidens we have that duty, on which King Spauk has insisted," Brunhilde argued.

"As you have observed, tomorrow I shall be queen, with great authority. Perhaps you'd like to live in the prison colony at the polar region and dine on grubs and blubber."

"We shall leave you then, as you insist, but please do hurry. King Spauk will be here soon and most impatient to take his pleasure."

The Baronesses retreated to the wedding suite, and Aurora bolted the door behind them. She bathed and dressed and then, with a heavy heart, returned to the wedding suite. Brunhilde and Daggmar made her wear a negligee of sensuous cut, and she tried to look resigned to her fate. But her look was misinterpreted as one of fear.

"Tsk, tsk, my child...I mean my queen," Brunhilde said, "be not afraid. Though King Spauk is not schooled in the ways of love...he's never had a woman, I'm sure that you can teach him to be gentle."

"Yes, for sure. It is a certainty," Daggmar chimed in, "and your duty, for all us Vikun ladies."

Aurora felt disgust bordering on nausea, but she steeled herself, now prepared to do what she felt she must.

"Sit here, dear queen," Daggmar said soothingly, "that Brunhilde may dress your hair and I may pat your neck and shoulders with attar of roses and musk...it is the King's favorite fragrance and will heighten his desire. More than that, it will make a frenzy of his passion."

Dutifully, Aurora sat on the edge of the bridal bed. Brunhilde, on one side, began to comb and fluff her hair, and Daggmar, on the other, began to rub her neck and shoulders with fragrant oil from a crystal flask.

Suddenly, Daggmar dropped the glass top and in her clumsiness to retrieve it, dropped the flask on Aurora's lap and spilled its contents everywhere. Daggmar cried out softly, as the King was due.

"You wretched drudge, you lumpish scullion, we'll have to start all over. Get a towel while I undress the girl," Brunhilde directed.

"No, no," Aurora cried out, trying to twist out of Brunhilde's iron grasp. Brunhilde held her till Daggmar returned and began to wipe Aurora's lap. Aurora squirmed again, to no avail.

"Oh," shouted Daggmar, as she felt a hard object at Aurora's thigh. She quickly pulled the negligee up Aurora's legs and revealed a little crystal dagger attached to her garter belt.

"Treachery, deceit...oh, the horror of it...against our noble king," Brunhilde wailed as she tore at the strap and wrenched the dagger loose.

"Oh, dearest queen, you don't know what you do," Daggmar cried in shock. Their words continued in a relentless torrent.

"You mustn't even think of such a thing."

"You must not harbor such a desire, for you're his no matter what."

"Should we call the guards, they'd kill us all."

"He'd torture you in ways you cannot imagine."

They ripped Aurora's gown from her and searched her head to toe.

"Now we must calm down and start again. The King is but moments away, and he will not be denied. You must accept your fate." They loosened their grip. Aurora pulled away and stood before them naked. Her humiliation was complete, but a serenity came over her. She knew what she had to do.

"Get Gurtrude, the chambermaid, quickly," Brunhilde commanded Daggmar. "She must clean up this mess and change the bed."

Daggmar hurried to the door and shortly returned with the maid, who began to tremble when she saw the Queen standing naked, her gown ripped from her, lying in shreds all over the floor. Eyes wide with fear, Gurtrude began bowing and curtsying.

"Foolish goose," Brunhilde shouted, "we've had a little accident, that is all. Change the sheets and wipe up this oil. Quickly now." The girl began to do as told, still trembling and averting her eyes from the naked Queen.

Composed, Aurora said, "I yield. I'll go and bathe again."

"We must accompany you. We cannot leave you alone now."

Aurora calmly replied, "I promise never again to attempt any harm against my lord Spauk. I swear it by my mother's grave in the Hall of Eternity. You shame and degrade me as you gaze upon my naked flesh. Is that not enough? It is, so you shall not and must not accompany me, for if you do, this time tomorrow, you will be in irons and on your way to the polar regions as I have promised."

Stymied, Brunhilde and Daggmar said nothing and made no move to follow as Aurora returned to the dressing room which housed the bath.

"Fear not," Aurora said as she closed the door behind her. "What I have to do, I shall do in a hurry."

Once inside, she bolted the door, turned on the water to fill the immense glass bath, ran to her trunk and pulled out her white satin gown, the one she wore at the ball when she first danced with Porch. He liked it so much, she had added a veil and train and wore it when they married. She picked up the crown of the Queen of Szidrous and affixed it to her hair. She pulled Spauk's heavy ring from her finger, then with three fingers reached into the jar of face cream, pulled out Porch's ring and put it on. Still holding the immense and hated ring that bound her to Spauk, she picked up the heavy orb from the dressing table. She went over to the picture window and pulled open the thermo-drapes. She gazed out at the beautiful evening star that Porch had told her was faraway Midlwurld. She looked at it sadly and said, "Forgive me, Aurelia, but I shall not be defiled."

Clasping her hands, she knelt in prayer with tears in her eyes, and asked to be forgiven and that her spirit be taken lovingly.

She rose, scratched a large circle on the glass with Spauk's heavy diamond, deposited that ring in the toilet as she passed and went to the bath that was now filled and overflowing. She got in carefully, immersed herself to her waist in the water, and pulled her skirt tight around her ankles. She took aim with the orb and threw it against the glass circle she had inscribed. As it broke the circle and fragmented the window, she lowered herself into the water. The words, "Porch, my beloved," formed on her lips and helped her breathe a great draught of water as she went under. The icy outside wind immediately formed a crust above her.

Several minutes before, in the bridal chamber where Brunhilde and Daggmar were waiting, there was a knock on the outside door. Both heard the singsong call, "It is I, sweet queen, your adoring husband, the king."

"Go quickly," Brunhilde directed Daggmar. "Keep him at bay."

Daggmar hurried over and said in loud voice, "Mighty King, your lady will be a moment more. She prepares herself most carefully."

"Open now, I shall not be denied. I am the king," Spauk shouted in a rage. His licentiousness had increased to the point of dementia.

Daggmar quaked with fear and could not move. Gurtrude, the chambermaid, scurried under the bridal bed. Brunhilde went to the door and opened it. Spauk rushed in and ran around in a frenzy, searching everywhere with eyes now slits of fire. He croaked, "Where is she? Where is the vixen?"

Then they heard the crash of glass in the bath. Spauk realized immediately what had happened. She had thwarted him. He went and sat down in the center of the room. His nose began to drip. Cold seeped into the chamber from under the locked door and Brunhilde and Daggmar then also guessed what Aurora had done.

Spauk shrieked, "Guards, Scrofulous." Berserkers poured in and Scrofulous followed. Spauk sullenly ordered, "Scrofulous, get the engineers and carpenters. Get the mortician."

Soon they all assembled. The engineers battered down the door to the bath and began to build a barrier in front of the shattered window. The cold became intense. Spauk began to shiver. Daggmar pulled quilts from the wedding bed and wrapped them around him.

Spauk said hoarsely, "Bring her out."

The mortician called his two assistants in with a stretcher and went into the bath. They returned with Aurora in peaceful repose, lying frozen on the sealskin, encased in a solid block of ice. Spauk looked at her without emotion. He saw her tiara and queenly dress. He saw Porch's ring on her finger and understood the totality of her rejection. He snarled, "Get rid of her. She has no uses now."

He said nothing as they removed the body. Brunhilde and Daggmar edged toward the outside door. Spauk nodded to the Berserkers, who grabbed the pair. He looked at them and said, "You failed."

Then he looked at Scrofulous and said softly, "Bring Kleaver with his ax, block and basket."

Soon Scrofulous returned with a dwarf, Kleaver, who wore a black hood with two eye holes. Kleaver, as wide as he was tall, rippled with muscles. He carried a huge two-bladed ax, a block and a basket.

Spauk said, "Set the block and basket here before my feet."

Then he nodded to the two Berserkers who held Daggmar. They straightened Daggmar's arms behind her and twisted them backwards to force her head down onto the block. Daggmar cried out in pain and when her neck was centered on the block, began to weep. Spauk looked at Kleaver and asked, "Is your ax sharp?"

"Yes, sire, both sides are sharp as razors," Kleaver replied.

"Then do your duty," said Spauk. In a mighty arc that began at his feet, Kleaver brought the ax behind him, over his head and squarely on through Daggmar's neck. Daggmar's head, spurting blood, rolled off the block into the basket. Scrofulous giggled loudly, but quickly stopped when Spauk gave him a threatening look. The Berserkers who had held Daggmar tight grabbed the ankles of the headless body and dragged it from the room.

Spauk next looked at the pair who held Brunhilde. They pulled her forward and began to straighten and twist her arms, but with a mighty heave of her stout arms, she sent both sprawling. As she did, her long twisted braid came down behind her back. She reached back and pulled it over her shoulder to the front. She then gave Spauk a haughty look and said, "If it must be the ax, very well, but I am a baroness and Vikun lady. I shall not be dragged around like some ignoble peasant."

She knelt down, laid her cheek on the wet red block, pulled her hair off her neck, turned and said to Kleaver, "Don't muss my hair."

Kleaver's ax began its arc, went around, cleft Brunhilde's head from her neck, and it too rolled into the basket. Kleaver then turned to Spauk and bowed. Spauk looked at him and around the room at all the others and said, "Get out."

Spauk continued to sit there. He pulled the quilts higher around his shoulders and spent the night there, impassive, looking at the bridal bed. Shortly before dawn, he cried out, "I want my nanny."

Then he slowly rose and left the suite. Ten minutes later, numb with both cold and fear, Gurtrude peeked out from under the bed and, seeing the coast was clear, wiggled out and also left. Hurriedly, she went to her room next to the kitchen, grabbed some furs and went to the provisioning sled outside the kitchen door. There, she slipped under the tarpaulin that covered it, wrapped herself in the furs, and lay as quiet as a mouse. An hour later, it began its scheduled run to Bifrost, which lay thirty miles down the mountain from Thrymheim.

CHAPTER 8

THE FUNERAL

Gurtrude counted it lucky that it was sleeting when the sleigh stopped at the royal warehouse in Bifrost. Few were on the street, and those who were had their heads down against the icy particles and wind. They paid her no attention, so she made it to the edge of town where her family lived. She told them what occurred the night before and during the days she hid under the bed. Then she was struck dumb with terror and did not recover for many days.

At first, they didn't believe her story; yet, apprehensive should such a tale get out, they hid her carefully. Would the Berserkers come to carry her off in the dread of night? Fearfully, they could do naught but wait and see.

The Mortician was struck numb with terror. "Dispose of her. She has no uses now," the King had said. Yet he could not bring himself to commit such a crime. She had royal Vikun blood and was queen of a brave people a world away. She lay serene within that block of ice, and even in the gloomy morgue had an aura of golden beauty about her. Would Kleaver come and take his head before first light? Tearfully, he could do naught but wait and see.

But something was wrong at Thrymheim. Rather than shining with the light of God-blessed nuptials, music and joy, it looked cold and forbidding on the high, dark mountain. People began wondering if something had gone awry, if something terrible had happened. Concerned, they began converging on the great kirk at Bifrost. Long lines of slowly moving folk filled the roads. They kept a vigil at the kirk, and many moved to the roads beneath the high mountain. Thrymheim was shrouded by fog during the day, and whenever the fog lifted, it looked leaden and dead. A chant took hold amongst them.

"King Spauk, King Spauk, come down. Deliver to us our queen, King Spauk." Nothing happened. Rumors took hold, first about Olaf.

"Cast into the wolven pit."

"No trial before the Council of Ten."

"Killed without his sword in hand."

"He'll never reach Valhalla."

Gradually the story of the dreadful things that happened at Thrymheim on the night of the wedding spread.

"How could she do such a thing?" they asked about Aurora.

Gurtrude came out of her coma and, surrounded by warriors day and night, repeated her eyewitness account.

"He was going to kill her consort, the one called the Interloper."

"The way he murdered Olaf."

"Sell her little daughter to the depraved debauchers on Cynn."

"She married him to save them both, then died to keep her virtue."

"Severed the heads of Brunhilde and Daggmar."

"We should have his head then, too. What kind of a king is he?"

"Without a trial, you say? What kind of a people are we?"

The throngs that stood before Thrymheim, which appeared dingy and dead, increased a hundred-fold, and their chanting did not cease.

"COME DOWN, SPAUK, COME DOWN—COME DOWN, SPAUK, COME DOWN. YOU HAVE BROUGHT TO US A HUNDRED YEARS OF MOURNING AND ONE THOUSAND YEARS OF SORROW. SPAUK—COME DOWN."

Thrymheim stayed dark and forbidden. At last, the Mortician, seeing the mood of the people, screwed up his courage and confessed to Odin's Scribe that he had not obeyed Spauk's order. The most noble and beautiful Queen still rested, frozen, in the purest Vikun water.

Odin's Scribe thundered, "We must conduct a Vikun funeral. She will rest forever beside her mother and her mother's mother on Ice Moon in the Hall of Eternity. Melt and purify the clearest amber gathered from northern seas and seal it well around the ice. It shall be her sarcophagus. Trim it with cedar wood and our finest gems, gold and silver. Build it fit for the queen who conquered an evil king and is now a legend for all the Vikun generations."

They laid Aurora in state in the town square under Yggdrasil, the World Tree sculpted in ice, before the week was out. The Vikuns came, young and old, night and day, through the bitter Ice World winter to pass the bier and pay homage to the queen they thought they'd gained. When they saw her resting serenely deep within the ice, not a one, from the hardiest warrior to the youngest child, passed without weeping. When the last had come and gone, twelve frost elk, black as night, drew the sledge of the dead into the square and reverently placed Aurora's body upon it. The sledge started out, preceded by a marching band of mourners dressed in somber black. Their music was a concatenation of grief, remorse and misery combined into a dirge of deep despair. The funeral procession headed toward the great spaceport, and the body was gently loaded there by the pallbearers into the finest Vikun spaceboat.

Odin's Scribe presided. He stretched out his arms and raised his eyes to the heavens. He called upon the gods to vote the spirit of this queen into Vingolf, the hall of goddesses. Surely if they did not, he said, Odin would rage, Thor would thunder, Freyja would weep, and Fenrir would howl till Ragnorak and the end of time.

Next he raised his arms, and the black ship's rockets fired. It slowly gained the sky, and six escorting launches took position alongside. Faster and faster the cortege rose till it was out of sight in the evening sky. As the burial party approached Ice Moon, the pallbearers donned space suits and removed Aurora's coffin. They rocketed down to the Hall of Eternity and placed her beside her mother and her mother's mother to rest in peace forever. As they did, the escorting longboats fired their lasers and ignited the ship that had carried her there. It veered off, flaming, on a course to the stars.

Down below, the Vikun mourners saw the fire and turned away. They returned to the road below Thrymheim and took up the chant, "Spauk, come down. Come down, Spauk." But Spauk did not come down.

CHAPTER 9

RETRIBUTION

High above the city on a rocky ledge, the man watched. He heard the tumult below Thrymheim. He watched the Vikuns file by the coffin. He watched the funeral procession and the rockets lift off to Ice Moon. He knew what had happened and went into exile of spirit, mind and body. The great white wolf was with him. It sensed the man's need for companionship. It sensed the eclipse of his soul. It sensed his sorrow and howled in anguish. The man mourned for many months, all through the fierce Vikun winter. Spring came and the ice broke on the river in the valley below the ledge.

It was then that hatred and rage enveloped the man. The hate was healthy, the rage salubrious. It burnt hot in his nostrils and acid in his throat. It sharpened his vision. It welled up from the darkest part of his soul. He had a monster to catch and kill.

Thus Porch's campaign began. One night, a valley away from Thrymheim, the royal hunting lodge, went up in flame, and a pack of wolven, led by a great white wolf, drove all the game into the mountains beyond the borders of the royal hunting preserve.

Scrofulous, who had become Spauk's eyes and ears, dutifully informed the King. "Mighty King," he whined, "the Interloper indeed escaped the fury of the thunder wolven. We found the body of the leader, its throat torn out, and several more, also dead, by the lava fountains. But worse than that, by some secret spell, he makes the others do his bidding. He burned down your hunting lodge, and the wolven drove the game far beyond recapture."

Scrofulous received a fury of lashes for his trouble. When Spauk caught his breath from that exertion, he said, "Call Kleaver."

Kleaver came posthaste. Spauk's eyes narrowed to slits as he slobbered, "Take a patrol, ten of your best. Find him. Bring him to me, alive if you can, dead if you must."

Kleaver went out to do the King's bidding. At dawn two days later, Spauk's lackeys opened the great iron gate to Thrymheim and found the patrol hanging by their feet from the lampposts, frozen stiff. Each had a strange indentation on his skull. The headsman's block on the walkway below had the great two-bladed ax struck deeply in. In front of the block, Kleaver's grinning head looked up from the basket.

Another report came in. The new wine in the royal winery flooded the floor, as the bungs on the casks had been pulled. The aged wine was soured, its casks pierced from above.

As winter lost its grip, avalanches more frequent than memory bore blocked roads, disrupting the King's commerce. As spring progressed, there seemed a calm in the course of destruction. But then all the calves and kids were found stillborn on the royal farms. Some said a strange substance was found at the salt licks. Others said no, the thunder wolven, led by a great white wolf, had so worried the cows, the nannies and the ewes that they could hardly feed or rest during the winter.

The royal granaries were found full of ergot and infested with rats, mice and vermin.

The royal fishing fleet was found scuttled in its harbor.

Spauk grappled with fear. He sputtered to Scrofulous, "Call out your full army. Come back with him dead, and you shall have all the royal mines. Not a one shall be left out."

Scrofulous led the dwarfs out, armed to the teeth. They crossed the woods and rivers, the mountains and valleys, to no avail. In the valleys, spring rains wiped out the trail, and on the mountains, blizzards wiped out all sign and track leading to their quarry. Before long, dwarfs snared by the foot and wafted upside down high in the trees froze in the wind. Others had their throats torn out by thunder wolven. The dwarfs continued their search until they were too few to count. Finally, only Scrofulous remained.

He returned to tell the King, "He breached and flooded the mines, then carried off one hundred cases of dynamite on the explosives sledge. Musk oxen pulled it up the mountain to the glacier and far volcano, where we know he has a lair and believe he waits."

Spauk sent messages to the Clans, hoping to bribe them to his side with promises of riches. The Chiefs responded by citing the rituals of mourning and told Spauk to come stand trial.

Stymied, Spauk brought in the space tramps he had hired as guards at the new spaceport. He promised them great riches to find and kill his tormentor. Shortly after they left the spaceport to do his bidding, explosions there, initiated in booster rockets, destroyed Spauk's longboat fleet, and those scurrilous creatures had no more luck than the dwarfs. Soon enough ambushes, rock slides and floods killed them all.

Panicking and fearful, Spauk called in his personal guard, the Berserkers. Composing himself, he said, "Go find him. Bring him to me. I'll pay your fee no matter what it is. Bring him in dead, and half the wealth of the kingdom is yours." He watched their greed and blood lust rise. So, with a scowl and narrowed eyes, he sputtered, "I'll add to that five hundred virgin milkmaids stolen from the countryside, stripped and chained to couches." His eyes darted around and he hissed, "Or trussed up tight with heavy leather, for however you might want to take your pleasure."

With a roar they went out and formed as a military force at the base of the castle. Presently, they found an obvious trail, as Porch had left it there. They shouted when they had him in sight. Porch led them on up the high mountains, staying just ahead. He reached the glacier, climbed it, and waited till they got to its base. He reached the volcano, climbed it, and waited till they got to its base. They were soon close behind, raging with blood lust because they knew he had nowhere else to go. He lit the fuse to the dynamite he had placed throughout the lava plug two weeks before.

The dynamite exploded and the lava plug vented with a roar. A great tongue of magma shot from the volcano's throat, and the Berserkers had but seconds to see their fiery death approach and feel it swallow them up. The volcano then belched relief from pent-up pressure and blew a plume of superheated steam into heavy ice-cold air above. The black sky protested with furious cascades of lightning and roaring thunder. Sleet pelted down and kept on coming till the lava froze over the Berserker army. When the lava tube was empty and only Vulcan's dim furnace seen within, Porch with the Great White Wolf came down to stand before its entrance and survey his retribution. Satisfied, he left. He still had more to do.

Far away in Bifrost, the people saw the volcano blow. Lightning ignited the sky from north to south, flashing from pole to pole. They heard the thunder roaring, rolling around them, reverberating endlessly. Then the pelting sleet arrived. They did not seek shelter but watched in veneration, scared to utter what they surely knew was true. They called on Odin's Scribe to say it, so he did. "The Interloper has become Thor and wielded Mjollnir, his mighty hammer, against the mountain. Worse than that, Fenrir, the wolven god, races back and forth at his feet."

The following day, the dam supplying electric power to Thrymheim blew. A wall of water surged down, filling the streets of Bifrost. It melted the ice statues remaining from the Vikun celebration, even Yggdrasil, the World Tree. The people sought refuge on roofs and other high places. Surely the dead Queen's consort was Thor.

Three days later, three men came out of the distant mountains, dressed in dirty, torn and blackened furs. Exhausted, they looked out from fearful faces, saying, "We were Berserkers, but no more. We'll never serve

Spauk again. We've thrown down our swords and cast off our armor. We stood at the base of the volcano, the last to start up. We saw it blow and the fiery lava consume our fellows. We ran back across the glacier and saw his shadow in the snow surrounded by an eerie hellish glow. He has become Thor."

The people said fearfully, "We know. Odin's Scribe has said that that is so." As they stood there, a messenger came running up and shouted, "The Szidrians have girded for war and all of Midlwurld has joined them. They have collected a mighty fleet and are coming, led by the man called Wizard, also known as No the Destroyer. It is said he brings a bomb, a cobalt bomb, a planet buster."

Odin's Scribe stood amidst the crowd, looked around and then raised his arm and pointed a finger toward the sky. Then he said, "Worse than that. He is the one-eyed Odin, disguised, who comes to avenge his son, mighty Thor."

Another Vikun, older even than Odin's Scribe, said in a tremulous voice, "I read the Old Norse Runes, the ones from Old Home in the far stars. They tell of Loki, the trickster god. Methinks him Spauk."

"We are lost. It is out of our hands," the Vikuns said. Again they went below Thrymheim and began their chant, "COME DOWN, SPAUK. SPAUK, COME DOWN. COME DOWN AND STAND BEFORE THE COUNCIL OF TEN."

In the Great Hall of Thrymheim, Spauk sat in the glow of a candle, bundled up in many robes and blankets, as there had been no heat or light since the dam had gone. He'd covered his ears against the cold but also so he would not hear them down below. He looked at the dwarf Scrofulous, the only one left.

"Sire," said Scrofulous, "they say come down and stand before the Council of Ten."

"But I am innocent," Spauk whimpered.

"Of course, but they say come down and present your case to the Council of Ten or face the Interloper here in the dark, alone."

Spauk shivered and looked around furtively, then a

crafty look came upon his face. "Yes, certainly, I am innocent. I meant no harm. I did it for the Vikun ladies and for future Vikun generations."

"Yes, sire," Scrofulous said brightly. "You did it for the little Vikun children you love so much, tee hee."

So Spauk went down to stand before the Council of Ten, and it was a good decision, for later that night Thrymheim was destroyed in a mighty explosion initiated in the castle's powder magazine.

CHAPTER 10
THE HEARING

The Wizard, Lord No, was in the Tower of Astral making stellar observations when Ragnor, with tears in his eyes and the shame of his people on his face, brought him news of the tragedy on Ice World. The Wizard took it stoically, for he knew the very nature of man in his fall from grace made life a tragedy. When Ragnor told him Sidrian forces were mobilizing and calling all of Midlwurld to join them, he visibly slumped.

He had grown old, and he carried the weight of his years on his shoulders. He knew a war between the two worlds and the good people inhabiting each would engender continuous enmity. No matter who won, hatred would pile on hatred with each succeeding generation, and war would continue, perhaps till the Vundercy sun itself grew old and died as a supernova, consuming all.

Then Ragnor, in his personal agony, said something cryptic. "I cannot believe a man of such perfidy and cruelty is a Vikun."

Immediately, the Wizard called in all accounts of what had occurred in the past hundred years on Midlwurld and what was known of Ice World. A computer analysis of these records told him what he needed to know. He also set his communication banks to monitor all transmissions made on Ice World. And so he heard the far-off Vikuns.

"Thor...the one-eyed Odin...Loki... It is out of our hands."

He thought to himself, *They cannot deal with the enormity of this tragedy and their part in it and so have retreated into the mythology that has sustained them through the generations.*

Thus he came to know what he would do.

One more time, he said to himself, *one more time.*

He gave the orders to depart. The Lord Chamberlain would command the fleet and orbit the Vikun planet on arrival. Ragnor and Shareem, king of the Desert Kingdom, would accompany him down to the planet.

The Vikun Chiefs met the Szidrian space shuttle at the Ice World spaceport. Greatly chastened by the tragedy, they felt disgrace and were full of shame. They were prepared for the worst.

Ragnor stepped out first. He said, "The Wizard, Lord No, comes so there may be peace between Ice World and Midlwurld. I, your brother Ragnor, swear it."

The Wizard then stepped out of the craft. He looked around sternly but said nothing for several minutes. He wore a great horned helmet covered with fur. Its long curving horns were plated with gold and spiraled high above the silvered helmet's base. His black ermine coat was girdled with a wide diamond-studded belt, on which his broadsword hung. Diverse jewels inlaid the broadsword scabbard. He bore a large round shield, and it too blazed with sparkling gems. A pair of heavy leather and steel boots completed his costume. It was meant to impress and set the stage for what was to come.

The Chieftains murmured among themselves, "Surely he is the All Father in disguise."

"It must be so: his furs are finer than any of ours, which I've always thought the best in all creation."

"And those gems sparkle with a fire that must have originated in Valhalla."

At last the Wizard spoke in a voice of great authority. "Our worlds have been at peace for a hundred years or so. Yes, at peace, since first we built the ships and longboats that ply the void between. Our interchange has been a harmony—of benefit to both. Yet now we have between us a tragedy of such dimension, a wrong of such proportion, that we are on the verge of war.

"Though you Vikuns are fierce warriors who stand above all others, today you have no fleet, while above you orbits a great armada that could bring on Ragnarok tomorrow. Yet we stand for peace."

The Wizard paused for effect while the Chieftains visibly sighed relief. Then he spoke again, "On this world, we lost a queen, a queen who came in peace, a lovely girl, guiltless, full of innocence and purity, dearly loved in all of Midlwurld. For this you bear the shame. Yet neither peace nor war can bring her back again."

Again, Lord No paused. The Vikun Chieftains, though stone faced, showed their anguish with the tears flowing freely down their cheeks.

He began again, "There is an evil, born forty years ago, that lurks among you. You know of whom I speak. A darkness pervades this world that must be exorcised before the peace of which I speak can be. You know of what I speak. Therefore, I will conduct a hearing, fairly heard, two weeks hence. Call it a trial if you'd rather. Set the time and place. I will be there, and you see that he is, too."

Lord No had finished speaking, so the Chieftains dispersed and Ragnor led the Szidrian party to waiting sleighs and to lodgings amongst his tribe. The next morning, Lord No called his delegation together and said, "I have a plan in which each of us has a critical role. Let's begin discussion, then set our course of action."

All day, the Szidrian delegation discussed the Wizard's plan and by nightfall were ready to carry out their missions. Concluding the discussion, the Wizard said, "I must go to the Marshes on the Eastern Sea to find one critical to our case. Ragnor, as you know this world better than any other, you must find Captain General Porch and bring him to the Hearing. I know his location, which I'll give to you, but go alone, for I fear he will kill any who accompany you.

"Harim, parlay with the Vikuns. They will accept you as a neutral. Ensure that Odin's Scribe is at the hearing and that the Chieftains bring their most learned men, Vikun historians, scientists and medical practitioners. Those who remain, ascertain that our equipment is tested and ready. Let's be off in the morning."

All left on schedule, and within a fortnight, the Wizard brought back the one he sought. Harim had secured a Vikun pledge that those requested would be present. But Ragnor had not yet returned with Captain General Porch.

Nevertheless, the Wizard said the Hearing would begin on the appointed day; and that day he gathered his delegation in the Great Hall of the People at the Allthing, the Vikun parliament. Commoners and nobles alike packed the Hall, as the Chieftains declared seating open to all to make the Hearing truly democratic.

On a platform at the front of the Hall, Spauk sat on a heavy throne to the right, because, like it or not, he still wore the king's ring. The Council of Ten sat to the left. There was space in the center for the advocates of both sides. The Vikuns put a table for the Szidrian delegation below the platform in the center of the Hall.

Lord No whispered to his compatriots who were gathered around him, "Ragnor will be here soon with Porch. I'm sure of that. But we must enter now, so we'll go in procession to make a proper impression and take our seats in the front of the Hall.

"Spauk's counselor will speak first. We will listen politely. When our turn comes, I will give them an omen to play on their fears, for the Vikuns are a superstitious lot. Let's proceed."

All eyes turned on them as they marched up the Hall. The Wizard led, wearing a hooded black cloak that extended to the floor. A small figure, the one he had gone to the Marshes to find, followed him. The figure hobbled a bit, and hooves could be seen below its cloak. Four carrying a large square box on a platform and two others with smaller devices followed. Then Harim Skarim Shareem came. Unlike the others, he wore a magnificent desert costume of colorful silks embroidered in gold and silver. The rest of the delegation, also cloaked and hooded, followed him.

The Vikuns speculated on the incongruity of the procession in whispered tones. When the delegation reached the table set for them, they sat, and all except the small figure following the Wizard pulled back their hoods to reveal grim faces.

Spauk said in a low, sullen voice, "Let the Hearing begin."

His counselor rose and began a long, legalistic harangue starting with the treaty between Spauk and Szid; going to the righteousness of Spauk's actions; and making the assertion that the noble Ice World king did what he did for the Vikun ladies and the little Vikun children he loved so much. He concluded with a flourish, bowed to Lord No, and with a sweep of his hand indicated that it was the Wizard's turn.

Lord No rose and dropped his cloak to reveal a dark blue gown with silver swirls and whorls and diverse figures of geometric design. Again, whispers pervaded the audience as he mounted the platform. Behind him, his men brought the large square box up, set it down, and opened it. The Wizard pushed a button and a crystal obelisk rose from inside. He called for four stools which he placed around its sides, and then called forth Odin's Scribe and the Desert King and beckoned the small hooded figure to join them. He seated Odin's Scribe opposite the hooded figure, and he took the stool opposite Harim. Then, from another box, he handed each a strange jeweled headband to wear, and told them to touch the obelisk base to complete a circuit.

Ready then, one of Ragnor's tribesmen darkened the Hall and he twisted a dial. Light emanated from the crystal, and a booming voice which seemed to come from nowhere and everywhere spoke. "Look to the Crystal Obelisk and the pendulum within. It ticks for you. It ticks for me. It ticks throughout eternity. It is the time from every place in universal space."

The voice softened, and as it did, light from the crystal rose up in shimmering curtains of greens and blues and veils of red. It undulated back and forth, faster and faster in a silent, shivering symphony. The Vikuns gasped throughout the Hall. One said, "It is our wondrous Northern Lights brought into this Hall."

"Only Odin the Allfather could do that," an aged Vikun observed, for he was never persuaded the beautiful Ice World Aurora was a natural phenomenon, no matter how many times he had been told.

An old woman sitting behind him corrected, "That is not so. The goddesses of Vingolf are speaking to us."

Another woman, sitting beside the first, had tears in her eyes and proclaimed, "They are telling us the girl's spirit has arrived. Yes, the one we lost, the one with the namesake of the lights."

All the women nearby began to weep piteously and then to wail. The lights began a furious dance, flashing hot, back and forth.

"Now Odin speaks," the old Vikun observed triumphantly, "so be silent and listen." They quieted down.

The booming voice spoke again. "Listen now and watch astutely while I wrest memories wrought in separate times and different places from these minds and weave them into the seamless story of deceit that spans both worlds."

The curtain of light calmed, dimming to flutter like a diaphanous veil in a gentle breeze, and then went out. It was replaced by a scene of sand, above which hovered a blazing sun. The people of Ice World were astonished, because most Vikuns had never seen a desert, nor even imagined one. They even thought they felt the heat.

Now a large, colorful and commodious tent appeared. It was Abdul's expeditionary tent. A rider on a camel-horse galloped up, leaped off and rushed into the tent. Abdul was there with his followers planning his campaign against the desert tribes that had not yet accepted his sovereignty.

"Excellency," the rider shouted, "the queen has born you a son."

Abdul looked up, smiling, and said, "We return at once."

The scene shifted to the great tent city of Toome at the Oasis of Oome and zoomed into Abdul's palace. Abdul had entered and was rushing to the Queen's chamber when the midwife intercepted him.

"Sire," she said, "you are twice blessed. You not only have a boy, but a daughter as well."

The King beamed, and as he reached his wife's side, one of the Queen's wet-nurses handed him the boy. Abdul frowned as he looked at the boy. The baby was long and gaunt, had a mottled skin, strange pointed ears, a long nose, and feet that looked like a duck's. He passed the child back to its wet-nurse and a handmaiden handed him the girl, who brought pleasure to his eyes. She was rosy cheeked and robust, with almond skin, little cherry lips, and beautiful big black eyes. He thought he saw her smile at him.

The metronome in the Obelisk ticked faster and faster, then slowed to another scene in Abdul's palatial tent. He was watching a maid give the babies a bath. The girl laughed and splashed, but the boy screamed and shivered. Sadly, Abdul shook his head and left.

Again the obelisk went fast forward to another scene. Abdul's tots were playing on the carpet at the foot of his throne. A huge spider crept up, the one the Desert People call a tarantula. The baby girl watched curiously as it crawled up her small foot and on up her leg. When it reached her little belly, she giggled, grabbed a spider leg, and held it out to her brother, who shrank back, screaming, then crawled off as fast as he could across the carpet.

The scene blinked off as though little time had passed, and now a great sandstorm raged. The Vikuns watched in awe. None had imagined sand could blow with the fury of a winter blizzard. The scene jumped inside a tent where Abdul was talking to his Grand Vizier.

Abdul, looking solemn, said, "I could not do it by my own hand, nor let another, because he is my flesh and blood, but if he inherits the crown, he will destroy the Desert Kingdom. We must trade him for another, a stalwart lad whom I'll make my foster son, but none must know. I have one a world away in mind." Now Abdul spoke in tones so hushed that not even the Obelisk could pick up the sound. Soon seven black hooded men hurried out.

That scene faded and a star field came into view. The power of the Obelisk was such that the Vikuns in the Allthing imagined themselves hurtling through space. Suddenly they were in the Old King's Hall at his murder. His queen, weeping, watched, clutching her little son to her breast. Then the Cutthroats, who had just killed the Old King, hidden in black wolven furs and helmets without horns, tore the child from her arms and ran out into the blizzard and the night.

Alarms rang throughout the Hall too late to save the King, but the Old King's personal guard now vowed to save his son. Mounting their horses, they picked up the Cutthroats' trail and raced out after them.

The Obelisk raced forward, and the Cutthroats were seen, halted, and clustered together with some others. They passed the heir of the Old King's throne to the group of men clad in black burnooses for ten bags of gold and another lad. The Old King's guard were hard upon this lot of plotters, so the Cutthroats stood to fight except for the one who carried the boy passed to them by Abdul's men. Abdul's men raced for their spacecraft, an early one of antiquated and flimsy design. The Old King's guard killed the Cutthroats quickly, then advanced toward the ship to capture Abdul's men. When they reached it, the craft was lifting off. As it did, twenty battle-axes pierced its thin outer skin. Still it rose, hovered for a minute, stricken, then fell to the ground, caught fire, exploded, and the Old King's heir was lost with all of Abdul's men.

The last Cutthroat, who carried the lad, rode on through the night, and the next day, too. He came to the Marshes on the Eastern Sea and felt he could lose his pursuers there, so he rode into the murky waters. He came to a cabin, really just a hut. There was a strange woman inside wearing goat hindquarters as pantaloons.

"Take off those bloomers that I may see what you're hiding there," the Cutthroat yelled.

"You'd find nothing hidden that you would want, no feet, nothing below the knees but stumps. You still want to see?" she retorted.

"Well, take this child and this gold to care for him. I'll have no more to do with either. They've brought a curse on me."

The Cutthroat handed the woman the child, threw a handful of gold coins on the dirt floor, ran to the door and paused. Looking back at the woman, as an afterthought, he said, "Take this ring as well. No doubt it too is damned."

He threw her the ring he'd wrenched from the chain around the little Prince's neck. Then he ran out, mounted his horse, and galloped away as fast as his horse could splash through the mire. The woman opened the blanket wound around the babe and exclaimed with joy, "My, what a pretty little boy."

She put him on a nearby table and bent down to pick up the gold. As she did, she heard a thunder of hoofbeats approaching. She picked up the coins as quickly as she could and dumped them with the ring into a stockpot of smelly fish she had bubbling over the fire in her hearth. Next she went to a potato bin near the table the boy lay on and dumped them out. She placed the boy at the bottom and covered him with potatoes. Then she sat down in a rocker beside the bin and began to peel potatoes. Soon the door burst open and several of the Old King's guard entered, swords drawn.

She looked up and said, "Would you care for supper? There is stew on the hearth, and I can cook up potatoes if the stew is not enough."

The men ignored her invitation, demanding, "Where is he? We saw the hoofprints in the snow outside."

"A man was here and had some stew, but he left when he heard you approach. Look around if you want, but he headed toward the sea."

"Did he have a boy with him?"

"I saw no one but a dwarf coming for supper. Would he do?"

Hurriedly, the guards looked around, went storming out, mounted their steeds and headed south. The woman lifted the boy out from under the potatoes, set him back on the table, and as she did, in came a dwarf derisively named Scrofulous. She turned to him and said, "Look at the pretty boy a man just gave to me. Hold him up. Now that he is mine, I have a ring on a chain to put around his neck."

The metronome in the crystal Obelisk began a high-speed chatter, then stopped, and there rode a youthful Spauk on a marsh ox pulled by the dwarf Scrofulous. Spauk wore royal robes bought at a costume shop on the road to Bifrost, but little did it matter, for he had on the ancient ring worn by all Vikun kings of Ice World since they came from Old Earth. Vikuns cheered as he rode up the Grand Avenue of Bifrost when they saw that ring on his finger.

"The Thurl has returned to claim the crown," they shouted.

"The Cutthroats never killed him, only forced him into hiding."

At last the scenes above the crowd in the Great Hall of the People faded. Ragnor's man returned the lights to normal, and Lord No lowered the Obelisk into its case. He rose, pulled off his Wizard robe, and stood before the Vikuns as Knight Commander of the Order of No.

He called out, "Odin's Scribe, by what authority do you know of those things that swirled above our heads?"

Odin's Scribe stood and replied, "I knew the Old King, that blessed man, and was there when all of it happened."

Lord No called out again, "And you, Harim Skarim Shareem, king of the Desert People, by what authority comes your images of Abdul and his followers?"

Harim Skarim Shareem then stood and replied, "I remember the events from the time I was a boy. Abdul died from remorse that the Old King's son was lost by his hand."

"And you, Goat Woman from the Marshes by the Eastern Sea, by what authority do you recall those things?"

Goat Woman pulled back her hood and revealed a haggard face. She croaked, "Because Lord Spauk was given to me, and I raised him from a baby. I am his nanny."

Lord No then turned to the people sitting in the Hall and said, "And it is the memories of you Vikuns, nothing else, that brought back the day Spauk rode into

Bifrost on the marsh ox, wearing that ancient ring and claiming the right to be your king. It was your assumption when you saw the ring that he was the long lost Thurl and the Old King's heir. That assumption is your gravest sin."

A loud murmur rose from the Vikuns sitting in the Hall, but Lord No continued, "Now for those of you who doubt or believe you have seen only magic, let science be the final judge."

He motioned two assistants to bring up the other instrument they had brought to the Hall. They placed it and a small box on a table and set up a screen. No opened the box, held up a vial, and went over to Odin's Scribe. "What is this?" he asked.

Odin's Scribe perused it very carefully and said, "It is the vial of blood Spauk sent to Szid when he made the blood oath to come to the aid of Midlwurld."

Then Lord No passed the vial to Spauk's lawyer, who took it and looked at it suspiciously. The Wizard asked, "Is it still sealed?"

"It is," Spauk's counselor admitted.

Lord No broke the seal, opened the vial, and poured several drops into the machine on the table. He then set the machine to whirling.

"This is a centrifuge, a fractionator. Your physicians sitting among you know it well," he said so all could hear. In a moment he stopped the device and projected an image of bands of fractionated blood up on the screen and said, "This is the biologic signature of the man you made your king."

Again he reached into the box and withdrew another vial. He handed it to Harim and asked, "Identify this, if you can, Harim Skarim Shareem, king of the Desert People."

Harim too looked at it carefully and said, "It is the Blood Oath made to Szid to come on call by our fabled Ruby Queen. I swear it by all that's holy."

Lord No handed the vial to Spauk's advocate for his inspection. When satisfied, the lawyer passed it back to Lord No, who did as he'd done before and fractionated the blood within. Then he displayed those bands beside

the first that were still up on the screen. Turning first to
the Council of Ten and then to the Vikuns in the Hall,
he said, "You see they match most closely."

He looked at Spauk, walked over to the throne and
pointed a finger at him. Spauk's eyes narrowed to slits
and his face grew florid as Lord No shouted, "This churl
you made your Thurl, and then your king because he
wore the ancient ring, has no right whatever to the Vikun
throne. He is the craven, unfit brother of the heroic Ruby
Queen. He is an impostor and usurper of the Old King's
throne."

The Wizard, having unraveled the forty-year deceit,
was finished. He turned to leave the platform, and as
he did, the dwarf Scrofulous leaped up screaming and
plunged a dagger deep into the Wizard's back. Lord No
fell heavily to the floor and rolled on his side. Bedlam
ensued. Vikun physicians rushed to the stricken man's
aid. Outraged Vikuns raced from the Council table,
grabbed the dwarf, who was still screaming, and threw
him to the floor, holding him there with boots on his
neck, arms and legs. One ripped the bloody dagger from
his hand. As the physicians tried to curb the flow of
blood from the Wizard's wound, the Vikuns who had
pinned Scrofulous picked him up to drag him from the
Hall. And in the confusion, Spauk slipped through a
curtain and out of the Hall.

An enraged Chieftain cried out, "Justice, justice now,
mete out justice now. Drag this hideous little troll to a
murderer's plot at the edge of Potter's Field. Tie him to
the Great Oak Shield that awaits assassins there."

So they dragged the murderous dwarf out of the
Hall to the edge of Bifrost and Potter's Field. There they
pinned him, spread-eagled, onto the massive shield that
rotated on an axle hammered through a great oak tree.
The shield was set to rolling. Then fifty Vikuns formed a
line at fifty paces, and each Vikun, one following another, ran forward ten and threw his ax with deft precision into the shield.

Meanwhile, Porch and Ragnor had entered the Hall.
Seeing the disarray that prevailed, they pushed their
way forward and saw Lord No lying there with doctors

all around. Lord No looked up and saw them, then said to those attending, "Don't try to move me. I broke my back when I fell. I am dying. Let me talk to my son."

As Porch came up, he reached feebly under his blouse, which the physicians had opened and pulled something from around his neck. Porch cast off his furs and knelt beside the old warrior. Lord No reached for the young man's hand and pressed the object into it. He smiled at Porch through half-closed eyes and said, "Death comes easy. My work is done. We are but a flicker in the stream of time."

He pulled his hand away from Porch's, and in the young man's palm rested a locket. It was companion to the one he'd lost so long ago. He looked at it in wonder, but only briefly, then turned his eyes back to Lord No. The old Wizard's eyes closed then, but with great effort, he said, "I am Jason. I always loved your mother. I never loved another."

Then he turned his head and died. Porch kissed his father's cheek and clutched his hand in desperation. Most of his world was gone. A deep sob rested in his throat as he thought to himself, *Oh, that this life could end.* Why had the Providence that spared him time and again take first his mother, then his bride, and now his father?

Porch knelt in his sorrow, at first not moving. Then he opened the locket to read, "seek out and find the Birthplace of Wonder." He read them over and over with tears in his eyes, until at last he felt a strong hand grasp his shoulder. He looked up into the stern eyes of Ragnor, and Ragnor said, "Life goes on. We have a monster to catch and kill. Spauk has escaped."

CHAPTER 11
PURSUIT

They searched for Spauk throughout the Vikun spring and well into the summer, not just Porch and Ragnor, but every able-bodied man. Each forest, city and town was scoured. They climbed the mountains and crossed the seas, all to no avail.

Then one night, Ragnor had a dream. He dreamt of the Wizard's Obelisk and the visions it projected. It was the battle forty years before between the Old King's Guard and the Cutthroats they cut down. He saw Abdul's flimsy longboat as it fell and then exploded. He saw a new longboat shoot up from the ashes. A dwarf was sitting on the ashes and laughing like a maniac. He looked like the murderous Scrofulous and said, "Hee-hee-hee, you've looked in every nook, you've searched in every cranny. But, hee-hee, you've overlooked his nanny."

Ragnor woke with a start and called to Porch, sleeping nearby, "I had a dream and silly it may seem, but it makes a lot of sense to me. I think Spauk has left Ice World. Let's get the men and follow."

Porch was up in a minute and the search party left at daybreak, headed for the Marshes by the Eastern Sea. When they arrived, they went to the Goat Woman's hut. Ragnor's hunch paid off. Although they did not find the Goat Woman, evidence abounded that there had been a recent flurry of activity. The hearth was torn apart and a shaft dug beneath. Inspection of the tunnel revealed that it had contained a treasure hurriedly removed, as bills and gems and coins of the realm lay scattered all around.

Ragnor said, "I suspect Spauk hid a treasure here, anticipating trouble. Let's search the forest near the old battleground and see if he left from there."

Examination of the site showed soil churned up over the snow and fresh char covering old. It was evident a rocket ship had blasted off several months before. So they returned to Bifrost convinced that Spauk had left the planet. The limited range ship Spauk had access to had but one place to go—Midlwurld.

Ragnor speculated darkly, "Could he be brazen enough, now proven Abdul's son, to lay claim to the throne of the Desert Kingdom?"

Porch's thought was worse, "–Or vengeful and brash enough to try to steal Aurora's child, my darling little princess?"

Hurriedly, they traveled back to Bifrost and radioed a warning to the Lord Chamberlain and Harim Skarim Shareem.

Since war had been averted, Orwell and Harim, both concerned with affairs of state, returned to Midlwurld with the Armada right after the Hearing. They took the Wizard's body in a golden casket to bury him as requested in his will, in a crypt beneath the Tower of Astral. He eschewed any monument but allowed a simple plaque at the tower's entrance and specified that it read:

JASON, LORD NO
KNIGHT COMMANDER OF THE ORDER OF NO
"He did his duty"

All knew this was enough for the children of generations to come to learn and recite his great deeds, then try to follow his example.

Soon the message came back from Midlwurld, "Aurelia is safe and well guarded. Hurry back, there is evidence that Spauk was here."

Porch and Ragnor took leave of the Vikuns. They had been left the shuttle in which they had first arrived, and carrying only two, it had plenty of range to return to Midlwurld. They landed at the Great Spaceport of

Nork without incident, to be greeted by both the Lord Chamberlain and Harim Skarim Shareem.

The Lord Chamberlain got right to the point—Spauk had been there, arriving before the Midlwurld Armada. He made an effort to gain the Desert Kingdom as Abdul's son and inheritor. Rebuffed by the Desert People, he made an abortive attempt to get the throne by kidnapping the little Princess Aurelia—to hold her as a ransom.

"Yes," Harim broke in, "he sent his agents late at night to Toome, but they were quickly captured. By dawn, my people buried them, naked, up to their necks in the sands of Soome and what the sun didn't do, the sand mites did. They lingered for a day and a half before they succumbed and died."

Then Orwell spoke again. "With the treasure he carried, he hired a crew of mutineers from an Indonesian ship headed for the Pleiades that stopped at Nork to resupply. He then fled with this opprobrious crew, most likely headed for the brothel world of Cynn. You'll soon be able to follow. We have under construction a fast cruiser of Earth design. As soon as they learned who and what the ship was for, the Union at Nork began working a double shift. It's been paid for with the indemnity Ice World paid to Szidrous for our terrible loss. Rightfully, Porch, it does belong to you."

Harim then said, "Come, let's ride to Toome and the Oasis of Oome so you may see your daughter." His men brought up the camel-horses.

Ragnor called out as Porch mounted, "I'll stay and hire a crew of warriors. Already, I'm told, there are many volunteers."

Porch found his daughter in the loving care of Victoria, sharing the Queen's quarters with one hundred warriors on guard day and night to assure her safety. The Priest, whom Porch had made her godfather, was there as well keeping constant vigilance. Though he yearned to take her up in his arms, he desisted, fearing he could never put her down and continue on his mission.

He returned to Nork and found Ragnor had a crew

assembled and the cutter had made a trial run above the planet. So they bade farewell to Midlwurld and headed for Cynn. Porch, the hunted, had become the hunter. In six months, the cutter came to orbit. Porch and Ragnor descended to the planet's surface with two dozen well-armed men. They found what they knew to be there: slavery, debauchery, drunkenness, murder, thievery and every kind of sin. Itinerants, spacefarers and riff-raff of every sort flooded the spaceport. Many had spent years in the void, some in a hypnotic stasis, others in cryogenic sleep, but all had been paid and savored the chance to wander about in a planet's true gravity. Some knew the planet's reputation. Others did not, but all were fleeced of their money and goods.

Porch, Ragnor and their landing party studied port records and ship manifests; they circled the planet searching for Spauk, questioning surly men. Highway men waylaid them, but they cut them down with laser pistols and slashing swords. At last they found firm evidence of Ice World coinage, showing Spauk had been there. He had fled when he learned of their coming. They left that sordid planet and went again into the void to track him down.

Spauk's path led them to Cynn's sister world of Slum, where people lived in ghettos. Crime was legal there, and woe to those who ventured off home turf. Invariably the injured parties found redress through the Association of Hit Men or Society of Vigilantes. Spauk didn't have the stomach to live there, so he came and quickly left.

His path then led to a planet called Greenpeace. Landing there, they found a world of woods and lakes and meadows. The Greenpower issued each man a forty-acre plot and said to him, "Be happy with your lot." Pioneers there lived on beans and rice and rabbit stew and an occasional fish or two, but not much more. Greenpower decreed it a crime to cut down a living tree or divert a stream from its journey to the sea. Spauk had not stayed there.

On they went, three years in all, to worlds of differing description, but Spauk remained elusive. At last they came to the water worlds of Naiad and Galatea in the Archimedes system, which lay at the edge of the star cluster. They asked of Spauk, and always got the answer, "Go see Dr. Tupology. He knows everything."

Finally they found a seashore where a small boat was beached. Boys called Sea Urchins and girls called Water Gamins frolicked on the sand and played in the surf. A boy called Lava-Lava came up and said, "I'll bet you're looking for Dr. Tupology."

Porch replied, "Yes. Do you know where he is?"

The boy continued, "Most certainly. He lives on that small island you see on the horizon. Get in the boat and we'll lead you there."

Porch and Ragnor climbed into the boat and took up the oars. The Sea Urchins ran to the water, dived into the surf, and, joined by the Water Gamins, began to swim to the island. Soon they landed. The Water Gamins and Sea Urchins took their leave and splashed into the waves to return to their pubescent pleasures on the larger island.

Right away, a maiden came out of a grass hut and said, "Dr. Tupology is surfing now, but he'll soon come in, as it's time for his lunch. Look there! He's coming now."

Porch gazed out to the high waves, and sure enough, saw a figure on a surfboard skimming in on a crest. He watched as the man skittered back and forth and at last reached the shore. Dr. Tupology dropped his board and, shaking water all over, came up to greet his visitors. He was tall and skinny, brown as a nut. He had an enormous shock of white hair and a beard to match.

He smiled, introduced himself and said, "Most invigorating, to say the least. Come with me and have some lunch. I'm sure it's ready."

As they walked to the hut, Ragnor and Porch told him who they were and whom they sought. While doing so, a bevy of maidens ran up to carry the board. Several more wiped Tupology dry with heavy beach towels. In the hut, a lunch of island fruit, nuts and cakes was spread on a woven mat. Tupology sat down, legs crossed, and invited them to do the same. As they ate, more maidens with lutes, feathered gourds, and bamboo sat behind the Doctor and began to play and sing island songs. Several more came up, sat down beside him and began to message his neck and shoulders.

He looked at Porch and Ragnor, very embarrassed, and said, pointing to one at a time, "This is Tawalani. She is Kikiloa, and she is Nineemi."

Ragnor nodded and Porch said hello.

Tupology, still flushed, said, "Mathematics is highly honored here. I'm sort of a hero and much sought out on arcane things."

Porch said, "Mathematics should always be honored, and you much more if you can tell us where the man we seek has gone."

Dr. Tupology replied, "We heard of that monster's terrible deeds well before he arrived with his murderous crew and mobilized our forces. We chased him then, ocean to ocean, island to island, until in haste he left."

"Yes," Porch said, "but where did he go?"

"He must go back, has to go back, can do no other than go back from whence he came. Let me explain."

Ragnor was looking rankled.

"Bear with me," Tupology said, looking at Ragnor's dagger. "All the suns in this star cluster that anchor living planets must reside on its surface because the cluster is much denser inside. Tidal forces from meandering stars sooner or later pull all inside planets apart. The surface is like a Mobius strip. The outside becomes the inside and the inside the outside. Take any direction and you are bound to return to your starting point. So take your star cruiser, cut across the cluster and sooner or later you will intercept the demon. He could be there by now, so hurry!"

CHAPTER 12

THE GOAT WOMAN

Six months later, Porch and Ragnor orbited Midlwurld. They identified the space cruiser in Szidrian code and descended to the surface in disguise, hoping they would not be found out until they determined if Spauk had returned there. When the shuttle landed, they cleared customs without being discovered and immediately went to the tavern at the terminal, as they knew that gossip, rumors and sometimes the truth abounded there. They found a table and sat down to get their bearings, but it was not long before three rugged Vikuns came up. Ragnor's hand went to his dagger. But one said quickly, "Ragnor, we'd know you anywhere. Stay your hand. It is I, Arnvid of Arnuval, with Askard and Olafson. We come in peace. We've been posted here by Odin's Scribe for many a day, awaiting your return."

The three did not recognize Porch, so they ignored him and another continued, "Come, my friend, we must talk—privately." Ragnor looked at Porch, who nodded his head, so he rose and went with the three to a corner table where they entered into quiet but intense conversation.

In a few minutes, he returned alone to where Porch was sitting and sat back down. He looked at Porch and said quietly, "They wish for me to return to Ice World. They say the tribes have split into factions and are on the verge of civil war. Odin's Scribe has tried to resolve their disputes, but he has been unsuccessful. He is very old, and failing. He fears that the tribes will be torn apart and war will come, that the terrible events of forty years ago could happen again. He said that only I have sufficient stature among the tribes to rule. He wants me to become the Thurl, and should the Allthing vote it so, the king."

Porch replied, "You must go."

"Yes," said Ragnor. He sat there for a minute, then took the dagger, Assassin, unhooked it from his belt, and laid it on the table in its sheath. He said to Porch, "When you find him, pull Assassin across his throat as I should have done years ago."

Then he rose and left.

Porch sat alone for several hours. He would miss Ragnor, a faithful companion, but he knew he must carry on until Spauk was found and destroyed. Finally he rose to leave. As he did he felt a trembling hand on his shoulder pushing him back down into the chair. Annoyed, he turned to confront whoever it was. He did not recognize the elfin figure standing there wrapped in a heavy hooded cloak, and so drew back. Then he saw the feet; hooves. It was the Goat Woman. He grabbed her and pushed her into the chair next to his, thinking she was his best chance to find Spauk.

"Sit," he commanded menacingly, drawing Ragnor's dagger from its sheath and holding it before her.

"Sir," she said, trembling, "please don't kill me. I tried to warn you, that I did indeed. Now I've been waiting for you."

"You know where he is, so tell me now."

"Buy me a whiskey, for I have a hacking cough," the Goat Woman replied shrilly, feigning a cough.

Porch signaled the waiter and ordered such.

Again she spoke. "You see, I raised him from a pup and treated him as my own all those years. Then he left me to die in those deep woods—yes, he did, by that dismal swamp."

The whiskey was set down and a gnarled hand reached out and withdrew it into the hood. Porch heard a gurgling swallow and the hand returned the glass to the table. Again the voice came from under the hood.

"Divine mercy be yours, sire. Another."

Porch ordered again, and when the waiter brought the drink, the Goat Woman downed it quickly and pushed the glass toward Porch.

"You've had enough," he said.

The Goat Woman whined, "Give strong drink to him that is ready to perish...let him drink...and remember his misery no more; Proverbs 31:67."

"...strong drink is raging and whosoever is deceived thereby is not wise; Proverbs 20:1. Now speak your piece, I have no time for foolishness."

"Mercy, sire, I am old and slow witted...I was forced...when he came to get the gold and jewels...and flee in the sky ship he had hidden...to go with him. Me, his old nanny, forced to go to all those worlds. He beat me, fed me leavings from his table, me, his old nanny who raised him from a babe...strange ears and all."

She fell silent.

"Go on," Porch demanded, running his finger along Assassin's edge.

"Mercy, great lord...cough, cough...I am so dry. I pulled some wires and made alarms sound and gauges go awry when the ship was orbiting here. He had to land. He traded the great ship he'd paid a pretty penny for, yes, he did, for a lesser one to get one fast. They call it a shuttle. I escaped and he fled again, but I know where he went..."

"Where, where? Tell me, and you shall have a bottle."

The Goat Woman leaned over conspiratorially and whispered into Porch's ear. "They say there is a place called Sanctuary on an inner planet in this star system. What do they call it? Damn, damn, ah, yes, Megadamn. He went there. It is a hot and fetid place, so I'm told. He was always cold, you know. Hee-hee-hee."

It was enough for Porch. Megadamn, yes, Spauk could go no farther in a shuttle. He rose to leave, sheathing Assassin, then he looked down at her and asked, "What will happen to you?"

"I'll go back to Ice World, I shall indeed. You saw those Vikuns who just left. I'll go with them. I have my ways. I do, indeed; they'll never know."

Porch signaled the waiter to bring a bottle, paid him, and hurried out. He went directly to Spaceport control, where he made inquiries of Megadamn. Most knew nothing. Many doubted the planet was inhabited. At last he found one man, a flight controller, who knew of it. "Yes," the man said, "I know of Megadamn. When I was young, I signed on to take two men and a cargo there. It is a dreadful place. Don't go there. You won't come back."

"Are there ships that go there now?"

"Only one—a sun sailer, the *Argosy*—takes a year or more. Some say there is a valuable trade. The Desert People are involved."

"Yes, but recently?" Porch persisted.

"Our scopes picked up a shuttle that went not long ago, but it was not identified, nor could anyone find it in the records. There is another who knows of Megadamn. He is a cargoman called Kane. He works at Shuttle Ramp B. Perhaps he could tell you more. I'll take you there if you like."

"Let's go."

They soon found Kane, and the Controller said, "This fellow wants to know about Megadamn. You bring consignments from there for the Desert People, do you not?"

"Yes," said Kane excitedly, anticipating some new orders. "I can get exotic fruits and nuts, medicines and drugs, and rare chocolates, yes, chocolates of extraordinary powers."

"No," said Porch. "I need to know of the planet itself. Are there good landing zones?"

Kane became suspicious, "Perhaps you're going to start an import business to compete with me. Well, listen well, I have exclusive rights here at Nork."

"No, no," Porch replied, shaking his head. "I'm searching for a man who's gone there. I'm going there myself."

"Well, he's as good as dead, and you will be, too," Kane retorted. "There is only one landing zone above the clouds, Mount Ararat. I helped build it years ago. But don't go there. Megadamn is a wet inferno. Danger lurks everywhere and..."

The Controller broke in, "I tried to tell him."

Kane said, "There is madness there."

CHAPTER 13
MEGADAMN

MacTavish, the caretaker, sat on a rock in front of the hut, blowing his pipes. He was playing *Annie Laurie*. His face turned hot pink as he blew, which contrasted vividly with his blue eyes, snow-white hair, and scraggly beard. The hut was a front for the entrance to cavernous underground processing and storage areas for the goods collected and shipped. There were also living quarters for MacTavish and Schwartz, the director of operations, and a few guest suites for the infrequent visitors who came to Megadamn. The only other building above ground was the Bijou. This theater with its glittering marquee was the most important edifice on the entire mountain, for without it, there would be no trade.

Both the Bijou and the hut were located on the small landing zone shaved off the top of Mount Ararat, the only mountain whose top stayed above the clouds on all of Megadamn. As he watched the billowy clouds roll by in endless procession below the mountain top, MacTavish felt he was on an island above a vast ocean.

He cleaned the pipes, put them down and opened the music case beside him. Taking out a clarinet, he began blowing *Ode to a Loon*. Its haunting strains added to his sense of peace. He thought back to his boyhood, when he'd stowed away on the Millenarian starship and headed away from Earth forever. There he met Schwartz, also a stowaway. They had been together ever since.

Suddenly, his reverie was interrupted. He saw the streak of a starship begin orbit in the blue-black sky above. Quickly, he put down the clarinet, wiped it off and put it in the case beside the flute. Rising with the case in hand, he hurried to the hut entrance. Just before he went inside, he shouted, "Schwartz, Schwartz, hurry. He's coming, he's coming."

In a few minutes, MacTavish emerged from the hut with Schwartz following. He was wearing a bright blue shako embellished with a blazing brass eagle and fat blue plume. His forty-button full dress coat was bright red, and he had crossed his chest with white canvas belts held in place with a gleaming brass breastplate which Tin Man always kept highly polished. His kilt topped high stockings and low silver-buckled shoes. MacTavish was extremely proud of his uniform collection. Tin Man had sewn and tailored forty-button full dress coats and fashioned shakos of just about every color in the spectrum for him. He also had the plaid of every clan he ever knew. So he was prepared to greet any visitor, wearing the colors of that particular visitor's homeland. He knew the man coming in was an American and he had chosen red, white and blue. He loved the skill that Tin Man had acquired; much better than that of the ham-handed Steel Soldier.

On the other hand, Schwartz wore what he always did when he went outside; namely, his wide- brimmed black Napoleonic hat and yellow slicker which extended all the way to his feet, covering his wading boots. MacTavish had never been able to convince Schwartz that it would not rain above the clouds and therefore Schwartz would not get wet. Schwartz had not cut his hair nor beard in all the years they had been on Megadamn, and in contrast to MacTavish's white hair and beard, his was jet black. He was wall-eyed to boot. Together, they were a memorable pair.

Over his slicker, Schwartz attached a snare drum at his side, and he carried two sticks to beat it. MacTavish led him to their parade positions about fifty yards from the landing pad. They lined up with Schwartz in back, awaiting the shuttle's arrival, watching its reflected light as it left the starship and came spiraling down.

They came to attention as it settled on the pad. The shuttle left as soon as the man jumped out. MacTavish raised a baton and ordered "Forward march" and then, quickly, "Right turn—march." Deftly, he stuck the baton into his white belt, and with Schwartz tapping out the rhythm, he raised his pipes and began to blow, "YANKEE DOODLE WENT TO TOWN, A RIDING ON A PONY..."

Porch, now out of the shuttle and standing on the landing pad, was flabbergasted at what he saw. He folded his arms and watched the pair approach. They were to his left, some yards away, when they reached a refrain. MacTavish ordered another left turn, and they marched right by. As they did, MacTavish saluted, baton to his brow. When they reached their starting position, the Caretaker gave another order. They did an about-face and started around their square all over again in the opposite direction. This time they played, "OH, I WISH I WAS IN THE LAND OF COTTON/OLD TIMES THERE ARE NOT FORGOTTEN...LOOK AWAY, LOOK AWAY..."

At last, they came to his front and stopped. MacTavish bowed gravely and introduced himself as the caretaker, then turned to Schwartz and introduced him as the director of operations. Porch introduced himself, whereupon MacTavish said, concerned, "We knew you were an American, but not whether you were a Yankee or a Rebel, so we did both."

Porch said, smiling, "Really neither, but I enjoyed both tunes."

After a few seconds of thought, MacTavish said, concerned, "Oh, if you're from the West, we can do *Home on the Range.*"

He raised his pipes and Schwartz quickly moved into line behind him, but Porch said, laughing, "No, no, that's quite all right. You're greeting was magnificent as it was."

It was the first time Porch had smiled or laughed in more than three years, and his heart went out to this goofy little man in the funny uniform and his strange companion. He said, kindly but firmly, "I'm looking for a man said to have come here. I am in a great hurry to find him."

MacTavish replied, "The hurrier you go here, the slower you end up. You need guides. We must summon them."

Schwartz asked quizzically, "Do you have specie?"

MacTavish looked at his companion with great disgust, but Porch handed Schwartz a small bag of coins. MacTavish then said, "You must have the 'gift,' though."

Porch was confused for a minute, then remembered the package Kane handed him as he left Nork, saying, "This is the gift for your guides. If you don't take it to them, you'll get nowhere."

He opened the small valise he had with him and pulled out the gift. He passed it to MacTavish, who smiled happily and opened it. It looked like two rolls of twentieth century celluloid in metal cans. He read the titles, and was further elated. He said, "We don't have this one. They haven't seen it."

He showed the films to Schwartz, then he looked at Porch and said, "We'll radio them right now. They should be here tomorrow. In the meantime, we'll show you the facility and have dinner. You'll be surprised. Tin Man is an excellent chef. Then you must get a night's rest. You can do nothing more until the guides come."

They led Porch into the hut, which was not as it appeared from the outside. A staircase led down to a modern elevator. They entered and started down, descending many levels. While moving, MacTavish allowed, "The ones who built this place put the entrance in. They did not want much activity on the surface, and anyway, there wasn't much room with the landing zone up there."

They stopped and the elevator doors opened to a large, well-lit chamber. Two robots stood there to greet them. MacTavish whispered, "I will introduce you. Shake their hands. They think they are just like us, except superior since they are made of metal."

He walked to the first and said, "Porch, this is Steel Soldier."

In a deep voice, Steel Soldier intoned gravely, "How do you do?"

His hand whirred out. Porch took it warily, shook it and returned Steel Soldier's greeting.

"Porch, this is Tin Man," MacTavish repeated.

"How do you do?" Tin Man chattered, his metal jaws creasing into a smile. Porch shook Tin Man's hand.

Steel Soldier was eight feet tall, of gunmetal color. His eyes appeared to be multifaceted lenses, as did Tin Man's. Tin Man, though, was only five feet tall and the color of brass. MacTavish said, matter-of-factly, "Steel Soldier is foreman of this enterprise, and Tin Man is the bookkeeper."

"We will show you around now," Steel Soldier intoned. He clumped off and Porch followed; then came MacTavish and Schwartz. Tin Man brought up the rear.

They went first to a receiving and sorting room. Chutes from the outside loomed above huge mounds of coconut-sized cacao beans. Machine like robots sorted, processed and packed these into crates for shipment. They sped up as Steel Soldier marched by. MacTavish said proudly, "Steel Soldier runs a tight ship."

Other robots put the crates on pallets and then conveyors which carried them to exit tunnels for shipment. There was a similar operation for bazil nuts big as melons.

"We process quite a volume," MacTavish said.

"It is very lucrative," said Schwartz.

"Come," Steel Soldier commanded, lumbering off down a corridor and into another chamber which had the look of a great kitchen. Huge cauldrons of boiling liquids and hot ovens stood in long rows, and again, robots tended operations. Tin Man chirped from the rear, "Here we do sugar and spice and everything nice."

"I taught him that," Schwartz chortled, slapping his knee.

Porch saw raw herbs, roots and exotic spices being processed. Down the line, raw material changed to flower petals and seed pods, and finished goods to food flavorings, perfumes and cosmetics.

"It's wondrous," Porch said to show appreciation for the tour.

"It's very lucrative," Schwartz replied.

They went up a level to a vast laboratory where yeast fermented in large vats, and fungi, algae and bacterial cultures grew in glass containers. Liquids flowed through filters and centrifuges whirled.

"Here we do pharmaceuticals," MacTavish said proudly.

"We make drugs for heart disease, mental illness and many types of bone debilitation, as well as cures for wholps and skags. We have preventatives for lopers and heeves."

"It's very lucrative," Schwartz said. They went up another level, toured and went up again. At last they reached the topmost level. They had shown him their whole operation except for one area that Steel Soldier said was off limits because of ongoing construction. The highest level had living quarters, a counting room and a treasury, as they called it, a parlor, dining room and a kitchen to which Steel Soldier and Tin Man retreated.

MacTavish said, "I'll take you to your quarters, where you can wash for dinner. We've prepared a feast for you, our honored guest, with delicacies in transit for many years from Old Earth."

"Yes," Schwartz added, his eyes bulging. "At great expense."

"Wash up, then come sit down. Everything will be ready."

Shortly, Porch entered the dining room, where he found MacTavish and Schwartz waiting. The table was set with silver candelabras, sterling, fine crystal and china on a damask tablecloth. They sat down, and Steel Soldier entered from the kitchen carrying a silver tray laden with peanut butter and Cheese Whiz sandwiches, Spam and Vienna sausage. Tin Man followed, carrying several pitchers of grape and strawberry Kool-aid. Both MacTavish and Schwartz were positively beaming. Porch smiled. He was very hungry, as were his hosts, so they ate and drank all set before them. When they finished, MacTavish wiped his mouth and proudly announced, "We have hot cocoa and Oreos for desert." This treat was duly brought and consumed.

Supper over, MacTavish said they should retire, and

he escorted Porch to his room. Porch fell asleep promptly and slept like a log, certain that he was on Spauk's trail.

During the night, anger, hatred and thirst for vengeance left him. He felt only duty driving him on, the duty to destroy a monster. Steel Soldier woke him late the next morning with breakfast. He ate, shaved, showered and dressed, then left his quarters to find his hosts. They were outside sitting in the dust, playing jacks and arguing heatedly. They ignored him.

"You were on threes'es," MacTavish accused.

"Was not, fours'es," Schwartz pouted.

"Were to."

"Was not."

Schwartz grabbed the jacks and put them in a slicker pocket. They both looked up, and MacTavish asked, "You want to play?"

"No," Porch replied, then asked, "Have the guides come?"

MacTavish rose and asked, "Would you rather play hopscotch? We have the squares laid out over on the landing pad." Before Porch could answer, he reached up, grabbed Porch's shirt and pulled him down so he could whisper in his ear. He said, conspiratorially, "Schwartz is easy to beat because he always wears those damn wading boots and steps on the lines."

Porch smiled and said, "I must get on with my search. Have the guides arrived yet?"

"Yes. The Prongs are in the theater. Look for yourself."

He looked and saw the marquee lights blinking brightly and asked, "What are they doing? When will they be out?"

MacTavish became agitated, "What are they doing? It's obvious. They're watching your gift, the movie you brought."

Schwartz looked at the yellow-gloved hands on his watch and said, "Mickey says they'll be finished with the third showing in a jiffy. They never watch a movie more than three times through."

MacTavish continued, "It's their pay for the cacao beans and bazil nuts, the herbs and spices. They won't work for anything but jungle movies from Old Earth. We've shown *Mowgli* and *Jungle Jim*. The females like *Sheena* a lot, but they all like *Tarzan* the best."

"Now, where is it you want to go?" MacTavish asked.

Porch replied, "I search for a man called Spauk who may have come here six months ago. He has a long nose and long pointed ears. He waddles when he walks."

"I saw him," Schwartz cried out, "he would not stay, but gave the Prongs three jungle films—a terrible way to spoil the natives."

"You never told me," MacTavish interrupted, horrified, "and you know that's against the rules."

"I couldn't stop him. He took up a stick to beat me when I tried. Fierce-looking men were with him. They left on the ship that brought him as soon as he went down in the clouds with the Prongs."

"You should've told me," MacTavish said sullenly.

"I didn't, 'cause I knew you'd be mad and withhold my promotion to assistant caretaker," Schwartz said sadly.

"Where is the place called Sanctuary?" Porch went on.

"Maybe nowhere—a myth, started by those who built this place to lure away the bad ones who come to steal the trade. Those who go never come back. They have to go through Satan's Garden."

"I must follow and find that man. He is a demon."

Looking terrified, the two got in line, and MacTavish said, "a one, a two, a three..." Then, moving like a pair of high school cheerleaders, they began to wave their arms in a rhythm. "MEGASAURUS—BRONTOSAURUS, TYRANNOSAURUS REX. RUN PELL MELL—FROM THE WET GREEN HELL, MEGADAMN'S A HEX. THUNDER LIZARD—FIRE DRAGON, MOUTHS A-SLASHING, TAILS A-THRASHING, DON'T BE BRAVE FOR A JUNGLE GRAVE, MEGADAMN'S A HEX."

They began again, "STEGASAURUS—HADRASAURUS, TYRANNOSAURUS REX..."

"Stop, stop," Porch cried out. "I cannot rest until I find him."

"Very well," MacTavish said resignedly. "Come into

the hut and we'll fix you up." Porch followed him to MacTavish's medicine chest, and the old man reached in and pulled out what looked like a jar of petroleum jelly and a respirator.

He said, "This is penicillium salve. Cover yourself head to foot and keep it on no matter how bad it gets to smelling. It will ward off the fungi and rot. Here, too, is a respirator. Wear it only when you get to the Field of Dreams, which some call Limbo and we call Satan's Garden. Should you not, your mind will fog with strange hallucinations. Then you'll be trapped and surely die."

"How 'bout a spare?" Porch suggested.

"Only one to a customer. We'll never see that one again," Schwartz broke in, his wall eye bulging.

Next, MacTavish took him to a closet and pulled out a green body suit. "Wear this, too, unless you don't mind toothy snails and blood-sucking leaches. Get dressed now. I'm sure the Prongs are waiting."

MacTavish went out. Porch bared himself, smeared on the pungent penicillium jelly, put on the body suit, and stuck the respirator in a pocket. Then he added his own war belt with laser pistols, sword and the dagger, Assassin. High boots impervious to slime came last, and he was ready to go. He stepped out of the hut where MacTavish and Schwartz were waiting.

"What about provisions?" Porch asked.

"Eat as the natives do, or they will feel insulted."

"Hark," said Schwartz, "I hear them coming now from the Bijou."

Hundreds of Prongs streamed out of the theater. They were pygmies, the tallest barely four feet. They were talking about the show.

"Shush," Schwartz cautioned, crossing his lips with a finger, "their leader is coming with several men. We cannot let them think we've been talking about them— they are very sensitive."

Several pygmies came up. They were wearing loin-cloths. Each carried a long blow gun, a quiver of darts, a knife at his side, and a small rolled pack on his back. The leader smiled.

"This is Um'gaawa," MacTavish said to Porch. Porch

took the pygmy's extended hand, and Um'gaawa shook Porch's fiercely and said, "Me glad meetchu, Papa."

MacTavish explained Porch's mission and where he wanted to go. He mentioned that Porch brought the gift Um'gaawa's people just saw.

Um'gaawa looked at Porch, laughed and clapped his hands, "You bringum good movie show, Papa. We take you. No sweat."

He turned to MacTavish and Schwartz and said, "Good-bye, Papa, we go now." Then he turned to Porch and said, "Come."

CHAPTER 14
LIMBO

Um'gaawa led Porch to a path at the edge of the escarpment. Porch noticed that Um'gaawa's entire tribe followed, fanning out to dozens of other paths leading down the mountain. Um'gaawa began to descend. The path appeared well traveled, with many switchbacks. The dirt and sand was soft beneath their feet. Very quickly, they reached the top of the clouds which enveloped them in a wet haze. That and the lush undergrowth which became thicker as they went down prevented them from seeing the other members of the tribe, and the pygmies were absolutely silent. Strangely, though, Porch felt their presence.

The air was acrid and heavy. He could smell traces of hydrogen sulfide, and there was sufficient nitrous oxide to make him feel giddy. Um'gaawa appeared unaffected, and MacTavish told him not to use the respirator until they reached the River Styx, and after that never to be without it. He wondered if he could hold out in this stuff. Soon they descended below the clouds and the fog dissipated.

The air cleared except for its wetness. It got hotter. The descent became less steep, and the vegetation more dense. The path was clear, though they were hemmed in on both sides by tree ferns and thick vines. They passed mineral chimneys and smoking fumeroles, built up over eons. They crossed flows of sulfides and iron compounds, some still warm. The incline gradually leveled to jungle floor. Above them a triple-tiered canopy grew to amazing height, preventing any sunshine from reaching the ground even during breaks in the cloud cover. Yet it was brighter than Porch had expected.

Flowers were abundant, and Porch caught glimpses of brilliantly colored birds flitting through the trees. Small mammals froze to look at the intruders before scampering away.

Um'gaawa called out creature's names when he saw them, and Porch noted their similarity to Earth animals; there were long-tailed raccoon-like cats, armadillos, rat-like creatures, and in the trees, lemurs, kinkajous and monkeys of endless variety. As they ambled along, Um'gaawa pulled leaves from a shiny bush and stuffed them into his mouth, chewing vigorously and every so often spitting them out. He handed Porch some, and Porch imitated him. The leaves were mildly narcotic. They eased his weariness, and he felt stronger.

They came to a clearing where all trees had been toppled and stripped of bark and leaves. A city of high mounds appeared directly in front of them. Porch continued on the path that led right through, but Um'gaawa grabbed him by the wrist and said, "No go, Papa."

He led him to a narrow path skirting the area, and as they passed one of the mounds on the edge, he pointed and said, "Lookie."

Porch looked over and saw an army of ants, each as big as his thumb, locked in deadly combat with an opposing army of termites the size of his big toe. As they trudged on, Um'gaawa got excited and pointed out cacao and bazil nut trees.

"Lookie, lookie, Papa," he shouted. He began to point to other plants, stopping and asking Porch to smell or taste them. They were reminiscent of the odors and flavors of the laboratories inside the mountain they had left behind.

Night was falling. At last Um'gaawa said, "We stoppee here."

They stopped, and the pygmy led Porch into the dense underbrush. He pulled several darts from his quiver, loaded his blow gun, aimed it at what Porch couldn't see, and blew a mighty blast. A monkey fell from an overhead branch. Um'gaawa did this a few more times and collected several birds and a rat-like mammal. He skinned and gutted them deftly, cut them up and put them on a spit along with some herbs, roots and mushrooms he'd gathered close by.

So intrigued was Porch with the little man's prowess that he was hardly aware of other pygmies coming together from all over. Soon a hundred or more gathered at what was to be their camp for the night. Each carried a game bird or animal. These too were cleaned and put on spits or with some water, and what were presumably vegetables were put into skin pots and boiled. The pygmies then pulled gourds from certain nearby vines. These proved full of oil which they poured over the branches and twigs they gathered. Then with the age-old method of metal against flint, they ignited the oil. Small fires began to appear all around.

"Me do easy, Papa," Um'gaawa said as he knelt down and lit his brush and twigs with a lighter, a prize possession probably obtained from Schwartz or MacTavish. He began to turn the spits he'd placed over the fire. Shortly, he took one off and handed it to Porch.

"Sheeshkebob," he said, his eyes dancing at the Old Earth word he'd learned. He motioned Porch to eat by pointing to his mouth and belly. Porch, hungry, went off a few yards and sat down to eat.

Um'gaawa shrieked and pulled him up and away, then, pointing to where Porch had sat, pulled a piece of meat off another spit and tossed it there. Tendrils from an adjacent fern-like plant moved to the meat and lifted it high to a pair of trap-like serrated leaves. These closed upon it.

Porch found another place to sit. It was beneath a tall tree and seemed mossy and clear of similar tendrils. Again, Um'gaawa pulled him away, then pointed up. Branches were dripping a fluid. Um'gaawa skewered an uncooked bird and held it under the dripping. Steam rose from its feathers where the drips hit, and Porch recognized strong, burning acid. Um'gaawa led him to a hollow in another tree and said, "This place OK, Papa."

He pushed him down, sat beside him and began eating his "sheeshkebob."

When they'd finished eating all Um'gaawa had prepared, the pygmy picked up the residue and took it to the fire. "No bringee ants, Papa," he said. He poured the remainder of the oil on the fire. It blazed up, and they both watched until it died. Then Um'gaawa said, "We sleepee now, Papa."

He lay down beside Porch and immediately fell off to sleep. All around the camp, the rest of the pygmies slept. Porch shrugged and soon followed them to sleep.

The next day and the one following were much like the first. They trudged along, stopped at night, built fires, killed and ate their roasted game, supplanted by roots and herbs, slept and were off again at dawn. Late the afternoon of the fourth day, they came to a swamp covered with bilious green algae. Um'gaawa plunged ahead and Porch followed. At times the water was waist deep to Porch and up to Um'gaawa's shoulders. They finally cleared the muck as night fell. Porch's boots and body suit protected him, but fat brown leeches covered Um'gaawa head to toe.

Reaching high ground, Porch looked around and, as the other Prongs came into view, he saw the creatures covered them as well. The Prongs settled down and spent an hour pulling these off each other, laughing and buzzing. They collected them, put them in the leather buckets they carried and boiled them into a broth which they consumed with gusto. Porch skipped supper that night.

The next day, they ascended some small hills and came to an escarpment edging a vast rift. It went north and south so far it seemed to split the planet itself. The clouds above also parted to let the hot sun through and reveal active volcanoes as far as they could see. They erupted so fiercely, Porch felt the planet was at war with itself. Thousands of feet below, Porch saw a river rushing along, picking its way past spewing geysers and fuming lava pools. But around these and up to the river, the land was quiet, and wide fields of high grass and clumps of fern trees persisted.

Um'gaawa began the descent and Porch followed. The way was easy, and several hours later they reached the bottom. Um'gaawa whispered to Porch, "Mokelembembe, Mokelembembe soon."

He whistled and began advancing through the grass. Porch imagined that he had called his tribe forward. Um'gaawa could not be seen above or through the grass, so Porch followed by watching the grass stir. They advanced for several hours. Every few minutes, Um'gaawa stopped, pulled down a head of grain and stuffed it into his mouth. Porch did likewise and relieved the hunger he felt from skipping supper the night before. They came to a fast-running stream where Um'gaawa stopped and indicated they should rest. The water was refreshing, though quite warm. At least it was clear of the green scum that floated in all the other water they'd had to drink since they'd left the mountain.

Suddenly, Um'gaawa stiffened. He put his head to the ground and began listening. A moment later, Porch picked it up, first a low rumbling, then the ground seemed to shake. Um'gaawa rose cautiously and motioned Porch up. Porch looked behind them and saw not fifty feet away the largest animal he'd ever seen lurching toward them. Its neck must have been eighty feet long, its massive body another fifty, and its tail as long as its neck. It was grazing as it moved, picking up huge swaths of grass. It was like the ancient megalosaurus that had roamed Earth millions of years before.

Amazed, Porch watched it intently, and a strong shove from behind bowled him over. Rolling after he hit the ground, he looked up to see another of the huge beasts. Its head, though small for the size of its body, was larger than he was, and it looked down at him dumbly. It sniffed him, then pulled away, ignoring his existence. Porch could not do the same, for if he had, the beast would have trampled him as it continued along its path right over where he'd been. He rolled aside desperately, then jumped up, moved farther away and bumped into Um'gaawa, who was laughing so hard tears filled his eyes.

After the dinosaur had ambled on, Um'gaawa whistled, indicating all should continue. Throughout the day, the Prongs met other huge beasts, but none so close as the first. Some animals had great upright plates on their backs, others spikes along their sides and tails, and still others horns or hoods on their heads.

They advanced far enough that day for Um'gaawa to call an early halt at a large clump of tree ferns. Soon the entire tribe gathered and began preparing their evening fare. The pygmies were more lighthearted than usual, glad to be out of jungle and swamp.

Suddenly, loud thrashing jolted the grove. Porch looked toward the source of the noise and saw tree ferns crashing down. Pygmies were running in every direction, yelling, "Mokelembembe, Mokelembembe."

A huge head appeared. Its tiny eyes darted all around looking for prey. As it crashed into full view, Porch saw tiny front claws that looked silly compared to its huge head and body, yet capable of grasping prey to shove into a great mouth full of long dagger-like teeth. Its neck was short compared to the other dinosaurs he'd seen. It stood over thirty feet, balancing on massive hind legs.

Porch stood his ground, thinking to kill the beast with his laser pistols, for with its speed and power it would no doubt catch, kill and eat many Prongs no matter how far they ran. The beast saw him and rushed over with gaping jaws and a hideous roar.

As the tyrannosaurus bent to snap him up, mouth wide open, Porch, set both laser pistols at full power, aimed them into its open jaws and fired. The terrible lizard came crashing down. It thrashed about and then, with a final twitch of its tail, died. Porch approached the beast to examine it, and several pygmies came up to examine Porch's wonderful weapons, which they had never seen before. But Um'gaawa began screaming in the Prong tongue to get away fast. Simultaneously, he grabbed Porch's arm to pull him away.

None too soon, for as they ran back, a giant pterodactyl landed. It folded its leathery wings, circled the fallen beast, leaped up on it, and with its long beak-like mouth full of sharp teeth, began tearing huge chunks from it. Many others quickly joined the first. All began ripping up flesh in a feeding frenzy.

Um'gaawa called the tribe to move on and find a new campsite before it was fully dark. They found a site and went about the business of preparing the evening meal as though nothing had occurred. Then they settled for the night.

Dawn came, but contrary to previous mornings, the Prongs were pensive and seemed fearful. By noon they had reached a wide, still, dirty brown river which had splotches of a cinnabar-colored algae from one bank to the other. Um'gaawa led Porch to the bank and quietly said, "No go, Papa, no go."

Porch looked around. Rather than staying dispersed as they had during the entire march, the whole tribe had gathered at the river bank behind Um'gaawa. Their eyes were wide and fearful, and they began to chant sadly and softly, "No go, Papa, no go."

Porch shook his head and said, "I must cross, I must."

Um'gaawa shrugged and motioned Porch to follow him, pointing to a half-submerged log a few yards away. He motioned Porch to stand on it, and he pulled a long pole from some nearby reeds. He got on the log behind Porch and pushed off. The log left the bank slowly and, with the lack of current, headed straight across. The Prongs on the bank behind them began to whimper and quietly sob.

Stiffly, Um'gaawa poled the log across the silent waters, a task made difficult because masses of the red algae stuck to the pole before slithering off. It grew hotter as they approached the far bank. At last the log bumped the bank with a soft thud. Porch hopped off and looked back at Um'gaawa. Again, Um'gaawa pleaded, "No go, Papa, no go." He too was crying.

Porch replied softly, "I must."

Um'gaawa said, "Good-bye, Papa," then turned and poled back to the other bank where his tribe waited.

Porch waited until Um'gaawa crossed, then waved silently as the Prongs disappeared into the jungle. He climbed the bank and stopped to look around. He stood at the edge of a jungle such as he'd never seen nor could perceive in the most horrible nightmare. An acrid mist rose all around. Then he remembered MacTavish saying, "Put on the respirator after you've crossed the river Styx."

He put it on. Swarms of mosquitoes, flies and gnats swarmed everywhere. Strange, batlike creatures and huge dragonflies flew about, feeding on them. The detritus of insects covered the jungle floor. Great pitcher plants, voodoo lilies and skunk cabbage that would shame those on Earth lined the path. Some simply smelt like rotting meat, attracting hordes of carrion beetles which the plants then consumed. Others captured prey with hot, fetid blasts of air. Still others sat like barrels, filled with digestive acids and emitting putrid smells to attract the insects. Victims buzzing in their death throes rent the air.

Porch looked up as he began to move away from the river and saw a maze of gnarled and crooked trees with intertwined branches further wrapped with thick vines. The leaves were black, and the supporting trunks sullen gray or ghostly white. Then he glimpsed the denizens of that dark place, and they stared back; they were troops of spider monkeys, a strange mutation different from any he had seen before. Their heads were almost hairless. Their faces, sunk and sallow with skin pulled taut, framed deep-set eyes mostly pupil, black as night. Their noses too were black and set above gumless mouths of bright white teeth. These features made them look like so many disembodied skulls set on black emaciated bodies that hardly could be seen. They chattered their annoyance of his transgression of their forest with a skeletal clatter that caused the soul to shiver, and they followed as he trudged on. The path was narrow and there was no other way, so he moved along silently till the end of the day.

At dark he remembered the small pouch of food pills he had brought from Midlwurld, and with his water purifier made these do for supper. He slept that night standing, leaning against a gnarled tree, for he dared not sit nor lie.

Morning greeted him with surroundings scarcely visible through the mist. He stretched his bones and shivered in the damp cold. Soon he knew it would be so hot his blood would nearly boil. So he began his journey, begging Providence to lead him to his quarry and his final joust with fate.

Almost imperceptibly the way led to a higher place, and a new feature appeared along his path. Huge webs were strung among the trees and every so often above the narrow trail itself. He noticed the mutant monkeys gave these wide margin. He picked up a chunk of wood and hurled it into the center of one. It did not break through, but stuck so fiercely that the mightiest blow of a long branch would not dislodge it. So he learned he must avoid these webs.

At mid-morning, still climbing, the path began to widen, and far ahead he saw a clearing. He hastened his pace, intent to reach it, for Schwartz had said he would find the man he sought in such a place, because that man would never reach the mythical city of Sanctuary. A chill not begotten of temperature embraced him. Instinctively he knew he'd reached the place called Limbo, the Field of Dreams and Satan's Garden.

Suddenly he heard a vine swish by, and before he could duck, a mutant spider monkey swung past and seized his respirator, chattering a taunting call. But its triumph didn't last, because, intent on its theft, it failed to see the web ahead and hurtled into its sticky strands. In a flick, the monkey spider lurking at its edge flashed down, seized the spider monkey, and injected it with paralyzing venom, then spun a tight cocoon around its convulsing body. As the monkey's spasms subsided, the spider injected eggs into this living larder and then retreated to its hiding place. Porch saw his respirator through the cocoon, beyond retrieval, still clutched tight in the monkey's hand.

No matter. He knew he must continue, so he tied the sweaty kerchief he carried to shield his nose and mouth from the mist and strode on, breathing as best he could. But the mist changed to a smoky powder, not moist at all, of particulate so fine he could not see it in his hand. And he trod on strange ashen-colored fungi which looked like dirty mossy snow. It seemed alive, moaning, as he crushed it down with every step of his heavy boots and it wafted more dirty dust into the air. He stumbled, feeling giddy, recovered and advanced farther into the field. He noticed whitish blobs covered with the fungi. They varied in height and seemed as if they were melted down from taller mounds. He stepped on one and heard a moan, stumbled against another and it too groaned. He went farther, felt woozy, and stopped by another nearby mound. They were becoming more abundant, and weird moans centered on each he passed. He stopped again to examine one more closely and nudged it with his foot. He saw a hole open at its center and the orifice formed the words, "Kill me, kill me quick."

He blinked, lurched back and came upon another mound, less decomposed. A pair of human eyes stared out at him from under the fungus. A pleading came from its orifice below, "Kill me. Kill me quick and end my torture. Use the pistols at your side."

Horrified, and thinking he was hallucinating, Porch asked, "I see your plight but understand not how such could happen. Are you a man?"

"I was. For years we've come, from Old Earth and other planets, too. One by one, in two's and three's, sometimes ten, all in all an army of men, seeking the riches fabled to lie beyond the jungles and swamps in a place called Zivola...or Sanctuary. Who cares what it's called? Only knaves seek Sanctuary, but here all are caught, ensnared in Satan's Garden and kept alive so this dread carpet can suck our substance—immobilized for a hundred years and more, paralyzed, with chugging hearts and pumping lungs—brains slowly drained through the ages so the fungal parasite can consume us every bit, and only then will oblivion bring peace and end our torment. Kill me, kill me now, I plead with thee. Use your sword. Plunge it into the hole you see."

Again Porch stumbled back, unsteady. He collected his wits and began to move on. He had to zigzag, for now, from everywhere, mouths on the mounds were calling, "Kill me—slay me—end my sorrow."

The din increased, then subsided as he passed. The mounds went back to labored breathing, pumping air in and out. Some had eyes as well as mouths, and then he saw an arm or two still free. Surely this was Satan's Garden. Now a darkness dimmed his eyes. He reeled back. A thousand hammers struck iron anvils in his head. Great swirls of color seized his brain. He fought to move, lurching, staggering. The ground began to undulate beneath his feet, yawing side to side. In his mind he was on a jet black ship riding the waves of a blood-red sea. Now the ground began to pitch, the ship turned bloody red, and the ocean black as night. Surely this was the Field of Dreams, unspeakable dreams, deadly dreams. He knew he was hallucinating.

Terrified, but with great force of will, he cleared his mind to stumble on. He came upon another mound. This time, he identified a face, a head, and as he surveyed the mound, a man. It was Spauk.

CHAPTER 15
RETRIBUTION

Just seeing the monster cleared his head. Spauk seemed to be sitting on a stump. Fungus covered him up to his chest. As Porch approached, Spauk spoke, "Ah, Interloper, you've come for your revenge. You've come to gloat. Perhaps you choose to kill me. Go ahead, for that would be the greatest gift that you could give me. If not, well, soon enough you'll sit beside me to hear my taunts for all eternity, though I did not mean the wench to die. Since none escape Satan's Garden, you've won nothing, never could, never will."

Porch pulled Lord No's great sword from its scabbard. He raised it slowly with both hands above his head. His muscles tensed as he gathered strength to bring down the devastating blow he'd so long hoped to strike. Suddenly, a blinding light penetrated the mist and he heard a voice, "Stay thy hand, my son."

He staggered back, wondering if he was hallucinating again. He lowered the sword and looked up, then brought a hand up to shield his eyes. He saw a figure of immense proportions arrayed in light. What was it? Who was it?—THE OLD ONE WHO MADE THE AGES—THE BIBLICAL GOD OF HIS YOUTH?

He staggered back again, sorely afraid, and wondered if he'd uttered such presumptive blasphemy against the Unknowable that it could never be forgotten nor forgiven.

"But who? Is it the Archangel Michael? It is so real."

Gathering his wits, he looked up again. The Phantasm shimmered in a blazing aureole and spoke again. "Who commissioned you to kill this man?"

Porch gasped, "Jason! Is that you, Jason? Why, it is you. From where have you come?"

"From a place called Splendor in a land called Glory. Now do not soil yourself with his blood. His fate is sealed. His doom is set. He'll never know love, and he won't feel hate, only the derisive laughter of voices up from hell— left in a place without direction to ponder his inhumanity.

"Here there is no up or down, no north and south, no east or west. There is no color, nor black and white, only a grayish sameness. For him, there is no substance. Time itself does not run. He is not now some dreaded demon, but simply a pathetic creature. So leave him to fulfill his fate."

Porch sheathed his sword and began to back away, but Spauk said, "So you won't kill me, then. I'm sorely disappointed, tee hee. I see you have Ragnor's dagger on your belt, the one they call Assassin. Long ago, above your world, Ragnor threatened to demonstrate its sharpness on my throat. Hand it to me now so while I'm able, I can complete his work."

Porch drew the dagger and dropped it at Spauk's feet. Slowly, Spauk reached down, but two inches from its hilt, his arm stopped, frozen in time and space as the fungi's fruiting bodies broke through his skin. Porch looked up again. The huge apparition had faded. The mist closed in around him till he could only see a grayness. He would go now. He would leave Satan's Garden, but he found that he could no longer move his feet.

CHAPTER 16
TIN MAN

"I was not programmed for this," Tin Man chirped.

"No matter," Steel Soldier intoned in reply. "The Director of Operations said, 'Do it,' so we must not fail. A mission is a mission. Where's your pride?" Steel Soldier continued on, crashing through the dense jungle, paying little heed to the brush and trees he ran over. Tin Man, much smaller, had great trouble keeping up. His legs were going like fury. Except for the pace that Steel Soldier set, the walking was easy because Steel Soldier leveled every hindrance they met. Tin Man was, however, backpacking the medicines, their fuel tablets and spare parts. Steel Soldier blasted through the termite city before Tin Man complained again.

"This is not in my job description," he whined.

"Shut up and march. You saw the Prongs. They waved us on. So march now, march on. Hup—tupp—three—four."

"Well, why must I carry all the supplies? Your back is broader."

"Because I am point man, security and navigator. You know the new arrival gave me the man finder and showed me how to work it, so silence. March," Steel Soldier thundered.

This was enough to keep Tin Man quiet throughout the night, but early the next morning they came to the river. Steel Soldier plunged in as though it wasn't there. Tin Man followed. When they reached the middle, the filthy water was up to Steel Soldier's waist, but Tin Man was completely submerged. They pressed on, rising out of the water when they reached the other bank. Leeches covered both. With a snap, crackle, pop they rid themselves of these with intense microwave bursts along their outer plates. Yet Tin Man was upset again.

"Look at me! Look at me! My beautiful golden shimmer changed to a dirty green patina which will soon turn black. I'll never be the same. It's just not fair," he tweeted shrilly.

"March. Hupp—tupp—three—four, left—right, left—right," Steel Soldier crackled.

"Easy for you to say—made of ultra steel."

Steel Soldier did not reply, so Tin Man continued, "Nothing but hupp—tupp—three—four, left—right, left—right. I had a good job but I left, I left, I left. I had a good job but I left."

Steel Soldier whirred his head around in a half circle, looked Tin Man directly in his photonic eyes and admonished him severely. "You've become a real smartass since you read that Old Earth stuff."

Really chastened, Tin Man shut up. Robots were never smartasses like humans. Drops of glycerin began flowing from his visuports down his metal cheeks, but thank goodness, Steel Soldier didn't see it happen. Soon they reached the escarpment above the great rift. Now even Steel Soldier became careful, because should either fall the thousands of feet to the bottom and hit the rocks below, not even their robotic durability would prevent them from becoming piles of junk. They made it safely and continued across the vast plain with only minor protest by the Mokelembembe for another interruption of their habitat.

The next morning they reached the River Styx. Steel Soldier hesitated when he heard the low moan behind him. Tin Man had not uttered a word since Steel Soldier had admonished him so severely. Now Steel Soldier felt something his feedback circuitry had never before signaled. He felt the pump under his steel breastplates thumping laboriously. Certain long dormant sensitivity algorithms directly connected to pump control had come into play. The thought came to him, *Have I treated my little friend too harshly?*

He swirled his head around and saw Tin Man ready to forge ahead, visusensors closed, with one hand holding his air intake shut and the other covering his speaker. He grabbed the smaller robot by the shoulder straps holding the supplies and lifted him high overhead. Then he turned and plunged into the river.

A good thing, too, he thought as the slime-infested waters rose to his own visusensors. Soon he had crossed, put Tin Man down, zapped the algae that enveloped him, and was on the way again. He felt better about himself after that.

Next he crashed through a dark forest of gnarled trees and great webs. Both perceived more light ahead. Steel Soldier stopped.

"Hark," he crackled, "the man finder is buzzing. Be alert. Its red warning light is flashing. We are close."

They came to a field of thick dusty matting which groaned beneath their feet as they tramped through it. They treaded amongst mounds that seemed to plead with them. Now the amber man finder light came on and both programmed their wide spectrum sensors to a 180 degree sweep. Within an hour, the man finder's green "immediate vicinity" light began flashing and it began buzzing.

Suddenly, Tin Man trumpeted with great elation, "There, there he is. I see him. Over there! Over there!"

He rushed to the spot and Steel Soldier followed. Porch stood before them unmoving, dazed, his breathing controlled by the fungi.

"Quickly," Steel Soldier thundered, "use the fungicide spray."

Tin Man already had it out and was spraying a ten-foot circle about the rigid man. The fungus turned black immediately and died. Steel Soldier was pleased with Tin Man's alacrity and seeming change in attitude, so he rasped softly, "Now we'll strip him."

He bent down, grabbed Porch's ankles, flipped him over and held him up by one ankle. Porch's boots came off in shreds except for the metal soles, which stayed in place. The fungal enzymes had just about dissolved the uppers. Tin Man pulled at Porch's body suit and it too shredded right off.

"Now the dermicidal soap and water," Steel Soldier coached, but once again Tin Man was ahead of him. He pulled the small drum of distilled water out of his backpack, turned on the spray hose, and was sponging the naked body with a soapy mixture. Steel soldier called for the syringe. Tin Man had it in hand.

"Thirty cubic centimeters in the gluteus maximus should be enough," Tin Man observed as he jammed the long needle full of penicillium into Porch's rump.

The naked body reacted violently, then went limp again. This done, Steel Soldier grabbed a towel from the backpack and dried it off. Tin Man covered it with penicillium salve. Steel Soldier took the body bag from Tin Man, flipped the body into it feet first, tied the bag loosely about the neck, and threw Porch over his shoulder.

"Mission accomplished. Let's go back," he intoned.

"I'll go first," Tin Man said happily.

The integrated circuits in his head began humming rapidly as he thought, *I found him, not Steel Soldier. Why, I'm a hero! Yes I am, not Steel Soldier. For sure, the Director of Operations will supply all the fuel tablets I need. And never again, when I miss an account number, will he set me below the clouds and turn me off, letting my plates tarnish, my joints rust, and lightning zap my circuits.*

He was so turned on he began to hum the music and patriotic marches MacTavish had taught him. He started with *The Battle Hymn of the Republic*. They reached the River Styx and he plunged right in; soon he was completely submerged. It didn't faze him. He came bubbling up on the far bank, singing *Semper Fidelis*.

Why, he thought, *Schwartz will not be so niggardly with the brass polish.* Oh, did he dare even think it? Yes, why not? He would ask for a complete new electroplating.

That thought really buoyed him up. He began to whistle *The Stars and Stripes Forever*. Even Steel Soldier, walking behind him, got into the act and began humming. When they got to the Mokelembembe, Tin Man was on Tchaikovsky's *1812 Overture*, whistling so loudly that the dinosaurs retreated to the farthest part of their range, and when Steel Soldier boomed the cannon part, even the tyrannosaurus stampeded. Then Tin Man began the most triumphant piece he'd ever heard, *The Marseillaise*.

CHAPTER 17
TUESDAY NORTH BEAR

Gradually the swirling in Porch's head diminished. He opened his eyes and the room came slowly into focus. He recognized it as the guest quarters on Mount Ararat. He was back. Memories of what had happened poured into his brain. He shuddered, then racked his brain to determine how he had gotten back. But he had no memory of that. A man sat at his bedside. At first, he didn't recognize him, then it came in a flash. It was the Priest. Incredulous, he asked, "Brother, what are you doing here?"

"I came to retrieve you. You've been quite sick, you know."

Further reality hit him, "Where is my daughter?"

The Priest evaded the question, saying, "If the spore had broached your blood-brain barrier, nothing would have saved you."

Porch asked again with growing suspicion, "Where is my daughter?"

Again, the Priest equivocated. "Fear not. She is safe."

Porch looked terrified and yelled, "Damn you. I trusted you. You took an oath. Where is Aurelia?" He looked around the room and saw his sword and pistol belt hanging in the corner. He started to rise and move toward them.

"Be not precipitous. Aurelia is safe, and I will take you to her shortly, but first I have something for you."

The Priest held out a pendant on a gold chain. Porch

took it and examined it. It was the locket—his mother's half locket, the one he'd lost long ago. He withdrew its mate from his neck and matched it. Puzzled, he decided that he could do no better than let the Priest tell his story. "Where did you get this?" he asked uneasily.

"I have safeguarded it for you for many years. I took it from the neck of a wanton creature in the Florida keys."

"Who are you?" Porch asked.

"First, about Aurelia. I sent her to Old Earth."

Porch slumped. His one vulnerability had been exploited. "Why?" he asked suspiciously. "She was with Victoria and Shareem."

"Yes, but after Spauk's agents tried to seize her, and even though the desert warriors made short work of them, Victoria was overwrought with fear. I persuaded her to let me send the child to Old Earth, where she would be absolutely safe. Victoria consented. I sent her by way of the new transporter at Nork with several bodyguards who came back and attested to her safety."

"Where did you send her on Earth?"

"To the Corporation."

"To the Corporation! My God! How could you do that to me?"

"It is time to end my masquerade."

The Priest took off his cap, opened the top buttons of his cassock, removed his clerical collar, and reached below his undershirt to pull off a layer of living skin. Then he removed the silicone implants that gave him the fat cheeks of a jolly friar. Beneath was another face, tan and gaunt, set off by piercing black eyes and an aquiline nose. Porch recognized the bear claw birthmark.

The Priest said in a different voice, "I am Inspector Tuesday North Bear. I have been tracking you for more than fourteen years. Only now is it appropriate to reveal myself and perform the duty I have sworn to carry out. I hereby arrest you in the name of the Corporation, and with the authority vested in me by the Space Academy and the Grand Fleet of the Western Alliance."

"In face of such treachery, how do I know you have Aurelia and that she is unharmed?"

"You don't and won't until she is returned to your arms. I must hold her as a ransom to your peaceful return."

"Very well," Porch sighed. "I've lived enough for ten, and I will return without resistance. I promise that."

"We leave immediately and you shall see the child soon enough, but know there will be a quarantine when we get there until we know the fungal spore is dead. It would devastate the Earth if carried there."

"Good enough. Now let me dress–I'm only in this nightshirt."

"That's suitable enough, for I have sent your belongings ahead. You may don your sword and pistols since I have your oath."

The Priest opened the door while Porch donned his belt. Steel Soldier was outside the door, waiting.

"Lead the way," Tuesday said to the robot, who then turned and clopped down the hall. He led them down several levels to the area which Porch remembered as designated off limits. Steel Soldier opened the door, and Porch saw the double bubble enclosure. He knew immediately that it was a transporter, most likely bootstrapped to Megadamn from Earth. Tuesday bade him enter and followed. Once inside, the Inspector said, "I've set the coordinates." He signaled Steel Soldier, who was already in the control booth. Porch saw the robot pull the lever. Then came the flash and bang he would well remember, for in Earth years, it was his thirty-second birthday.

CHAPTER 18
REUNION

Porch felt he could eat nails. It was the eighty-ninth day of his quarantine. He had not seen Tuesday since they materialized on Earth, presumably at the Corporation. He assumed the Inspector too had been isolated. He well agreed with the quarantine. Just the thought that he might still harbor the deadly fungus and contaminate Earth or infect Aurelia left him in a cold sweat.

When they emerged, armed guards fully protected in contamination gear whisked him away and put him in an isolation chamber which looked like a space station or, for that matter, an ancient naval decompression chamber. The chamber had a double lock entrance, only one viewport, and looked brand new. Perhaps it had been brought in hurriedly. It had three rooms and a large bath. It was completely self-contained, with its own air recycling and filtration system and lacked for nothing in the way of comfort. One room was a medical examining station, and he was examined every day by a doctor or med-technician. The air filters too were replaced daily, which he thought part of the inspection procedures.

Late on the eighty-ninth day of his quarantine, the double lock opened and a man in street clothes entered. Porch recognized him immediately, though he appeared much older. It was the Lawyer, and he said, "It is good to see you again after so many years. Your quarantine is over and the Chairman will see you at nine o'clock tomorrow morning."

Porch acknowledged the Lawyer's statement with a nod, but did not speak. The Lawyer took this as an affront, so he spoke again, "I am still your advocate, and I assure you the circumstance of tomorrow's meeting will differ from your first appointment. My men will bring the things of yours we transported from the Vundercy system in right away. We have inventoried, repaired and cleaned, or polished and shined your apparel. I'll say good night now and escort you tomorrow."

Porch had a restless night. Tomorrow he would see his daughter. Tomorrow would bring the final showdown with the Corporation. As he slept fitfully, he decided he would not go as a supplicant but as a man of substance with dignity and pride intact. If he could not raise his daughter himself, at least they must assure him that she would be returned to her people on Midlwurld.

When morning came, he dressed in his black uniform as a captain general of the Order of No. He put on his many decorations and his sword belt. He was ready when the Lawyer entered. He did not know if the Lawyer had been briefed about his exploits during his long odyssey, but on the trip to the palazzo, he noted a deference in the man's demeanor. Apparently, he had chosen his costume well.

As the brougham glided along the road, memories flashed back as he saw the tall wrought iron fence, the main gate with the red griffins on its pillars, and the Lombardy poplars which still graced the broad avenue leading to the palazzo. They passed the biofarms. He saw the diminutive deer grazing on the designer grass. They passed the swamp where he evaded his captors long ago. He saw the mammoths, the aurochs and the ibex. The magnificent palazzo came into view, and as they crossed the guard bridge, he imagined he saw a flash of tawny orange in the pampas grass, but it could have been an illusion. They rounded the great circular drive with the beautiful pink marble fountain.

The brougham stopped at the grand staircase, and before he knew it, they were up the wide staircase, past the massive bronze and glass doors, and into the huge lobby. Everything seemed the same. The grand chandelier, the Founder's portrait, and his successors' portraits were there. That of beautiful Francesca hung on the far wall. She was so striking; he remembered it well. But it had been moved from the anteroom above.

"Please, let's go up. Its almost time," the Lawyer said. He led Porch up the grand staircase and into the Chairman's anteroom. This had changed. Paintings by French impressionists and twenty-first century Modernists and paneling of butternut replaced the dark mahogany paneling and Renaissance masterpieces. Lighter floral carpet on creamy tile replaced the thick pile rugs on the dark oak floor. Flowering plants flourished under new skylights, replacing Greek and Roman statuary. The heavy leather sofas and chairs were gone, making way for lighter furniture upholstered in rich silk brocades. Even the background music was different. Mozart's violin concertos replaced Verdi's operas. This puzzled Porch, but only for a moment, as the Lawyer bade him follow him into the Chairman's inner sanctum. He entered. Again, change. A new light ambiance replaced the imperial aura. But two things had not changed. There was the immense mahogany desk and behind it, turned to the French windows, the huge high-backed leather chair.

"He is here," the Lawyer said to the chair. Porch stopped before the desk and waited. As the chair turned, Porch was stunned—for sitting in it was Bonnie, Bonnie Brightwood, or rather Bonnie Brightwood...Petersen. She looked at him joyfully for a few seconds, then smiled and said, "Ah, my sweet errant Grub has returned, now an heroic knight, a mighty eagle. You look resplendent."

Porch asked evenly, "Where is my daughter?"

Bonnie turned to her right and called out softly, "Aurelia, your daddy is here." Slowly, a side door to Porch's left opened and a little golden-haired girl shyly entered and looked around, then fixed her eyes on him. She wore a blue silk dress and was carrying a Barbie doll. Porch thought his heart would stop; she was no longer a baby.

She was a miniature Aurora. He dropped to one knee

as she timidly approached, and when she got up to him, she looked at him carefully and asked, "Are you my daddy?"

Great wet tears flowed from Porch's eyes as he replied, "Yes, my darling. Yes, my darling little princess."

Aurelia came up to his face and peered into it. She saw what seemed to be great distress, so patted his cheek and said, "Don't cry, Daddy. I'll take care of you."

Then she dropped her doll, put her little arms around his neck and hugged him. He held her tight for a long time, kissing her, saying softly, over and over again, "My darling, oh, my darling little Aurelia." At last, he released her and held her out so he could look at her again. In a few seconds, she broke free and bent over to pick up her doll. She held it out to him and said, "See my dolly. Aunt Bonnie gave her to me. I love Aunt Bonnie."

Groping for words, Porch asked, "What is her name? She is a nice dolly."

Aurelia replied, "Her name is Bonnie, too. She is in the Space Service. See her yun...uniform." Suddenly she looked over her shoulder. A young boy had entered the room. She shouted with glee, "Neils, Neils, will you play with me?" She hesitated and looked back at Porch. Then she went over, took the lad's hand, brought him over to Porch and said solemnly, "Neils, this is my daddy. You have a mommy and I have a daddy."

She looked at Bonnie and asked, "May I go play with Neils?"

Bonnie looked at Porch and hesitated, then said, "Yes, my darling. I need to talk with your father."

Neils bowed and shook Porch's hand gravely. Then Aurelia hugged him again, gave him a peck, and turned toward Neils, who took her hand and led her from the room. Porch rose, took a cloth and wiped his eyes.

Bonnie spoke carefully, "You have been exonerated. After thorough investigation by both the Space Academy and the Corporation, all charges have been dropped. The Space Academy has issued an honorable discharge in your name, declaring your going AWOL was due to circumstances beyond your control." Then she paused and looked over at the Lawyer and said, "I wish to speak to this man alone."

He left immediately. After he was gone, she looked back at Porch and said, "Come and sit on the sofa with me."

Once seated, she looked at Porch and said, "You look well... I have a full report from Inspector Tuesday... It tells of all that you have done...and all that you have suffered. I am so sorry." Carefully, she awaited his response.

After a moment, he looked at her and said, "Thank you...and Bonnie... May I call you Bonnie?"

"Of course." She smiled.

"I am grateful to you for returning Aurelia to me...for caring for her and for all you have done to clear my name and secure my pardon."

"Belisarius is dead...now for several years. In many ways, he was a great man. He had his faults, terrible faults. He went to any length to protect his family...the family he never had, until he married Francesca. His family was Francesca, the Corporation and Werewick...in that order. As he had no heirs, the Corporation Board of Directors elected me to the Chair...so I've tried to put a human face on the megalith. I reopened your case. Many came forward to testify, no longer fearful. It was a terrible smirch on the Academy."

They talked on for an hour, carefully, feeling each other out. At last, Bonnie looked at her watch and said, "The morning is gone. Come, we'll have lunch with the children. Then we'll talk some more, perhaps in the garden."

"Oh," Porch said as he got up, "where is Admiral Petersen? I served with him, though he may not know it."

Bonnie replied sadly, "Admiral Petersen is dead. I have been a widow for ten years."

CHAPTER 19

THE GARDEN

After lunch, Bonnie led Porch to the garden. As they strolled, she said, "This is a beautiful place."

"Yes," Porch replied. "Years ago, after I was captured and tried, this was my refuge. They allowed me an hour a day to exercise. It was from here that I escaped."

He thought of another garden in another place. Bonnie almost read his thoughts, saying, "Aurelia is a beautiful child, compassionate and gentle. Her mother would be proud."

Porch replied, "She is a miniature Aurora to me."

They strolled on silently when Bonnie said, "Take my arm... I was devastated when the Admiral died. He never knew he had a son. After the child was born, I could hardly bear to look at him. But now he grows into the image of his gallant father...and I know how much I'm blessed. I love him for the son he is, for the golden memory he wakes in me with each smile, each move he makes."

There was silence again, then, deep in thought, Bonnie continued, "Sven was killed in a test of the super transporter. The Corporation bought the original model from the Israelis, from the inventor, one Absalom, a strange old man... They thought him tetched...that they could do better, upgrade it...and kept him away. All went well in four tests. My husband and four of his men were scheduled for the fifth...to be sent to an asteroid used for the Mars Project. There was an error in one of the tenth order tensors. They say the wormhole bounced off... Absalom was brought in. After examining everything, he said they bounced into another universe... But there was a great burn on the asteroid. I think Absalom tried to soften my loss and give me hope, but I know my husband died."

Again, silence. Porch could not find words to express his sorrow.

"Poor Absalom," Bonnie mused, "he took the accident so hard, believing it somehow his fault, but the Corporation engineers had pushed him aside...Yet he found the error and fixed the machine."

They continued to walk, a bond developing between them. At the end of the path, they turned back. But then Porch stopped and looked at the ground on the side of the path. He imagined that he saw a burn smudge.

"What is it?" Bonnie asked.

"There was an old man who made a diversion for me by burning down a garden shack as I escaped. He had been at the Academy. His name was Gideon. He was a sweet old man. I suppose they killed him after they found out he helped me."

Bonnie smiled, "No, he wasn't even implicated. Nobody dared touch him. Come with me. I have something to show you."

She led Porch to a well-kept but secluded side path. They came to its end near the great old apple tree. Before them, side by side, lay three highly polished oblong granite gravestones. Black roses surrounded the left stone which bore the inscription—

BELISARIUS XAVIER BELISARIUS

15 SEPTEMBER 2180—15 MARCH 2269

The second stone, decorated with white roses, was inscribed—

FRANCESCA MARIA BELISARIUS

22 FEBRUARY 2204—16 APRIL 2240

and the far stone, adorned with red roses, bore the inscription—

GIDEON ZACHARIAH BELISARIUS

2 SEPTEMBER 2176—15 MARCH 2264

Porch brightened when Bonnie said, "Gideon was Belisarius' older brother."

They started back and Bonnie continued, "I am resigning from the Corporation. My work is about finished. Belisarius built the company into an international megagiant, but in his final years he became an old man trapped in old ideas. When I took over, I saw the Corporation too had grown old...inflexible, evil. The directors see this now, so we are splitting the colossus up, going public, transferring units to stockholders and employees. When this is finished, Neils and I will leave, so stay awhile with Aurelia...to get reacquainted. Do you know what you want to do or where you will go?"

Porch hesitated, then said, "I have given it no thought, none at all. I just want her with me. I can show her Old Earth, as the emigrants call it...the places I've been. Someday we should return to Midlwurld, but I couldn't bring myself to do that right now."

They came to the end of their walk, and the day came to its end. In the days that followed, they saw each other occasionally. Bonnie was busy completing corporate restructuring. Porch spent most days with Aurelia—days of delight. Her laughter had a healing power. When he and Bonnie were together, they bantered about the present, avoiding the painful past. Soon each found the other in the garden more often. Yet both held their thoughts about the future close.

About a month after they first had talked, Bonnie told Porch she had a surprise for him, a formal dinner in his honor that evening. At her insistence, he accepted. She told him the guest list would be limited and, of course, he was to bring Aurelia.

CHAPTER 20

STAR MAN

Porch entered the dining room promptly at eight, with Aurelia in tow. She was very excited about the party. He became excited, too, as the first person he saw was Bo Bokasi. Bokasi wore the three stripes of a full commander in the Space Service and had Olivia O. Olive on his arm. He grinned broadly when he saw Porch and walked rapidly over to greet him. His peg leg did not inhibit him, but rather served to enhance his formidable or, as some would say, fierce appearance. He had not adopted modern prosthetics, but retained the highly ornate oaken peg the ERTS had carved for the mighty BOKS. The giant grabbed Porch in a mighty bear hug and did not let go until Olivia began pounding him on the back and saying loudly, "Bertram, that's just enough. Where is your decorum?."

Porch gave Olivia, now Mrs. Bertram Beauregard Bokasi and fully in charge of Bo, a gentle hug and a kiss. Then he lifted Aurelia up to greet them both. Aurelia gave them a friendly smile. Porch noticed a touch of regal aplomb in her greeting, felt both pride and sorrow, and wondered if such had been bred into her. The little Princess had never asked of Aurora, nor had he dared broach the subject.

Their reunion was interrupted by Miriam, with Absalom trailing.

"Portch, Gottenyu! Bubelah! Bubelah," she yelled as she too crushed him in a hug, followed by a plethora of kisses and tears. Then she spotted Aurelia and swept her up, totally distracted in enchantment, princess or not, shouting, "The little darling, Chotchke, Bubee, my sweetheart kinderlach."

"Aurelia did not protest, which gave Porch a chance to greet Absalom. The old man appeared full of anguish, but he recognized Porch, which seemed to give him confidence, so he stammered, "The fault was in the tensor setting...I was not there to stop them...I found it when they let me look.

Another universe... They are endless... He was cast into another universe, he and his four men...they are endless...don't you know...expanding to grow old and die, then contracting to find renewal...a bubbling froth...from forever to forever, don't you know? But I fixed it and I tested it... and I fixed them, too."

Porch gave the old man a hug and patted him on the shoulder. Then Absalom continued, "The wolf came down from the north...seeking, looking, always looking...guards feared he would kill the Chairman's game...so said kill him. The Chairman said no...Trap him and put him to stud...but the wolf was canny...would die if not be free. I found him first... He followed...seemed to know...led him to the bubble and put a sensor probe with a release around his neck... He seemed to know...sent him to the Cold World...released the sensor...brought it back. Then I knew I'd fixed it and fooled them, and the Great White Wolf was free...don't you see?"

Porch was dumbstruck for a minute, then once more he grasped the old man's shoulder and said, "Yes, I see. I see now more than I thought I'd ever see, and am forever in your debt."

At last, Absalom smiled and seemed relaxed. Porch felt a tap on his own shoulder, a laugh, and heard the words, "Joe, Joe Smith, It's good to see you again. We thought you were lost at sea."

Porch turned and with a broad smile greeted Captain, now Colonel, Ironwood. They shook hands vigorously, and Porch said, "It's so good to see you again, sir."

Ironwood replied, "It's John, John Ironwood, please, and this is my wife, Cecilia."

Cecilia was a pretty little redhead. Porch took her hand and bowed. A waiter came up with drinks. Ironwood took two, and handed one to Porch. Then he raised his glass and said, "To the Flotilla and the valiant Admiral who led her."

Porch raised his own glass and replied, "Aye."

Then he asked, "Wasniak and Carruthers?"

Ironwood looked down at his glass and said, "Lieutenant Wasniak was killed in a foray against resurgent pirates off Neptune."

Porch said, "I am so sorry. He was a good man and high spirit."

"The Assault Sergeant Major retired after that incident. Yes, Carruthers and his seven brothers run a hotel in Jamaica—Kingston Town, for retired spacefarers, particularly those from the Fleet."

Bonnie came up to talk to her old classmate. She had Bokasi on her arm. She gave Ironwood and his Mrs. a hug, Porch a kiss on the cheek, and asked, "John, do you remember when these two thought they had to fight to defend this lady's honor?"

"Most certainly. I thought we'd lose Bokasi."

Ironwood raised his glass again and they toasted their days at the Academy. Then Porch saw Nogales, friend of his Southwest boyhood. At first, Nogales was happy, then he saddened, saying, "Harry, el paso sobre el rio–he passed over the river."

Porch's eyes glistened. Harry, his foster father, who loved him so much and taught him so much, died of old age on his ranch, No Sech Place, in west Texas. Harry commissioned Nogales to give his last regards to his ward, to tell him he crossed the river with no regrets. Nogales gave Harry's will to Porch. All Harry had, he wrote, passed to his boy, Porch. Nogales said the ranch prospered. Water had come back to the great aquifer. Porch said he had suspected Harry had passed away and regretted he missed his final days. Then he said, "Amigo, you were his faithful friend and the ranch shall pass to you, for I will not pass that way again. I'll see to that." Nogales protested, but Porch insisted. It was an emotional moment.

Then Porch saw Inspector Tuesday hanging back from the revelry. When Tuesday saw he'd caught his old quarry's eye, he looked away. Seeing this, Porch went over, and when he saw those black eyes level up to his, he said, "Inspector, you had no recourse but to do what you did, but Brother, we saw too much and fought too long together to be other than faithful friends."

Tuesday's hard face softened. He smiled and said to Porch, "I hoped to part from you that way, for my days in law enforcement have ended."

"Where will you go from here?" Porch asked.

"I'm going back to Bountiful, where Maria Many Coup, the one they call the Algonquin Woman, waits for me."

Bonnie, delighted with the reunion, happily called them all to dinner. Porch looked around for Aurelia, and saw her with Neils. He had her hand and was tugging lightly on her arm to escort her to the table. She seemed a bit petulant. As Porch came up to her, Neils released her hand and stood aside. Porch said, "Aurelia, my darling, you seem a bit unhappy."

She looked at him and asked, "Daddy, why are you hugging all these people?"

He replied, "Oh, my little darling, these are old friends whom I've not seen for a long, long time."

She admonished him, "Daddy, your hugs are for me."

Taken aback, he stammered, "Of course, always."

She looked up at him again and asked fearfully, "Daddy, are you going to leave me again?"

Porch gulped, and understood her fretfulness. So he bent down, kissed her, and whispered, "Oh, my little darling, I shall never leave you again."

She seemed relieved and brightened, then looked around for Neils, who had stayed nearby. She took his hand and let him lead her to the table. When they reached their seats, Neils bowed, somewhat awkwardly, pulled her chair out for her, and when she was seated, helped her pull up to the table. Aurelia thanked him and then giggled at his grave sobriety. But Neils didn't mind, for he had long range plans. He fully intended to win her heart.

Bonnie seated Porch to her right, with Ironwood to her left and the others interspersed around the table, which was small enough to allow cross conversation. A small orchestra played the latest from Broadway musicals during the dinner, songs Bonnie dearly loved. Neils and Aurelia were seated opposite and quickly wrapped themselves in their own world. All enjoyed the dinner, which seemed to end before they knew it. As it did, Miriam rose and proposed a toast. "To the reunion, the good health of all, and future good fortune."

Then Bokasi rose, saying, "There is a song that must now be sung."

With that, Olivia rose, and both went over by the orchestra. Soon her hauntingly beautiful voice had them enraptured, "STARMAN—STARMAN, YOU CAME WITH LIGHTNING, WIND AND THUNDER—TO TAKE ME TO YOUR WORLD OF WONDER "

Bokasi's deep baritone took up as Olivia faded, "OH, LITTLE ONE, MY PRECIOUS ONE—IT IS MY HEART THAT YOU HAVE WON."

Both knew Porch loved that song written so long ago, even though it expressed the pathos of his life. They paused and looked at him. Porch motioned them to continue, so Olivia's voice rose again. "RODE AWAY ON A BLAZING ROCKET—LEFT BUT A MEMORY IN A GOLDEN LOCKET," and Bo came in, "LOOK NEAR TO HER, LOOK NEAR TO HER—CAN YOU MEND A HEART SO BROKEN—WITH BUT A LOCKET AS A TOKEN."

They came to the last refrain, which Olivia began. "DO YOU WONDER, EVER WONDER—WHERE IS THE BIRTHPLACE OF WONDER."

Bo replied, "YES, I WONDER—ALWAYS WONDER—WHERE IS THE BIRTHPLACE OF WONDER."

Olivia and Bo returned to quiet conversation at the table. In a moment, Porch discreetly excused himself and went out through the French doors to the terrace to take in some fresh air. Once again, he could look at the stars. Behind him, he heard his dinner partners entreat Bo and Olivia to sing some more, and he heard some more songs from Olivia's long ago production. It was very enjoyable.

After awhile, Bonnie came out and stood beside him. She too gazed up at the sparkling beauty of the stars in the moonless sky, and said, "It is beautiful. The stars twinkle like bright diamonds this midsummer night."

Porch gave a start, recalling it was on a midsummer night fifteen years before that he began his epic flight from the Academy. Bonnie saw this and said, "Perhaps we have come full circle."

Just then, Aurelia interrupted, calling from the terrace doors. She was with Miriam. She said, "Daddy, I'm sleepy. Can Aunt Miriam take me to bed? She said she would tell me some stories."

"Yes, of course, my darling."

Then she ran over, hesitated when she saw Bonnie, and turned to give her a hug. Bonnie lifted her up, gave her a squeeze, kissed her on her neck, and put her down. Then she turned to Porch, looked up at him, and asked, "Daddy, do you have a hug left in your arms for me?"

As Porch picked her up, tears came to his eyes. He hugged her tight and she kissed him, patted his cheek, and said, "Good night, Daddy."

"Good night, Little One, pleasant dreams," Porch replied, setting her down. Both watched her skip back over to Miriam and go out.

Porch looked at Bonnie and smiled. She returned his smile and asked, "Do you have a hug left in your arms for me?"

Porch took her in his arms, put his lips to hers, and kissed her tenderly.

EPILOGUE

FIFTEEN YEARS LATER

The letter began:

"Old Friend,

Forgive me–it's been so many years, but I am not a man of 'Belles Lettres' as you are, so bear with me. I have read all your books: *Slave Ship; Jason, Lord No; The Ruby Queen; The Great White Wolf* and *ERTSONG*, to name a few. I liked *ERTSONG* the best. They are very popular on Old Earth, and it is hard to get a copy, they sell out so fast. The Fleet Bookstore has promised me the first copy of your latest, *Megadamn–the Forbidden Planet*. I suspect you'll write several about that fearful place. But its gravity was good to us when it slung our lifeboat back to Midlwurld. Write of the Prongs. Tell us a tale of Tin Man, Steel Soldier, and those two crazy old coots.

The kids are on their own now, one in law, one in medicine, two in music, and the youngest girl doing postgrad in mathematics, so Olivia has time on her hands and is after me to retire, and I have decided to do so in six months.

Old Earth is peaceful–an autumn world, somewhat dull. Our most adventurous people emigrate, which is good, as population growth is again a problem. Though the Federation has compressed the Mars Project schedule again, it will still be several hundred years before that planet may be colonized. Now our biochemists are studying the feasibility of developing an organic and chemical stew to counteract the harsh atmosphere of Venus and make it habitable. The seventy Earth atmospheres at the surface make me think they've gone off the deep end, but with the exponential advances in science–who knows?

But I'm wandering. Write me of your life. Are you happy? Are you well? Olivia and I are considering the 'Grand Galactic Tour,' so tell me–would we be disappointed? Could we come see you?"

Porch stopped reading, took pen in hand and began a response.

Dear Bo,

Yes, it has been too many years, but everything now is like yesterday to me. Yes, we are very happy. Life is rugged here on Rim World at the Galaxy edge. We miss Old Earth, but we feel like pioneers and wouldn't have it any other way.

We have indulged ourselves and built a large and well-appointed lodge, so come when you can and stay as long as you will. We have a garden–planted in a piece of Old Earth, ten cubic yards of rich Earth loam transported through the wormhole at a king's ransom. But Bonnie insisted and wouldn't have it any other way. We grow tomatoes, squash, radishes, cucumbers, lettuce, melons and sweet ears of corn, all from seeds she carried here from Old Earth.

She sends her love. Right now she's in her studio painting a portrait of the twins. Neils is here on furlough from the Fleet, and Aurelia will not let him out of her sight. Recently, we went to Aurelia's graduation from the Great University at Land's End, the Wizard's legacy on Midlwurld to the people there, and to fetch her back. She graduated cum laude in anthropogenic archeology with a minor in music. The people of Szidrous want her back as their queen. That is her choice, but when I see her and Neils together, I see a different future.

It was the first time I had returned to that solar system. I went alone to Ice Moon and the Hall of Eternity to visit 'my long ago darling.' Bonnie understood my need to do that, for we've found solace in each other and have built a comfortable and enduring love.

Aurora sleeps there in a state of grace, and I would swear that as I knelt and placed roses by her bier that through the ice I saw a tint of color come back to her cheeks and a slight smile to her lips, as though she was pleased with me and how my life came out.

Aurelia and Neils came into the study to go to the viewport, and his thoughts were interrupted. He lifted his pen and smiled at them. Then he went back to Bokasi's letter and reviewed several lines. He lifted his pen again.

"You ask of the 'Grand Tour,' and would you be disappointed–never. There are wonders out there: star clusters alive with life whose worlds see heavens of starry sparkle, red and blue giants, supergiants, brown dwarfs, too. There are swirling double stars and trinary systems that dance an incomprehensible jig. Great whorls of gas reflect brilliant greens, blues and reds. Shock waves born in milliseconds journey out untold millennia to make new stars in great cascades of fire that only the centuries see.

There are so many worlds throughout the void that I cannot count them: water worlds of sand and sea, of perfumed island archipelagos; icy worlds of frosted air and hoary forests; worlds of steamy jungle; and desiccated desert. There are new worlds just forming life and old worlds with vintage civilizations. Come see. Visit us."

Again Porch set down his pen to read Bokasi's letter. There were several pages left. He came to the end and read the scrawl: "As ever, Bo," and then underneath, "FLEET ADMIRAL, COMMANDING: COMBINED EARTH FLEETS."

But there was more–"P.S. Did you ever find the Birthplace of Wonder?"

Porch pushed back from the desk, and as he looked up, his eye caught Neils and Aurelia. Neils was looking through the scope, a duplicate of the Wizard's in the

Tower of Astral. He pointed to M-31, the Milky Way's great sister galaxy in Andromeda, amazingly clear from Rim World. Aurelia looked up at him adoringly. Porch overheard him say, "...someday." He smiled and again picked up his pen to write, writing, "Yes, there are wonders, wonders everywhere, but the birthplace of wonder rests in the human heart. As ever, Porch."

APPENDICES

TIME LINE

100 MILLION YEARS AGO ~ Civilization of the Ancients
6000 YEARS AGO ~ Recruitment of Tunkus from middle
   Asia.
1014 AD ~ Vikuns travel with Ancients to Ice World

TWENTY-FIRST CENTURY ~ Twenty Worst Century rav-
   ages of nature.
   2010 Corporation founded by Guiseppi.
   2010 Moon Base
   2018 First mission to Mars
   2019 All spectra telescope base, sun orbit, each sta-
      tion equidistant
   one from the other at Earth distance from the Sun
   2020 First space laboratory/factory
   2023-2040 Gigantic earthquakes ravish Mississippi
      area.
   2050 Founder's son, Bruno, born.
   2053 Willow Wind Commune established.
   2060 Thaddeus P. Winter's first emigration
   2080 Founder dies, son, Bruno, CEO
   2090 Second emigration

TWENTY-SECOND CENTURY 2100 Founder's grandson,
   Silvano, born.
   2102 Federal Paperwork Reduction Act of 2102
   2130 Founder's son dies, grandson, Silvano, CEO
   2130 Third Emigration
   2140 Great-grandson of founder, Urbano, born.

2158 Beehive originally launched as *USS Lincoln*
2170 Founder's grandson dies at 70. Great-grand-
    son, Urbano, CEO.
2173 Great-great-grandson of founder, Dominic,
    born.
2180 Fourth emigration
2185 Belisarius born.
2196 Harry born

TWENTY-THIRD CENTURY
2201 Great-grandson, Urbano, dies at 61. Great-
    great-grandson, Dominic, CEO, at age 28.
2204 Founder's line of male succession broken,
    Francesca born
2218 Harry graduates from Harvard and MIT
2219 Harry graduates from Wharton School of Fi-
    nance
2220 Francesca's bastard son, Werewick, born
2222 Harry marries Dulcie
2223 Harry marries Druscilla
2223 Francesca marries Werewick to give the child
    a name.
2224 Harry marries Dorcas
2224 Francesca rehabilitated.
2225 Harry's great trek west
2226 Werewick Senior dies.
2228 Great-great-grandson of founder, Dominic,
    dies at 55.
2229 Francesca marries Belisaurius X. Belisaurius
2230 Fifth emmigration
2237 Jason's great voyage
2237 Jason to marry Amilee
2237 26 June, Jason and Amilee consummate their
    love
2238 March, Porch born
2238 GREAT BLIZZARD ON THE WESTERN PLAINS
    (October)
2238 October Porch is a foundling, Amilee dies in
    desert
2238 13th year of Harry's self-imposed exile
2239 Bountiful burnt out by Corporation.

2240 Francesca killed in high-speed auto accident. Belisarius CEO.

2254 June, Porch enters Space Academy. Meets Bo Bokasi.

2254-2255 July to February, Torment

2255 March, Duels

2255 April, Brigade rejuvenation

2255 15 June, Off Campus Day

2255 21 June, Midsummer's Night Festival

2255 21 June, Report to Werewick

2255 22 June, Flight

2255 30 June, Bonnie Brightwood graduates from Space Academy

2255 30 July, Ensign Brightwood joins space fleet

2255 Porch is 17 plus three months

2255 June, 326th All Star Game

2255 July, Porch captured.

2255 Sept., Porch brought before Chairman

2255 Oct., Porch's trial. Found guilty.

2255 31 Oct., Porch escapes, heads East.

2255 2 Nov., Millenarian encounter, outfits himself, and heads North.

2256 1 Jan, Tuesday commissioned to bring in Porch

2256 1 July, Lt.Brightwood is assigned to Admiral Peterson's staff on the Mars Project. Meets Petersen.

2256 1 Aug., Ensign Olive joins her.

2256 31 Oct., Shrieker demonstration at Coliseum in LA

2256 3 Nov., Admiral and Bonnie reassigned.

2256 4 Nov., Porch encounter with Fenrir. Heads east and south.

2257 April, Porch reaches Academy, recovers locket. Heads to Bountiful.

2257 June, Porch reaches Bountiful, meets Purity Wyndotte

2257 31 June, Porch escapes from Bountiful

2257 July, Tuesday reaches the Academy

2257 September 20, Bonnie meets Petersen at Corp Hq.

2257 3 October, Fateful meeting in Tukanon's bunker

2257 October, Porch reaches Georgia.

2257 3 November, Porch meets Hackstraw and Bernouli.

2257 1 Dec., Quarterly meeting of Corporation Board of Directors

2257 5 Dec., Tuesday reaches Bountiful

2257 3 Dec., The trio reaches the keys.

2257 4 Dec., Shanghaied

2258 Feb., Loaded into shuttle and flown to Beehive as slaves.

2258 March, Tuesday reaches the Keys

2258 1 May, Operation Griffinslayer scheduled to commence.

2258 2 May, Tukanon destroyed.

2258 1 July, Chairman proposes Bonnie join the Corporation

2258 Sept., Tuesday reaches the pit in Amazonia

2258 10 Nov., Porch kills Grolub; rescued in Petersen's attack.

2259 2 Feb., *USS Constitution* orbits Earth, shuttles to Diego Garcia

2259 17 Feb., Porch leaves Diego Garcia by lifeboat

2259 26 Apr., Porch reaches Seychelles

2259 27 Apr., Wet monsoon starts

2259 1 June, Porch reaches Israel

2259 30 June, Bokasi graduates from Academy

2259 1 Sept., Porch in time machine, emerges on Midlwurld at Nork.

2260 1 Sept., Leaves Nork, meets Priest, travels to Tower of Astral. Porch meets the Wizard, Lord No.

2260 10 Sept., Mission to Ruby Queen.

2260 10 Oct., Combat with Red Eric

2260 13 Oct., Sojourn with ERTS begins

2260 20 Nov., Condor-steeds fly Porch back to Szid

2260 26 Nov., Porch dropped on Aurora's balcony is smitten with Aurora

2261 1 Mar., Inspection complete; King Szidrous' Birthday Ball

2261 1 Mar., Porch twenty-three

2261 2 Mar., Throgs land on Midlwurld

2261 3 Aug., Porch's flight to ERTFOREST, meets Bokasi.

2261 23 Aug., Throg vanguard is defeated.

2261 25 Aug., Spauk forced to return to Ice World

2261 1 Sept., Main force discovered.

2261 30 Dec., Diversion of Throg main force into Nemesis.

2262 1 Mar., Porch twenty-four

2262 20 Mar., Porch and Bokasi get back to Midlwurld

2262 10 Apr., Porch meets Aurora in the garden

2262 1 June, Porch marries Aurora

2263 2 June, Aurelia born

2264 2 Jun, Aurelia's first birthday

2264 8 July, Porch and Aurora leave for Ice World

2264 2 Aug., Arrive at Ice World

2264 4 Aug., Porch seized and Aurora put in high tower

2264 5 Sept., Aurora sees Olaf murdered, Porch threatened

2264 7 Sept., Aurora agrees to annul marriage to Porch and marry Spauk

2264 17 Sept., Aurora marries Spauk, commits suicide

2264 20 Oct., Aurora is laid in state

2264 22 Dec., Aurora's funeral procession to Ice Moon

2265 25 May, Porch begins his raids

2265 1 Sept., Lord No to Ice World

2265 15 Sept., The Hearing, Lord No murdered, Spauk escapes

2265 1 Dec., Return to Midlwurld following Spauk

2266 10 Feb., Pursuit to Cynn

2266 10 July, orbit Cynn

2269 1 July, Land on Galatea, led to Dr. Tupology by Water Gamins

2270 10 Jan., Porch and Ragnor return to Midlwurld

2270 20 Jan., Porch lands on Megadamn. Meets MacTavish and Schwartz.

2270 27 Jan., Porch finds Spauk in limbo

2270 1 Feb., Steel Soldier and Tin Man rescue Porch

2270 1 Mar., Tuesday reveals himself and apprehends Porch.

2270 1 Mar., Immediate return to Earth via bootstrapped transporter.

2270 1 Mar., Porch's thirty-second birthday

2270 1 Mar. to 1 June, quarantine at Corporation Hq

2270 1 Jun, Porch brought before the new Chairman, Bonnie Brightwood Reunited with Aurelia

2270 August, Reunion, eventual marriage to Bonnie Brightwood.

2285 Epilogue, Letter from Admiral Bokasi, response detailing life as writer and pioneer on Rim World. Reveals Birthplace of Wonder.

CHARACTERS

- Abdul'a'bool'bool'emir: The Ruby Queen's Father
- Absalom: Inventor Of Transporter
- Ajax: Porch's Dog, Son Of Hercules
- Amilee: Porch's Mother
- Arnvid Of Arnuval: Vikun Chieftain
- Askard Of Skaggerack: Vikun Chieftain
- Astra: Aurora's Mother
- Aurelia: Porch's And Aurora's Daughter
- Aurora: Princess, Porch's Beloved First Wife, Daughter Of King Szidrous
- Baldor: Vikun Chieftain
- Bathsheba: The Ruby Queen's Great Female Panther
- Becky: The Little Girl At The Millenarian Commune.
- Belisarius X Belisarius: Chairman Of Corp. And Porch's Nemesis;
- Bernouli: Porch's And Hackstraw's Companion
- Bertram Beauregard (Bo) Bokasi: Porch's Academy Roommate
- Big Boogie: Leader Of The Throgs
- Big Gywn: Porch's First Friend On Midlwurld
- Brobdingnagia: Ruby Queen's Grand Vizier
- Bonnie Brightwood: Porch's Company Commander And Second Wife
- Boks: Panther God Of The Erts
- Brunhilde: Vikun Baroness, Aurora's Handmaiden
- Bruno: Founder's Son
- Caleb: One Of Three Brothers In Bountiful
- Carruthers: Assault Master Sergeant, *Uss Constitution* Assault Team 1.

- Cheeko: Tchako's Assistant Squad Leader And Minion
- Cevello: Corporation Doctor
- Dagmar: Vikun Baroness, Aurora's Handmaiden
- Dominic: Great Great Grandson Of Founder
- Donaldson Rotter: ZVS Heavy Anchor
- Dorcas: Harry's Third Wife
- Dorfman: Member Of Operetta Music Team
- Druscilla: Harry's Second Wife
- Dulcie: Harry's First Wife
- Dunsmore: Member Of Operetta Music Team
- Dunston: Member Of Operetta Music Team
- El Raton: Sheriff Lobo's Deputy
- Ertsinger: Ert Historian, Keeper Of The Ert Stories
- Ess: Warewick's Bodyguard And Corporation Investigator, Tall, Long Face
- Fenrir: The Great White Wolf
- Flight-Leader: One Of The Erts Who Finds Porch On The Desert
- Francesca: Beautiful And Wild Daughter Of Founder's Great Grandson
- Forward Observer: Erts Leader At Fringe
- Fufi Fondle: Shrieker High Priestess
- Gee: Ess's Companion; Werewick's Bodyguard, Massive, Short, Flat Face
- Genuine Ginger: Palacio Prostitute
- Gideon: Academy Handyman And Corporation Gardener; Belisarius Brother
- Giuseppi: Founder
- Goat Woman: Spauk's Nanny
- Gommorah: Warewick's Fierce Hound
- Good Medicine, The: Erts Doctor
- Granny Gronx: Hill Country Midwife And Healer
- Greedy Gretchen: Palacio Prostitute
- Grubol: Nonose, Master Of Slaves.
- Gurtrude: A Vikun Chambermaid Who Carries The True Story Of Spauk To The Clans
- Hackstraw: Porch's And Bernouli's Companion
- Harim Skarim Shareem: Captain Of The Queen's Own Camel Horse; Palace Guard
- Harry, Alias Ole Mulemilk: Porch's Adoptive Father

- Hedda: Machine Gunner Who Took Husband's Place After He Was Killed
- Hercules: Harry's Huge Dog, Ajax's Sire
- Hodel: Proprietor Of Hodel's Hostel
- Hulda: One Of The Vikun Ladies
- Hunter-Man: One Of The Erts Who Finds Porch On The Desert
- Inez Garcia Valdez: 83rd President Of The United States.
- Captain Ironwood: Bokasi's Swordsman Instructor
- Jason, Alias Wizard, Alias Lord No: Amilee's Lover And Porch's Father
- Jethro: One Of Three Brothers In Bountiful
- Josh: The Old Millenarian Farmer
- Kamakasi Kawasaki: Samurai Tight End
- Kane: Megadamn Concessionaire At Nork
- Little Weejie: Big Gywn's Companion
- Lobo: Sheriff Of Pecado
- Lu: Great King Of Northern Kingdom
- Luther: The Ruby Queen's Great Male Panther
- Mactavish: Caretaker Of Megadamn
- Maria Many Coup: Tuesday North Bear's Algonquin Woman
- Mendel: Szidrian Tailor Who Made Porch's Uniforms
- Mephistopheles: Harry's Black Cat
- Mokelembembe: Dinasours Inhabiting Great Rift Valley On Megadamn
- Mortician: Vikun Who Retrieved Aurora's Body After Her Suicide
- Mortimer: Harry's Huge Snake
- Mulatto, The: Slaver Responsible For Shanghais
- Mungo: One Of Three Brothers In Bountiful
- Neils: Bonnie Brightwood's Son By Sven Petersen
- Nogales: Harry's Friend, Postman And Mayor Of Pecado
- Oberon, Mineas: Major Werewick's Real Father
- Odin's Scribe: Vikun Shaman
- Olaf: Vikun Chieftain
- Orwell, Lord Chamberlain: Of Szidrous, Next In Authority To The King.
- Ouregard: Chief Of The Erts
- Owl; Harry's Pet

- Out-Guards: Ert-Guards Responsible For Warnings Of Intrusion Into Ertforest
- Paglio: Singer At King Szidrous' Ball
- Peaches: Caracabana Prostitute
- Petersen, Sven, Admiral: Mars Project Head And Bonnie's First Husband
- Pixie: Caracabana Prostitute
- Porch: A Foundling, Son Of Amilee And Jason
- Preacher Wyndotte:; Leader Of Bountiful Community
- Purity: Preacher Wyndotte's Granddaughter
- Purple The Pimp: Works The Whores At The Palacio In Pecado
- Pussycat: Caracabana Prostitute
- Ragnor: Vikun Chieftain
- Rashid: Porch's Guide To The City Of Toome
- Rasputin: Immigrant Bicycle Man Who Carried The Priest Back To The Fortress
- Root -Woman: Ert Apothecary
- Rumermong: Space Worker And Occupant Of Mama Mia's
- Samurai: Nickname Of Tokyo U Football Team
- Scab: One Of Scrofulous' Band Of Dwarfs
- Scar: One Of Scrofulous' Band Of Dwarfs
- Schwartz: Mactavish's Assistant On Megadamn
- Scout: One Of The Erts Who Found Porch On The Desert
- Scrofolous: Spauk's Dwarf Retainer
- Scruff; One Of Scrofulous Band Of Dwarfs
- Seven Sumo: Tokyo University's Fabled Line
- Short: One Of Scrofulous' Band Of Dwarfs
- Shu: Son Of Lu, A Wastrel King Of Northern Kingdom,
- Silvano: Founder's Grandson
- Snort: One Of Scrofulous' Band Of Dwarfs
- Sodom: Werewick's Huge Hound
- Spauk: Lord Of Ice World
- Steel Soldier: Robot Foreman On Megadamn
- Stomper: One Of Scrofulous' Band
- Stonehead: One Of Scrofulous' Band
- Stoop: One Of Scrofulous' Band
- Stubble: One Of Scrofulous' Band
- Stuff: One Of Scrofulous' Band

- Stump: One Of Scrofulous' Band
- Sushi: Tokyo U Quarterback
- Sweet Sue: Palacio Prostitute
- Szid: King Of Szidrous; Octogenarian, Senile And Frail
- Taleberry: Space Worker At Nork
- Tang: Tukanon's American Agent.
- Throgs: Warriors Devolved From Ancient Tunkus; The Scourge
- Tin Man: Steel Soldier's Robot Companion
- Tuckerman, Tobias T.: Wandering Minstrel Who Becomes Purity's Husband.
- Tuesday North Bear: Detective Tracking Porch
- Tukanon: Dictator Of Central Asian Autonomy
- Tukanon's Aide: The Corporation Mole
- Turg: The Ruby Queen's First Husband
- Twins: Bonnie's And Porch's Offspring
- Ulysses: Porch's Dog, Son Of Hercules
- Urbano: Founder's Great Grandson
- Ward, Lt.: Cmdr, Red Assault Team, Killed Off Neptune.
- Wasniak: Captain Ironwood's Orderly And Big Mouth
- Winter, Thaddeus P.: Leader Of Millinariians, First Emigration
- Winter, Thaddeus P. Iv: Leader Of Millenarians On Midlworld
- Wolven: Ice World Wolves
- Wu: Chief Astrologer Of Northern Kingdom

About The Author

Jonathan Holman acquired a fondness for literature and love for the diversity of the English language while attending the Landon School in Bethesda, Maryland. He graduated from the US Military Academy in 1951 and is a veteran of the Korean War and Viet Nam.

He holds a master's degree in mechanical engineering from the University of Southern California, another in military art and science and has had a lifetime interest in the natural sciences. He is a landscape and still life painter. He and his wife, Virginia, live in Sierra Vista, Arizona.